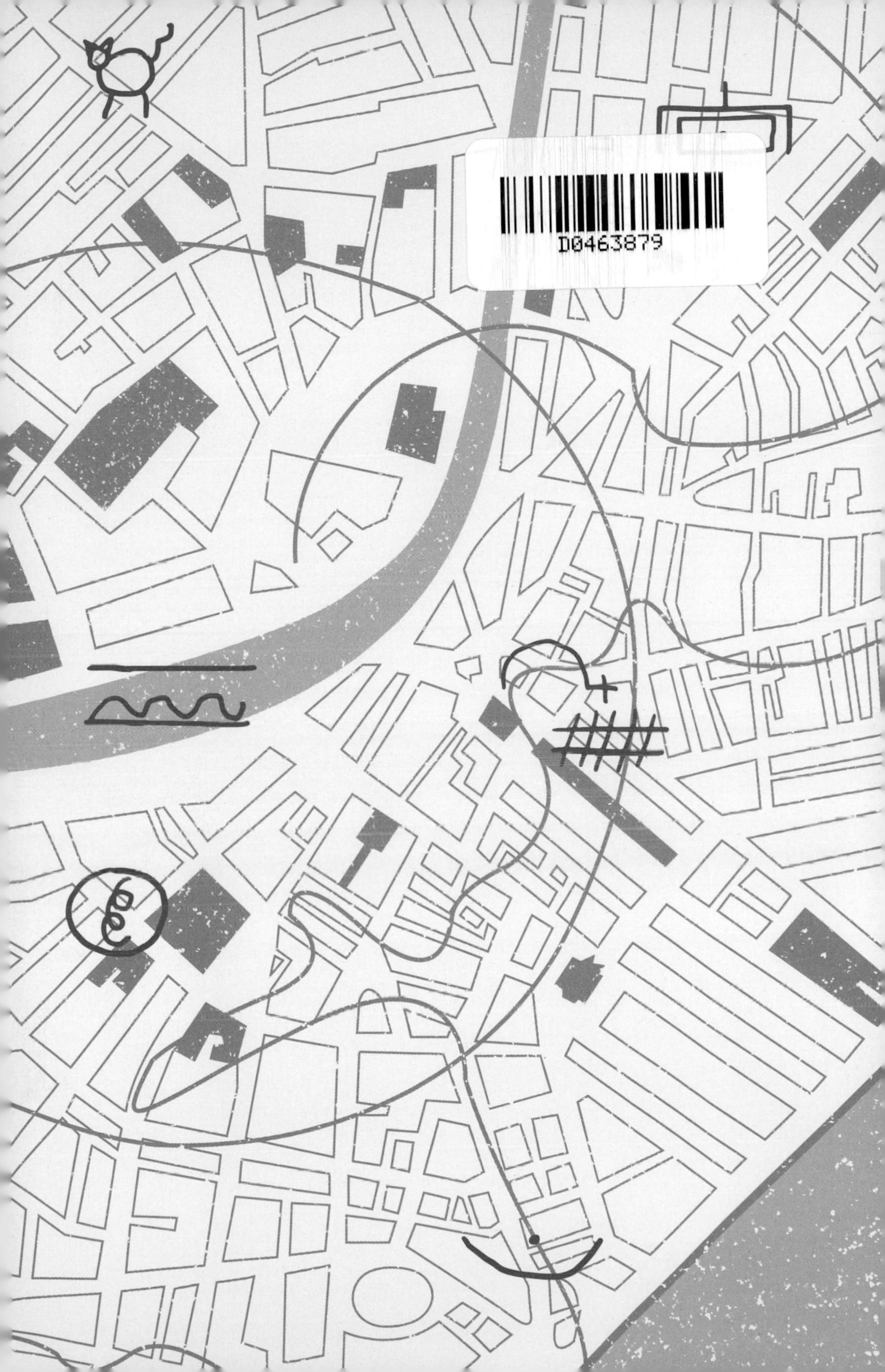

SOUPY LEAVES HOME™

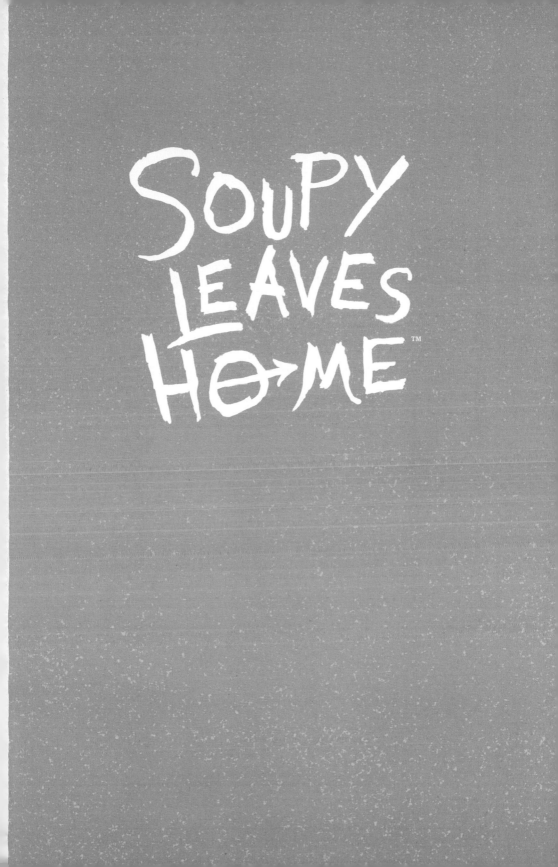

For all the Pearls in the world.
—Cecil Castellucci

To Tita, the kindest person I've known.
—Jose Pimienta

SOUPY LEAVES HOME™

Written by **Cecil Castellucci**

Illustrated by **Jose Pimienta**

Lettered by **Nate Piekos of Blambot®**

DARK HORSE BOOKS

President & Publisher **Mike Richardson**
Editor **Shantel LaRocque**

First Edition:
Assistant Editor **Katii O'Brien**
Designer **Sarah Terry**
Digital Art Technician **Christianne Goudreau**

Second Edition:
Designers **Jen Edwards and Kathleen Barnett**
Digital Art Technician **Adam Pruett**

*Special thanks to Sierra Hahn, Kel McDonald, Joe Infurnari, the
MacDowell Colony, and to all the mentors who've taken us under their wings.*

Neil Hankerson Executive Vice President • **Tom Weddle** Chief Financial Officer • **Randy Stradley** Vice President of Publishing • **Nick Mcwhorter** Chief Business Development Officer • **Dale Lafountain** Chief Information Officer • **Matt Parkinson** Vice President of Marketing • **Vanessa Todd-Holmes** Vice President of Production and Scheduling • **Mark Bernardi** Vice President of Book Trade and Digital Sales • **Ken Lizzi** General Counsel • **Dave Marshall** Editor in Chief • **Davey Estrada** Editorial Director • **Chris Warner** Senior Books Editor • **Cary Grazzini** Director of Specialty Projects • **Lia Ribacchi** Art Director • **Matt Dryer** Director of Digital Art and Prepress • **Michael Gombos** Senior Director of Licensed Publications • **Kari Yadro** Director of Custom Programs • **Kari Torson** Director of International Licensing • **Sean Brice** Director of Trade Sales

To find a comics shop in your area, visit comicshoplocator.com

Published by Dark Horse Books
A division of Dark Horse Comics LLC
10956 SE Main Street
Milwaukie, OR 97222

DarkHorse.com

Library of Congress Cataloging-in-Publication Data
Names: Castellucci, Cecil, 1969- writer. | Pimienta, Jose, illustrator. |
    Piekos, Nate, letterer.
Title: Soupy leaves home / written by Cecil Castellucci ; illustrated by
    Jose Pimienta ; lettered by Nate Piekos of Blambot.
Description: Second edition. | Milwaukie, OR : Dark Horse Books, 2020. |
    Audience: Grades 7-9 | Summary: In 1932 a teenage girl Pearl Plankette
    runs away from her abusive father, changes her identity to a boy named
    Soupy, and meets a hobo named Ramshackle who takes her under his wing as
    they hop trains, care for each other, and learn about themselves.
Identifiers: LCCN 2020010214 (print) | LCCN 2020010215 (ebook) | ISBN
    9781506722054 (hardcover) | ISBN 9781616554316 (trade paperback) | ISBN
    9781630083144 (ebook)
Subjects: LCSH: Graphic novels. | CYAC: Graphic novels. |
    Runaways--Fiction. | Homeless persons--Fiction. | Coming of
    age--Fiction.
Classification: LCC PZ7.7.C375 So 2020 (print) | LCC PZ7.7.C375 (ebook) |
    DDC 741.5/973--dc23
LC record available at https://lccn.loc.gov/2020010214
LC ebook record available at https://lccn.loc.gov/2020010215

First edition: April 2017
Ebook ISBN 978-1-63008-314-4
Trade Paperback ISBN 978-1-61655-431-6

Second edition: August 2021
Ebook ISBN 978-1-50672-251-1
Hardcover ISBN 978-1-50672-205-4

1 3 5 7 9 10 8 6 4 2
Printed in China

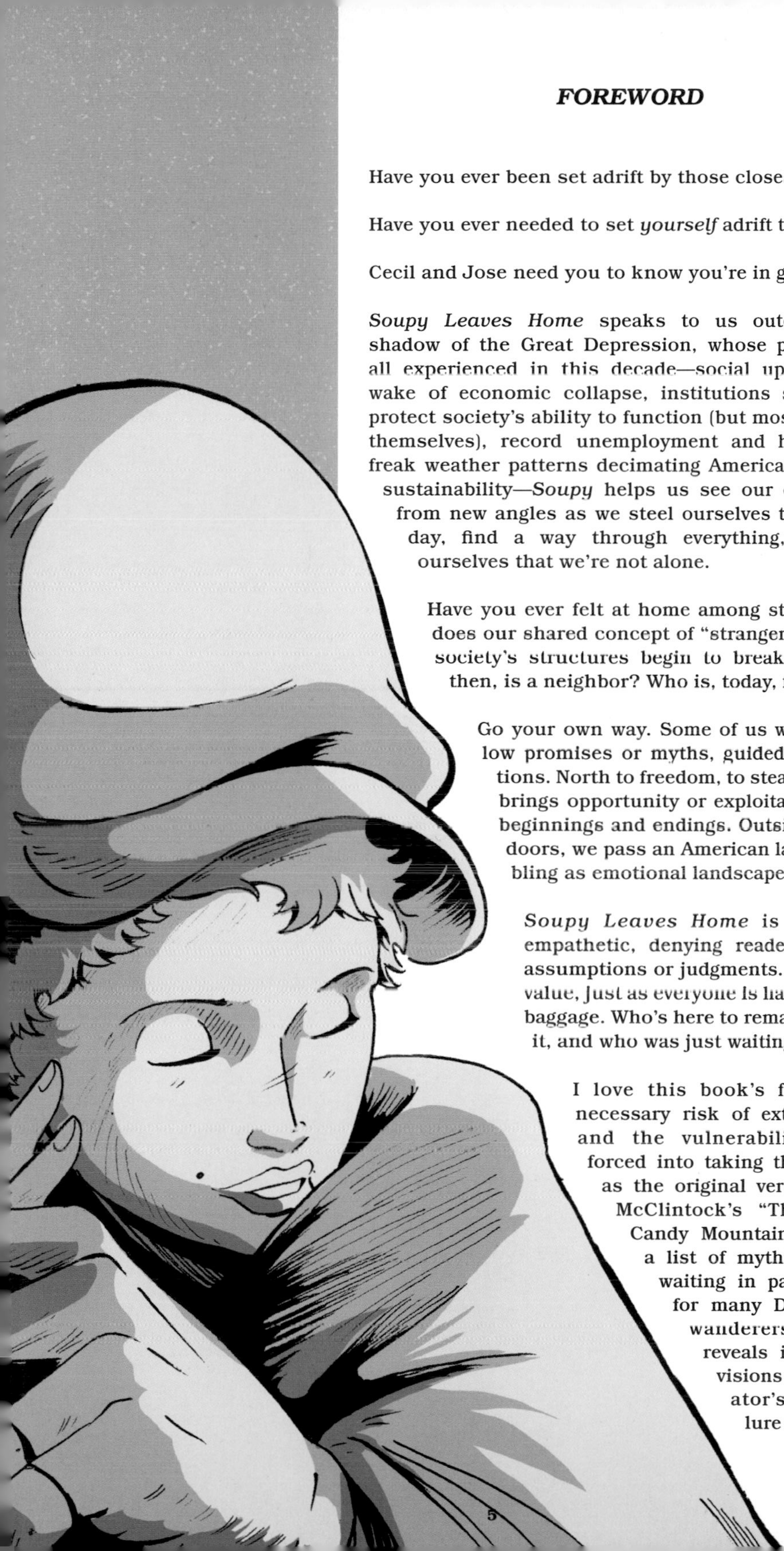

FOREWORD

Have you ever been set adrift by those closest to you?

Have you ever needed to set *yourself* adrift to survive?

Cecil and Jose need you to know you're in good company.

Soupy Leaves Home speaks to us outcasts. In the shadow of the Great Depression, whose parallels we've all experienced in this decade—social upheaval in the wake of economic collapse, institutions scrambling to protect society's ability to function (but mostly protecting themselves), record unemployment and homelessness, freak weather patterns decimating America's agricultural sustainability—*Soupy* helps us see our own situation from new angles as we steel ourselves to get up each day, find a way through everything, and remind ourselves that we're not alone.

Have you ever felt at home among strangers? How does our shared concept of "stranger" evolve when society's structures begin to break down? Who, then, is a neighbor? Who is, today, for you?

Go your own way. Some of us will always follow promises or myths, guided by constellations. North to freedom, to steadiness. South brings opportunity or exploitation. West for beginnings and endings. Outside the boxcar doors, we pass an American landscape doubling as emotional landscape.

Soupy Leaves Home is patient and empathetic, denying readers any quick assumptions or judgments. Everyone has value, just as everyone is haunted by their baggage. Who's here to remain tethered to it, and who was just waiting to let go?

I love this book's focus on the necessary risk of extending trust, and the vulnerability of being forced into taking that risk. Just as the original version of Harry McClintock's "The Big Rock Candy Mountain," describing a list of mythical promises waiting in parts unknown for many Depression-era wanderers, ultimately reveals its fantastical visions to be a predator's attempt to lure a transient child into his orbit. Such lofty promises often crumble upon examination, but there's also danger in refusing to seek out the promise of something better.

The transient underground depicted within these pages regularly grapples with grifters and opportunists, but largely chooses the risk of welcoming the stranger. Indeed, Soupy's new crew insists upon it. Viewed through the lens of its characters, this story is post-apocalyptic. Its survivors are building something together, at times anarchist and egalitarian, at other times a mirror of America writ large, prey to exploitation and corruption. That dynamic forces a central hobo rule: "Don't take advantage of someone who is in a vulnerable situation."

Cecil's writing is made for the comics page, anticipating where Jose will take it, and her prose works in rhythmic blocks that push the stage flair of her stories. I love seeing Jose's room to soar with her script, having been given maximum space for visual interpretation. Her scriptwriting is a dream for cartoonists who are drawn to their characters' rich, subjective, complicated internal experiences.

Jose's use of color-as-structure in *Soupy*, particularly in a period piece which wouldn't necessarily require it, was eye-opening and influential on my own work. Through Jose, color becomes storyteller, signpost, and character. We allow his chromatic guides to carry us safely through, watching for its shifts like symbols etched onto fences and boxcars in faraway towns.

I write this at the close of a tense week, during an immensely consequential election in a nation on the precipice between democracy and authoritarianism. You and I each make tentative plans as we wait to see if our social structures can, and will, prevail. One day, then the next. For each of us, the American promise of self-determination requires confronting the hollowness of myth, cautiously approaching the Big Rock Candy Mountain.

We're all living through a global pandemic which has brought a partial shuttering of society, and of possible futures. Plans made are not to gamble on our dreams, not to seek our future selves, but simply to get by. To stay alive and healthy each day must sometimes be enough. What gets lost in the small choices we make throughout each day? Our personal decisions help support and sustain each other, keeping each other well and alive for another day.

Dreams have to wait, right?

Some dreams still keep us awake at night, even when we've left them in the dust—and they *should*. Listen to Soupy, Ramshackle, and everyone you meet along the way when they share themselves with you. Let their stories remind you that there *is* a future worth building, and that we must look out for each other in order to overcome the risks all around us.

Nate Powell, November 2020

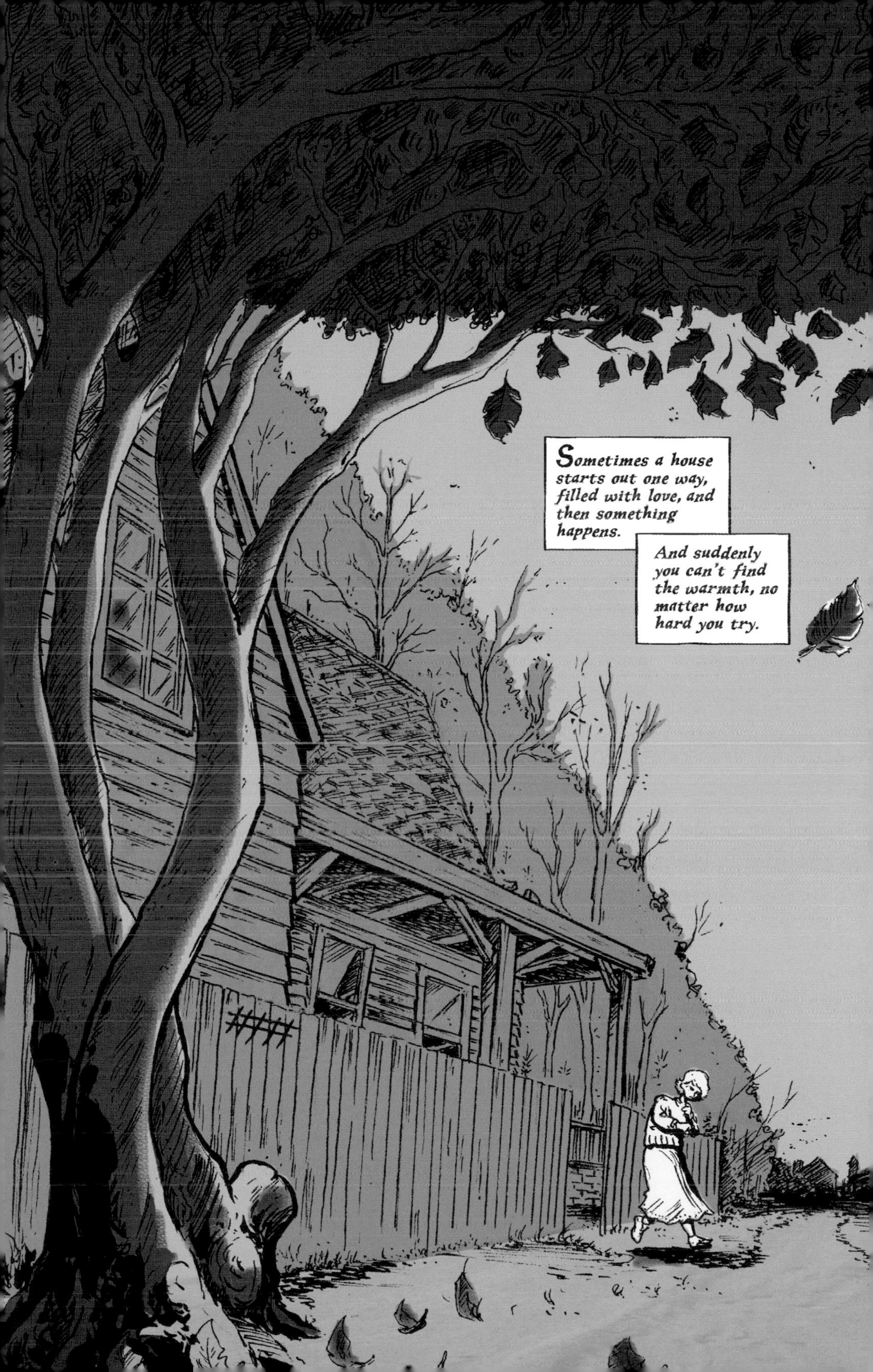
Sometimes a house starts out one way, filled with love, and then something happens.
And suddenly you can't find the warmth, no matter how hard you try.

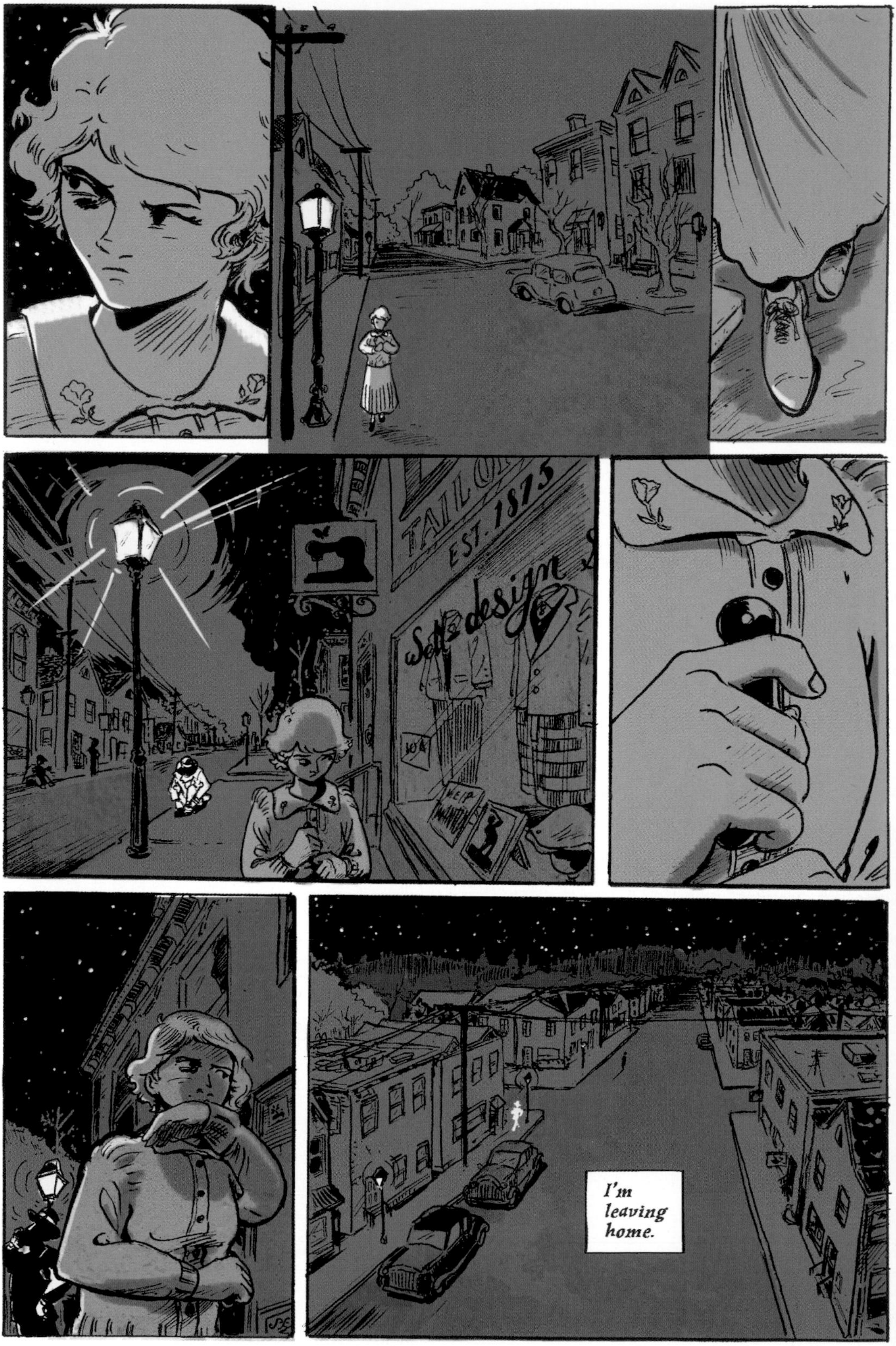
EST. 1875
I'm leaving home.

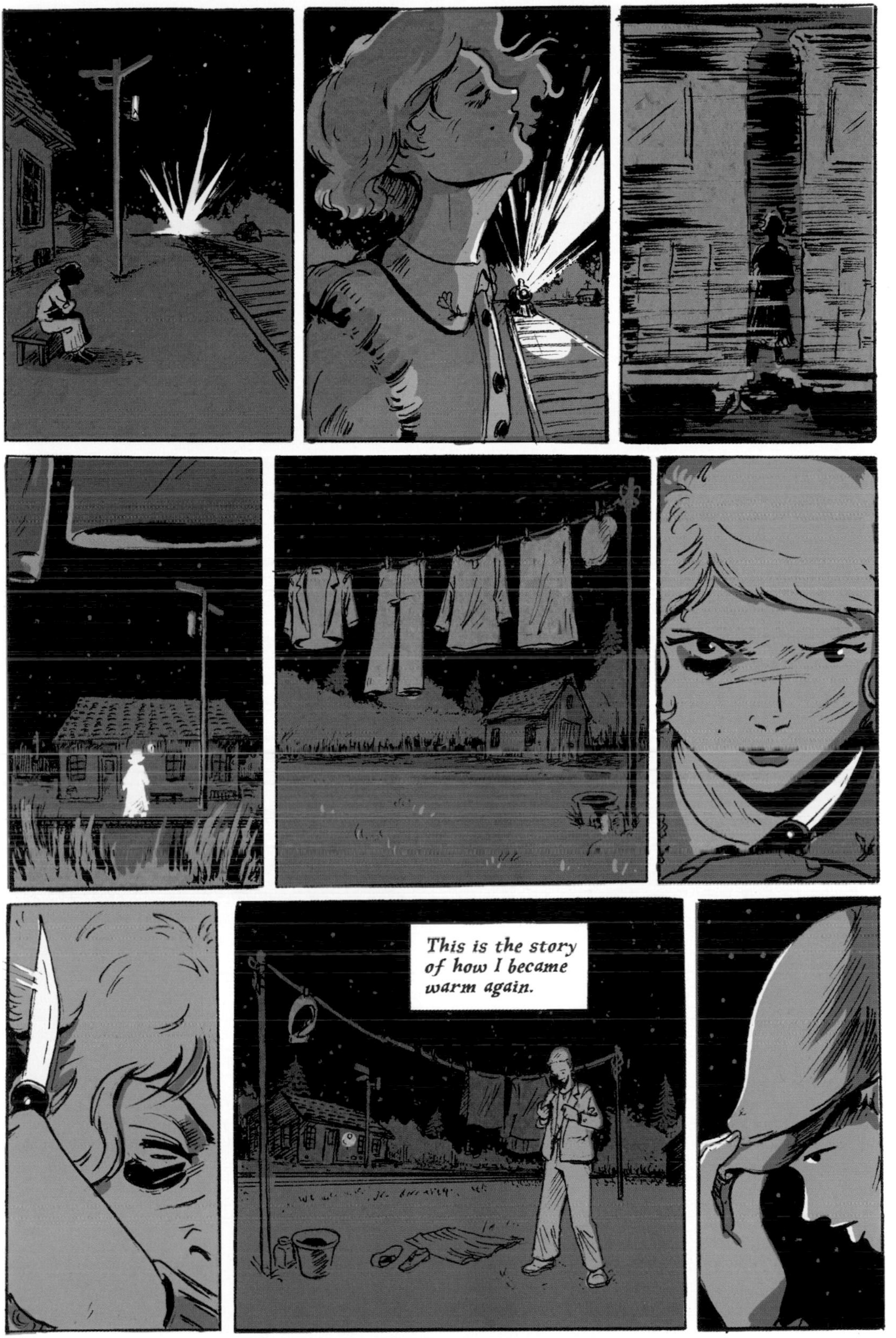
This is the story
of how I became
warm again.

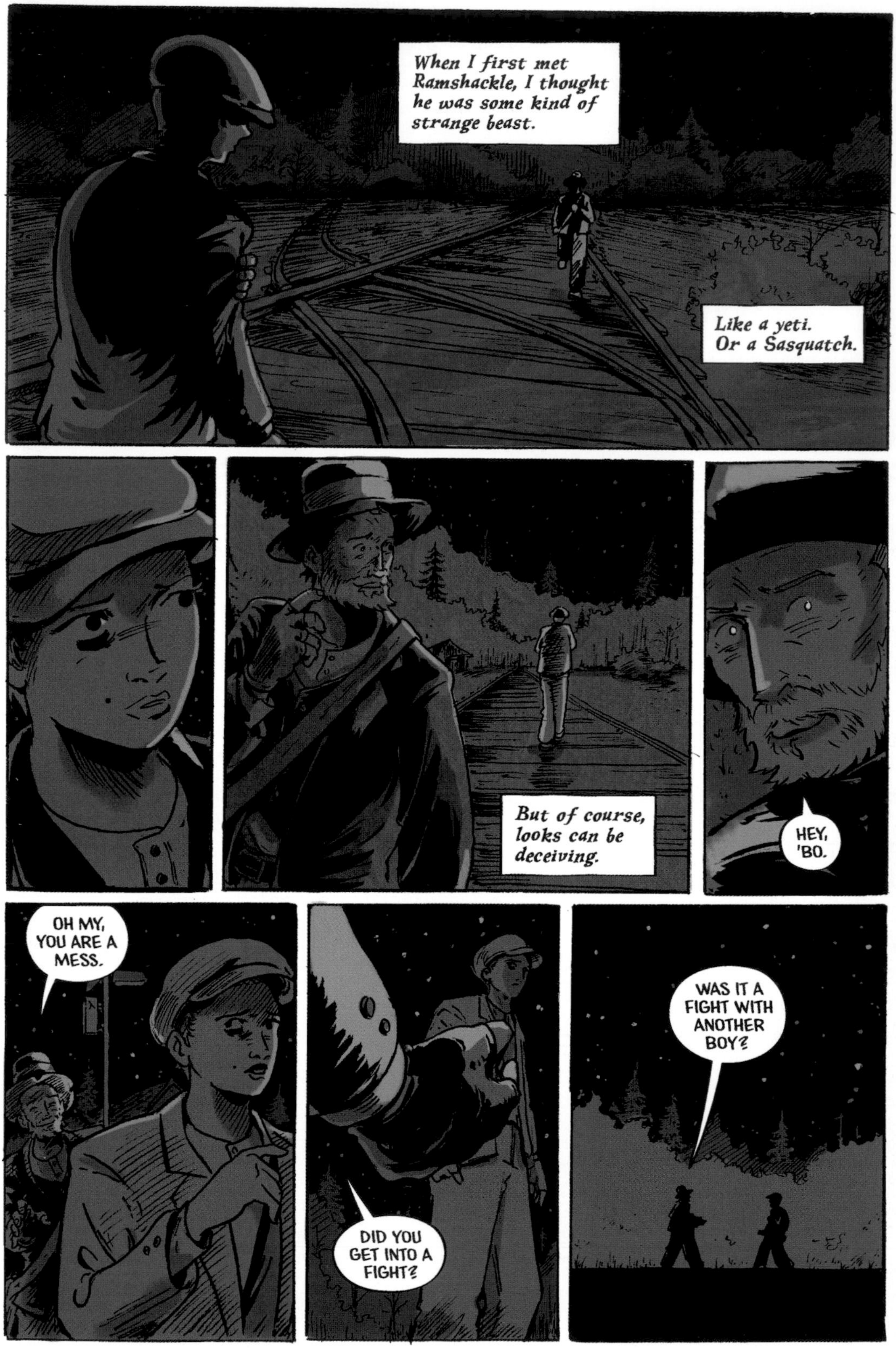
When I first met Ramshackle, I thought he was some kind of strange beast.
Like a yeti. Or a Sasquatch.
But of course, looks can be deceiving.
HEY, 'BO.
OH MY, YOU ARE A MESS.
DID YOU GET INTO A FIGHT?
WAS IT A FIGHT WITH ANOTHER BOY?

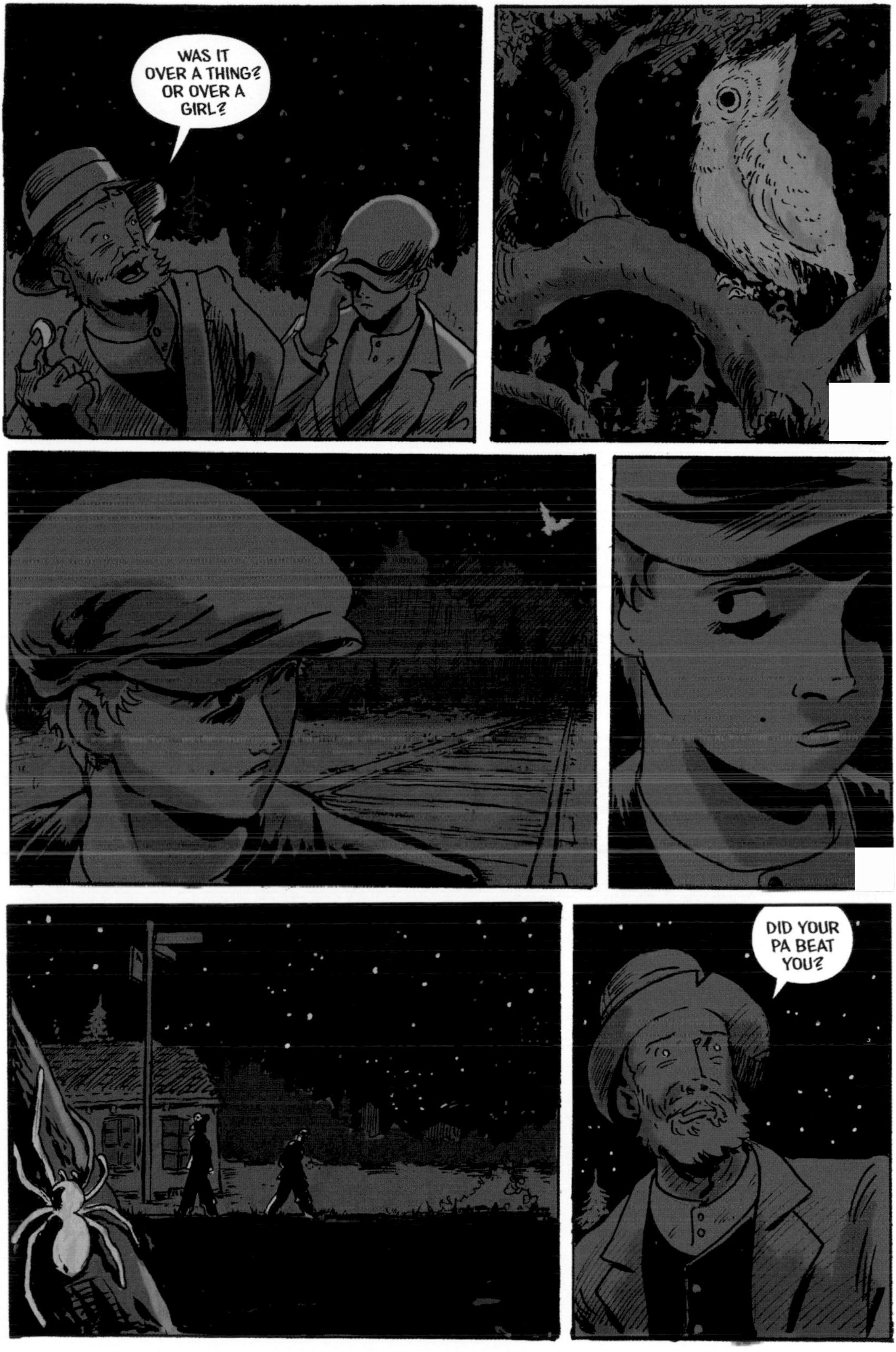
WAS IT OVER A THING? OR OVER A GIRL?
DID YOUR PA BEAT YOU?

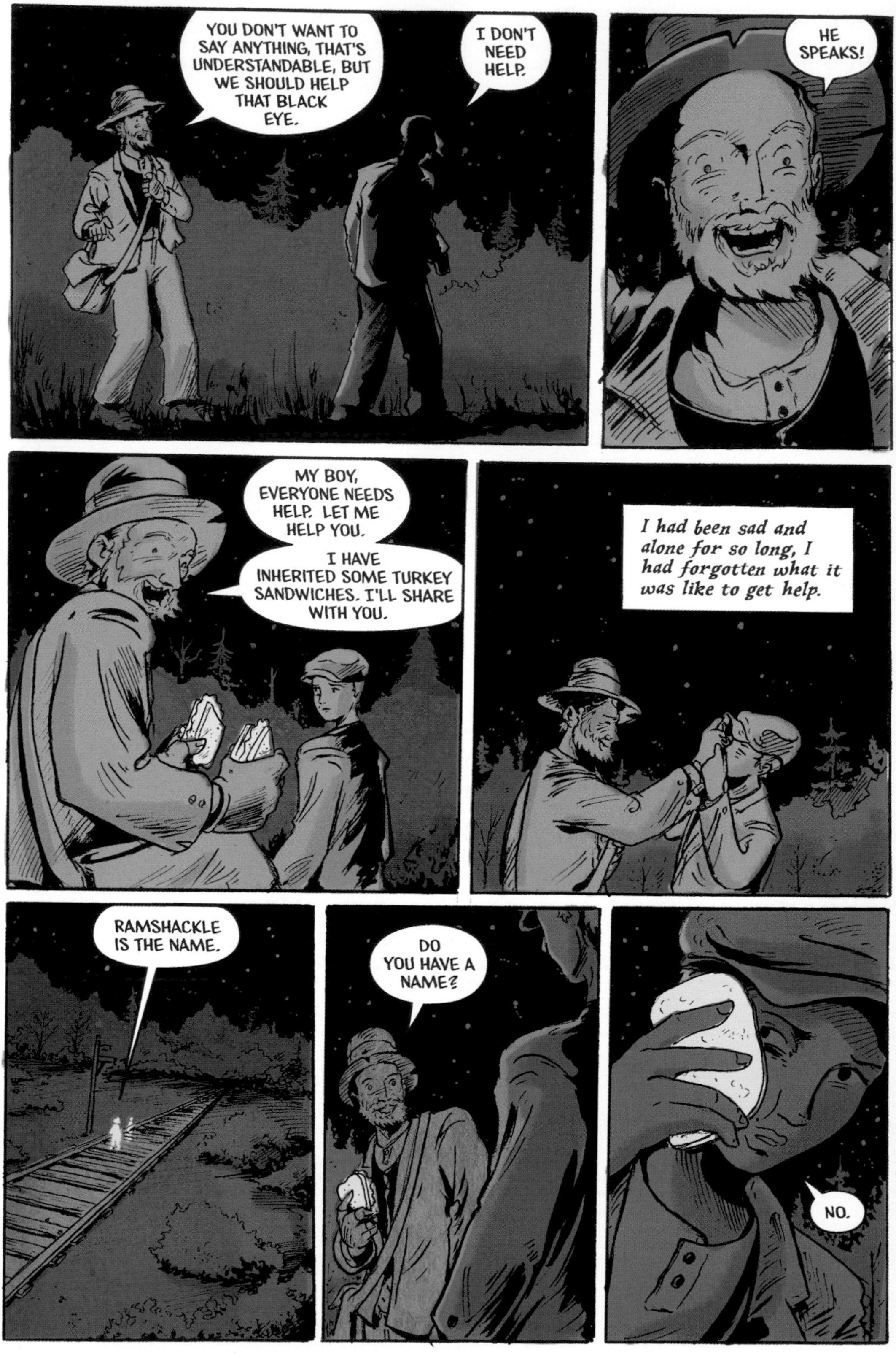
YOU DON'T WANT TO SAY ANYTHING, THAT'S UNDERSTANDABLE, BUT WE SHOULD HELP THAT BLACK EYE.
I DON'T NEED HELP.
HE SPEAKS!
MY BOY, EVERYONE NEEDS HELP. LET ME HELP YOU.
I HAVE INHERITED SOME TURKEY SANDWICHES. I'LL SHARE WITH YOU.
I had been sad and alone for so long, I had forgotten what it was like to get help.
RAMSHACKLE IS THE NAME.
DO YOU HAVE A NAME?
NO.

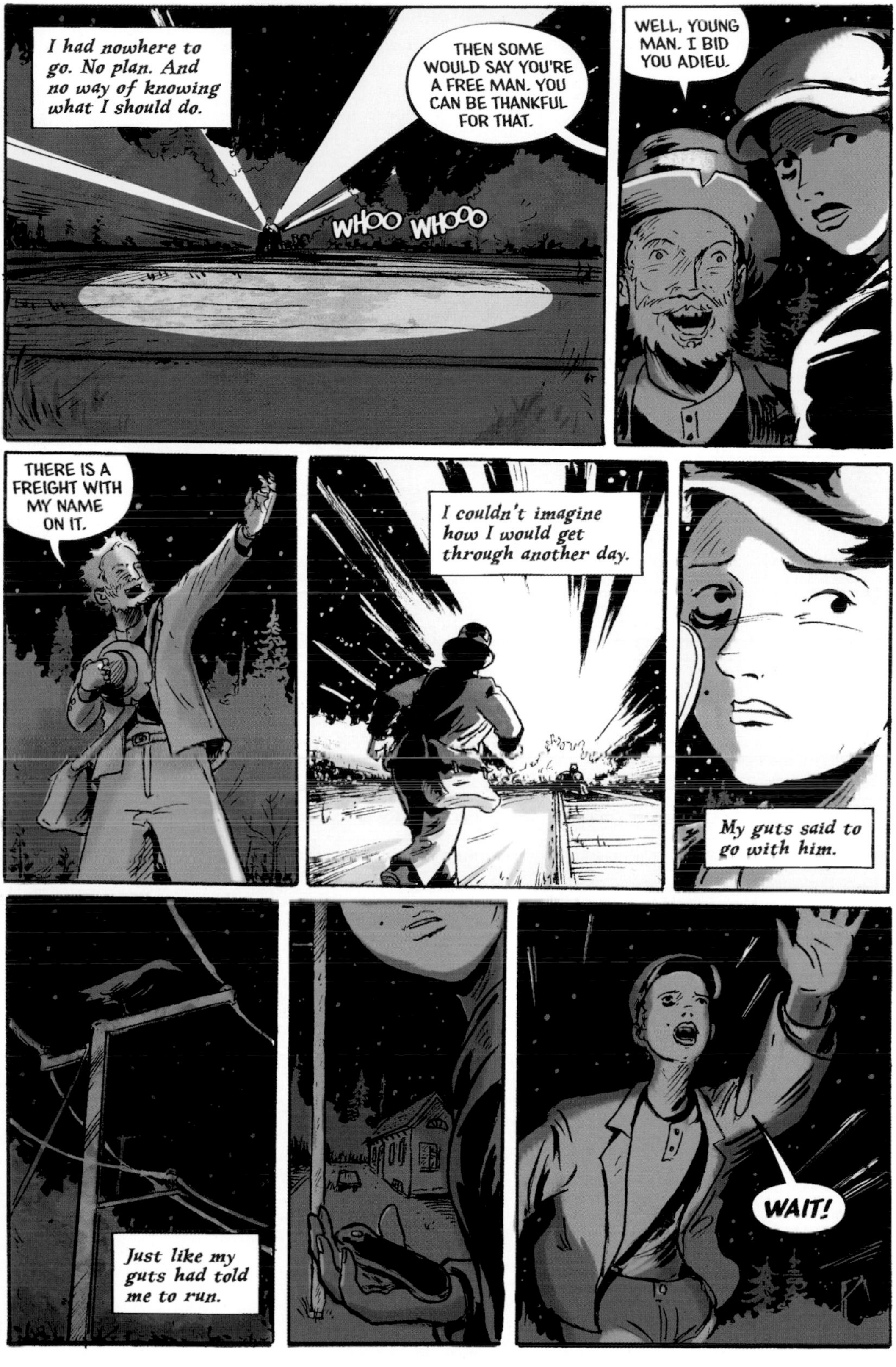
I had nowhere to go. No plan. And no way of knowing what I should do.
THEN SOME WOULD SAY YOU'RE A FREE MAN. YOU CAN BE THANKFUL FOR THAT.
WHOO WHOOO
WELL, YOUNG MAN. I BID YOU ADIEU.
THERE IS A FREIGHT WITH MY NAME ON IT.
I couldn't imagine how I would get through another day.
My guts said to go with him.
Just like my guts had told me to run.
WAIT!

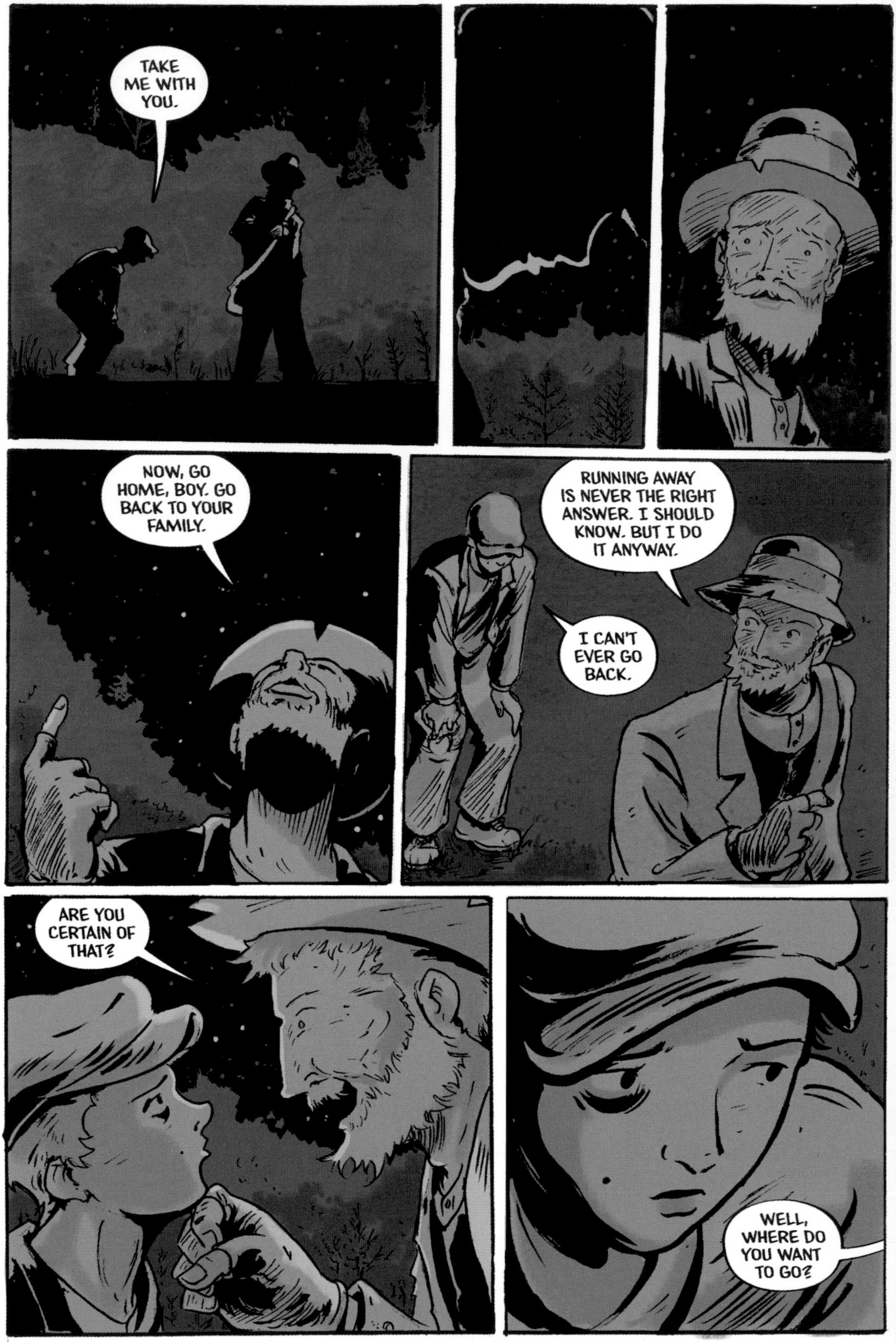
TAKE ME WITH YOU.
NOW, GO HOME, BOY. GO BACK TO YOUR FAMILY.
RUNNING AWAY IS NEVER THE RIGHT ANSWER. I SHOULD KNOW. BUT I DO IT ANYWAY.
I CAN'T EVER GO BACK.
ARE YOU CERTAIN OF THAT?
WELL, WHERE DO YOU WANT TO GO?

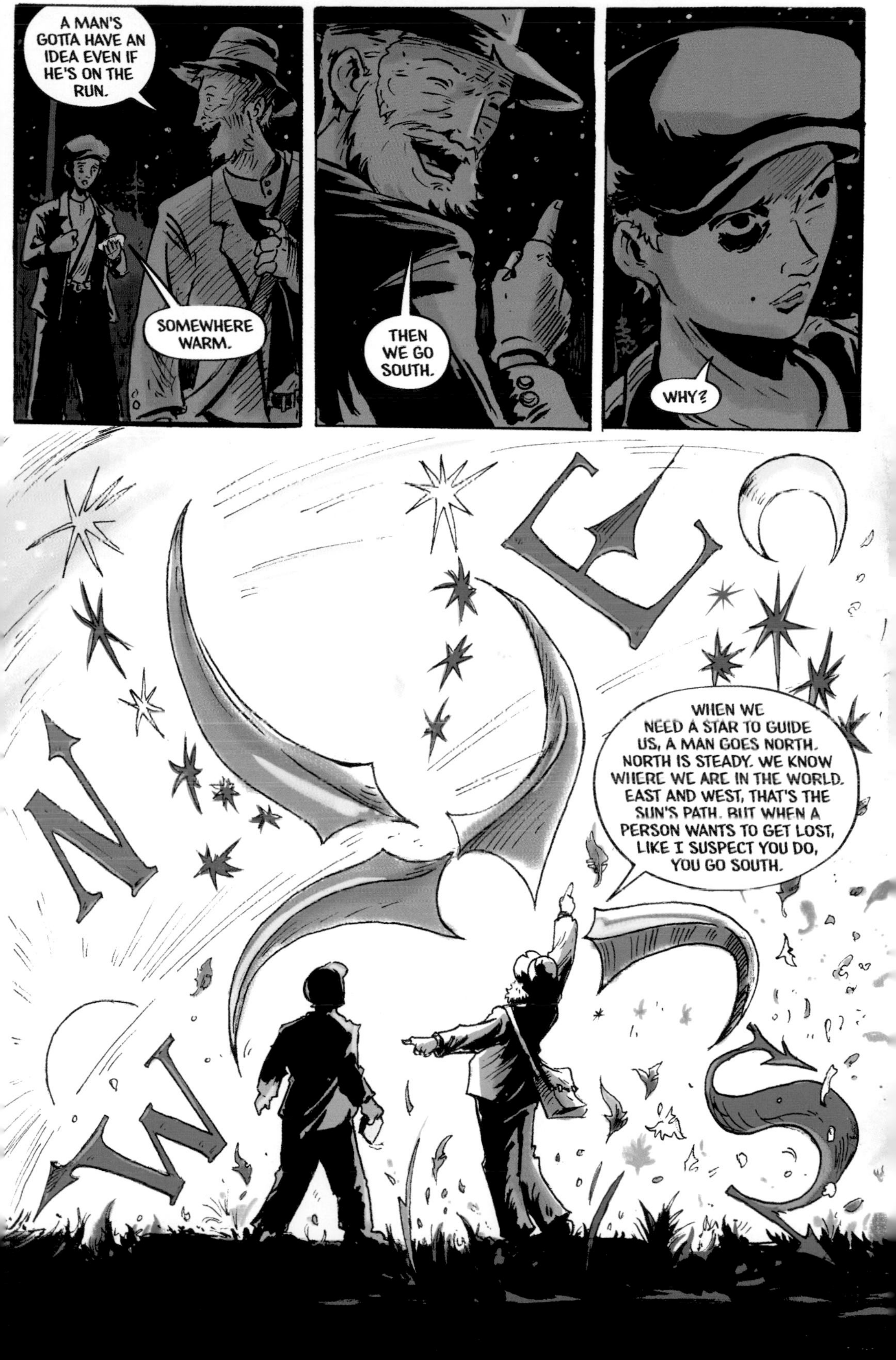
A MAN'S GOTTA HAVE AN IDEA EVEN IF HE'S ON THE RUN.
SOMEWHERE WARM.
THEN WE GO SOUTH.
WHY?
N
E
S
W
WHEN WE NEED A STAR TO GUIDE US, A MAN GOES NORTH. NORTH IS STEADY. WE KNOW WHERE WE ARE IN THE WORLD. EAST AND WEST, THAT'S THE SUN'S PATH. BUT WHEN A PERSON WANTS TO GET LOST, LIKE I SUSPECT YOU DO, YOU GO SOUTH.

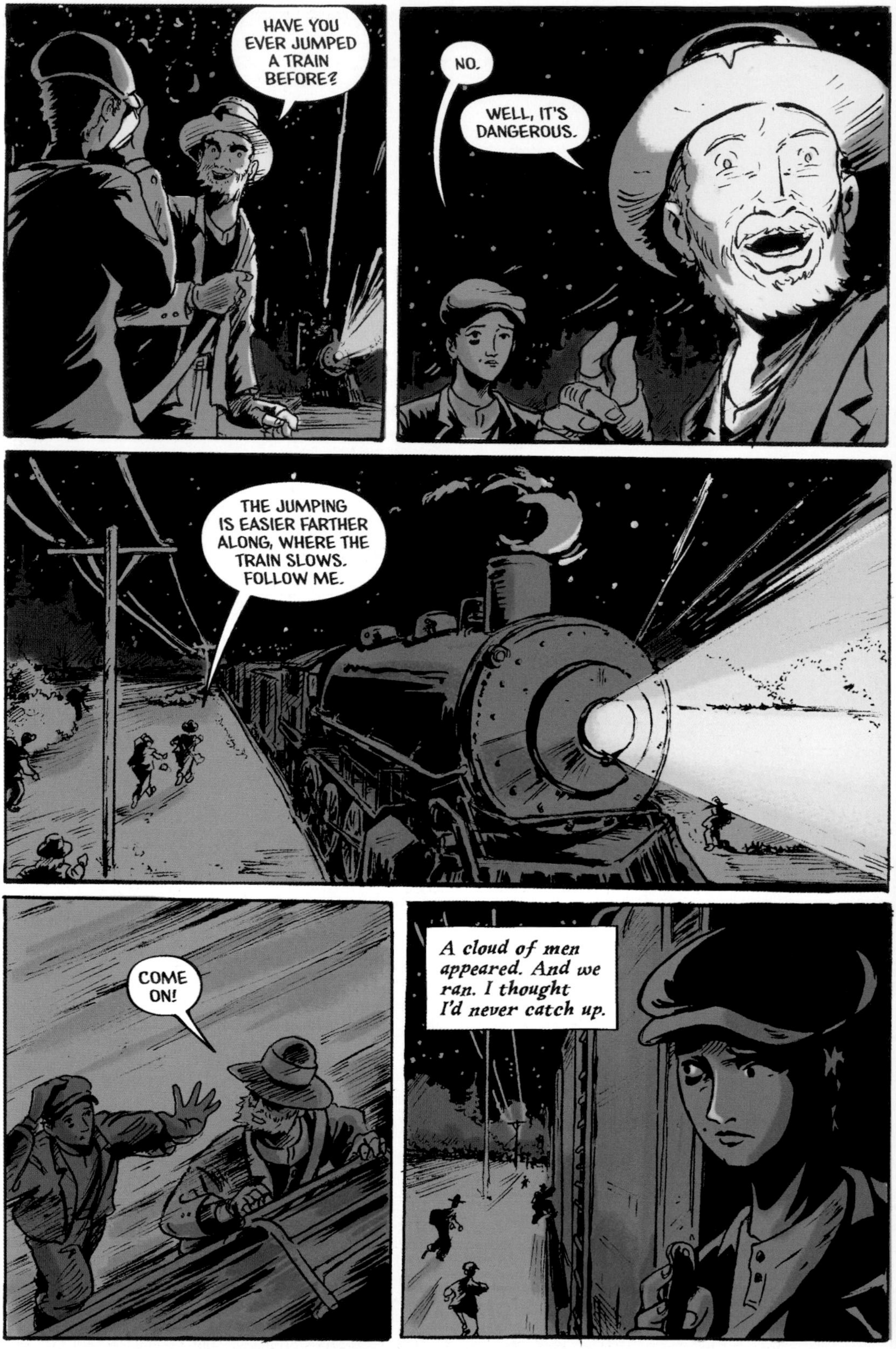
HAVE YOU EVER JUMPED A TRAIN BEFORE?
NO.
WELL, IT'S DANGEROUS.
THE JUMPING IS EASIER FARTHER ALONG, WHERE THE TRAIN SLOWS. FOLLOW ME.
COME ON!
A cloud of men appeared. And we ran. I thought I'd never catch up.

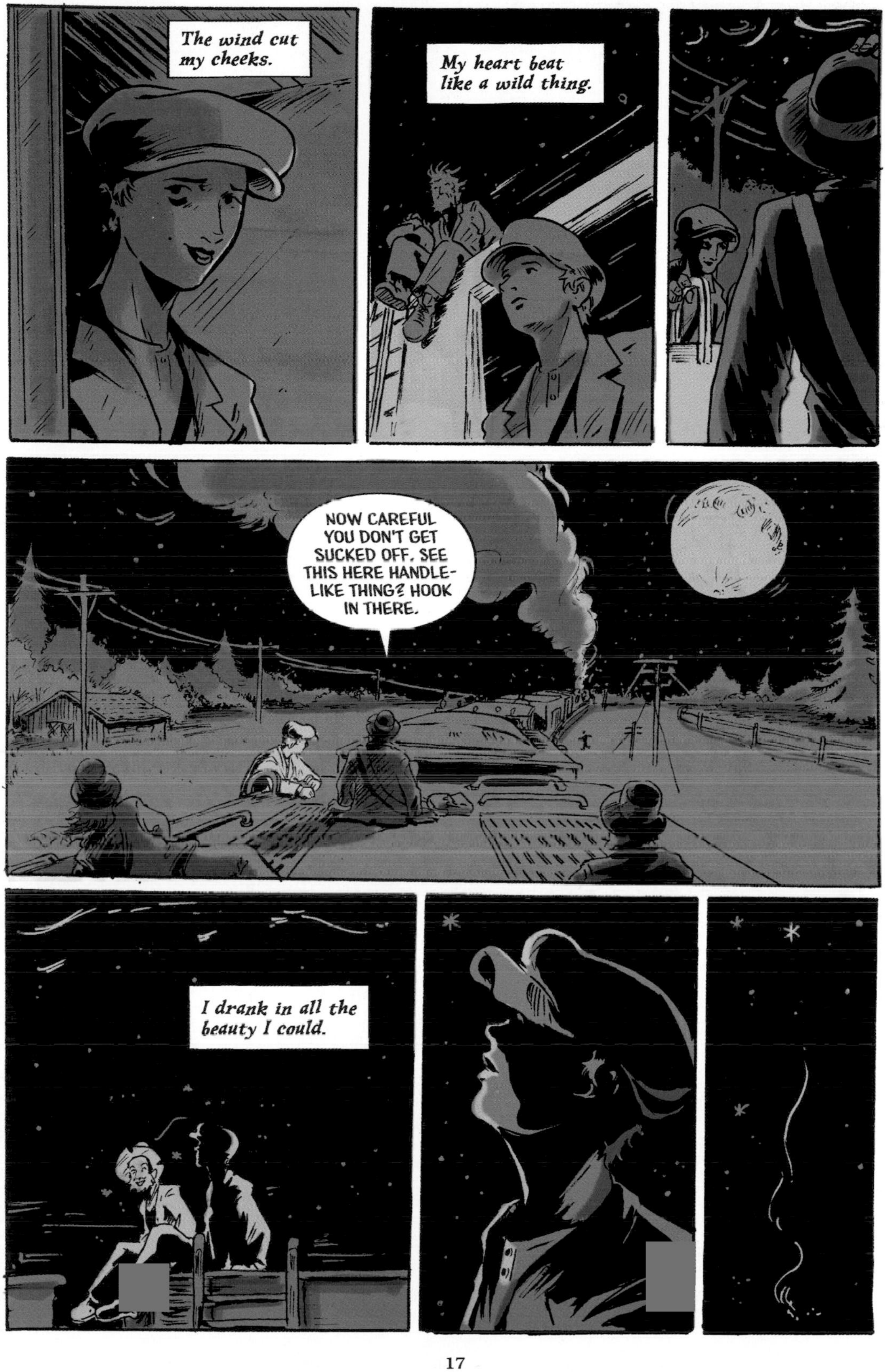
The wind cut my cheeks.
My heart beat like a wild thing.
NOW CAREFUL YOU DON'T GET SUCKED OFF. SEE THIS HERE HANDLE-LIKE THING? HOOK IN THERE.
I drank in all the beauty I could.

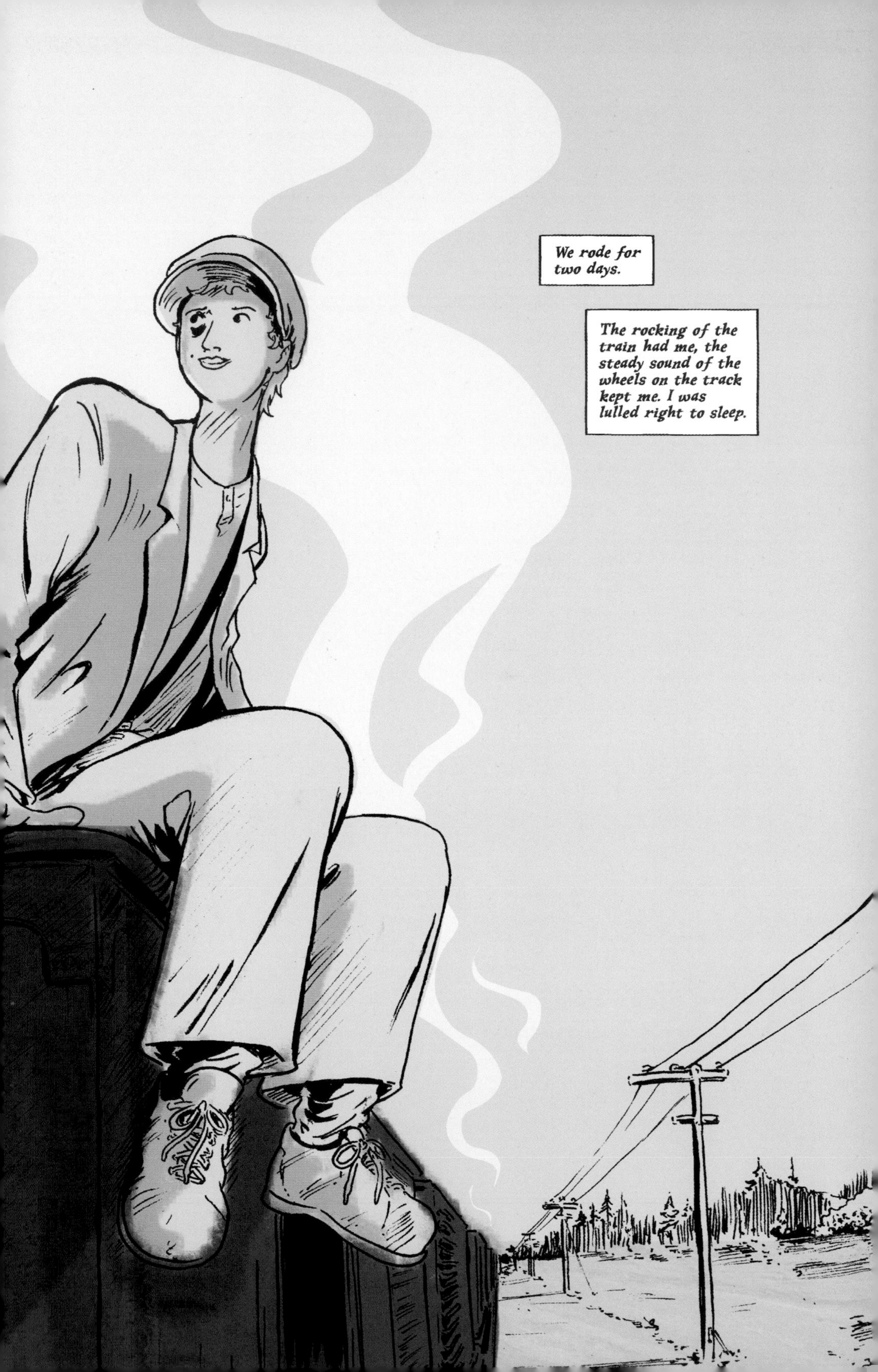
We rode for two days.
The rocking of the train had me, the steady sound of the wheels on the track kept me. I was lulled right to sleep.

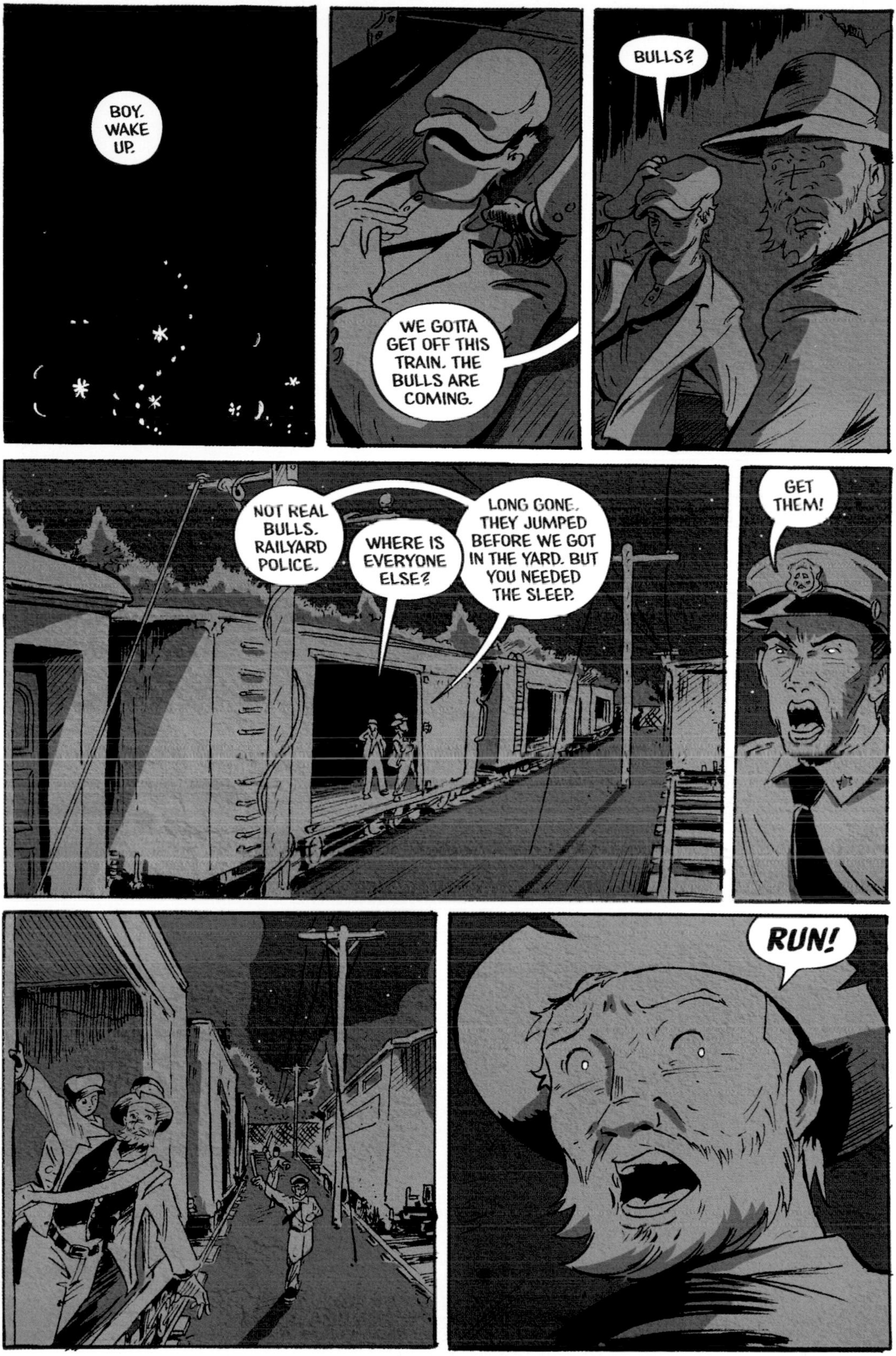
BOY. WAKE UP.
WE GOTTA GET OFF THIS TRAIN. THE BULLS ARE COMING.
BULLS?
NOT REAL BULLS. RAILYARD POLICE.
WHERE IS EVERYONE ELSE?
LONG GONE. THEY JUMPED BEFORE WE GOT IN THE YARD. BUT YOU NEEDED THE SLEEP.
GET THEM!
RUN!

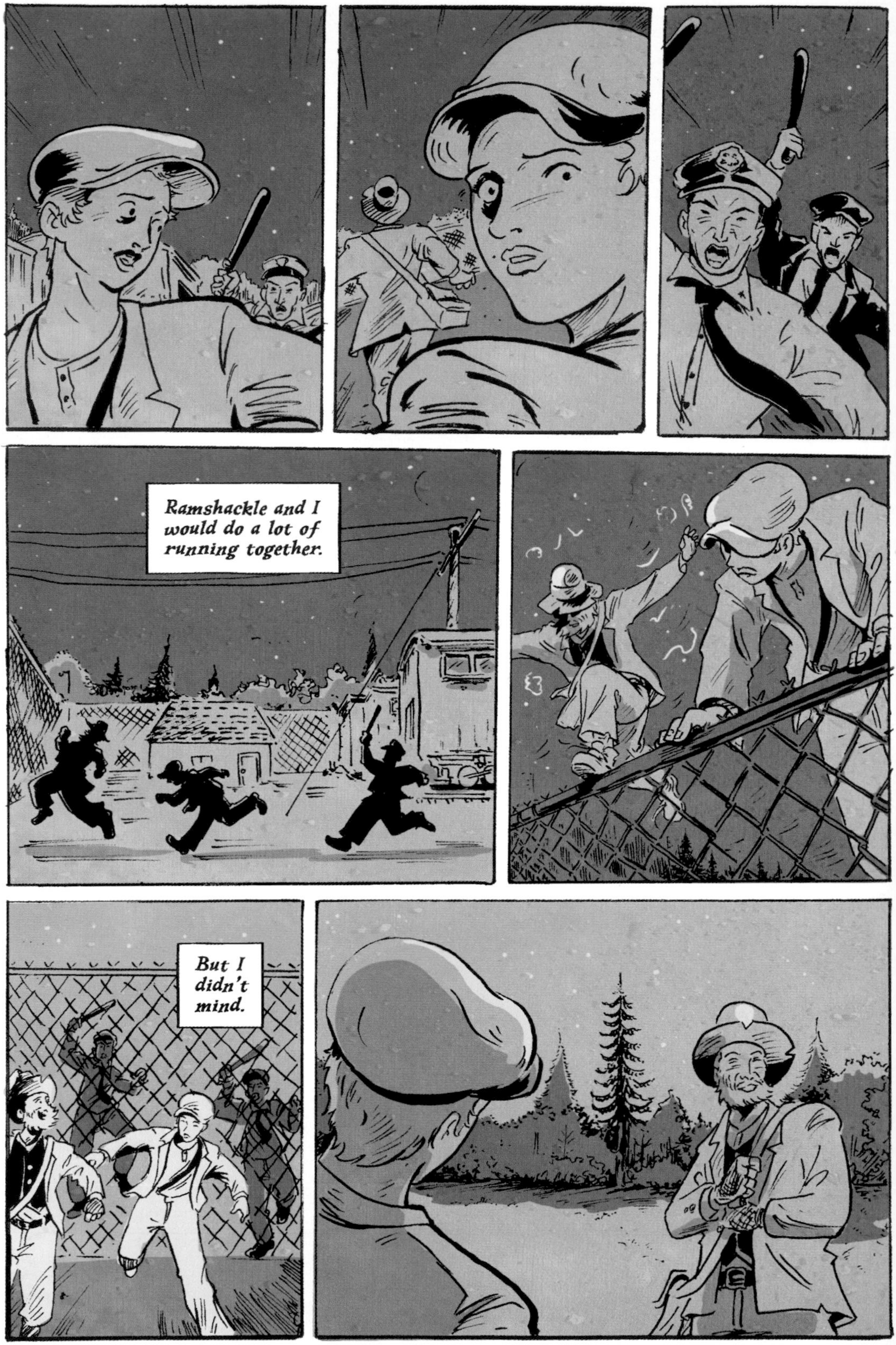
Ramshackle and I would do a lot of running together.
But I didn't mind.

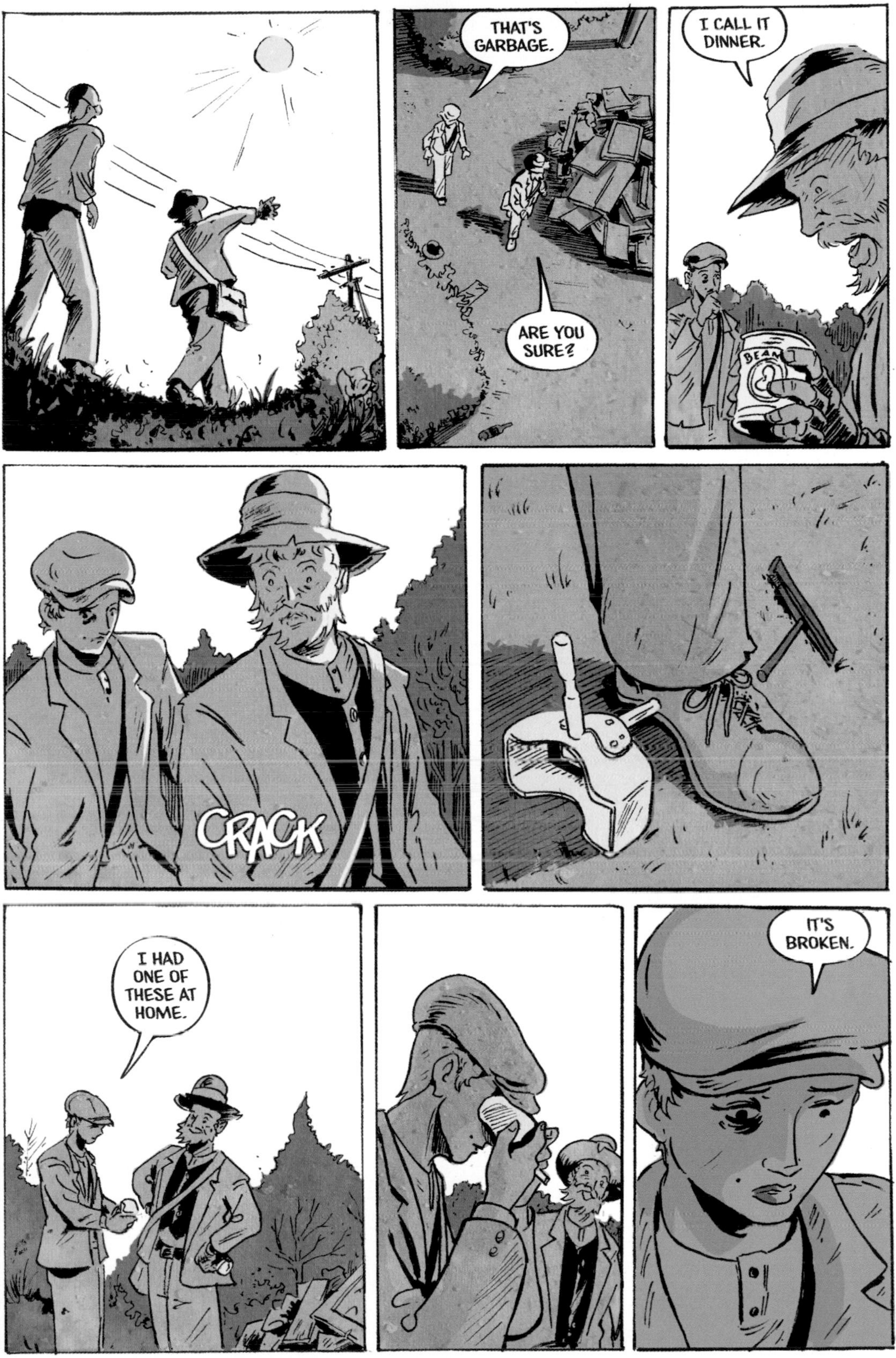
THAT'S GARBAGE.
ARE YOU SURE?
I CALL IT DINNER.
BEANS
CRACK
I HAD ONE OF THESE AT HOME.
IT'S BROKEN.

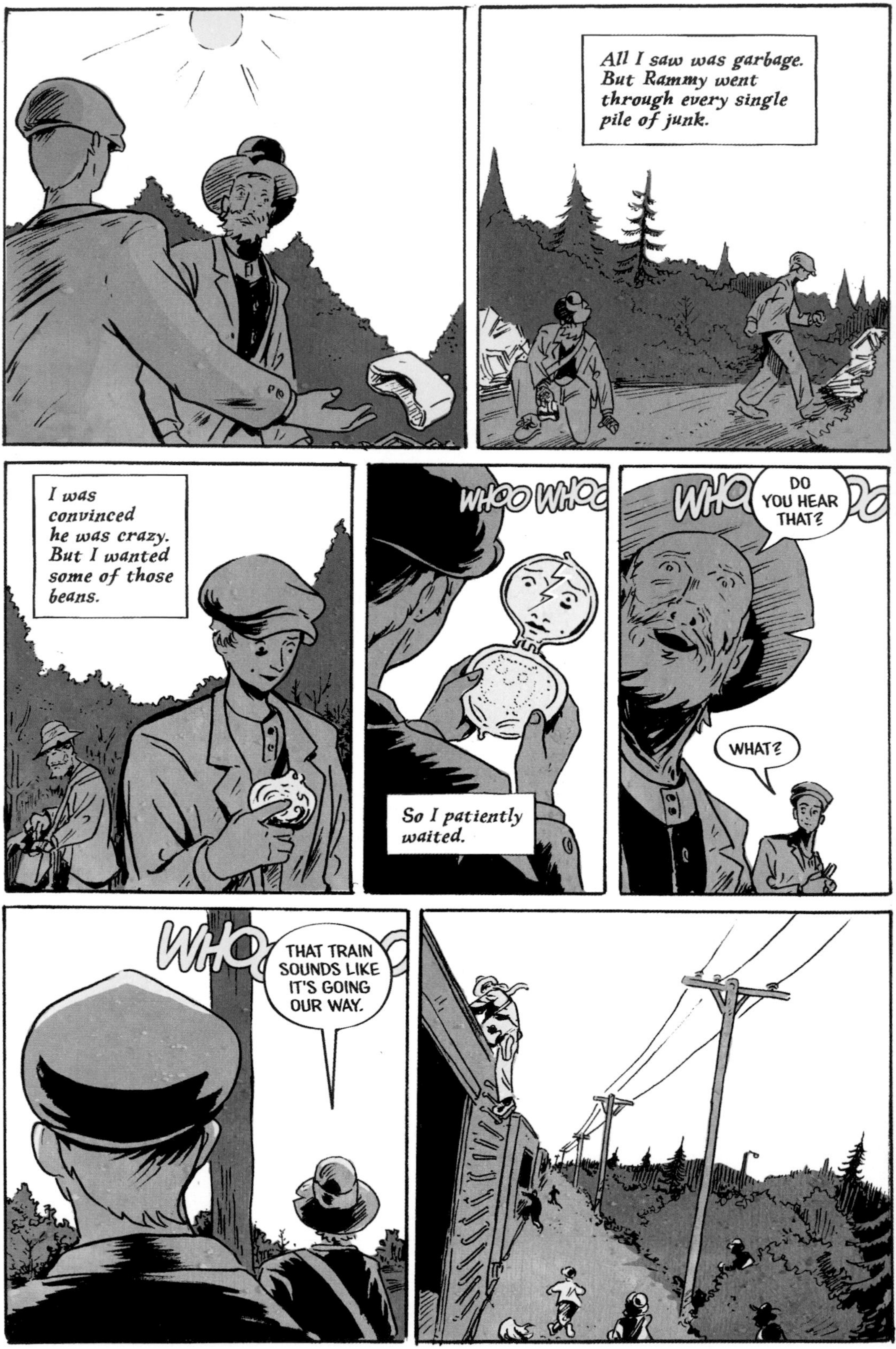
All I saw was garbage. But Rammy went through every single pile of junk.
I was convinced he was crazy. But I wanted some of those beans.
WHOO WHOO
So I patiently waited.
DO YOU HEAR THAT?
WHAT?
THAT TRAIN SOUNDS LIKE IT'S GOING OUR WAY.

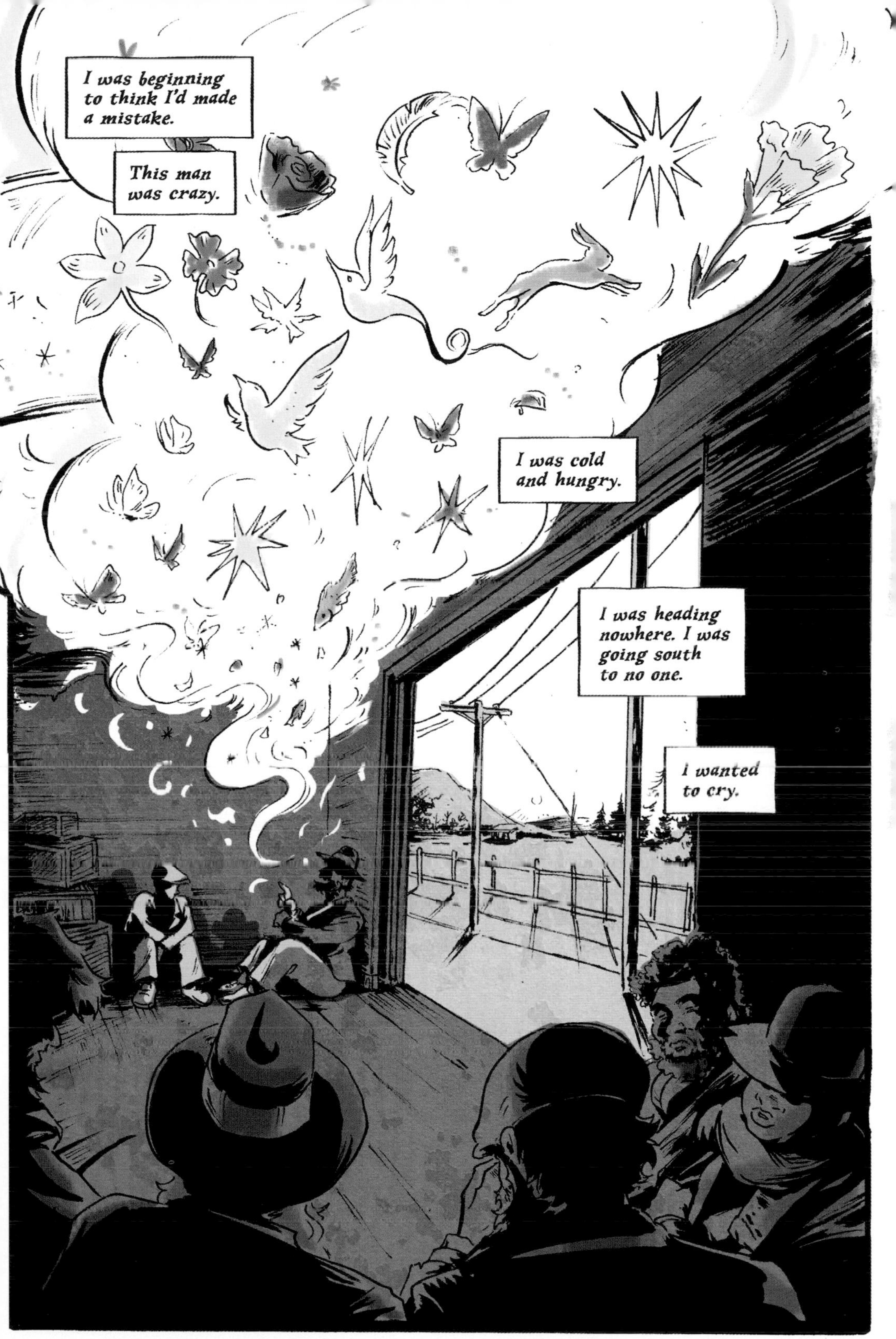
I was beginning to think I'd made a mistake.
This man was crazy.
I was cold and hungry.
I was heading nowhere. I was going south to no one.
I wanted to cry.

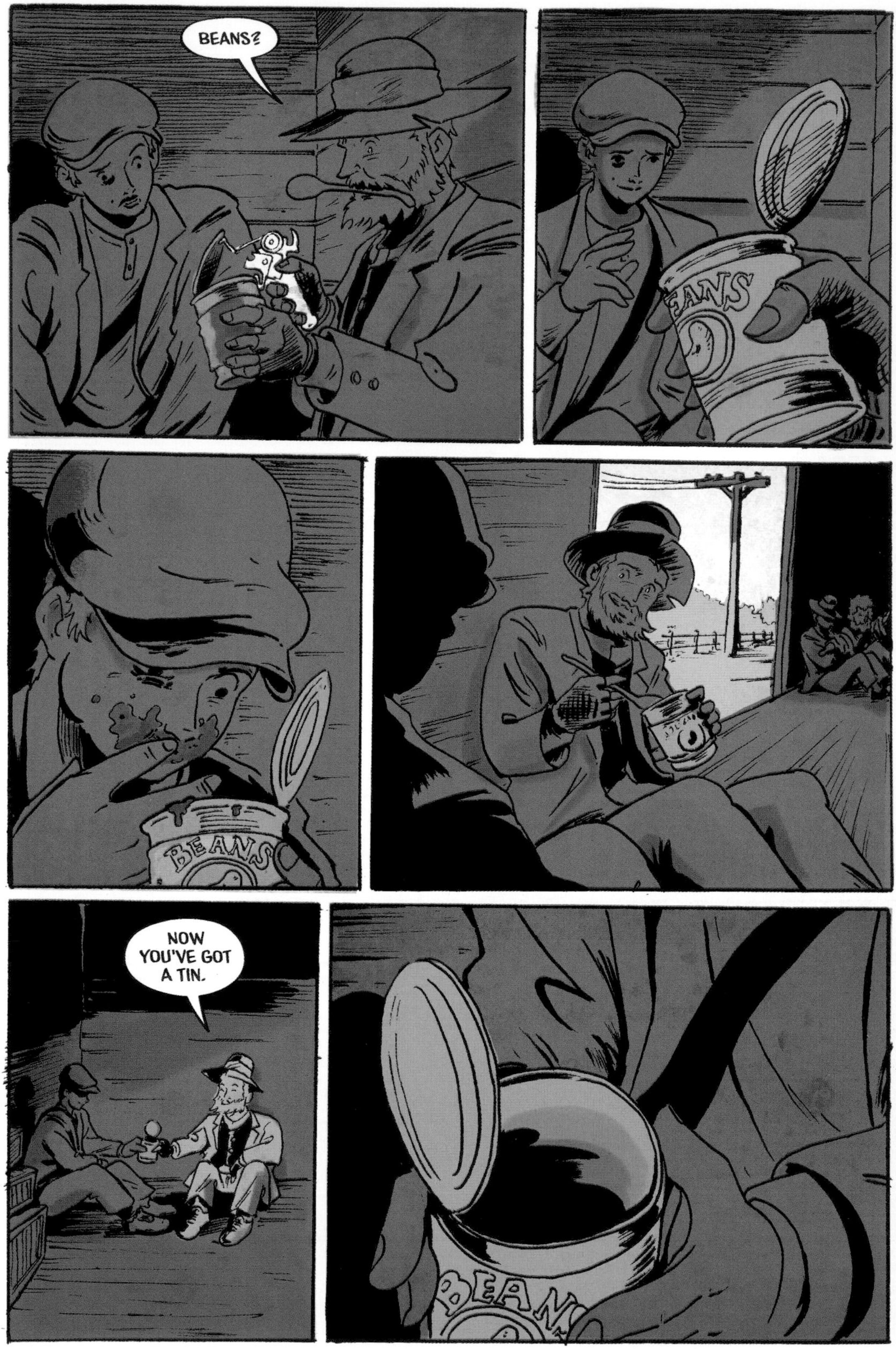
BEANS?
BEANS
BEANS
NOW YOU'VE GOT A TIN.
BEAN

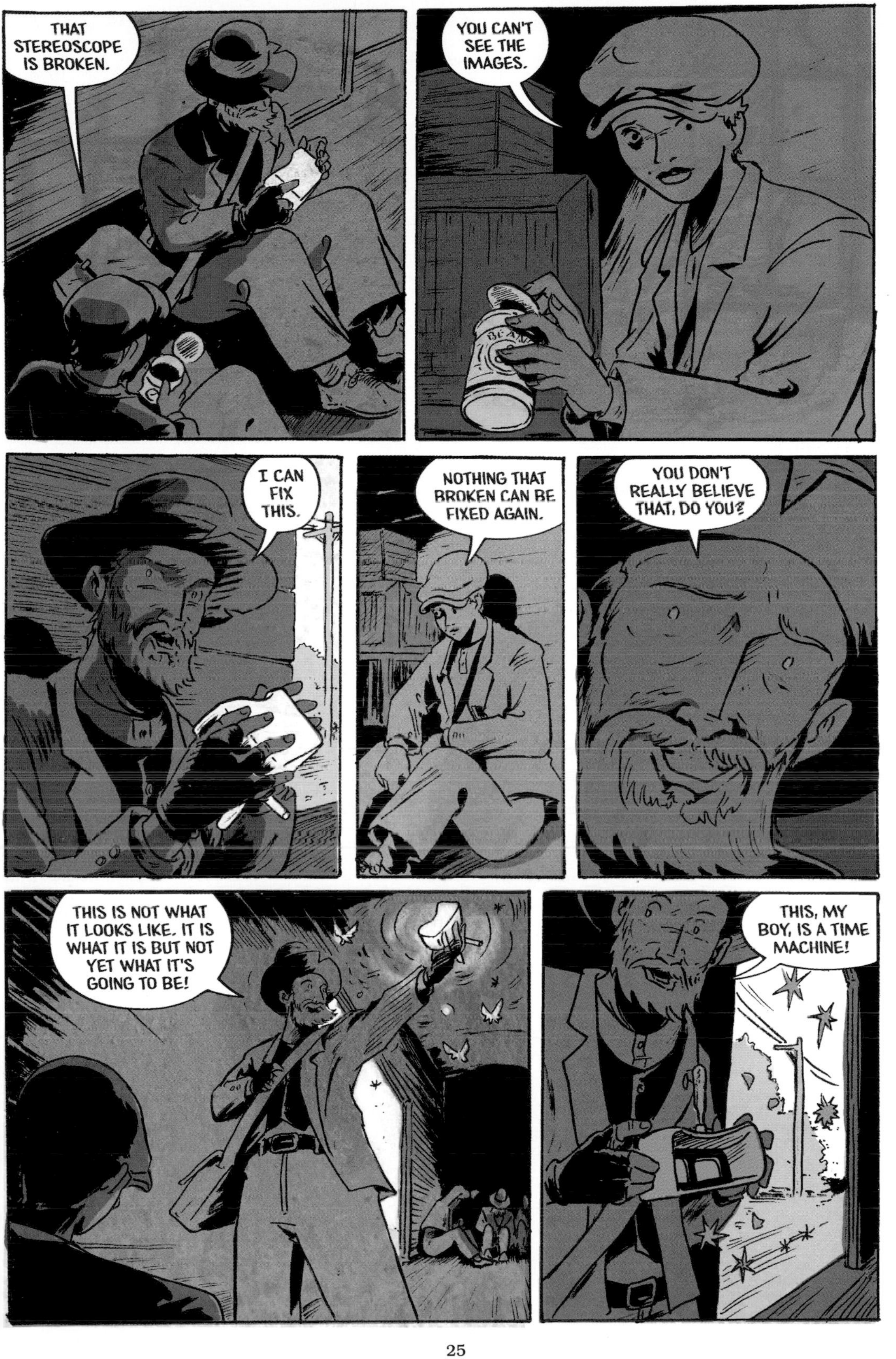
THAT STEREOSCOPE IS BROKEN.
YOU CAN'T SEE THE IMAGES.
I CAN FIX THIS.
NOTHING THAT BROKEN CAN BE FIXED AGAIN.
YOU DON'T REALLY BELIEVE THAT, DO YOU?
THIS IS NOT WHAT IT LOOKS LIKE. IT IS WHAT IT IS BUT NOT YET WHAT IT'S GOING TO BE!
THIS, MY BOY, IS A TIME MACHINE!

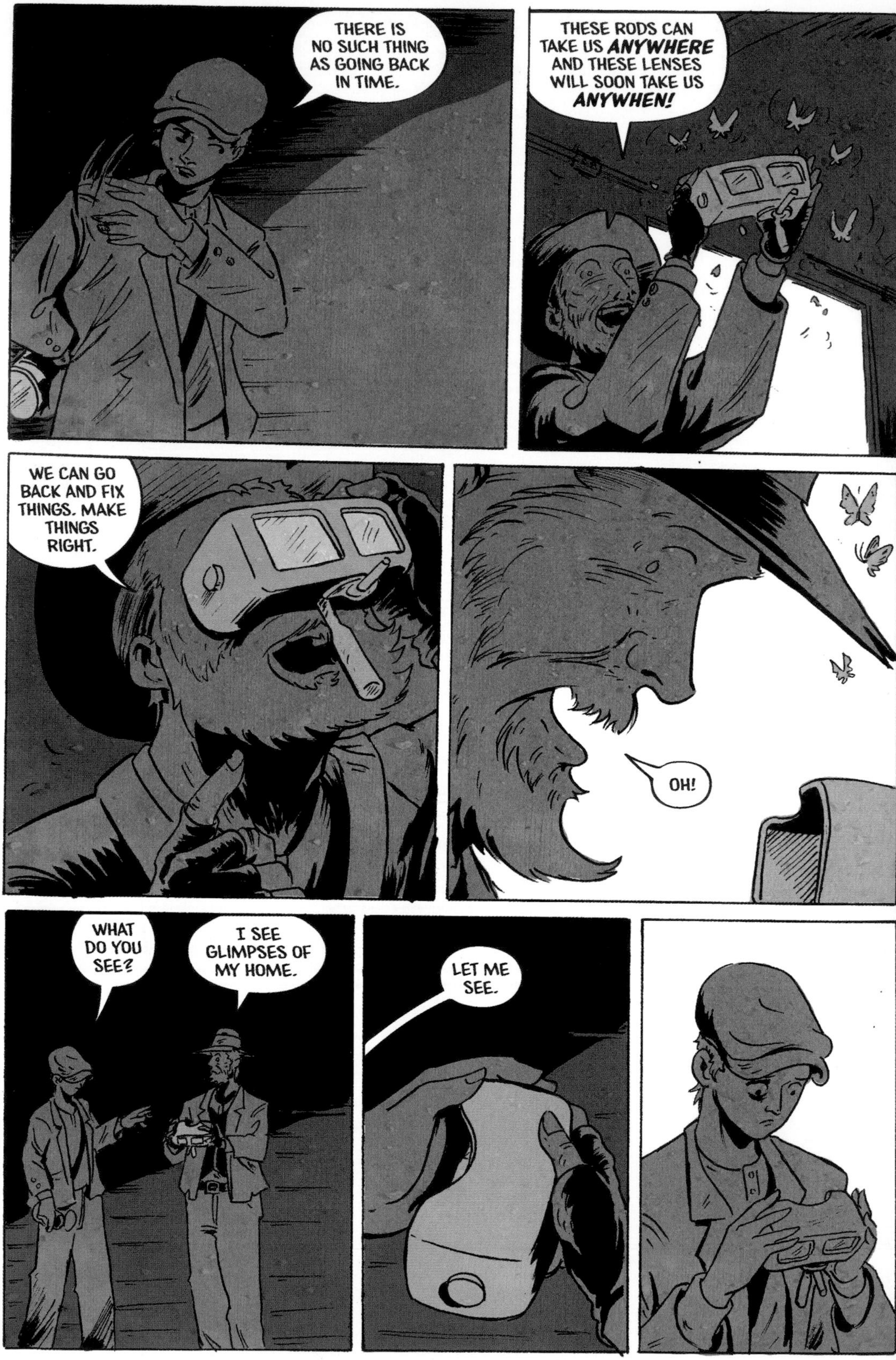
THERE IS NO SUCH THING AS GOING BACK IN TIME.
THESE RODS CAN TAKE US ANYWHERE AND THESE LENSES WILL SOON TAKE US ANYWHEN!
WE CAN GO BACK AND FIX THINGS. MAKE THINGS RIGHT.
OH!
WHAT DO YOU SEE?
I SEE GLIMPSES OF MY HOME.
LET ME SEE.

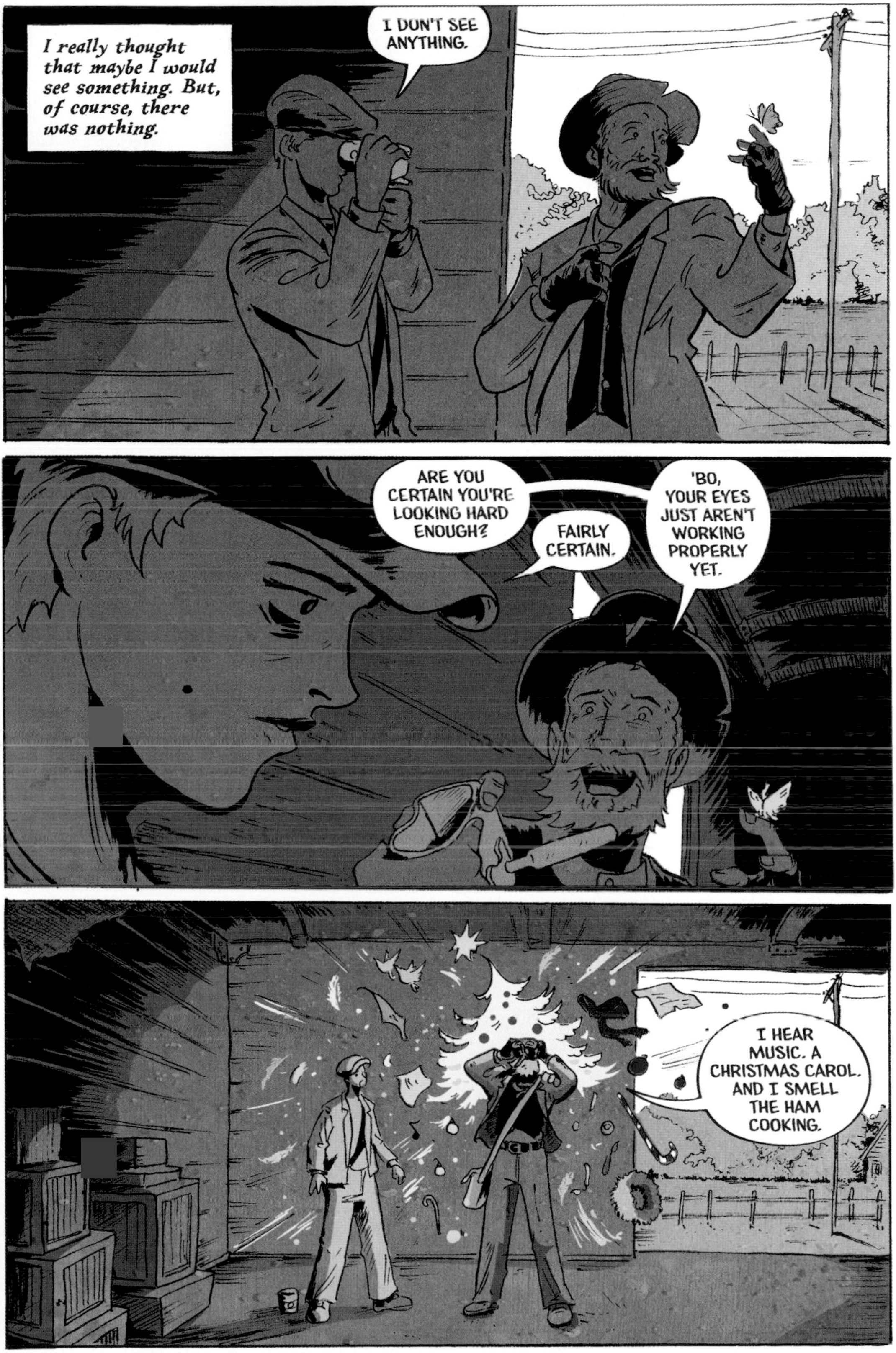
I really thought that maybe I would see something. But, of course, there was nothing.
I DON'T SEE ANYTHING.
ARE YOU CERTAIN YOU'RE LOOKING HARD ENOUGH?
FAIRLY CERTAIN.
'BO, YOUR EYES JUST AREN'T WORKING PROPERLY YET.
I HEAR MUSIC. A CHRISTMAS CAROL. AND I SMELL THE HAM COOKING.

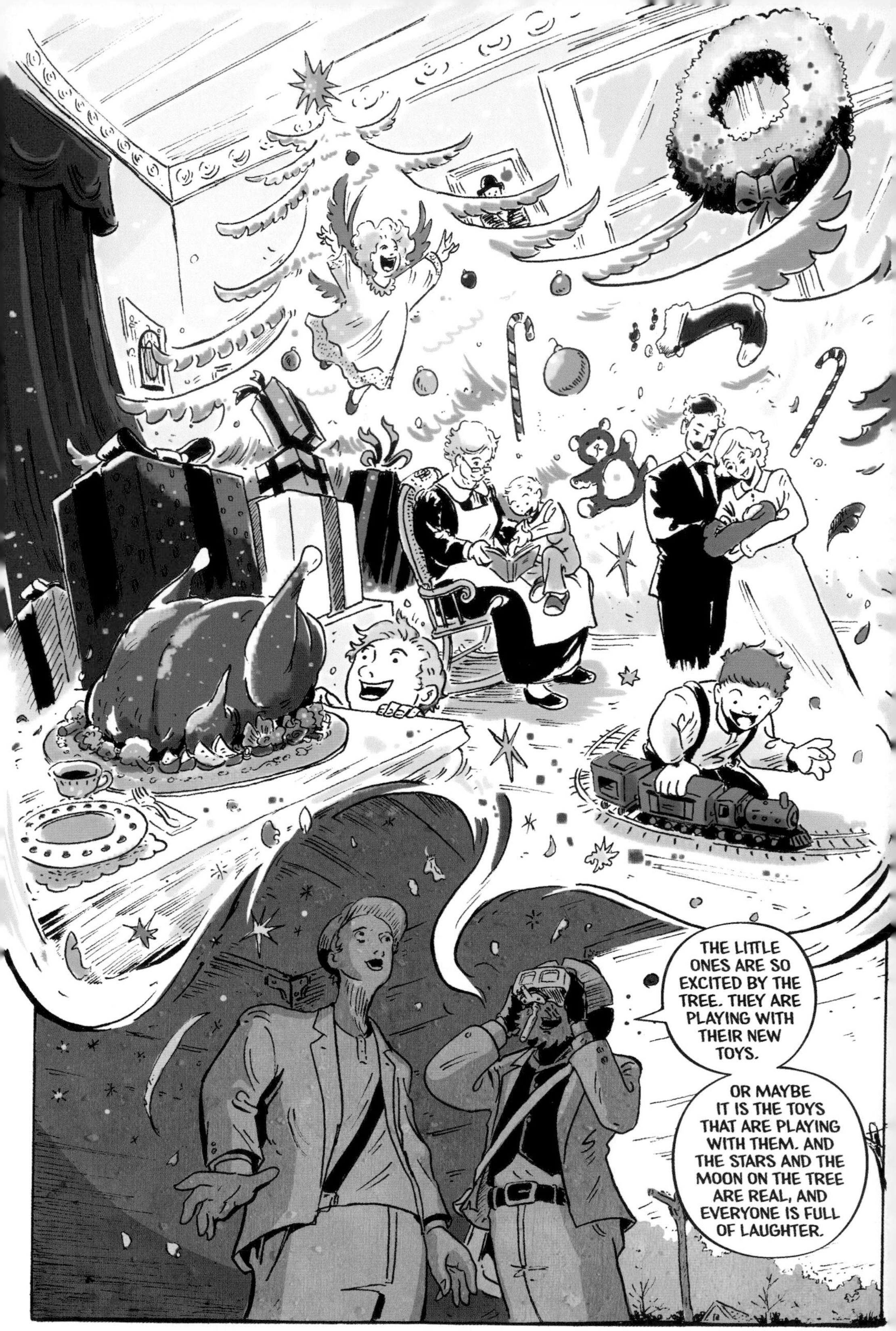
THE LITTLE ONES ARE SO EXCITED BY THE TREE. THEY ARE PLAYING WITH THEIR NEW TOYS.
OR MAYBE IT IS THE TOYS THAT ARE PLAYING WITH THEM. AND THE STARS AND THE MOON ON THE TREE ARE REAL, AND EVERYONE IS FULL OF LAUGHTER.

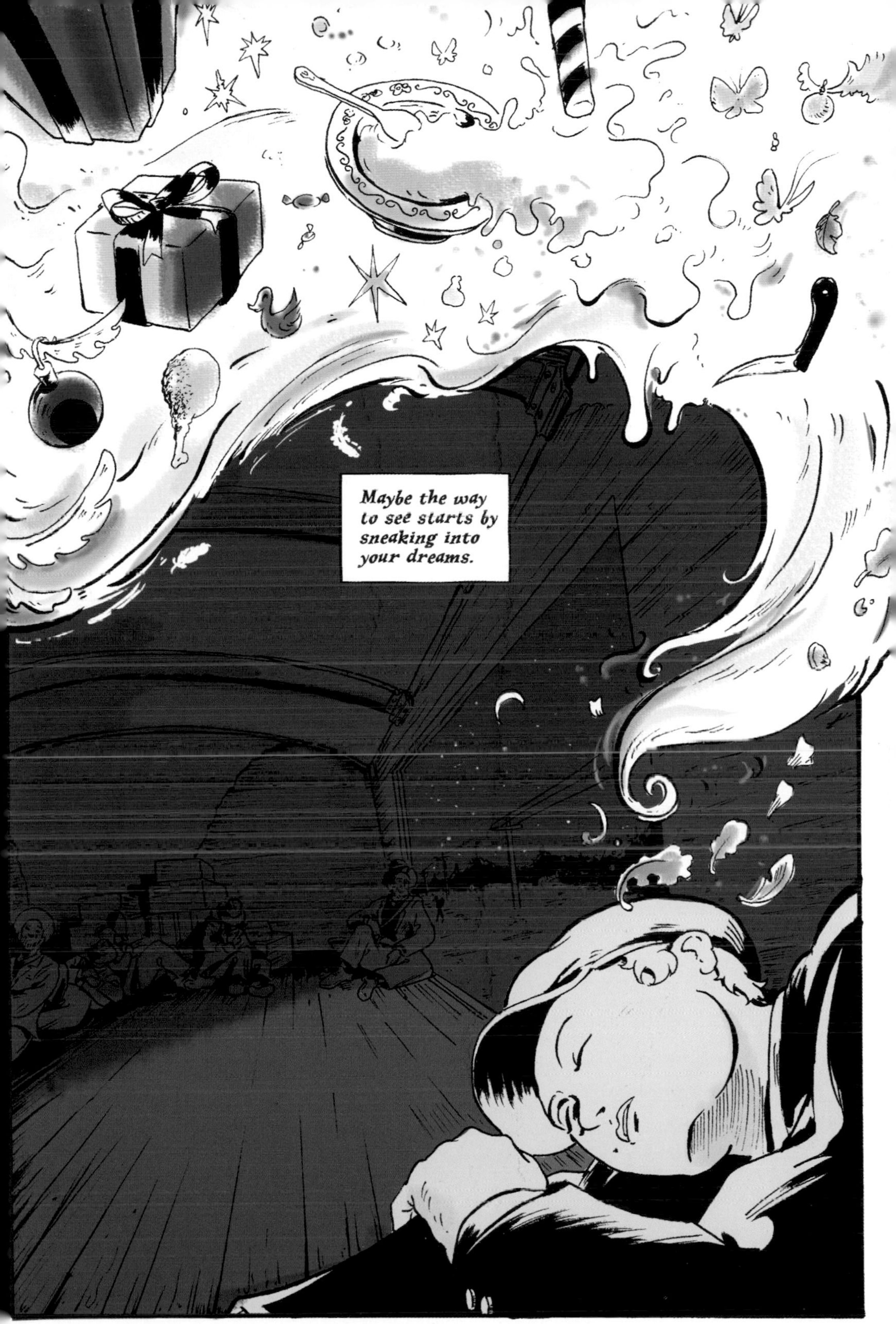
Maybe the way to see starts by sneaking into your dreams.

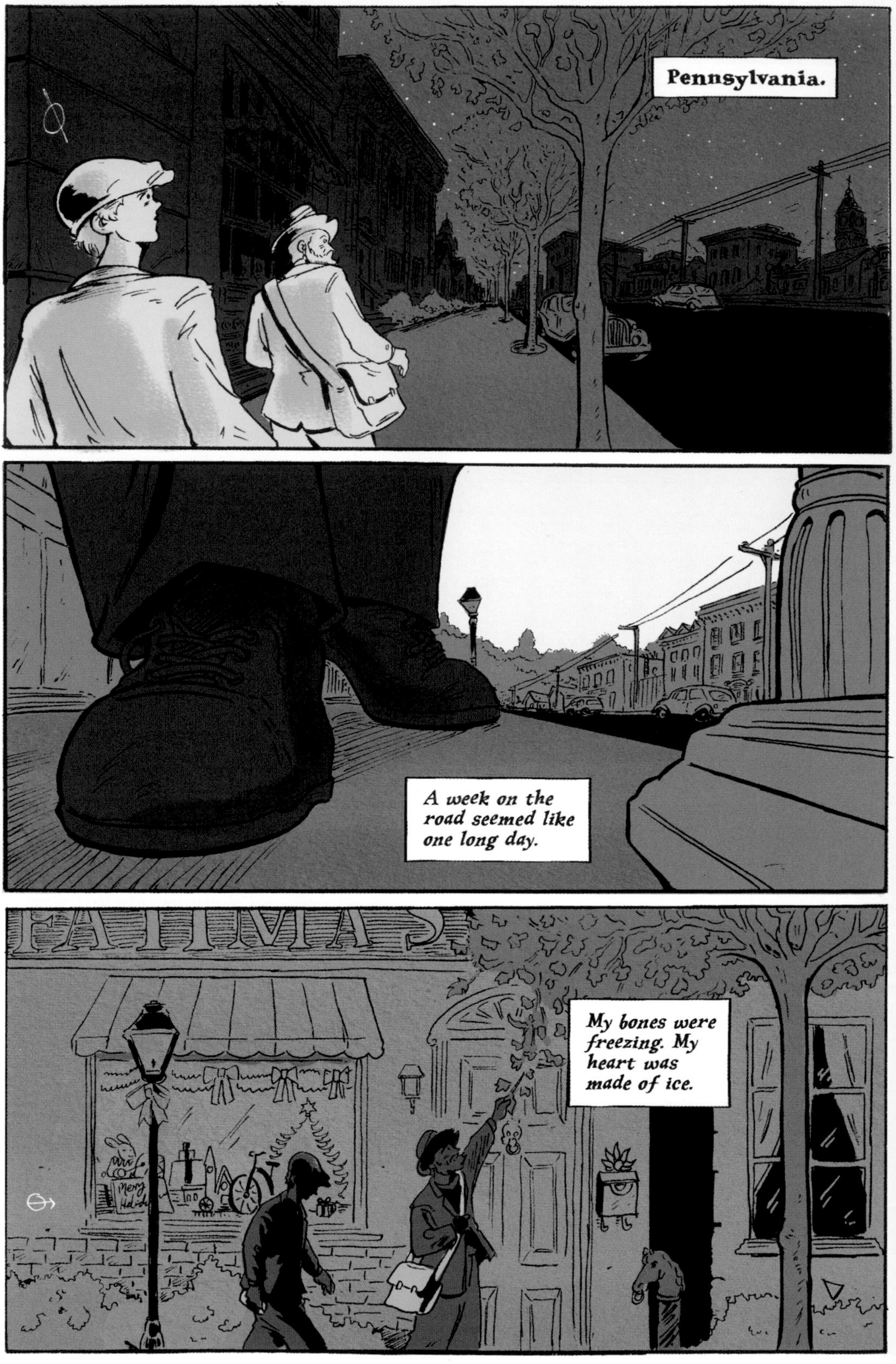
Pennsylvania.
A week on the road seemed like one long day.
FATIMAS
Merry Holid
My bones were freezing. My heart was made of ice.

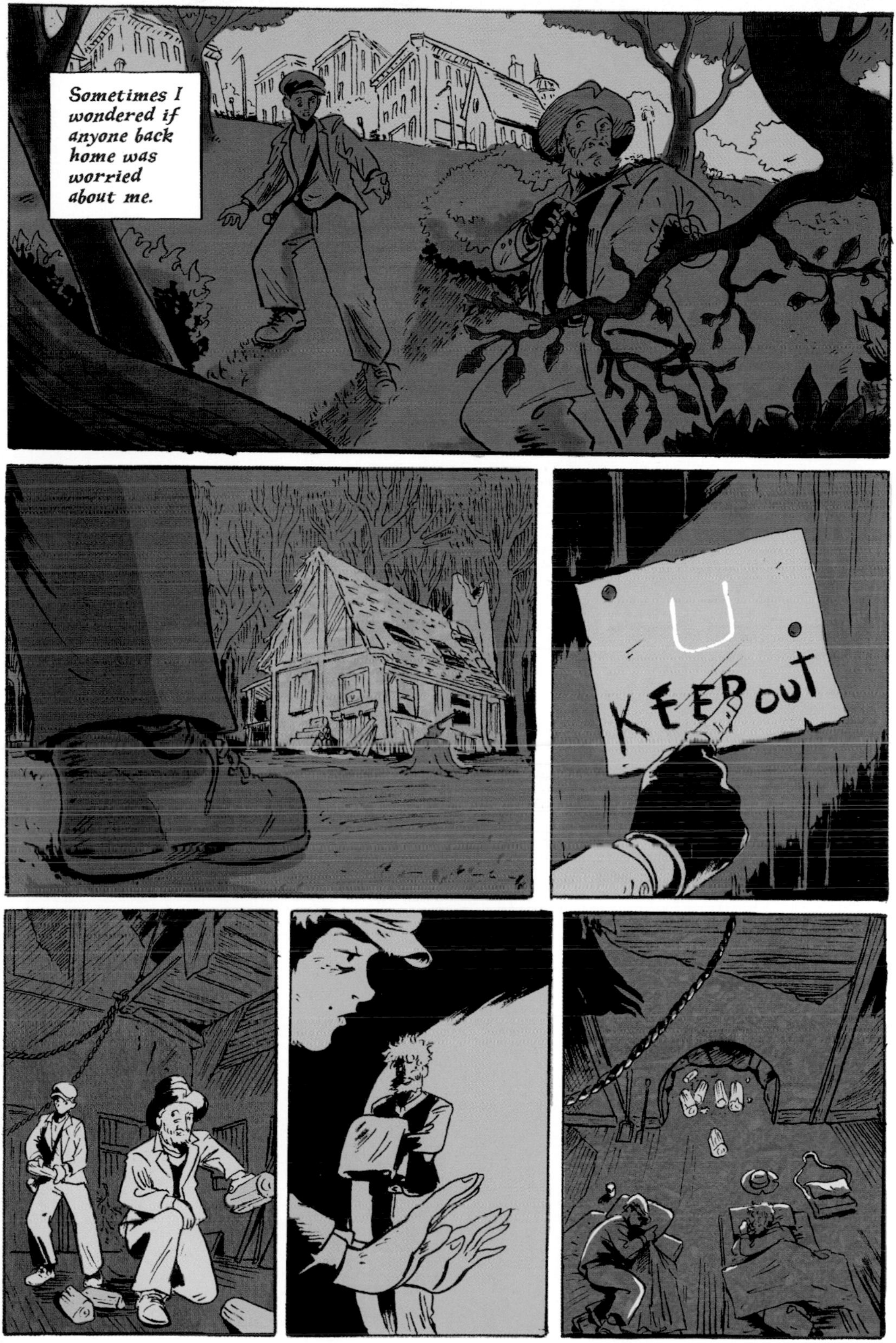
Sometimes I wondered if anyone back home was worried about me.
KEEP OUT

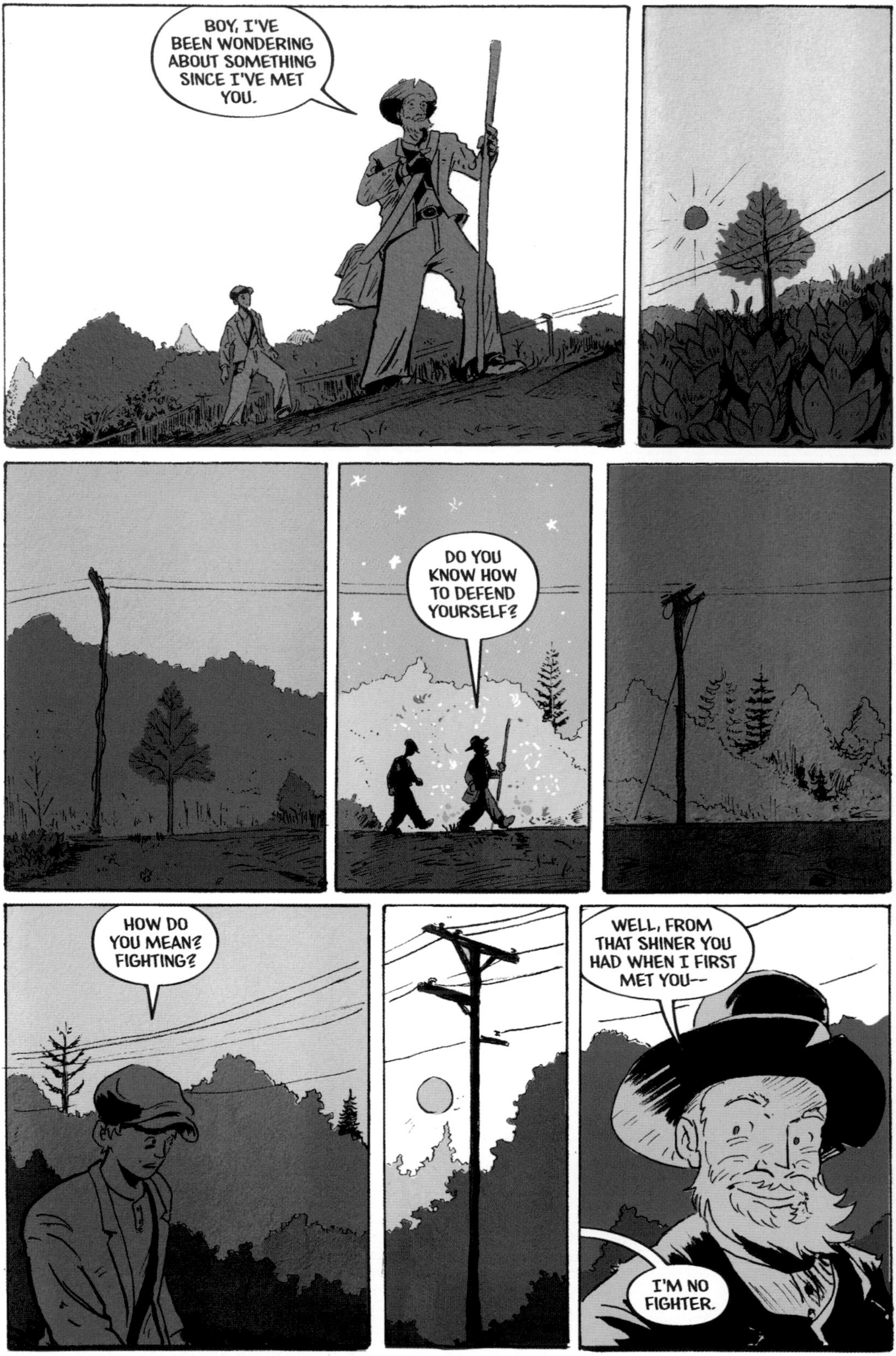
BOY, I'VE BEEN WONDERING ABOUT SOMETHING SINCE I'VE MET YOU.
DO YOU KNOW HOW TO DEFEND YOURSELF?
HOW DO YOU MEAN? FIGHTING?
WELL, FROM THAT SHINER YOU HAD WHEN I FIRST MET YOU--
I'M NO FIGHTER.

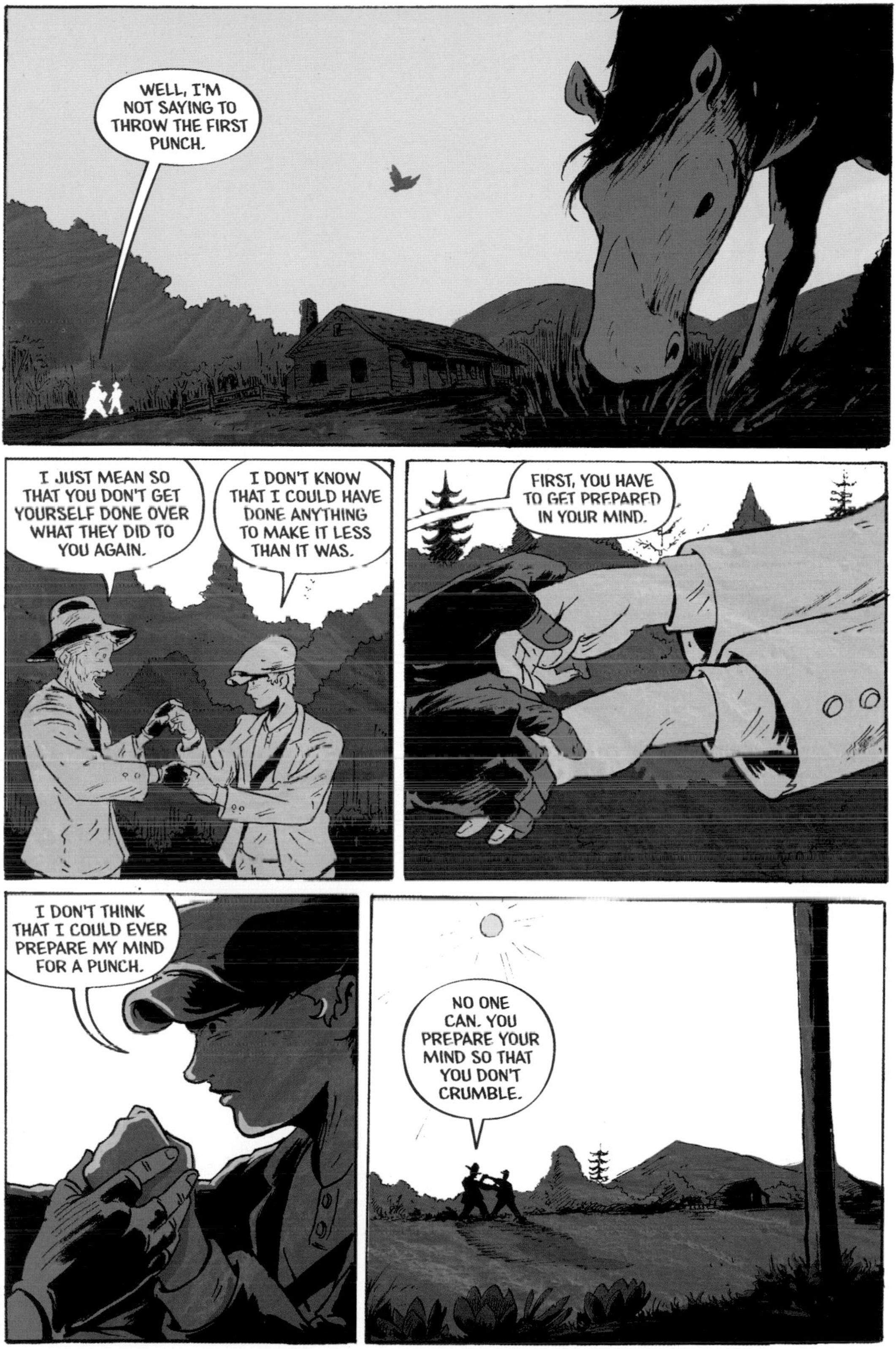

WELL, I'M NOT SAYING TO THROW THE FIRST PUNCH.
I JUST MEAN SO THAT YOU DON'T GET YOURSELF DONE OVER WHAT THEY DID TO YOU AGAIN.
I DON'T KNOW THAT I COULD HAVE DONE ANYTHING TO MAKE IT LESS THAN IT WAS.
FIRST, YOU HAVE TO GET PREPARED IN YOUR MIND.
I DON'T THINK THAT I COULD EVER PREPARE MY MIND FOR A PUNCH.
NO ONE CAN. YOU PREPARE YOUR MIND SO THAT YOU DON'T CRUMBLE.

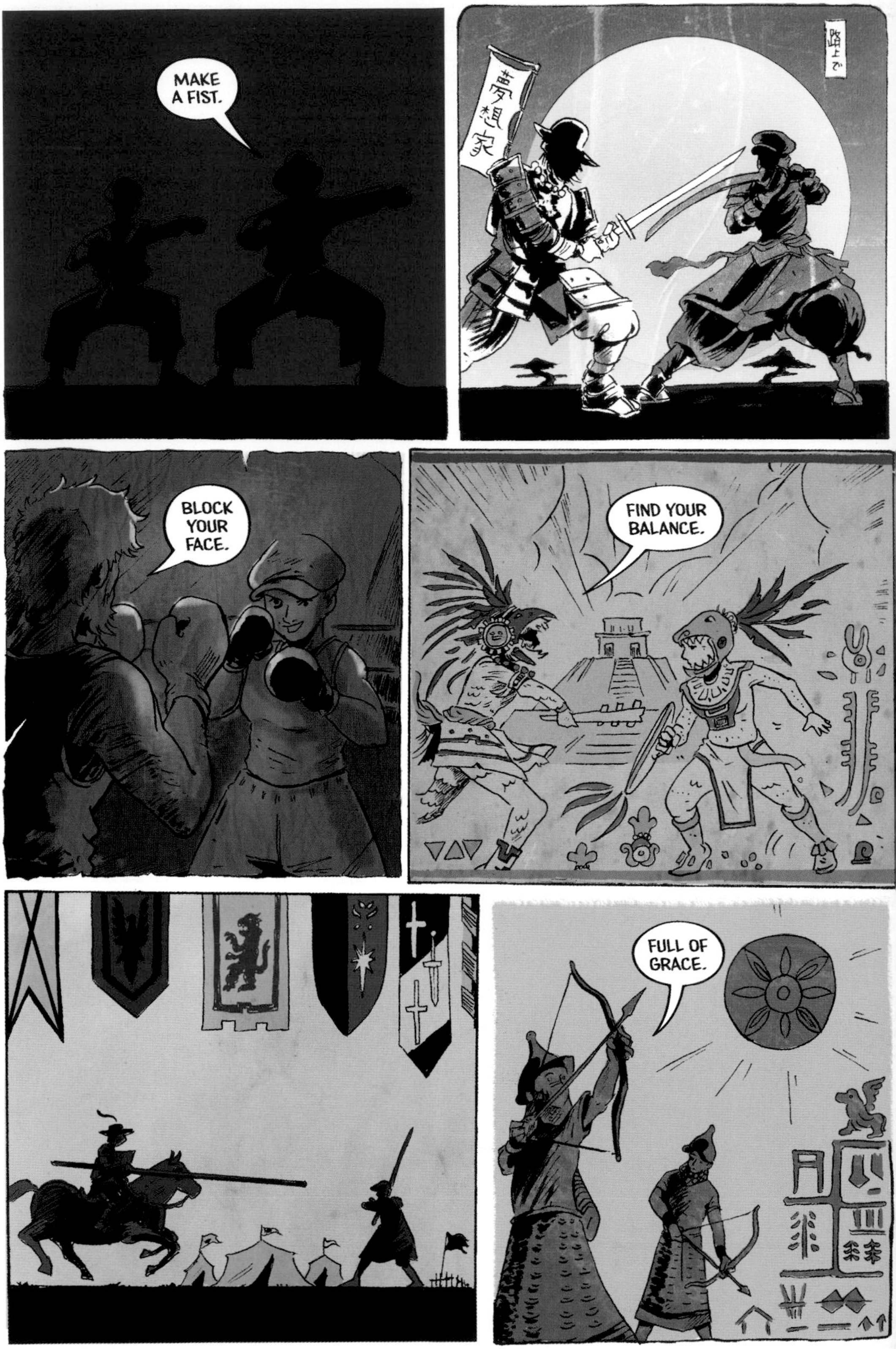
MAKE A FIST.
路上で
夢想家
BLOCK YOUR FACE.
FIND YOUR BALANCE.
FULL OF GRACE.

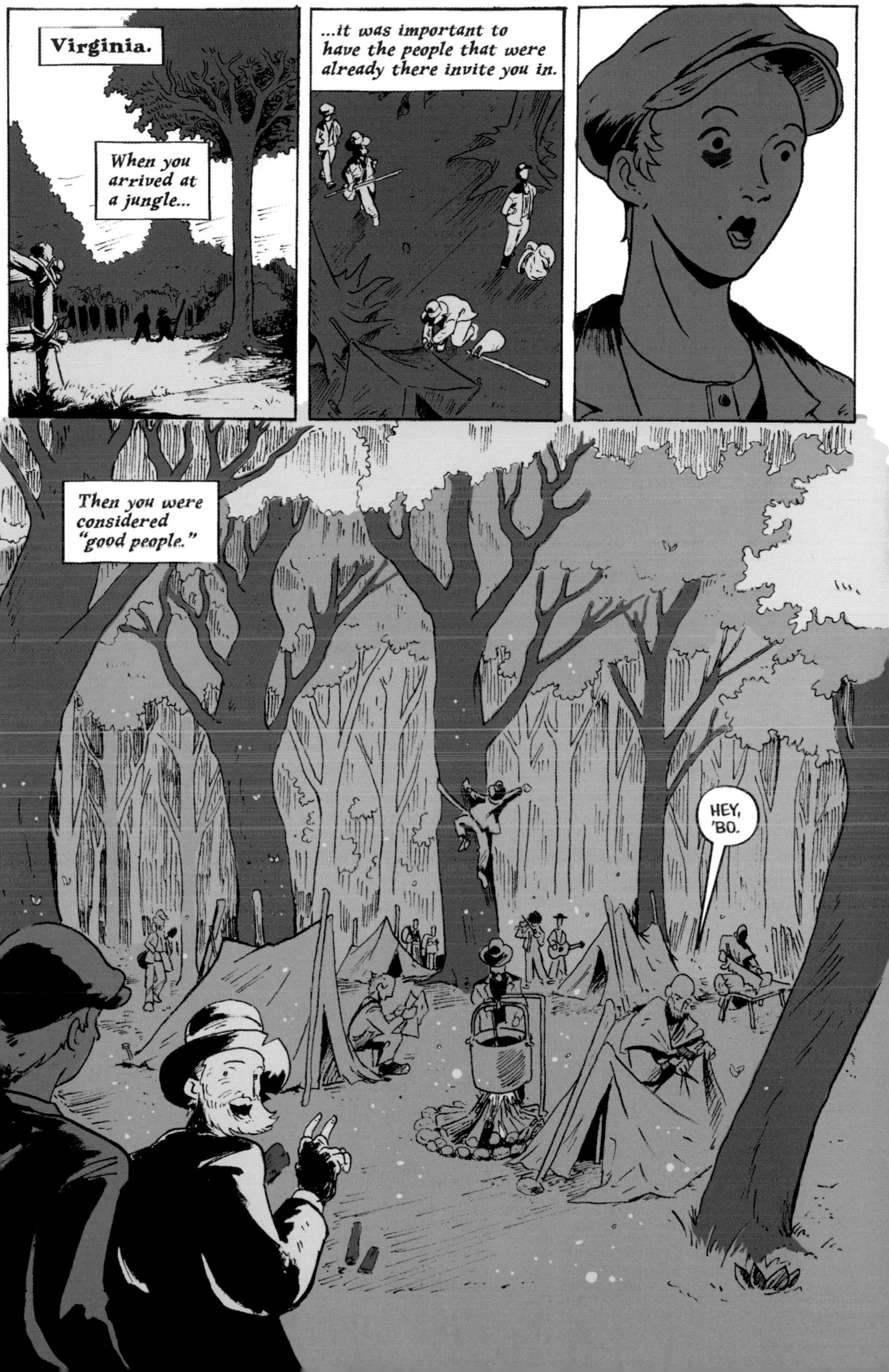
Virginia.
When you arrived at a jungle...
...it was important to have the people that were already there invite you in.
Then you were considered "good people."
HEY, 'BO.

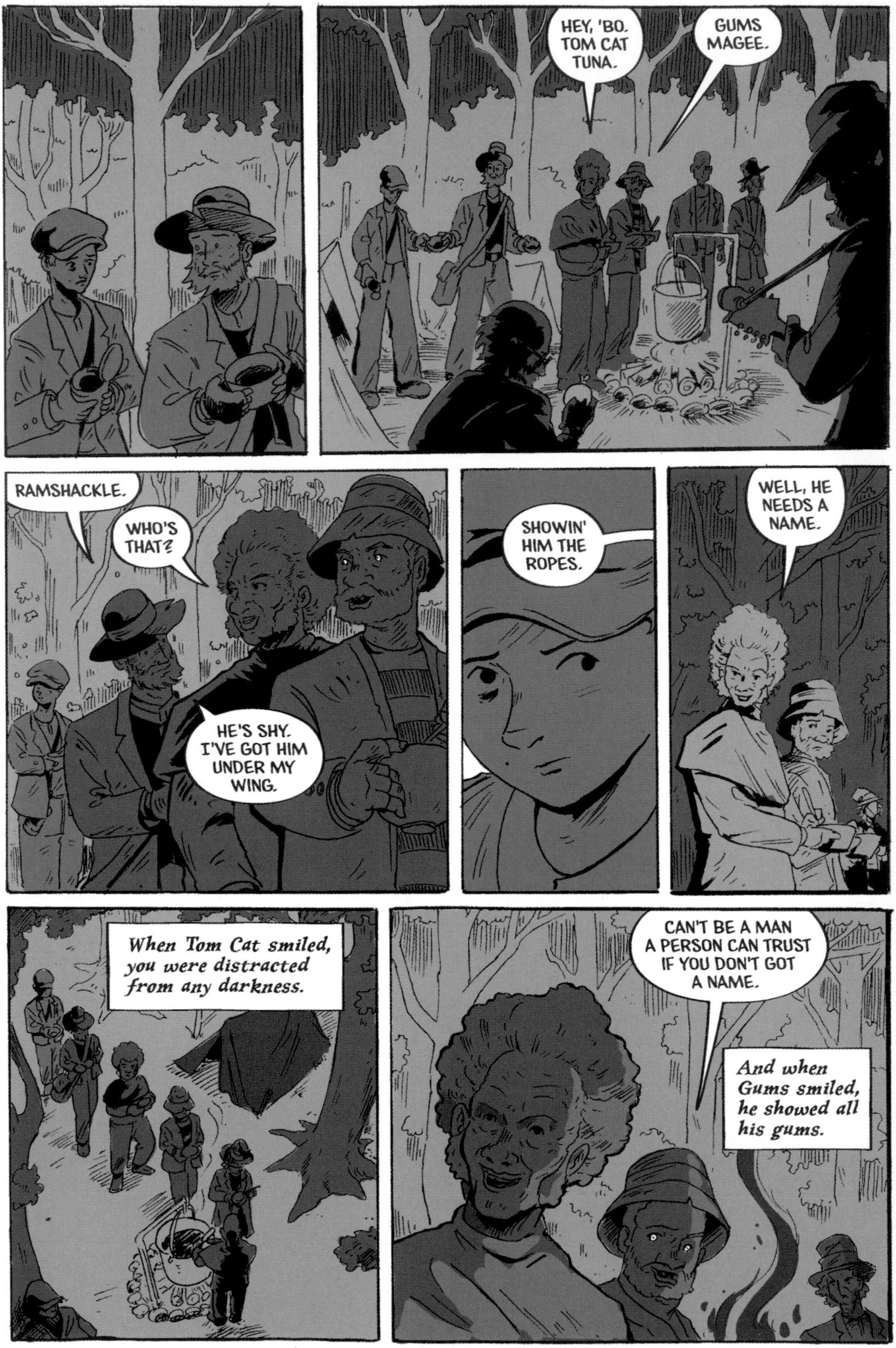
HEY, 'BO. TOM CAT TUNA.
GUMS MAGEE.
RAMSHACKLE.
WHO'S THAT?
HE'S SHY. I'VE GOT HIM UNDER MY WING.
SHOWIN' HIM THE ROPES.
WELL, HE NEEDS A NAME.
When Tom Cat smiled, you were distracted from any darkness.
CAN'T BE A MAN A PERSON CAN TRUST IF YOU DON'T GOT A NAME.
And when Gums smiled, he showed all his gums.

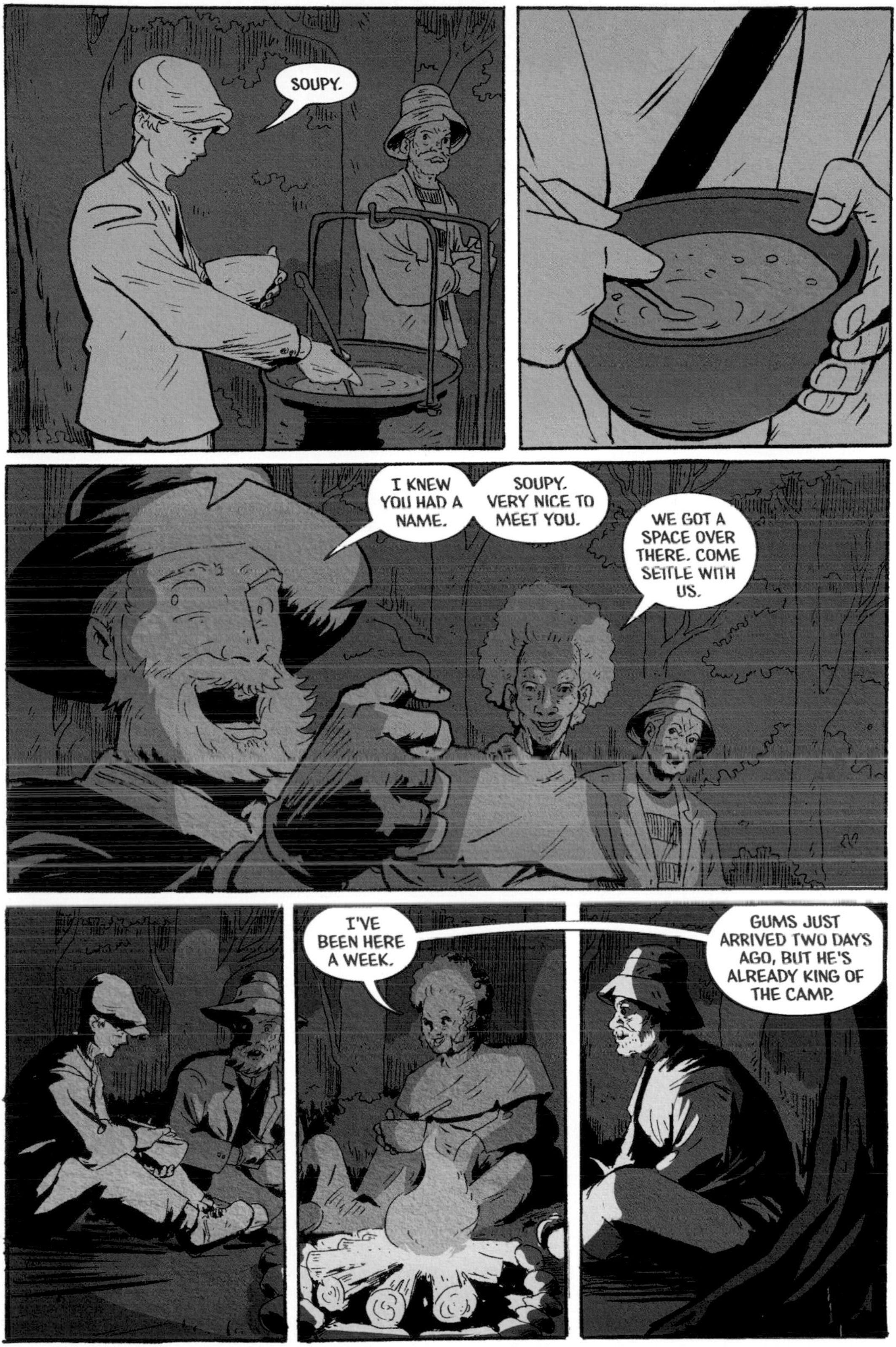
SOUPY.
I KNEW YOU HAD A NAME.
SOUPY. VERY NICE TO MEET YOU.
WE GOT A SPACE OVER THERE. COME SETTLE WITH US.
I'VE BEEN HERE A WEEK.
GUMS JUST ARRIVED TWO DAYS AGO, BUT HE'S ALREADY KING OF THE CAMP.

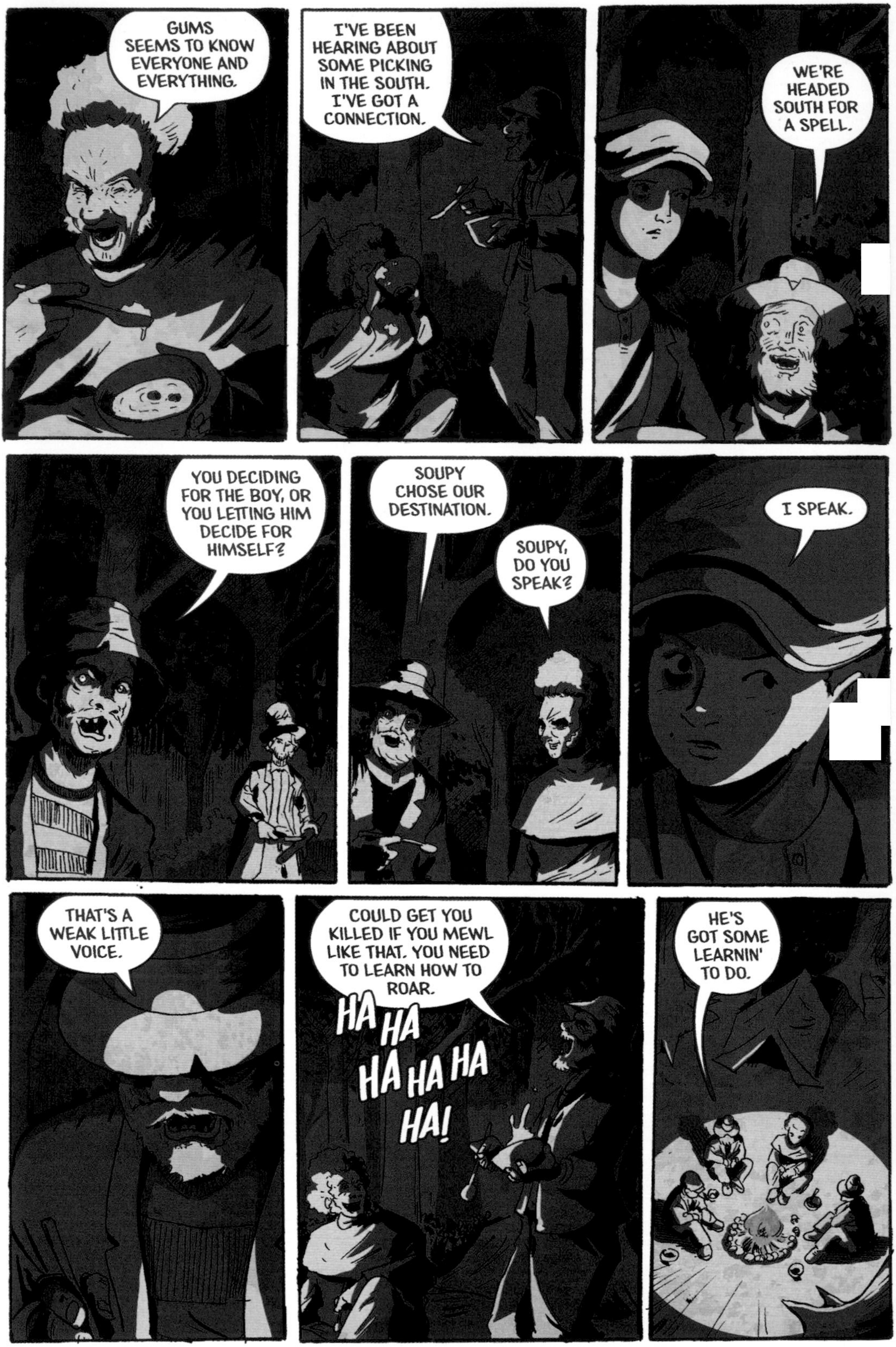

GUMS SEEMS TO KNOW EVERYONE AND EVERYTHING.
I'VE BEEN HEARING ABOUT SOME PICKING IN THE SOUTH. I'VE GOT A CONNECTION.
WE'RE HEADED SOUTH FOR A SPELL.
YOU DECIDING FOR THE BOY, OR YOU LETTING HIM DECIDE FOR HIMSELF?
SOUPY CHOSE OUR DESTINATION.
SOUPY, DO YOU SPEAK?
I SPEAK.
THAT'S A WEAK LITTLE VOICE.
COULD GET YOU KILLED IF YOU MEWL LIKE THAT. YOU NEED TO LEARN HOW TO ROAR.
HA HA HA HA HA HA!
HE'S GOT SOME LEARNIN' TO DO.

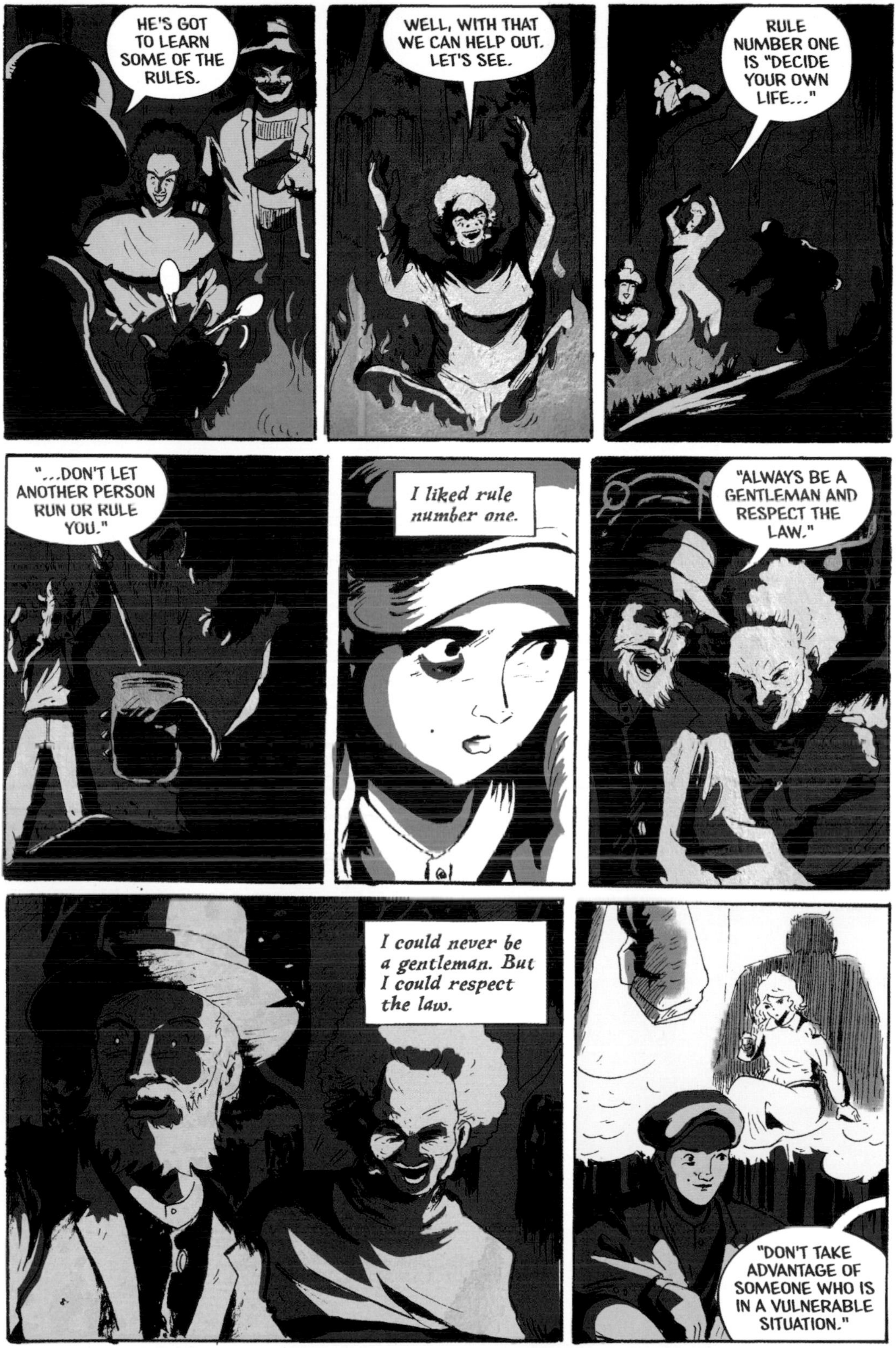
HE'S GOT TO LEARN SOME OF THE RULES.
WELL, WITH THAT WE CAN HELP OUT. LET'S SEE.
RULE NUMBER ONE IS "DECIDE YOUR OWN LIFE...
"...DON'T LET ANOTHER PERSON RUN OR RULE YOU."
I liked rule number one.
"ALWAYS BE A GENTLEMAN AND RESPECT THE LAW."
I could never be a gentleman. But I could respect the law.
"DON'T TAKE ADVANTAGE OF SOMEONE WHO IS IN A VULNERABLE SITUATION."

RULES TAKEN FROM "CODE OF THE ROAD," THE ETHICAL CODE CREATED BY TOURIST UNION #63 AT THE ANNUAL HOBO CONVENTION IN THE LATE 1880'S.

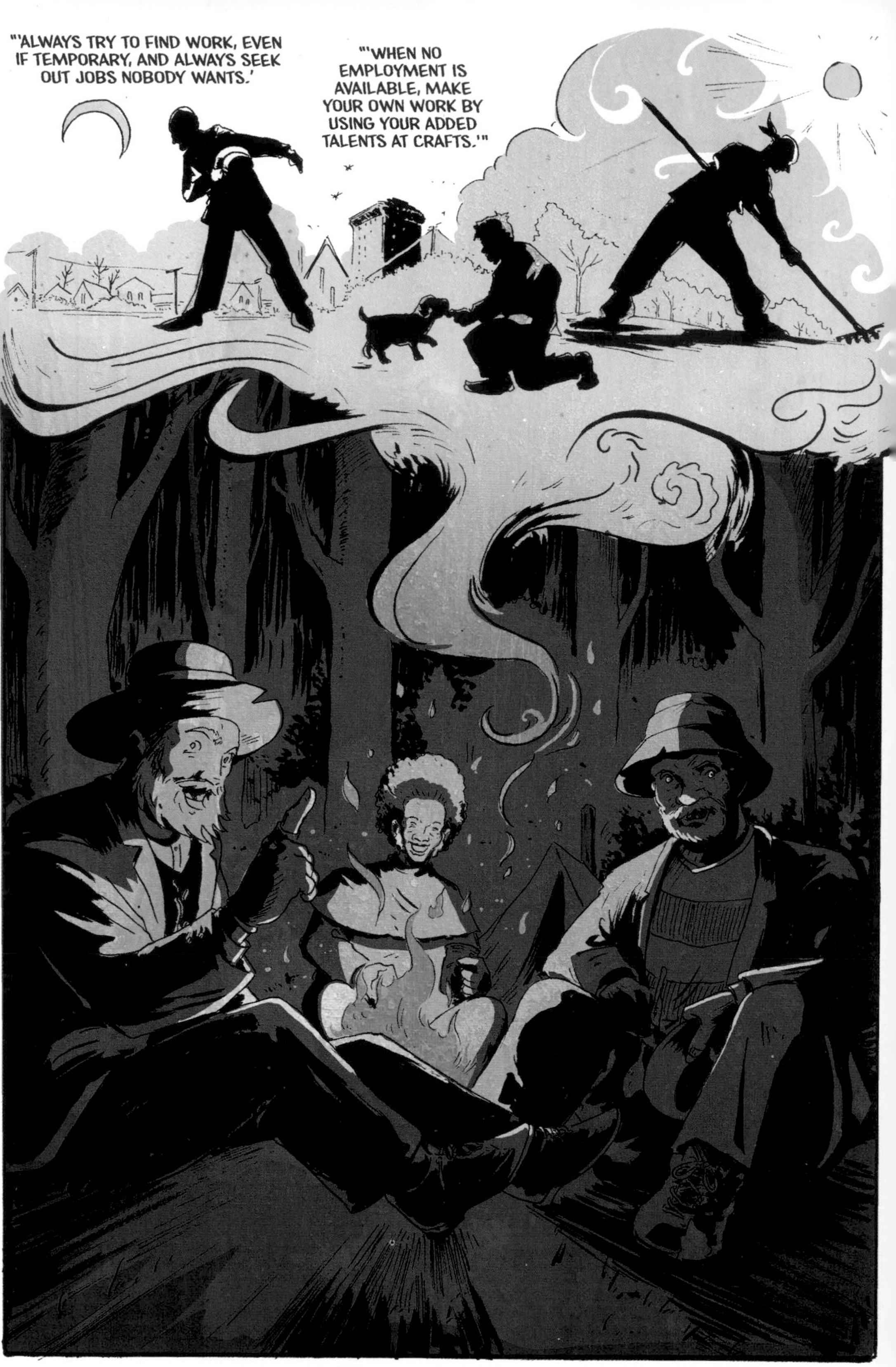
"'ALWAYS TRY TO FIND WORK, EVEN IF TEMPORARY, AND ALWAYS SEEK OUT JOBS NOBODY WANTS.'
"'WHEN NO EMPLOYMENT IS AVAILABLE, MAKE YOUR OWN WORK BY USING YOUR ADDED TALENTS AT CRAFTS.'"

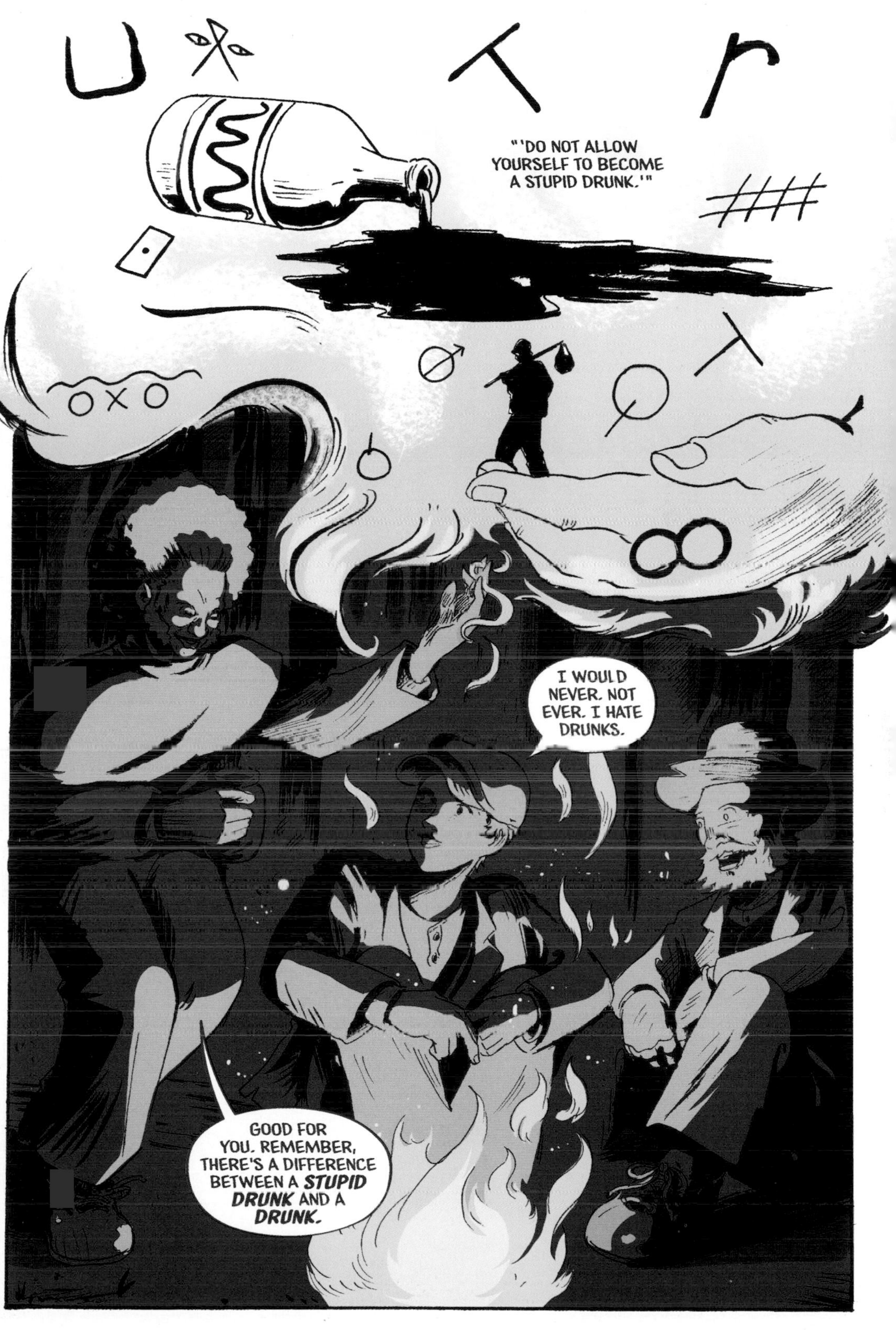
"'DO NOT ALLOW YOURSELF TO BECOME A STUPID DRUNK.'"
I WOULD NEVER. NOT EVER. I HATE DRUNKS.
GOOD FOR YOU. REMEMBER, THERE'S A DIFFERENCE BETWEEN A ***STUPID DRUNK*** AND A ***DRUNK.***

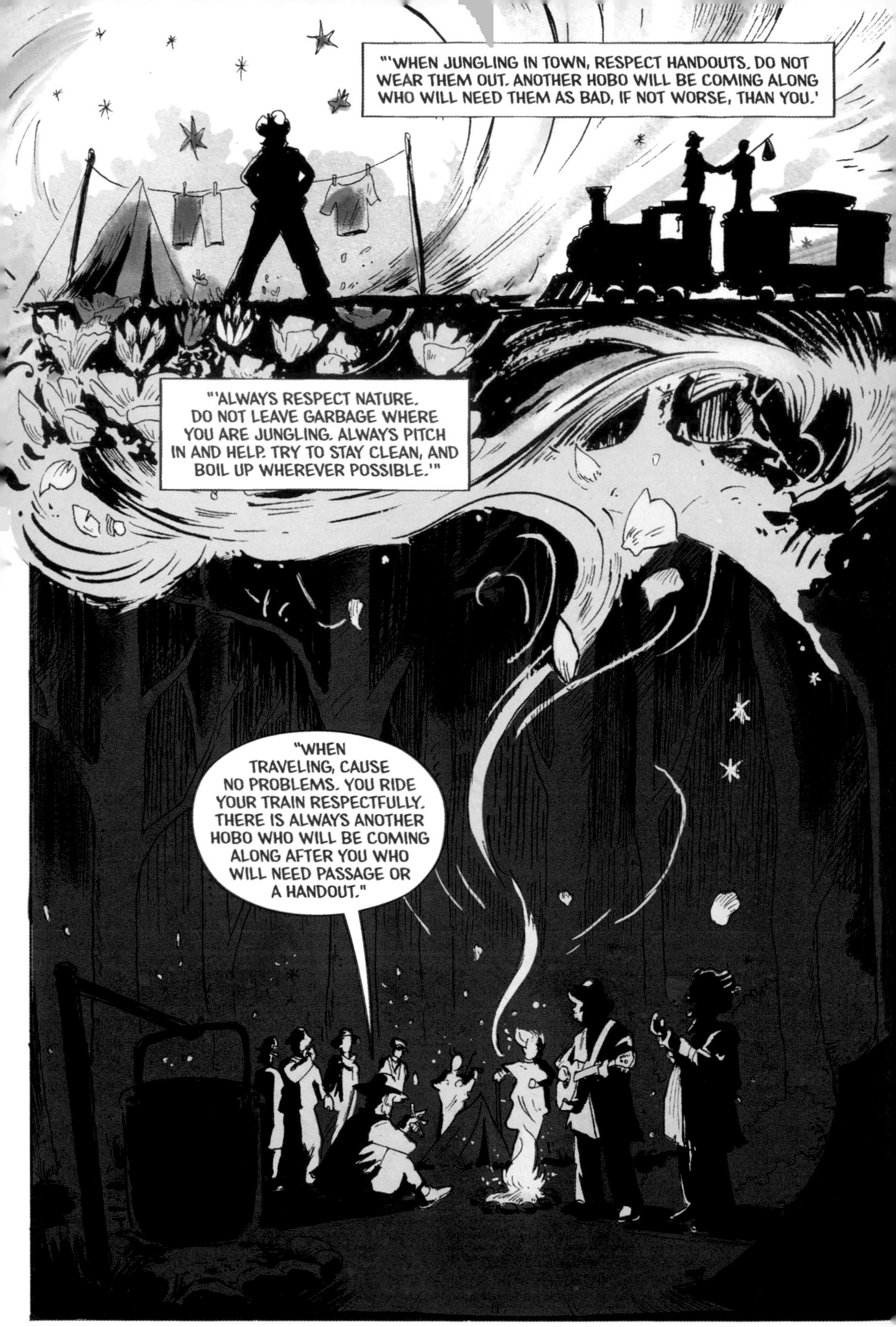
"'WHEN JUNGLING IN TOWN, RESPECT HANDOUTS. DO NOT WEAR THEM OUT. ANOTHER HOBO WILL BE COMING ALONG WHO WILL NEED THEM AS BAD, IF NOT WORSE, THAN YOU.'
"'ALWAYS RESPECT NATURE. DO NOT LEAVE GARBAGE WHERE YOU ARE JUNGLING. ALWAYS PITCH IN AND HELP. TRY TO STAY CLEAN, AND BOIL UP WHEREVER POSSIBLE.'"
"WHEN TRAVELING, CAUSE NO PROBLEMS. YOU RIDE YOUR TRAIN RESPECTFULLY. THERE IS ALWAYS ANOTHER HOBO WHO WILL BE COMING ALONG AFTER YOU WHO WILL NEED PASSAGE OR A HANDOUT."

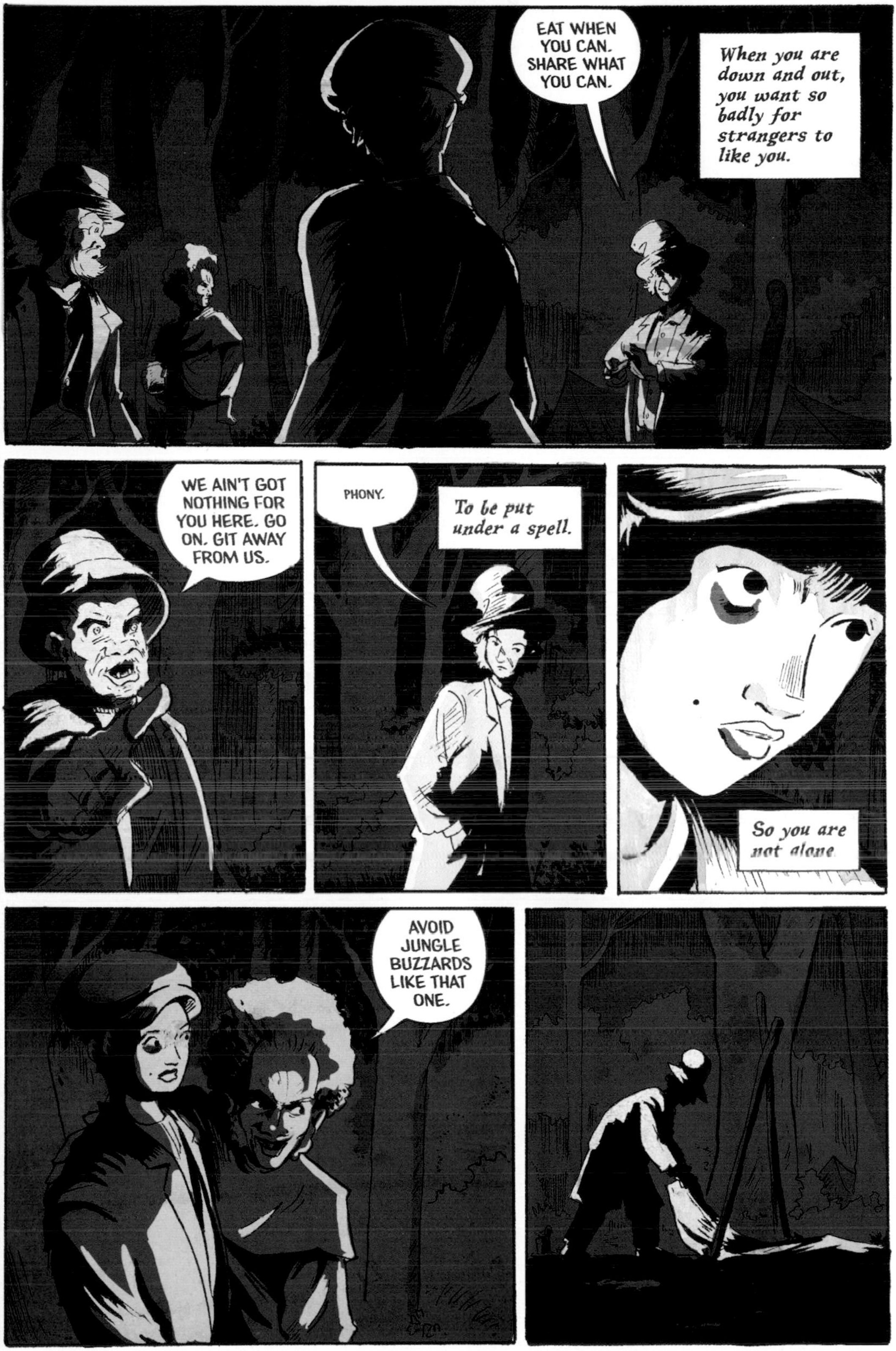
EAT WHEN YOU CAN. SHARE WHAT YOU CAN.
When you are down and out, you want so badly for strangers to like you.
WE AIN'T GOT NOTHING FOR YOU HERE. GO ON. GIT AWAY FROM US.
PHONY.
To be put under a spell.
So you are not alone.
AVOID JUNGLE BUZZARDS LIKE THAT ONE.

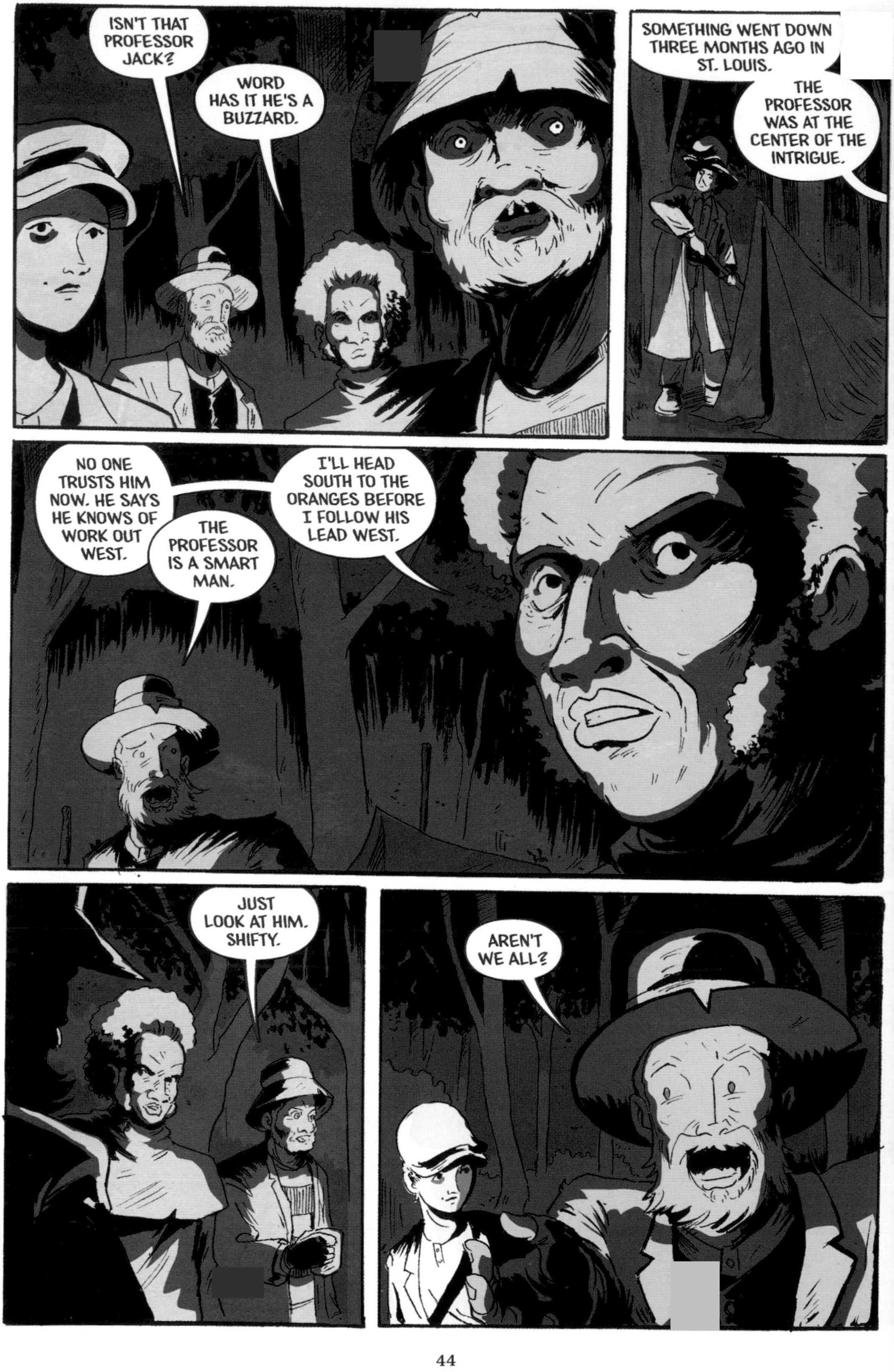
ISN'T THAT PROFESSOR JACK?
WORD HAS IT HE'S A BUZZARD.
SOMETHING WENT DOWN THREE MONTHS AGO IN ST. LOUIS.
THE PROFESSOR WAS AT THE CENTER OF THE INTRIGUE.
NO ONE TRUSTS HIM NOW. HE SAYS HE KNOWS OF WORK OUT WEST.
I'LL HEAD SOUTH TO THE ORANGES BEFORE I FOLLOW HIS LEAD WEST.
THE PROFESSOR IS A SMART MAN.
JUST LOOK AT HIM. SHIFTY.
AREN'T WE ALL?

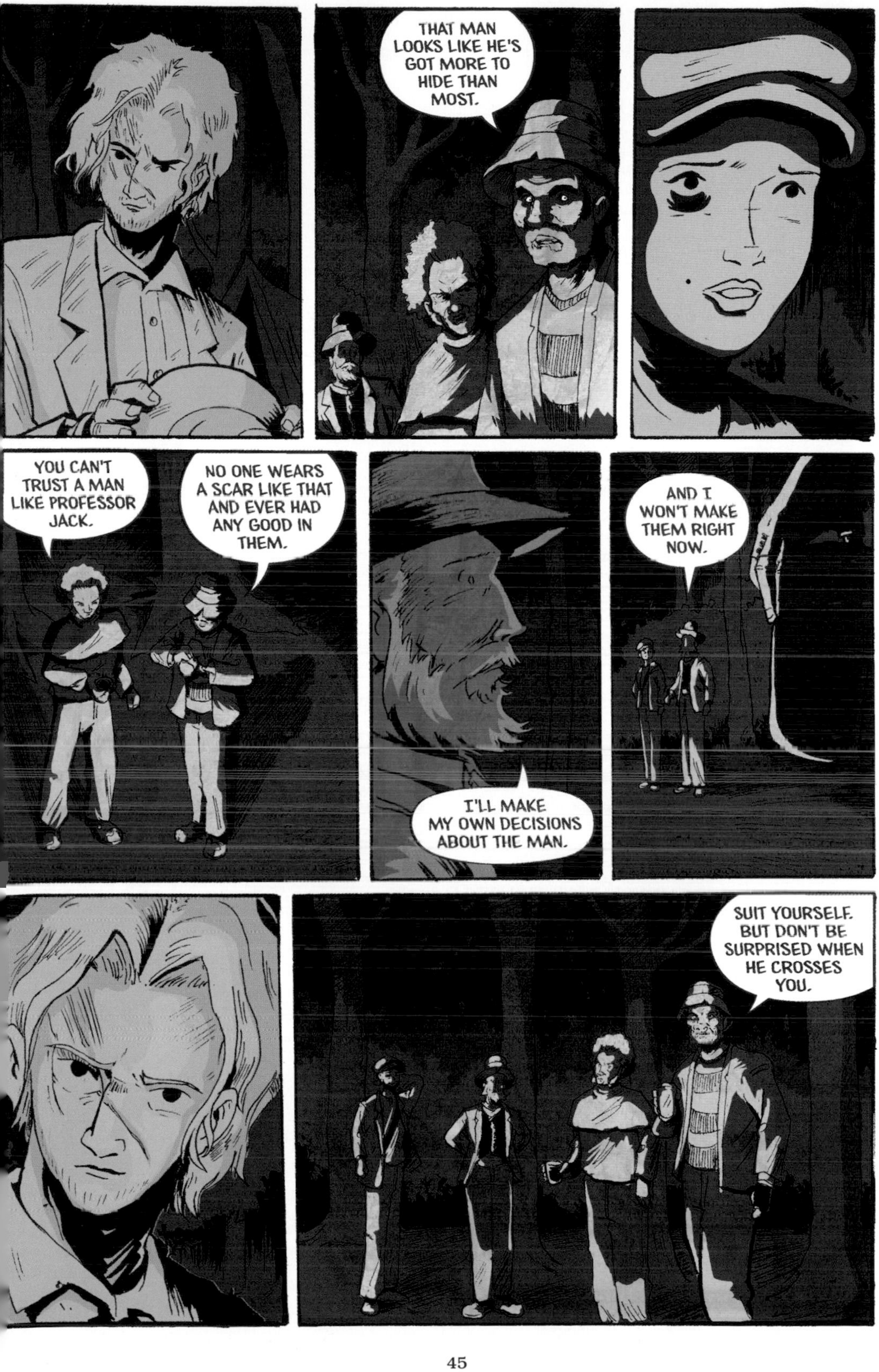
THAT MAN LOOKS LIKE HE'S GOT MORE TO HIDE THAN MOST.
YOU CAN'T TRUST A MAN LIKE PROFESSOR JACK.
NO ONE WEARS A SCAR LIKE THAT AND EVER HAD ANY GOOD IN THEM.
I'LL MAKE MY OWN DECISIONS ABOUT THE MAN.
AND I WON'T MAKE THEM RIGHT NOW.
SUIT YOURSELF. BUT DON'T BE SURPRISED WHEN HE CROSSES YOU.

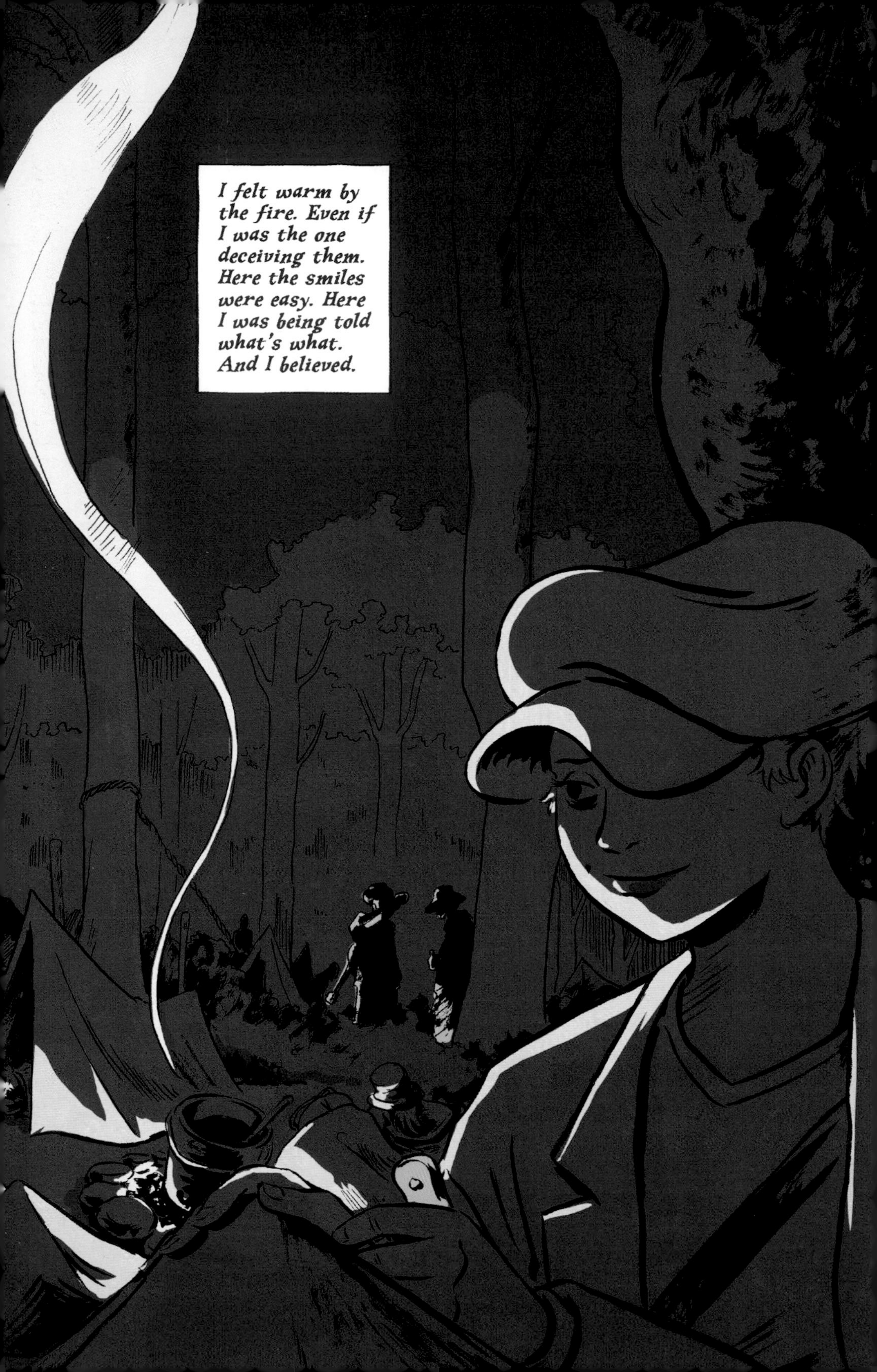
I felt warm by the fire. Even if I was the one deceiving them. Here the smiles were easy. Here I was being told what's what. And I believed.

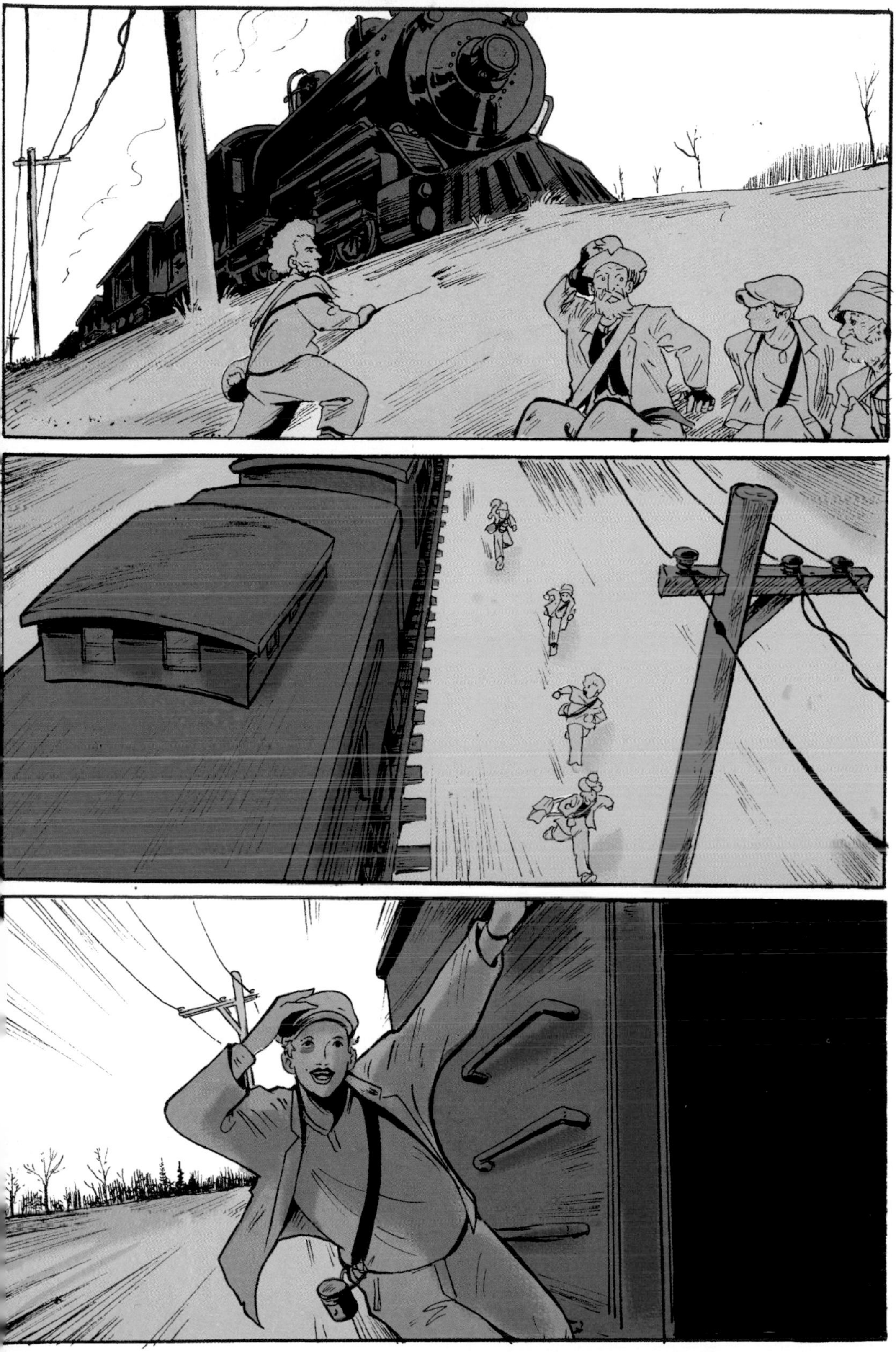

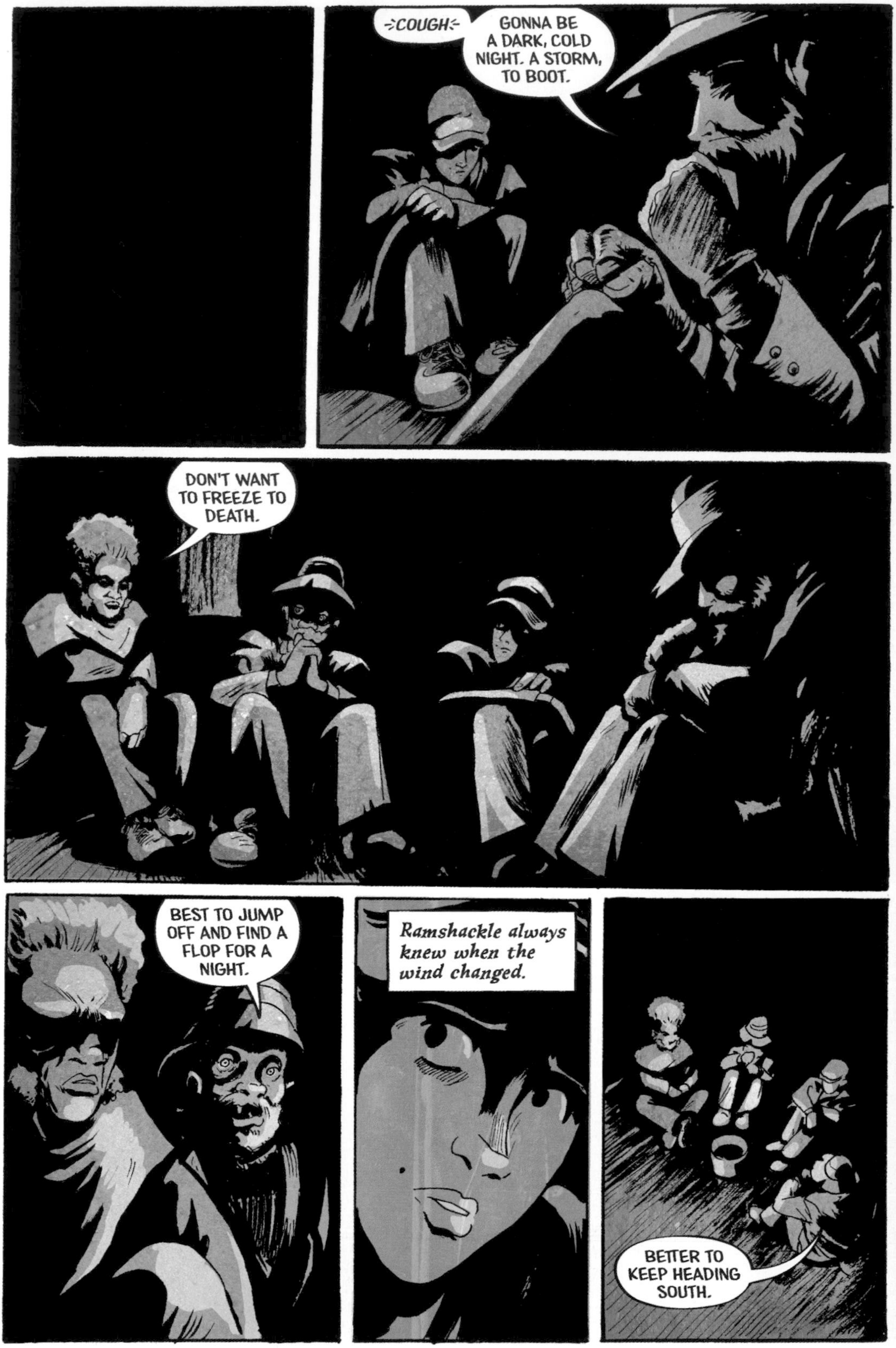

-COUGH-
GONNA BE A DARK, COLD NIGHT. A STORM, TO BOOT.
DON'T WANT TO FREEZE TO DEATH.
BEST TO JUMP OFF AND FIND A FLOP FOR A NIGHT.
Ramshackle always knew when the wind changed.
BETTER TO KEEP HEADING SOUTH.

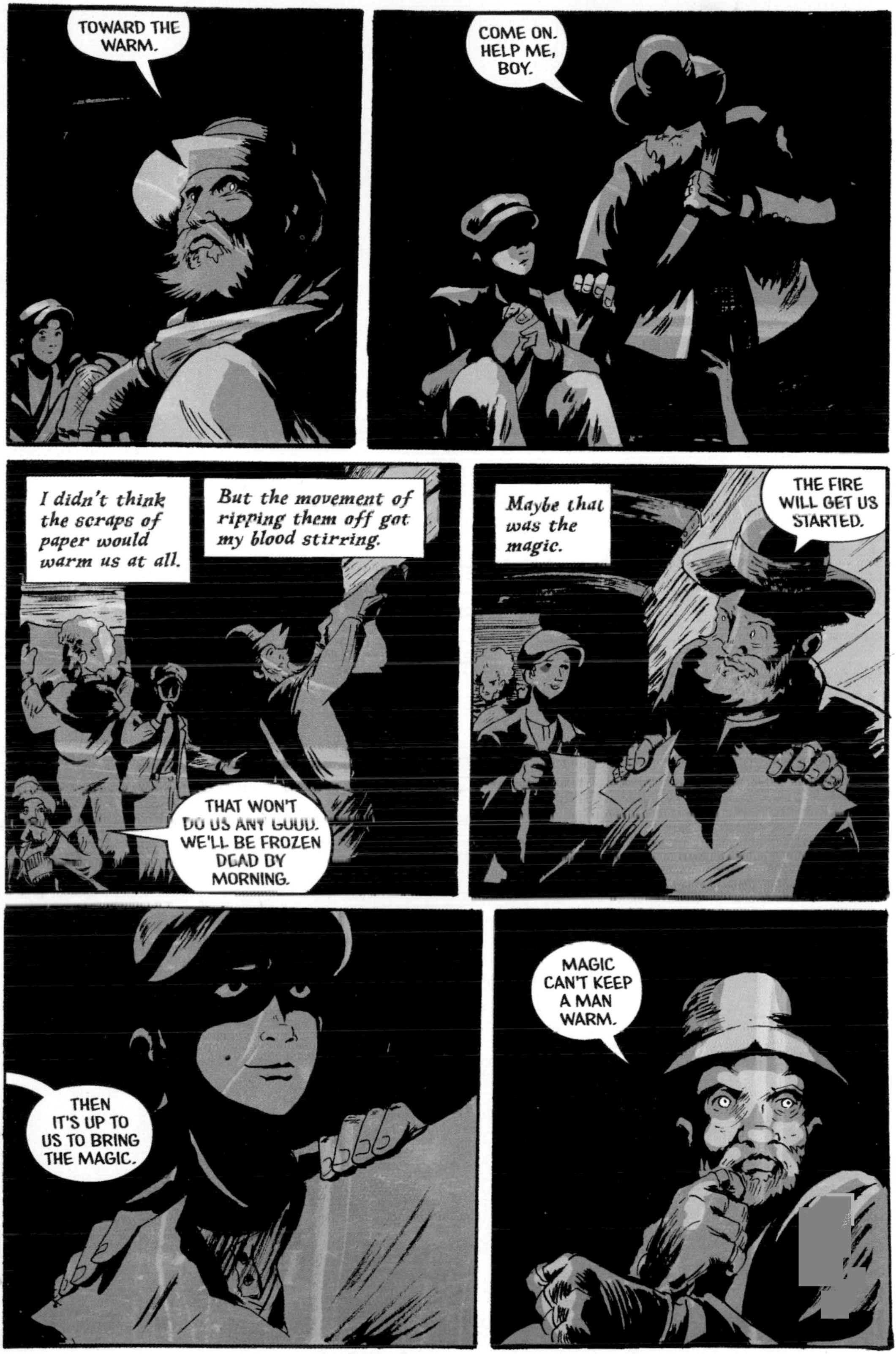
TOWARD THE WARM.
COME ON. HELP ME, BOY.
I didn't think the scraps of paper would warm us at all.
But the movement of ripping them off got my blood stirring.
THAT WON'T DO US ANY GOOD. WE'LL BE FROZEN DEAD BY MORNING.
Maybe that was the magic.
THE FIRE WILL GET US STARTED.
THEN IT'S UP TO US TO BRING THE MAGIC.
MAGIC CAN'T KEEP A MAN WARM.

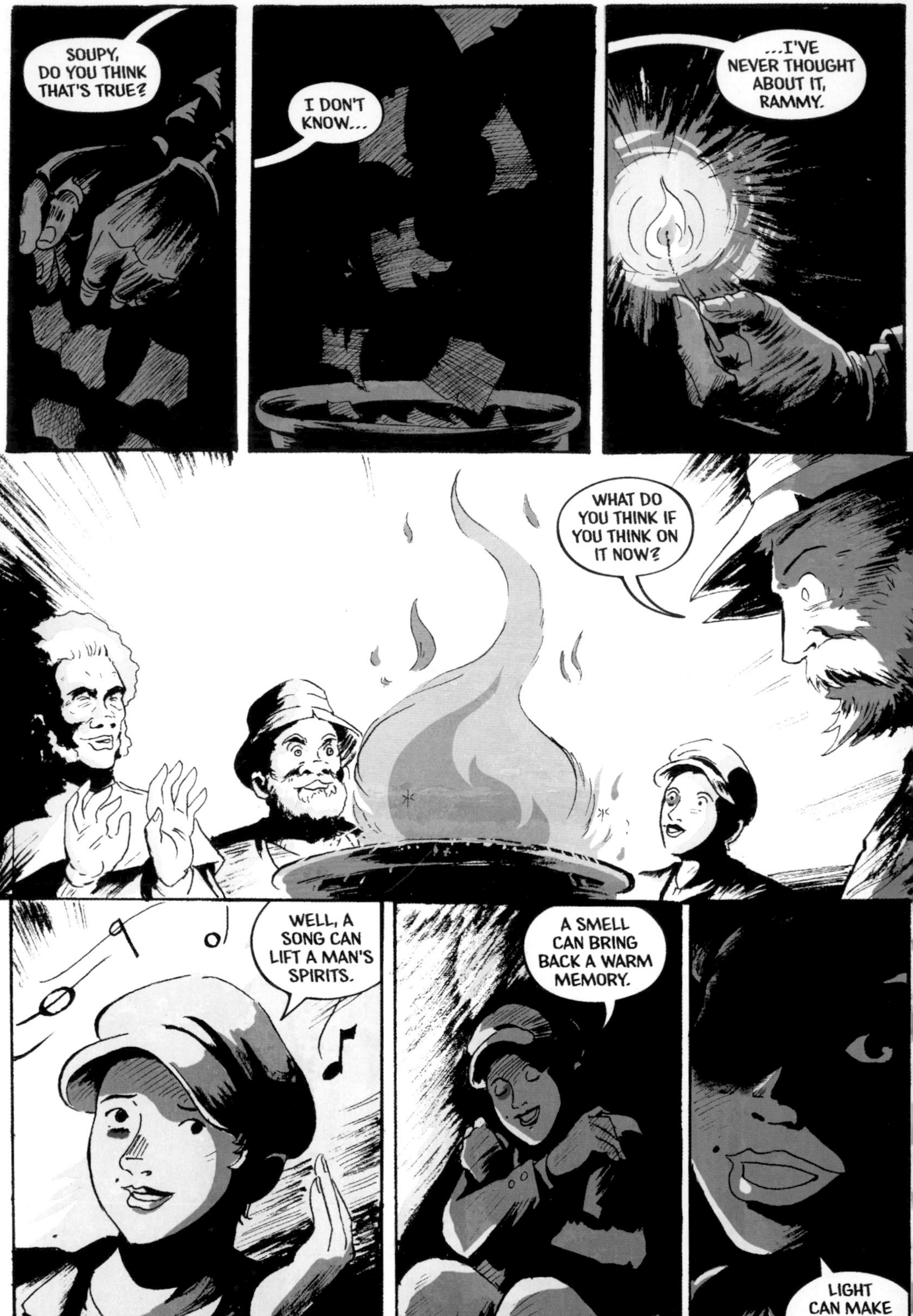
SOUPY, DO YOU THINK THAT'S TRUE?
I DON'T KNOW...
...I'VE NEVER THOUGHT ABOUT IT, RAMMY.
WHAT DO YOU THINK IF YOU THINK ON IT NOW?
WELL, A SONG CAN LIFT A MAN'S SPIRITS.
A SMELL CAN BRING BACK A WARM MEMORY.
LIGHT CAN MAKE A DARK TIME BETTER.

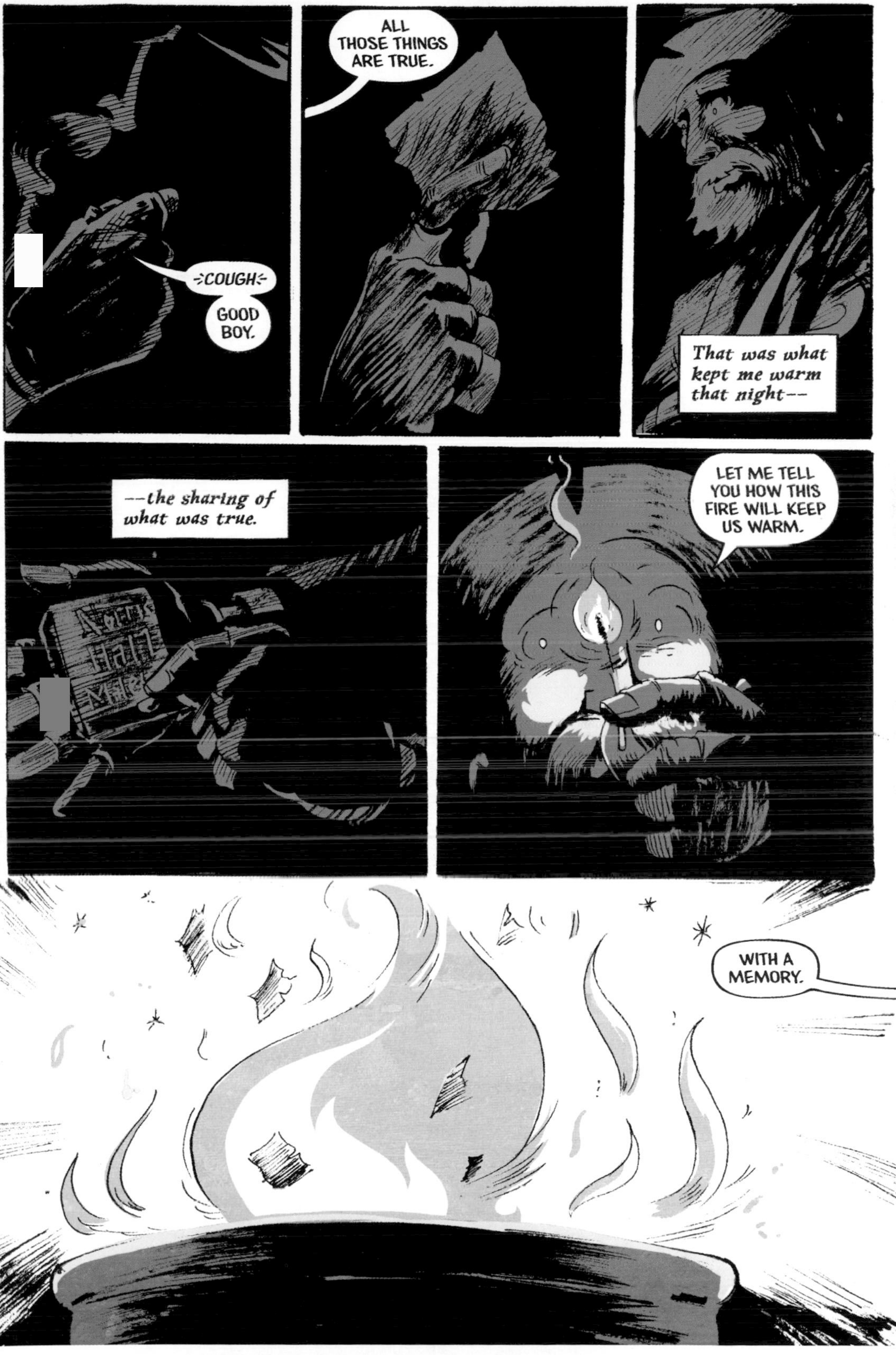

-COUGH-
GOOD BOY.
ALL THOSE THINGS ARE TRUE.
That was what kept me warm that night--
--the sharing of what was true.
LET ME TELL YOU HOW THIS FIRE WILL KEEP US WARM.
WITH A MEMORY.

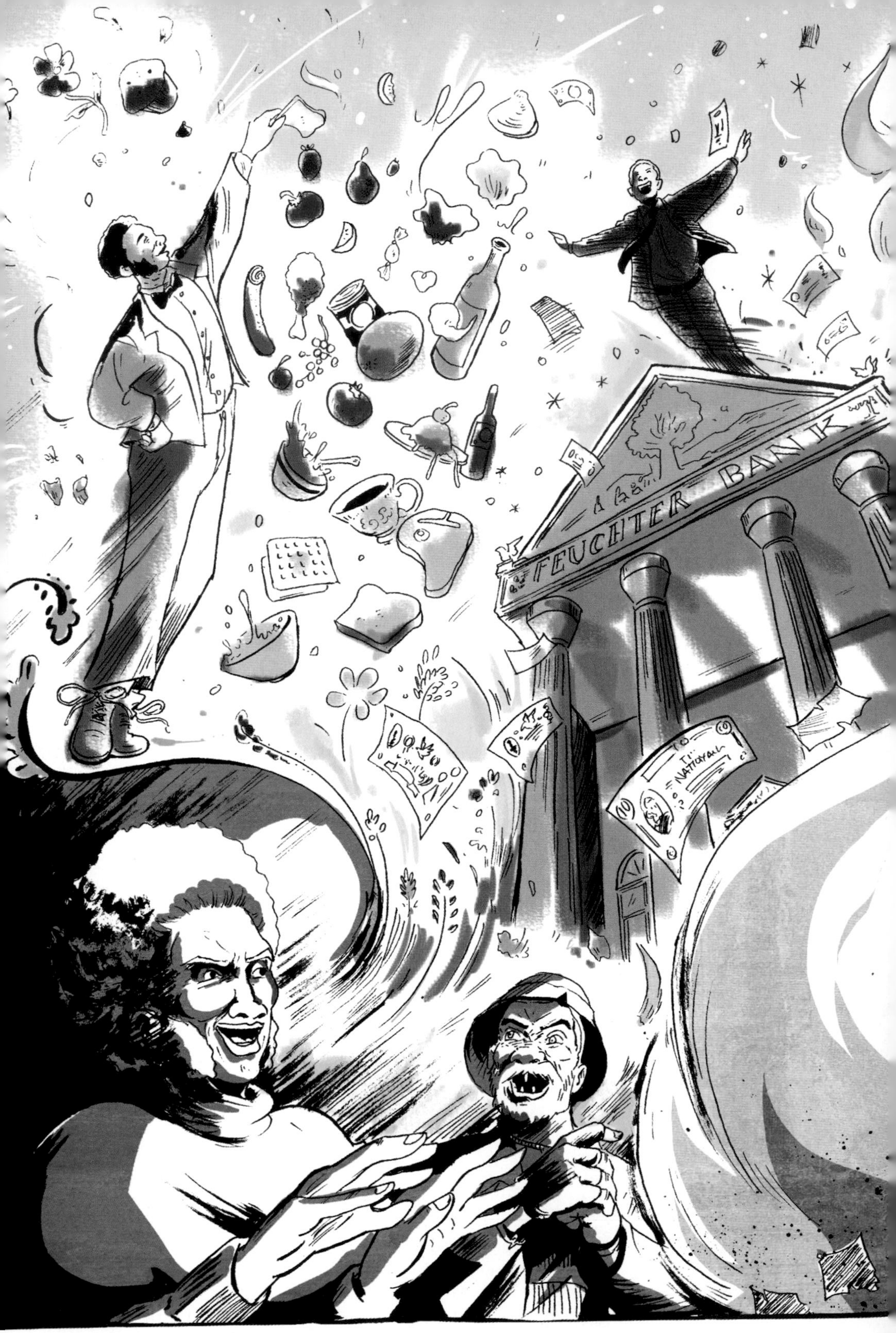
FEUCHTER BANK

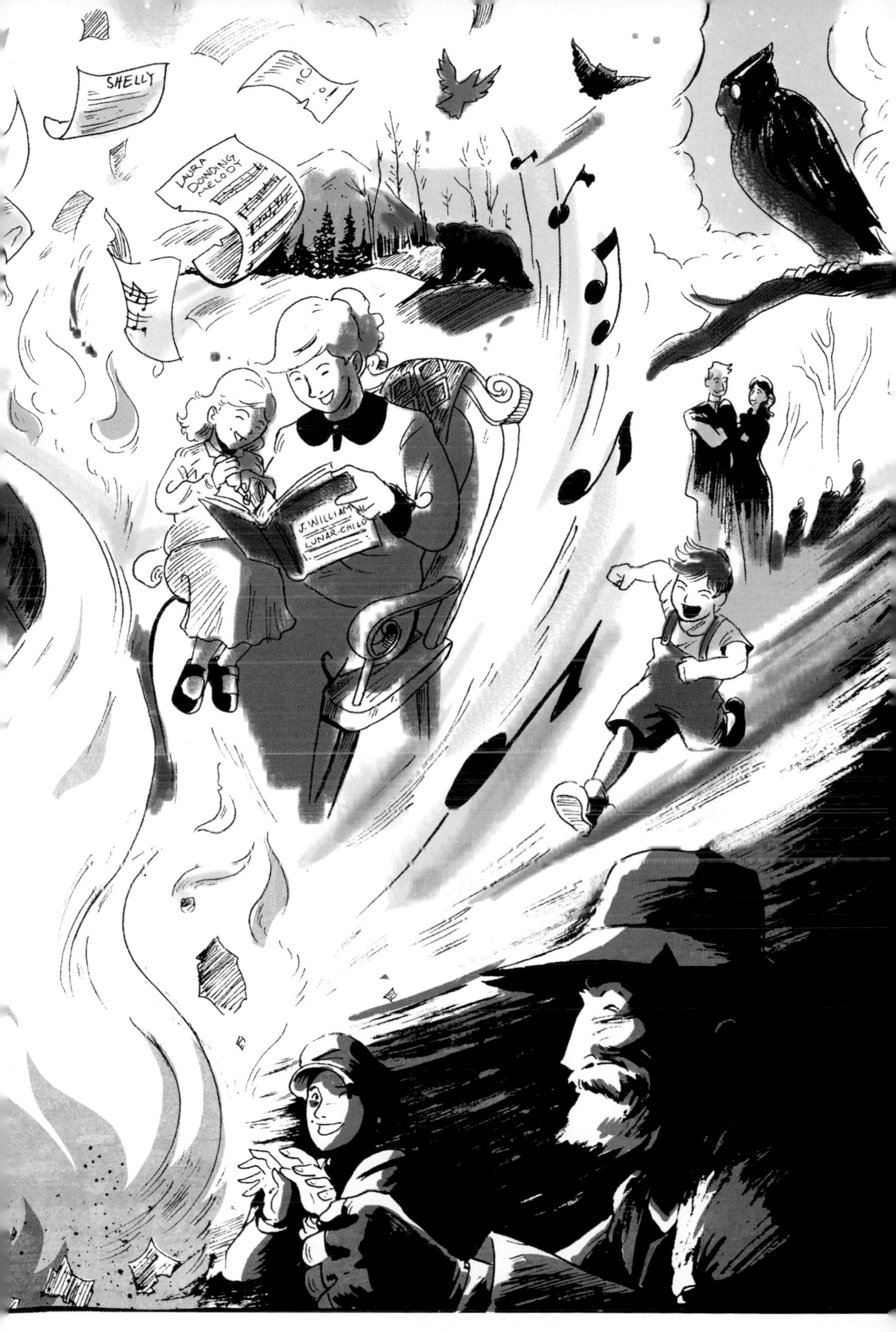

SHELLY
LAURA DOWNING MELODY
J. WILLIAM LUNAR-CHILD

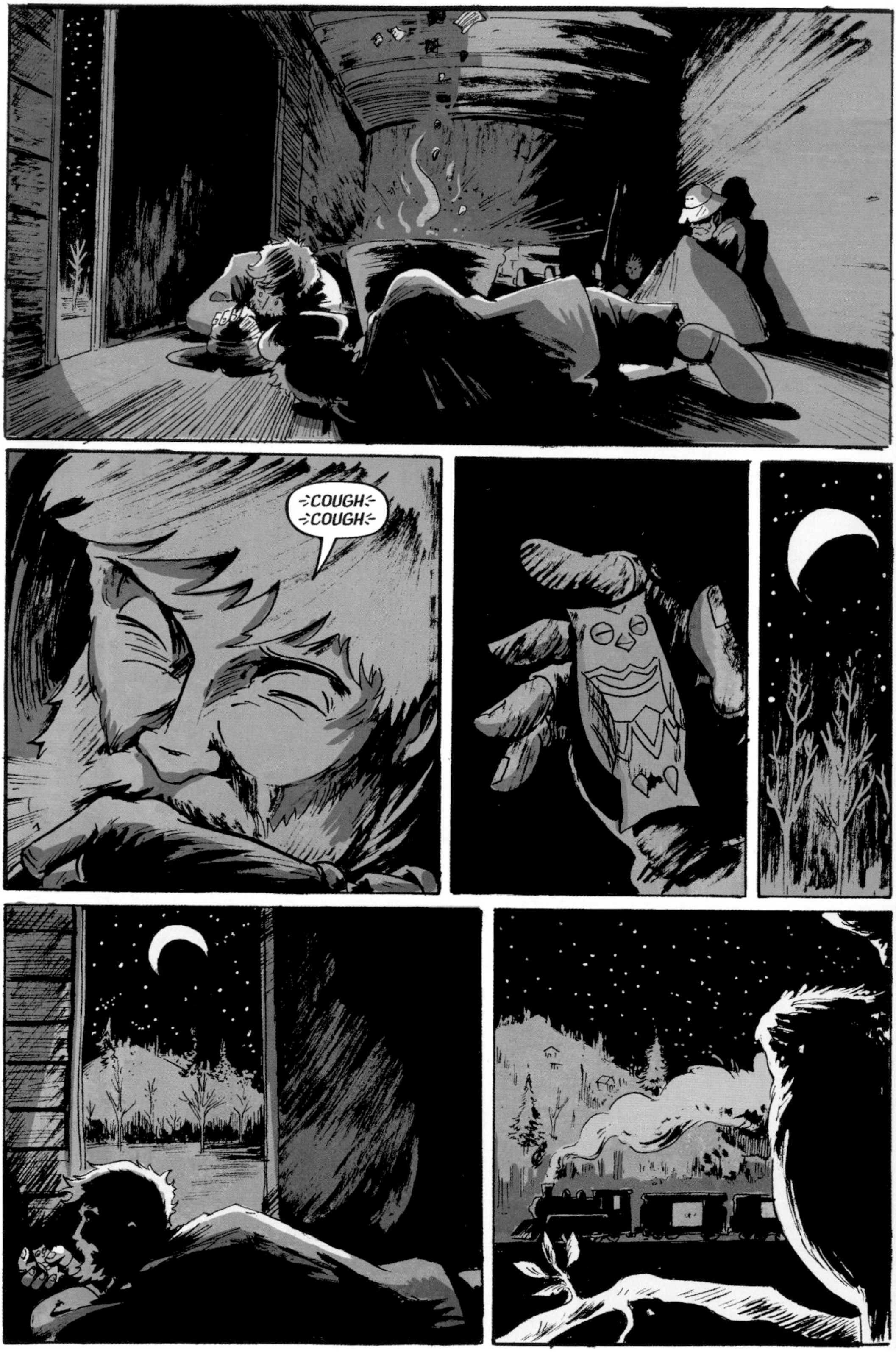
COUGH
COUGH

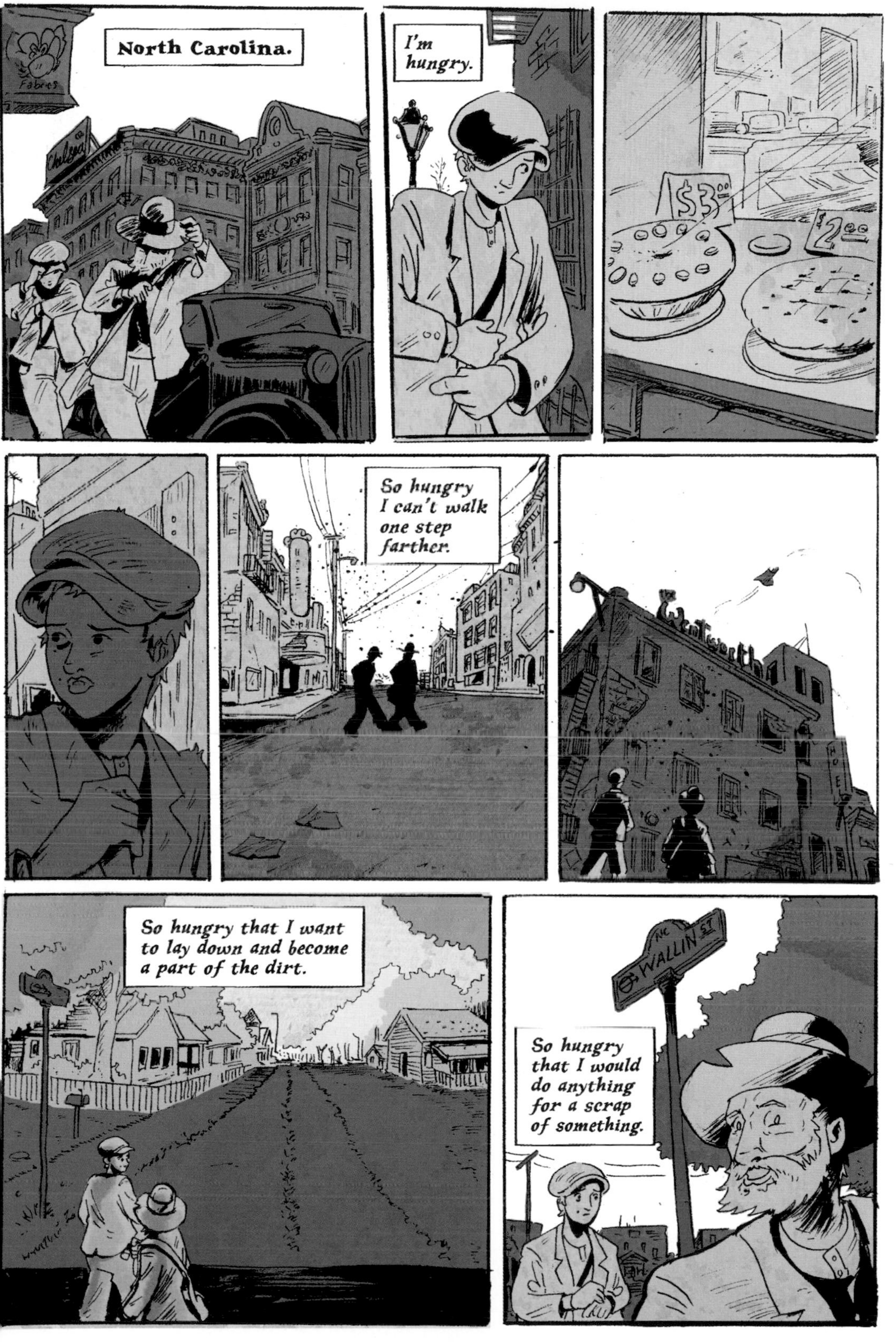
North Carolina.
I'm hungry.
$3.00
$2.00
So hungry I can't walk one step farther.
So hungry that I want to lay down and become a part of the dirt.
WALLIN ST
So hungry that I would do anything for a scrap of something.

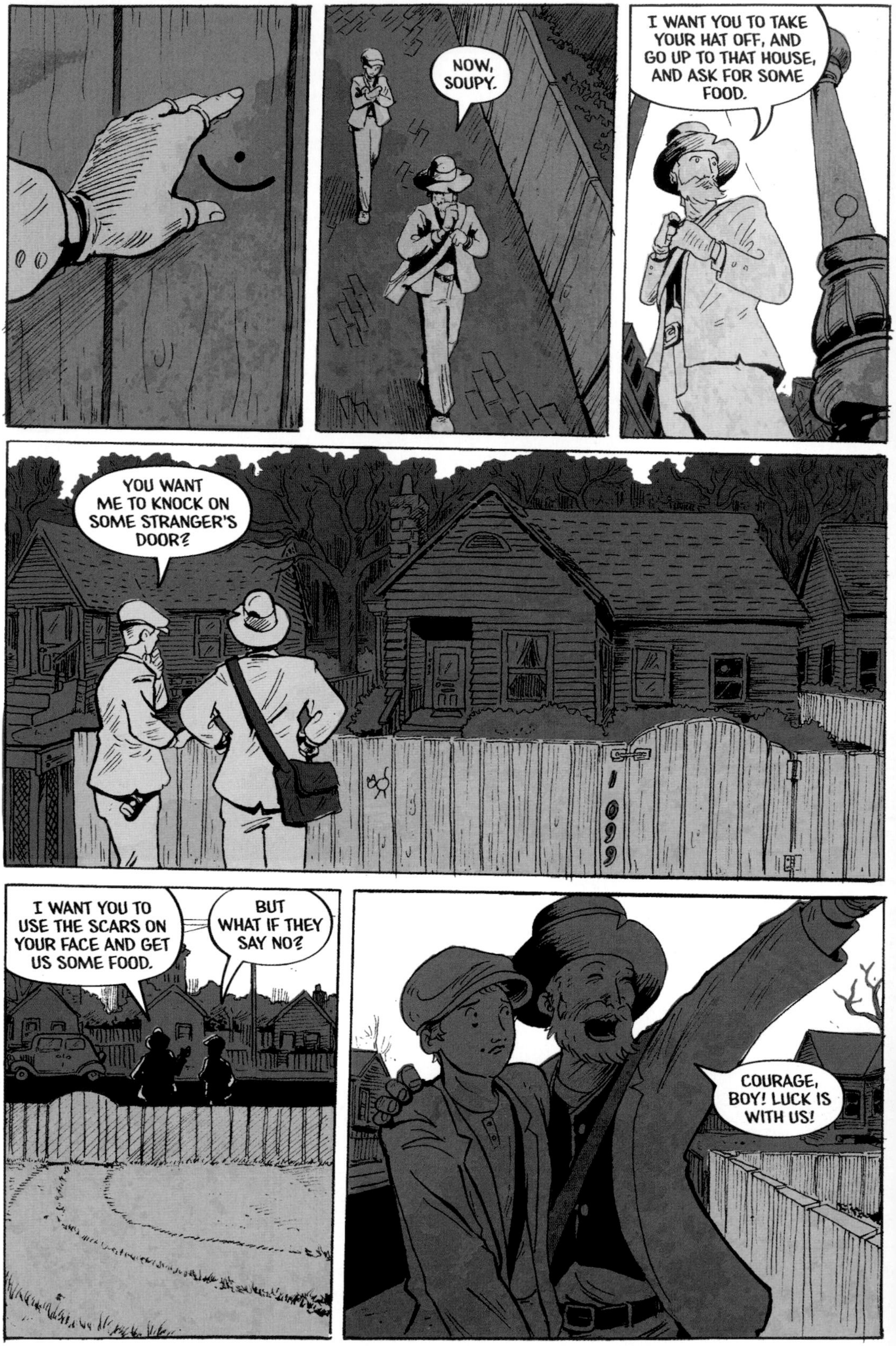
NOW, SOUPY.
I WANT YOU TO TAKE YOUR HAT OFF, AND GO UP TO THAT HOUSE, AND ASK FOR SOME FOOD.
YOU WANT ME TO KNOCK ON SOME STRANGER'S DOOR?
I WANT YOU TO USE THE SCARS ON YOUR FACE AND GET US SOME FOOD.
BUT WHAT IF THEY SAY NO?
COURAGE, BOY! LUCK IS WITH US!

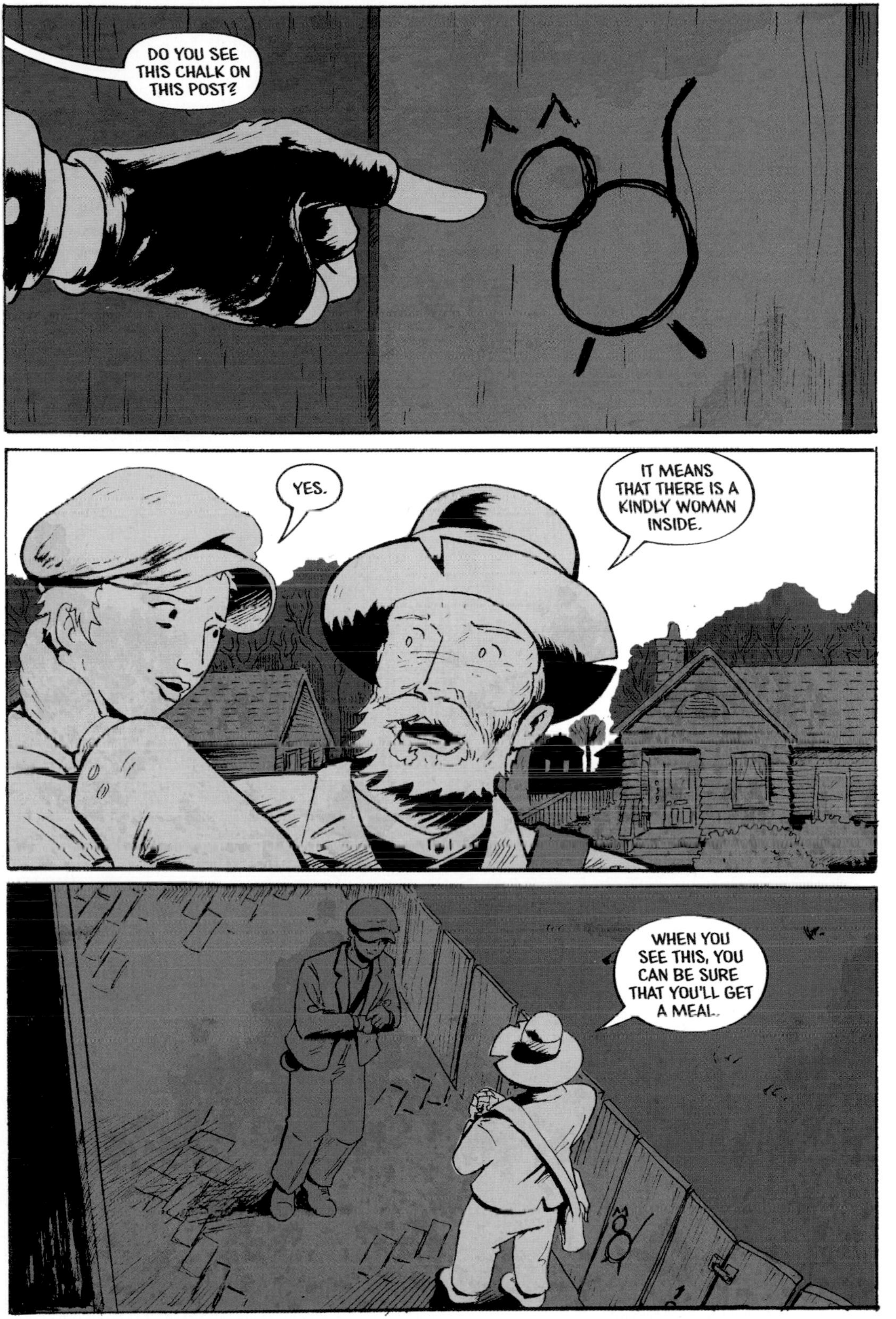
DO YOU SEE THIS CHALK ON THIS POST?
YES.
IT MEANS THAT THERE IS A KINDLY WOMAN INSIDE.
WHEN YOU SEE THIS, YOU CAN BE SURE THAT YOU'LL GET A MEAL.

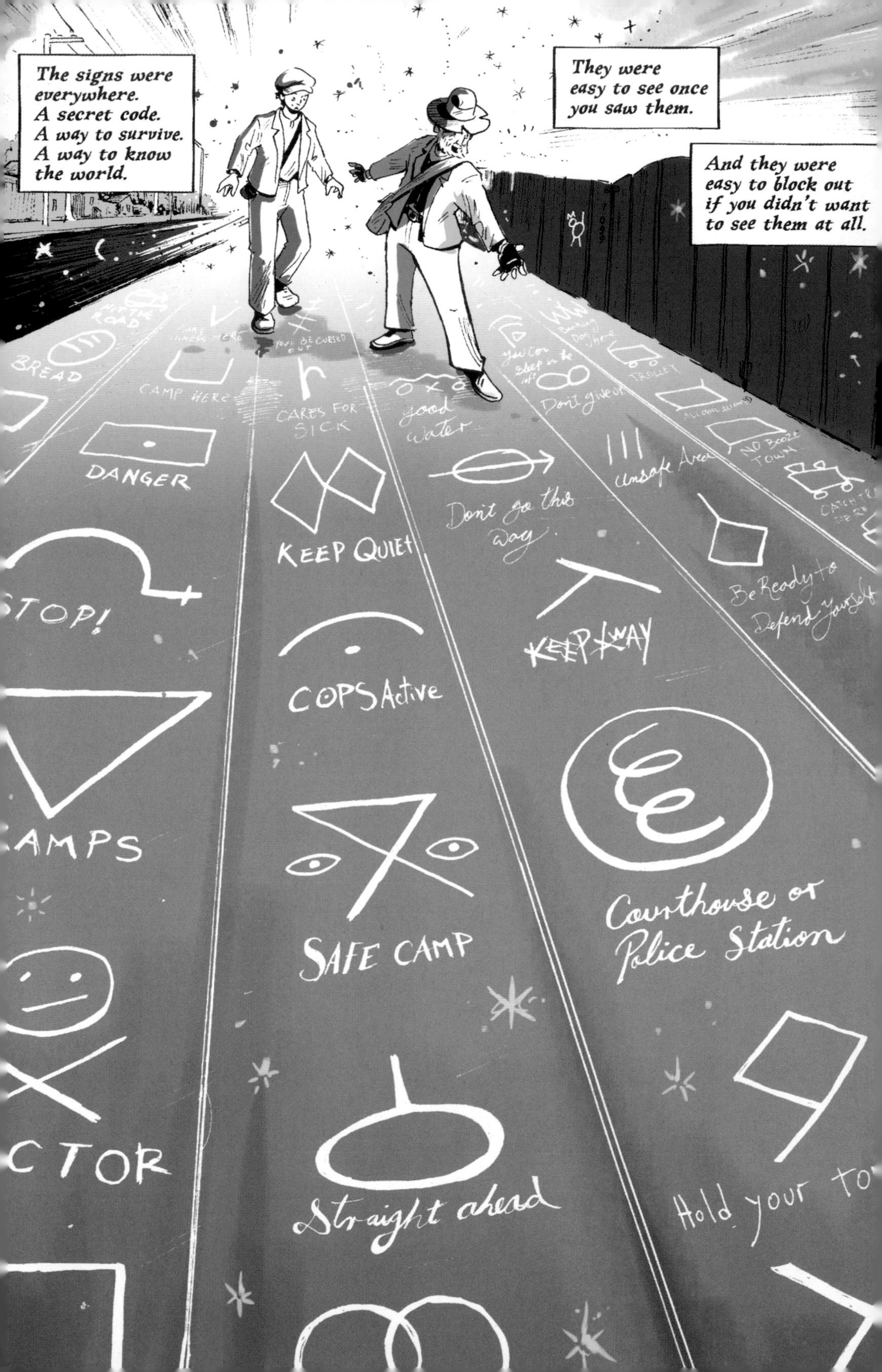
The signs were everywhere. A secret code. A way to survive. A way to know the world.
They were easy to see once you saw them.
And they were easy to block out if you didn't want to see them at all.
HIT THE ROAD
YOU'LL BE CURSED OUT
BREAD
CAMP HERE
CARES FOR SICK
good water
you can sleep in the loft
Don't give up
TROLLEY
NO BOOZE TOWN
DANGER
KEEP QUIET
Don't go this way
Unsafe Area
TOP!
KEEP AWAY
Be Ready to Defend Yourself
COPS Active
AMPS
SAFE CAMP
Courthouse or Police Station
CTOR
Straight ahead
Hold your to

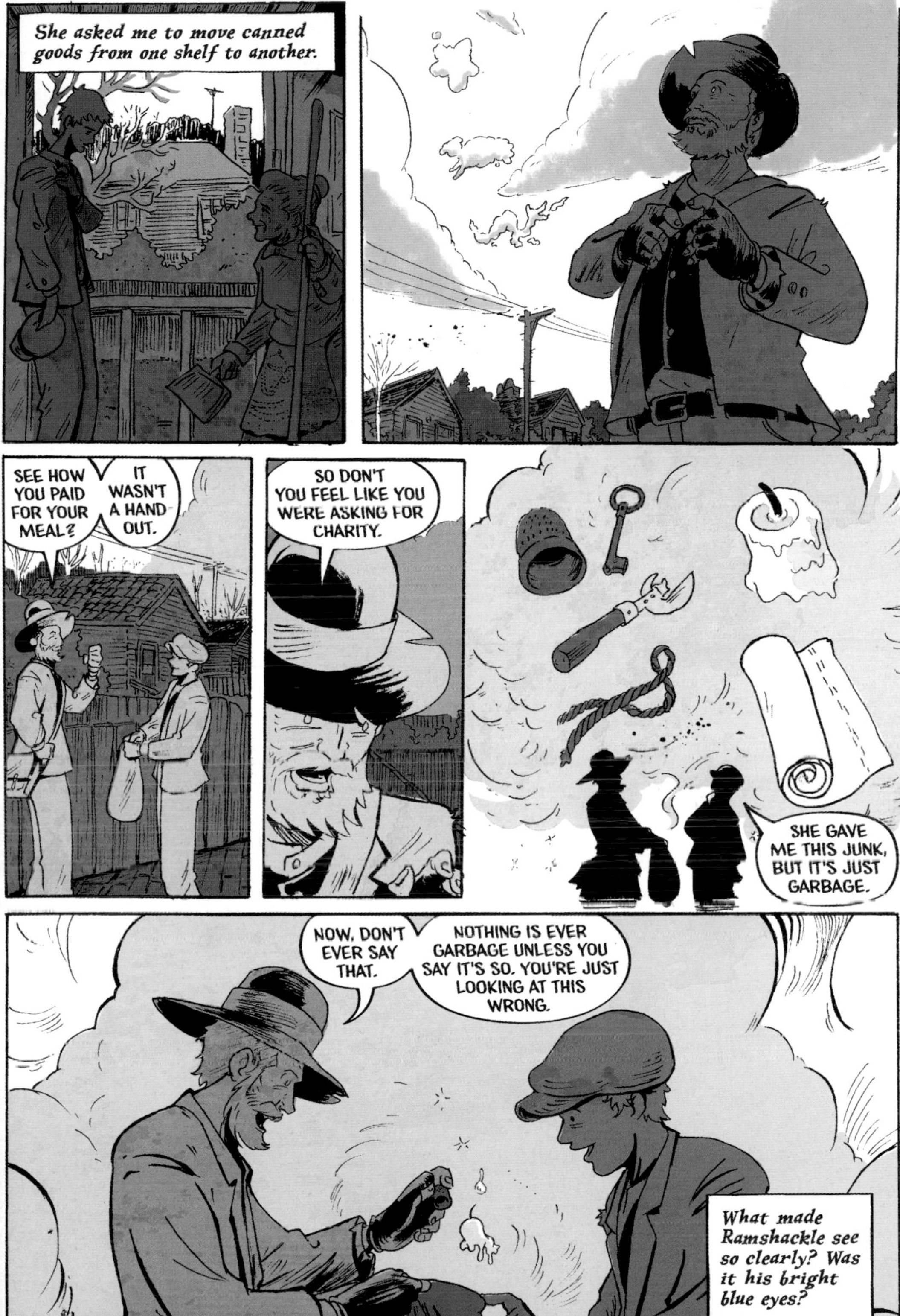
She asked me to move canned goods from one shelf to another.
SEE HOW YOU PAID FOR YOUR MEAL?
IT WASN'T A HAND-OUT.
SO DON'T YOU FEEL LIKE YOU WERE ASKING FOR CHARITY.
SHE GAVE ME THIS JUNK, BUT IT'S JUST GARBAGE.
NOW, DON'T EVER SAY THAT.
NOTHING IS EVER GARBAGE UNLESS YOU SAY IT'S SO. YOU'RE JUST LOOKING AT THIS WRONG.
What made Ramshackle see so clearly? Was it his bright blue eyes?

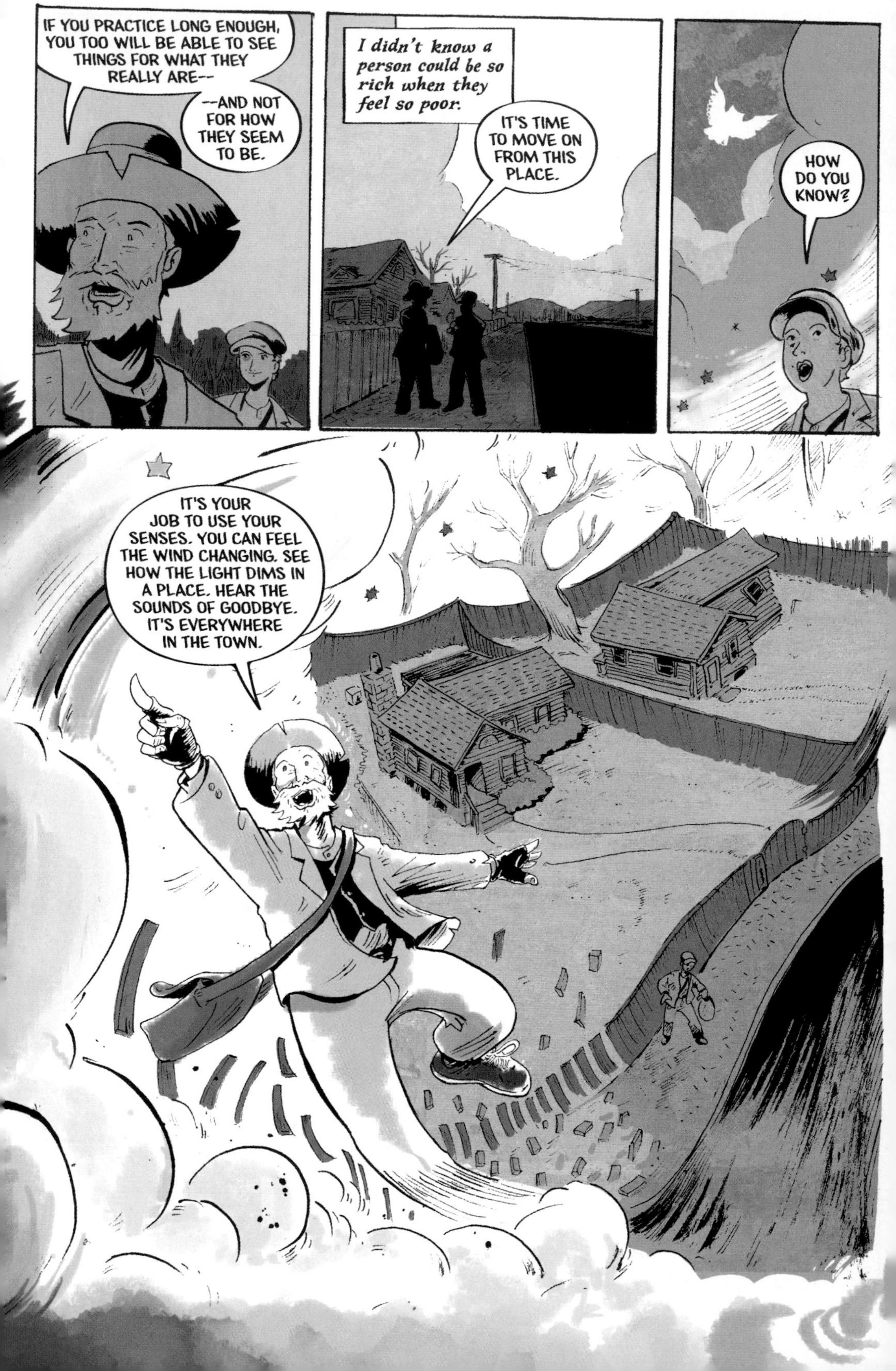
IF YOU PRACTICE LONG ENOUGH, YOU TOO WILL BE ABLE TO SEE THINGS FOR WHAT THEY REALLY ARE--
--AND NOT FOR HOW THEY SEEM TO BE.
I didn't know a person could be so rich when they feel so poor.
IT'S TIME TO MOVE ON FROM THIS PLACE.
HOW DO YOU KNOW?
IT'S YOUR JOB TO USE YOUR SENSES. YOU CAN FEEL THE WIND CHANGING. SEE HOW THE LIGHT DIMS IN A PLACE. HEAR THE SOUNDS OF GOODBYE. IT'S EVERYWHERE IN THE TOWN.

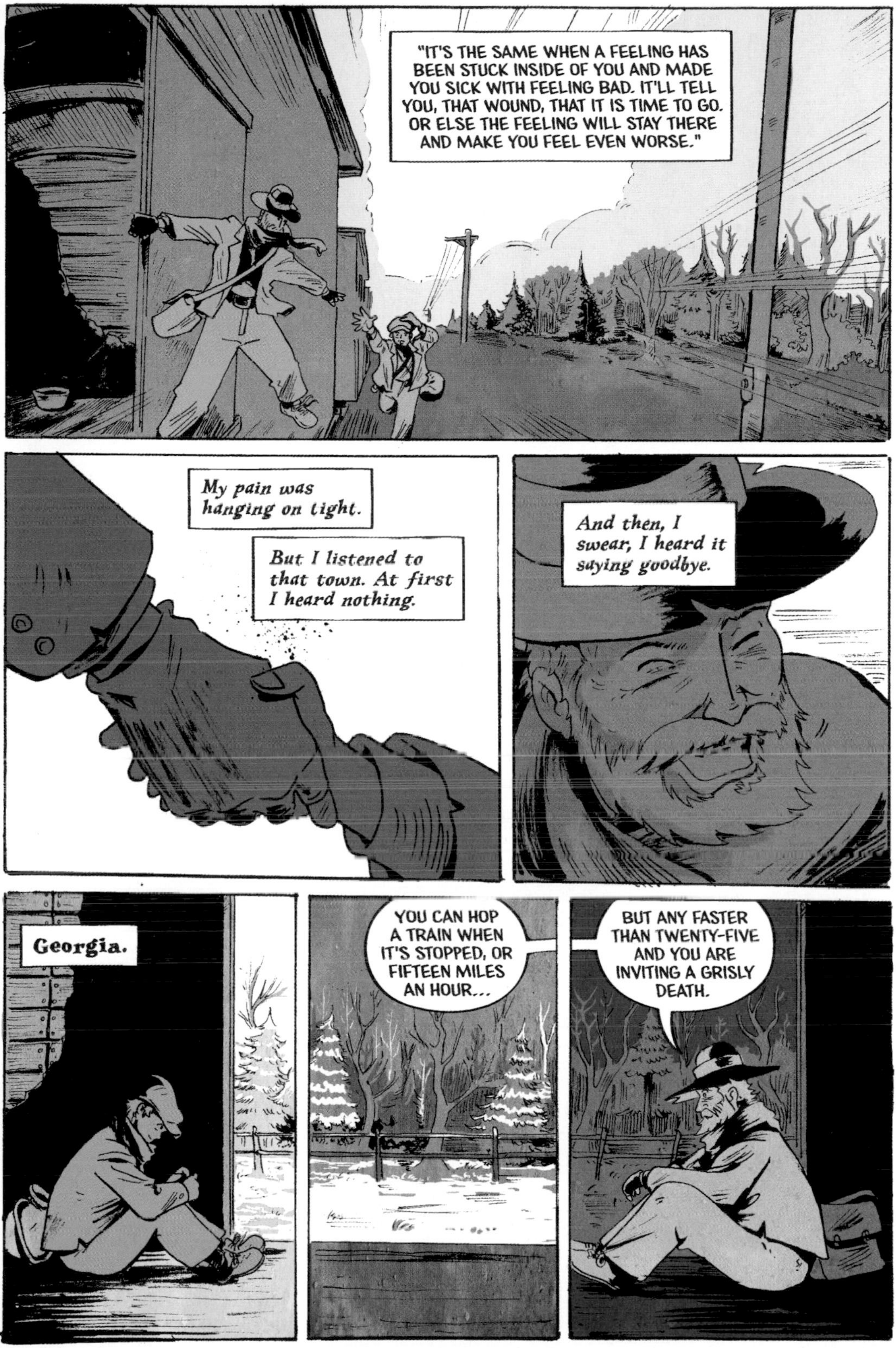
"IT'S THE SAME WHEN A FEELING HAS BEEN STUCK INSIDE OF YOU AND MADE YOU SICK WITH FEELING BAD. IT'LL TELL YOU, THAT WOUND, THAT IT IS TIME TO GO. OR ELSE THE FEELING WILL STAY THERE AND MAKE YOU FEEL EVEN WORSE."
My pain was hanging on tight.
But I listened to that town. At first I heard nothing.
And then, I swear, I heard it saying goodbye.
Georgia.
YOU CAN HOP A TRAIN WHEN IT'S STOPPED, OR FIFTEEN MILES AN HOUR...
BUT ANY FASTER THAN TWENTY-FIVE AND YOU ARE INVITING A GRISLY DEATH.

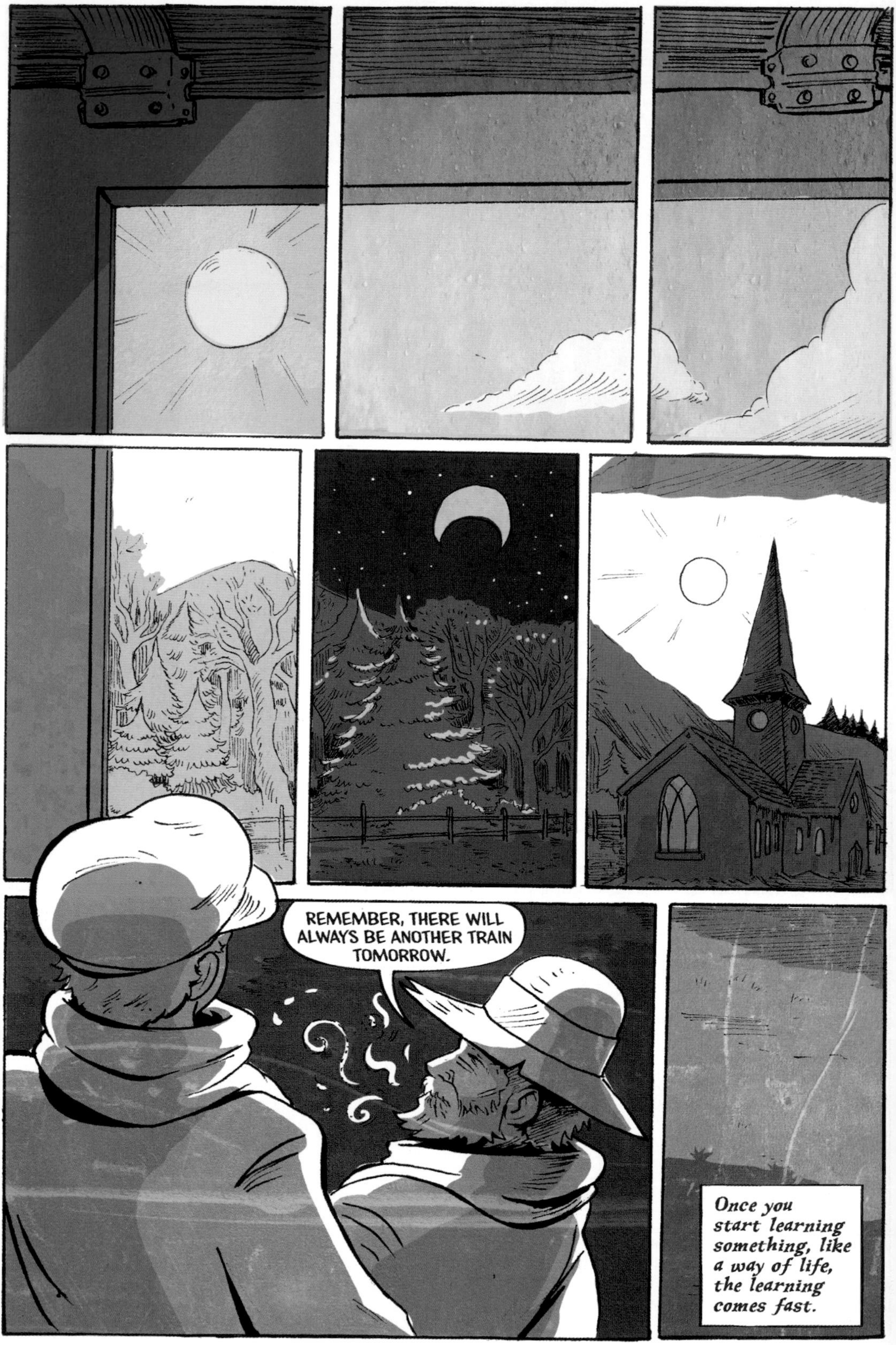
REMEMBER, THERE WILL ALWAYS BE ANOTHER TRAIN TOMORROW.
Once you start learning something, like a way of life, the learning comes fast.

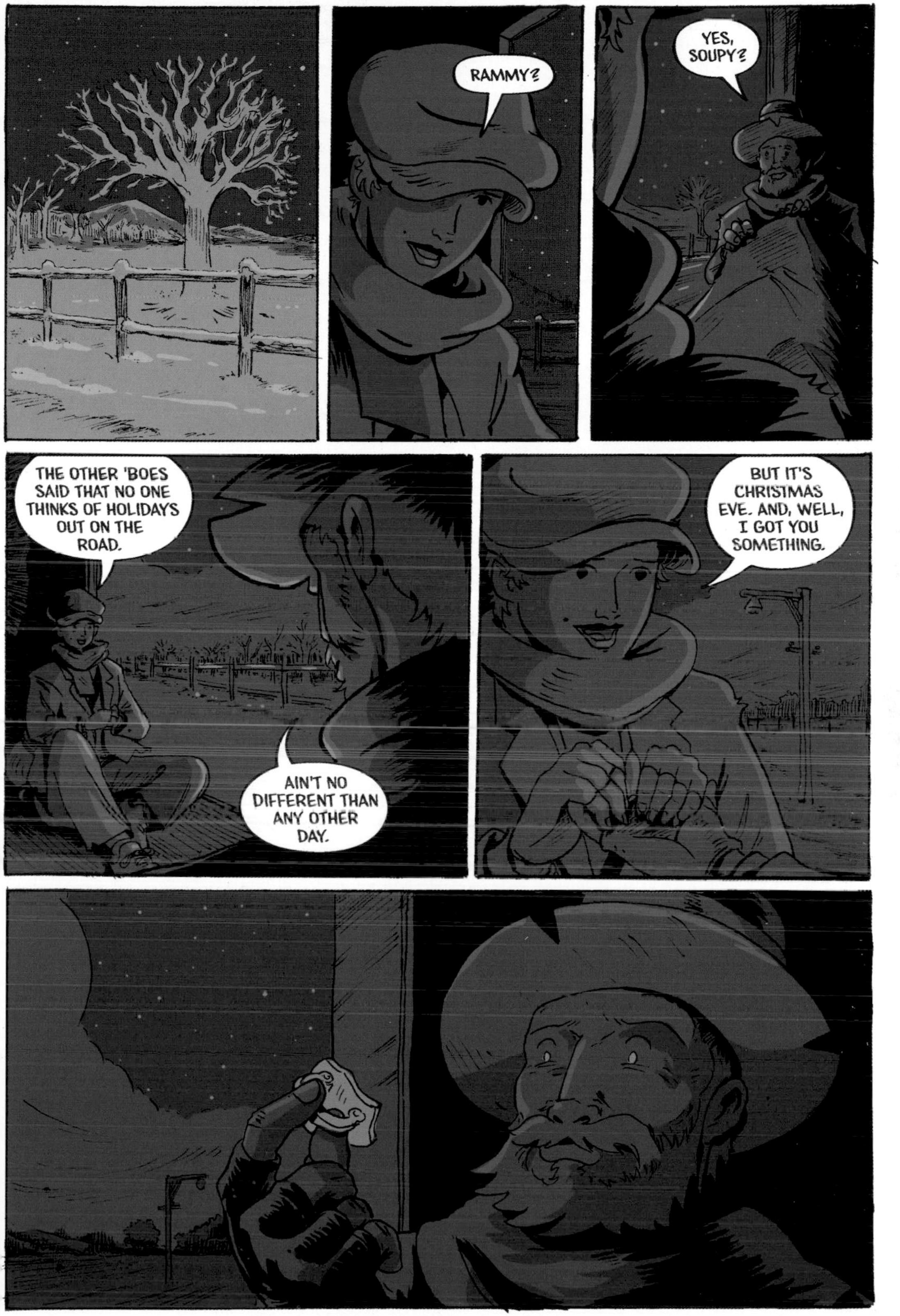
RAMMY?
YES, SOUPY?
THE OTHER 'BOES SAID THAT NO ONE THINKS OF HOLIDAYS OUT ON THE ROAD.
AIN'T NO DIFFERENT THAN ANY OTHER DAY.
BUT IT'S CHRISTMAS EVE. AND, WELL, I GOT YOU SOMETHING.

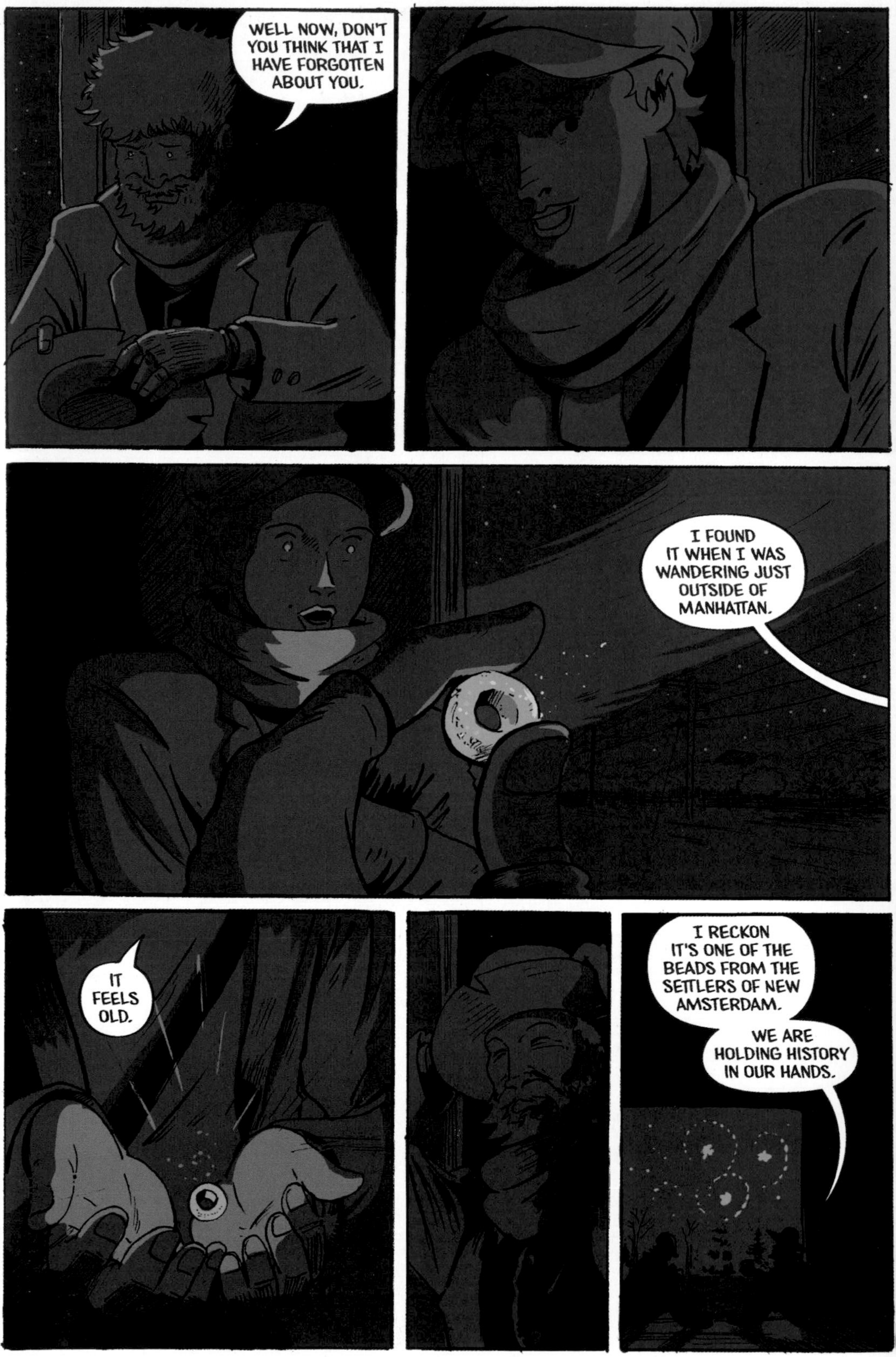
WELL NOW, DON'T YOU THINK THAT I HAVE FORGOTTEN ABOUT YOU.
I FOUND IT WHEN I WAS WANDERING JUST OUTSIDE OF MANHATTAN.
IT FEELS OLD.
I RECKON IT'S ONE OF THE BEADS FROM THE SETTLERS OF NEW AMSTERDAM.
WE ARE HOLDING HISTORY IN OUR HANDS.

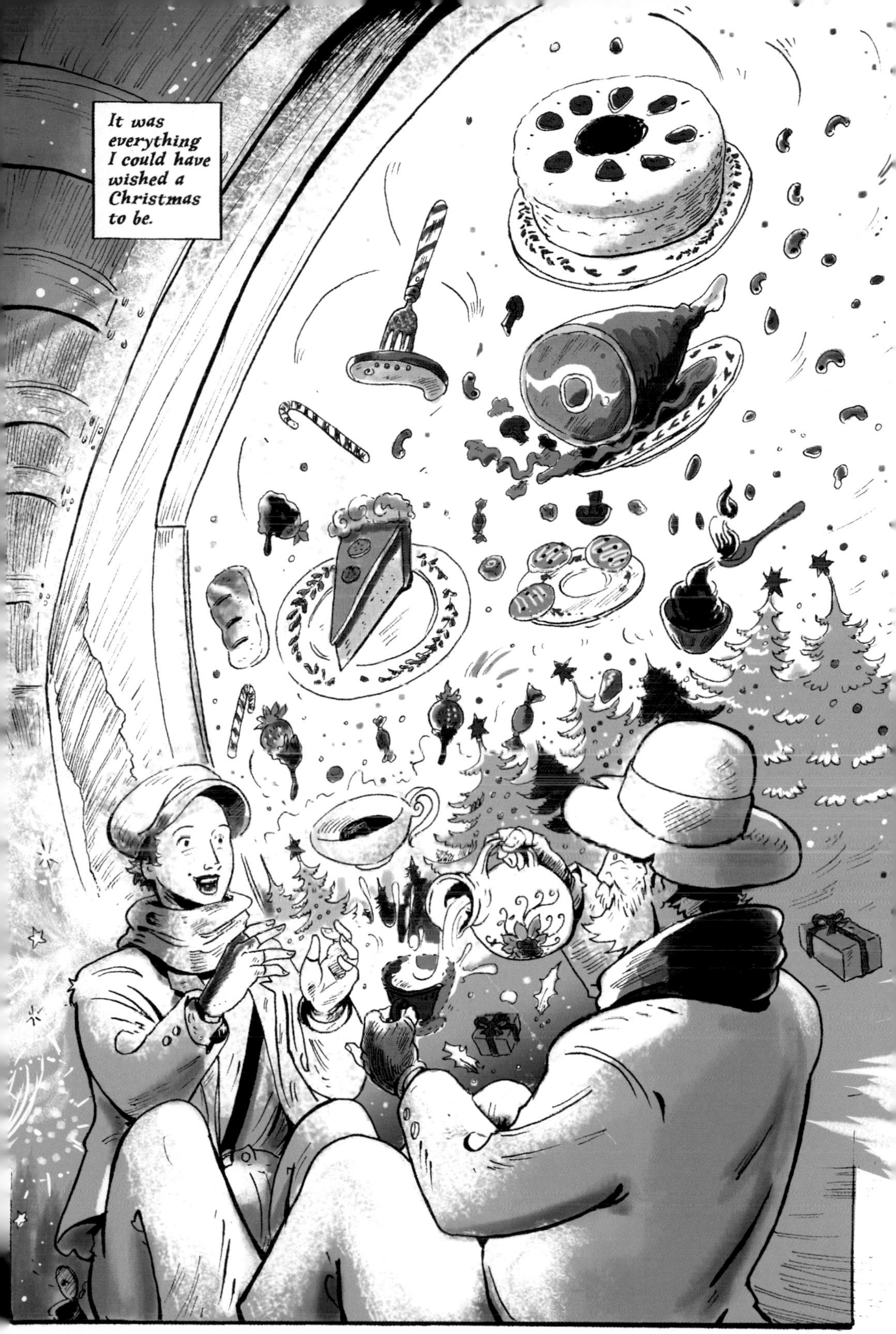
It was everything I could have wished a Christmas to be.

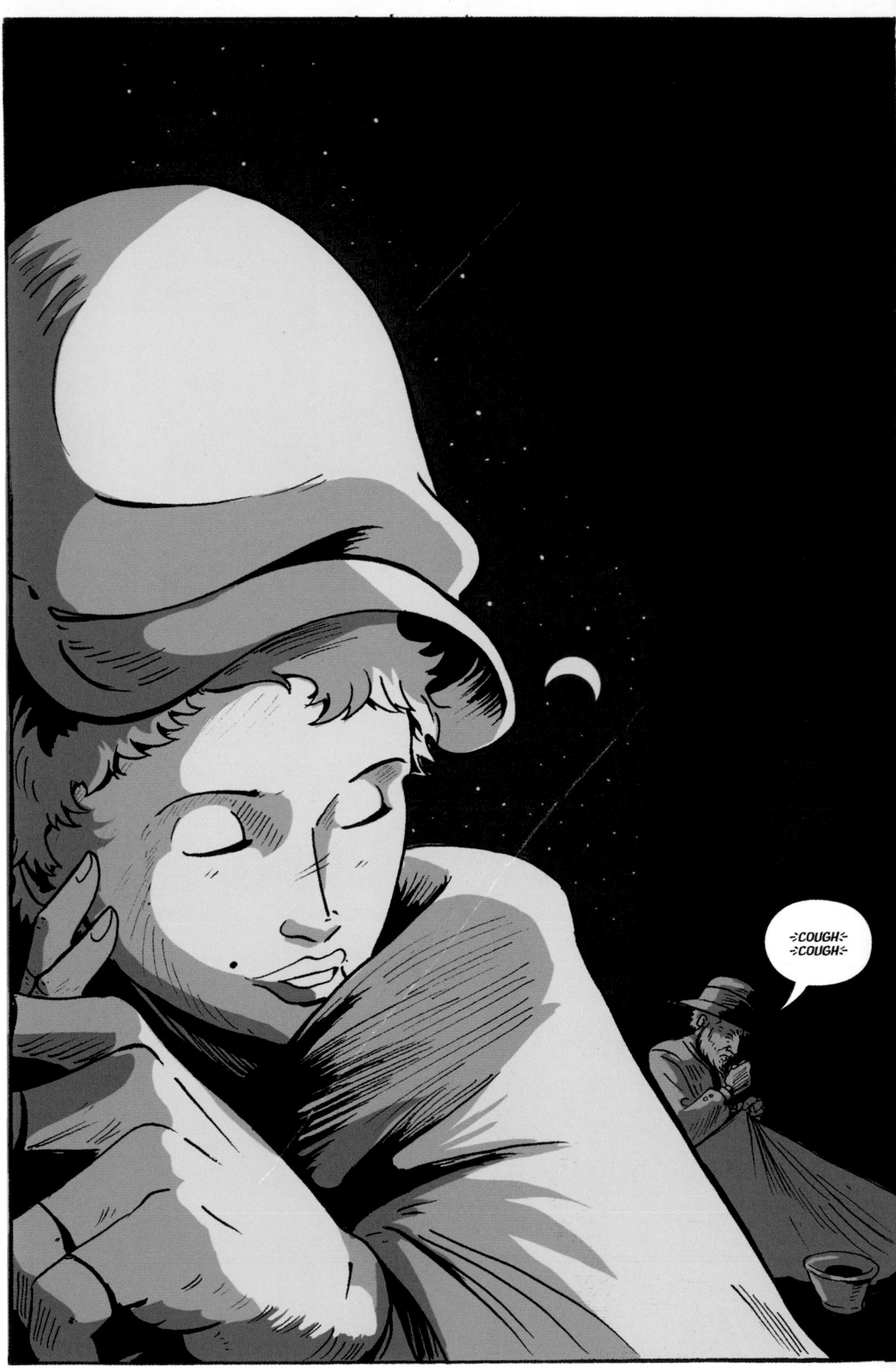
COUGH COUGH

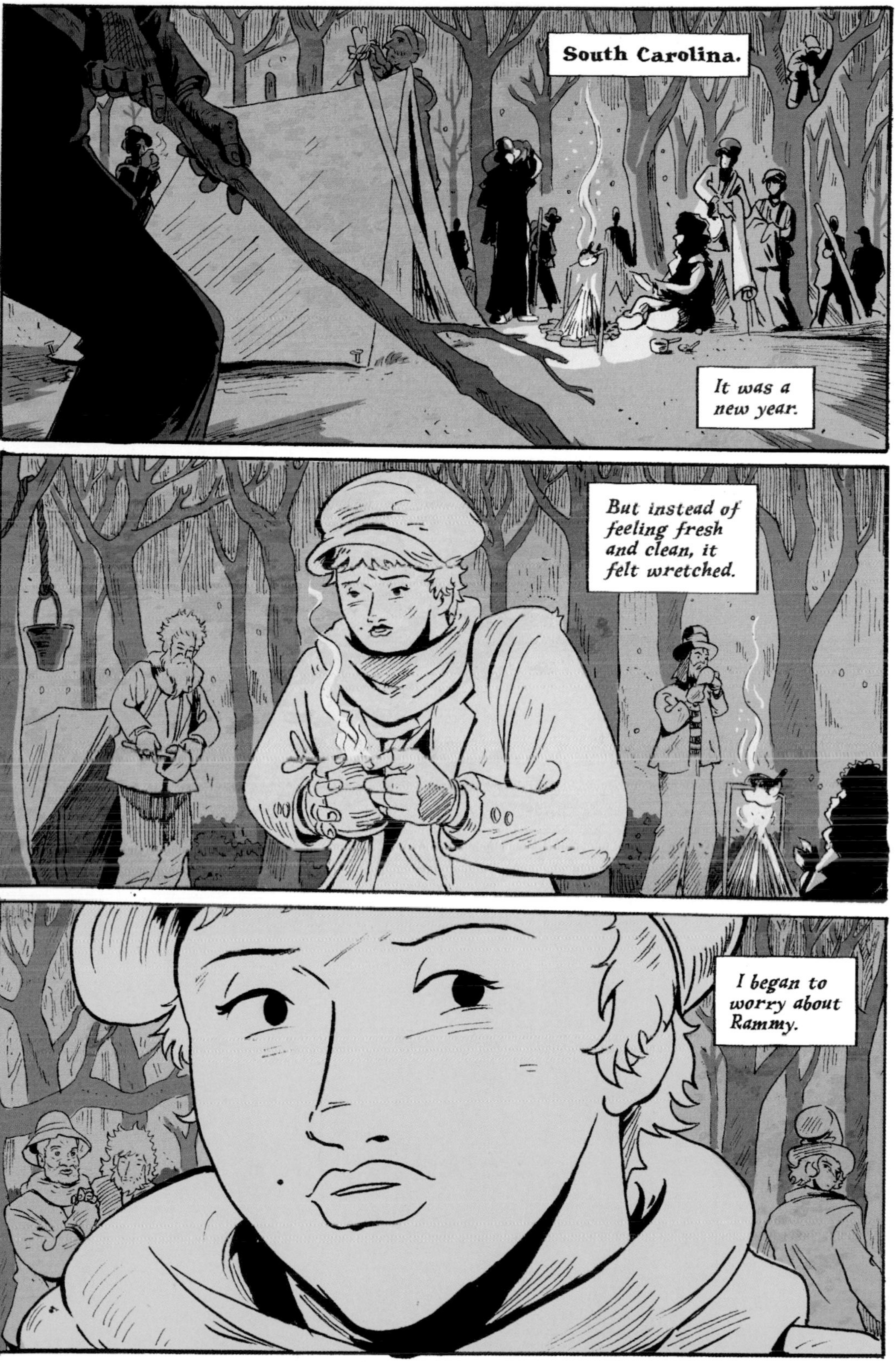
South Carolina.
It was a new year.
But instead of feeling fresh and clean, it felt wretched.
I began to worry about Rammy.

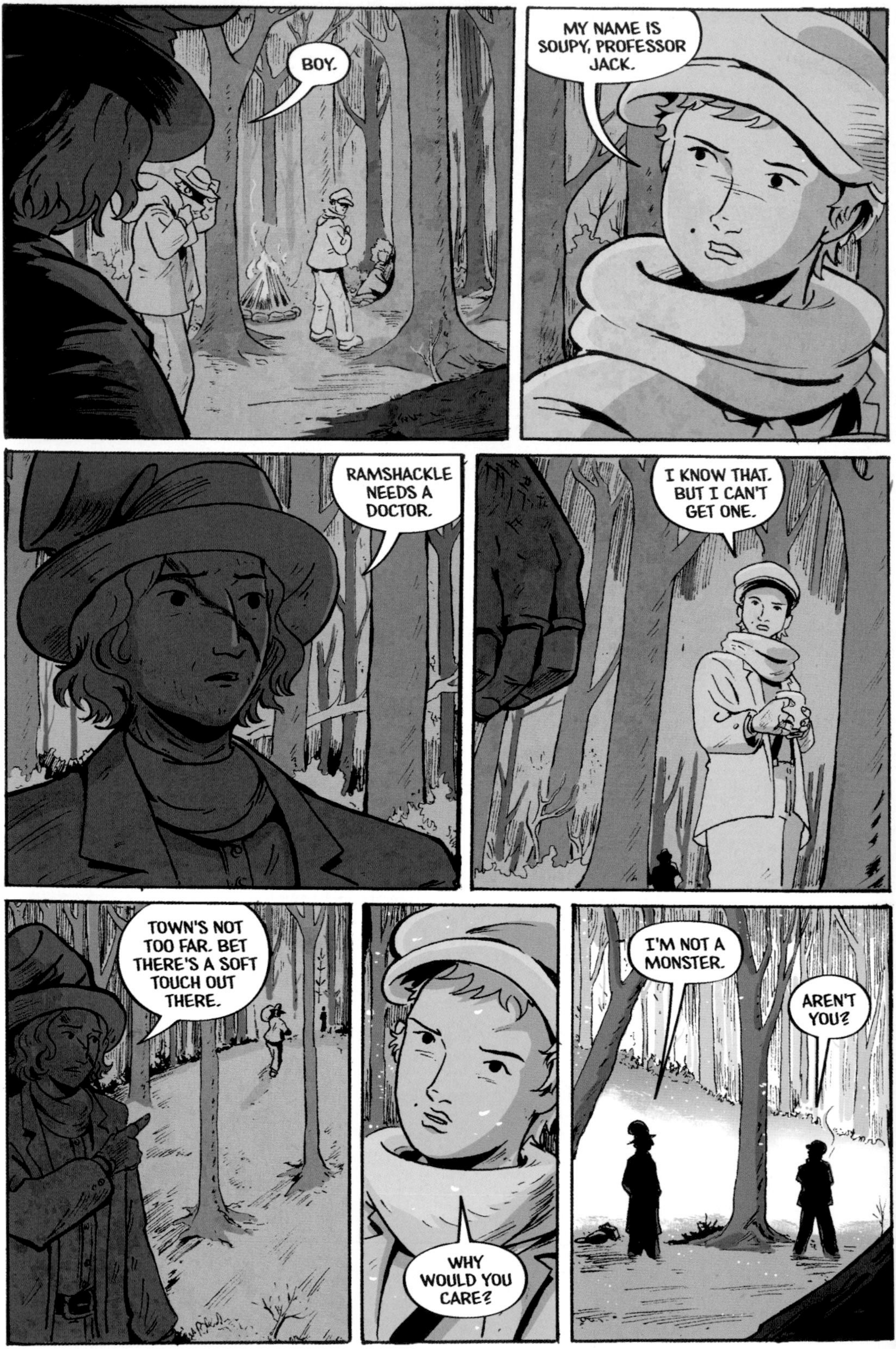
BOY.
MY NAME IS SOUPY, PROFESSOR JACK.
RAMSHACKLE NEEDS A DOCTOR.
I KNOW THAT. BUT I CAN'T GET ONE.
TOWN'S NOT TOO FAR. BET THERE'S A SOFT TOUCH OUT THERE.
WHY WOULD YOU CARE?
I'M NOT A MONSTER.
AREN'T YOU?

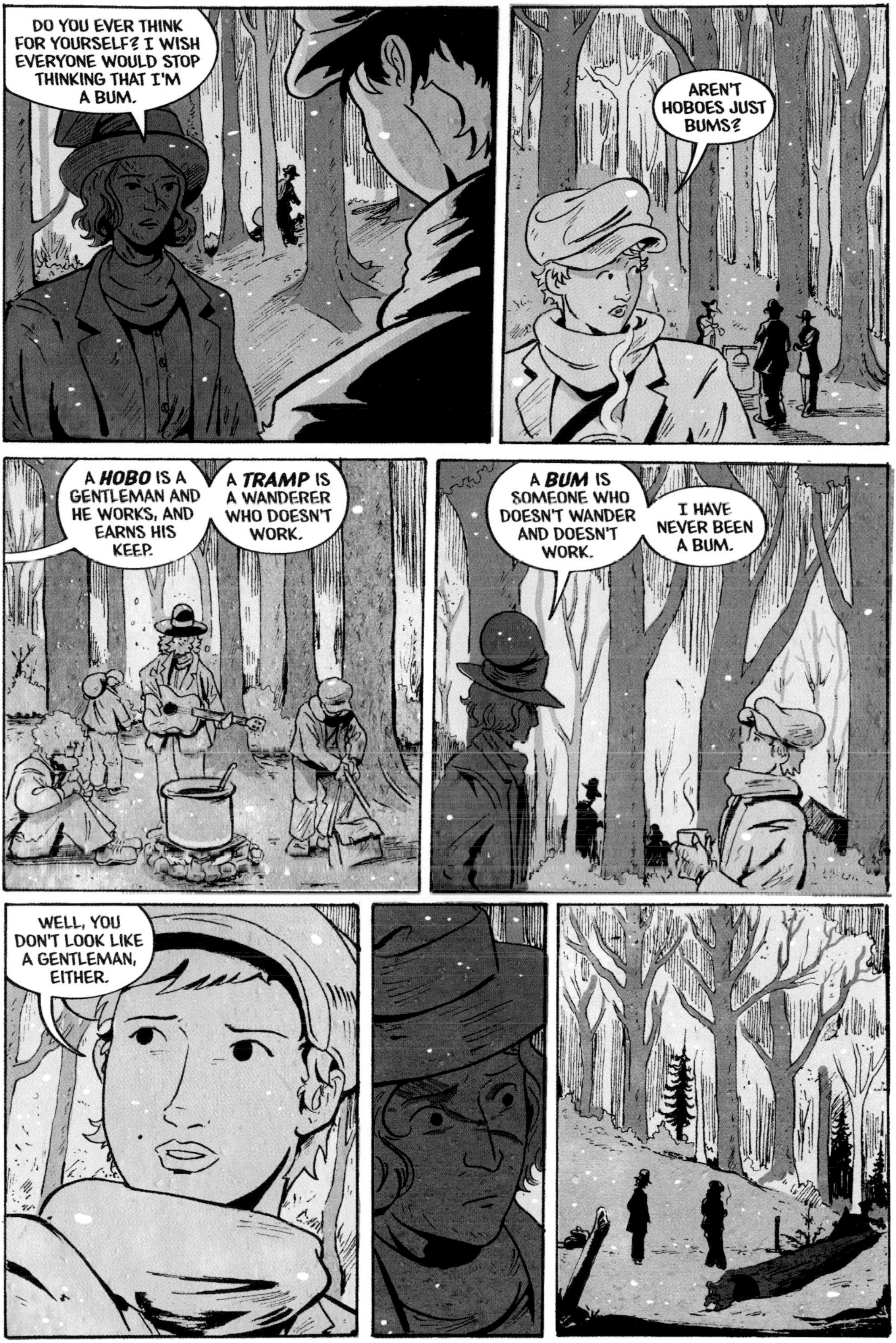
DO YOU EVER THINK FOR YOURSELF? I WISH EVERYONE WOULD STOP THINKING THAT I'M A BUM.
AREN'T HOBOES JUST BUMS?
A *HOBO* IS A GENTLEMAN AND HE WORKS, AND EARNS HIS KEEP.
A *TRAMP* IS A WANDERER WHO DOESN'T WORK.
A *BUM* IS SOMEONE WHO DOESN'T WANDER AND DOESN'T WORK.
I HAVE NEVER BEEN A BUM.
WELL, YOU DON'T LOOK LIKE A GENTLEMAN, EITHER.

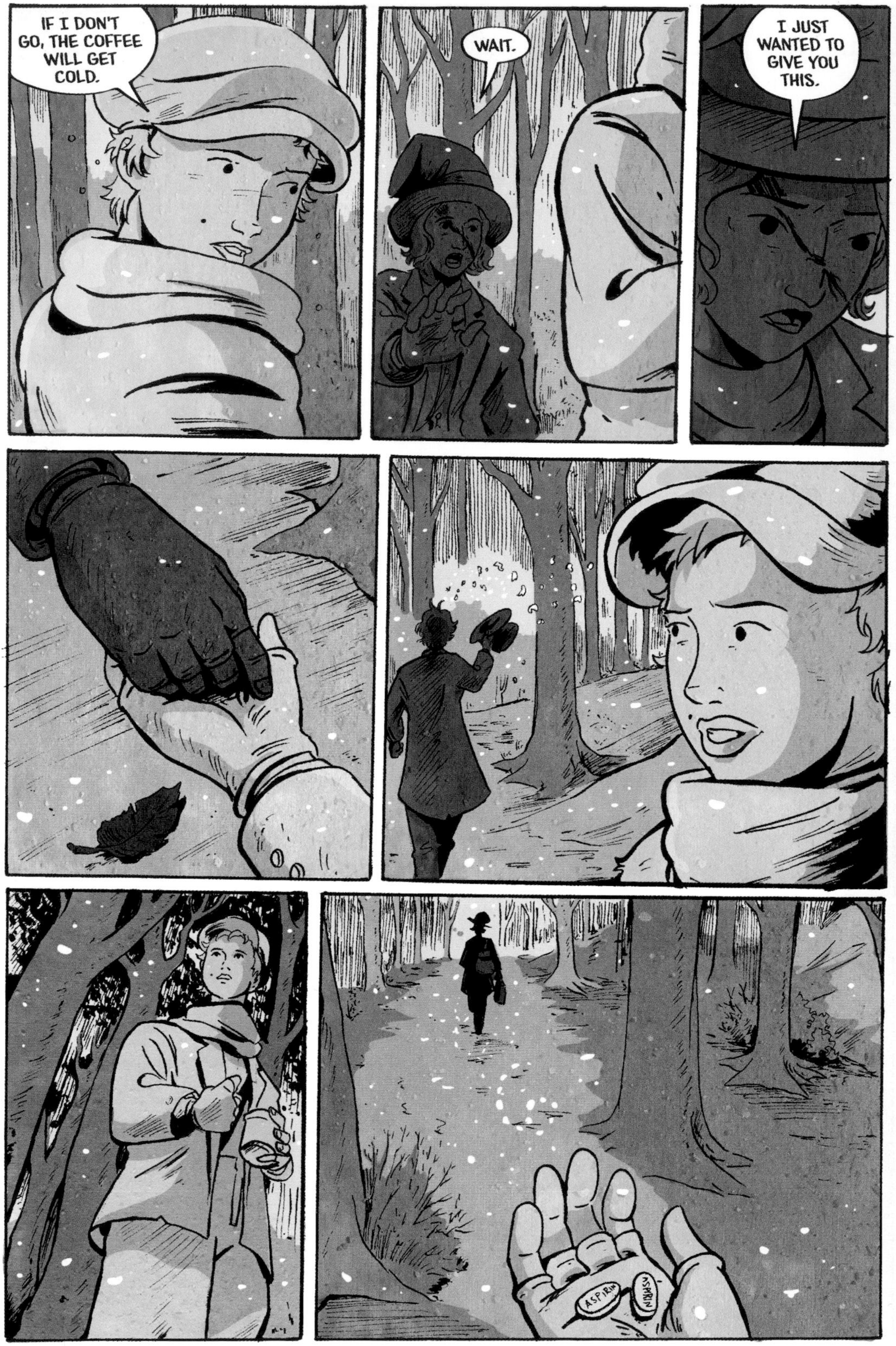
IF I DON'T GO, THE COFFEE WILL GET COLD.
WAIT.
I JUST WANTED TO GIVE YOU THIS.
ASPIRIN
ASPIRIN

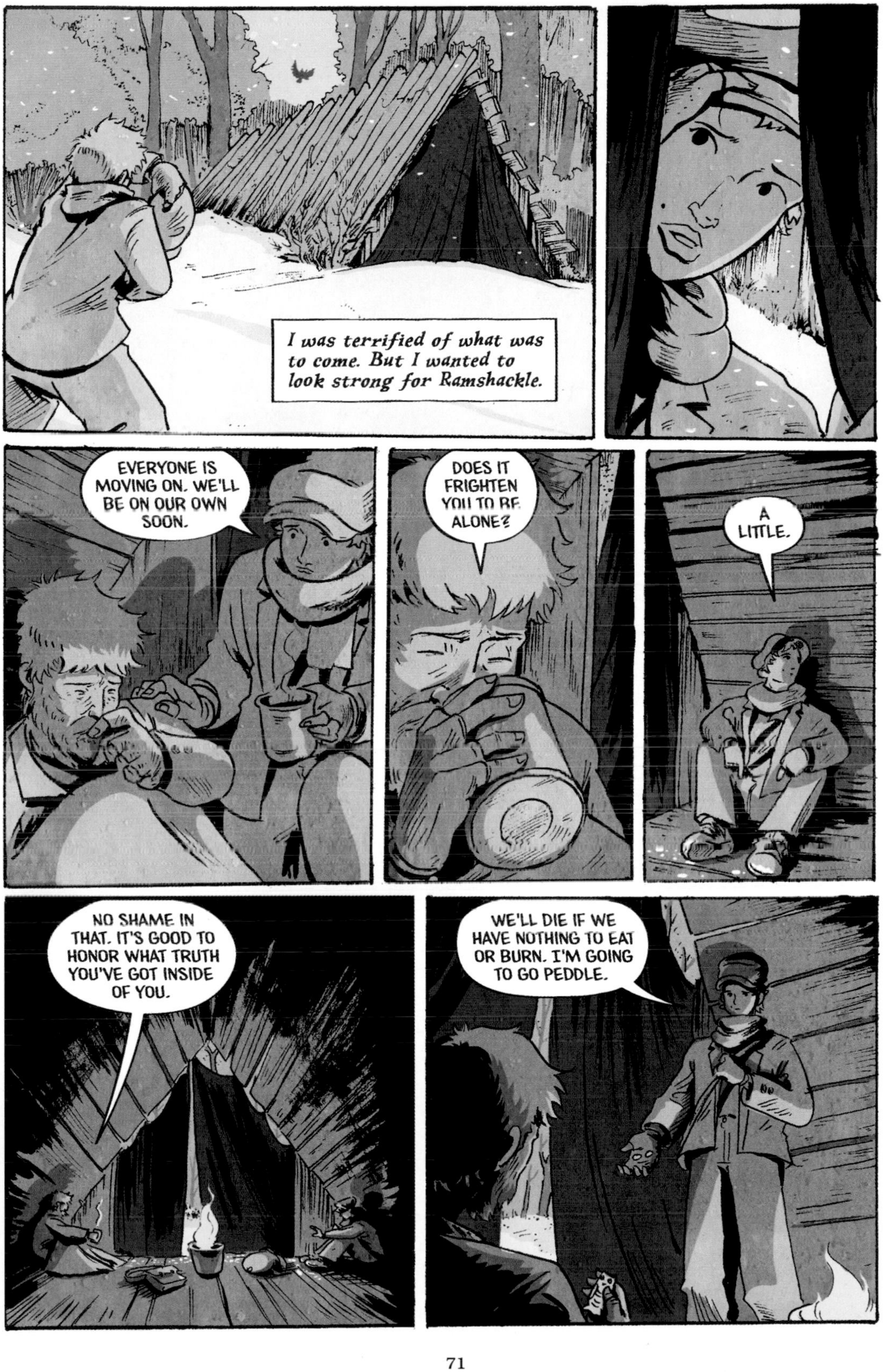
I was terrified of what was to come. But I wanted to look strong for Ramshackle.
EVERYONE IS MOVING ON. WE'LL BE ON OUR OWN SOON.
DOES IT FRIGHTEN YOU TO BE ALONE?
A LITTLE.
NO SHAME IN THAT. IT'S GOOD TO HONOR WHAT TRUTH YOU'VE GOT INSIDE OF YOU.
WE'LL DIE IF WE HAVE NOTHING TO EAT OR BURN. I'M GOING TO GO PEDDLE.

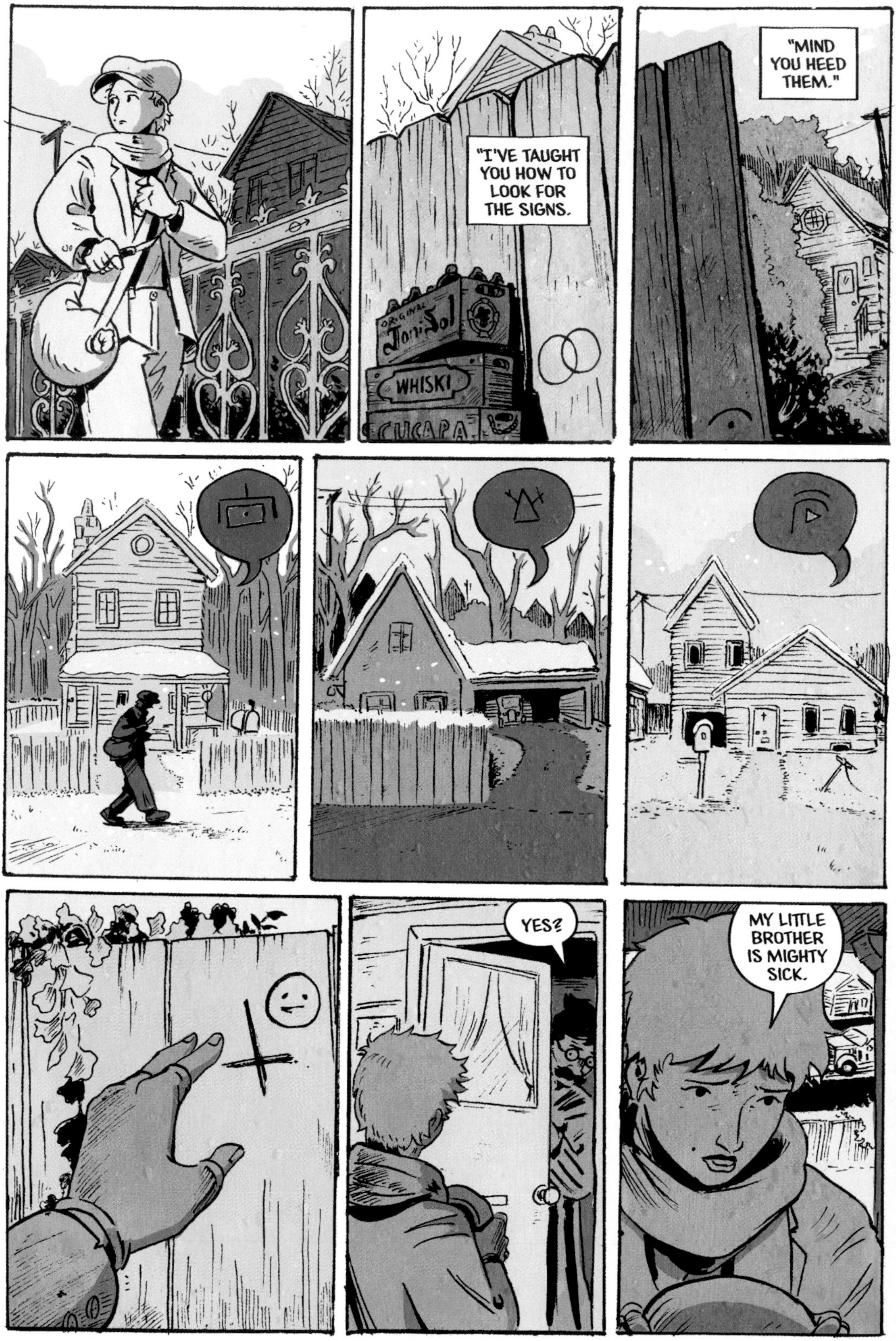
"I'VE TAUGHT YOU HOW TO LOOK FOR THE SIGNS.
ORIGINAL
WHISKI
CUCAPA
"MIND YOU HEED THEM."
YES?
MY LITTLE BROTHER IS MIGHTY SICK.

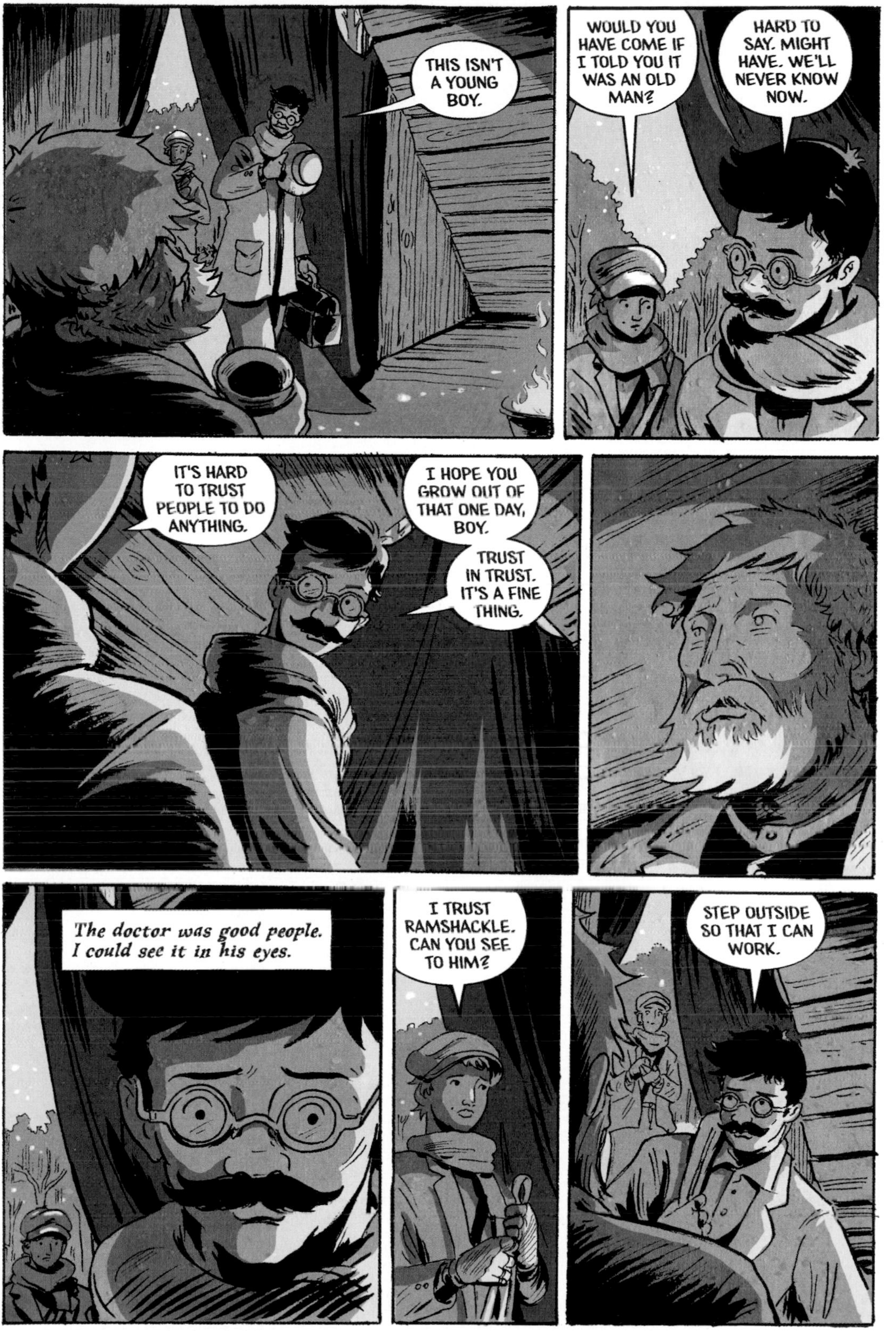
THIS ISN'T A YOUNG BOY.
WOULD YOU HAVE COME IF I TOLD YOU IT WAS AN OLD MAN?
HARD TO SAY. MIGHT HAVE. WE'LL NEVER KNOW NOW.
IT'S HARD TO TRUST PEOPLE TO DO ANYTHING.
I HOPE YOU GROW OUT OF THAT ONE DAY, BOY.
TRUST IN TRUST. IT'S A FINE THING.
The doctor was good people. I could see it in his eyes.
I TRUST RAMSHACKLE. CAN YOU SEE TO HIM?
STEP OUTSIDE SO THAT I CAN WORK.

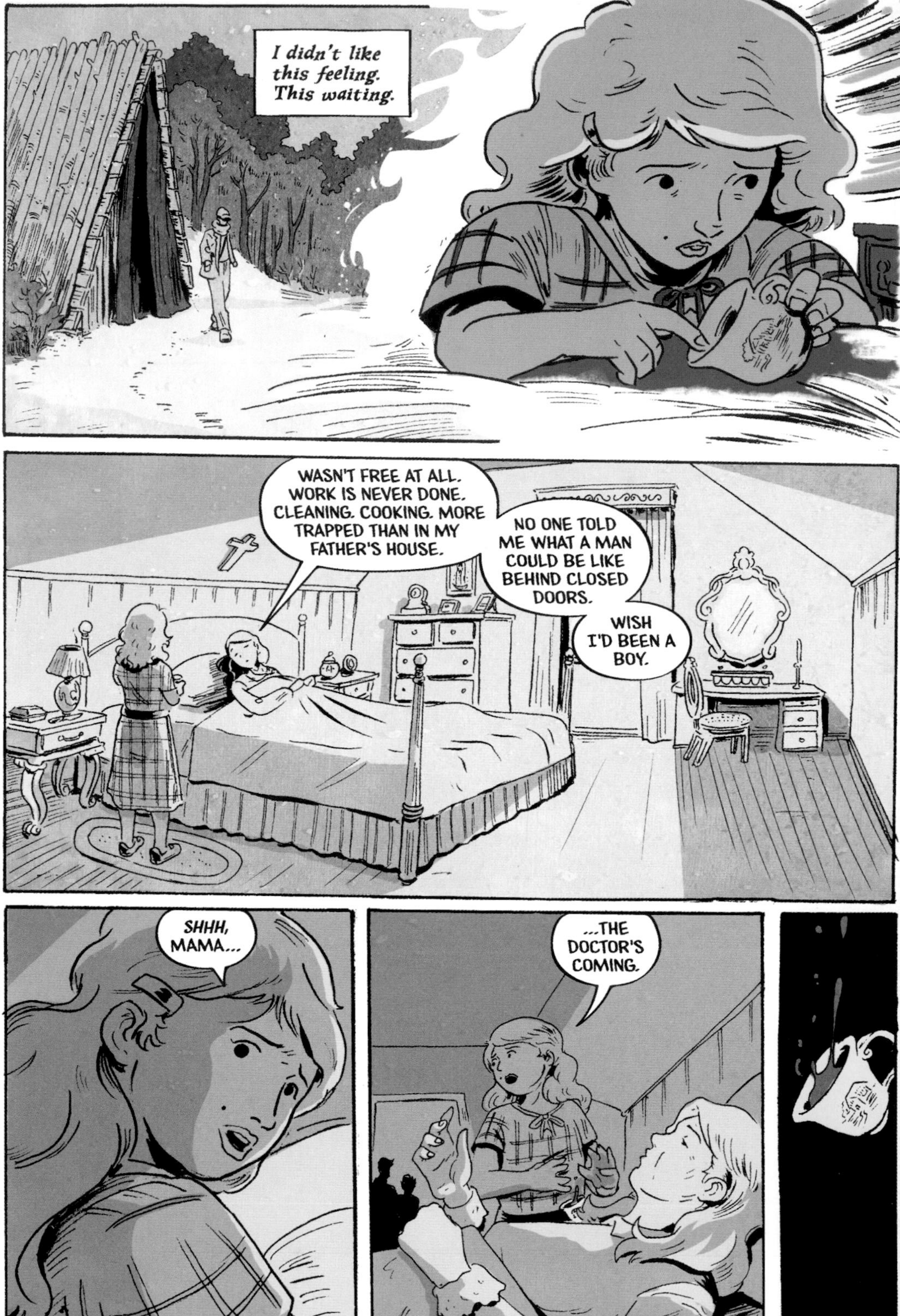
I didn't like this feeling. This waiting.
WASN'T FREE AT ALL. WORK IS NEVER DONE. CLEANING. COOKING. MORE TRAPPED THAN IN MY FATHER'S HOUSE.
NO ONE TOLD ME WHAT A MAN COULD BE LIKE BEHIND CLOSED DOORS.
WISH I'D BEEN A BOY.
SHHH, MAMA...
...THE DOCTOR'S COMING.

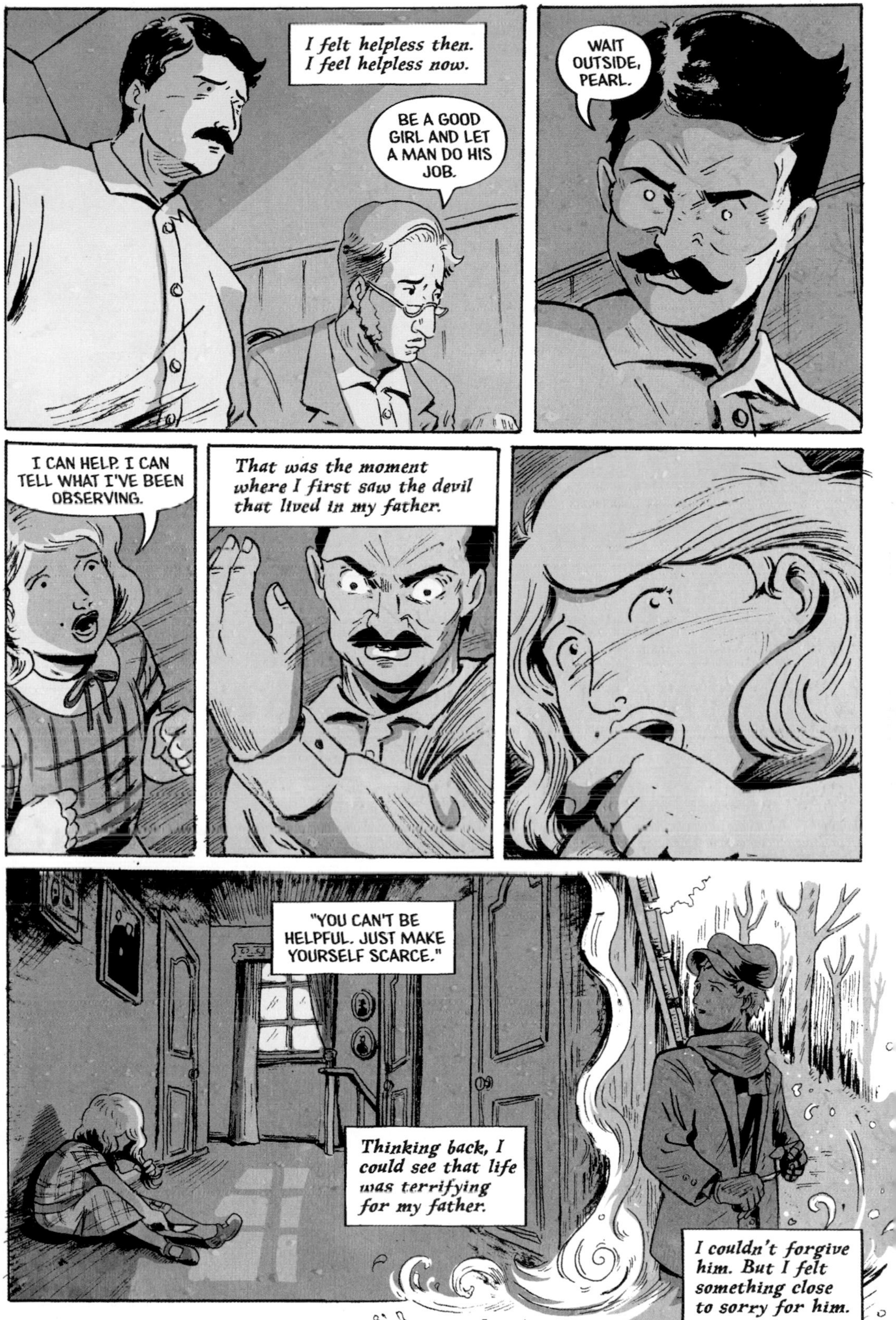

I felt helpless then. I feel helpless now.
BE A GOOD GIRL AND LET A MAN DO HIS JOB.
WAIT OUTSIDE, PEARL.
I CAN HELP. I CAN TELL WHAT I'VE BEEN OBSERVING.
That was the moment where I first saw the devil that lived in my father.
"YOU CAN'T BE HELPFUL. JUST MAKE YOURSELF SCARCE."
Thinking back, I could see that life was terrifying for my father.
I couldn't forgive him. But I felt something close to sorry for him.

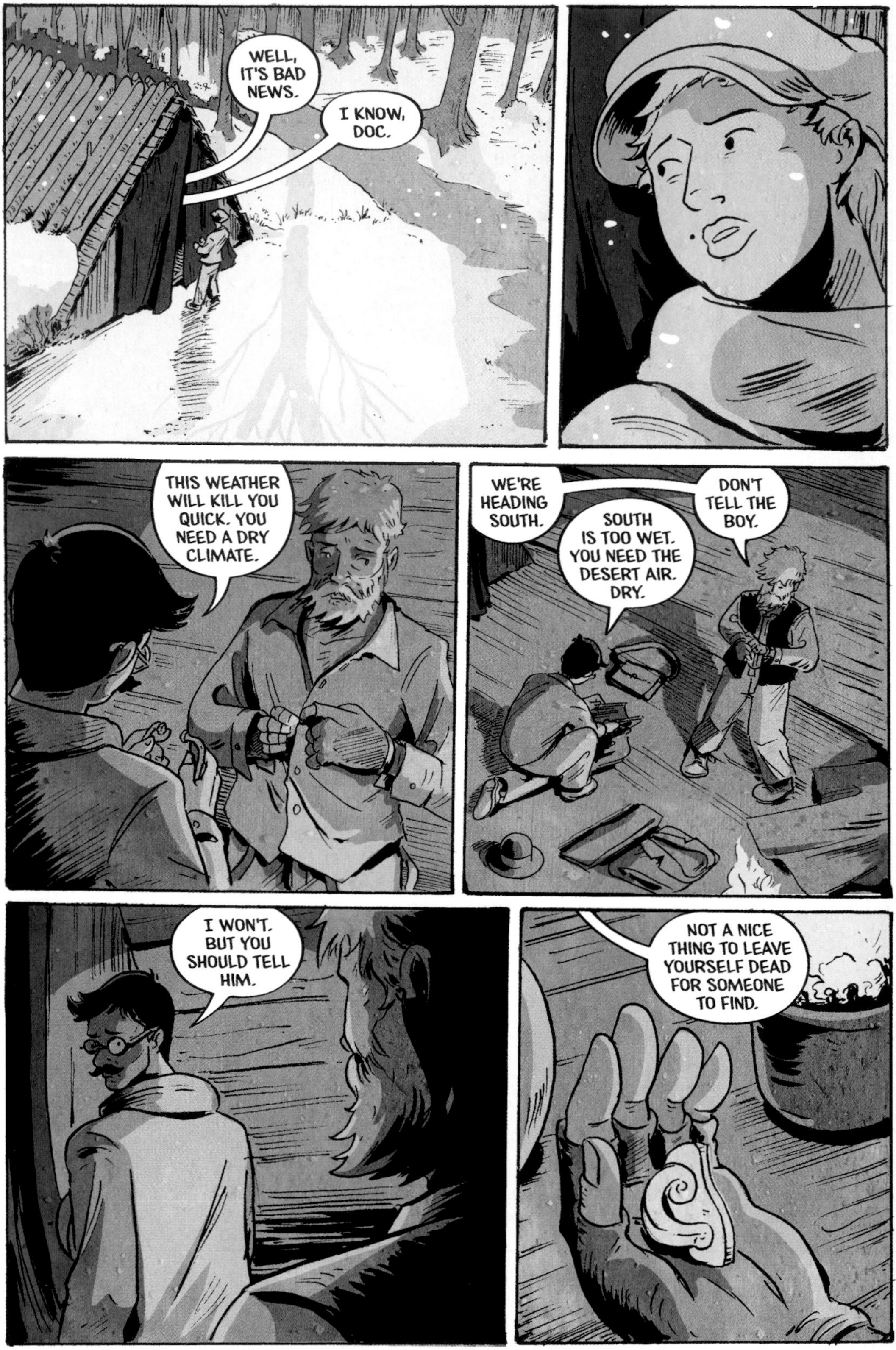
WELL, IT'S BAD NEWS.
I KNOW, DOC.
THIS WEATHER WILL KILL YOU QUICK. YOU NEED A DRY CLIMATE.
WE'RE HEADING SOUTH.
DON'T TELL THE BOY.
SOUTH IS TOO WET. YOU NEED THE DESERT AIR. DRY.
I WON'T. BUT YOU SHOULD TELL HIM.
NOT A NICE THING TO LEAVE YOURSELF DEAD FOR SOMEONE TO FIND.

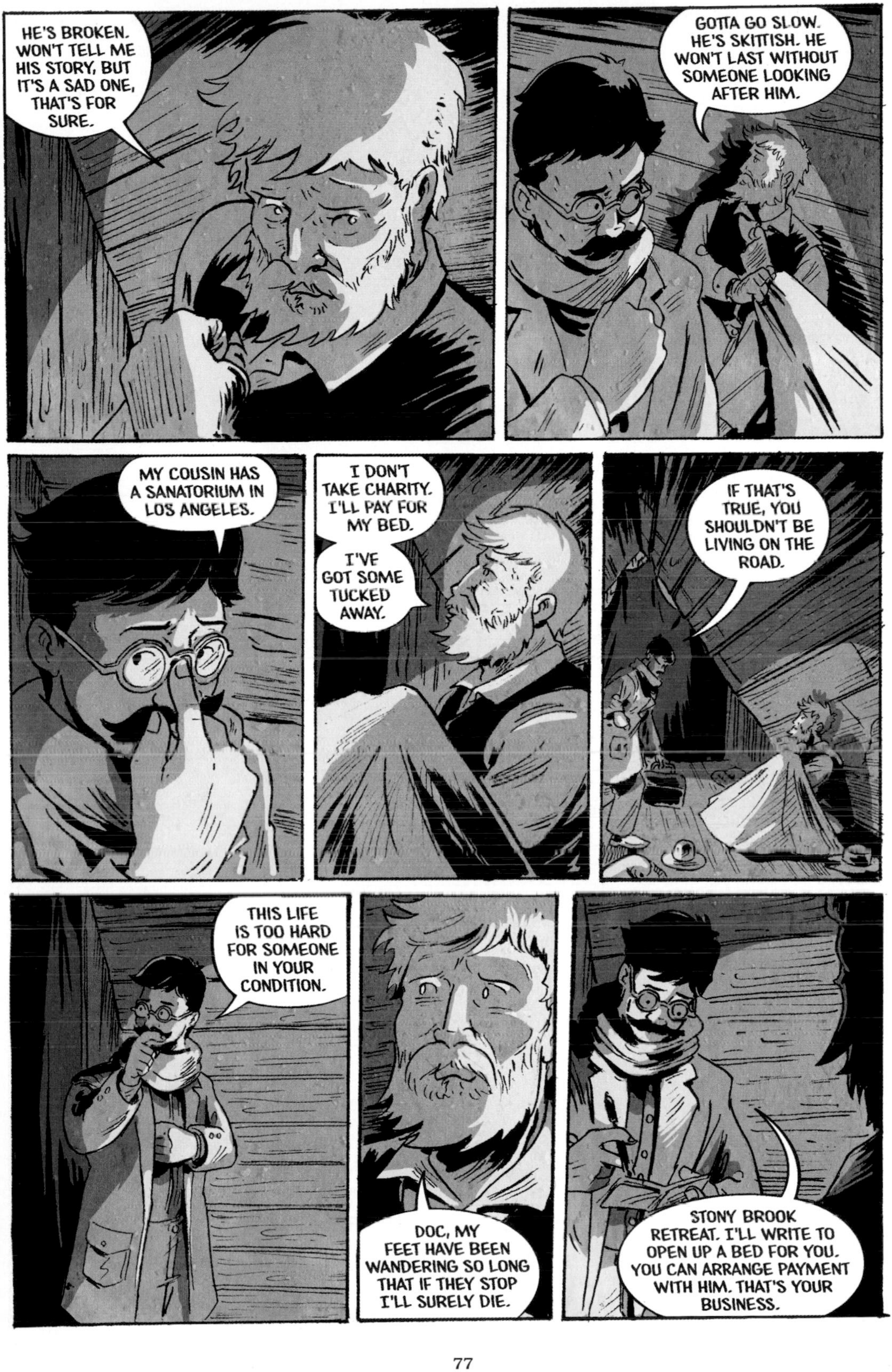
HE'S BROKEN. WON'T TELL ME HIS STORY, BUT IT'S A SAD ONE, THAT'S FOR SURE.
GOTTA GO SLOW. HE'S SKITTISH. HE WON'T LAST WITHOUT SOMEONE LOOKING AFTER HIM.
MY COUSIN HAS A SANATORIUM IN LOS ANGELES.
I DON'T TAKE CHARITY. I'LL PAY FOR MY BED.
I'VE GOT SOME TUCKED AWAY.
IF THAT'S TRUE, YOU SHOULDN'T BE LIVING ON THE ROAD.
THIS LIFE IS TOO HARD FOR SOMEONE IN YOUR CONDITION.
DOC, MY FEET HAVE BEEN WANDERING SO LONG THAT IF THEY STOP I'LL SURELY DIE.
STONY BROOK RETREAT. I'LL WRITE TO OPEN UP A BED FOR YOU. YOU CAN ARRANGE PAYMENT WITH HIM. THAT'S YOUR BUSINESS.

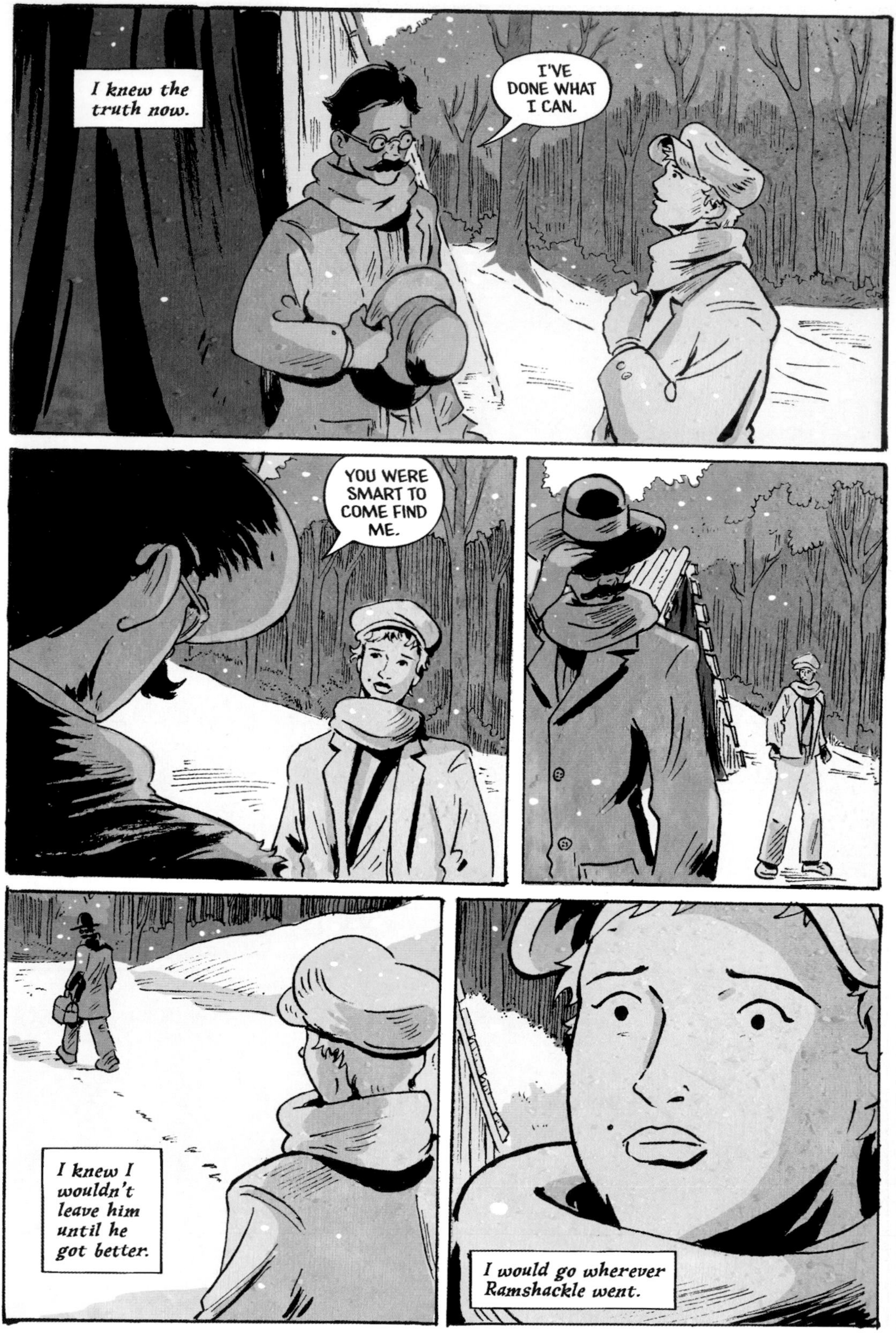
I knew the truth now.
I'VE DONE WHAT I CAN.
YOU WERE SMART TO COME FIND ME.
I knew I wouldn't leave him until he got better.
I would go wherever Ramshackle went.

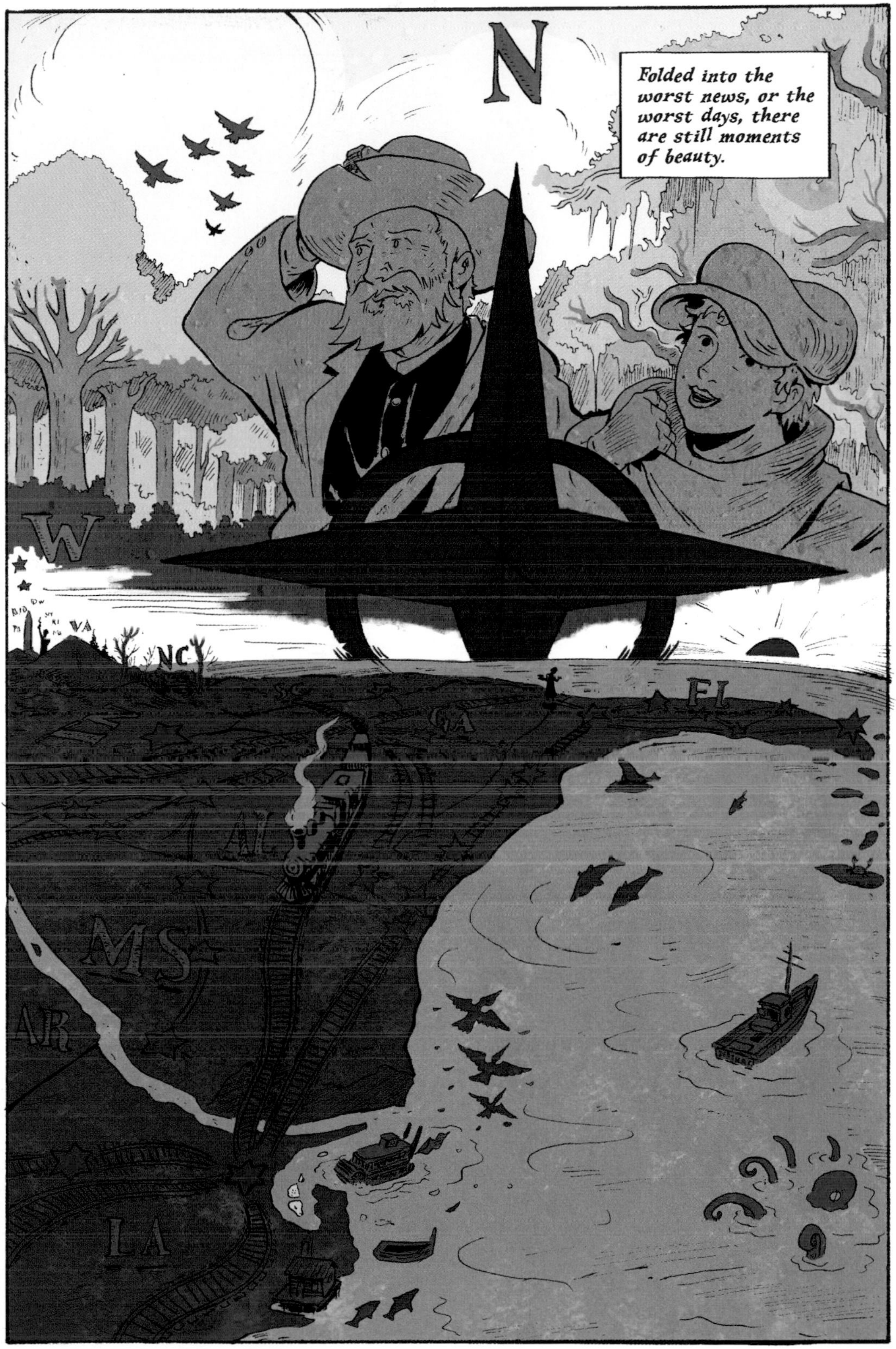
N
Folded into the worst news, or the worst days, there are still moments of beauty.
W
VA
NC
FL
GA
AL
MS
AR
LA

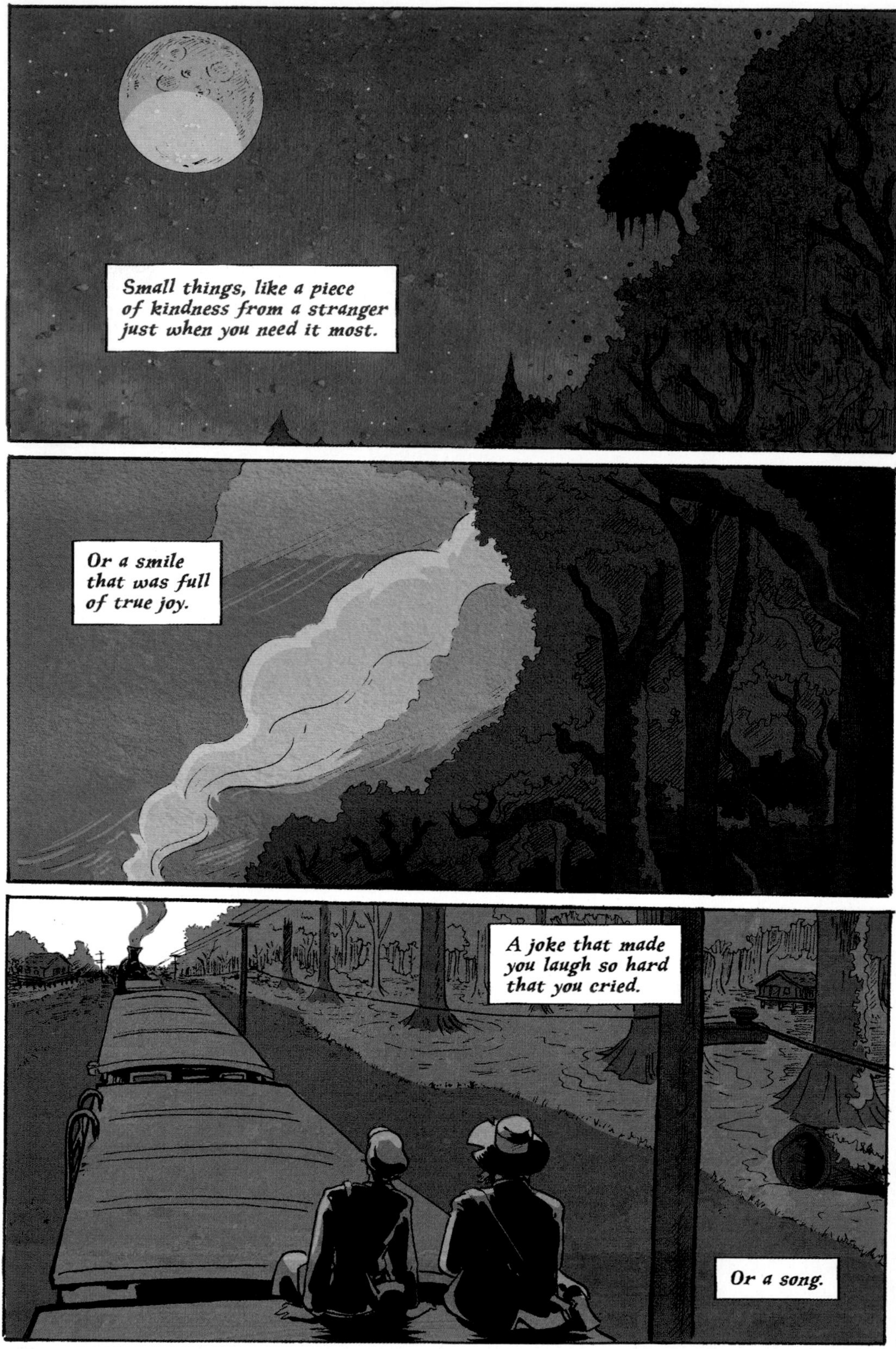
Small things, like a piece of kindness from a stranger just when you need it most.
Or a smile that was full of true joy.
A joke that made you laugh so hard that you cried.
Or a song.

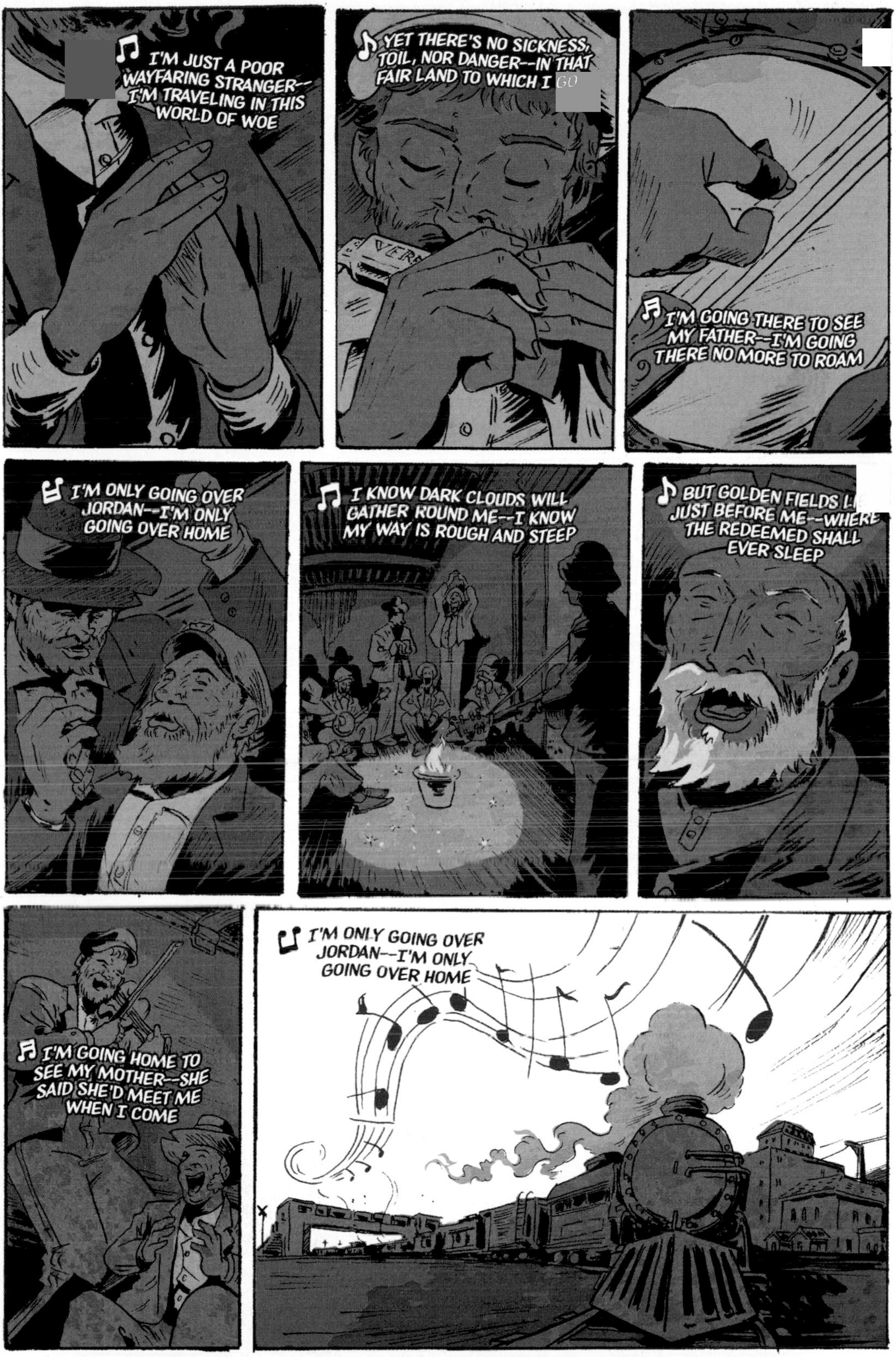
I'M JUST A POOR WAYFARING STRANGER--I'M TRAVELING IN THIS WORLD OF WOE
YET THERE'S NO SICKNESS, TOIL, NOR DANGER--IN THAT FAIR LAND TO WHICH I GO
I'M GOING THERE TO SEE MY FATHER--I'M GOING THERE NO MORE TO ROAM
I'M ONLY GOING OVER JORDAN--I'M ONLY GOING OVER HOME
I KNOW DARK CLOUDS WILL GATHER ROUND ME--I KNOW MY WAY IS ROUGH AND STEEP
BUT GOLDEN FIELDS L
JUST BEFORE ME--WHERE THE REDEEMED SHALL EVER SLEEP
I'M GOING HOME TO SEE MY MOTHER--SHE SAID SHE'D MEET ME WHEN I COME
I'M ONLY GOING OVER JORDAN--I'M ONLY GOING OVER HOME

"THE WAYFARING STRANGER," ALSO KNOWN AS "POOR WAYFARING STRANGER," IS AN AMERICAN FOLK AND GOSPEL SONG BELIEVED TO HAVE ORIGINATED IN THE EARLY 19TH CENTURY.

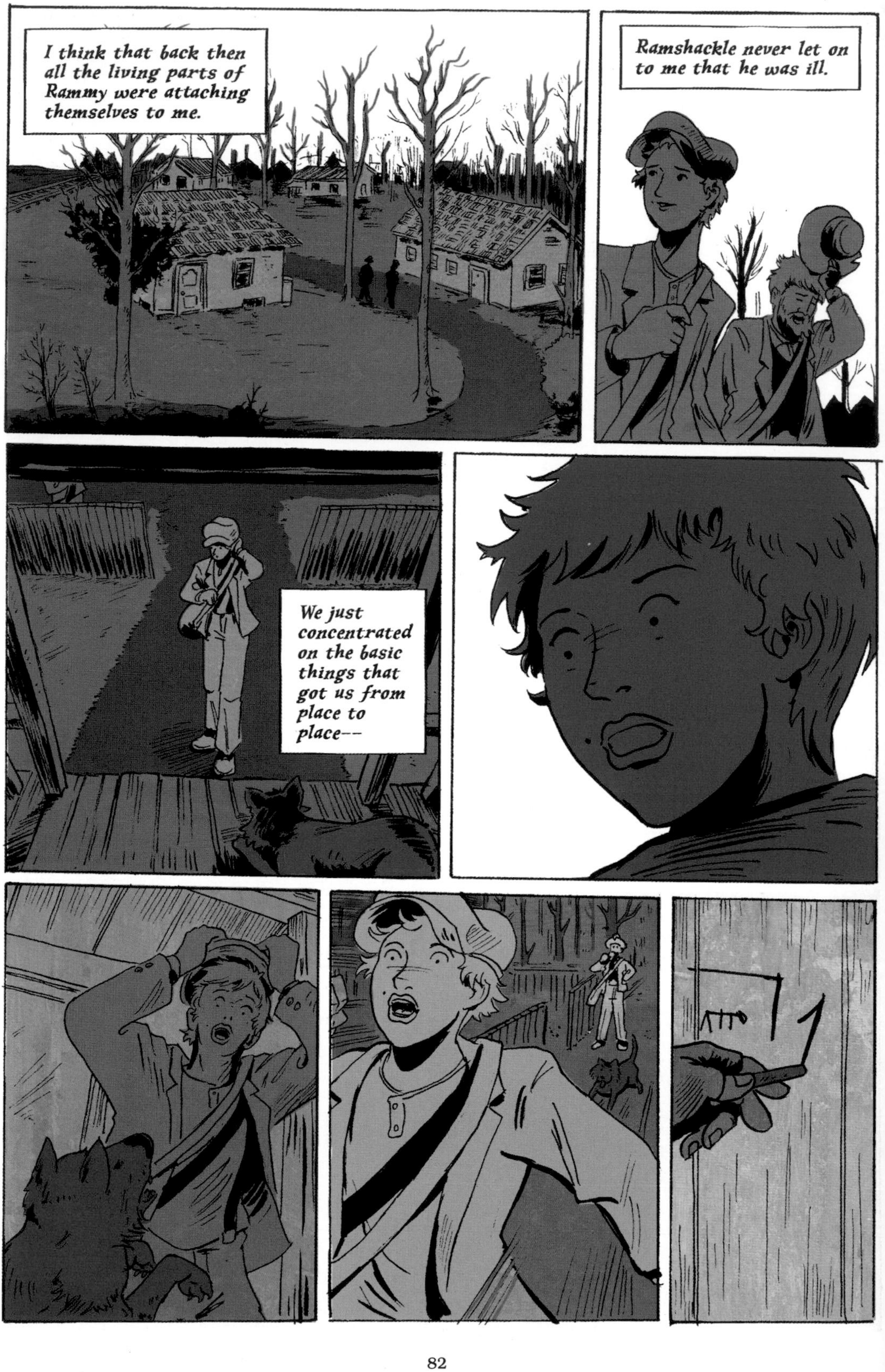
I think that back then all the living parts of Rammy were attaching themselves to me.
Ramshackle never let on to me that he was ill.
We just concentrated on the basic things that got us from place to place--

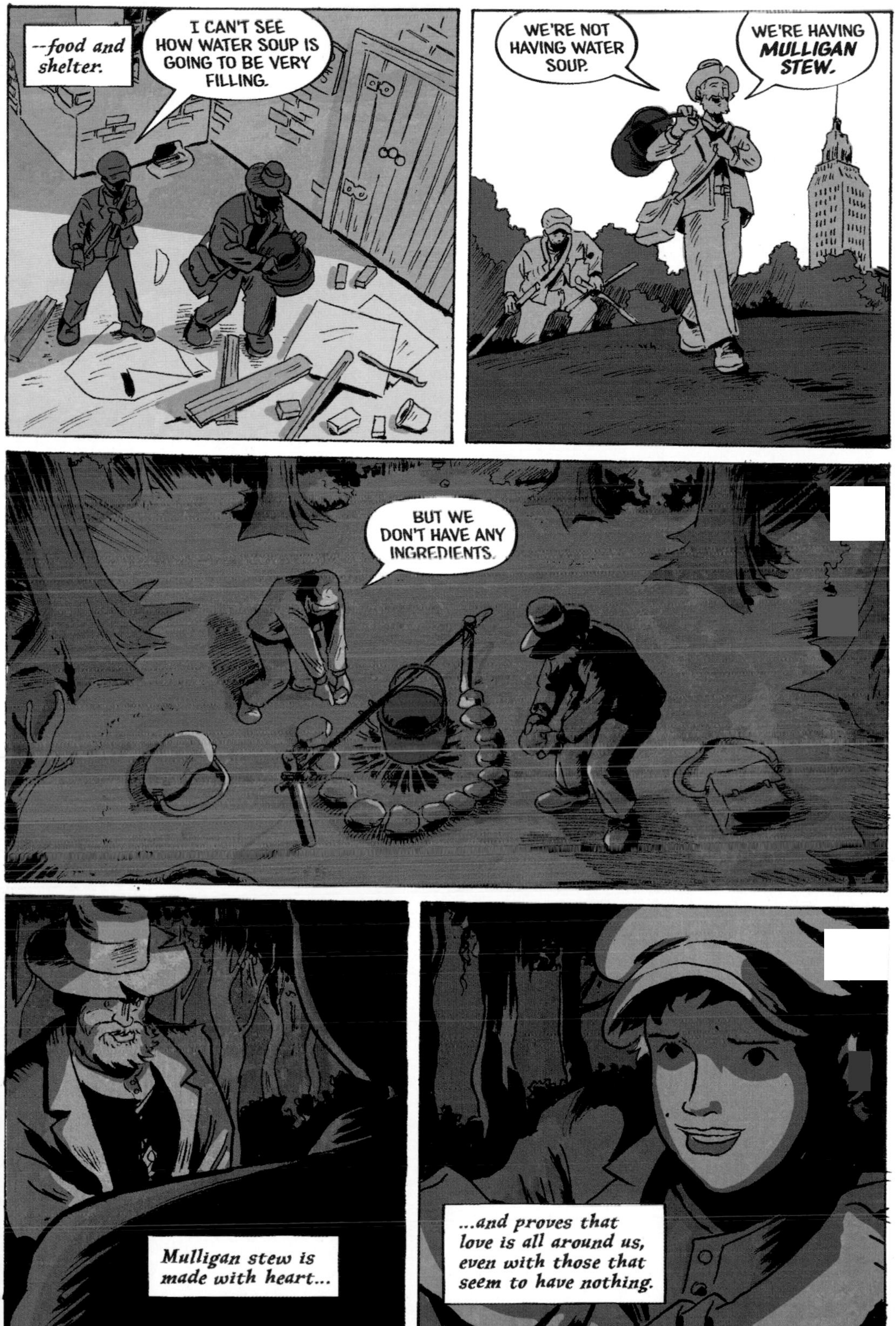
--food and shelter.
I CAN'T SEE HOW WATER SOUP IS GOING TO BE VERY FILLING.
WE'RE NOT HAVING WATER SOUP.
WE'RE HAVING MULLIGAN STEW.
BUT WE DON'T HAVE ANY INGREDIENTS.
Mulligan stew is made with heart...
...and proves that love is all around us, even with those that seem to have nothing.

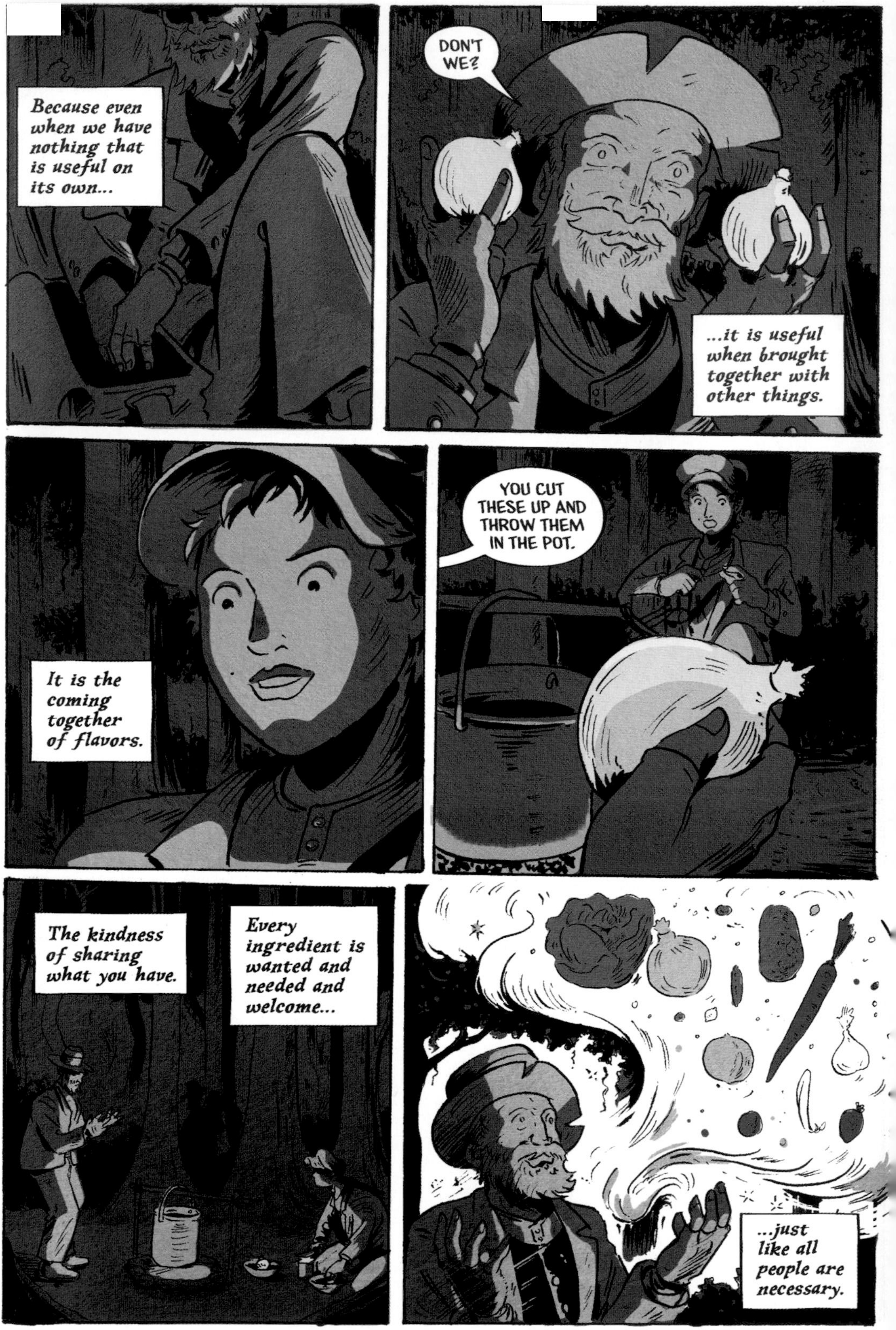

Because even when we have nothing that is useful on its own...
DON'T WE?
...it is useful when brought together with other things.
It is the coming together of flavors.
YOU CUT THESE UP AND THROW THEM IN THE POT.
The kindness of sharing what you have.
Every ingredient is wanted and needed and welcome...
...just like all people are necessary.

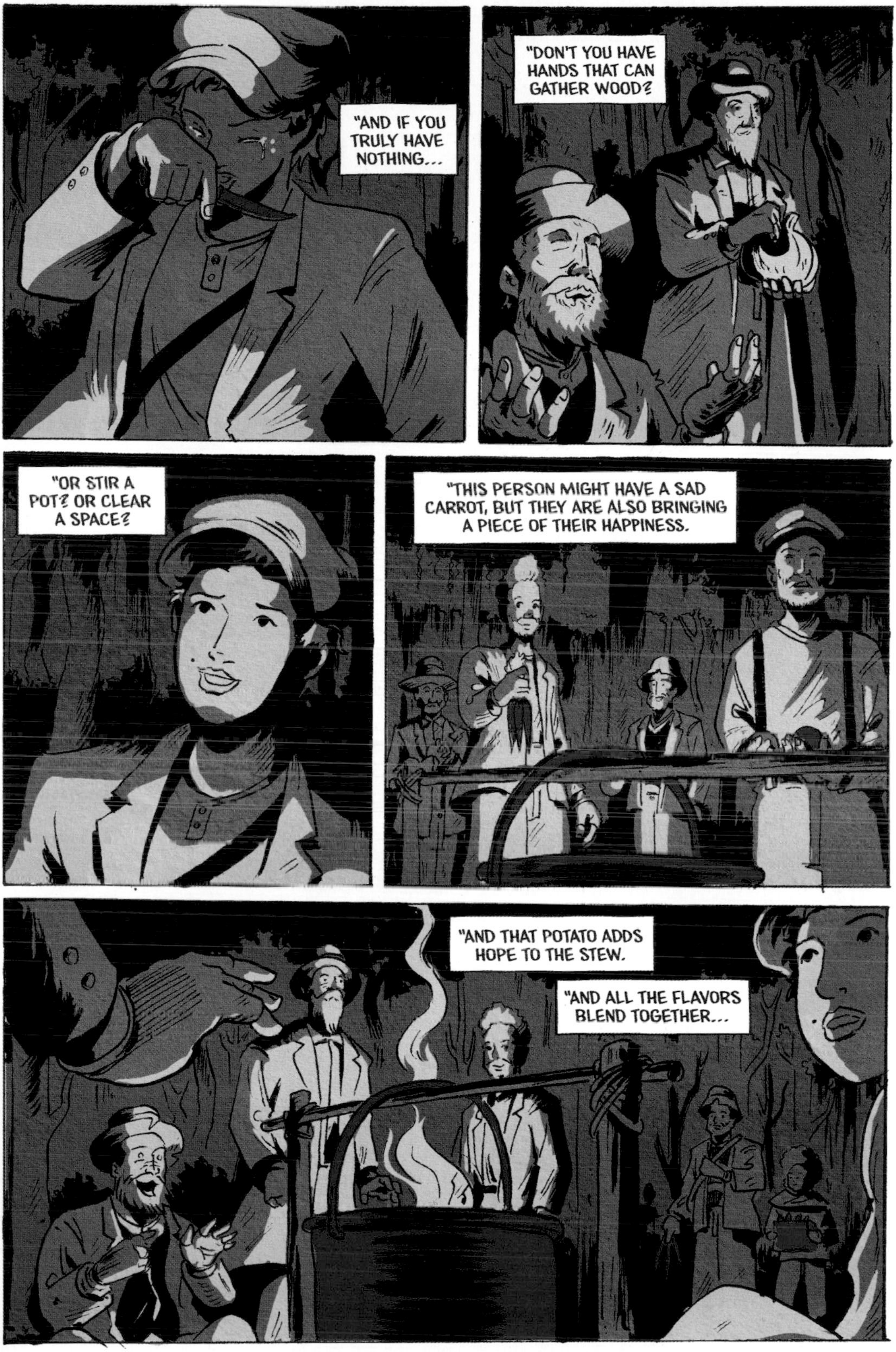
"AND IF YOU TRULY HAVE NOTHING...
"DON'T YOU HAVE HANDS THAT CAN GATHER WOOD?
"OR STIR A POT? OR CLEAR A SPACE?
"THIS PERSON MIGHT HAVE A SAD CARROT, BUT THEY ARE ALSO BRINGING A PIECE OF THEIR HAPPINESS.
"AND THAT POTATO ADDS HOPE TO THE STEW.
"AND ALL THE FLAVORS BLEND TOGETHER...

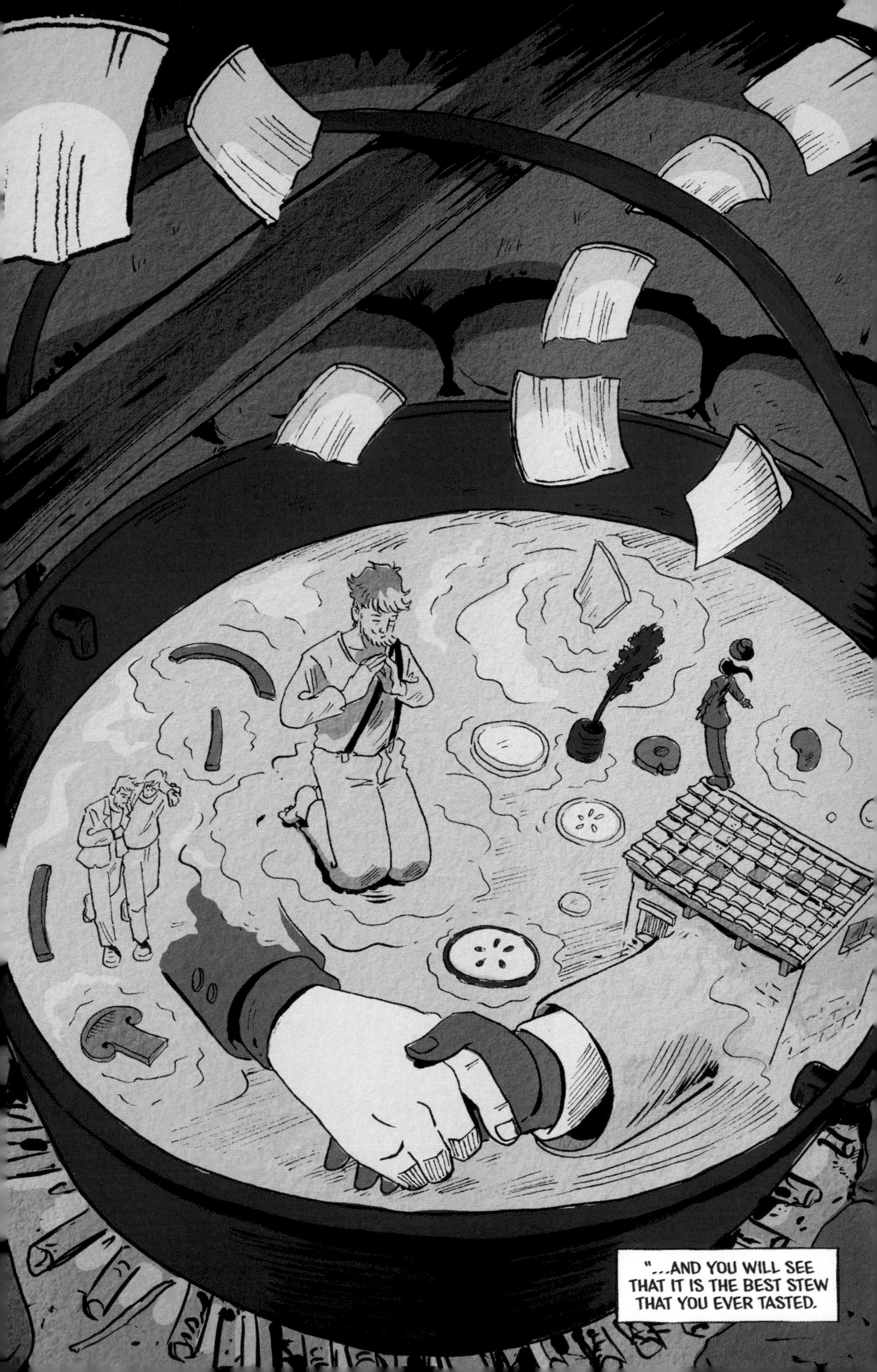
"...AND YOU WILL SEE THAT IT IS THE BEST STEW THAT YOU EVER TASTED.

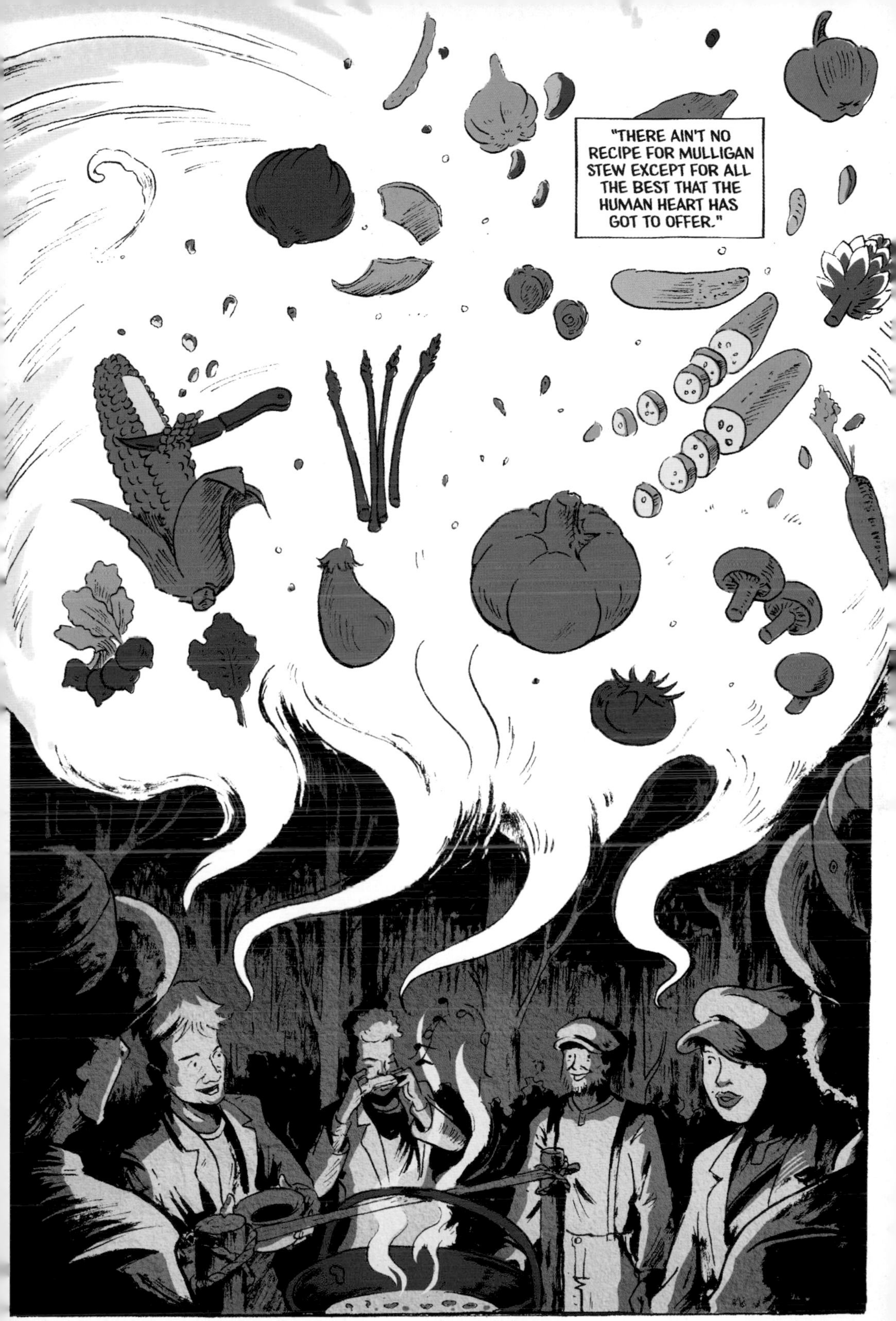
"THERE AIN'T NO RECIPE FOR MULLIGAN STEW EXCEPT FOR ALL THE BEST THAT THE HUMAN HEART HAS GOT TO OFFER."

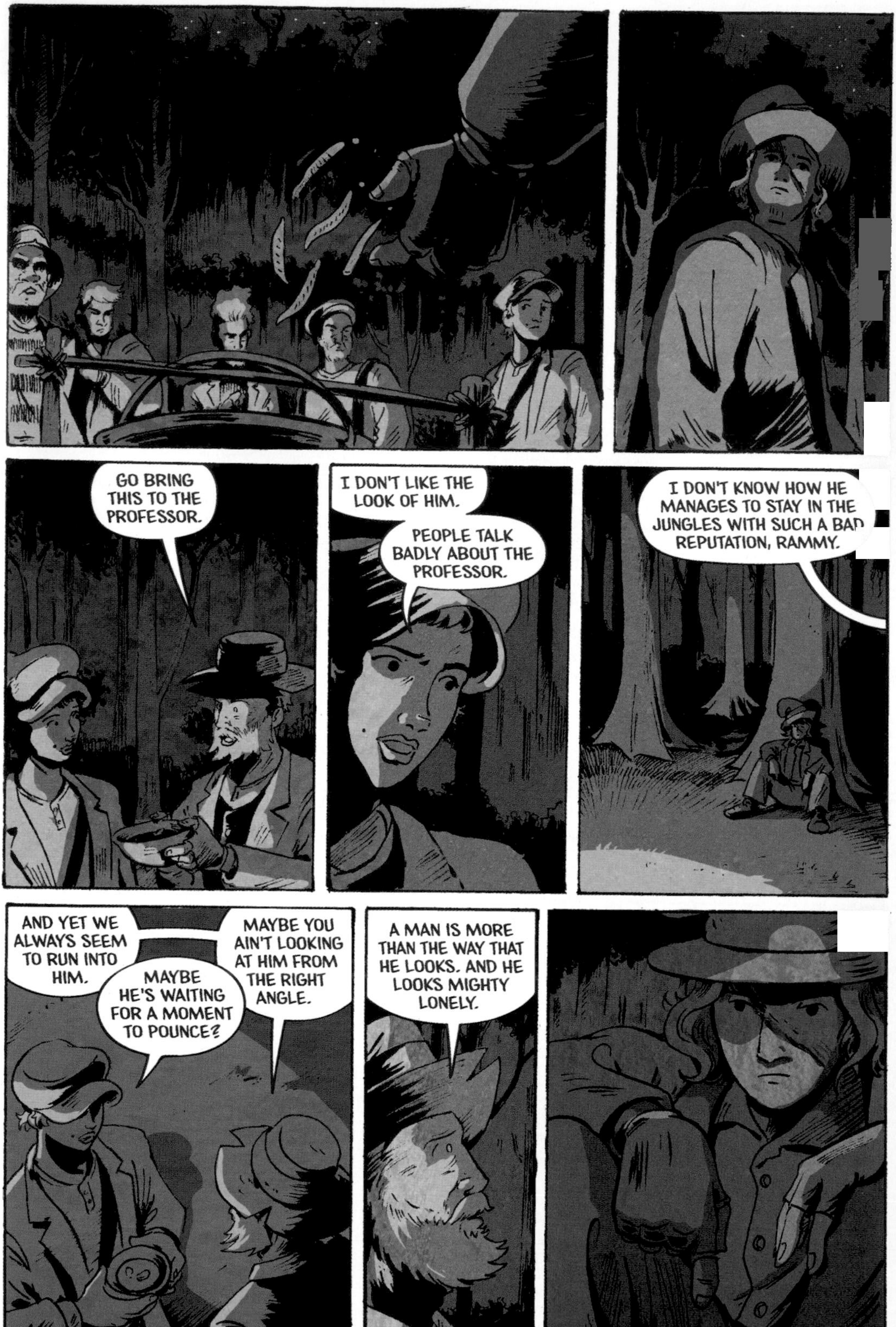
GO BRING THIS TO THE PROFESSOR.
I DON'T LIKE THE LOOK OF HIM.
PEOPLE TALK BADLY ABOUT THE PROFESSOR.
I DON'T KNOW HOW HE MANAGES TO STAY IN THE JUNGLES WITH SUCH A BAD REPUTATION, RAMMY.
AND YET WE ALWAYS SEEM TO RUN INTO HIM.
MAYBE HE'S WAITING FOR A MOMENT TO POUNCE?
MAYBE YOU AIN'T LOOKING AT HIM FROM THE RIGHT ANGLE.
A MAN IS MORE THAN THE WAY THAT HE LOOKS. AND HE LOOKS MIGHTY LONELY.

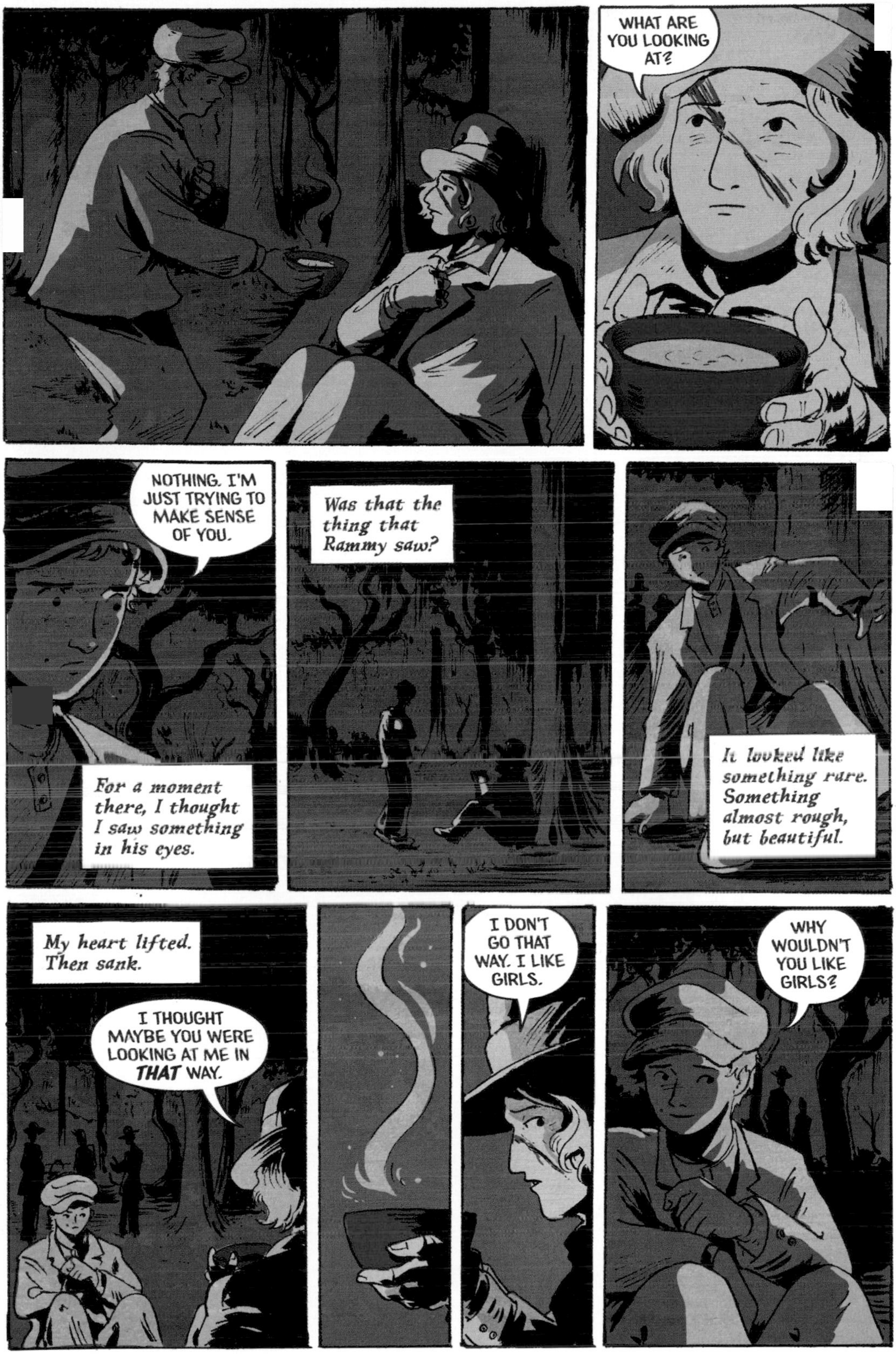

WHAT ARE YOU LOOKING AT?
NOTHING. I'M JUST TRYING TO MAKE SENSE OF YOU.
For a moment there, I thought I saw something in his eyes.
Was that the thing that Rammy saw?
It looked like something rare. Something almost rough, but beautiful.
My heart lifted. Then sank.
I THOUGHT MAYBE YOU WERE LOOKING AT ME IN THAT WAY.
I DON'T GO THAT WAY. I LIKE GIRLS.
WHY WOULDN'T YOU LIKE GIRLS?

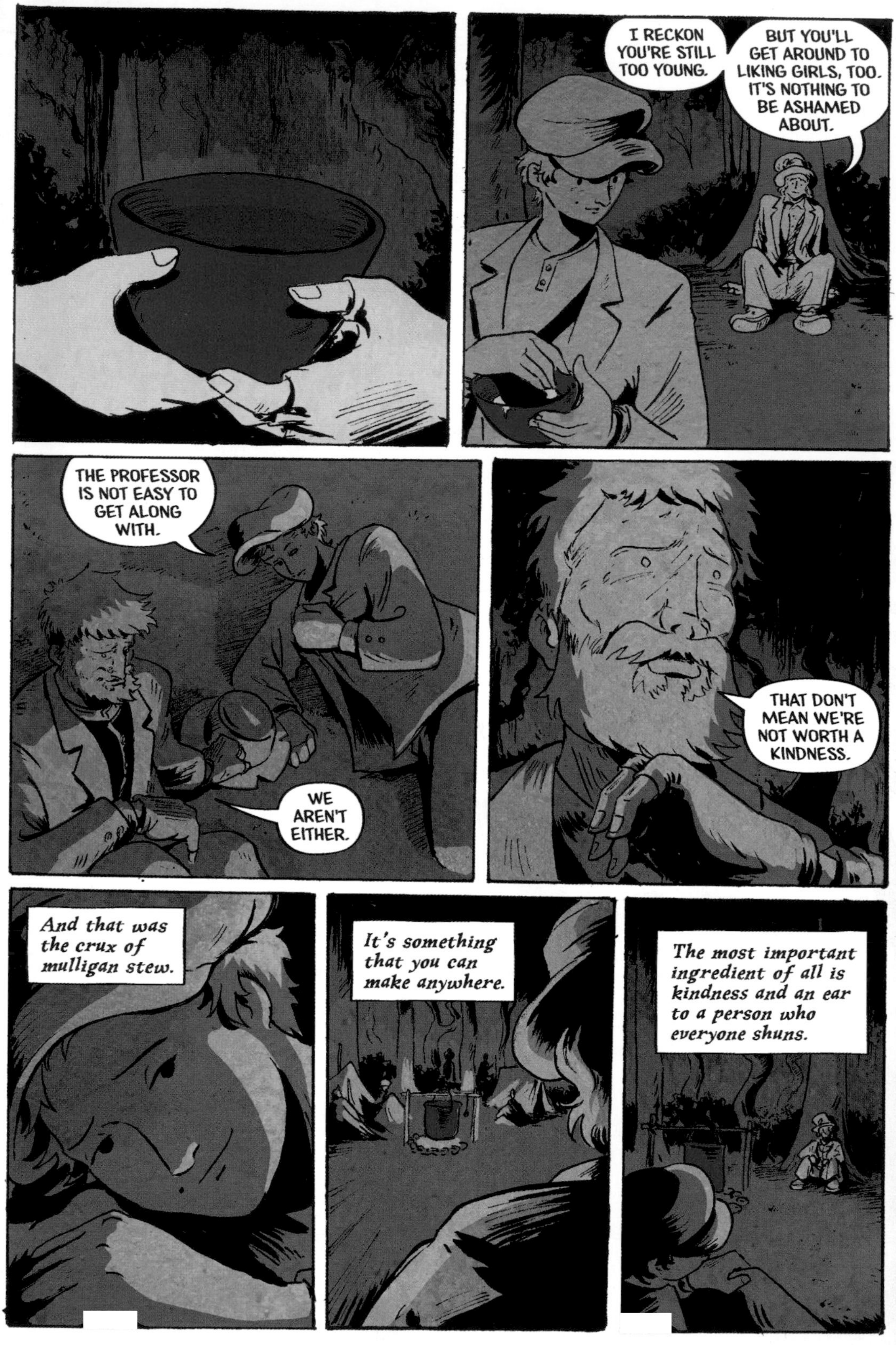
I RECKON YOU'RE STILL TOO YOUNG.
BUT YOU'LL GET AROUND TO LIKING GIRLS, TOO. IT'S NOTHING TO BE ASHAMED ABOUT.
THE PROFESSOR IS NOT EASY TO GET ALONG WITH.
WE AREN'T EITHER.
THAT DON'T MEAN WE'RE NOT WORTH A KINDNESS.
And that was the crux of mulligan stew.
It's something that you can make anywhere.
The most important ingredient of all is kindness and an ear to a person who everyone shuns.

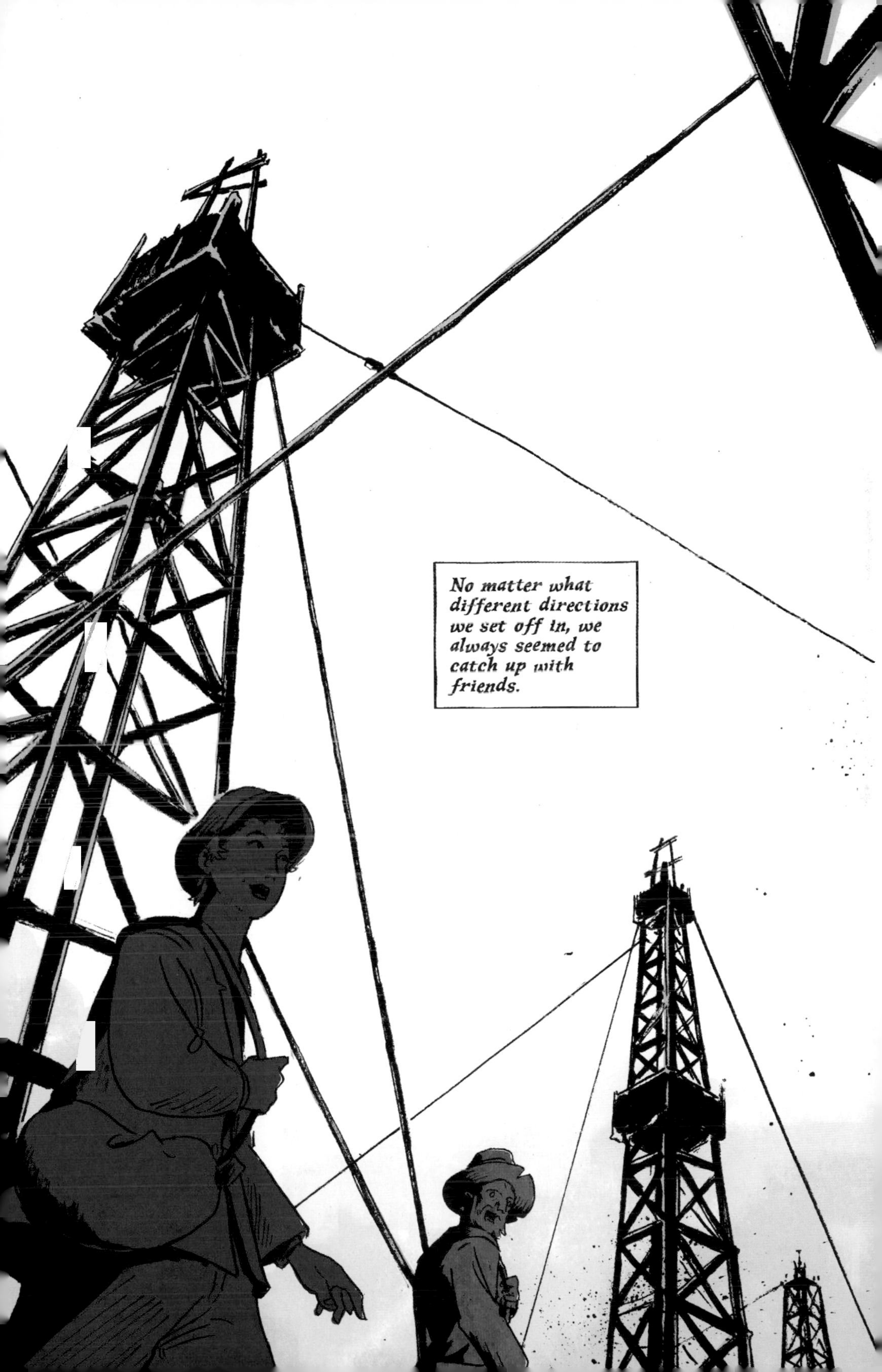
No matter what different directions we set off in, we always seemed to catch up with friends.

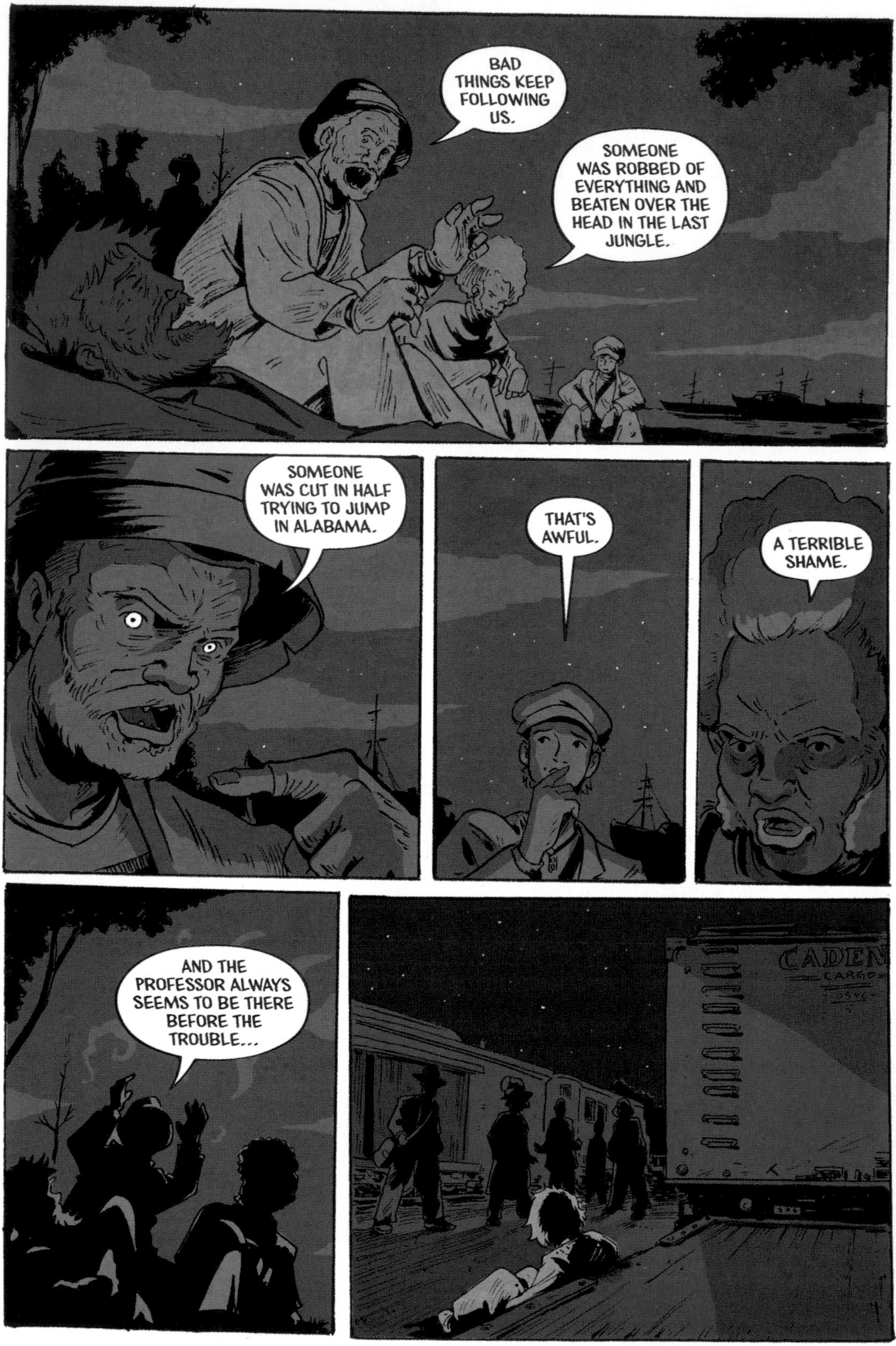
BAD THINGS KEEP FOLLOWING US.
SOMEONE WAS ROBBED OF EVERYTHING AND BEATEN OVER THE HEAD IN THE LAST JUNGLE.
SOMEONE WAS CUT IN HALF TRYING TO JUMP IN ALABAMA.
THAT'S AWFUL.
A TERRIBLE SHAME.
AND THE PROFESSOR ALWAYS SEEMS TO BE THERE BEFORE THE TROUBLE...

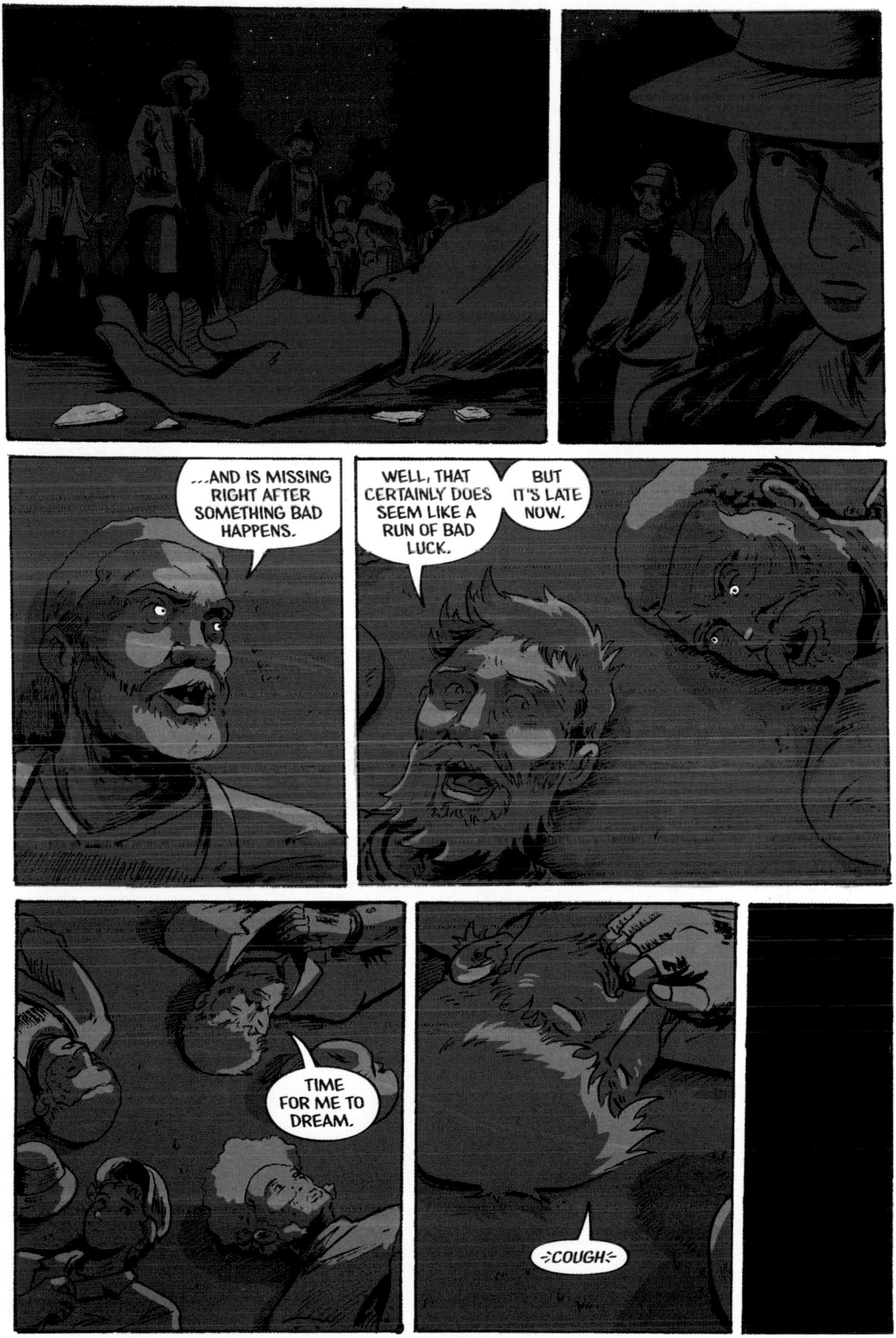
...AND IS MISSING RIGHT AFTER SOMETHING BAD HAPPENS.
WELL, THAT CERTAINLY DOES SEEM LIKE A RUN OF BAD LUCK.
BUT IT'S LATE NOW.
TIME FOR ME TO DREAM.
COUGH

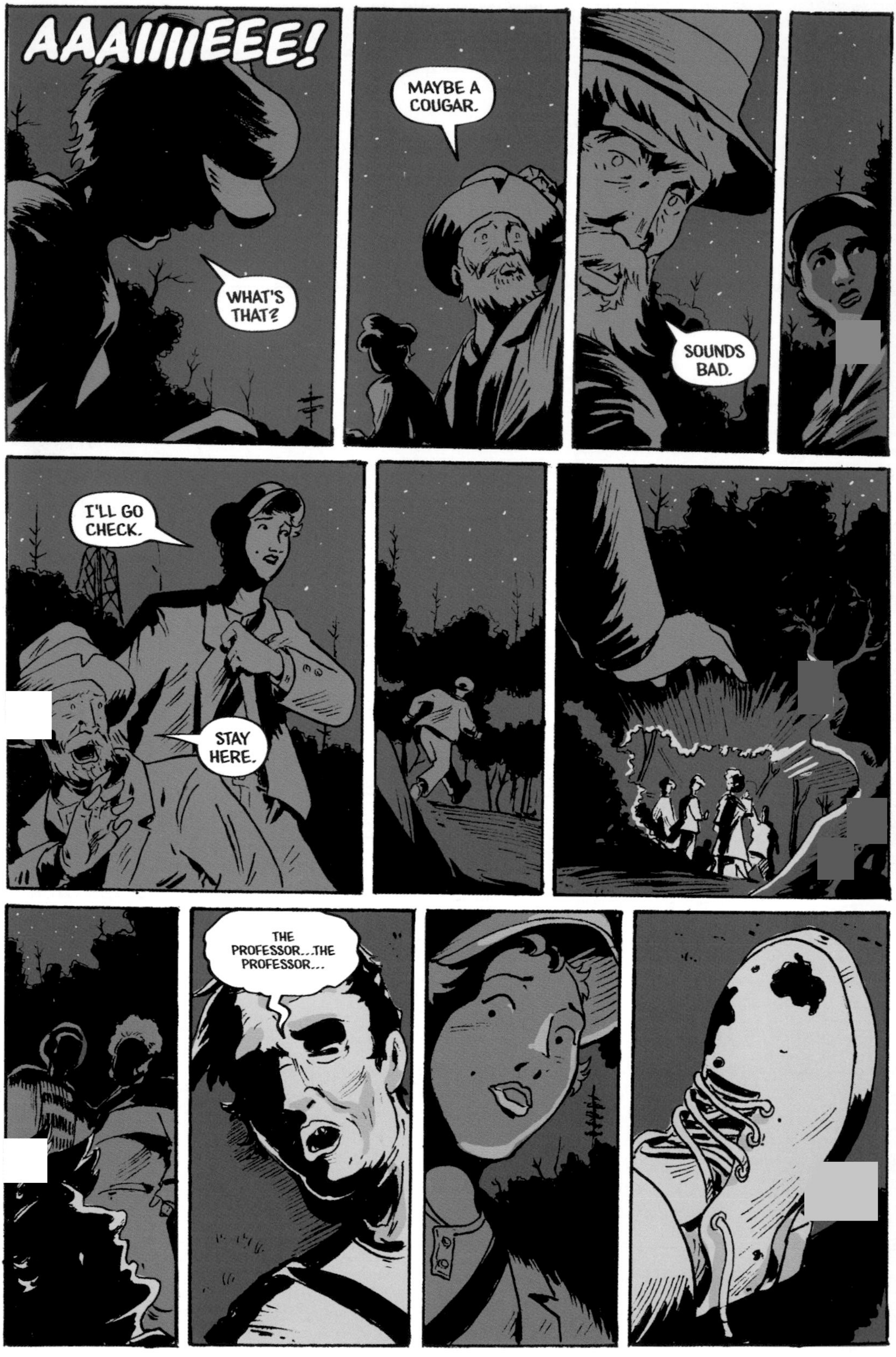
AAAIIIIEEE!
WHAT'S THAT?
MAYBE A COUGAR.
SOUNDS BAD.
I'LL GO CHECK.
STAY HERE.
THE PROFESSOR... THE PROFESSOR...

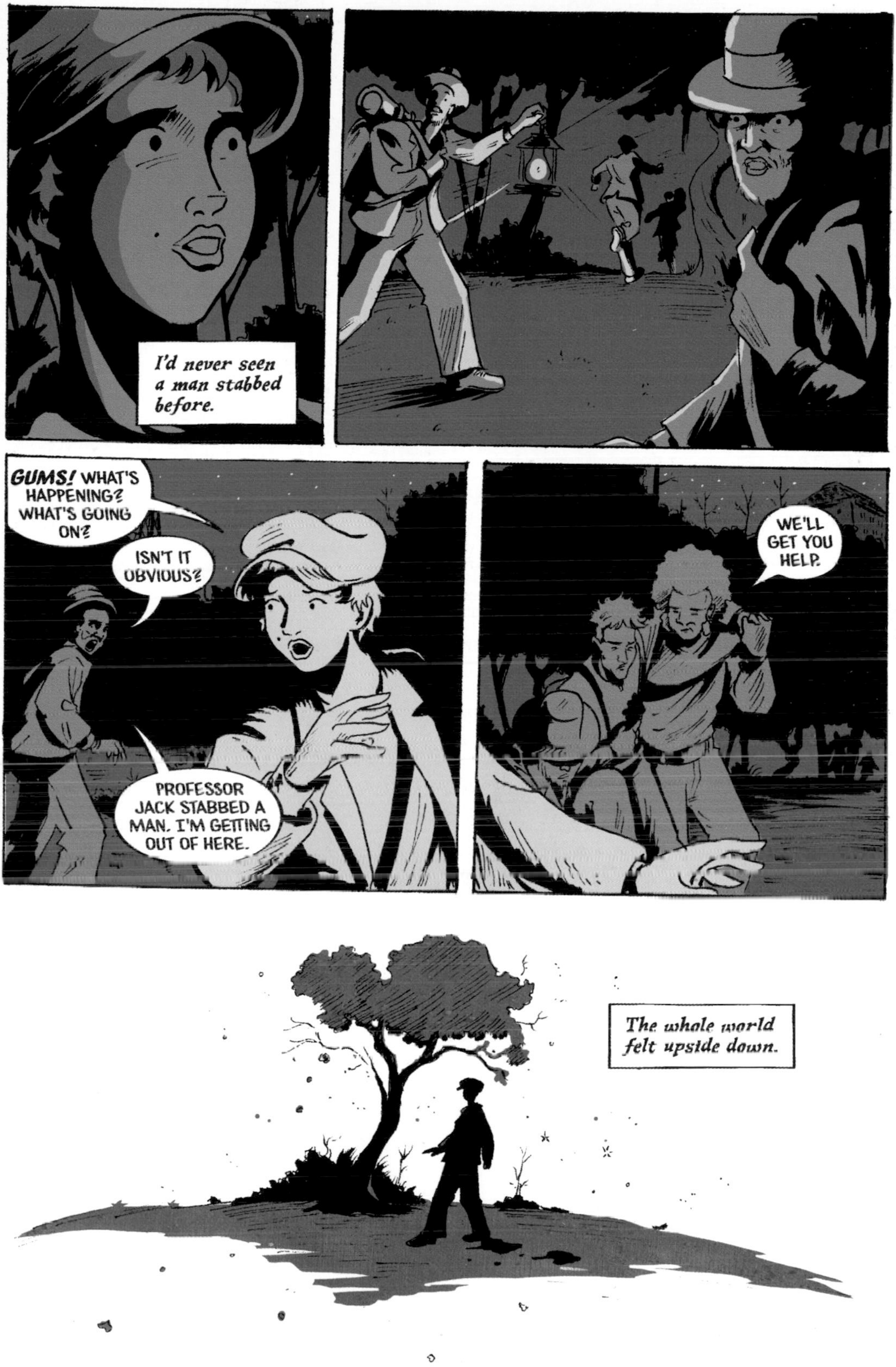
I'd never seen a man stabbed before.
GUMS! WHAT'S HAPPENING? WHAT'S GOING ON?
ISN'T IT OBVIOUS?
PROFESSOR JACK STABBED A MAN. I'M GETTING OUT OF HERE.
WE'LL GET YOU HELP.
The whole world felt upside down.

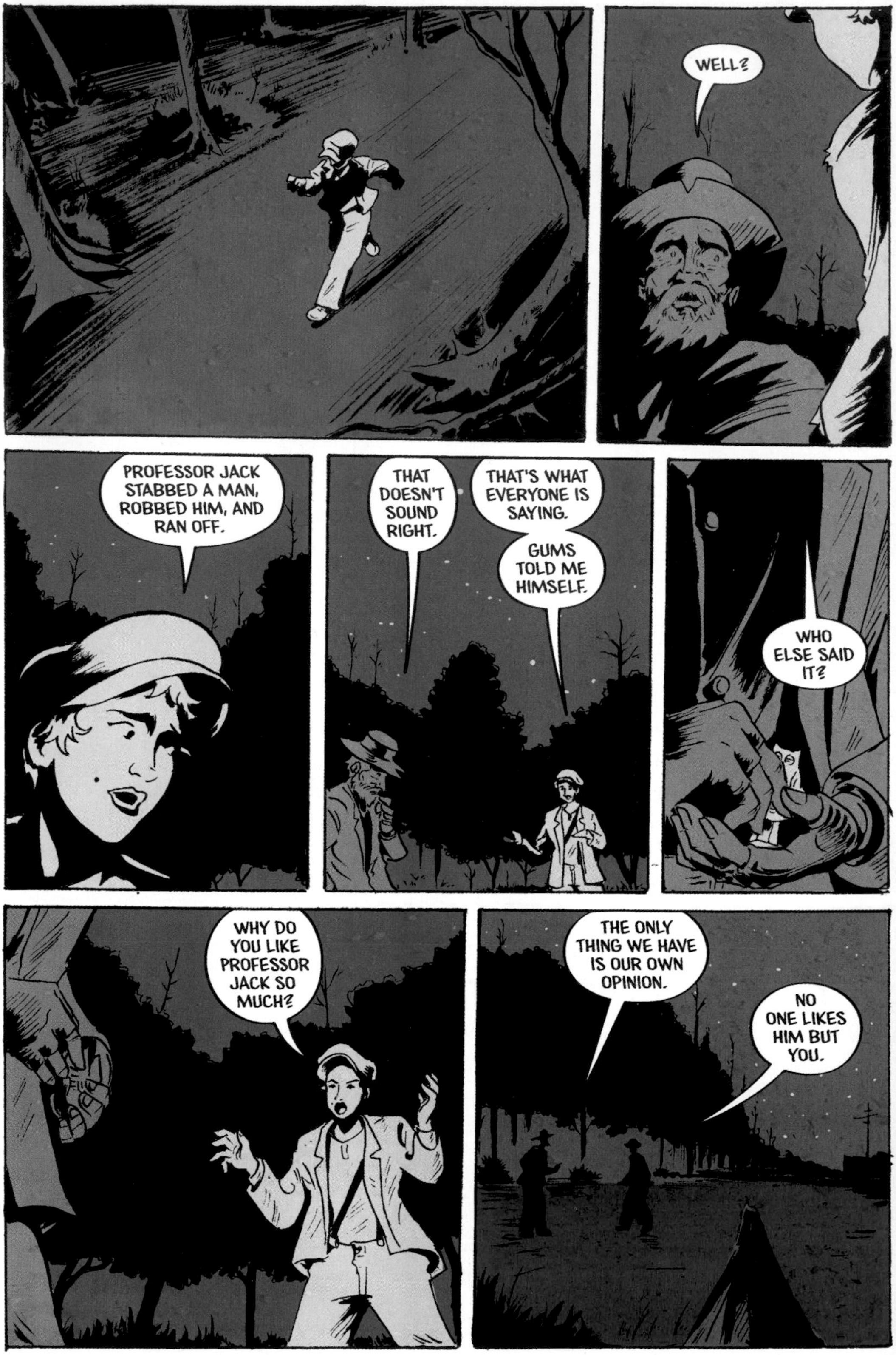
WELL?
PROFESSOR JACK STABBED A MAN, ROBBED HIM, AND RAN OFF.
THAT DOESN'T SOUND RIGHT.
THAT'S WHAT EVERYONE IS SAYING.
GUMS TOLD ME HIMSELF.
WHO ELSE SAID IT?
WHY DO YOU LIKE PROFESSOR JACK SO MUCH?
THE ONLY THING WE HAVE IS OUR OWN OPINION.
NO ONE LIKES HIM BUT YOU.

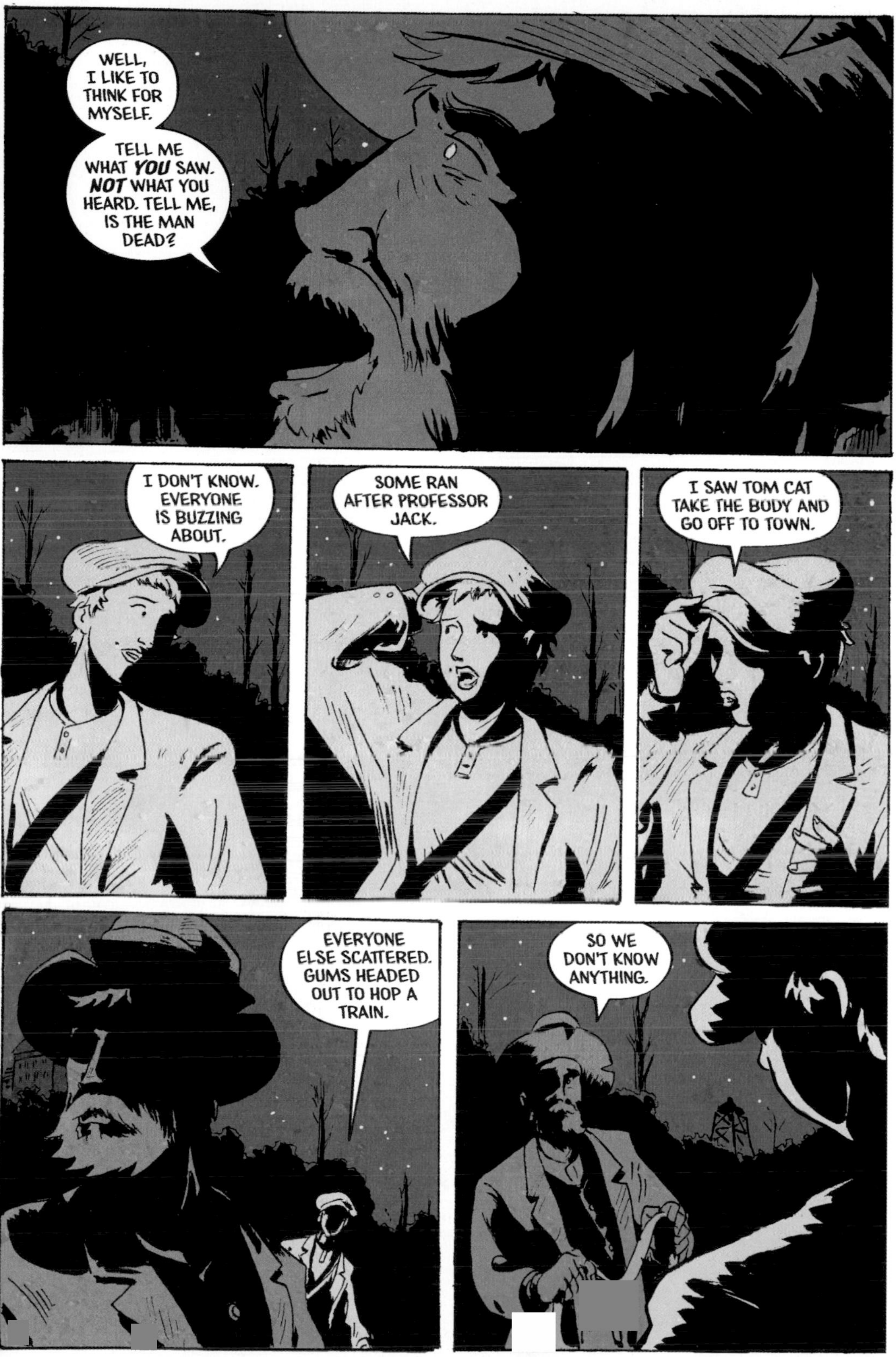
WELL, I LIKE TO THINK FOR MYSELF.
TELL ME WHAT *YOU* SAW. *NOT* WHAT YOU HEARD. TELL ME, IS THE MAN DEAD?
I DON'T KNOW. EVERYONE IS BUZZING ABOUT.
SOME RAN AFTER PROFESSOR JACK.
I SAW TOM CAT TAKE THE BODY AND GO OFF TO TOWN.
EVERYONE ELSE SCATTERED. GUMS HEADED OUT TO HOP A TRAIN.
SO WE DON'T KNOW ANYTHING.

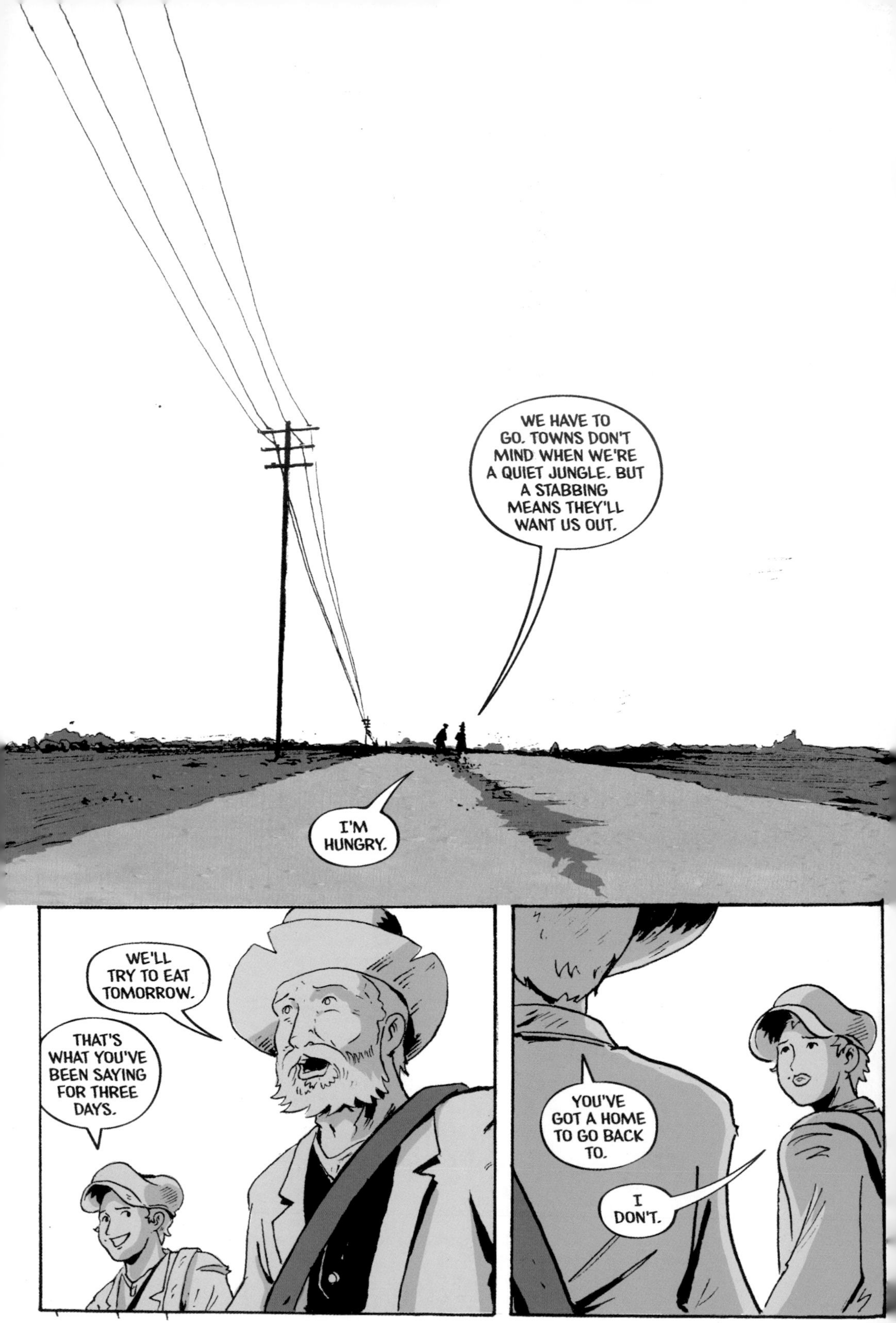
WE HAVE TO GO. TOWNS DON'T MIND WHEN WE'RE A QUIET JUNGLE. BUT A STABBING MEANS THEY'LL WANT US OUT.
I'M HUNGRY.
WE'LL TRY TO EAT TOMORROW.
THAT'S WHAT YOU'VE BEEN SAYING FOR THREE DAYS.
YOU'VE GOT A HOME TO GO BACK TO.
I DON'T.

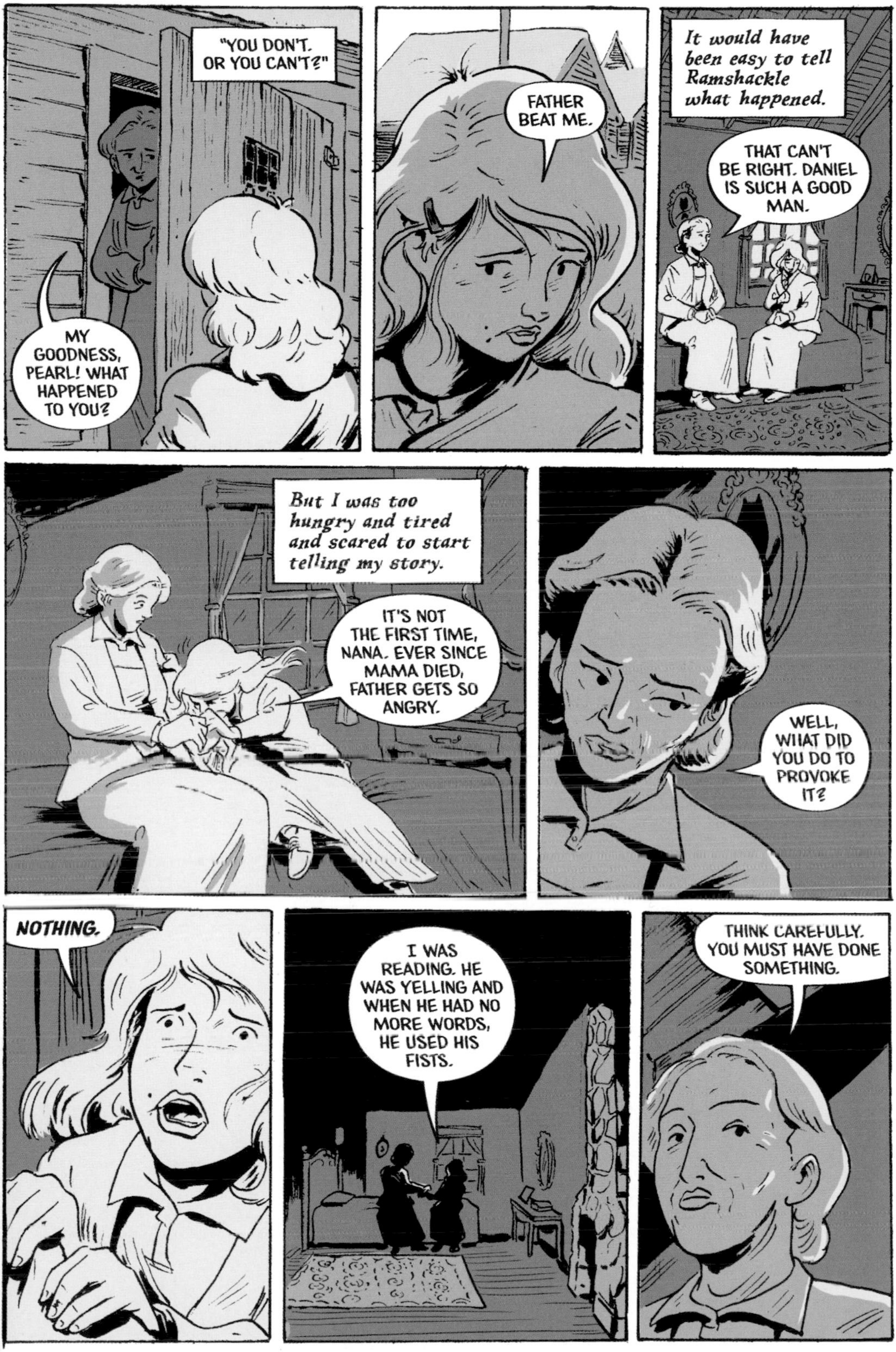
"YOU DON'T. OR YOU CAN'T?"
MY GOODNESS, PEARL! WHAT HAPPENED TO YOU?
FATHER BEAT ME.
It would have been easy to tell Ramshackle what happened.
THAT CAN'T BE RIGHT. DANIEL IS SUCH A GOOD MAN.
But I was too hungry and tired and scared to start telling my story.
IT'S NOT THE FIRST TIME, NANA. EVER SINCE MAMA DIED, FATHER GETS SO ANGRY.
WELL, WHAT DID YOU DO TO PROVOKE IT?
NOTHING.
I WAS READING. HE WAS YELLING AND WHEN HE HAD NO MORE WORDS, HE USED HIS FISTS.
THINK CAREFULLY. YOU MUST HAVE DONE SOMETHING.

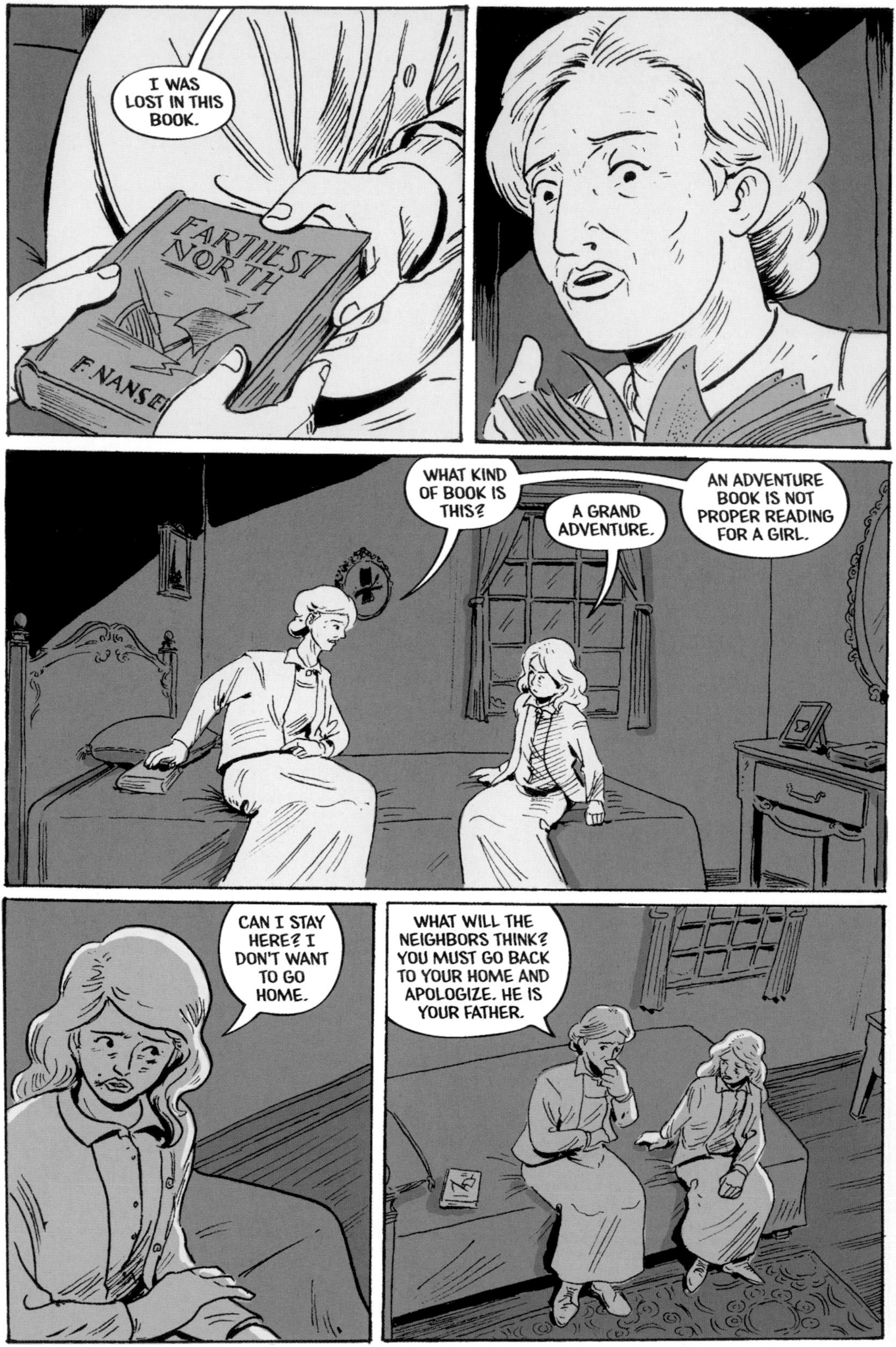
I WAS LOST IN THIS BOOK.
FARTHEST NORTH
F. NANSE
WHAT KIND OF BOOK IS THIS?
A GRAND ADVENTURE.
AN ADVENTURE BOOK IS NOT PROPER READING FOR A GIRL.
CAN I STAY HERE? I DON'T WANT TO GO HOME.
WHAT WILL THE NEIGHBORS THINK? YOU MUST GO BACK TO YOUR HOME AND APOLOGIZE. HE IS YOUR FATHER.

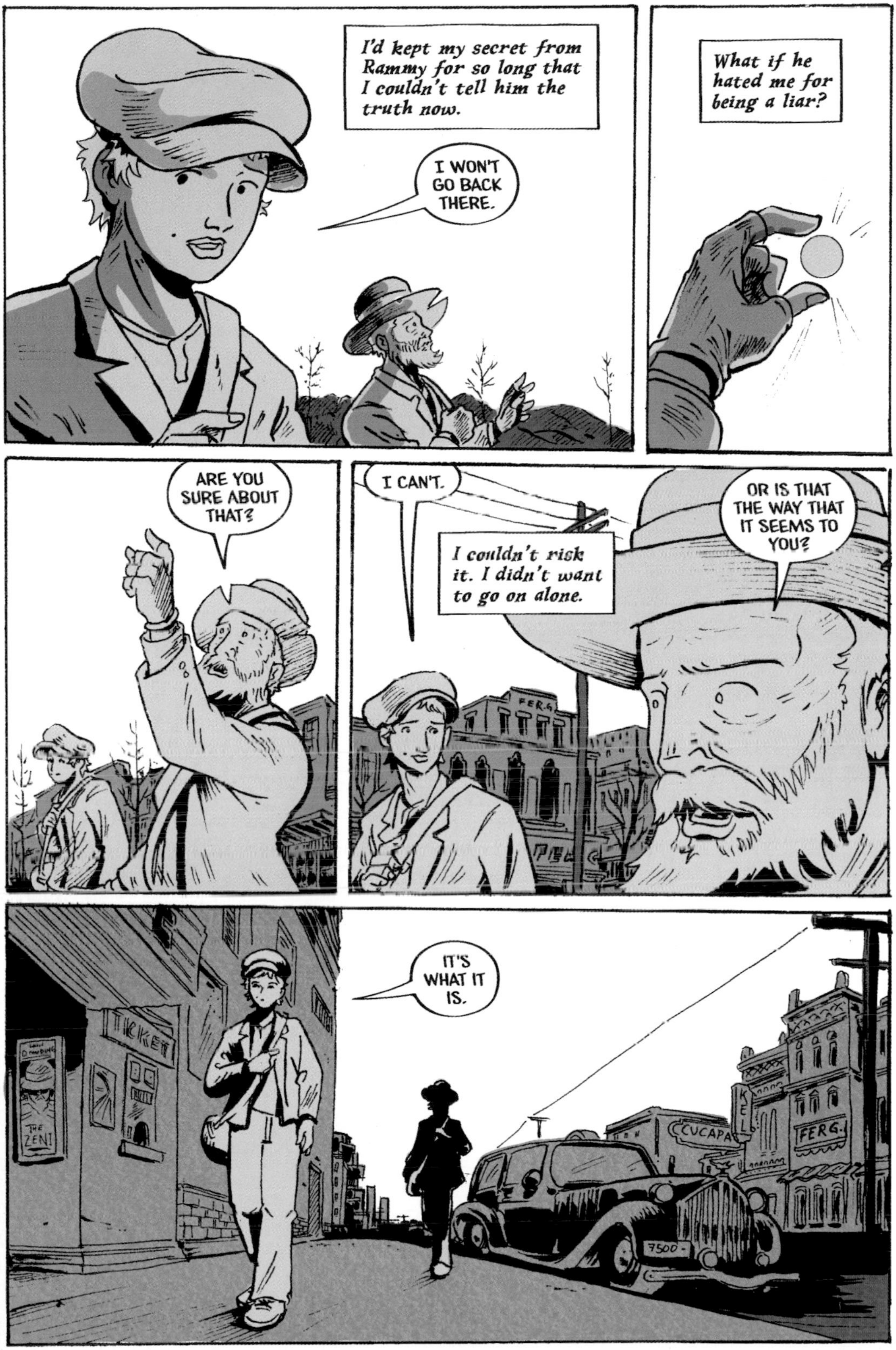
I'd kept my secret from Rammy for so long that I couldn't tell him the truth now.
I WON'T GO BACK THERE.
What if he hated me for being a liar?
ARE YOU SURE ABOUT THAT?
I CAN'T.
I couldn't risk it. I didn't want to go on alone.
OR IS THAT THE WAY THAT IT SEEMS TO YOU?
FERG.
IT'S WHAT IT IS.
TICKET
THE ZENI
CUCAPA
FERG.
7500

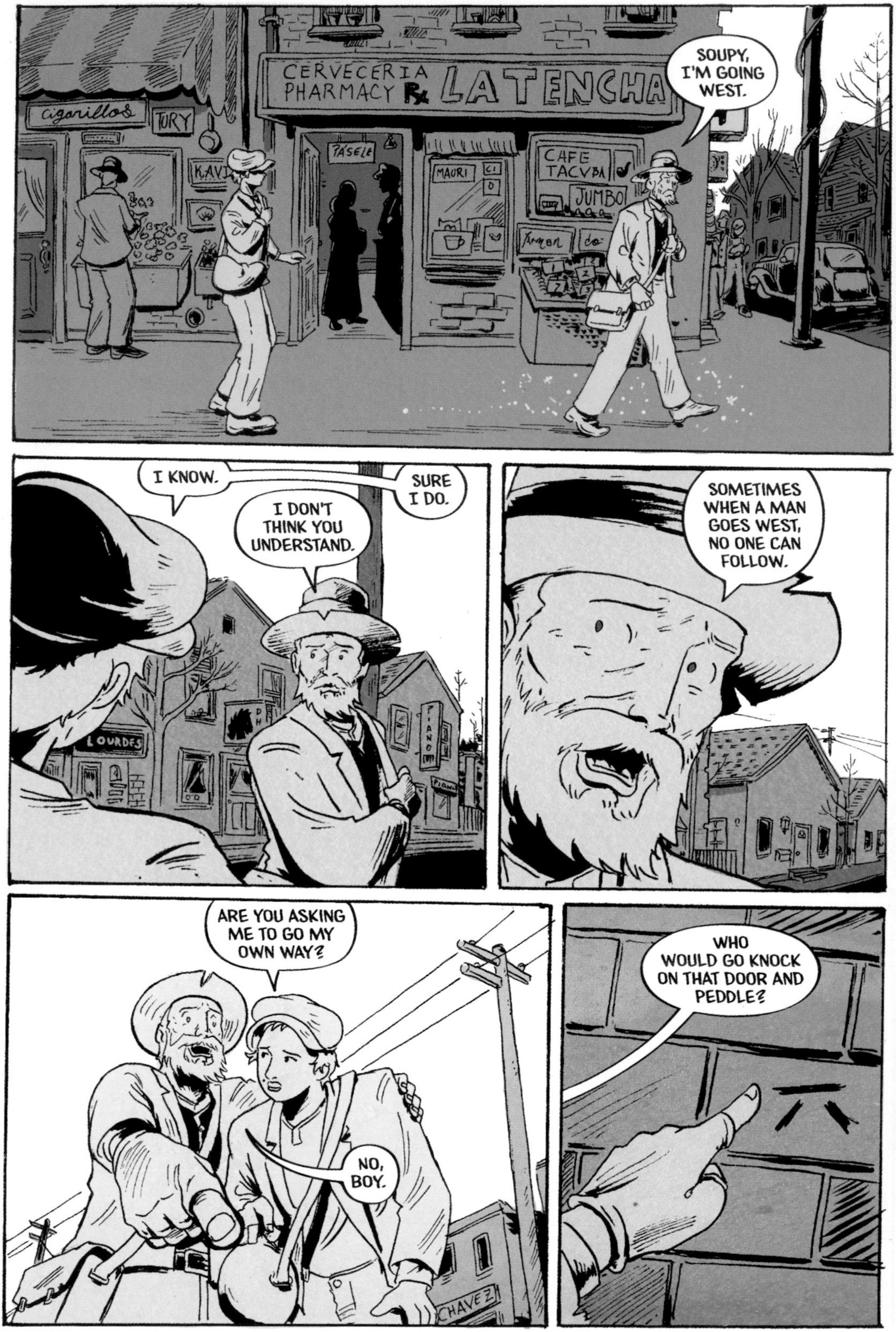
CERVECERIA
PHARMACY ℞
LATENCHA
cigarillos
TURY
PÁSELE
KAVI
MAURI
CAFE TACUBA
JUMBO
SOUPY, I'M GOING WEST.
I KNOW.
I DON'T THINK YOU UNDERSTAND.
SURE I DO.
LOURDES
PIANO
SOMETIMES WHEN A MAN GOES WEST, NO ONE CAN FOLLOW.
ARE YOU ASKING ME TO GO MY OWN WAY?
NO, BOY.
CHAVEZ
WHO WOULD GO KNOCK ON THAT DOOR AND PEDDLE?

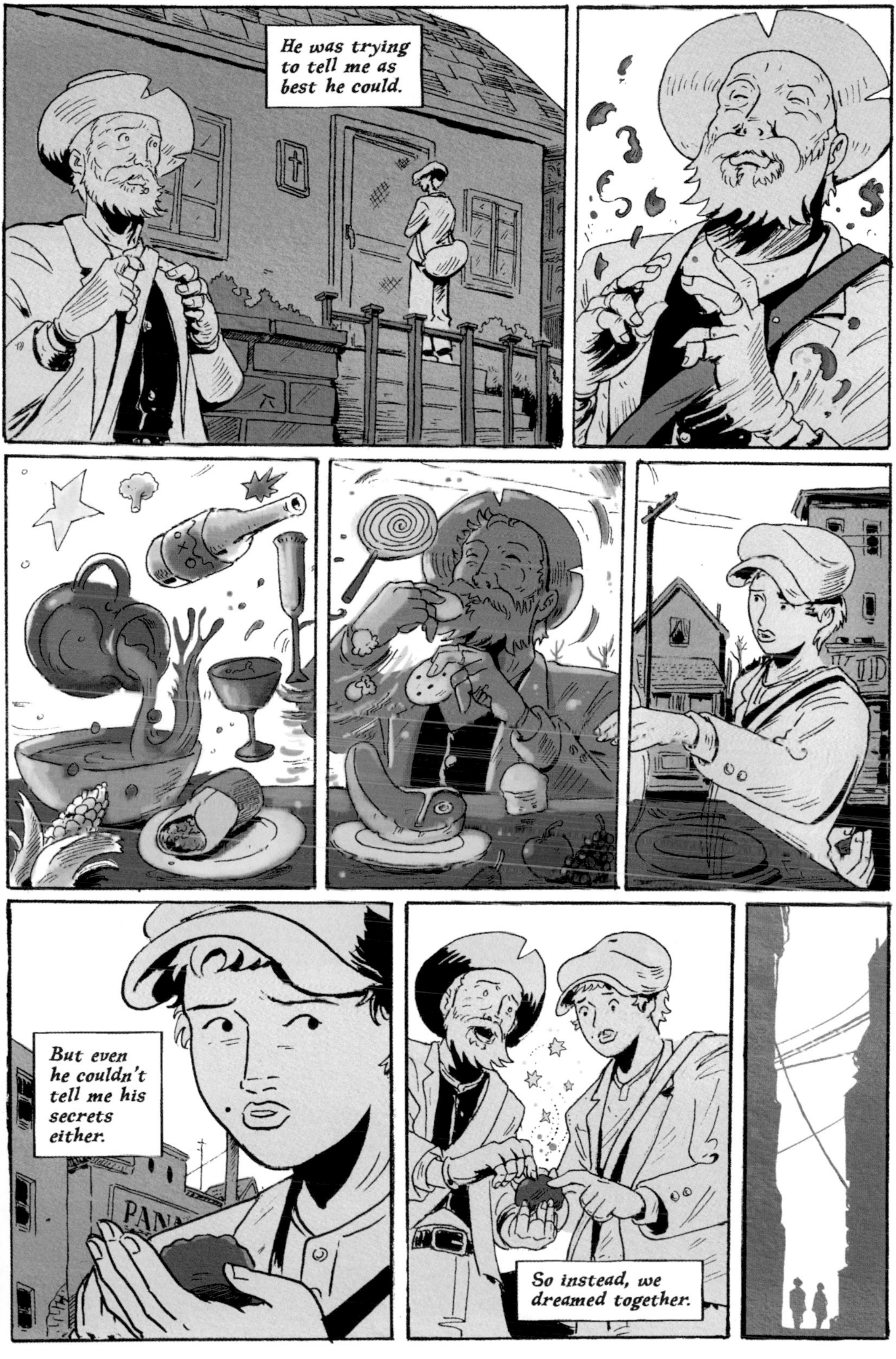
He was trying to tell me as best he could.
But even he couldn't tell me his secrets either.
PANA
So instead, we dreamed together.

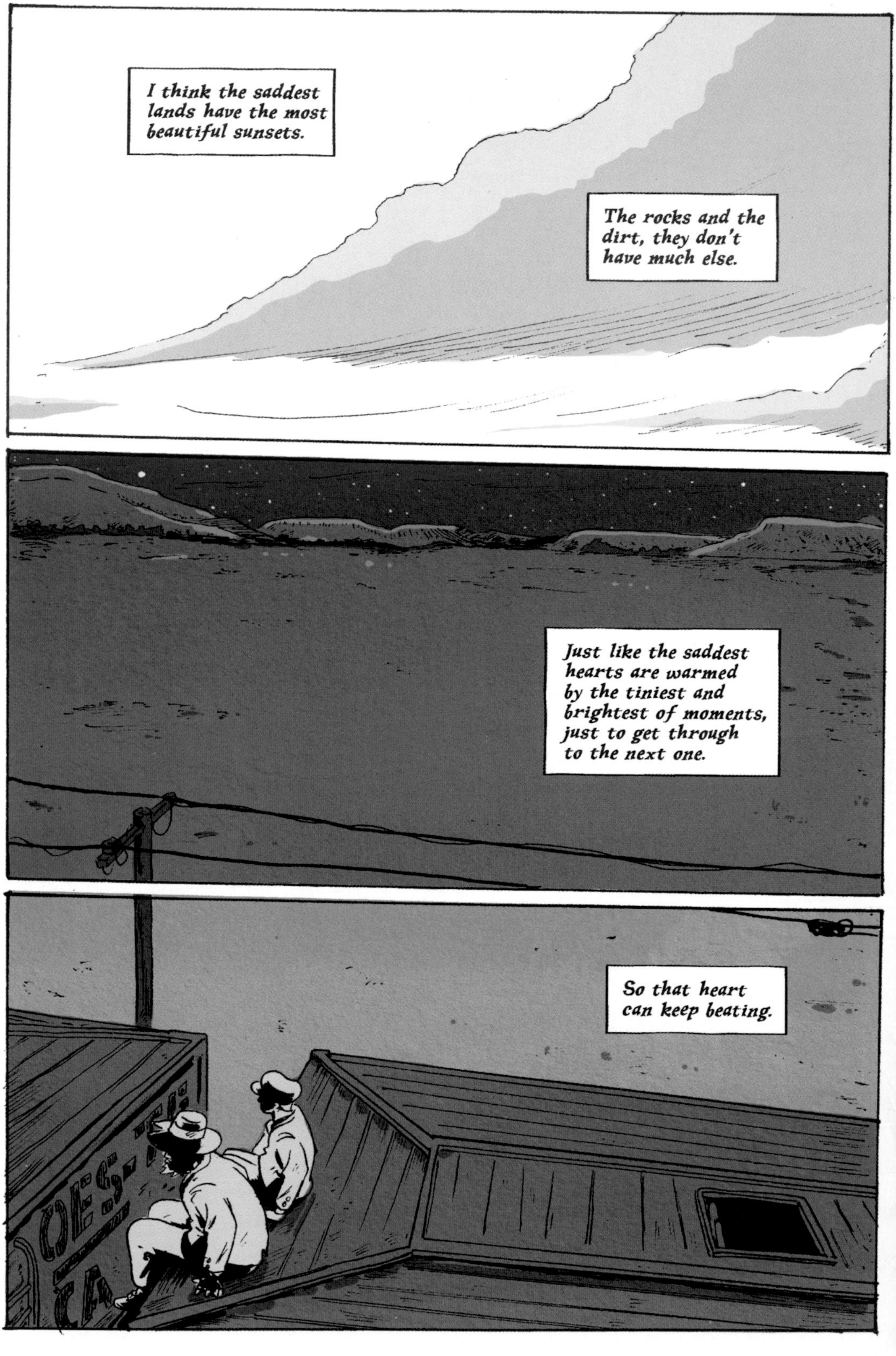
I think the saddest lands have the most beautiful sunsets.
The rocks and the dirt, they don't have much else.
Just like the saddest hearts are warmed by the tiniest and brightest of moments, just to get through to the next one.
So that heart can keep beating.

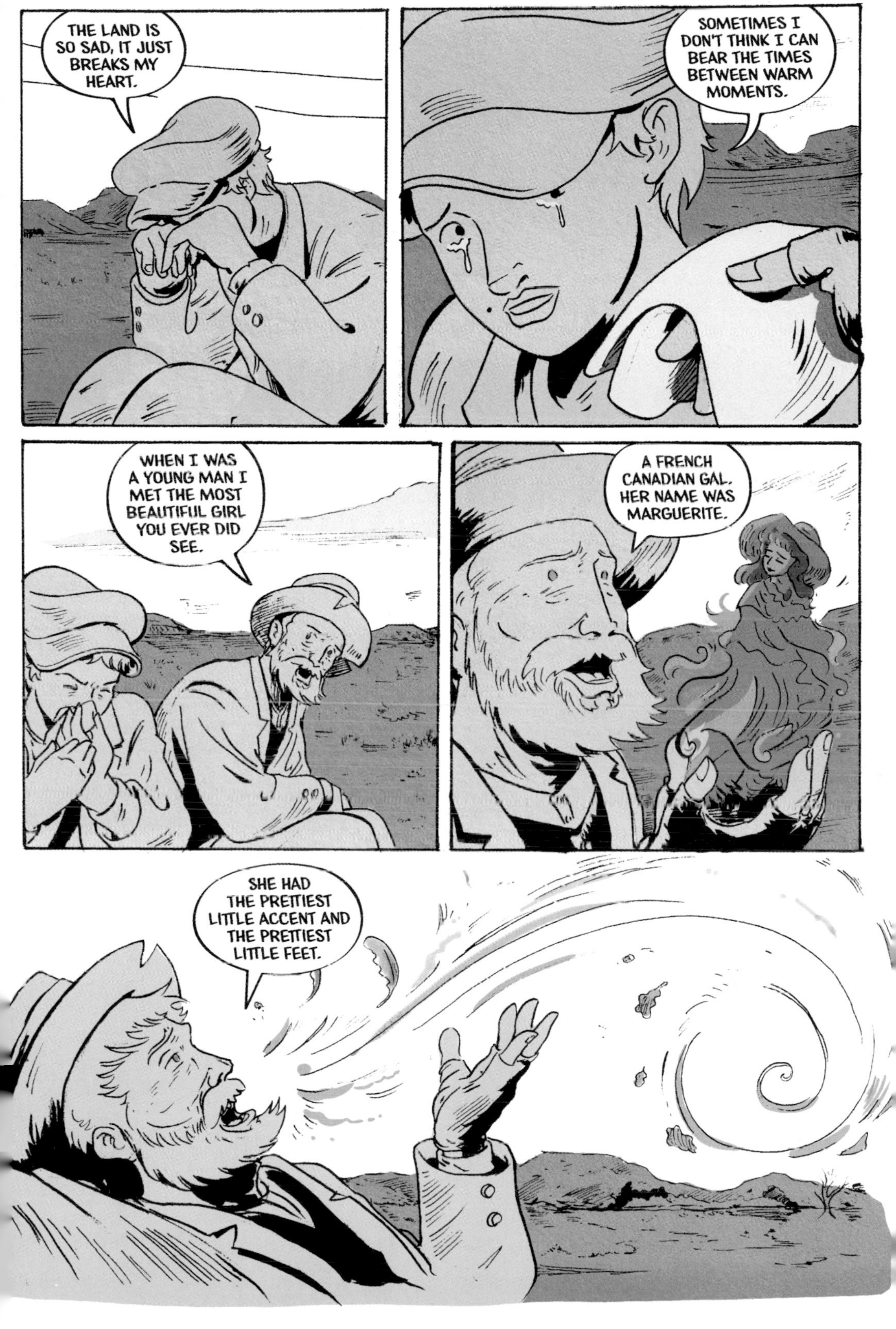
THE LAND IS SO SAD, IT JUST BREAKS MY HEART.
SOMETIMES I DON'T THINK I CAN BEAR THE TIMES BETWEEN WARM MOMENTS.
WHEN I WAS A YOUNG MAN I MET THE MOST BEAUTIFUL GIRL YOU EVER DID SEE.
A FRENCH CANADIAN GAL. HER NAME WAS MARGUERITE.
SHE HAD THE PRETTIEST LITTLE ACCENT AND THE PRETTIEST LITTLE FEET.

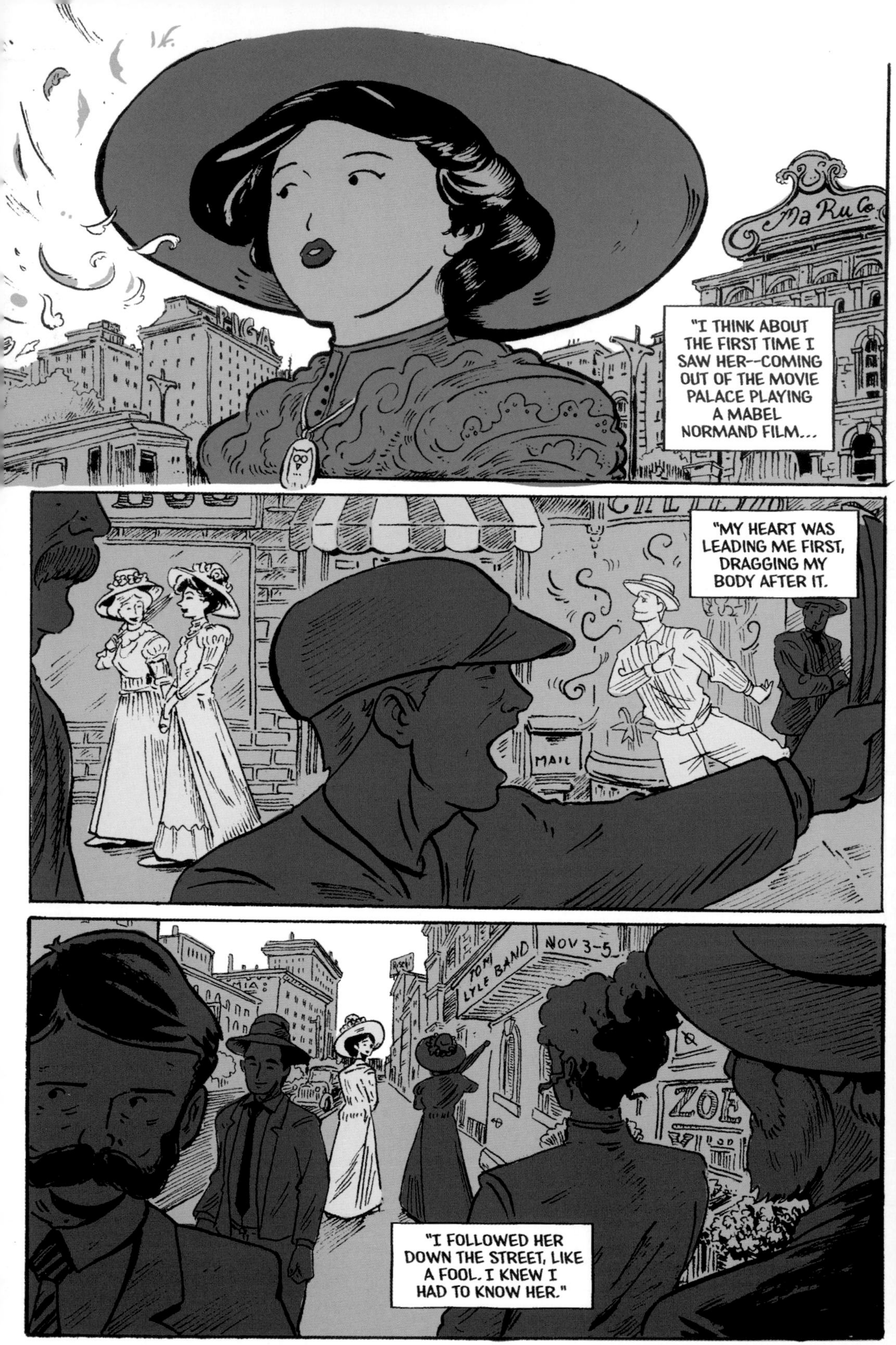
Ma Ru Co
"I THINK ABOUT THE FIRST TIME I SAW HER--COMING OUT OF THE MOVIE PALACE PLAYING A MABEL NORMAND FILM...
"MY HEART WAS LEADING ME FIRST, DRAGGING MY BODY AFTER IT.
MAIL
TONI LYLE BAND
NOV 3-5
ZOE
"I FOLLOWED HER DOWN THE STREET, LIKE A FOOL. I KNEW I HAD TO KNOW HER."

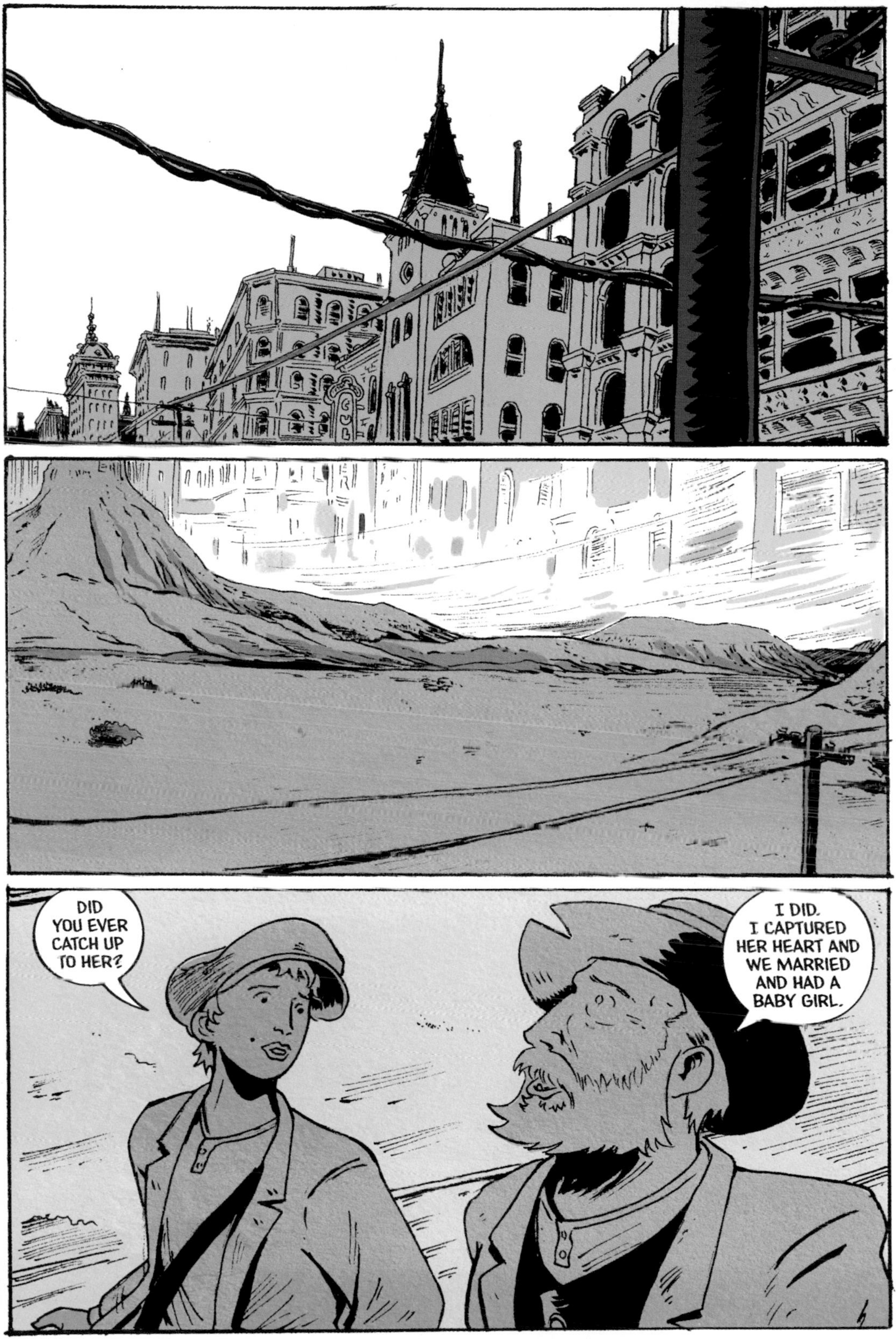
DID YOU EVER CATCH UP TO HER?
I DID. I CAPTURED HER HEART AND WE MARRIED AND HAD A BABY GIRL.

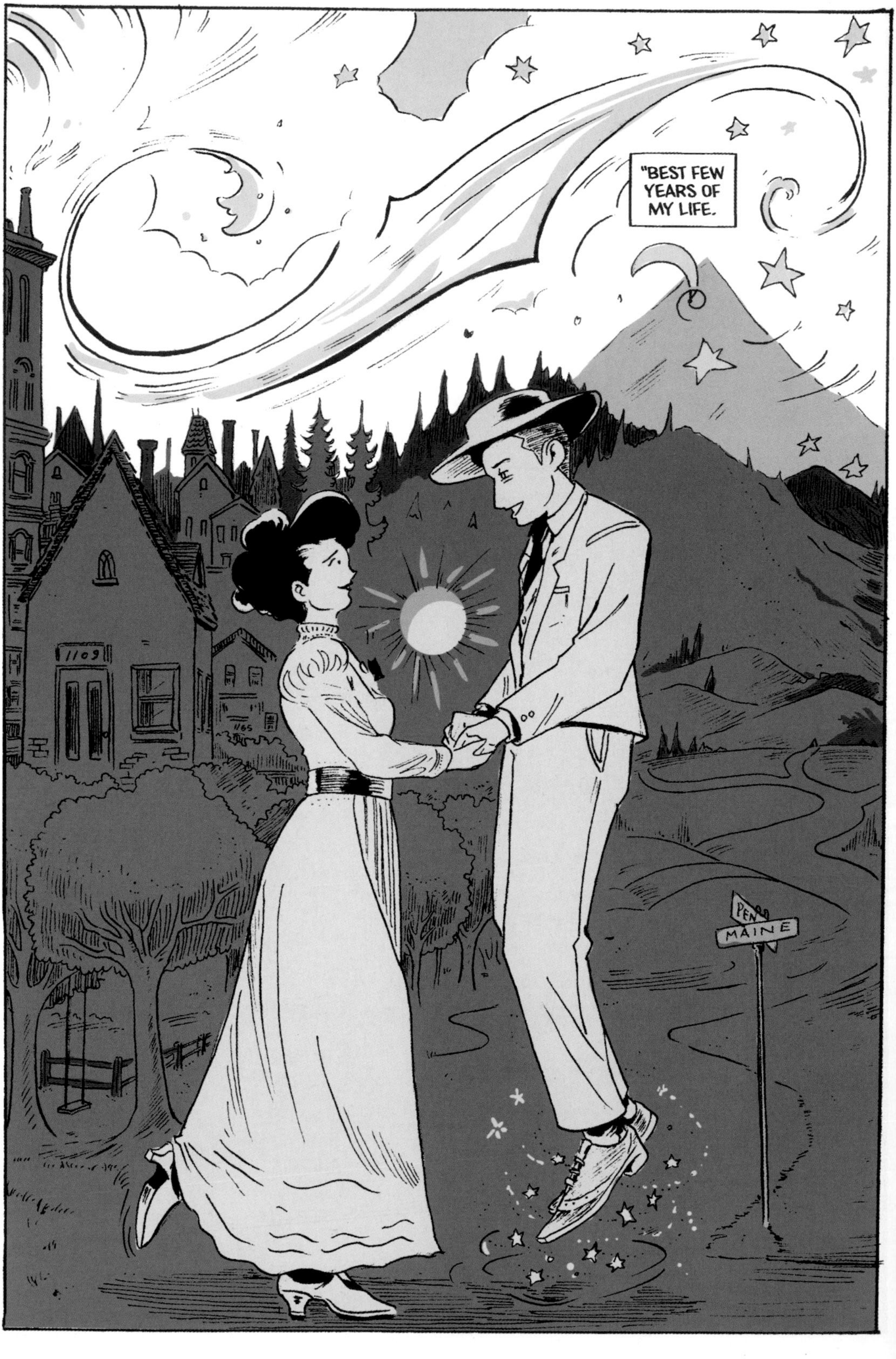
"BEST FEW YEARS OF MY LIFE.
1109
1165
PEN
MAINE

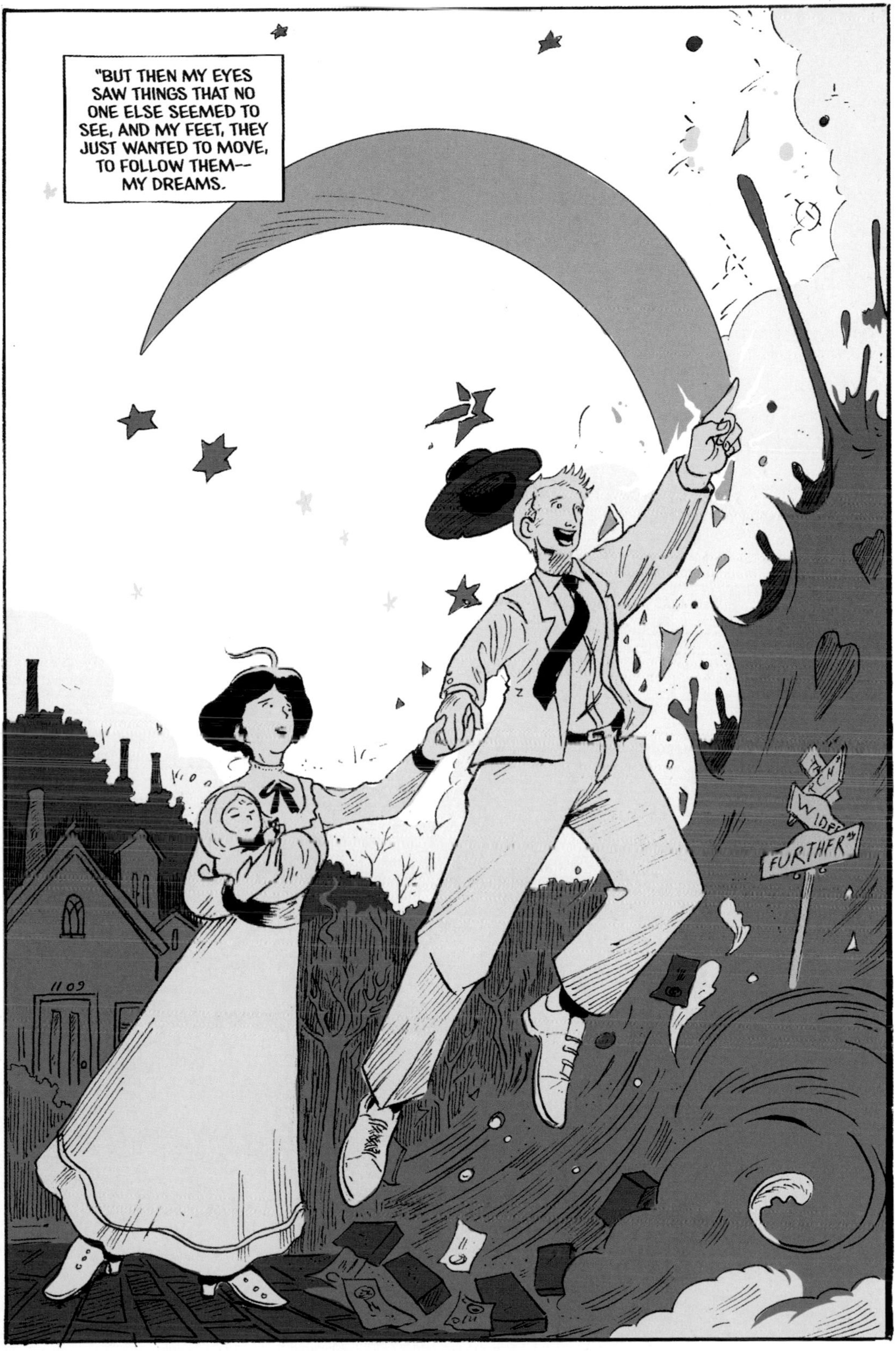
"BUT THEN MY EYES SAW THINGS THAT NO ONE ELSE SEEMED TO SEE, AND MY FEET, THEY JUST WANTED TO MOVE, TO FOLLOW THEM-- MY DREAMS.
1109
FURTHER

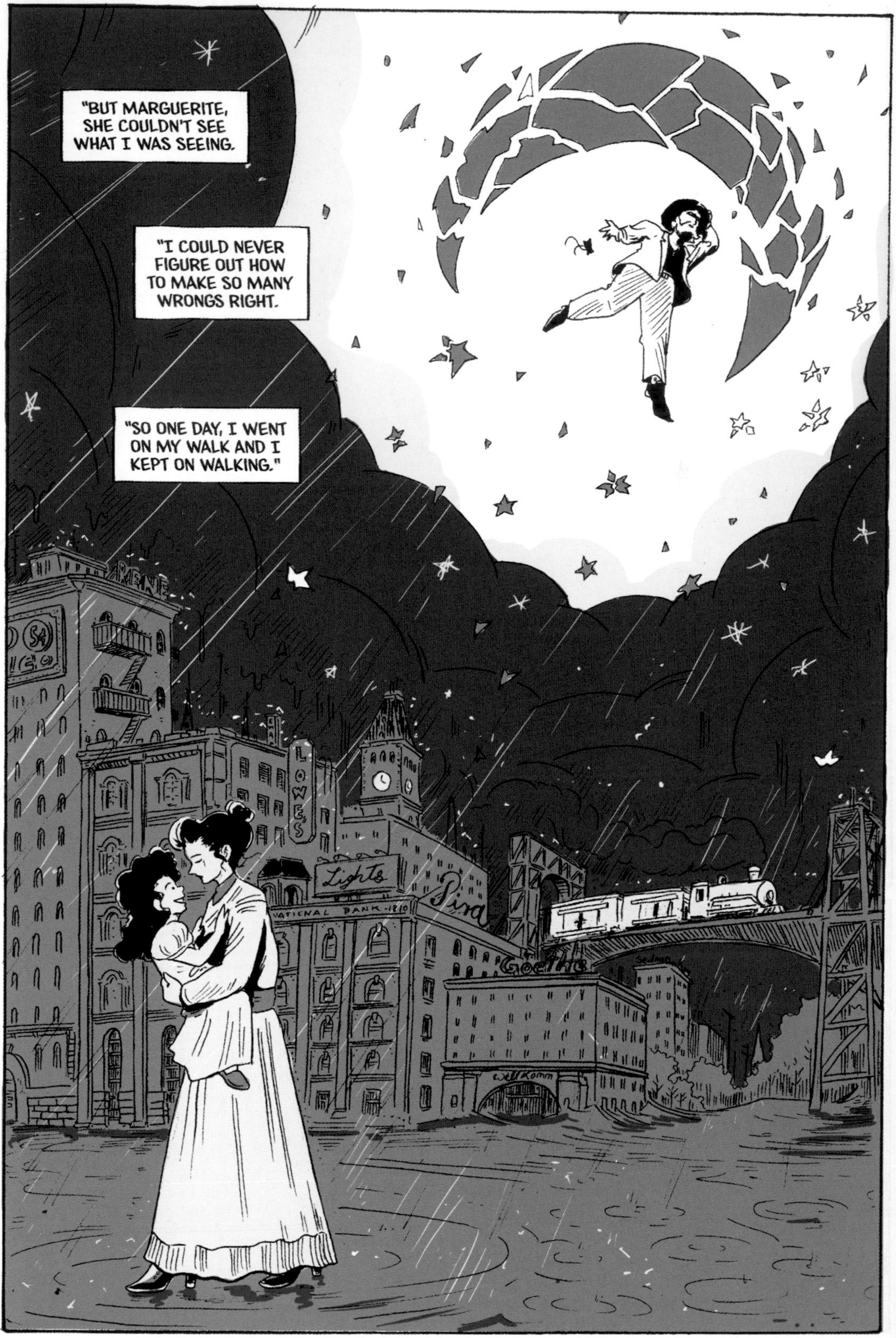
"BUT MARGUERITE, SHE COULDN'T SEE WHAT I WAS SEEING.
"I COULD NEVER FIGURE OUT HOW TO MAKE SO MANY WRONGS RIGHT.
"SO ONE DAY, I WENT ON MY WALK AND I KEPT ON WALKING."
LOWE'S
Lights
Goethe

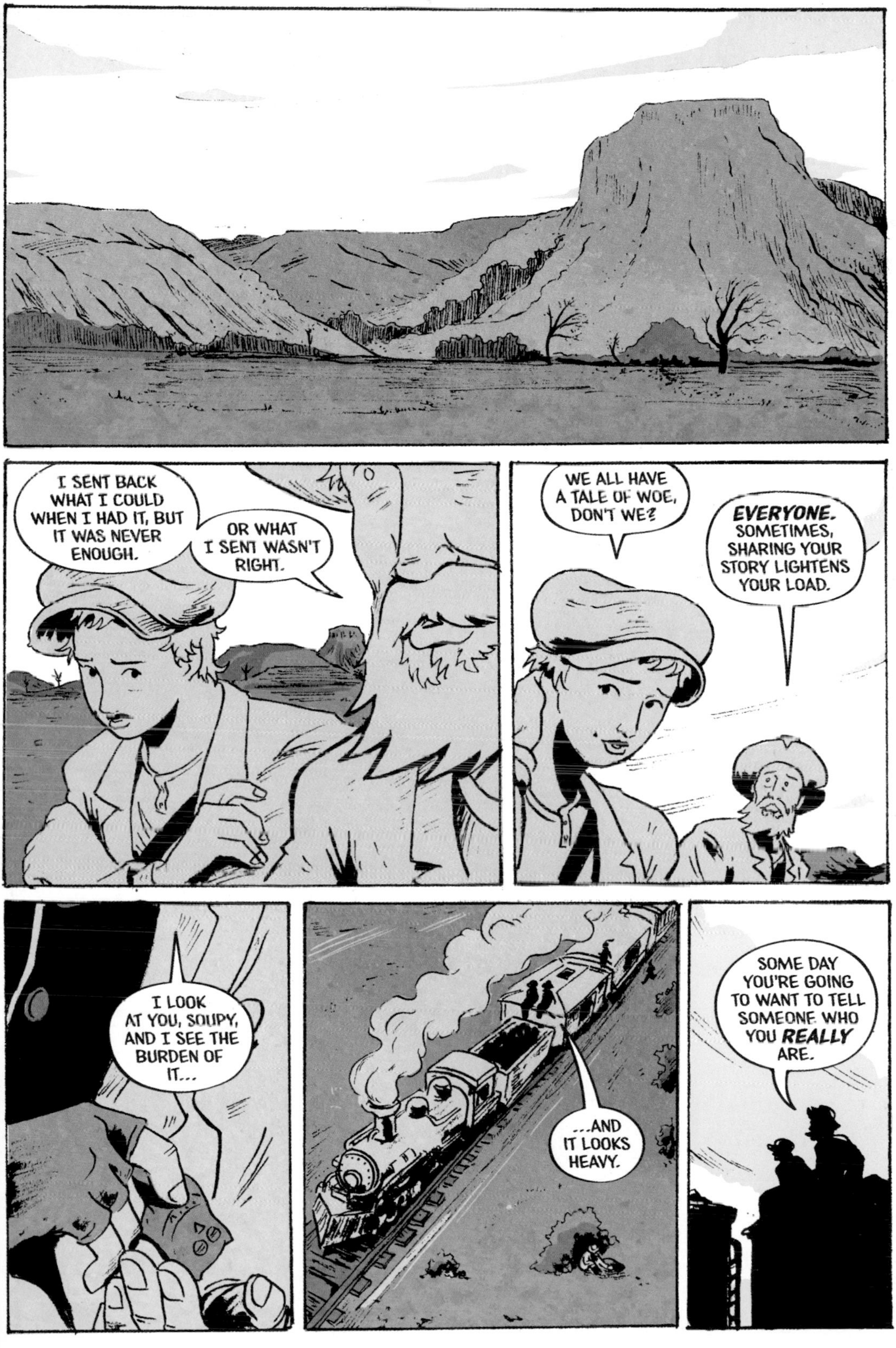

I SENT BACK WHAT I COULD WHEN I HAD IT, BUT IT WAS NEVER ENOUGH.
OR WHAT I SENT WASN'T RIGHT.
WE ALL HAVE A TALE OF WOE, DON'T WE?
EVERYONE. SOMETIMES, SHARING YOUR STORY LIGHTENS YOUR LOAD.
I LOOK AT YOU, SOUPY, AND I SEE THE BURDEN OF IT...
...AND IT LOOKS HEAVY.
SOME DAY YOU'RE GOING TO WANT TO TELL SOMEONE WHO YOU **REALLY** ARE.

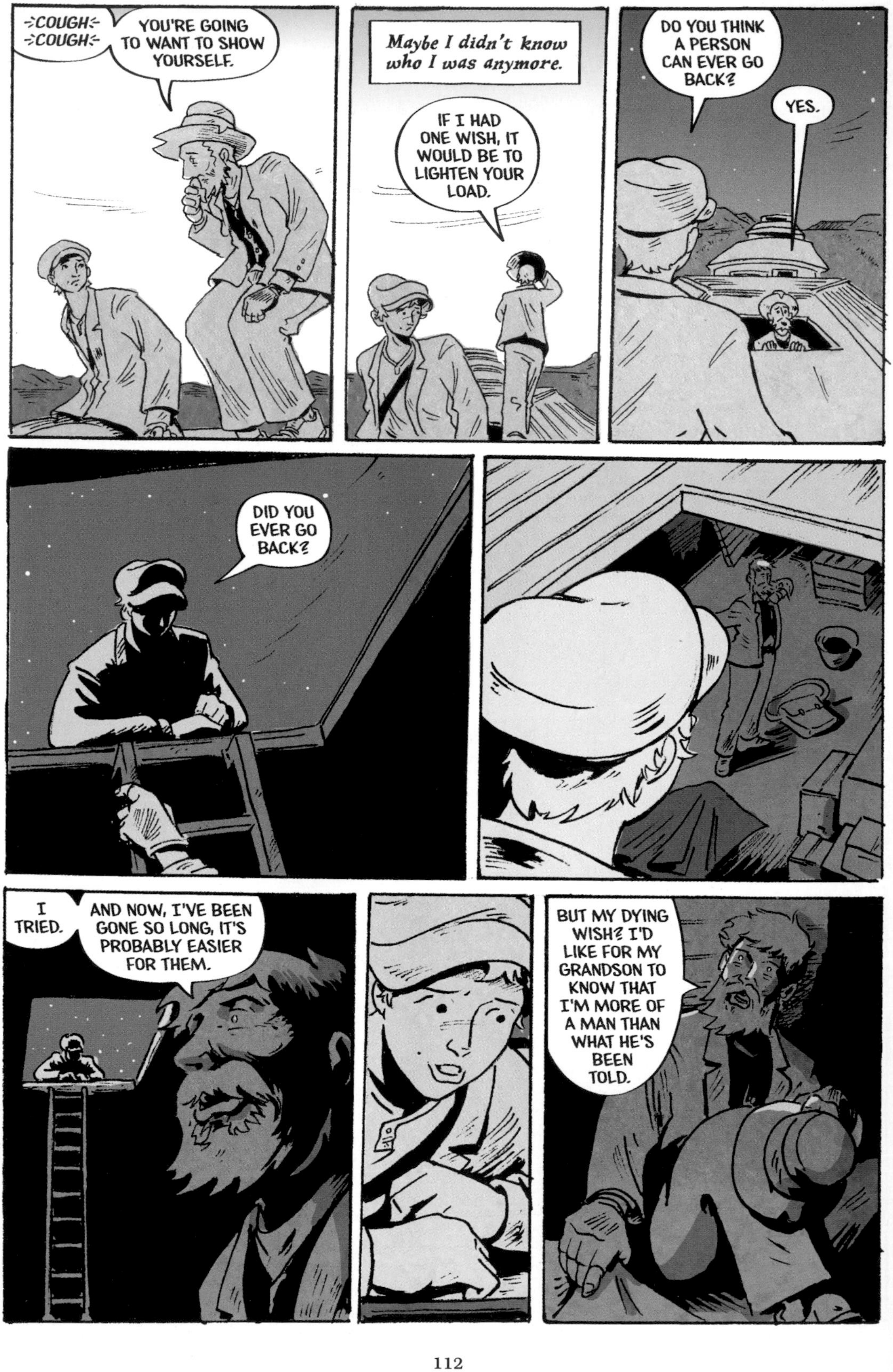

COUGH
COUGH
YOU'RE GOING TO WANT TO SHOW YOURSELF.
Maybe I didn't know who I was anymore.
IF I HAD ONE WISH, IT WOULD BE TO LIGHTEN YOUR LOAD.
DO YOU THINK A PERSON CAN EVER GO BACK?
YES.
DID YOU EVER GO BACK?
I TRIED.
AND NOW, I'VE BEEN GONE SO LONG, IT'S PROBABLY EASIER FOR THEM.
BUT MY DYING WISH? I'D LIKE FOR MY GRANDSON TO KNOW THAT I'M MORE OF A MAN THAN WHAT HE'S BEEN TOLD.

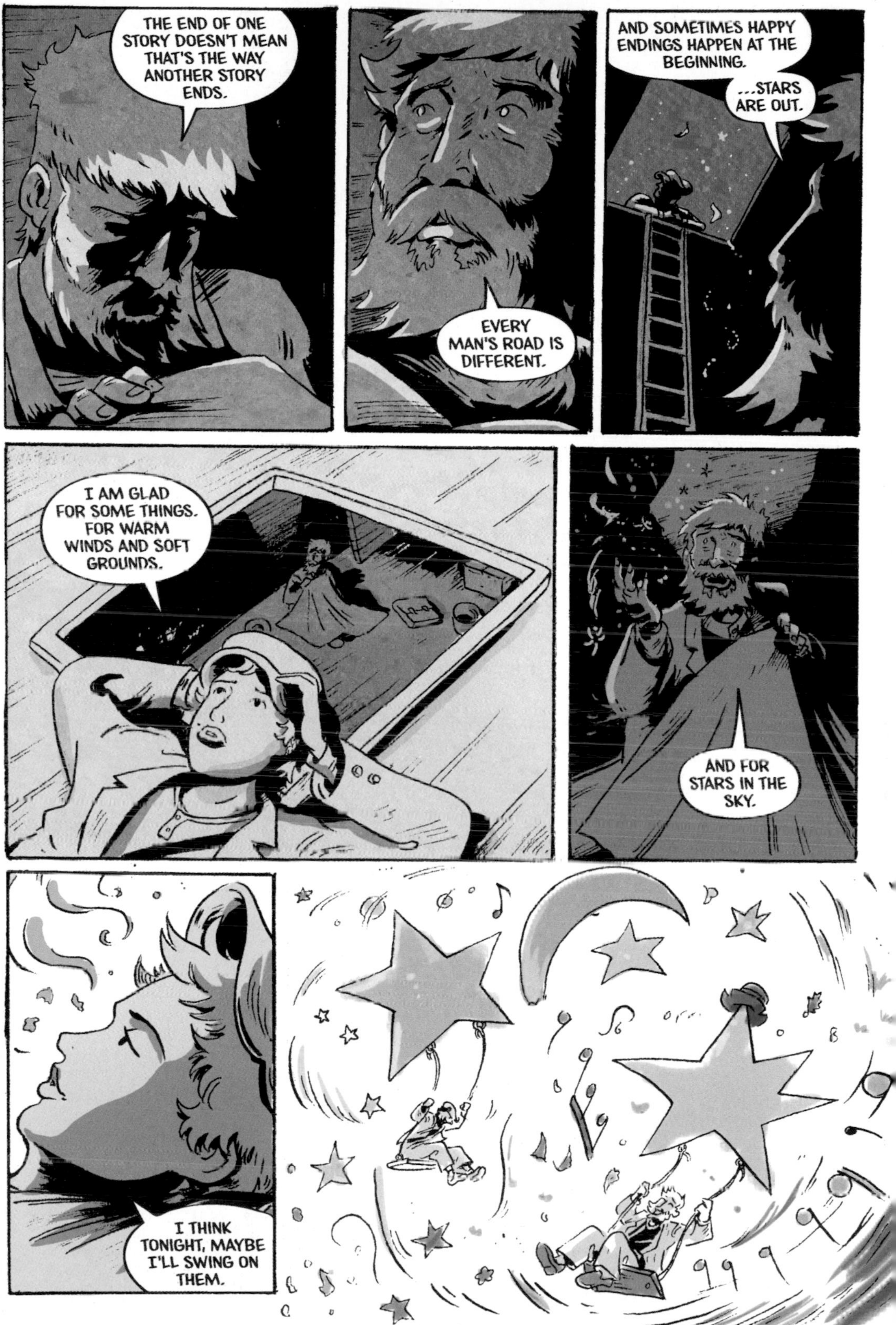
THE END OF ONE STORY DOESN'T MEAN THAT'S THE WAY ANOTHER STORY ENDS.
EVERY MAN'S ROAD IS DIFFERENT.
AND SOMETIMES HAPPY ENDINGS HAPPEN AT THE BEGINNING.
...STARS ARE OUT.
I AM GLAD FOR SOME THINGS. FOR WARM WINDS AND SOFT GROUNDS.
AND FOR STARS IN THE SKY.
I THINK TONIGHT, MAYBE I'LL SWING ON THEM.

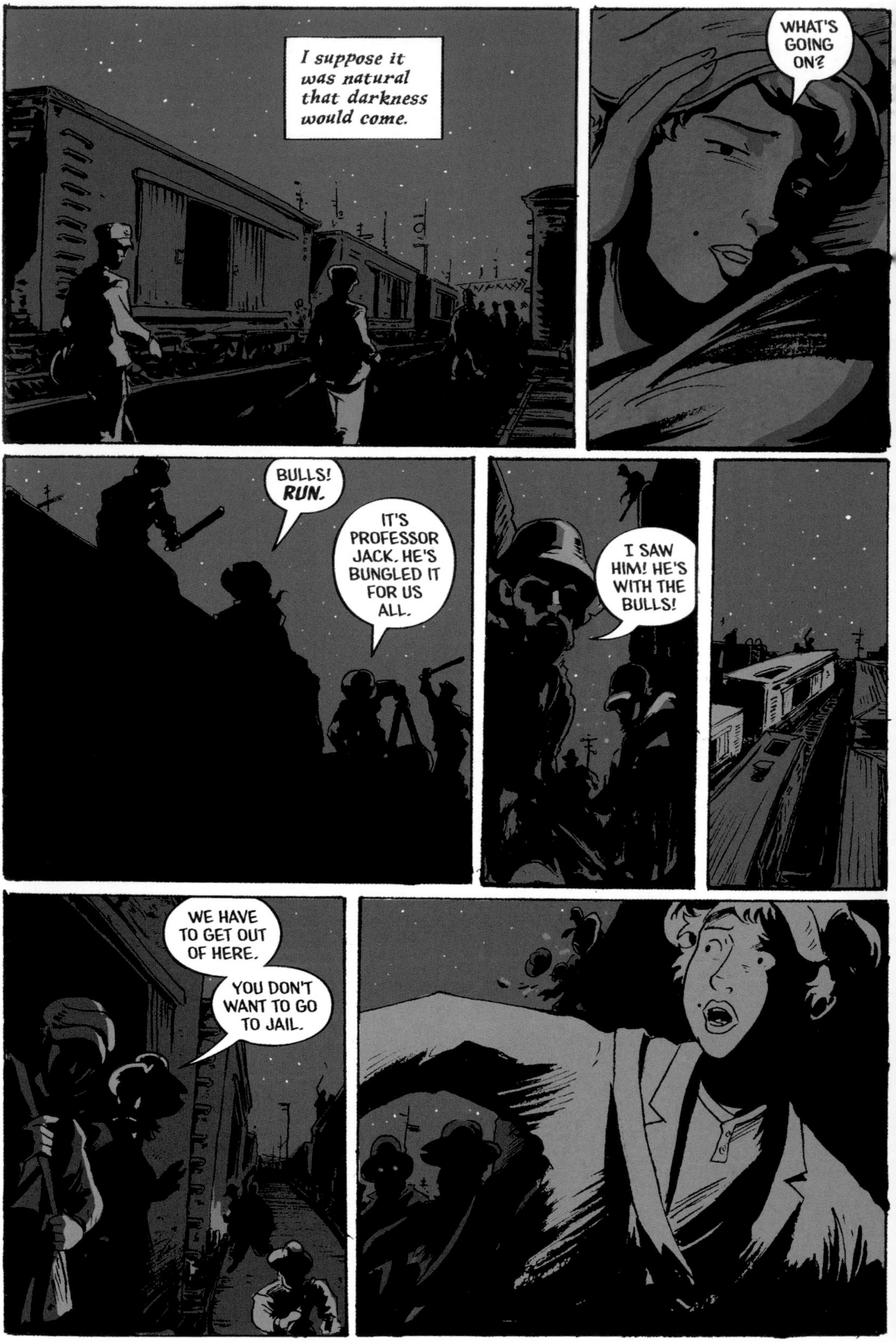
I suppose it was natural that darkness would come.
WHAT'S GOING ON?
BULLS! RUN.
IT'S PROFESSOR JACK. HE'S BUNGLED IT FOR US ALL.
I SAW HIM! HE'S WITH THE BULLS!
WE HAVE TO GET OUT OF HERE.
YOU DON'T WANT TO GO TO JAIL.

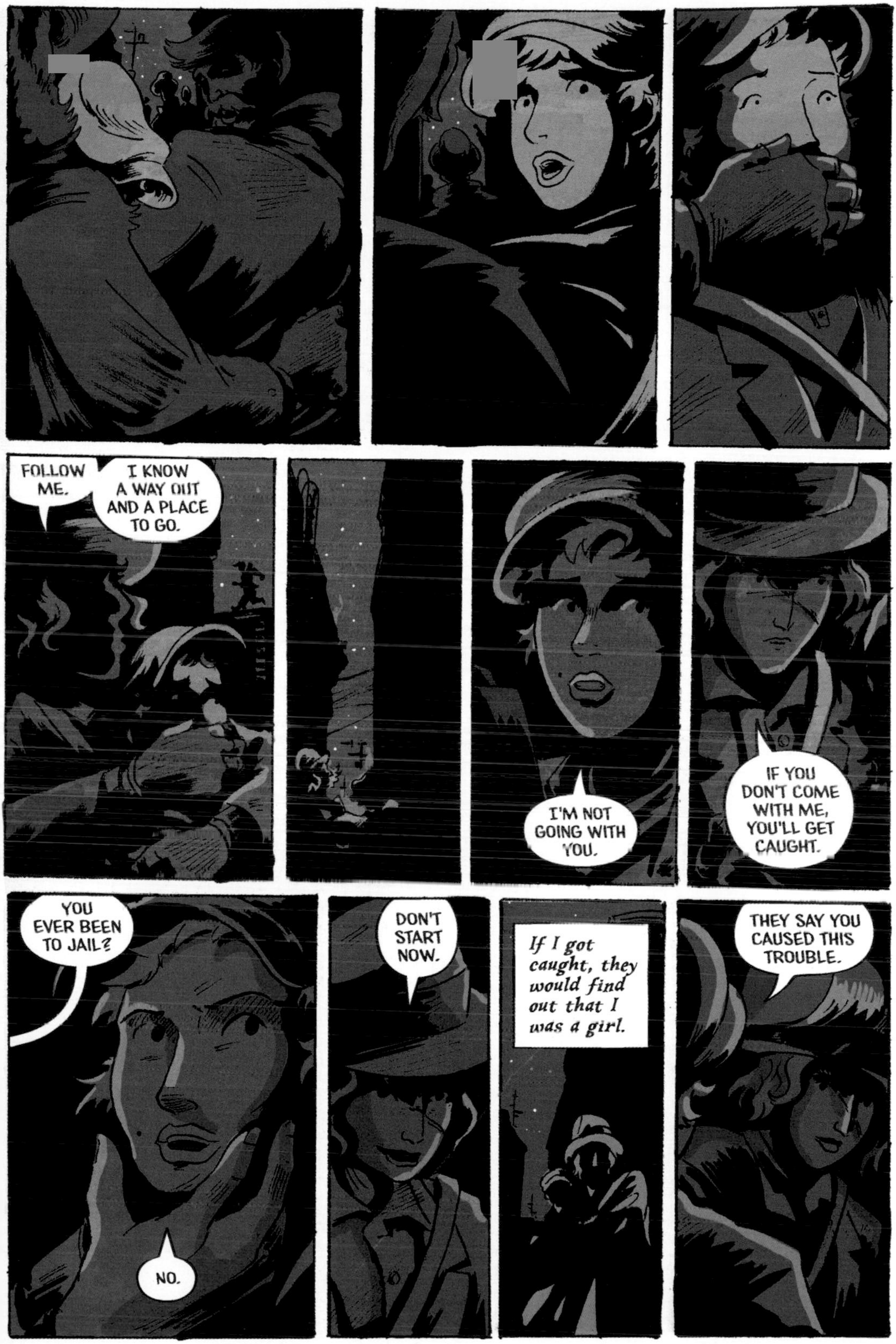
FOLLOW ME.
I KNOW A WAY OUT AND A PLACE TO GO.
I'M NOT GOING WITH YOU.
IF YOU DON'T COME WITH ME, YOU'LL GET CAUGHT.
YOU EVER BEEN TO JAIL?
NO.
DON'T START NOW.
If I got caught, they would find out that I was a girl.
THEY SAY YOU CAUSED THIS TROUBLE.

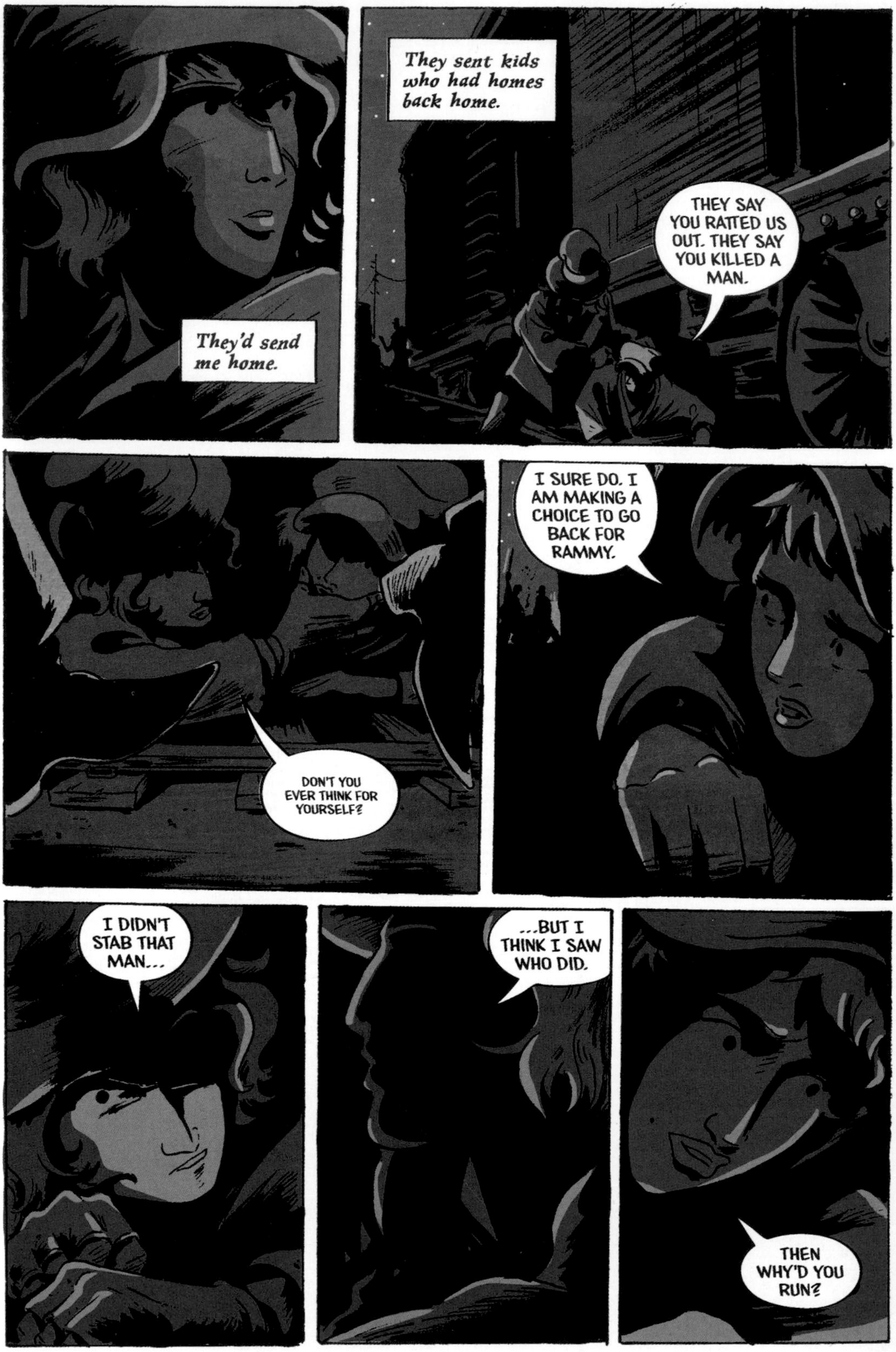
They'd send me home.
They sent kids who had homes back home.
THEY SAY YOU RATTED US OUT. THEY SAY YOU KILLED A MAN.
DON'T YOU EVER THINK FOR YOURSELF?
I SURE DO. I AM MAKING A CHOICE TO GO BACK FOR RAMMY.
I DIDN'T STAB THAT MAN...
...BUT I THINK I SAW WHO DID.
THEN WHY'D YOU RUN?

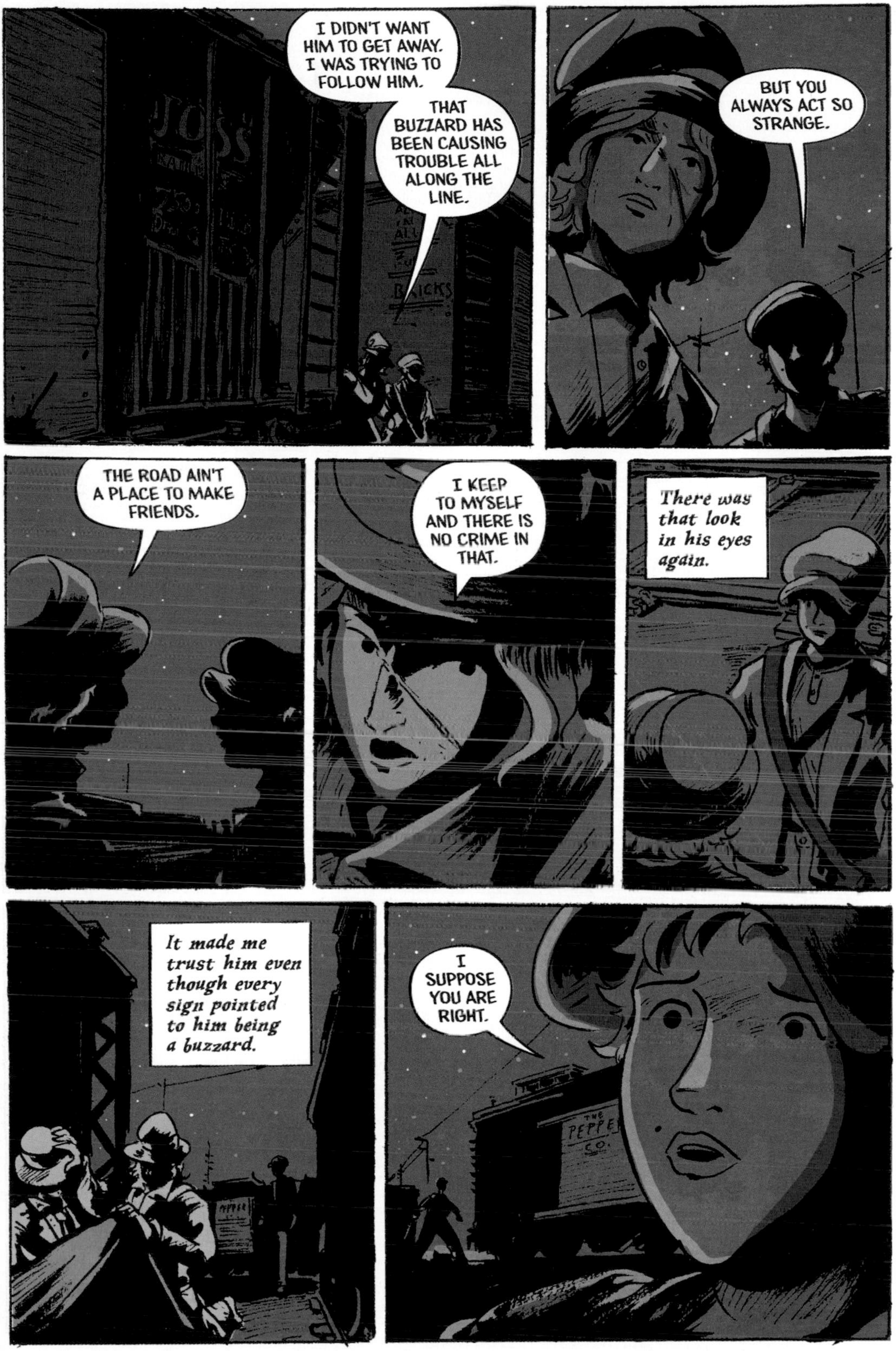

I DIDN'T WANT HIM TO GET AWAY. I WAS TRYING TO FOLLOW HIM.
THAT BUZZARD HAS BEEN CAUSING TROUBLE ALL ALONG THE LINE.
BUT YOU ALWAYS ACT SO STRANGE.
THE ROAD AIN'T A PLACE TO MAKE FRIENDS.
I KEEP TO MYSELF AND THERE IS NO CRIME IN THAT.
There was that look in his eyes again.
It made me trust him even though every sign pointed to him being a buzzard.
I SUPPOSE YOU ARE RIGHT.

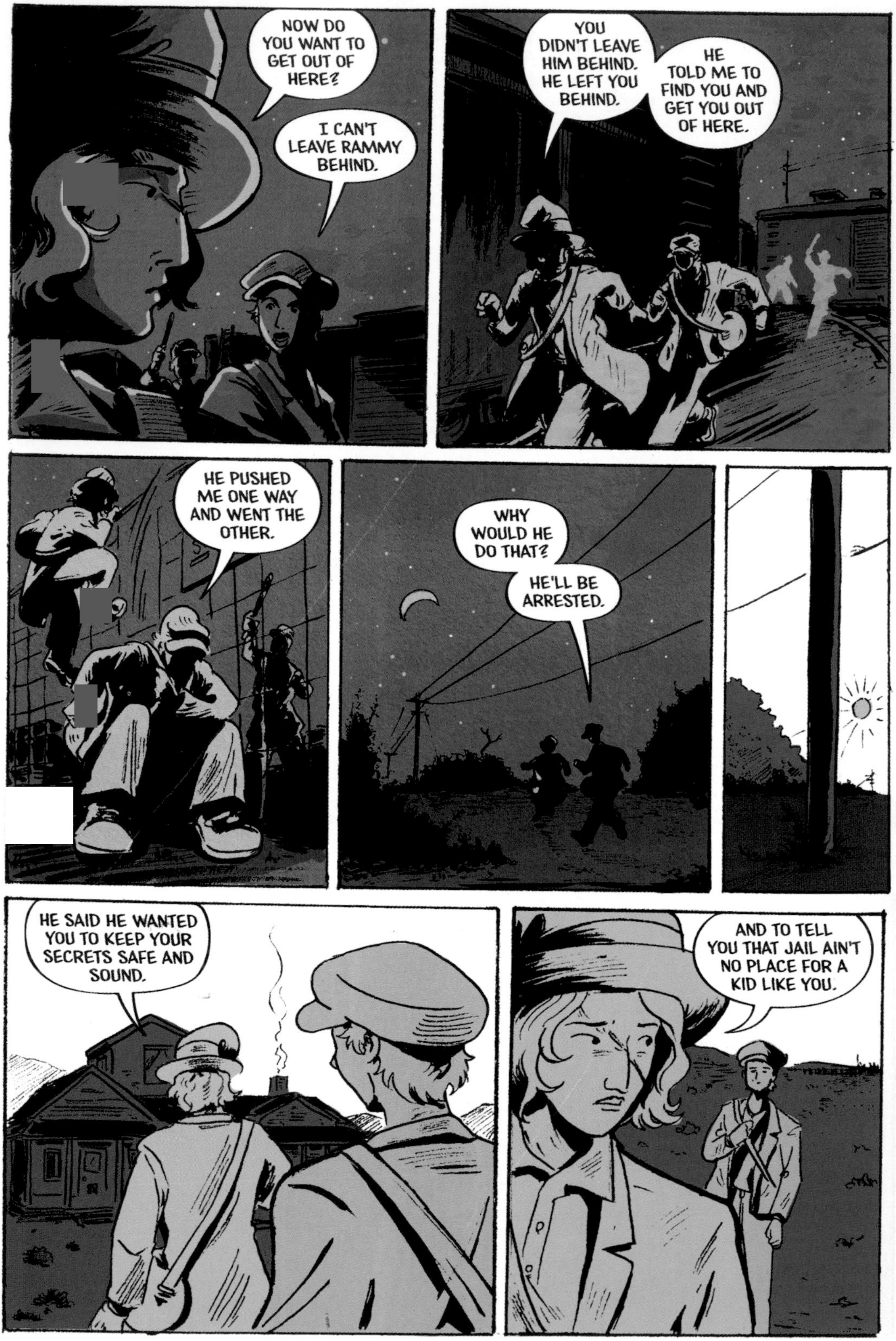
NOW DO YOU WANT TO GET OUT OF HERE?
I CAN'T LEAVE RAMMY BEHIND.
YOU DIDN'T LEAVE HIM BEHIND. HE LEFT YOU BEHIND.
HE TOLD ME TO FIND YOU AND GET YOU OUT OF HERE.
HE PUSHED ME ONE WAY AND WENT THE OTHER.
WHY WOULD HE DO THAT?
HE'LL BE ARRESTED.
HE SAID HE WANTED YOU TO KEEP YOUR SECRETS SAFE AND SOUND.
AND TO TELL YOU THAT JAIL AIN'T NO PLACE FOR A KID LIKE YOU.

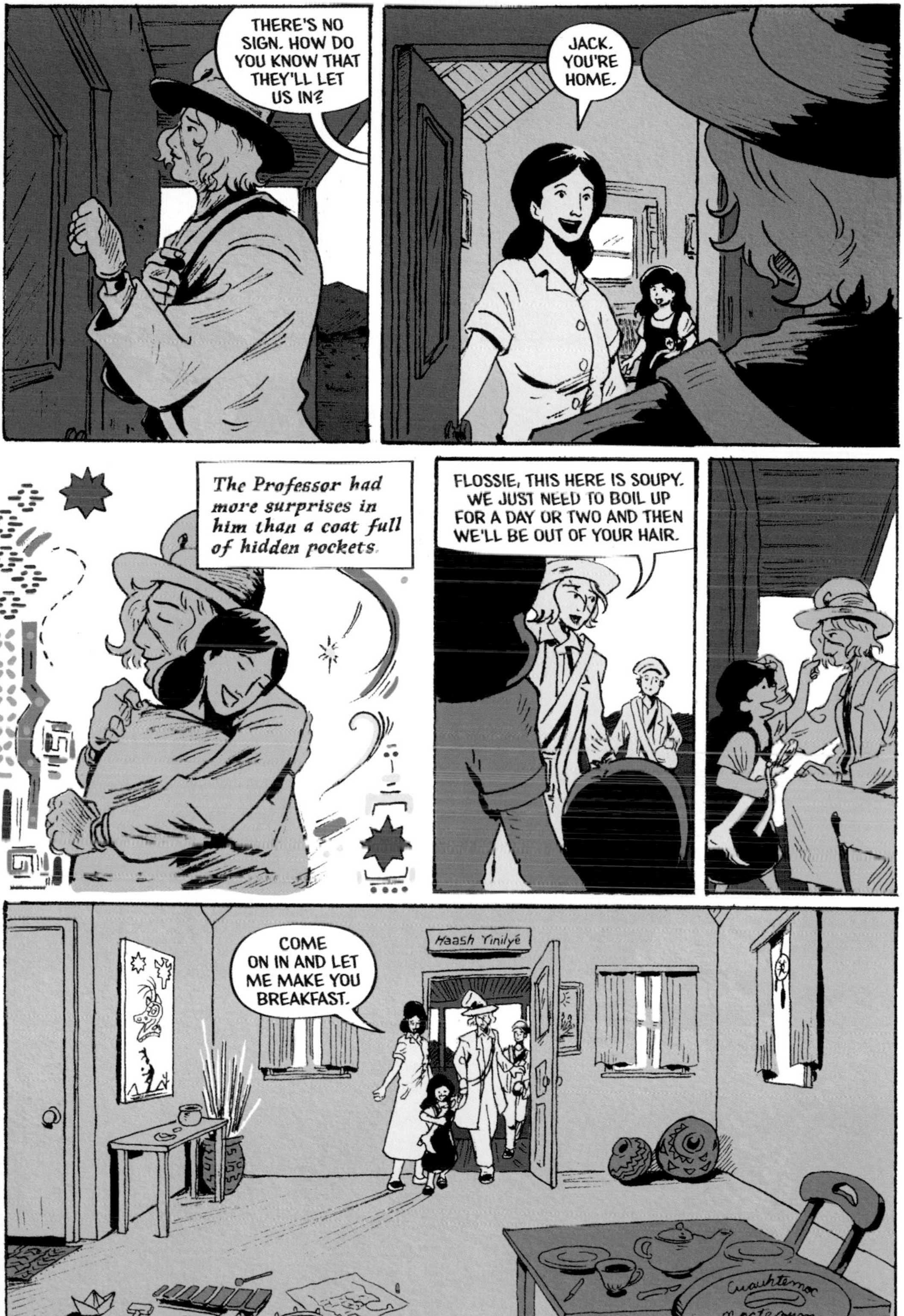
THERE'S NO SIGN. HOW DO YOU KNOW THAT THEY'LL LET US IN?
JACK. YOU'RE HOME.
The Professor had more surprises in him than a coat full of hidden pockets.
FLOSSIE, THIS HERE IS SOUPY. WE JUST NEED TO BOIL UP FOR A DAY OR TWO AND THEN WE'LL BE OUT OF YOUR HAIR.
COME ON IN AND LET ME MAKE YOU BREAKFAST.
Haash Yinilyé
Cuauhtemoc
Moctezuma

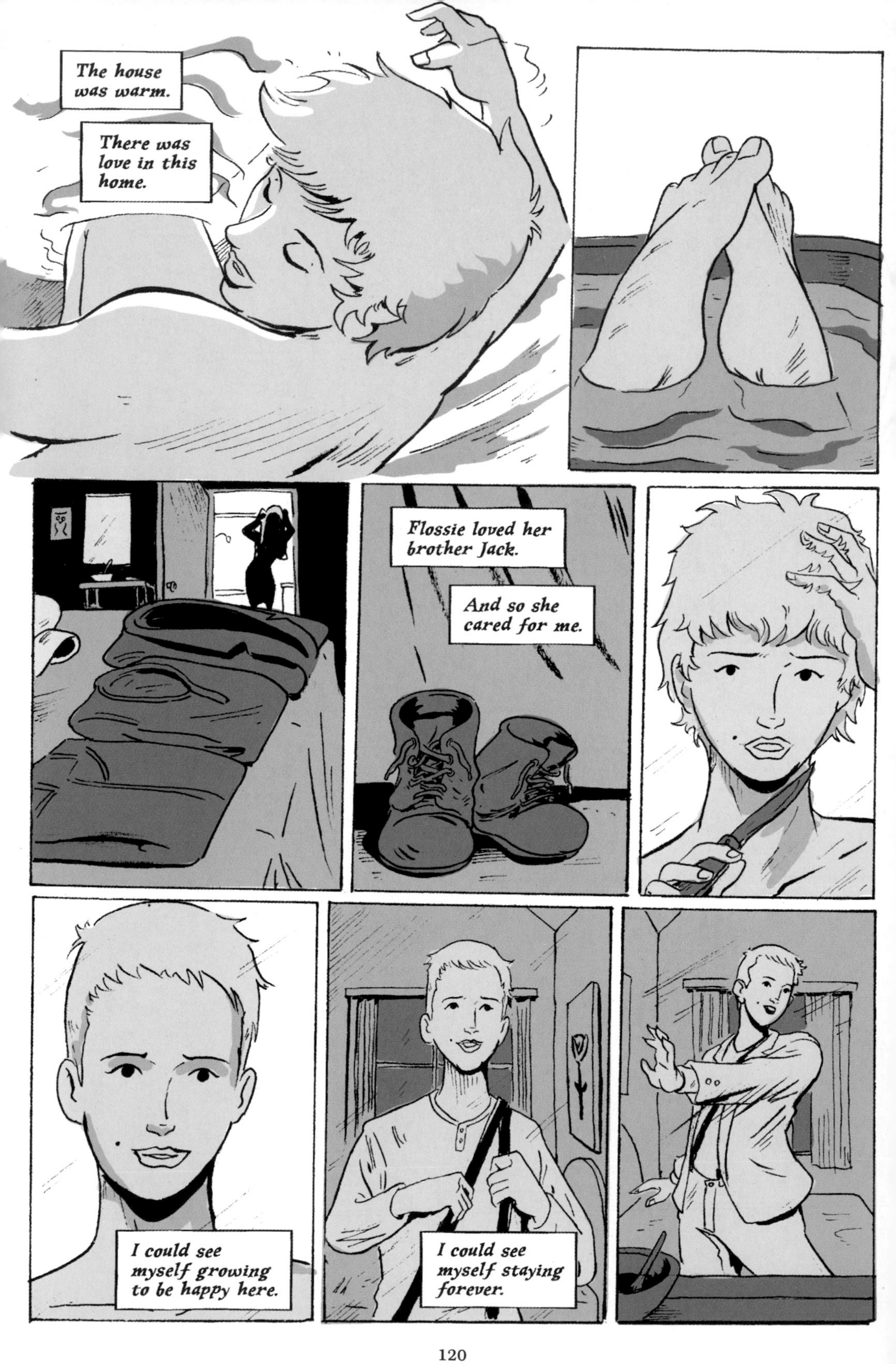
The house was warm.
There was love in this home.
Flossie loved her brother Jack.
And so she cared for me.
I could see myself growing to be happy here.
I could see myself staying forever.

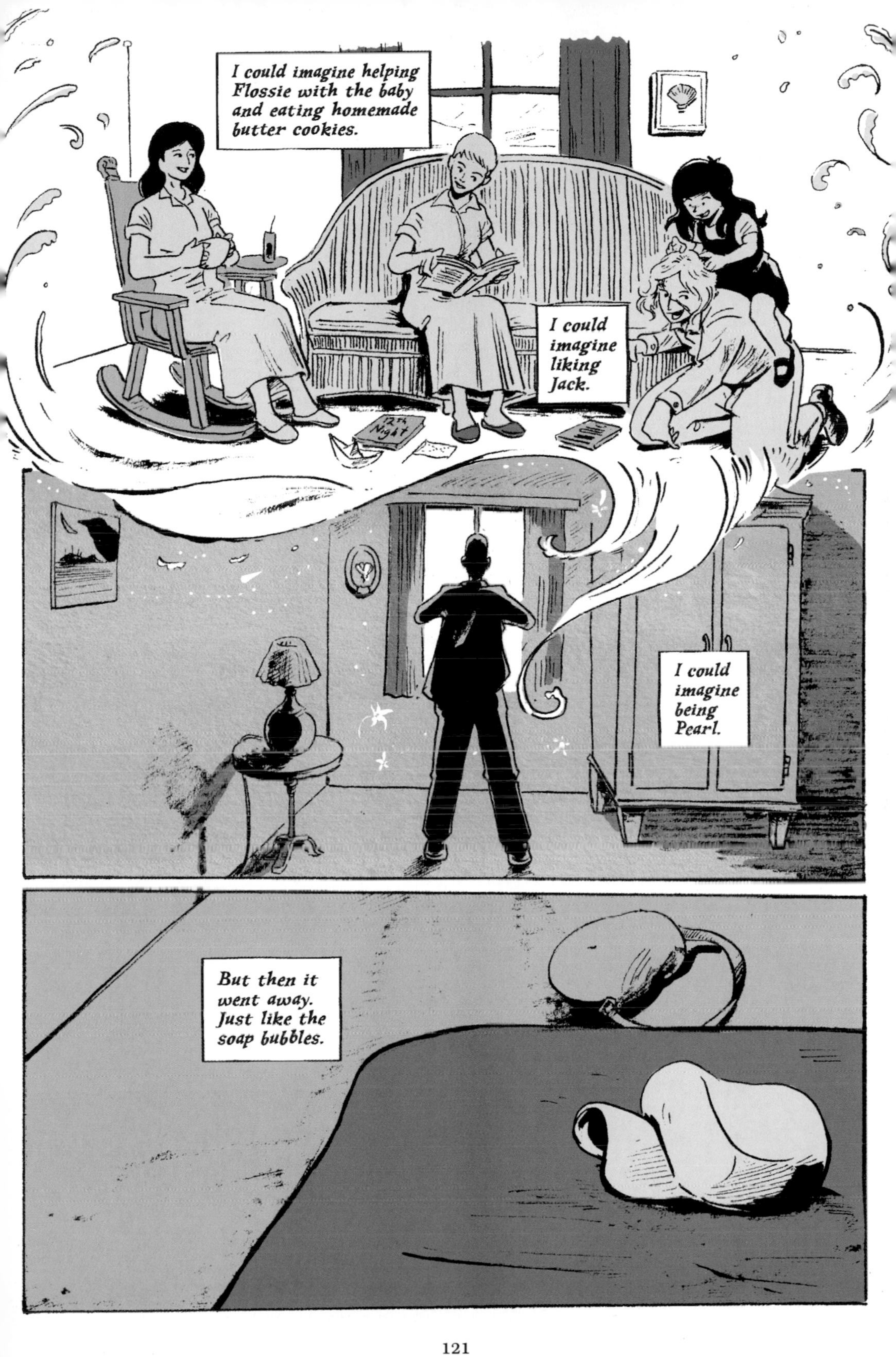
I could imagine helping Flossie with the baby and eating homemade butter cookies.
12th Night
I could imagine liking Jack.
I could imagine being Pearl.
But then it went away. Just like the soap bubbles.

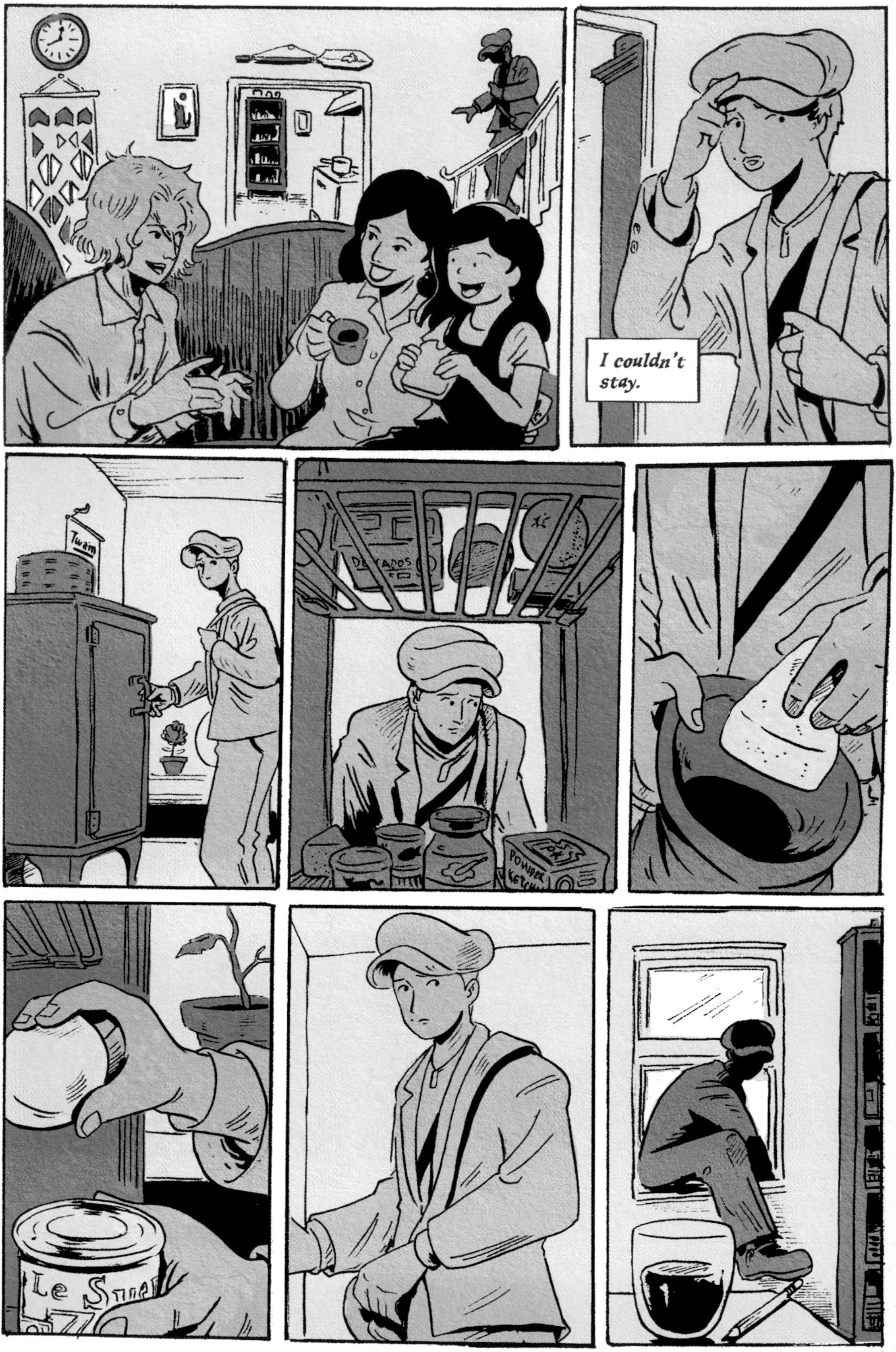
I couldn't stay.
Twain

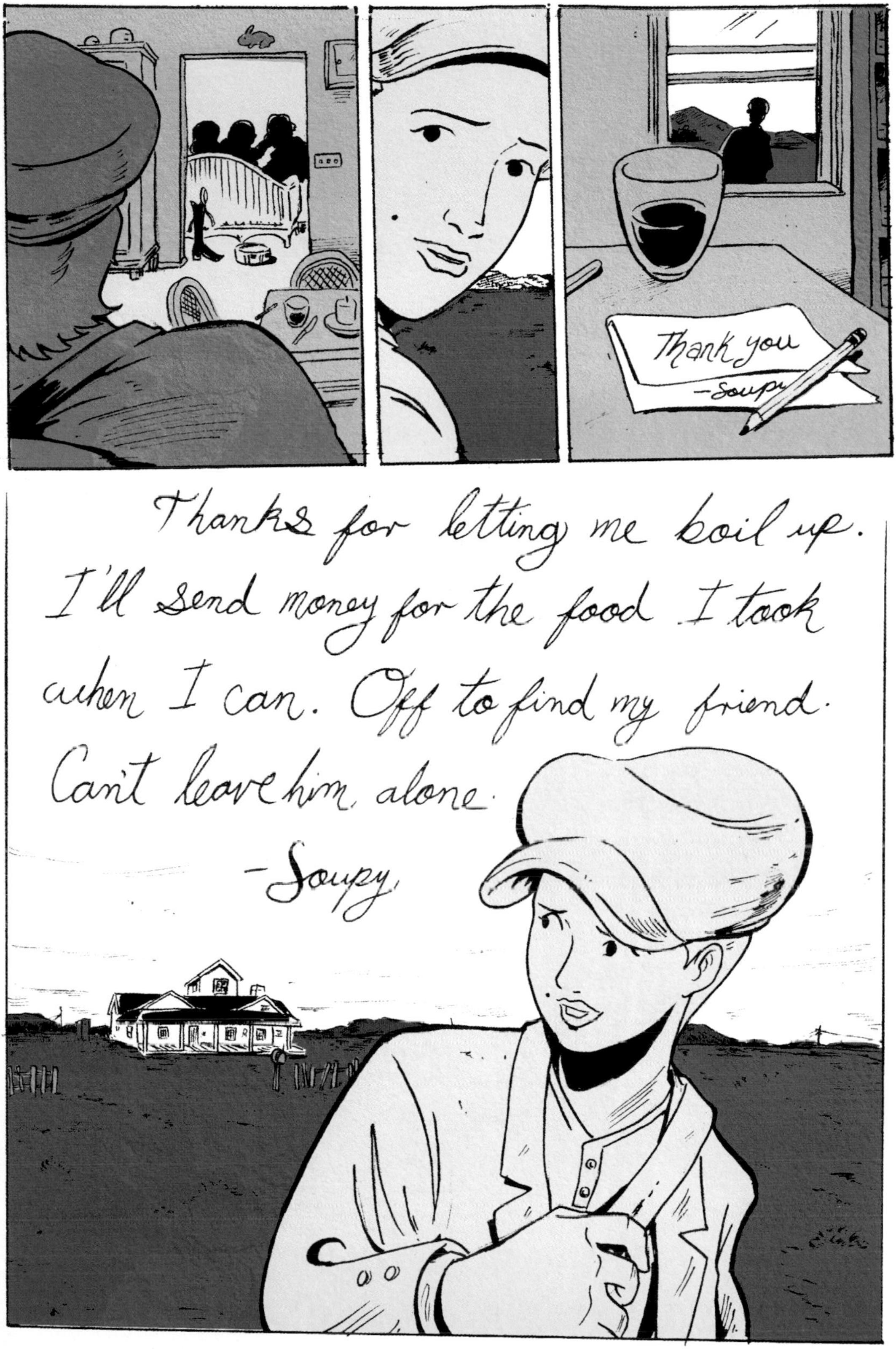
Thank you
-Soupy
Thanks for letting me boil up.
I'll send money for the food I took
when I can. Off to find my friend.
Can't leave him alone.
-Soupy

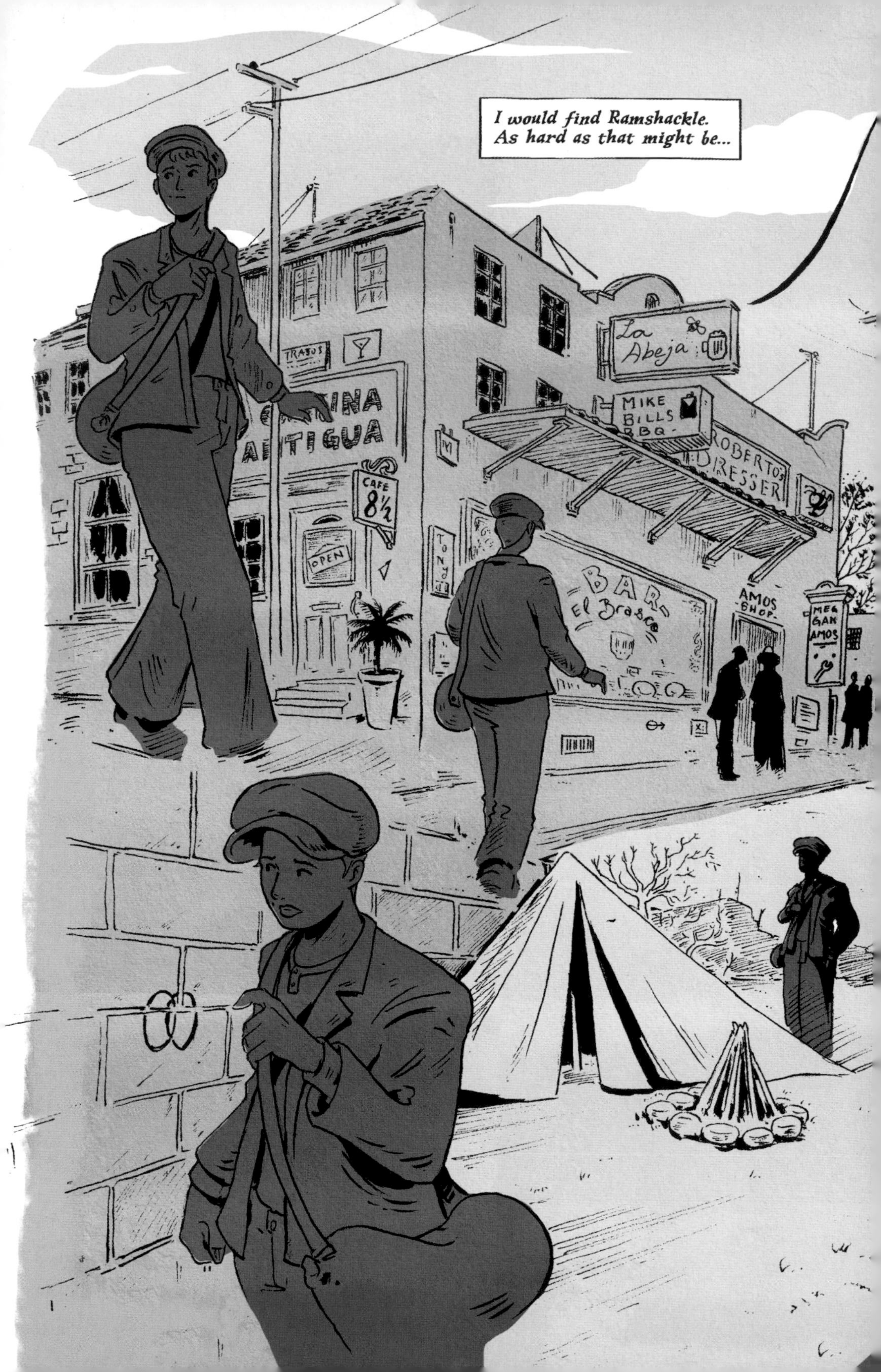
I would find Ramshackle.
As hard as that might be...
La Abeja
MIKE BILLS BBQ
ROBERTO'S DRESSER
CAFE 8½
OPEN
BAR El Brasco
AMOS SHOP
MEG GAN AMOS

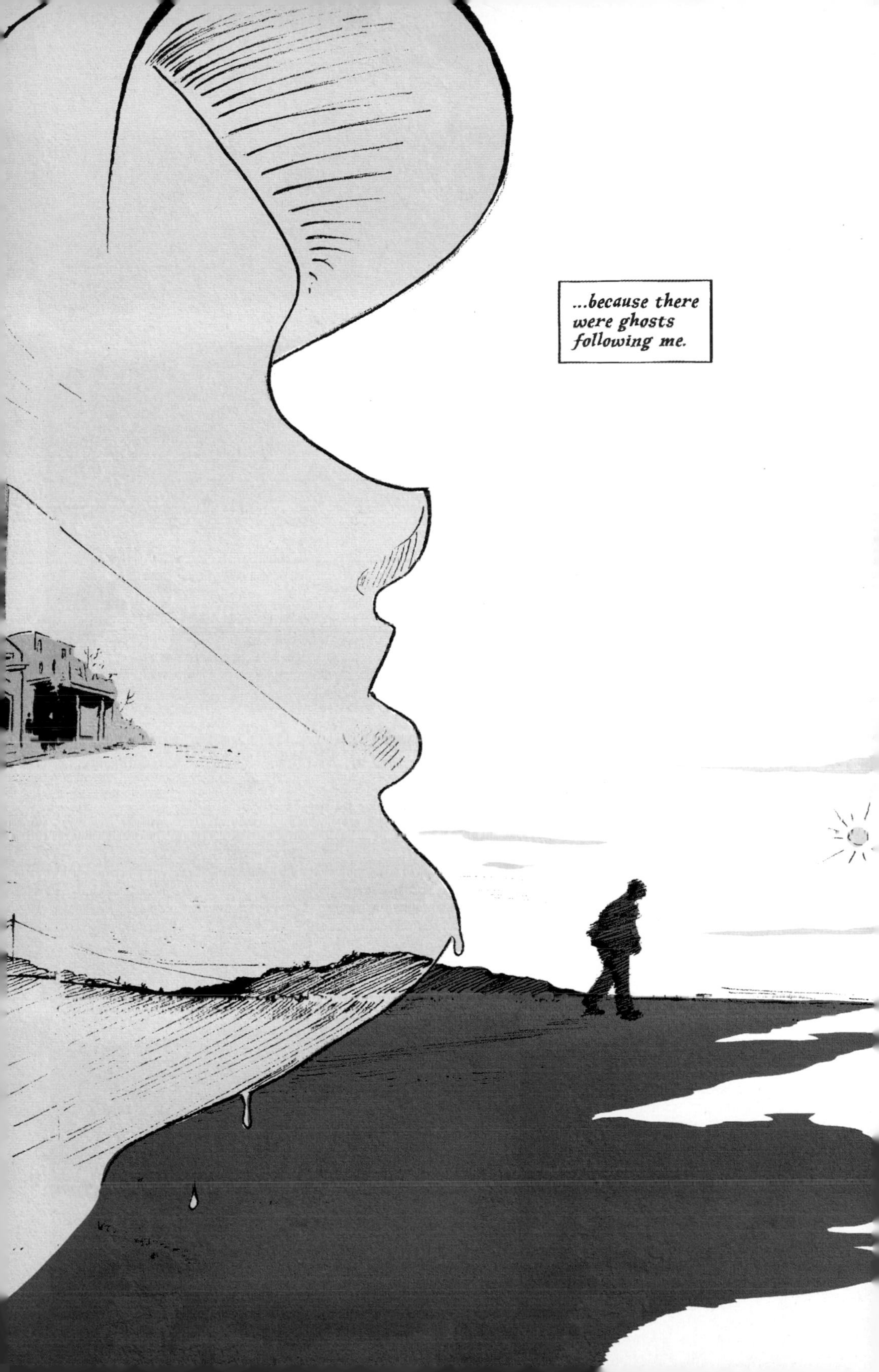
...because there were ghosts following me.

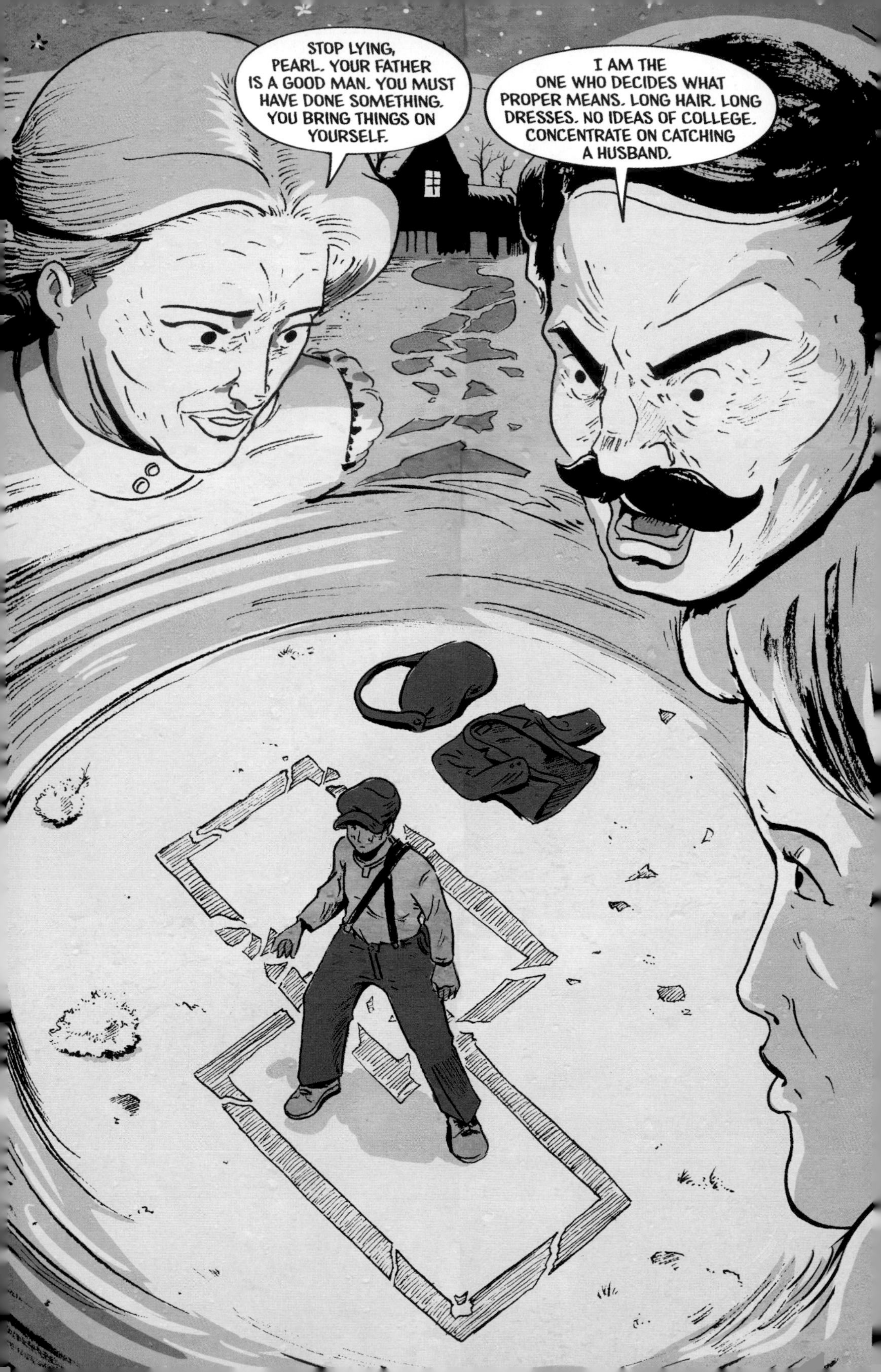
STOP LYING, PEARL. YOUR FATHER IS A GOOD MAN. YOU MUST HAVE DONE SOMETHING. YOU BRING THINGS ON YOURSELF.
I AM THE ONE WHO DECIDES WHAT PROPER MEANS. LONG HAIR. LONG DRESSES. NO IDEAS OF COLLEGE. CONCENTRATE ON CATCHING A HUSBAND.

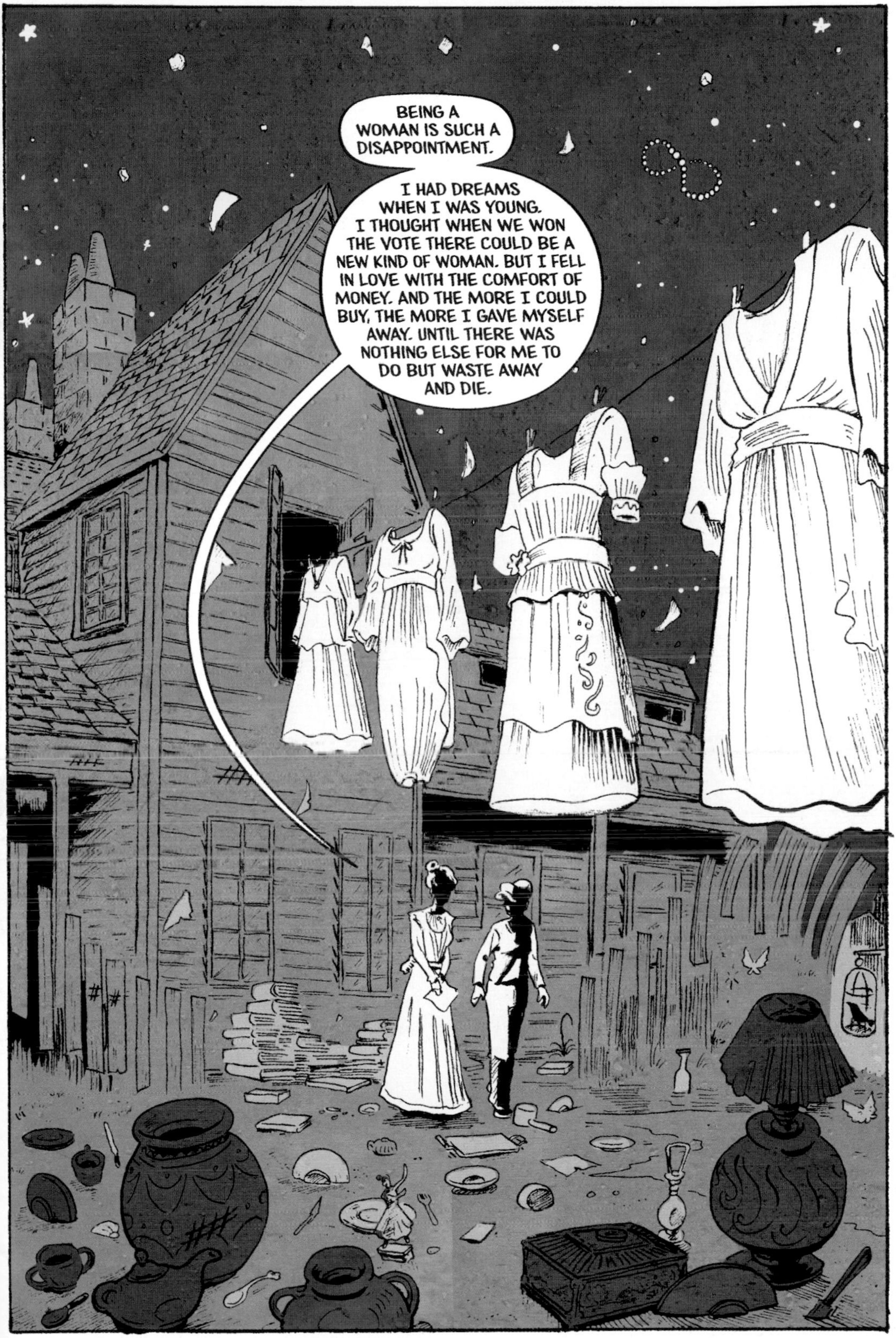
BEING A WOMAN IS SUCH A DISAPPOINTMENT.
I HAD DREAMS WHEN I WAS YOUNG. I THOUGHT WHEN WE WON THE VOTE THERE COULD BE A NEW KIND OF WOMAN. BUT I FELL IN LOVE WITH THE COMFORT OF MONEY. AND THE MORE I COULD BUY, THE MORE I GAVE MYSELF AWAY. UNTIL THERE WAS NOTHING ELSE FOR ME TO DO BUT WASTE AWAY AND DIE.

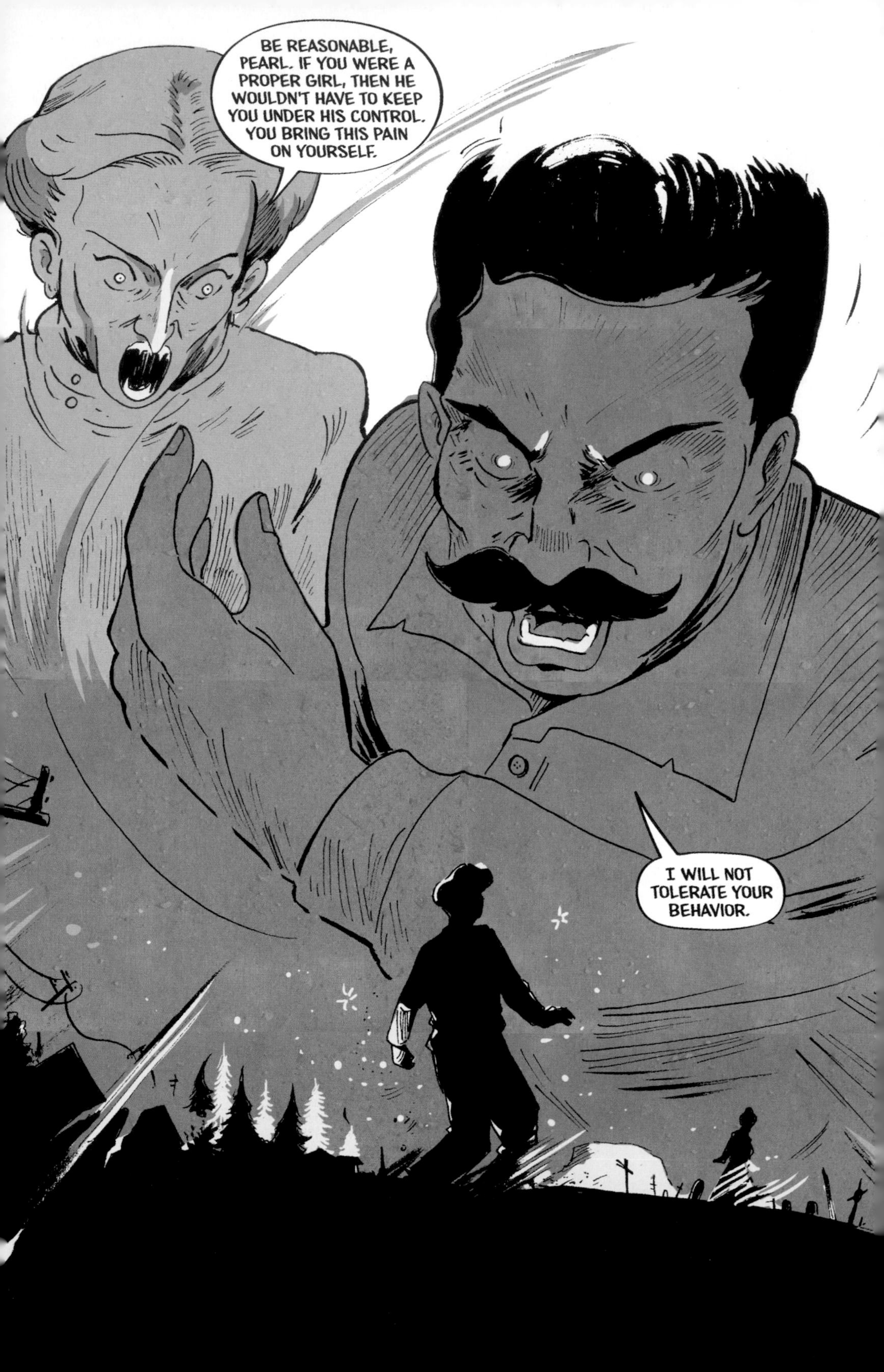
BE REASONABLE, PEARL. IF YOU WERE A PROPER GIRL, THEN HE WOULDN'T HAVE TO KEEP YOU UNDER HIS CONTROL. YOU BRING THIS PAIN ON YOURSELF.
I WILL NOT TOLERATE YOUR BEHAVIOR.

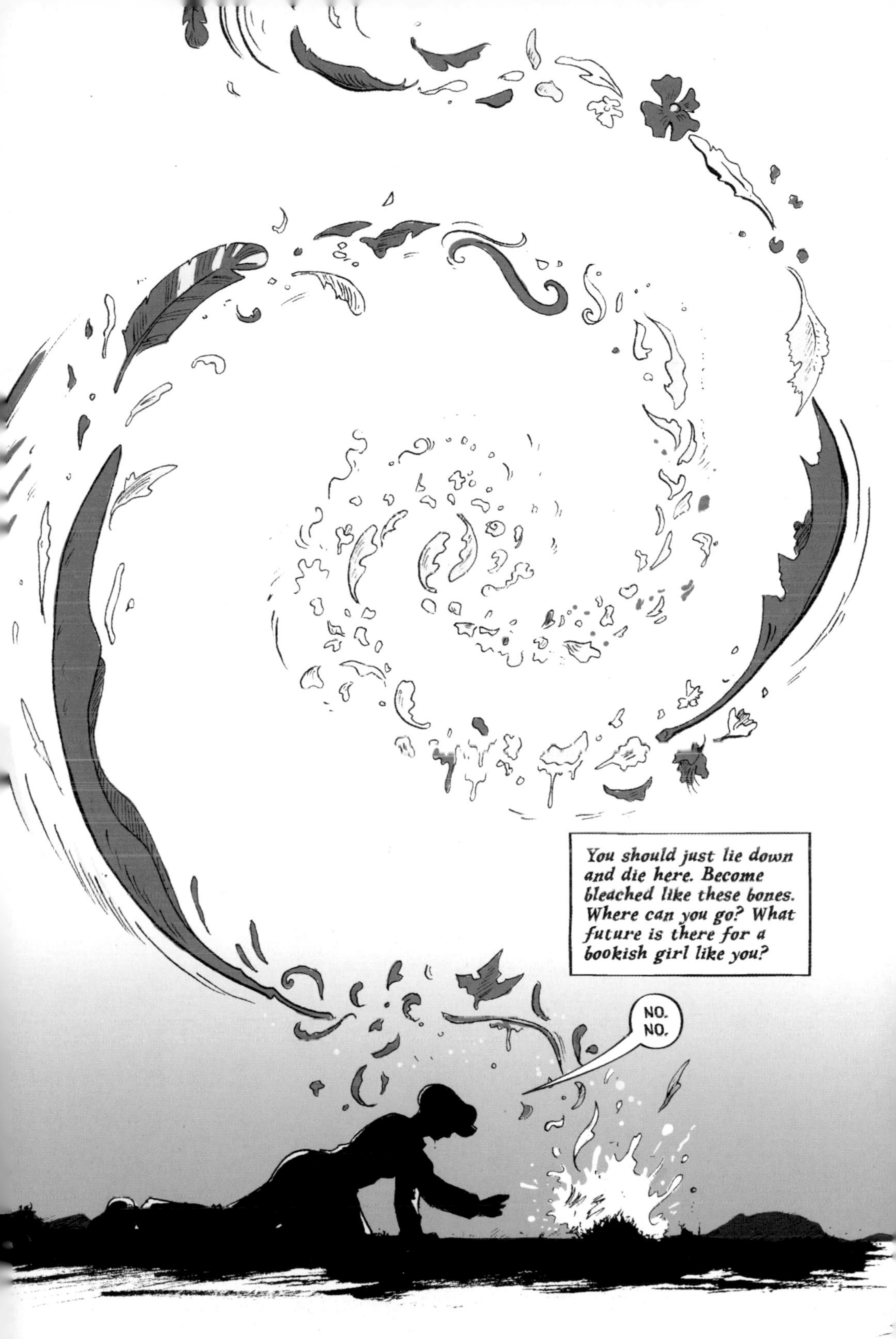
You should just lie down and die here. Become bleached like these bones. Where can you go? What future is there for a bookish girl like you?
NO. NO.

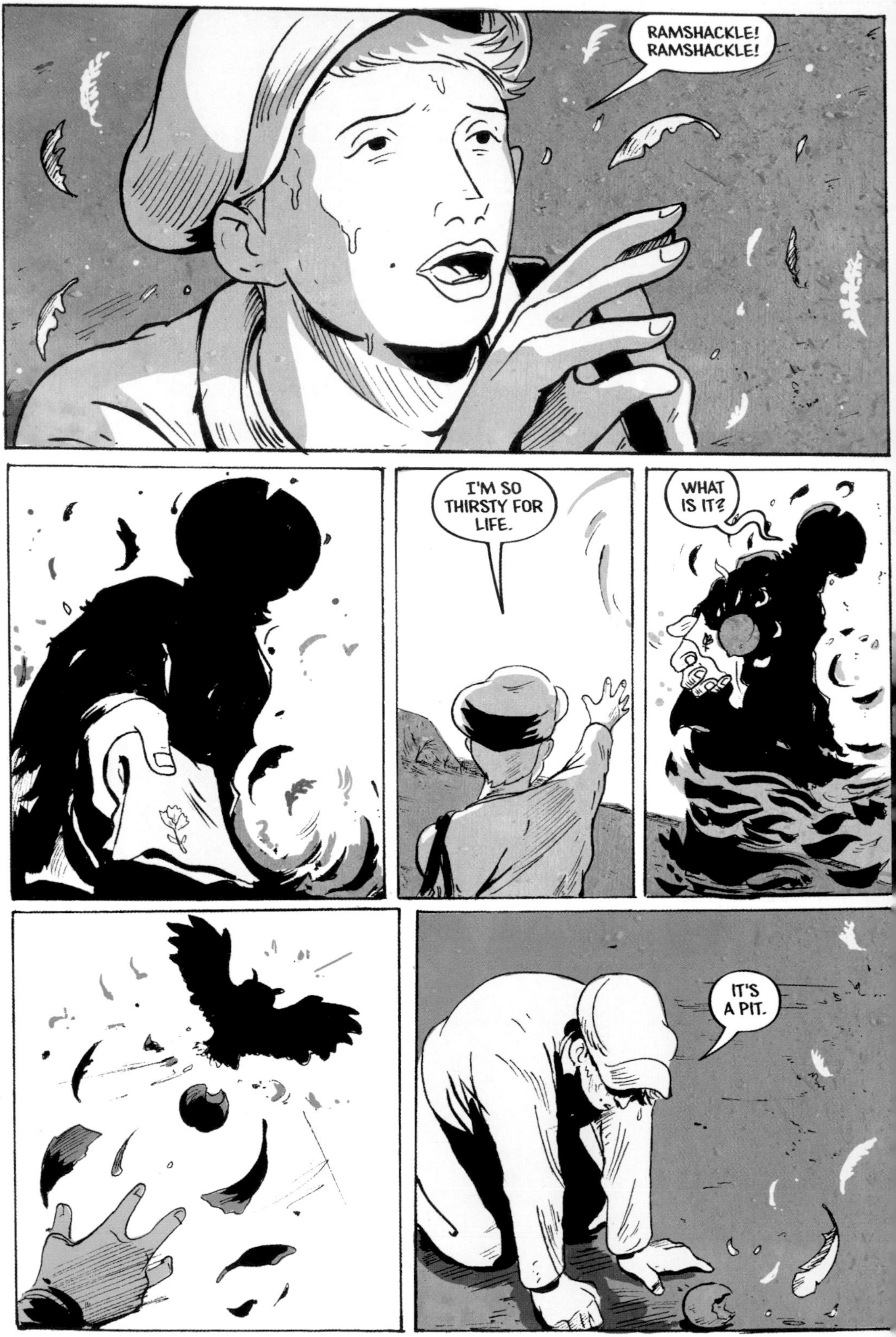
RAMSHACKLE!
RAMSHACKLE!
I'M SO THIRSTY FOR LIFE.
WHAT IS IT?
IT'S A PIT.

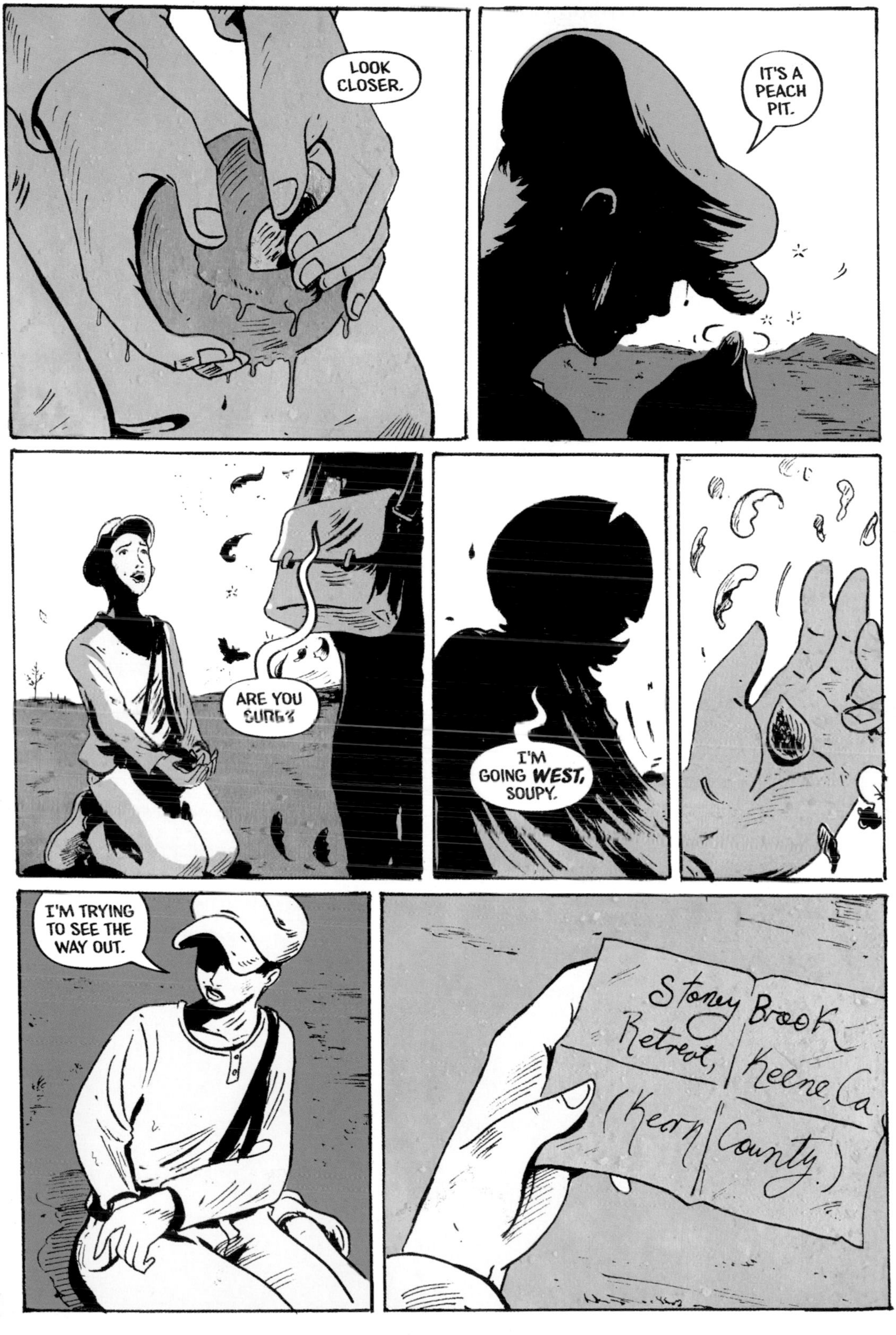

LOOK CLOSER.
IT'S A PEACH PIT.
ARE YOU SURE?
I'M GOING WEST, SOUPY.
I'M TRYING TO SEE THE WAY OUT.
Stoney Brook Retreat, Keene, Ca (Keorn County)

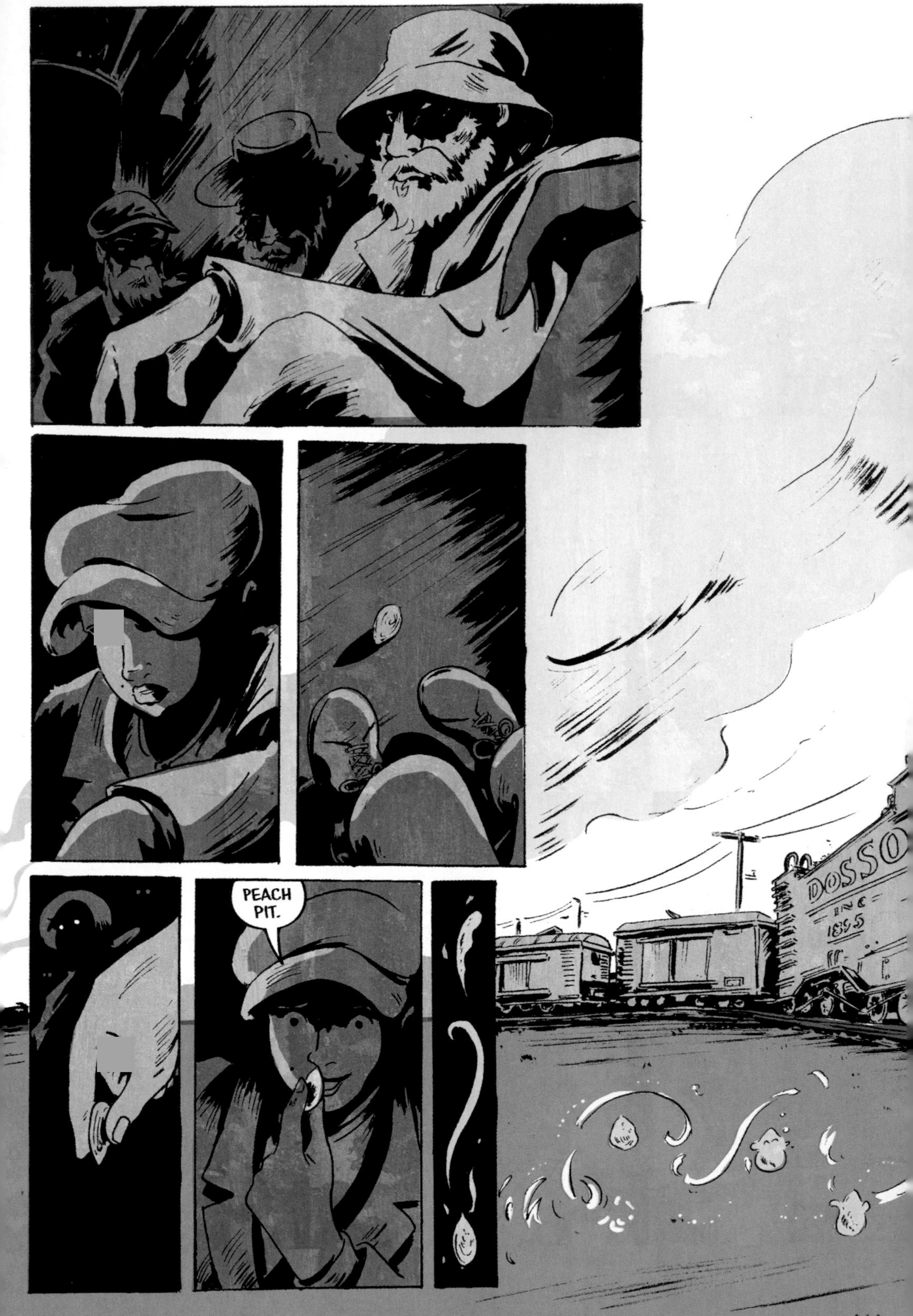
PEACH PIT.
DOSSO
INC
1895

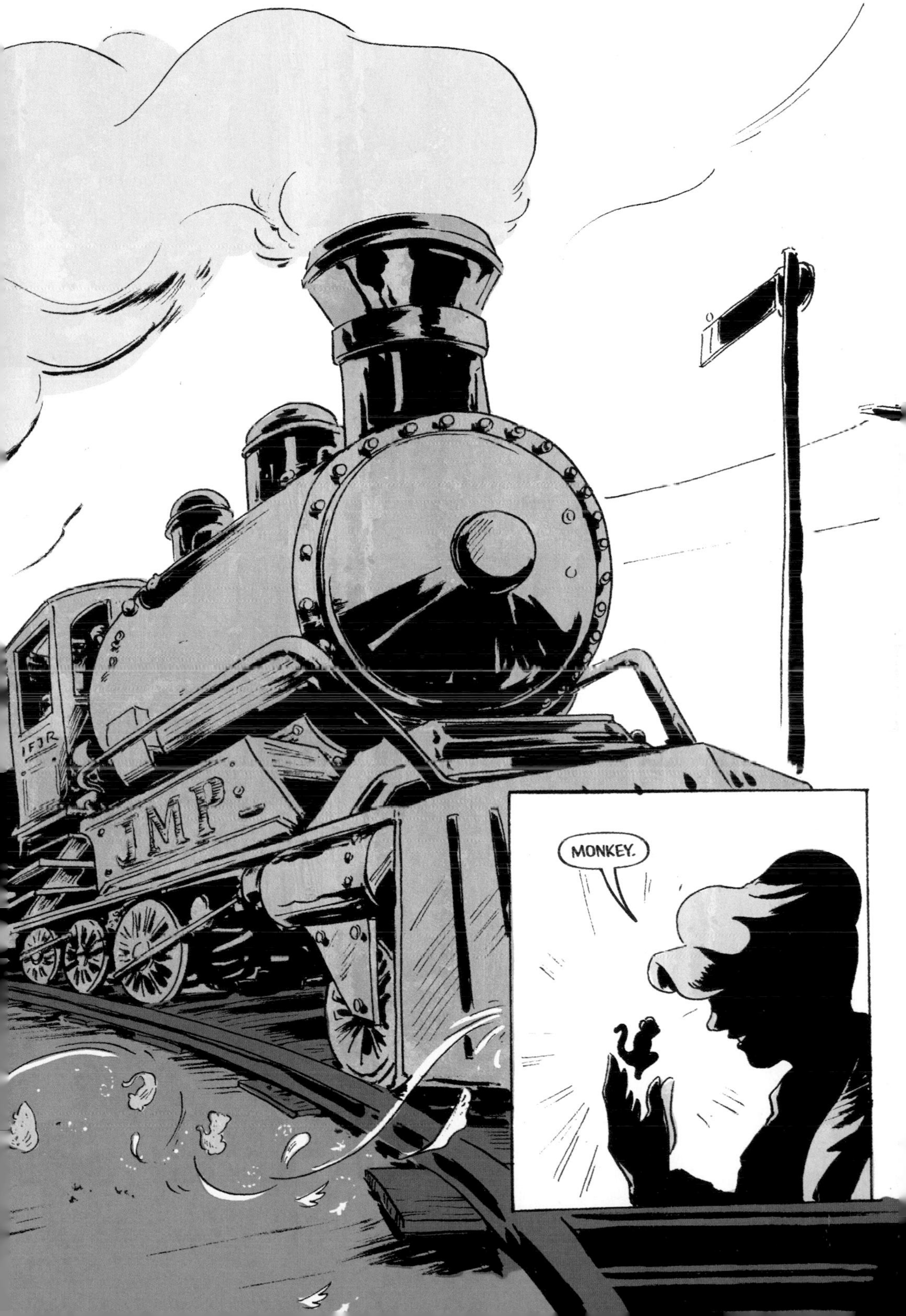

IFJR
JMP
MONKEY.

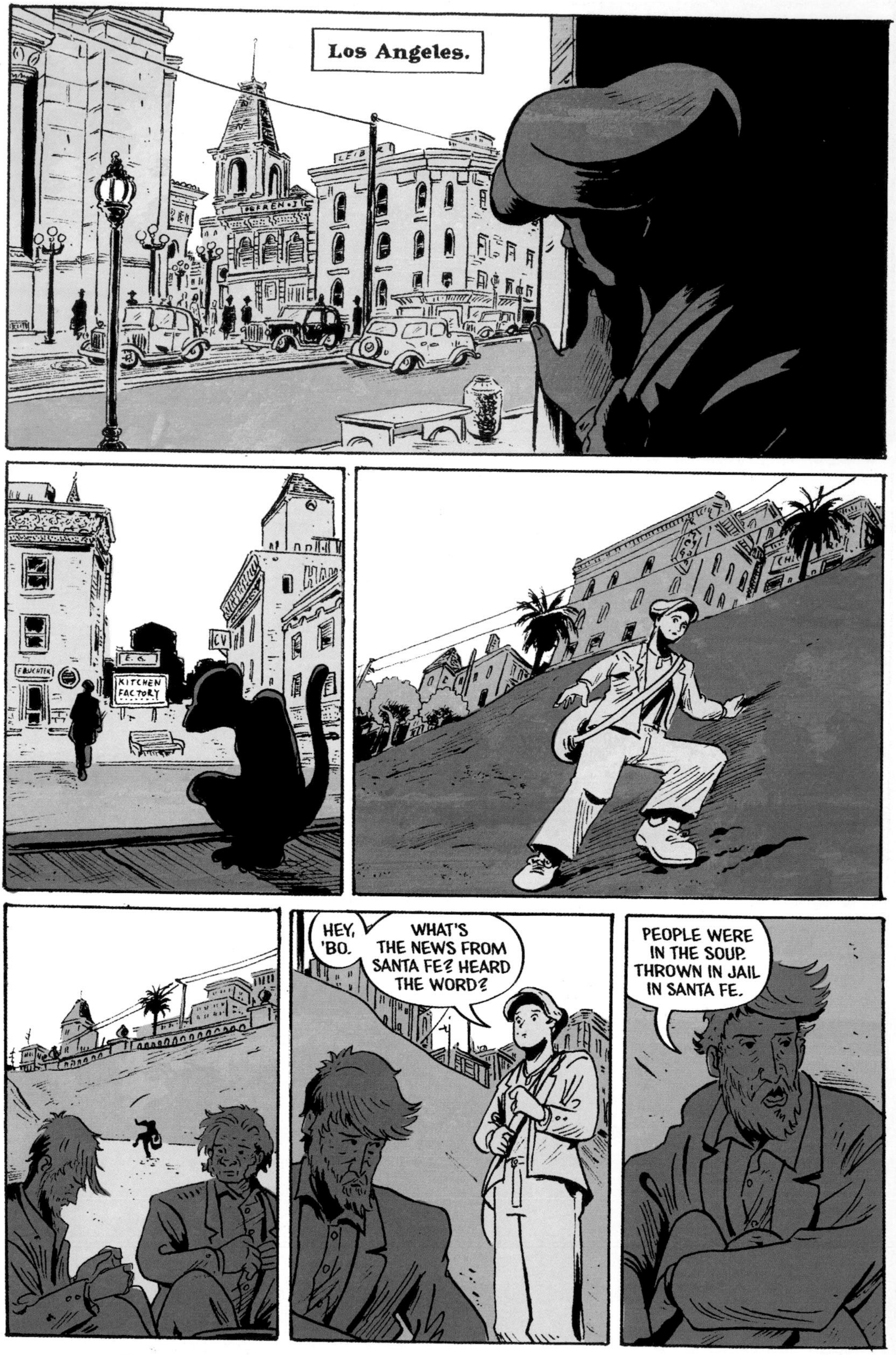
Los Angeles.
KITCHEN FACTORY
HEY, 'BO.
WHAT'S THE NEWS FROM SANTA FE? HEARD THE WORD?
PEOPLE WERE IN THE SOUP. THROWN IN JAIL IN SANTA FE.

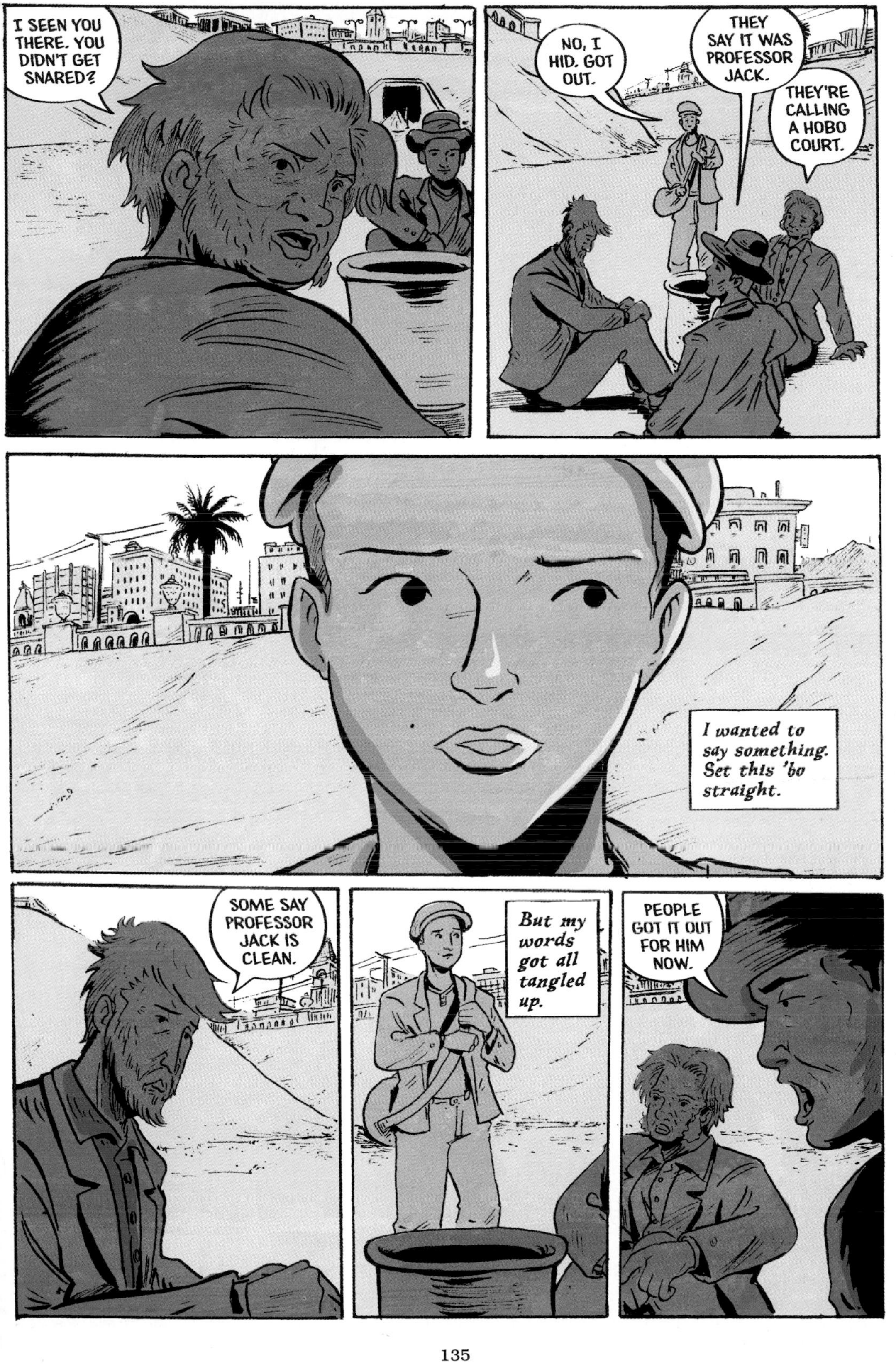

I SEEN YOU THERE. YOU DIDN'T GET SNARED?
NO, I HID. GOT OUT.
THEY SAY IT WAS PROFESSOR JACK.
THEY'RE CALLING A HOBO COURT.
I wanted to say something. Set this 'bo straight.
SOME SAY PROFESSOR JACK IS CLEAN.
But my words got all tangled up.
PEOPLE GOT IT OUT FOR HIM NOW.

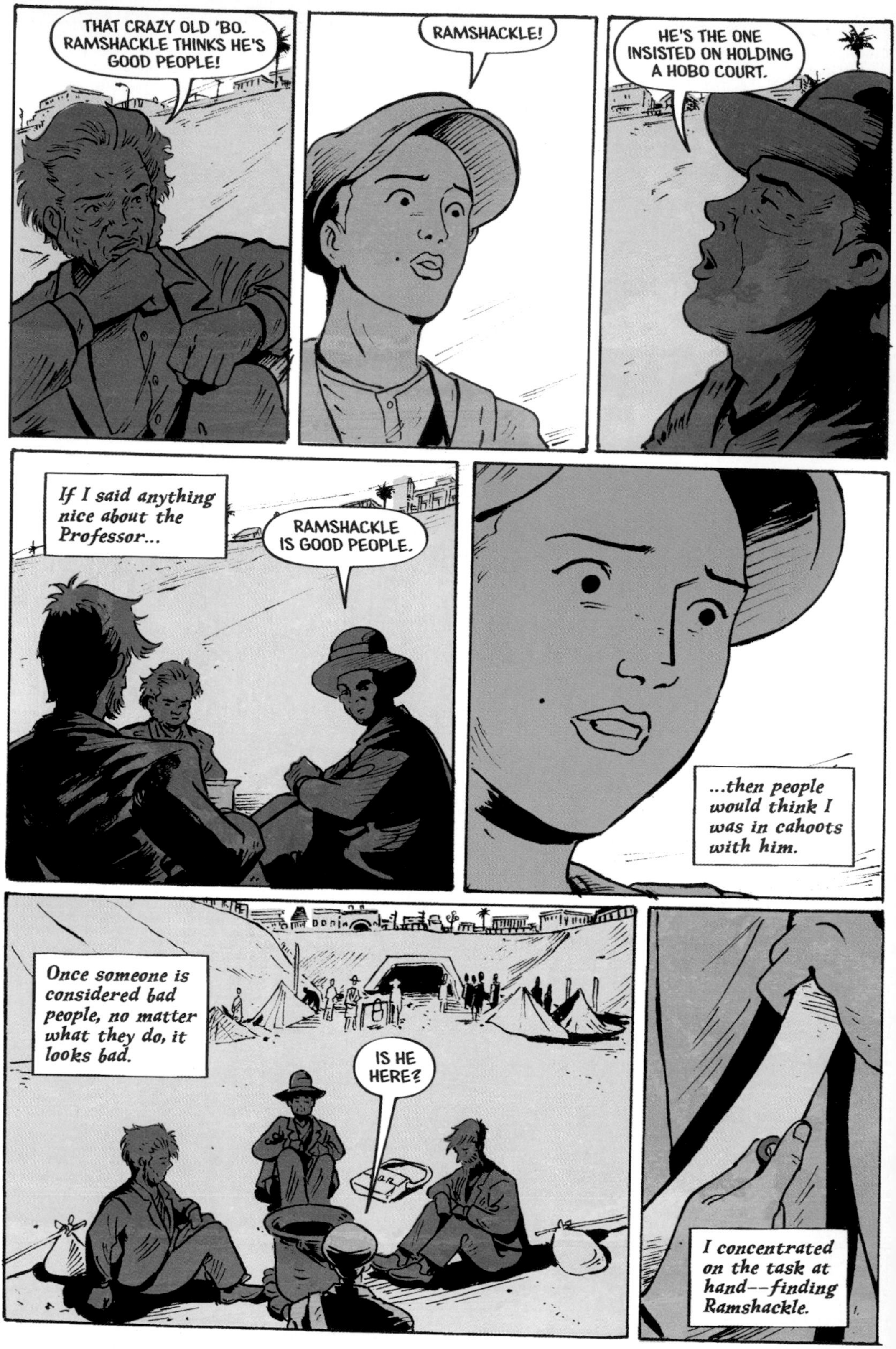
THAT CRAZY OLD 'BO. RAMSHACKLE THINKS HE'S GOOD PEOPLE!
RAMSHACKLE!
HE'S THE ONE INSISTED ON HOLDING A HOBO COURT.
If I said anything nice about the Professor...
RAMSHACKLE IS GOOD PEOPLE.
...then people would think I was in cahoots with him.
Once someone is considered bad people, no matter what they do, it looks bad.
IS HE HERE?
I concentrated on the task at hand--finding Ramshackle.

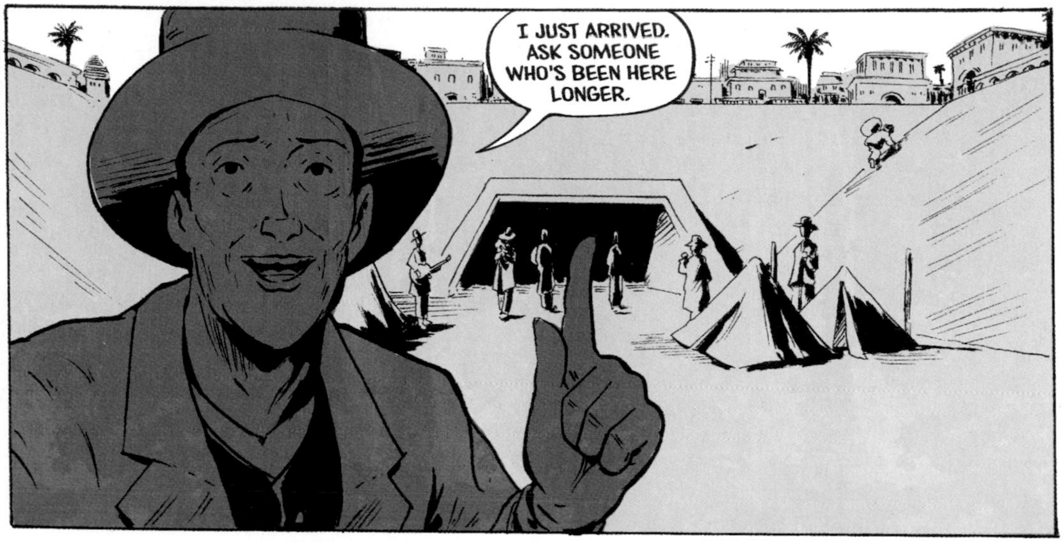
I JUST ARRIVED. ASK SOMEONE WHO'S BEEN HERE LONGER.

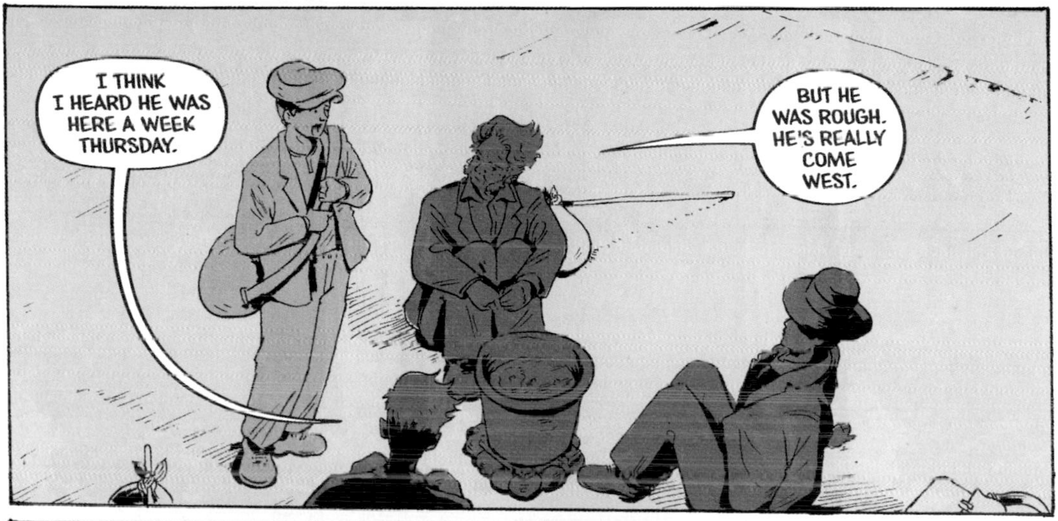
I THINK I HEARD HE WAS HERE A WEEK THURSDAY.
BUT HE WAS ROUGH. HE'S REALLY COME WEST.

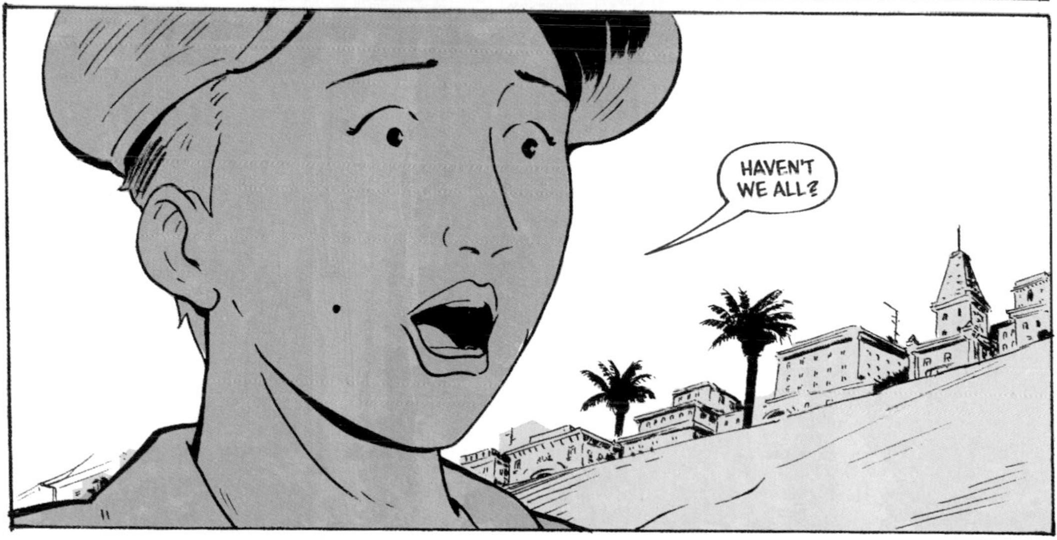
HAVEN'T WE ALL?

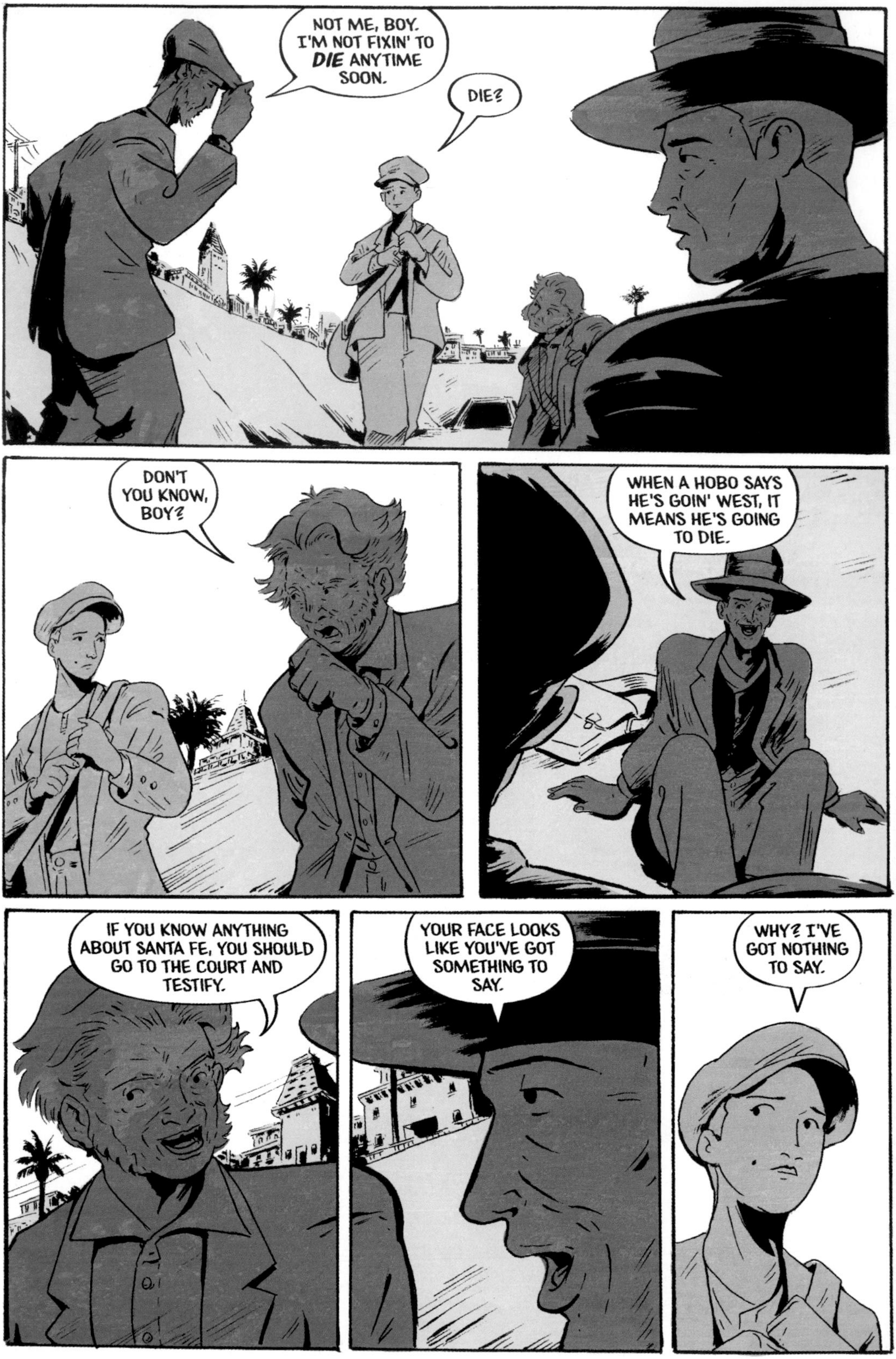
NOT ME, BOY. I'M NOT FIXIN' TO *DIE* ANYTIME SOON.
DIE?
DON'T YOU KNOW, BOY?
WHEN A HOBO SAYS HE'S GOIN' WEST, IT MEANS HE'S GOING TO DIE.
IF YOU KNOW ANYTHING ABOUT SANTA FE, YOU SHOULD GO TO THE COURT AND TESTIFY.
YOUR FACE LOOKS LIKE YOU'VE GOT SOMETHING TO SAY.
WHY? I'VE GOT NOTHING TO SAY.

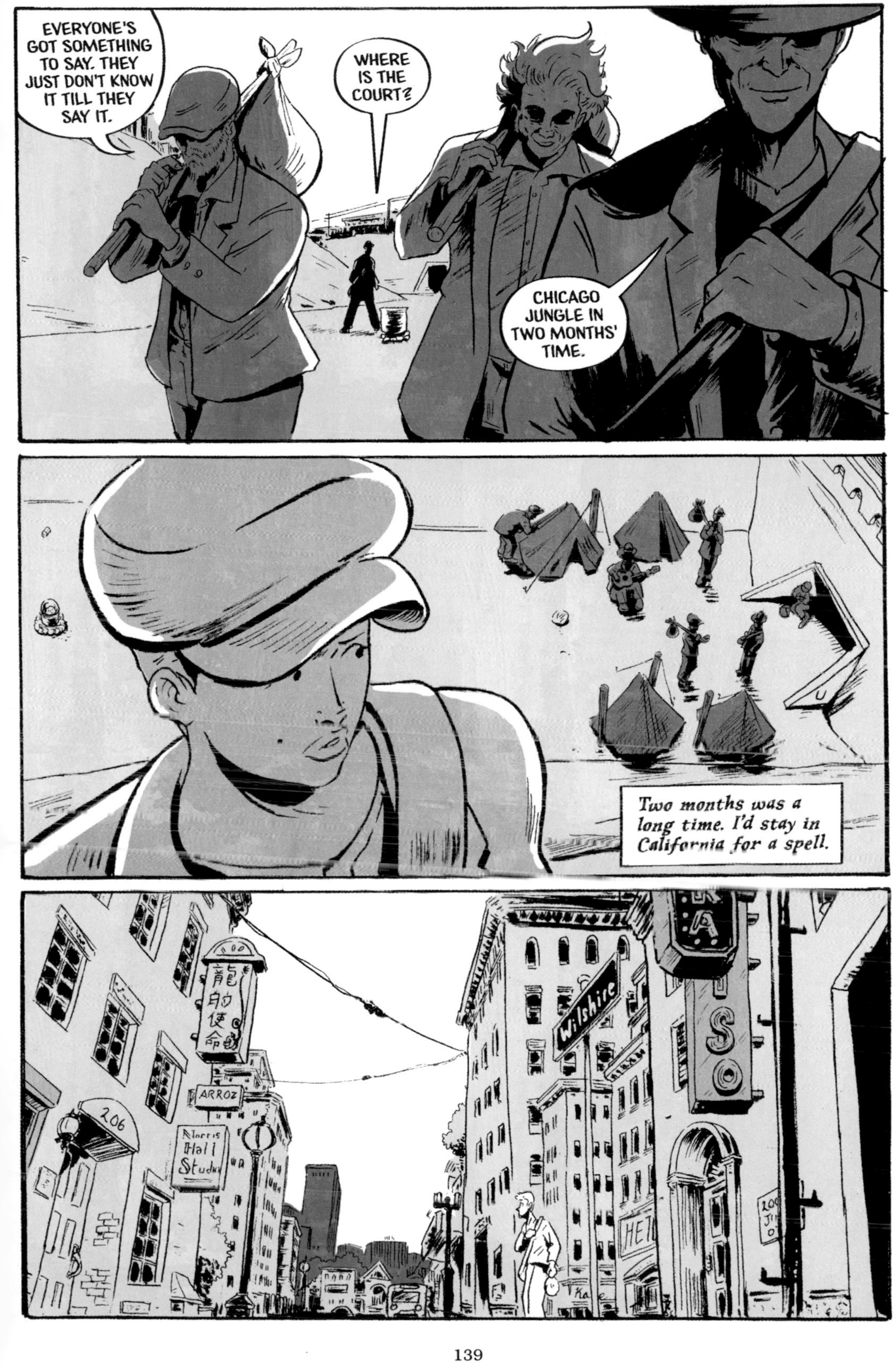
EVERYONE'S GOT SOMETHING TO SAY. THEY JUST DON'T KNOW IT TILL THEY SAY IT.
WHERE IS THE COURT?
CHICAGO JUNGLE IN TWO MONTHS' TIME.
Two months was a long time. I'd stay in California for a spell.
ARROZ
206
Wilshire

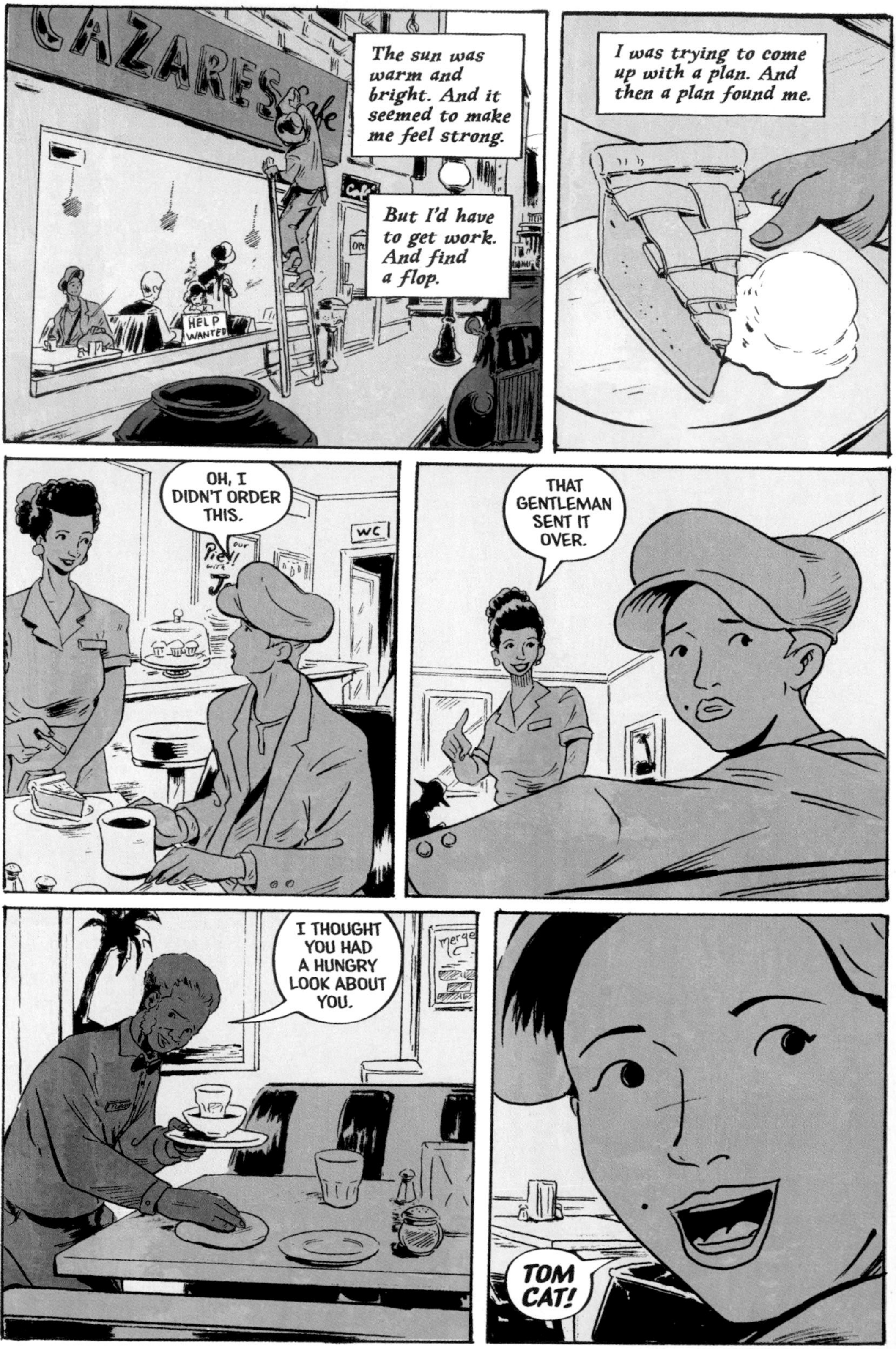
CAZARES Cafe
The sun was warm and bright. And it seemed to make me feel strong.
But I'd have to get work. And find a flop.
HELP WANTED
I was trying to come up with a plan. And then a plan found me.
OH, I DIDN'T ORDER THIS.
WC
THAT GENTLEMAN SENT IT OVER.
I THOUGHT YOU HAD A HUNGRY LOOK ABOUT YOU.
TOM CAT!

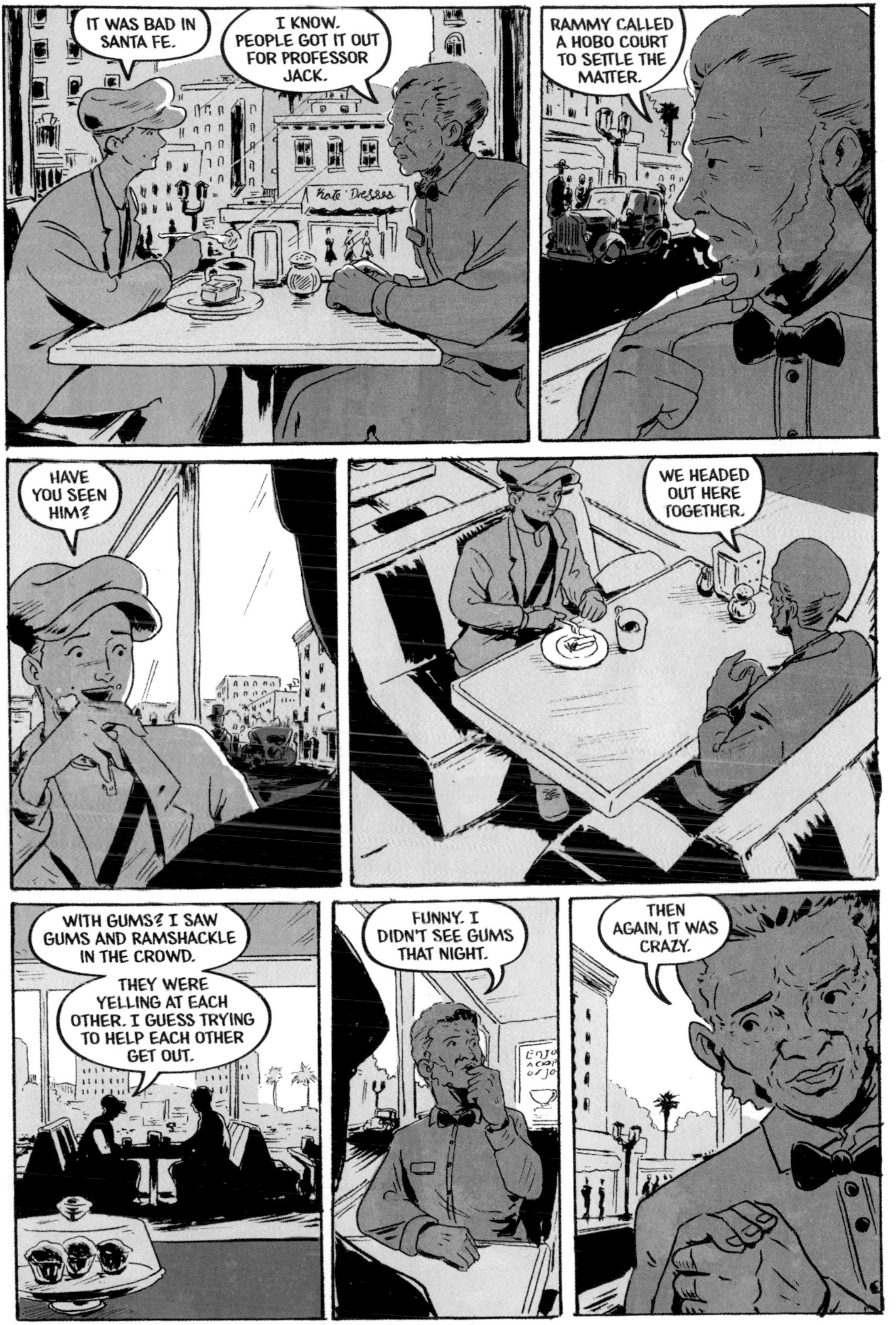
IT WAS BAD IN SANTA FE.
I KNOW. PEOPLE GOT IT OUT FOR PROFESSOR JACK.
Kate' Dresses
RAMMY CALLED A HOBO COURT TO SETTLE THE MATTER.
HAVE YOU SEEN HIM?
WE HEADED OUT HERE TOGETHER.
WITH GUMS? I SAW GUMS AND RAMSHACKLE IN THE CROWD.
THEY WERE YELLING AT EACH OTHER. I GUESS TRYING TO HELP EACH OTHER GET OUT.
FUNNY. I DIDN'T SEE GUMS THAT NIGHT.
THEN AGAIN, IT WAS CRAZY.

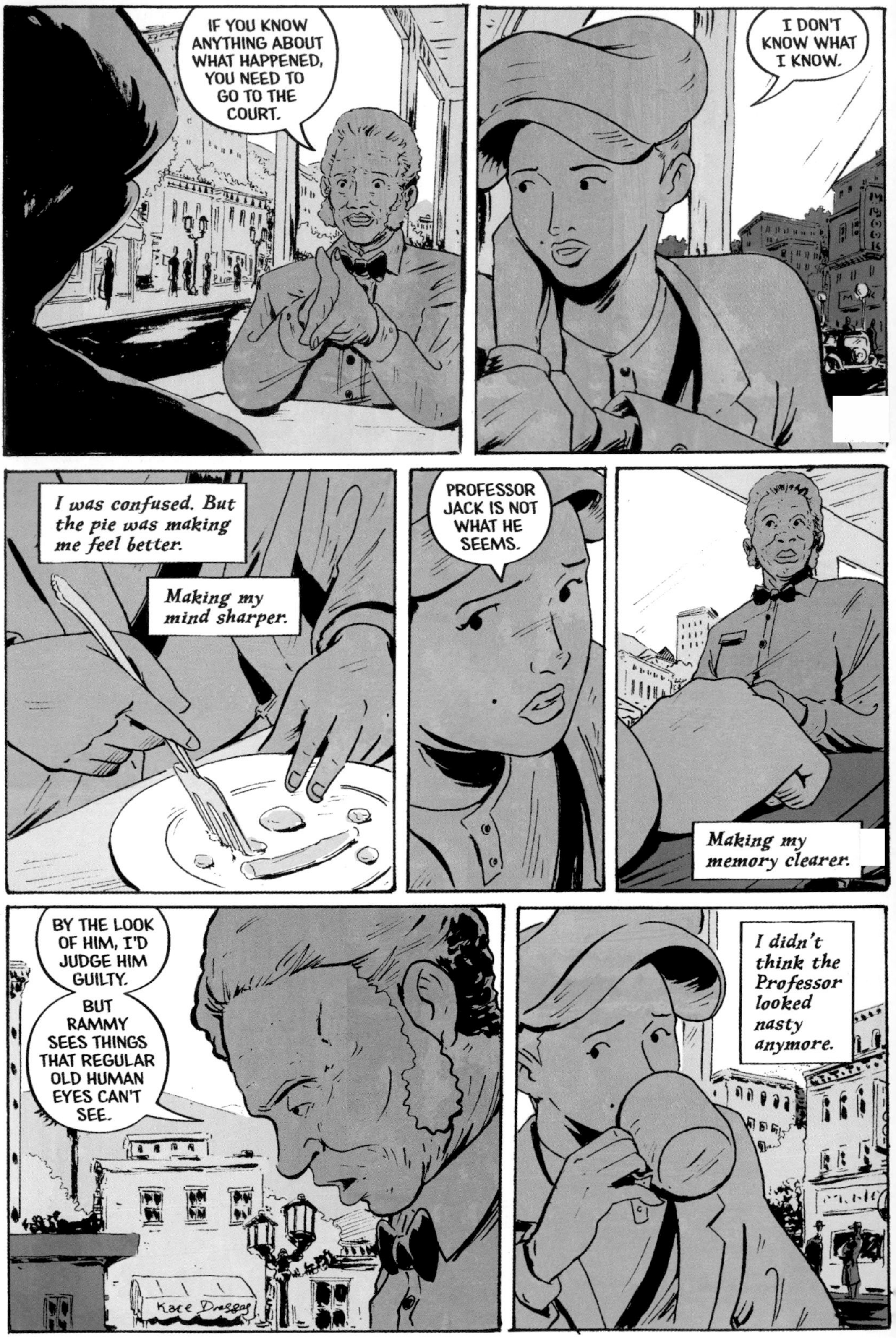
IF YOU KNOW ANYTHING ABOUT WHAT HAPPENED, YOU NEED TO GO TO THE COURT.
I DON'T KNOW WHAT I KNOW.
I was confused. But the pie was making me feel better.
Making my mind sharper.
PROFESSOR JACK IS NOT WHAT HE SEEMS.
Making my memory clearer.
BY THE LOOK OF HIM, I'D JUDGE HIM GUILTY.
BUT RAMMY SEES THINGS THAT REGULAR OLD HUMAN EYES CAN'T SEE.
Kate Driggs
I didn't think the Professor looked nasty anymore.

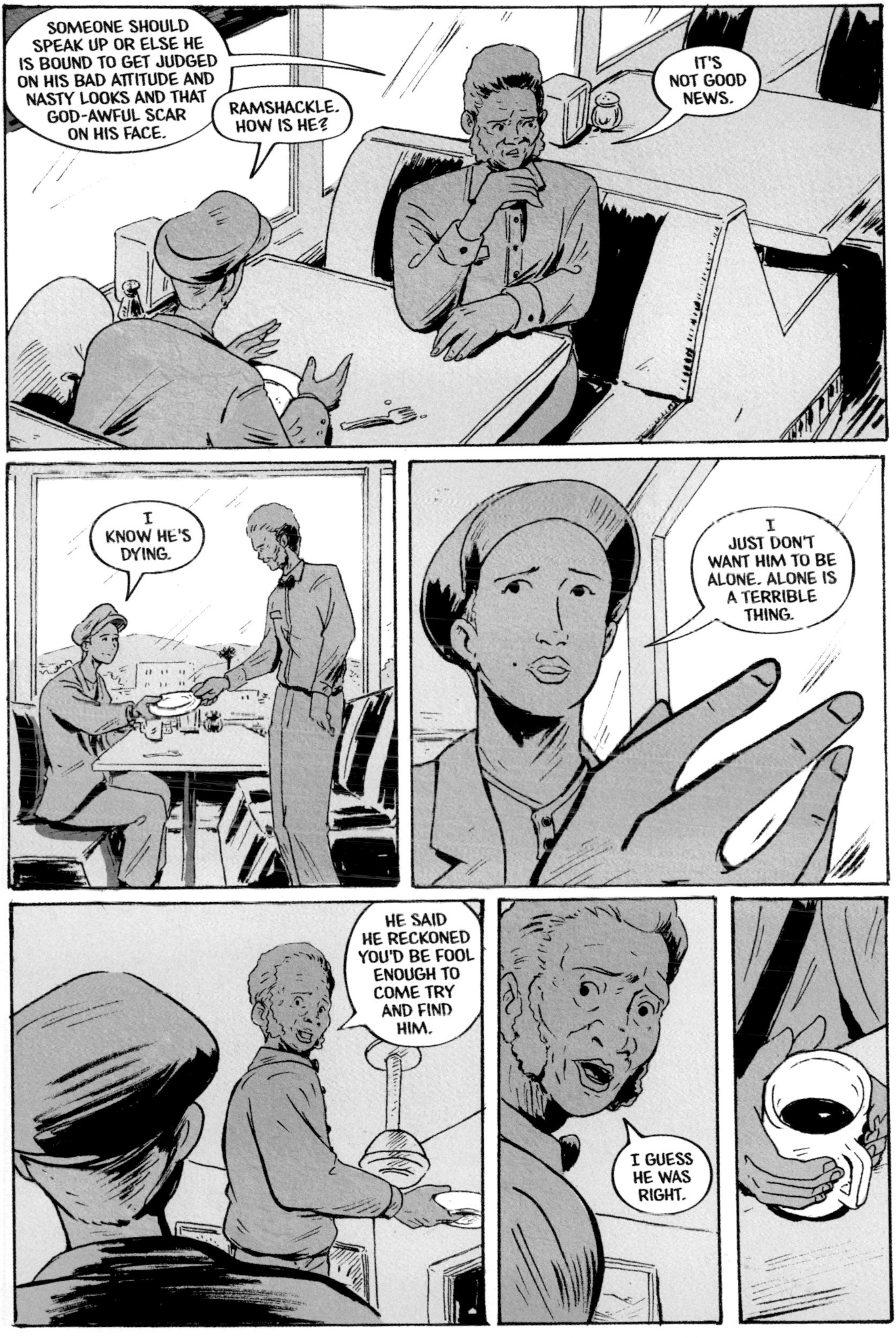
SOMEONE SHOULD SPEAK UP OR ELSE HE IS BOUND TO GET JUDGED ON HIS BAD ATTITUDE AND NASTY LOOKS AND THAT GOD-AWFUL SCAR ON HIS FACE.
RAMSHACKLE. HOW IS HE?
IT'S NOT GOOD NEWS.
I KNOW HE'S DYING.
I JUST DON'T WANT HIM TO BE ALONE. ALONE IS A TERRIBLE THING.
HE SAID HE RECKONED YOU'D BE FOOL ENOUGH TO COME TRY AND FIND HIM.
I GUESS HE WAS RIGHT.

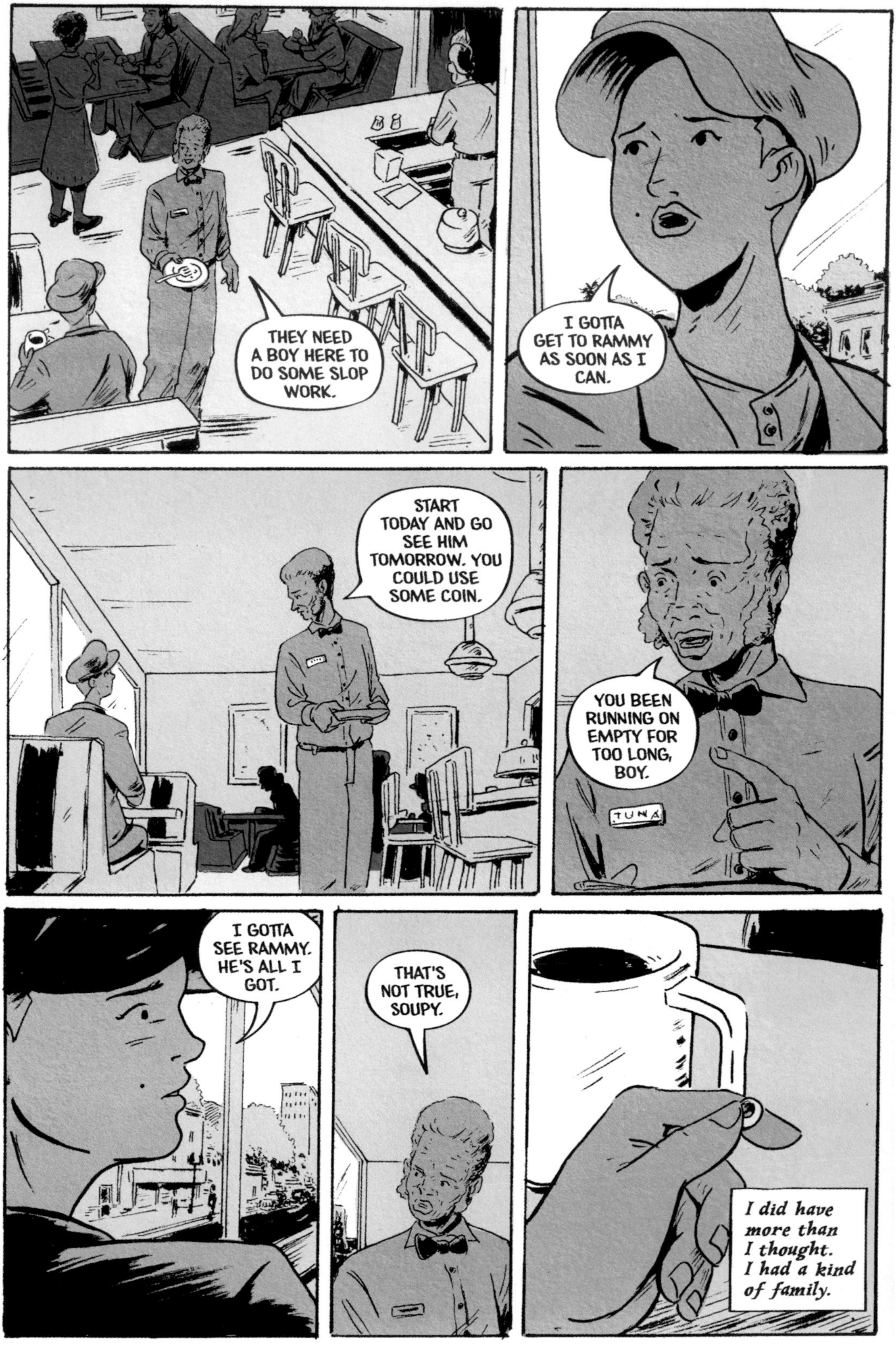
THEY NEED A BOY HERE TO DO SOME SLOP WORK.
I GOTTA GET TO RAMMY AS SOON AS I CAN.
START TODAY AND GO SEE HIM TOMORROW. YOU COULD USE SOME COIN.
YOU BEEN RUNNING ON EMPTY FOR TOO LONG, BOY.
TUNA
I GOTTA SEE RAMMY. HE'S ALL I GOT.
THAT'S NOT TRUE, SOUPY.
I did have more than I thought. I had a kind of family.

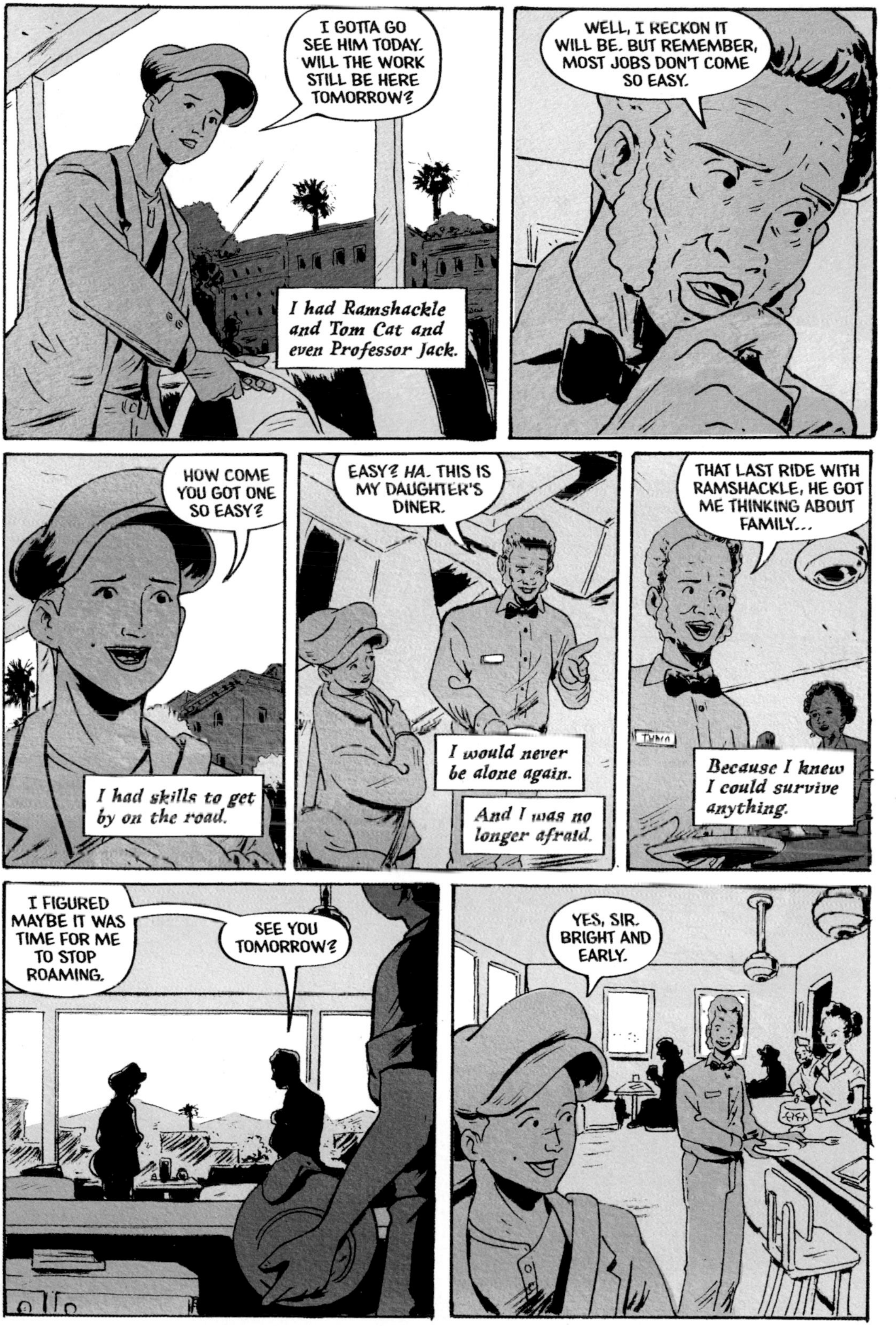
I GOTTA GO SEE HIM TODAY. WILL THE WORK STILL BE HERE TOMORROW?
I had Ramshackle and Tom Cat and even Professor Jack.
WELL, I RECKON IT WILL BE. BUT REMEMBER, MOST JOBS DON'T COME SO EASY.
HOW COME YOU GOT ONE SO EASY?
I had skills to get by on the road.
EASY? HA. THIS IS MY DAUGHTER'S DINER.
I would never be alone again.
And I was no longer afraid.
THAT LAST RIDE WITH RAMSHACKLE, HE GOT ME THINKING ABOUT FAMILY...
Because I knew I could survive anything.
I FIGURED MAYBE IT WAS TIME FOR ME TO STOP ROAMING.
SEE YOU TOMORROW?
YES, SIR. BRIGHT AND EARLY.

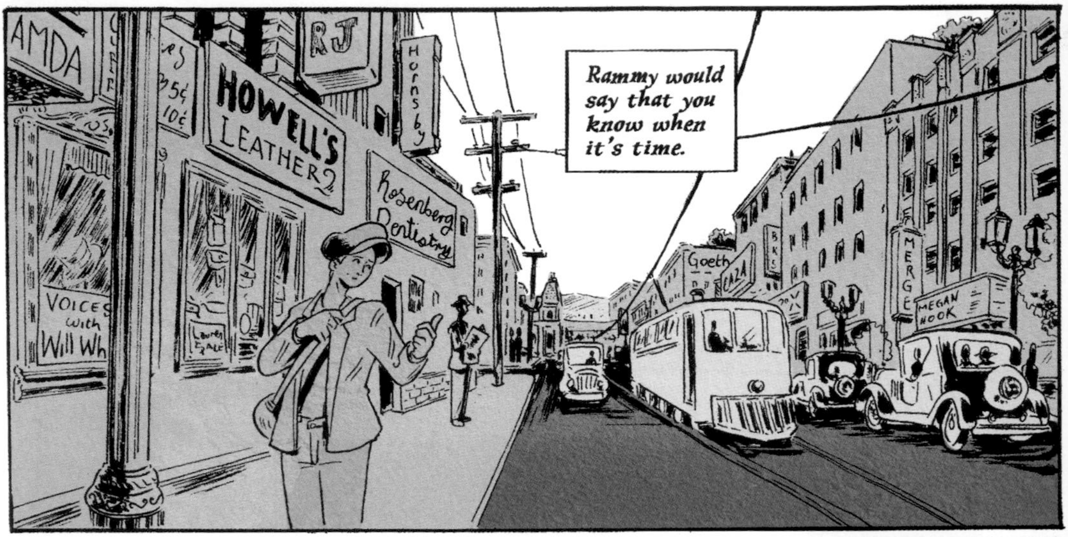
AMDA
RJ
HOWELL'S
LEATHER 2
Hornsby
Rosenberg Dentistry
VOICES with Will Wh
Goeth
MERGE
MEGAN HOOK
Rammy would say that you know when it's time.

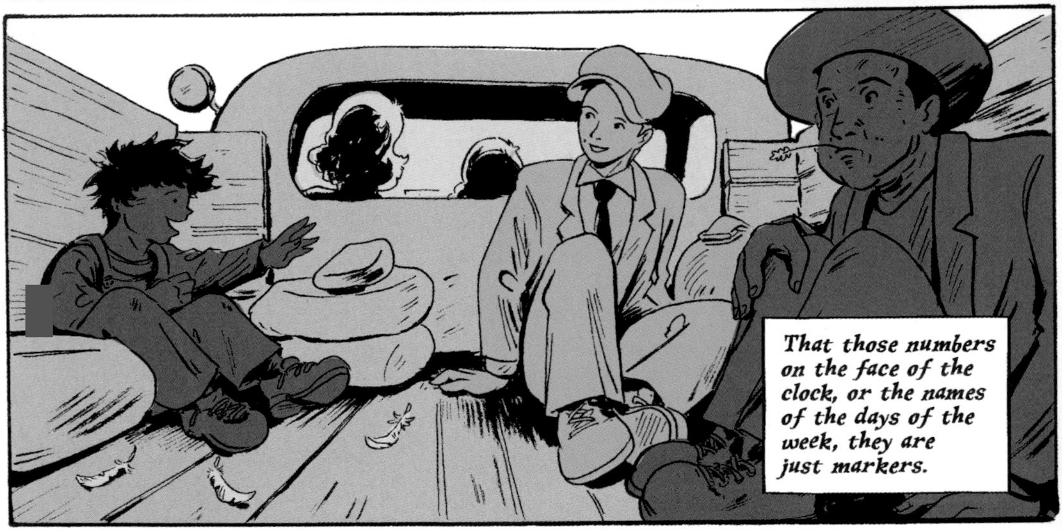
That those numbers on the face of the clock, or the names of the days of the week, they are just markers.

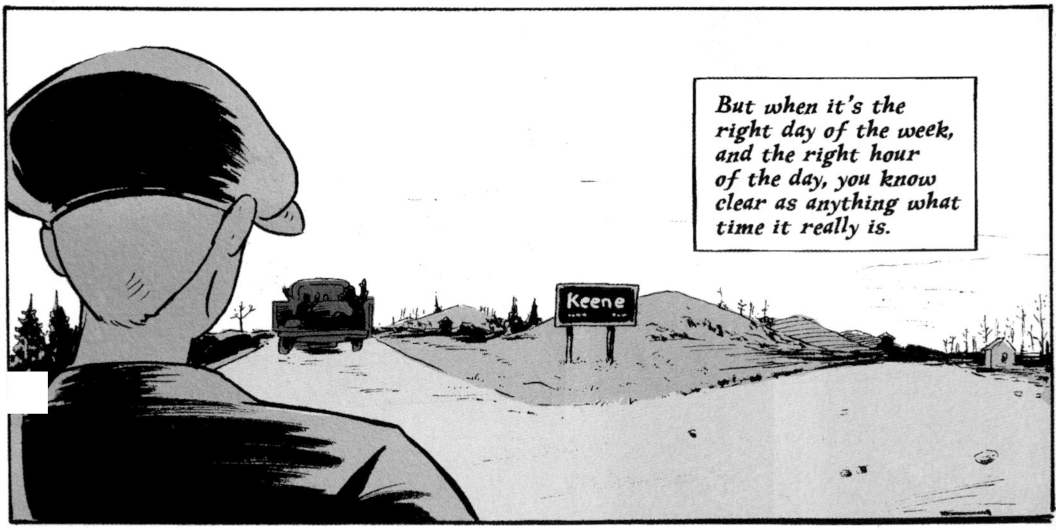
But when it's the right day of the week, and the right hour of the day, you know clear as anything what time it really is.
Keene

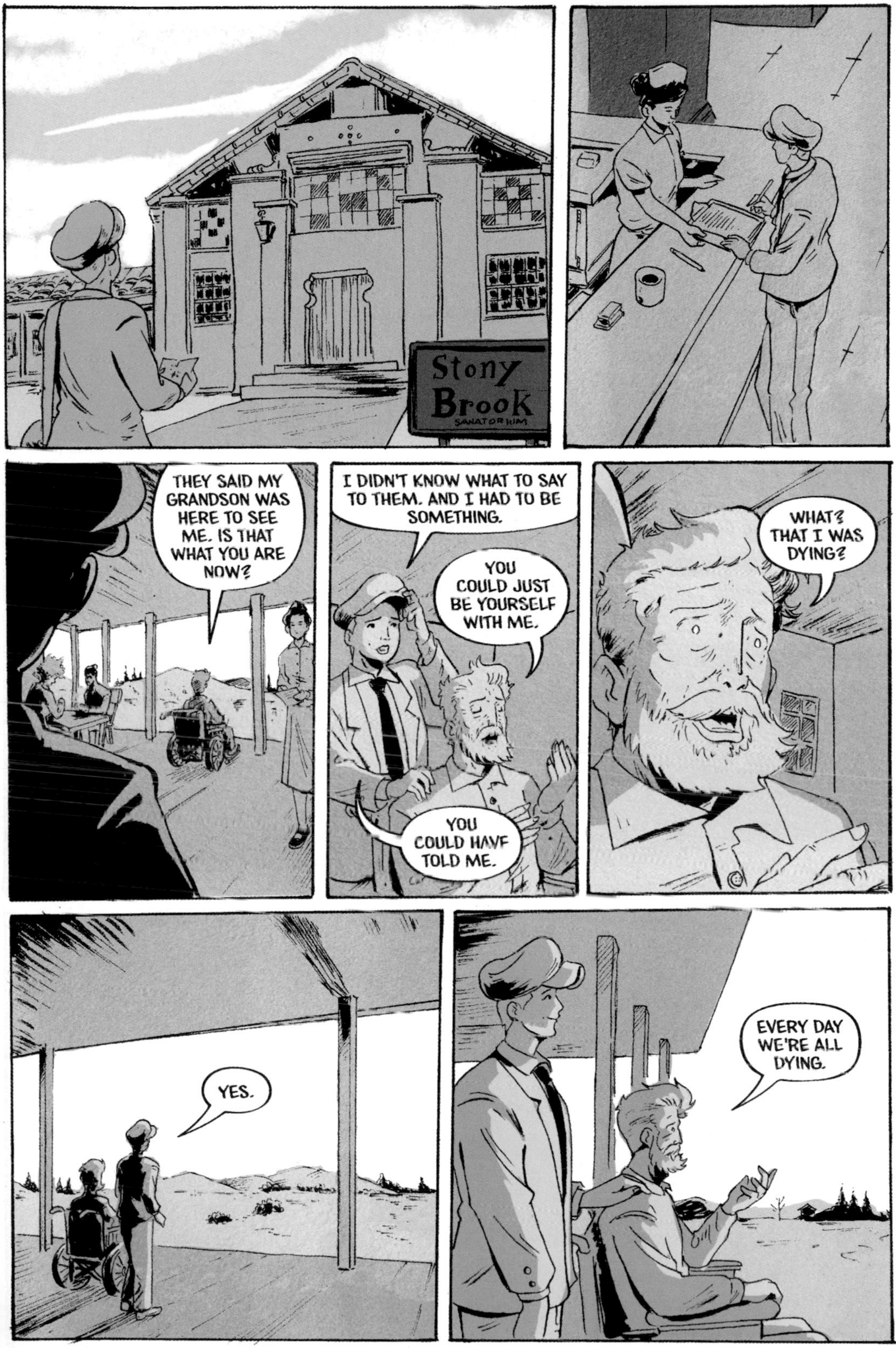
Stony
Brook
SANATORIUM
THEY SAID MY GRANDSON WAS HERE TO SEE ME. IS THAT WHAT YOU ARE NOW?
I DIDN'T KNOW WHAT TO SAY TO THEM. AND I HAD TO BE SOMETHING.
YOU COULD JUST BE YOURSELF WITH ME.
YOU COULD HAVE TOLD ME.
WHAT? THAT I WAS DYING?
YES.
EVERY DAY WE'RE ALL DYING.

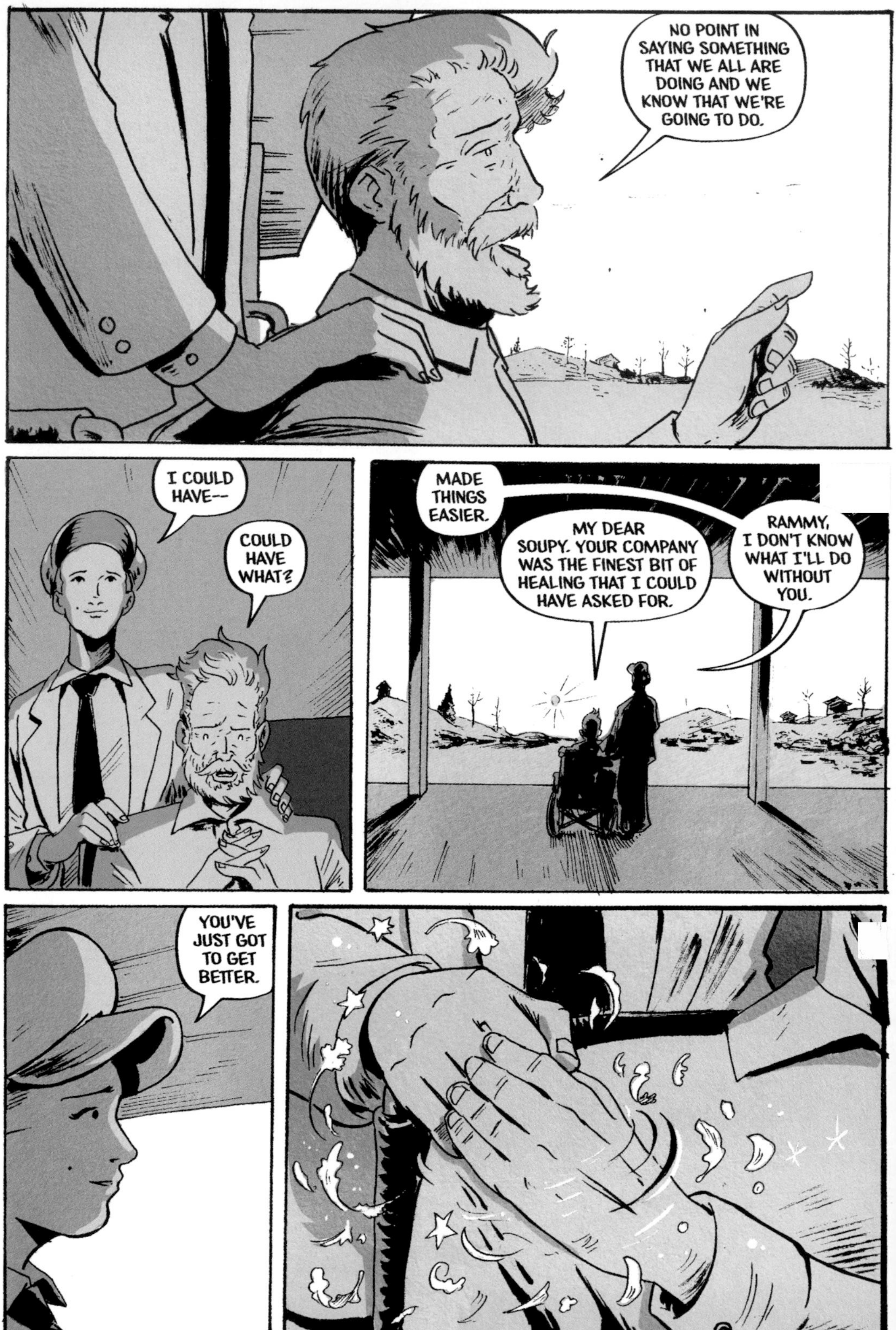
NO POINT IN SAYING SOMETHING THAT WE ALL ARE DOING AND WE KNOW THAT WE'RE GOING TO DO.
I COULD HAVE--
COULD HAVE WHAT?
MADE THINGS EASIER.
MY DEAR SOUPY. YOUR COMPANY WAS THE FINEST BIT OF HEALING THAT I COULD HAVE ASKED FOR.
RAMMY, I DON'T KNOW WHAT I'LL DO WITHOUT YOU.
YOU'VE JUST GOT TO GET BETTER.

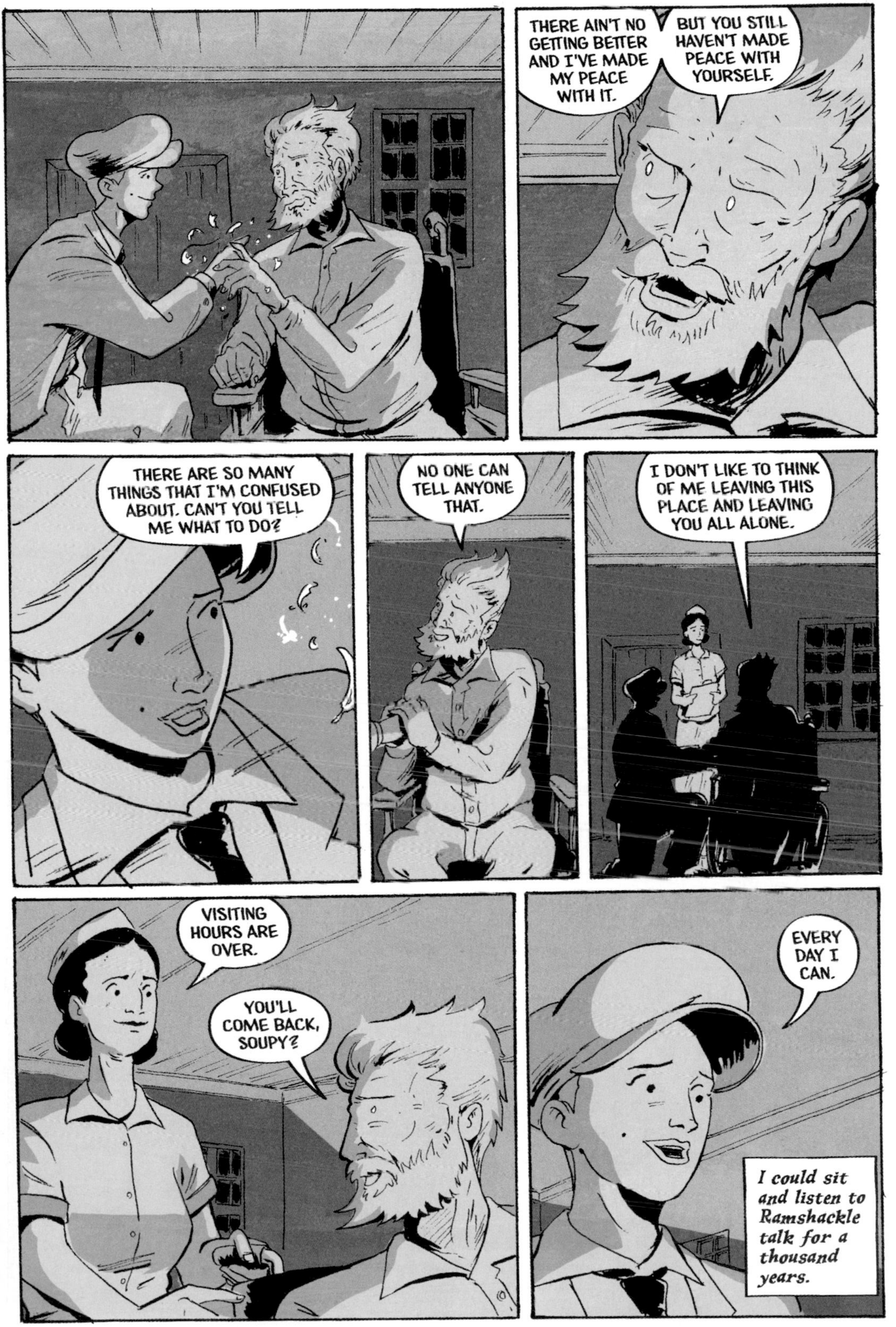
THERE AIN'T NO GETTING BETTER AND I'VE MADE MY PEACE WITH IT.
BUT YOU STILL HAVEN'T MADE PEACE WITH YOURSELF.
THERE ARE SO MANY THINGS THAT I'M CONFUSED ABOUT. CAN'T YOU TELL ME WHAT TO DO?
NO ONE CAN TELL ANYONE THAT.
I DON'T LIKE TO THINK OF ME LEAVING THIS PLACE AND LEAVING YOU ALL ALONE.
VISITING HOURS ARE OVER.
YOU'LL COME BACK, SOUPY?
EVERY DAY I CAN.
I could sit and listen to Ramshackle talk for a thousand years.

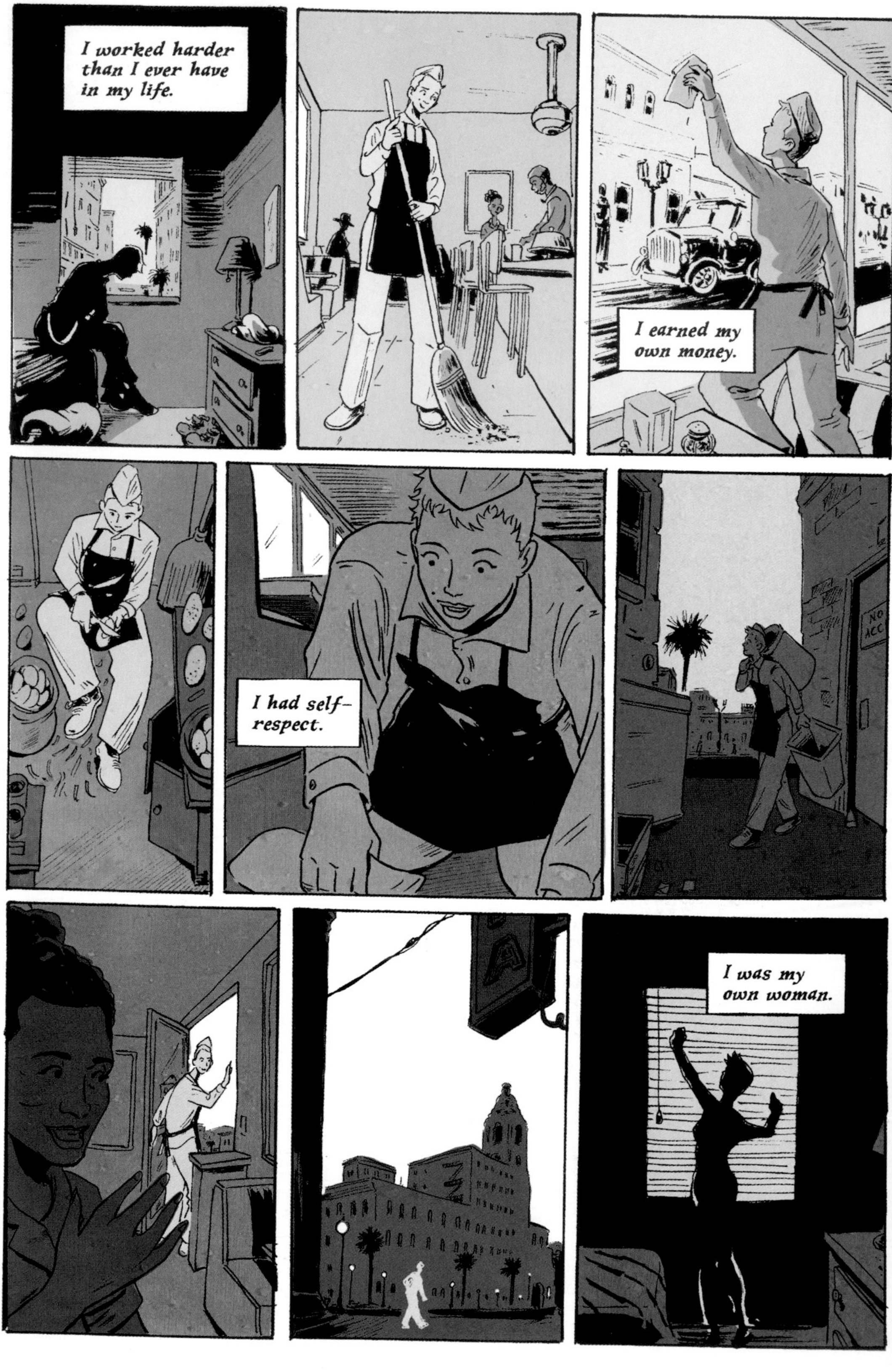
I worked harder than I ever have in my life.
I earned my own money.
I had self-respect.
NO ACC
I was my own woman.

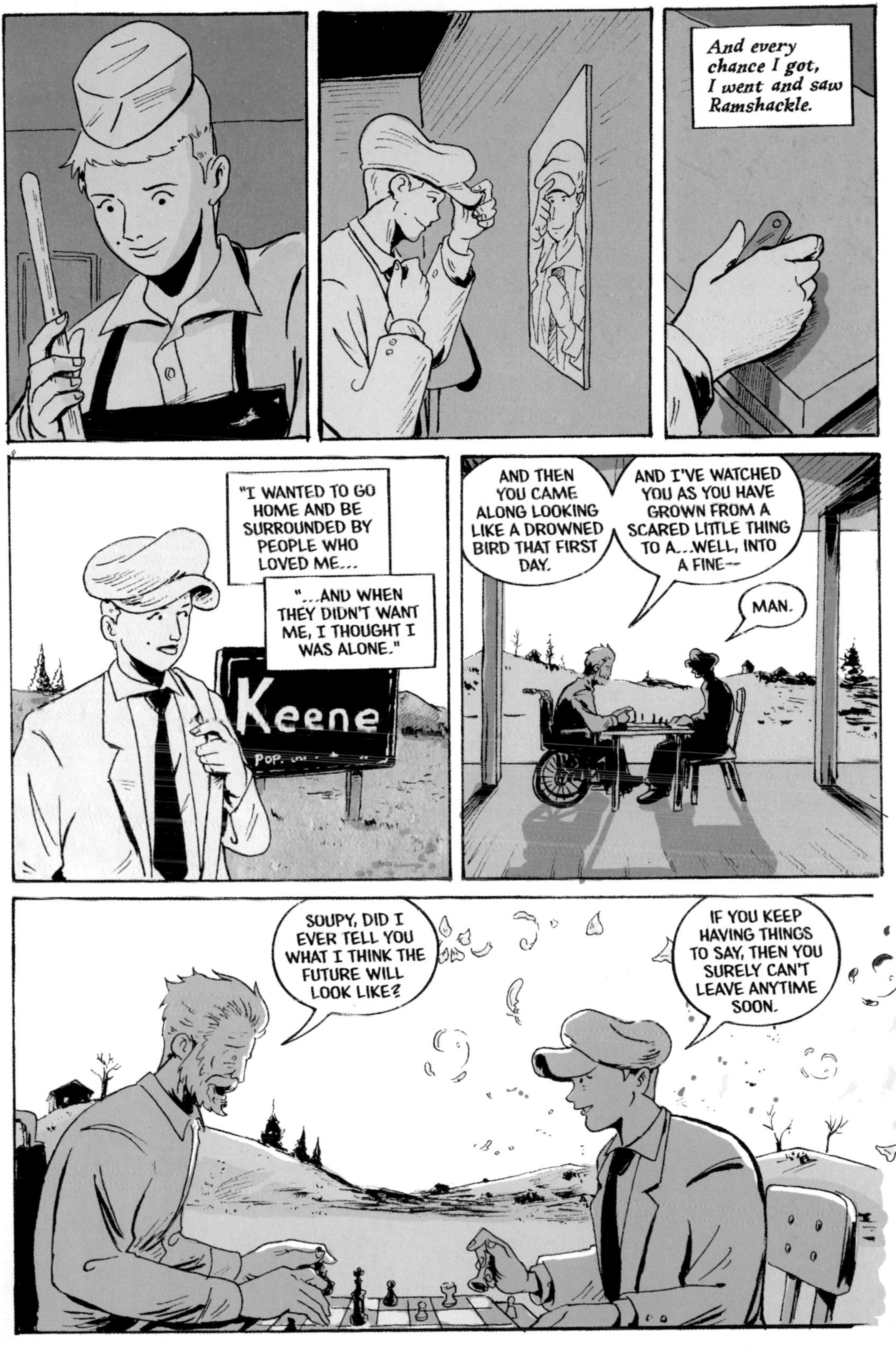
And every chance I got, I went and saw Ramshackle.
"I WANTED TO GO HOME AND BE SURROUNDED BY PEOPLE WHO LOVED ME...
"...AND WHEN THEY DIDN'T WANT ME, I THOUGHT I WAS ALONE."
Keene
POP.
AND THEN YOU CAME ALONG LOOKING LIKE A DROWNED BIRD THAT FIRST DAY.
AND I'VE WATCHED YOU AS YOU HAVE GROWN FROM A SCARED LITTLE THING TO A...WELL, INTO A FINE--
MAN.
SOUPY, DID I EVER TELL YOU WHAT I THINK THE FUTURE WILL LOOK LIKE?
IF YOU KEEP HAVING THINGS TO SAY, THEN YOU SURELY CAN'T LEAVE ANYTIME SOON.

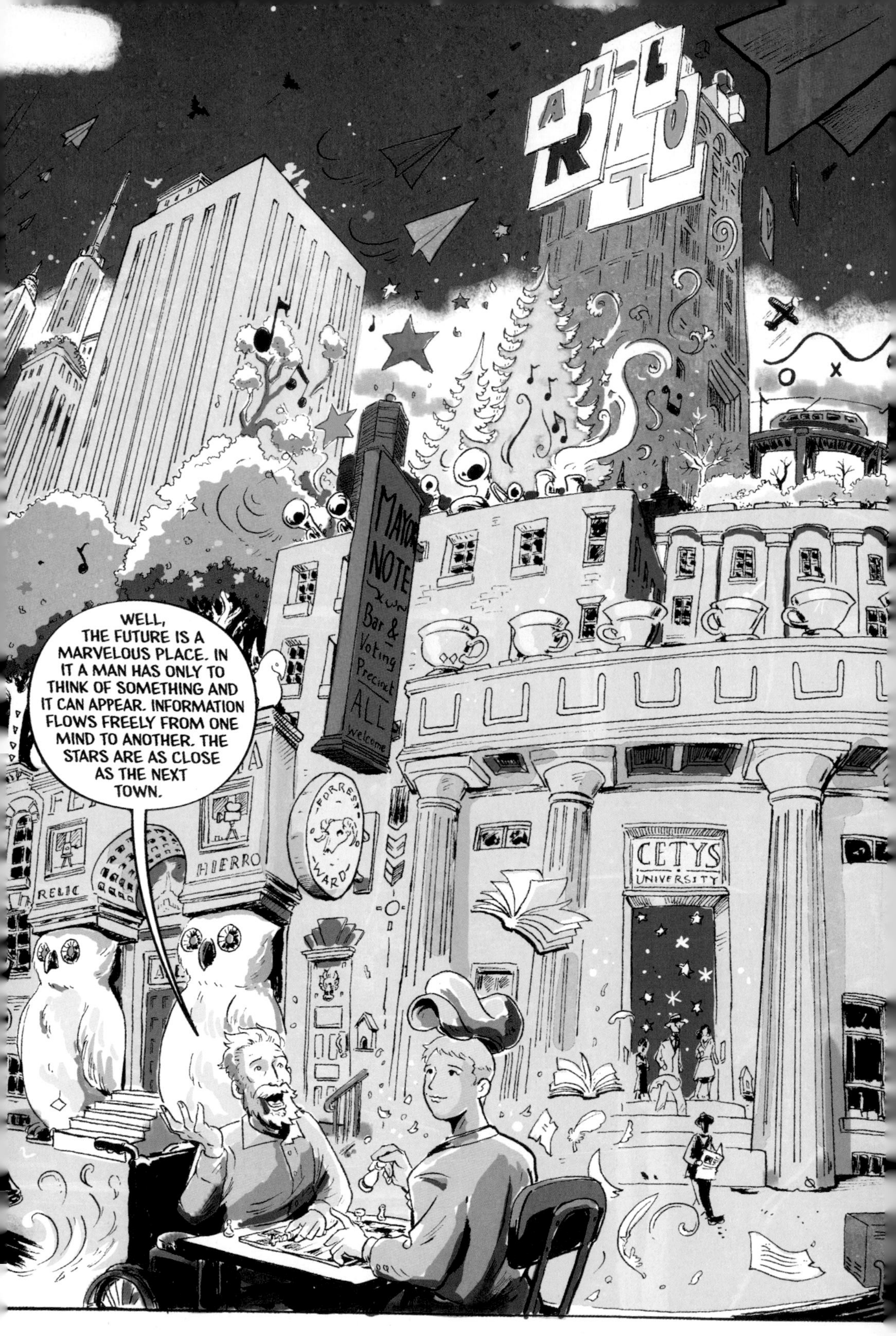
WELL, THE FUTURE IS A MARVELOUS PLACE. IN IT A MAN HAS ONLY TO THINK OF SOMETHING AND IT CAN APPEAR. INFORMATION FLOWS FREELY FROM ONE MIND TO ANOTHER. THE STARS ARE AS CLOSE AS THE NEXT TOWN.
MAYOR NOTE
Bar & Voting Precinct
ALL welcome
FORREST WARD
CETYS UNIVERSITY
HIERRO
RELIC

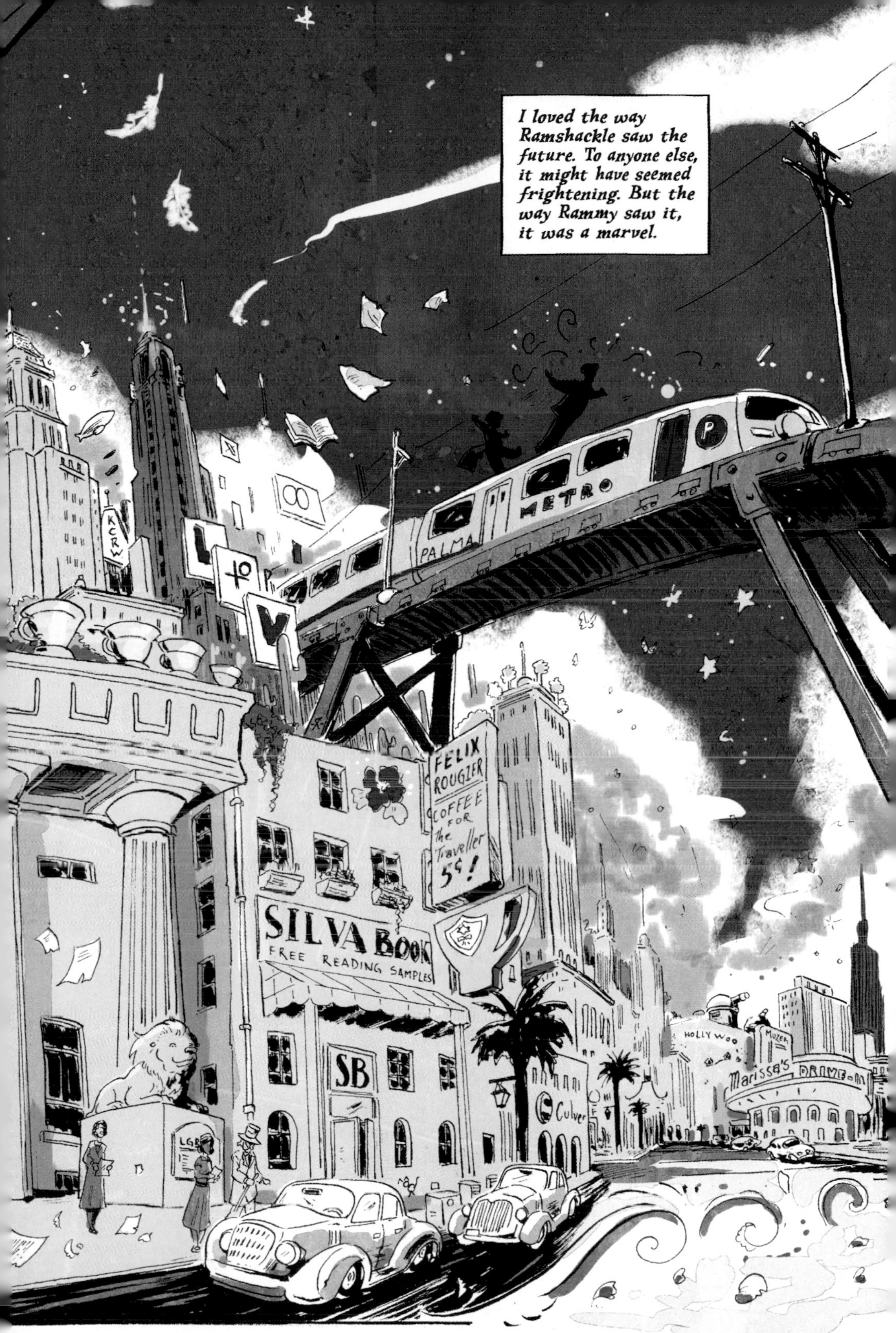
I loved the way Ramshackle saw the future. To anyone else, it might have seemed frightening. But the way Rammy saw it, it was a marvel.
KCRW
METRO
PALMA
P
FELIX ROUGIER
COFFEE FOR the Traveller 5¢!
SILVA BOOK
FREE READING SAMPLES
SB
Culver
Marissa's
DRIVE-IN

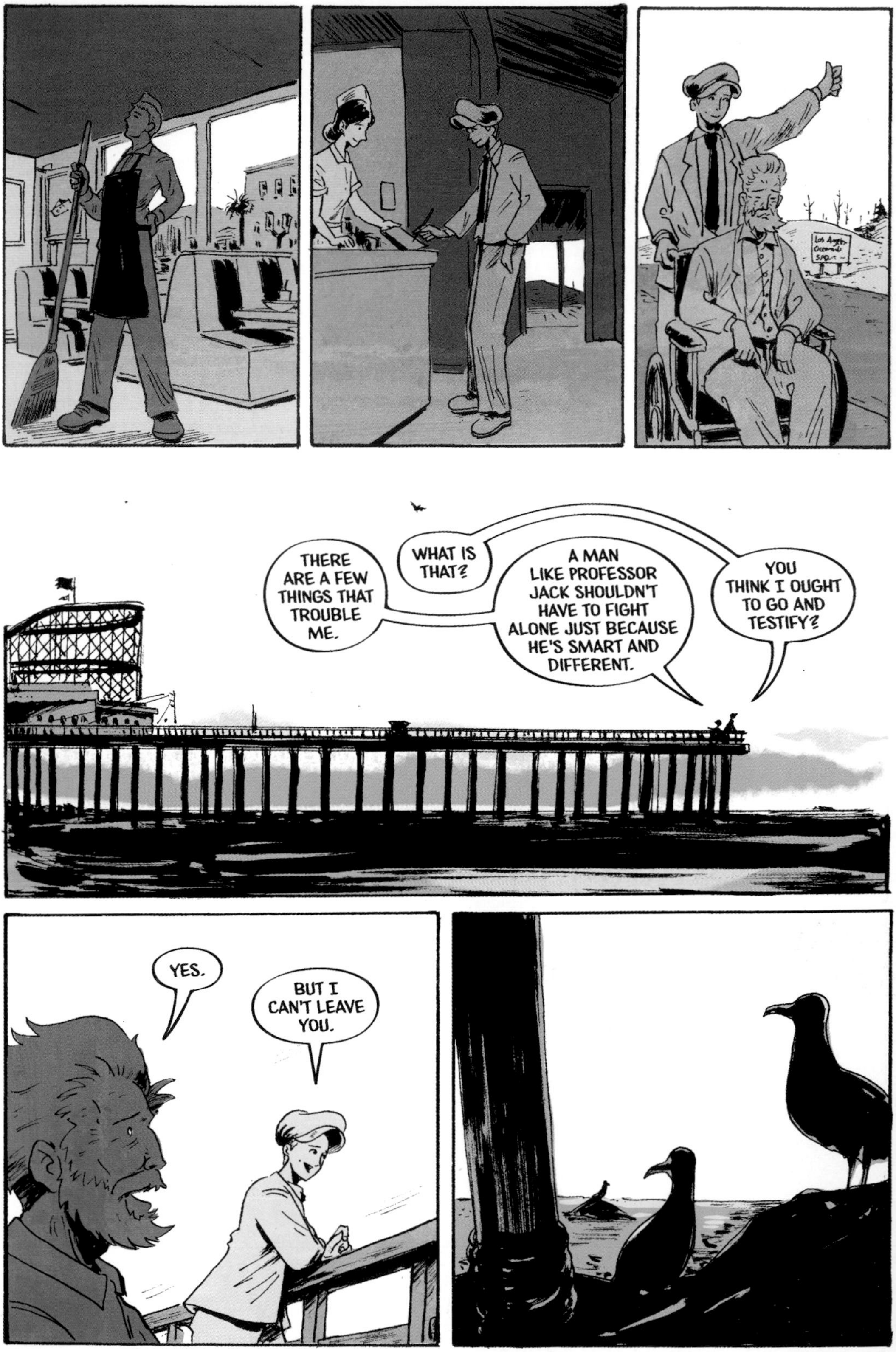
THERE ARE A FEW THINGS THAT TROUBLE ME.
WHAT IS THAT?
A MAN LIKE PROFESSOR JACK SHOULDN'T HAVE TO FIGHT ALONE JUST BECAUSE HE'S SMART AND DIFFERENT.
YOU THINK I OUGHT TO GO AND TESTIFY?
YES.
BUT I CAN'T LEAVE YOU.

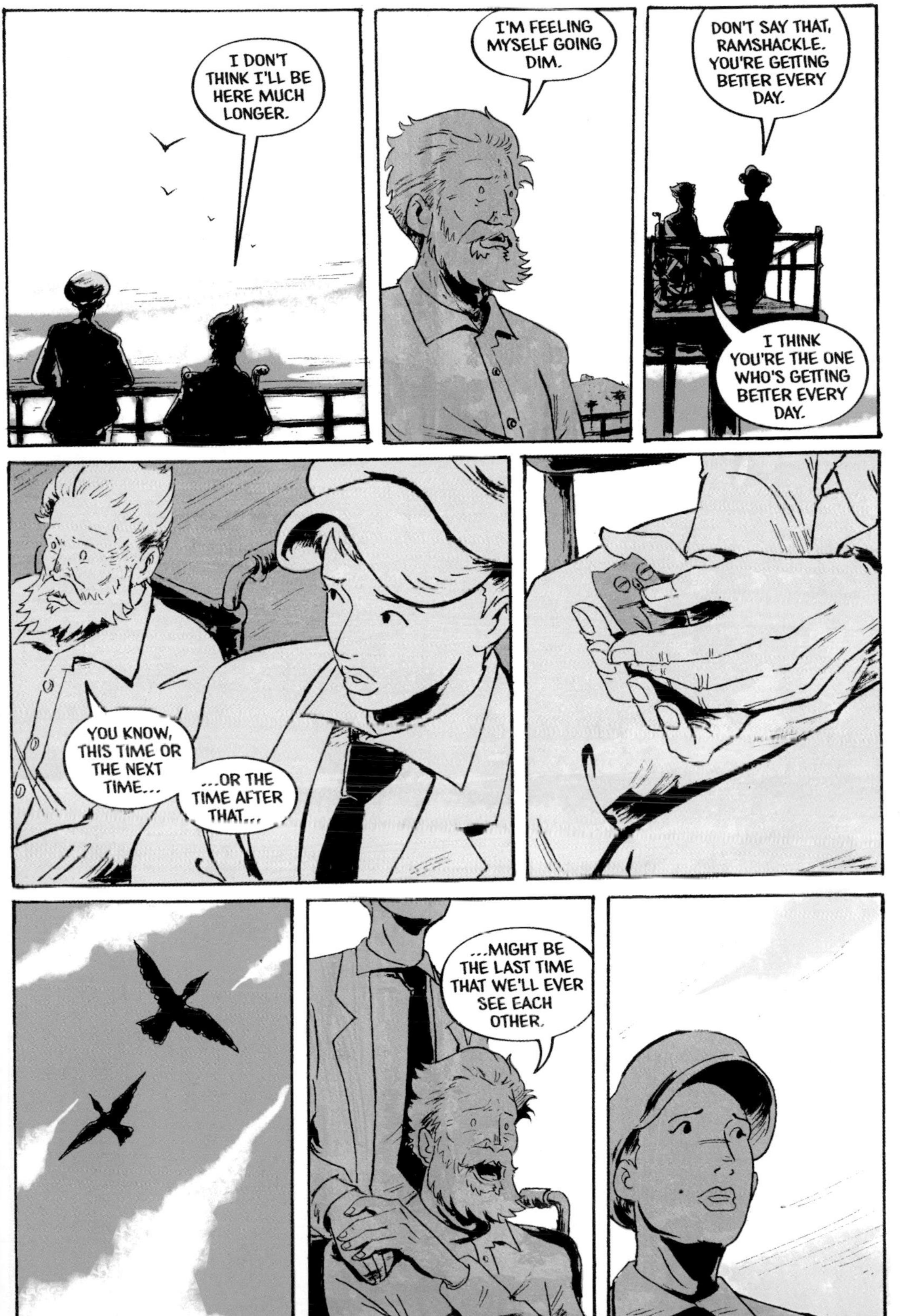
I DON'T THINK I'LL BE HERE MUCH LONGER.
I'M FEELING MYSELF GOING DIM.
DON'T SAY THAT, RAMSHACKLE. YOU'RE GETTING BETTER EVERY DAY.
I THINK YOU'RE THE ONE WHO'S GETTING BETTER EVERY DAY.
YOU KNOW, THIS TIME OR THE NEXT TIME...
...OR THE TIME AFTER THAT...
...MIGHT BE THE LAST TIME THAT WE'LL EVER SEE EACH OTHER.

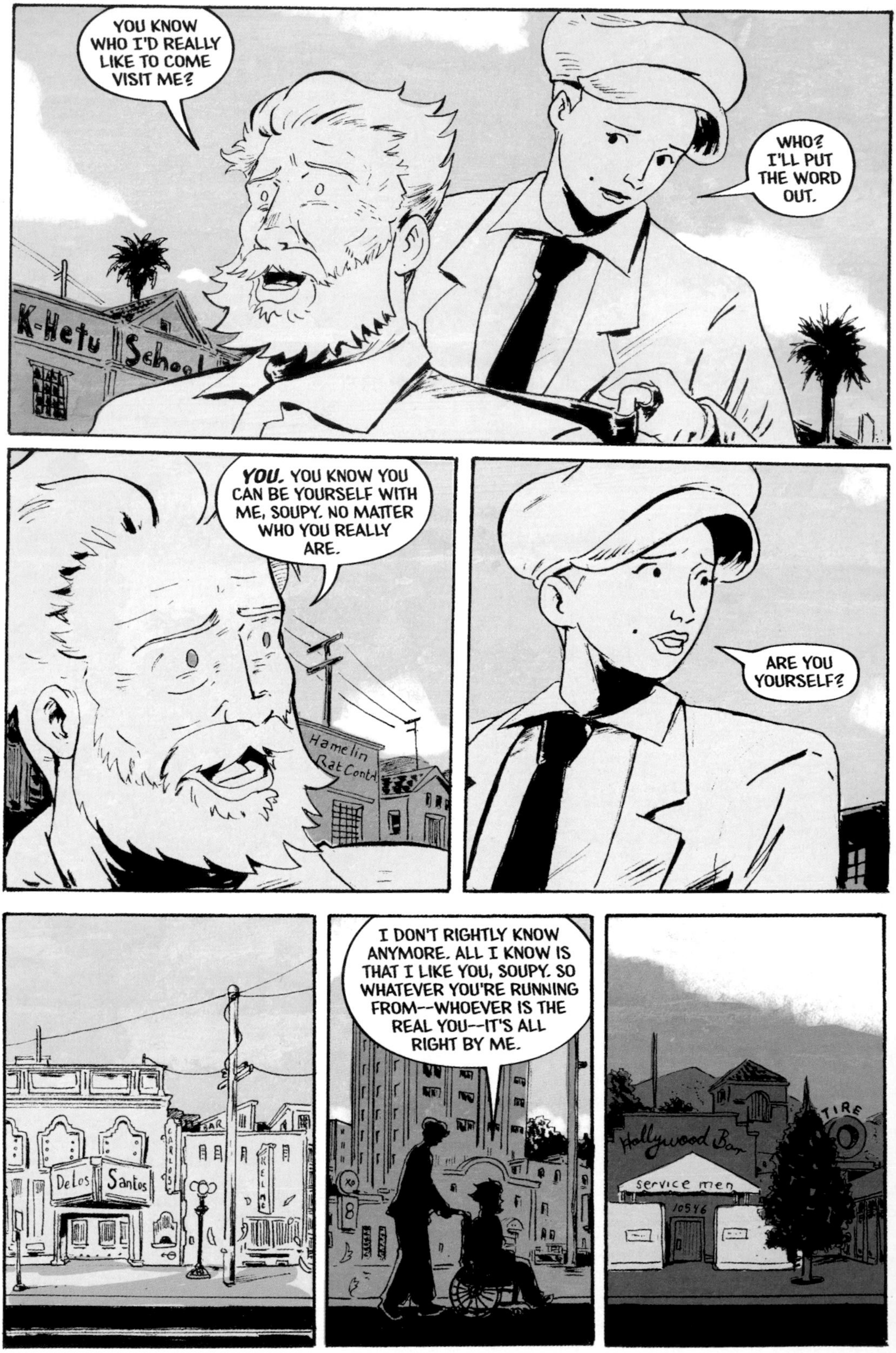
YOU KNOW WHO I'D REALLY LIKE TO COME VISIT ME?
WHO? I'LL PUT THE WORD OUT.
K-Hetu School
YOU. YOU KNOW YOU CAN BE YOURSELF WITH ME, SOUPY. NO MATTER WHO YOU REALLY ARE.
Hamelin Rat Contl
ARE YOU YOURSELF?
DeLos Santos
I DON'T RIGHTLY KNOW ANYMORE. ALL I KNOW IS THAT I LIKE YOU, SOUPY. SO WHATEVER YOU'RE RUNNING FROM--WHOEVER IS THE REAL YOU--IT'S ALL RIGHT BY ME.
Hollywood Bar
service men
10546
TIRE

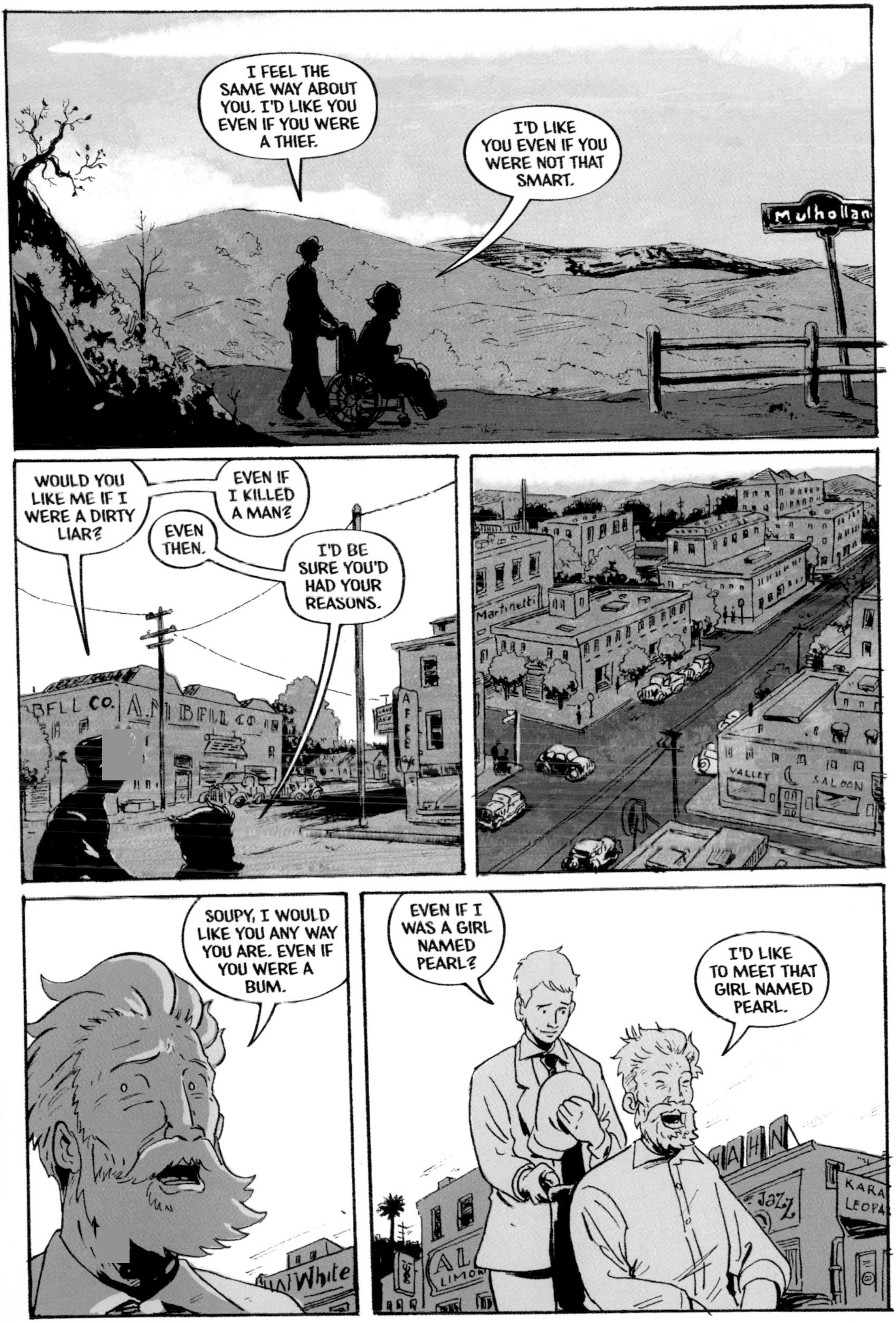
I FEEL THE SAME WAY ABOUT YOU. I'D LIKE YOU EVEN IF YOU WERE A THIEF.
I'D LIKE YOU EVEN IF YOU WERE NOT THAT SMART.
WOULD YOU LIKE ME IF I WERE A DIRTY LIAR?
EVEN IF I KILLED A MAN?
EVEN THEN.
I'D BE SURE YOU'D HAD YOUR REASONS.
Martinelli
VALLEY SALOON
SOUPY, I WOULD LIKE YOU ANY WAY YOU ARE. EVEN IF YOU WERE A BUM.
White
EVEN IF I WAS A GIRL NAMED PEARL?
I'D LIKE TO MEET THAT GIRL NAMED PEARL.
Jazz

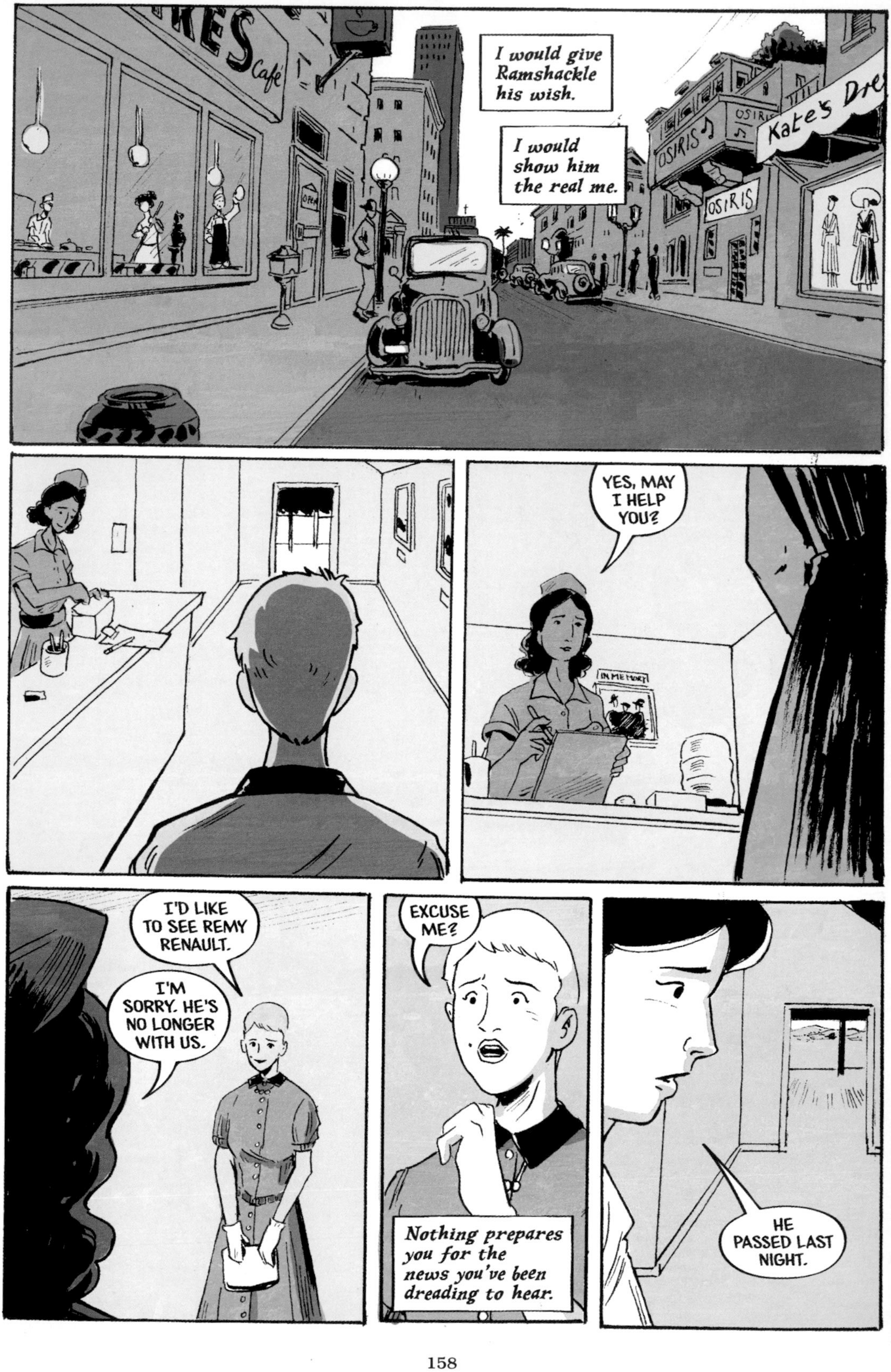
Café
I would give Ramshackle his wish.
I would show him the real me.
OPEN
OSIRIS
OSIRIS
OSIRIS
Kate's Dre
YES, MAY I HELP YOU?
IN MEMORY
I'D LIKE TO SEE REMY RENAULT.
I'M SORRY. HE'S NO LONGER WITH US.
EXCUSE ME?
Nothing prepares you for the news you've been dreading to hear.
HE PASSED LAST NIGHT.

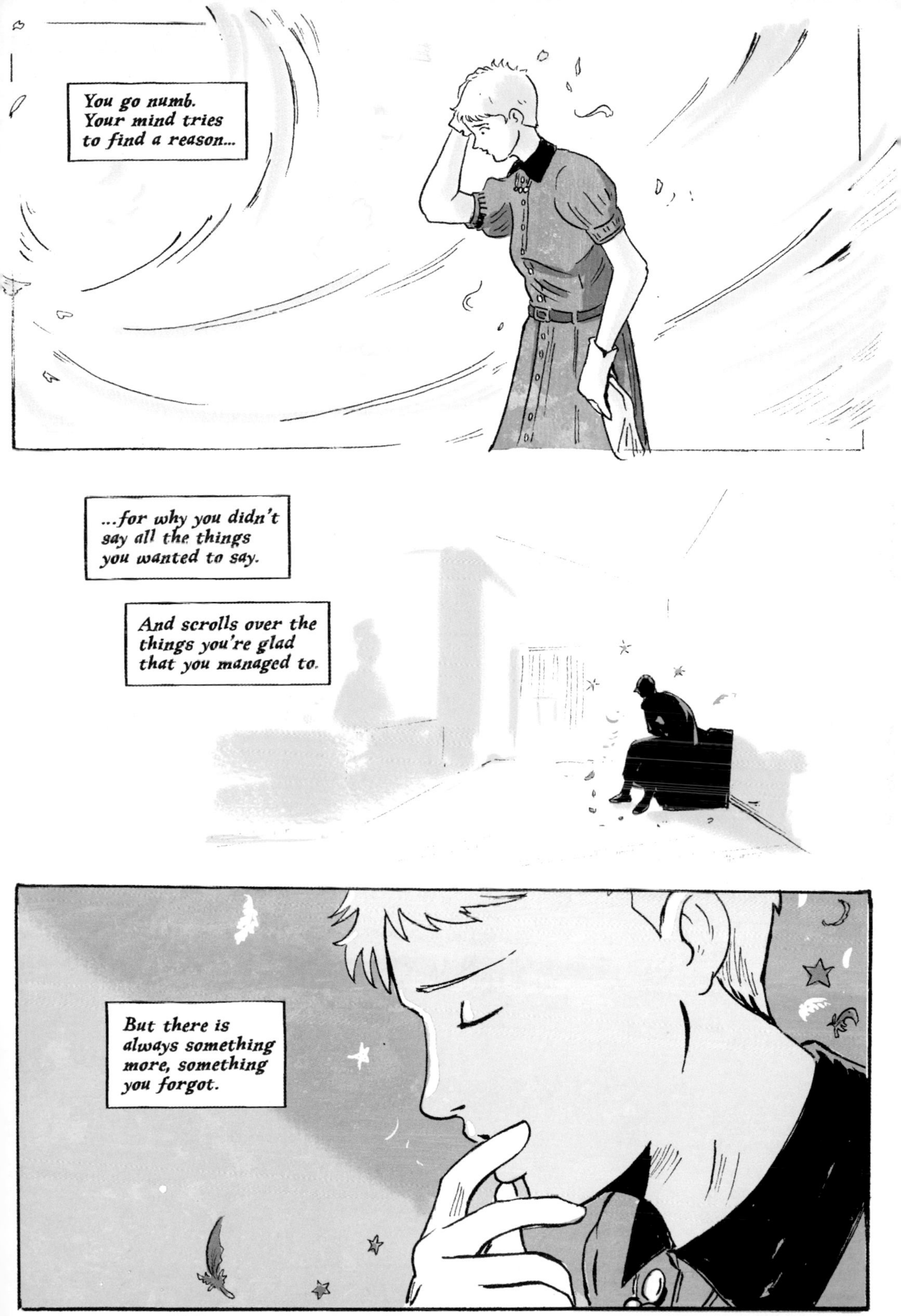
You go numb. Your mind tries to find a reason...
...for why you didn't say all the things you wanted to say.
And scrolls over the things you're glad that you managed to.
But there is always something more, something you forgot.

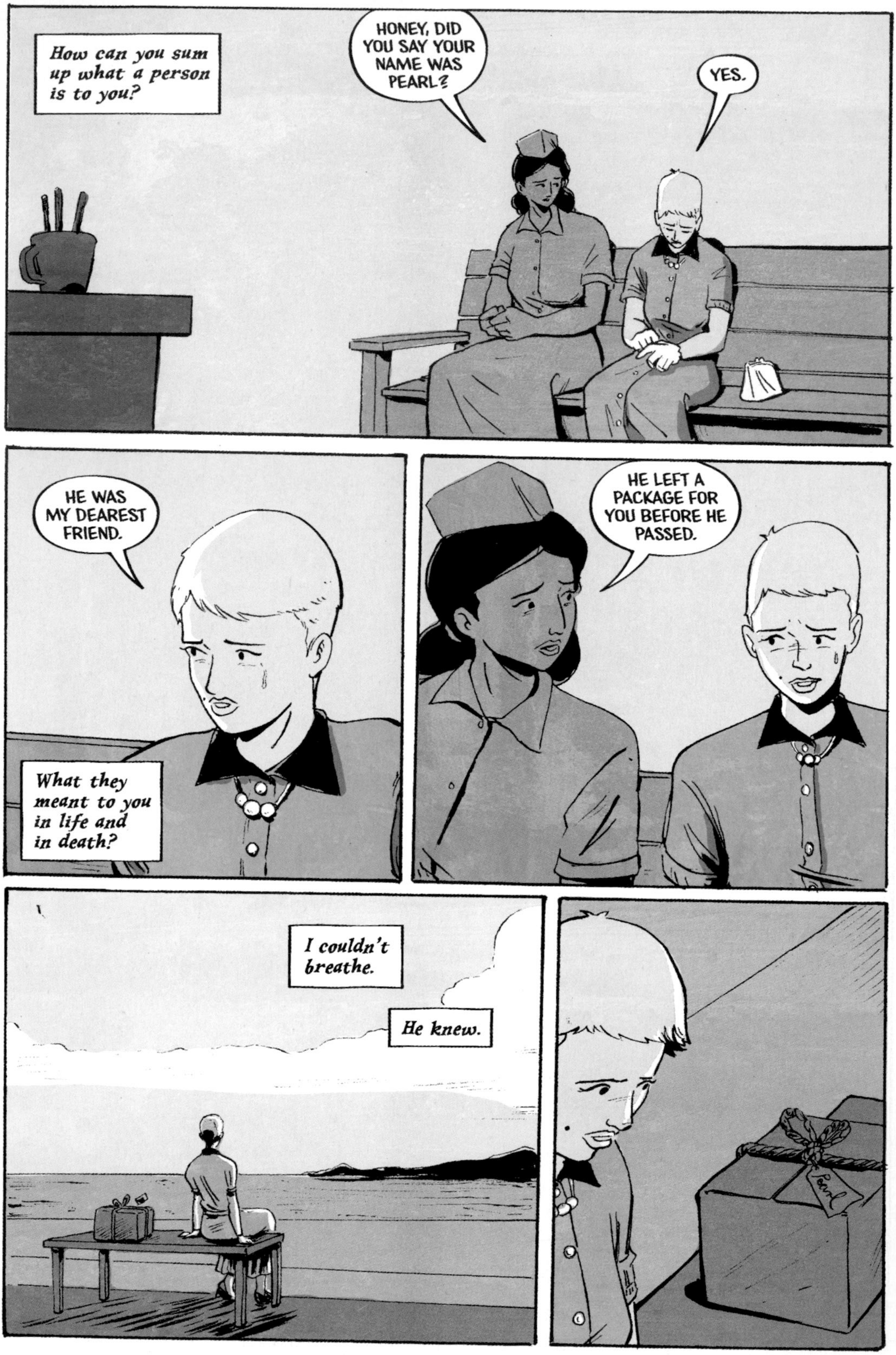
How can you sum up what a person is to you?
HONEY, DID YOU SAY YOUR NAME WAS PEARL?
YES.
HE WAS MY DEAREST FRIEND.
What they meant to you in life and in death?
HE LEFT A PACKAGE FOR YOU BEFORE HE PASSED.
I couldn't breathe.
He knew.
Pearl

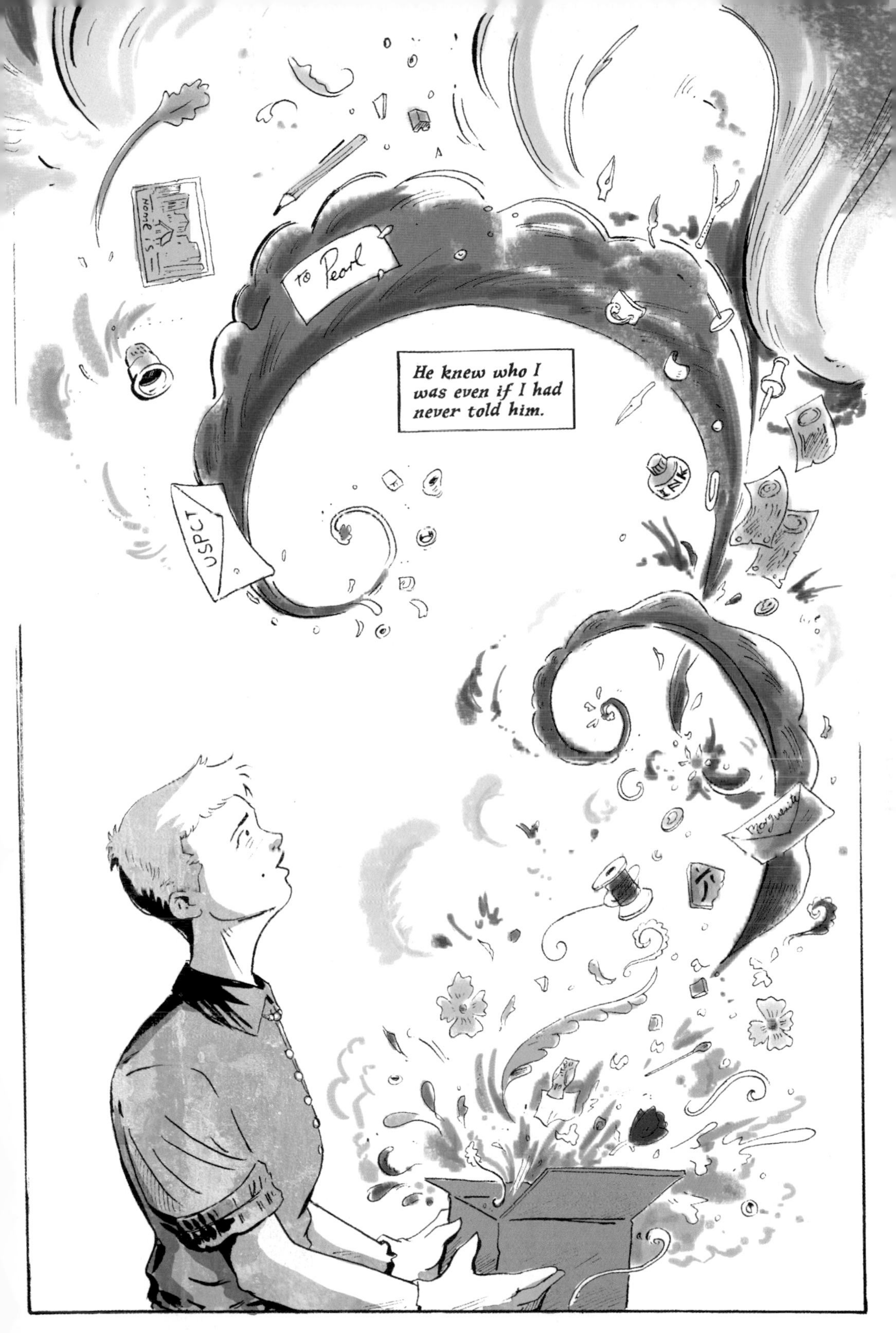
to Pearl
He knew who I was even if I had never told him.
USPCT
INK

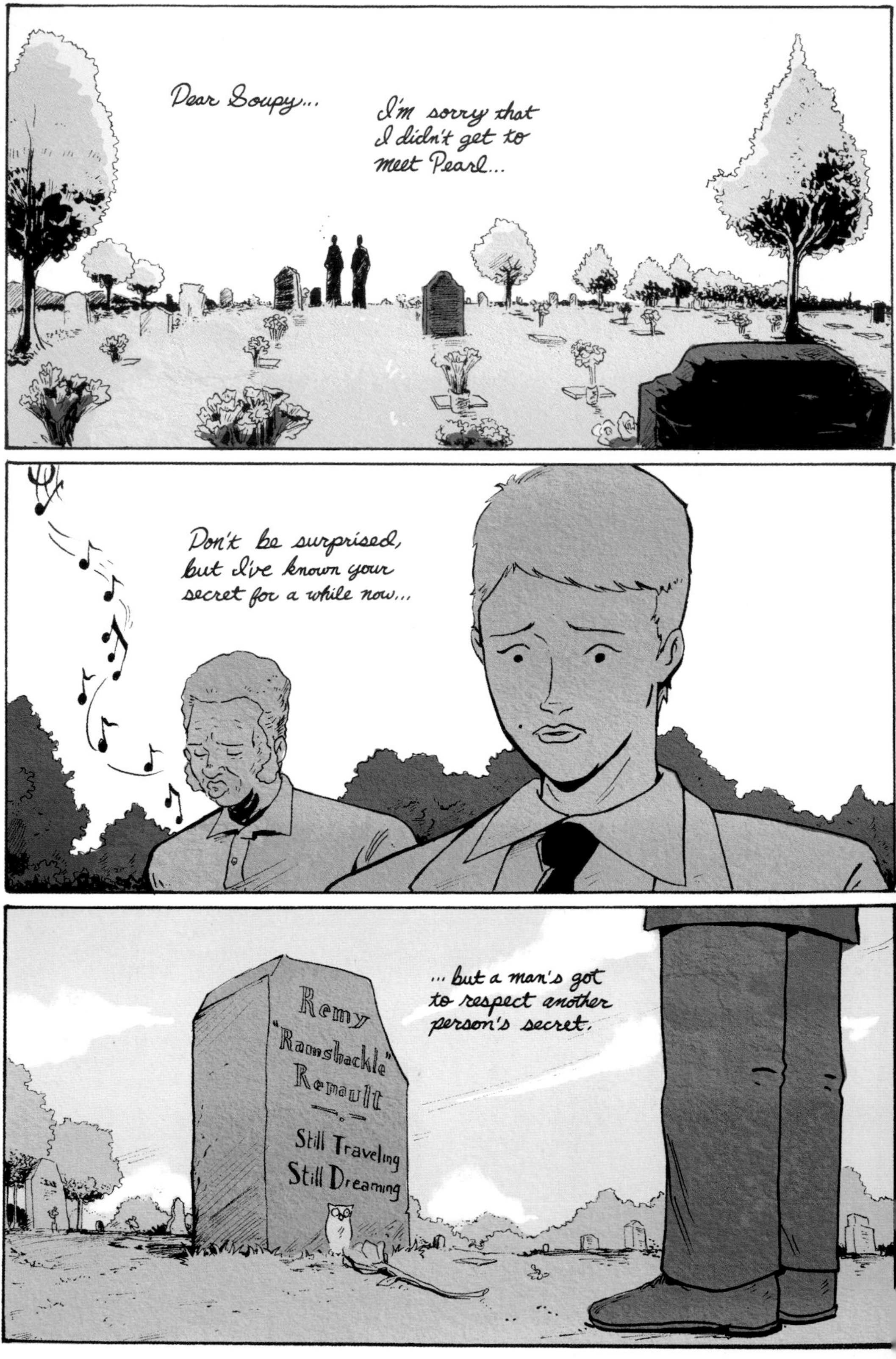
Dear Soupy...
I'm sorry that I didn't get to meet Pearl...
Don't be surprised, but I've known your secret for a while now...
Remy "Ramshackle" Renault
Still Traveling Still Dreaming
...but a man's got to respect another person's secret.

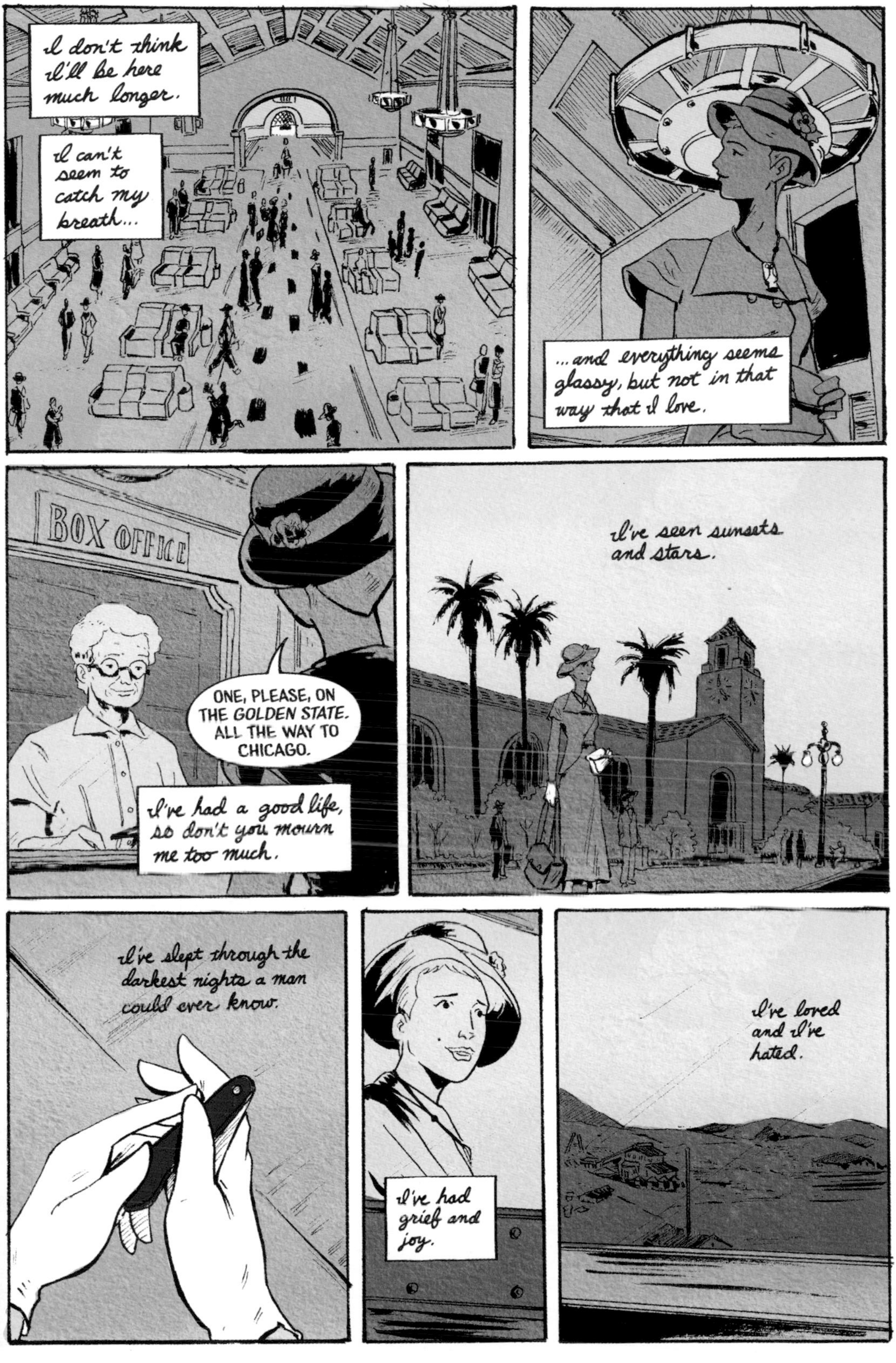
I don't think I'll be here much longer.
I can't seem to catch my breath...
...and everything seems glassy, but not in that way that I love.
BOX OFFICE
ONE, PLEASE, ON THE GOLDEN STATE. ALL THE WAY TO CHICAGO.
I've had a good life, so don't you mourn me too much.
I've seen sunsets and stars.
I've slept through the darkest nights a man could ever know.
I've had grief and joy.
I've loved and I've hated.

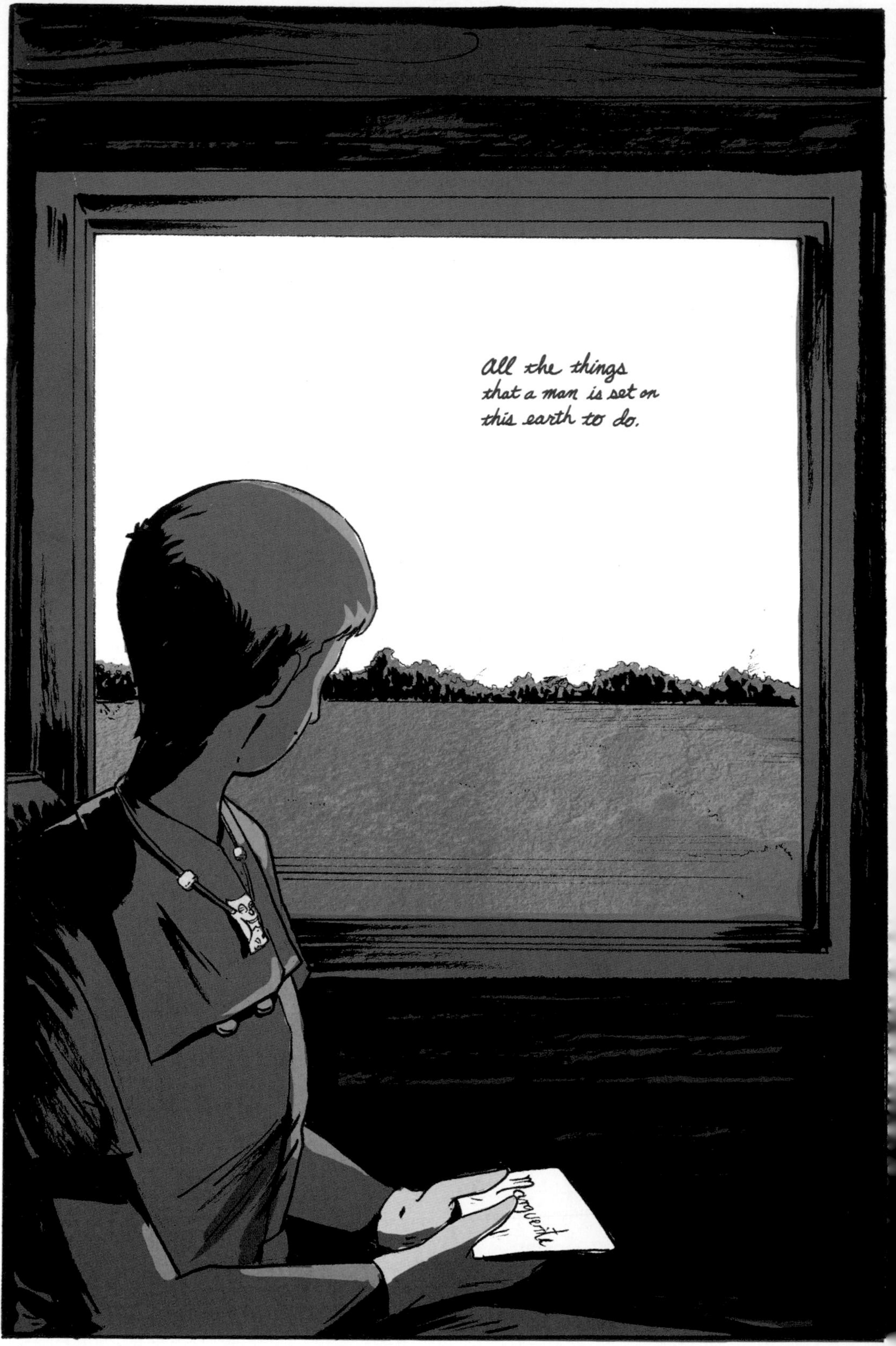
All the things
that a man is set on
this earth to do.
Marguerite

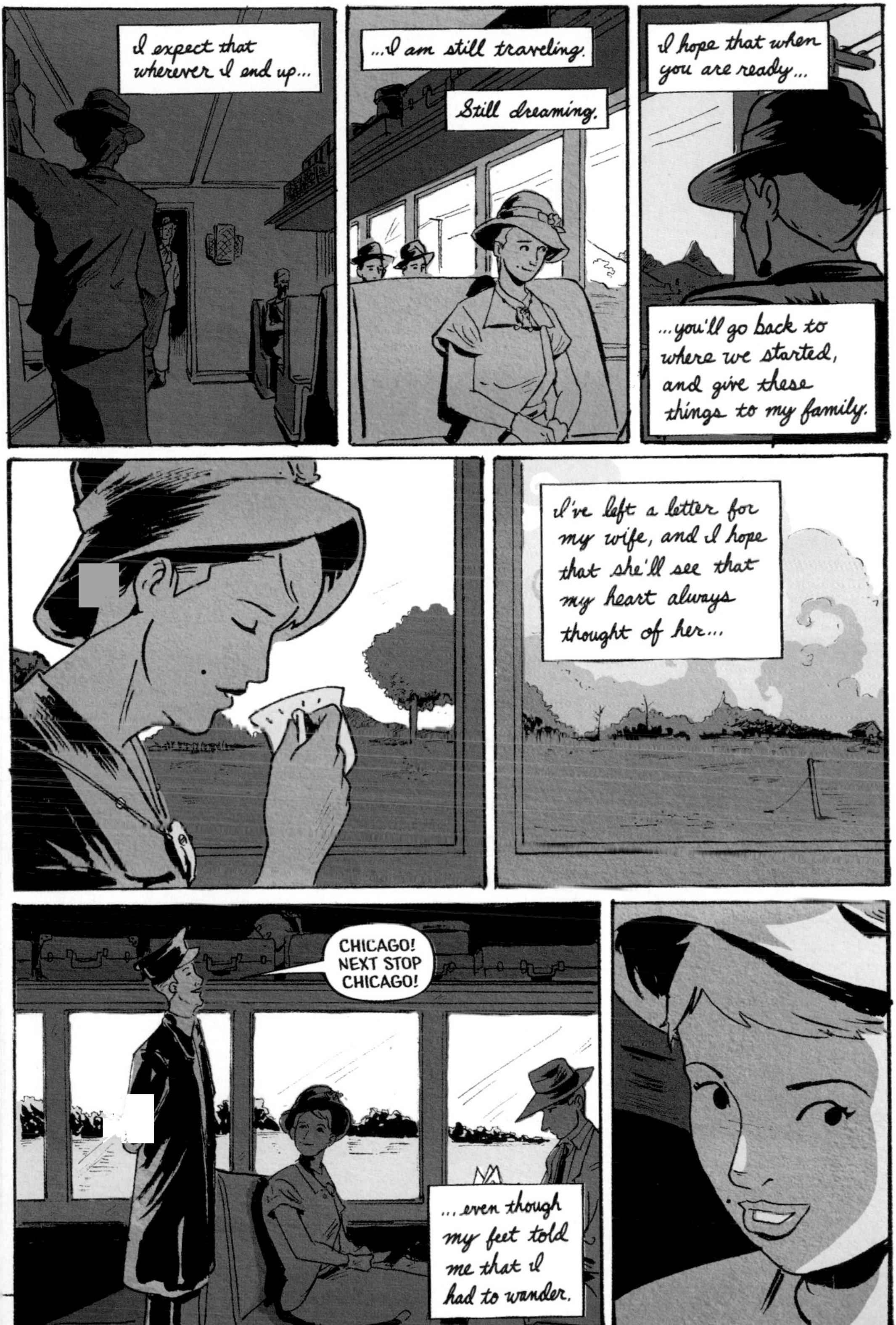
I expect that wherever I end up...
...I am still traveling.
Still dreaming.
I hope that when you are ready...
...you'll go back to where we started, and give these things to my family.
I've left a letter for my wife, and I hope that she'll see that my heart always thought of her...
CHICAGO! NEXT STOP CHICAGO!
...even though my feet told me that I had to wander.

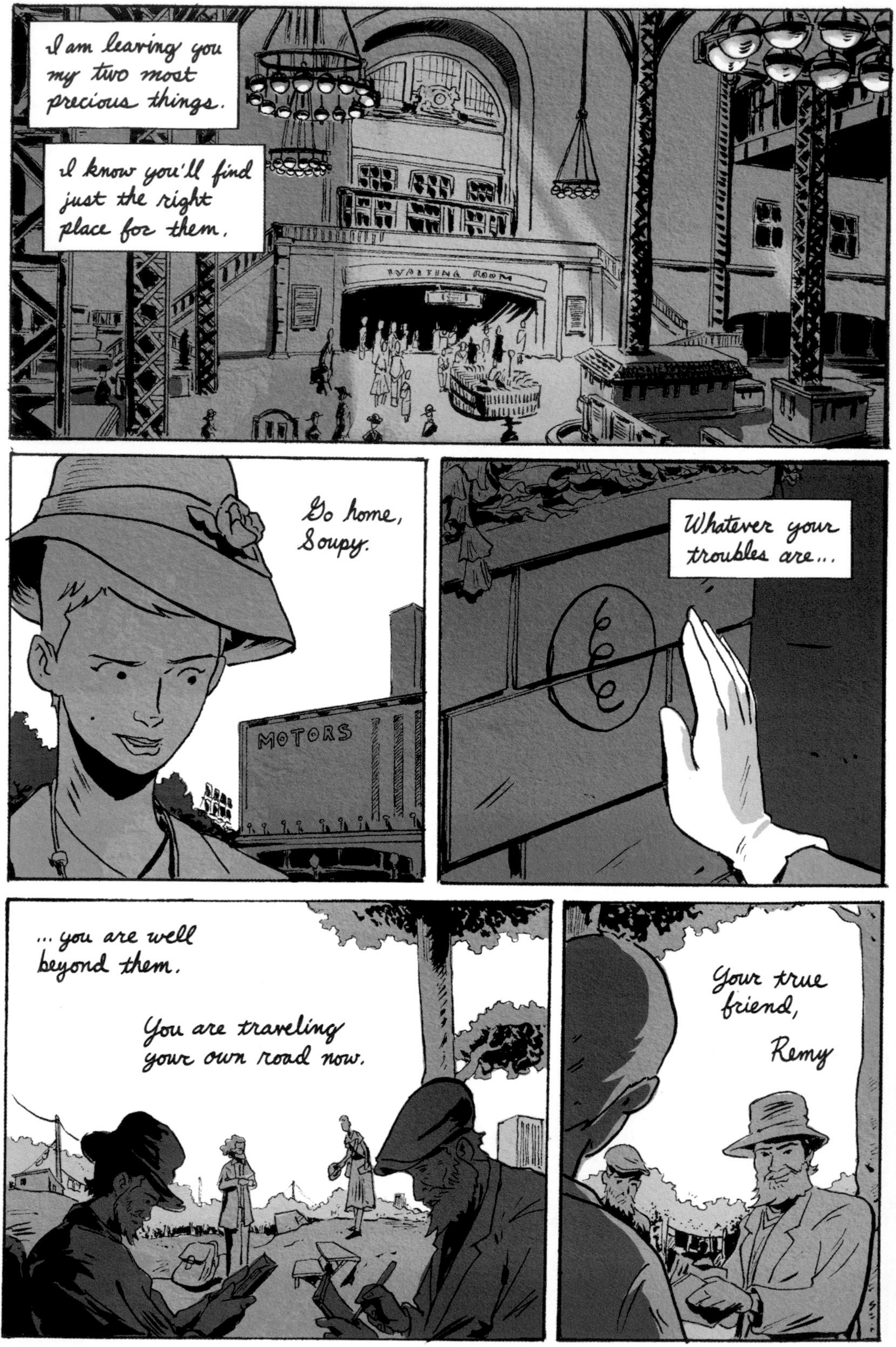
I am leaving you my two most precious things.
I know you'll find just the right place for them.
WAITING ROOM
Go home, Soupy.
MOTORS
Whatever your troubles are...
... you are well beyond them.
You are traveling your own road now.
Your true friend,
Remy

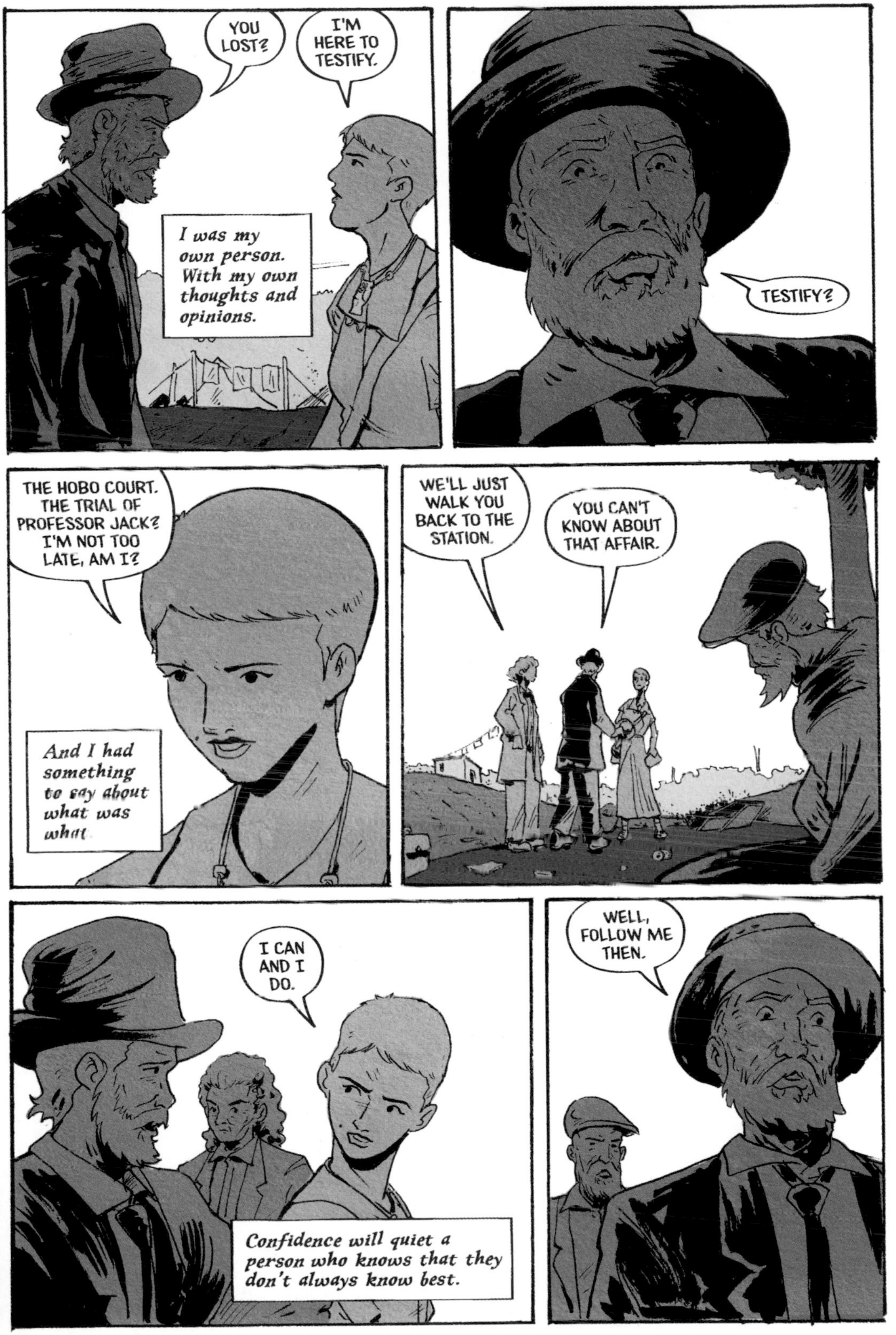
YOU LOST?
I'M HERE TO TESTIFY.
I was my own person. With my own thoughts and opinions.
TESTIFY?
THE HOBO COURT. THE TRIAL OF PROFESSOR JACK? I'M NOT TOO LATE, AM I?
And I had something to say about what was what.
WE'LL JUST WALK YOU BACK TO THE STATION.
YOU CAN'T KNOW ABOUT THAT AFFAIR.
I CAN AND I DO.
Confidence will quiet a person who knows that they don't always know best.
WELL, FOLLOW ME THEN.

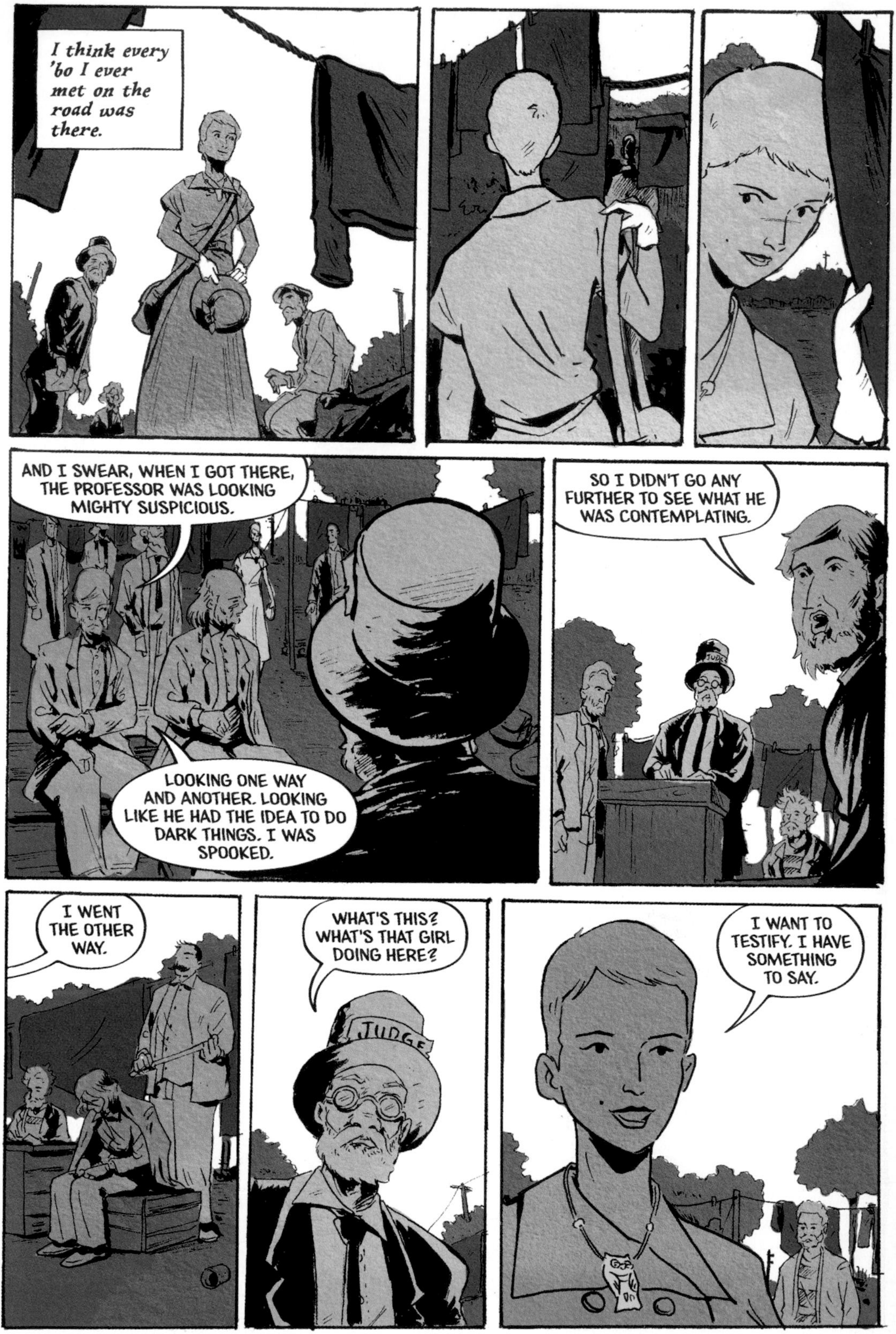
I think every 'bo I ever met on the road was there.
AND I SWEAR, WHEN I GOT THERE, THE PROFESSOR WAS LOOKING MIGHTY SUSPICIOUS.
LOOKING ONE WAY AND ANOTHER. LOOKING LIKE HE HAD THE IDEA TO DO DARK THINGS. I WAS SPOOKED.
SO I DIDN'T GO ANY FURTHER TO SEE WHAT HE WAS CONTEMPLATING.
JUDGE
I WENT THE OTHER WAY.
WHAT'S THIS? WHAT'S THAT GIRL DOING HERE?
JUDGE
I WANT TO TESTIFY. I HAVE SOMETHING TO SAY.

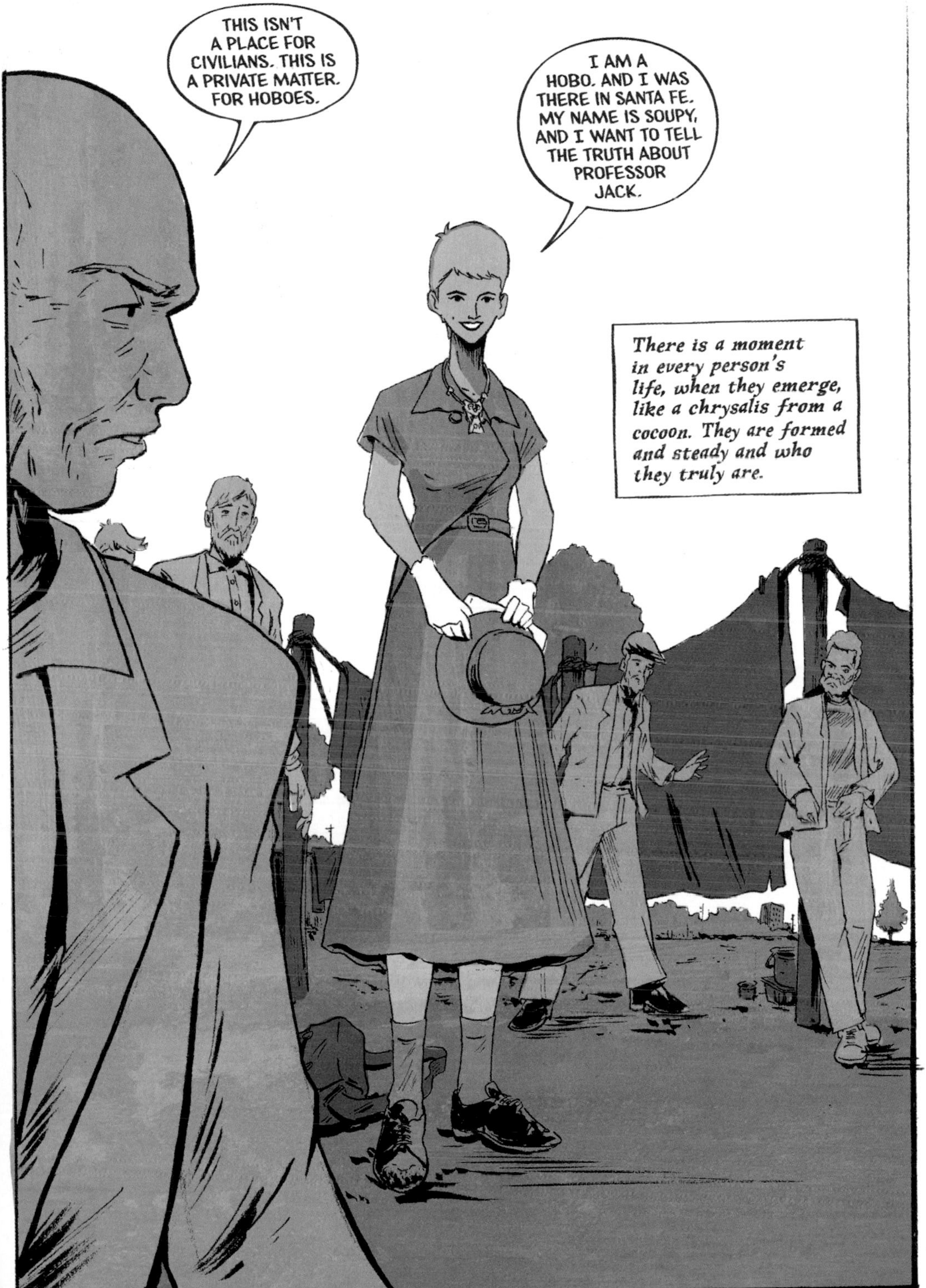
THIS ISN'T A PLACE FOR CIVILIANS. THIS IS A PRIVATE MATTER. FOR HOBOES.
I AM A HOBO. AND I WAS THERE IN SANTA FE. MY NAME IS SOUPY, AND I WANT TO TELL THE TRUTH ABOUT PROFESSOR JACK.
There is a moment in every person's life, when they emerge, like a chrysalis from a cocoon. They are formed and steady and who they truly are.

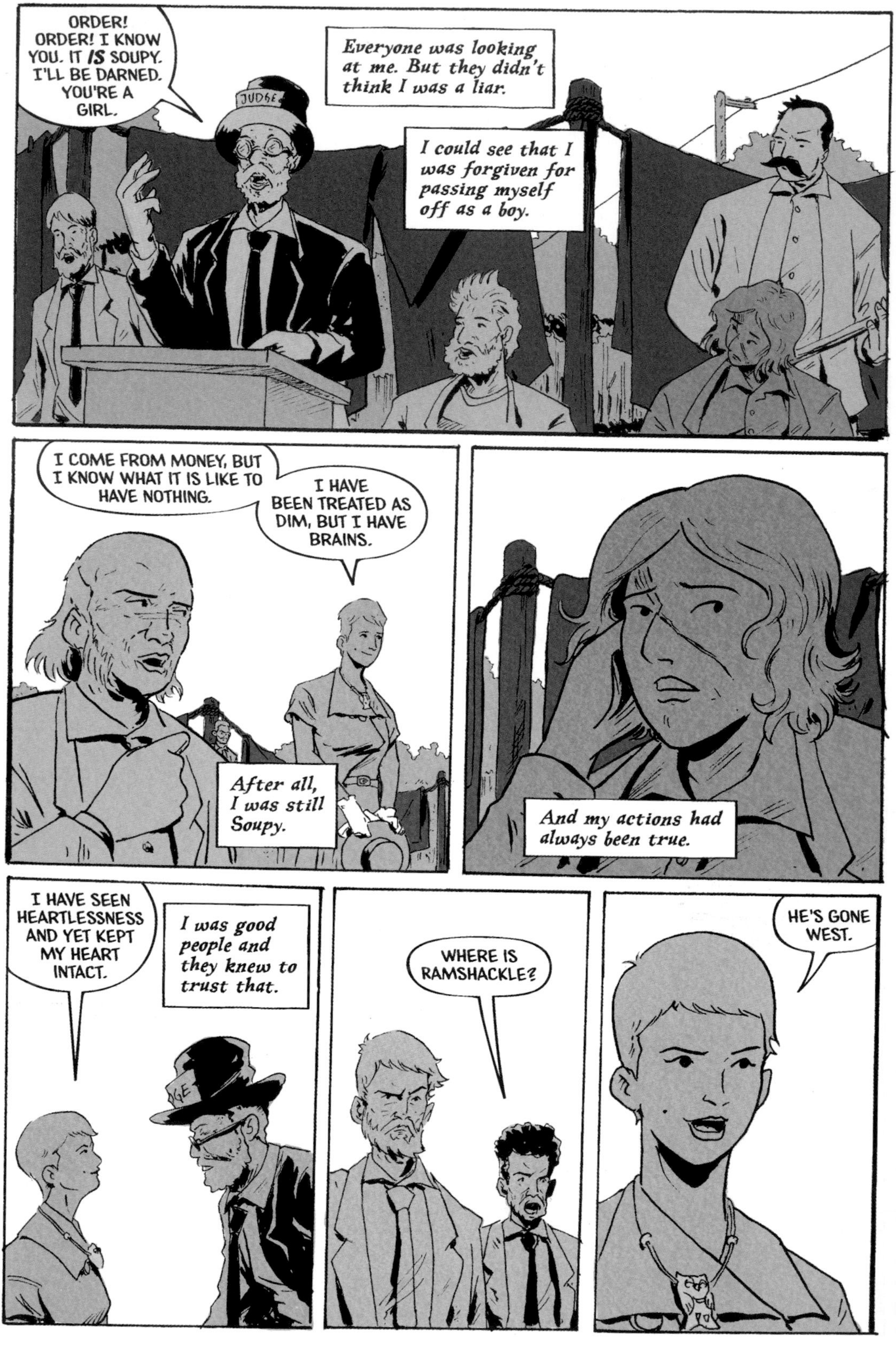
ORDER! ORDER! I KNOW YOU. IT *IS* SOUPY. I'LL BE DARNED. YOU'RE A GIRL.
JUDGE
Everyone was looking at me. But they didn't think I was a liar.
I could see that I was forgiven for passing myself off as a boy.
I COME FROM MONEY, BUT I KNOW WHAT IT IS LIKE TO HAVE NOTHING.
I HAVE BEEN TREATED AS DIM, BUT I HAVE BRAINS.
After all, I was still Soupy.
And my actions had always been true.
I HAVE SEEN HEARTLESSNESS AND YET KEPT MY HEART INTACT.
I was good people and they knew to trust that.
WHERE IS RAMSHACKLE?
HE'S GONE WEST.

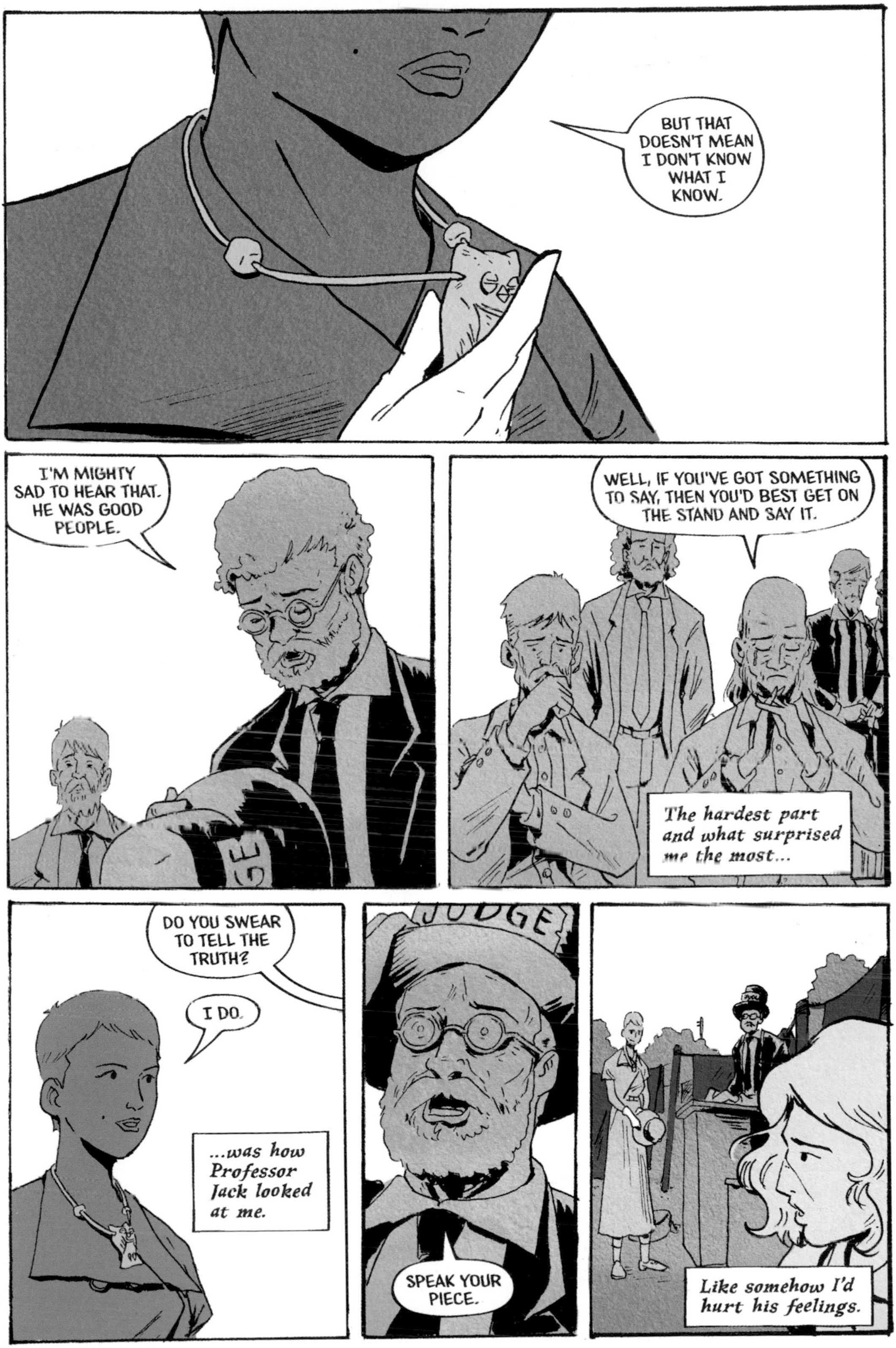
BUT THAT DOESN'T MEAN I DON'T KNOW WHAT I KNOW.
I'M MIGHTY SAD TO HEAR THAT. HE WAS GOOD PEOPLE.
WELL, IF YOU'VE GOT SOMETHING TO SAY, THEN YOU'D BEST GET ON THE STAND AND SAY IT.
The hardest part and what surprised me the most...
DO YOU SWEAR TO TELL THE TRUTH?
I DO.
...was how Professor Jack looked at me.
JUDGE
SPEAK YOUR PIECE.
Like somehow I'd hurt his feelings.

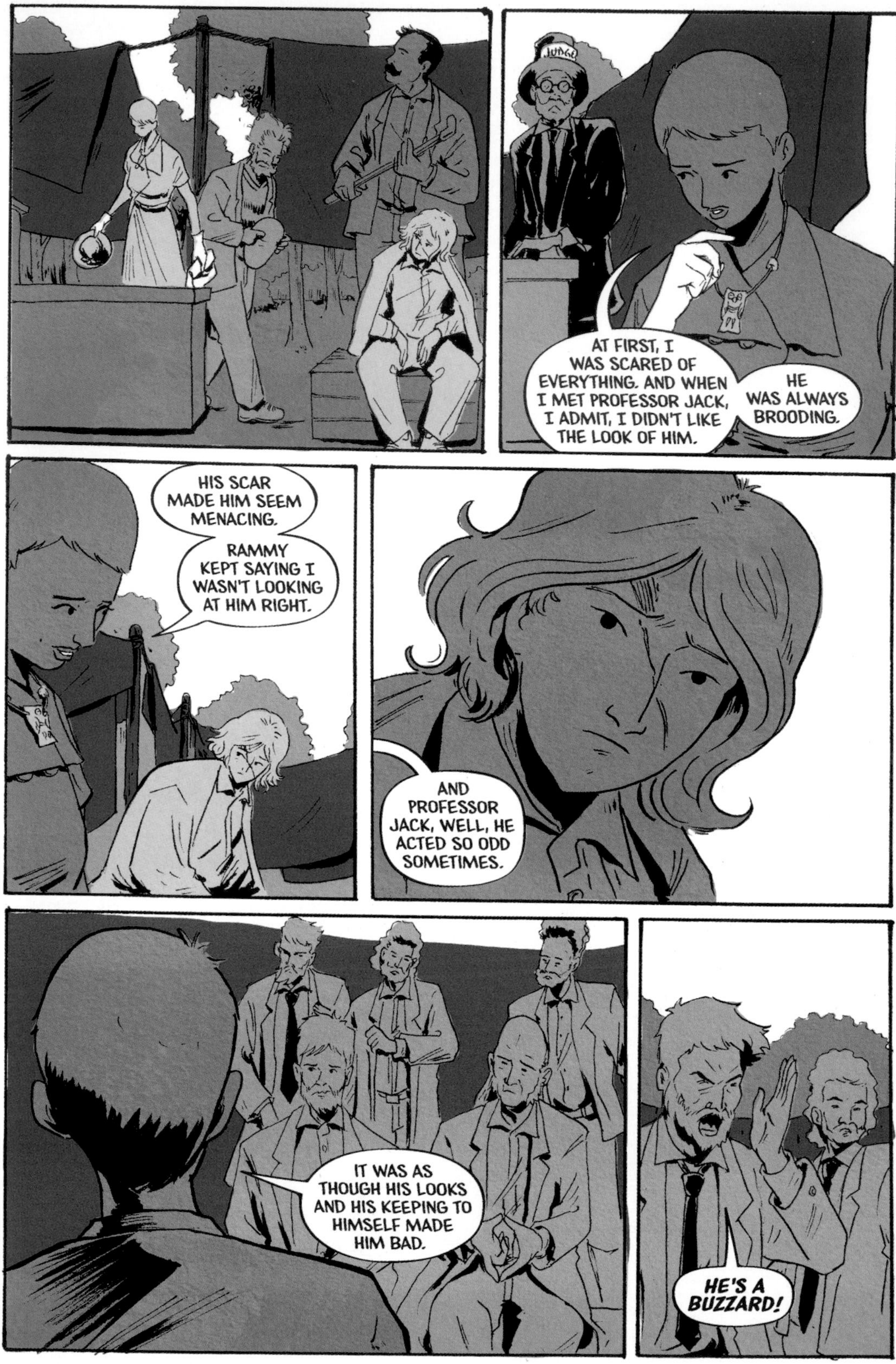
JUDGE
AT FIRST, I WAS SCARED OF EVERYTHING. AND WHEN I MET PROFESSOR JACK, I ADMIT, I DIDN'T LIKE THE LOOK OF HIM.
HE WAS ALWAYS BROODING.
HIS SCAR MADE HIM SEEM MENACING.
RAMMY KEPT SAYING I WASN'T LOOKING AT HIM RIGHT.
AND PROFESSOR JACK, WELL, HE ACTED SO ODD SOMETIMES.
IT WAS AS THOUGH HIS LOOKS AND HIS KEEPING TO HIMSELF MADE HIM BAD.
HE'S A BUZZARD!

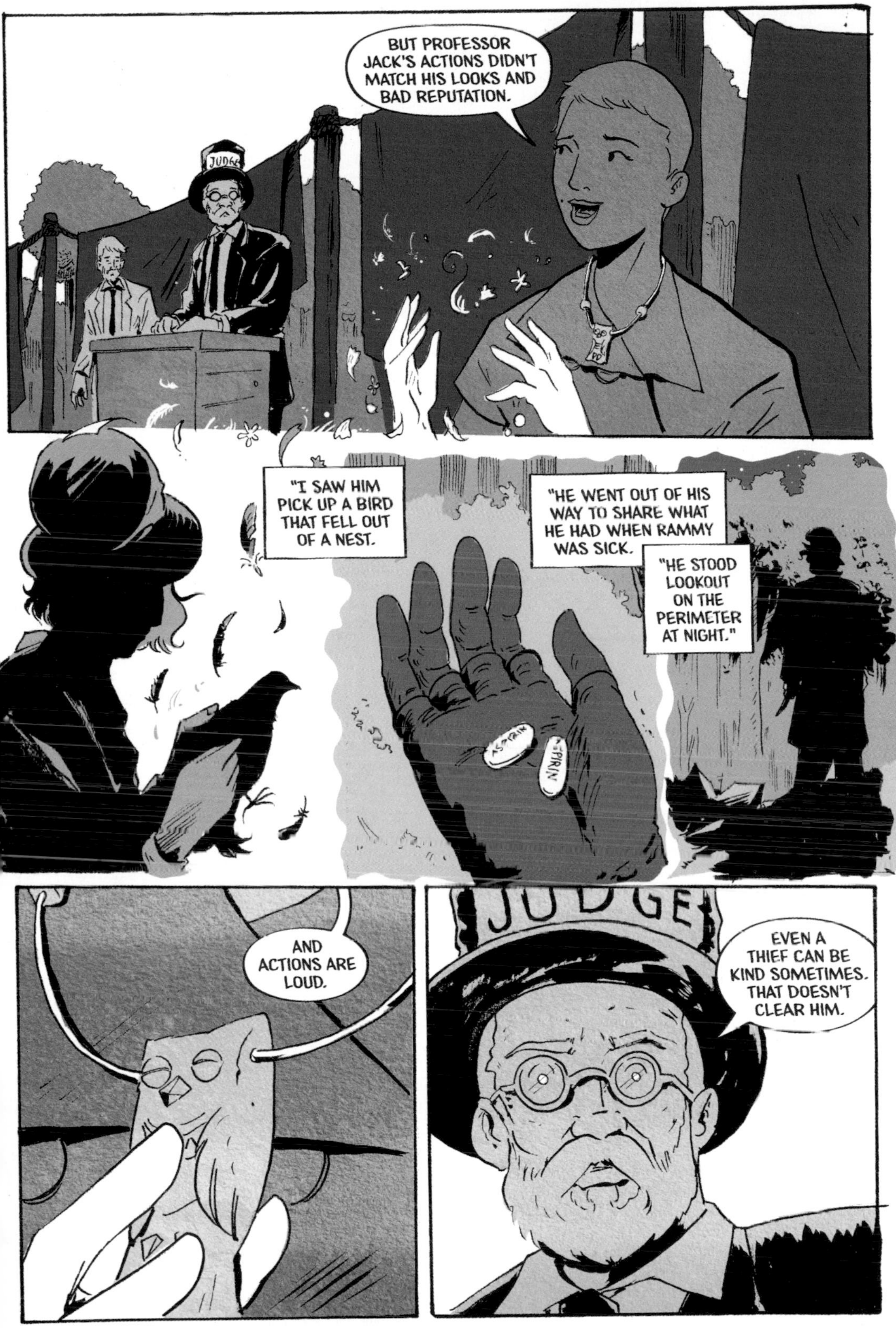
BUT PROFESSOR JACK'S ACTIONS DIDN'T MATCH HIS LOOKS AND BAD REPUTATION.
JUDGE
"I SAW HIM PICK UP A BIRD THAT FELL OUT OF A NEST.
"HE WENT OUT OF HIS WAY TO SHARE WHAT HE HAD WHEN RAMMY WAS SICK.
"HE STOOD LOOKOUT ON THE PERIMETER AT NIGHT."
AND ACTIONS ARE LOUD.
JUDGE
EVEN A THIEF CAN BE KIND SOMETIMES. THAT DOESN'T CLEAR HIM.

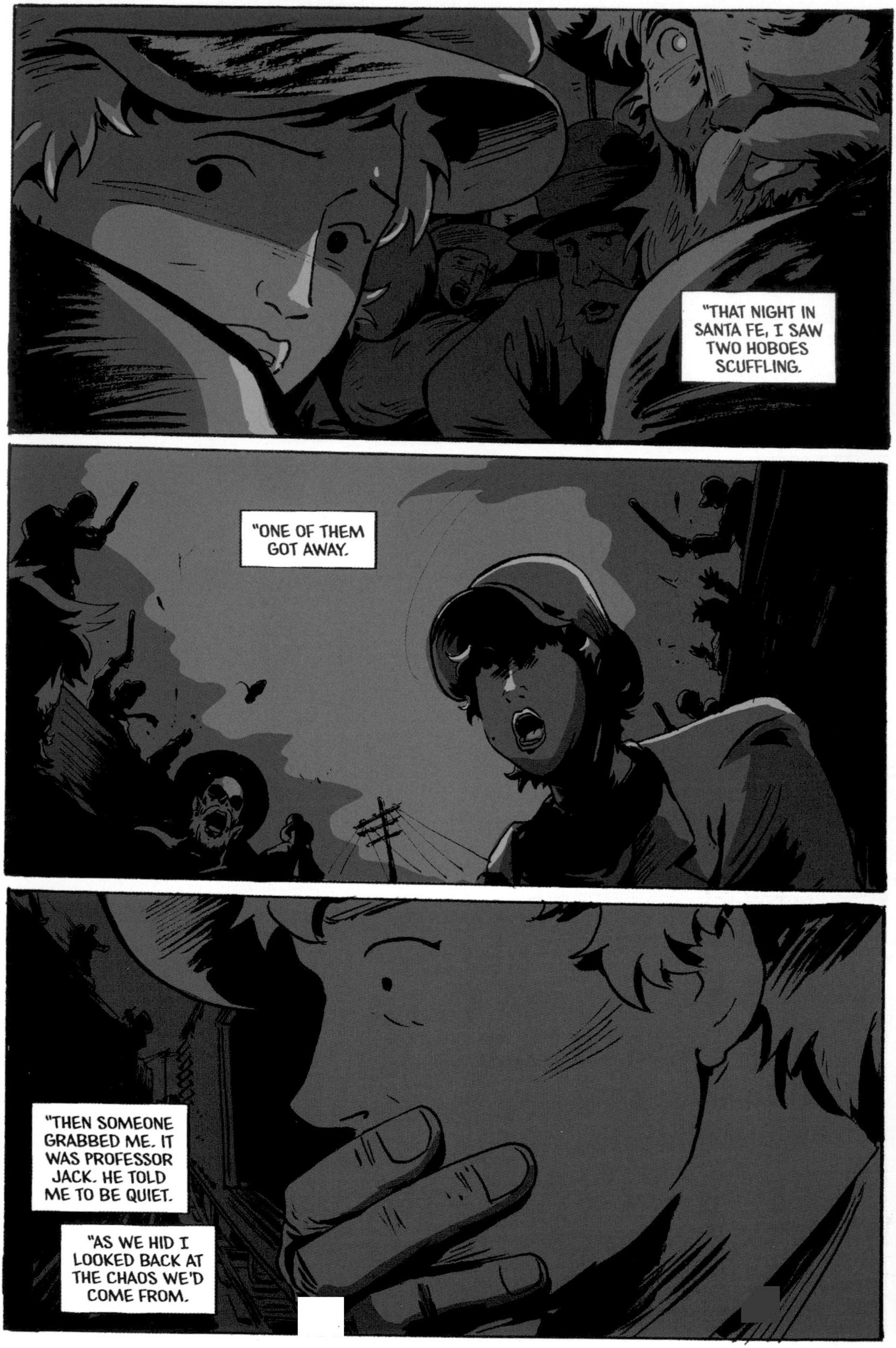
"THAT NIGHT IN SANTA FE, I SAW TWO HOBOES SCUFFLING.
"ONE OF THEM GOT AWAY.
"THEN SOMEONE GRABBED ME. IT WAS PROFESSOR JACK. HE TOLD ME TO BE QUIET.
"AS WE HID I LOOKED BACK AT THE CHAOS WE'D COME FROM.

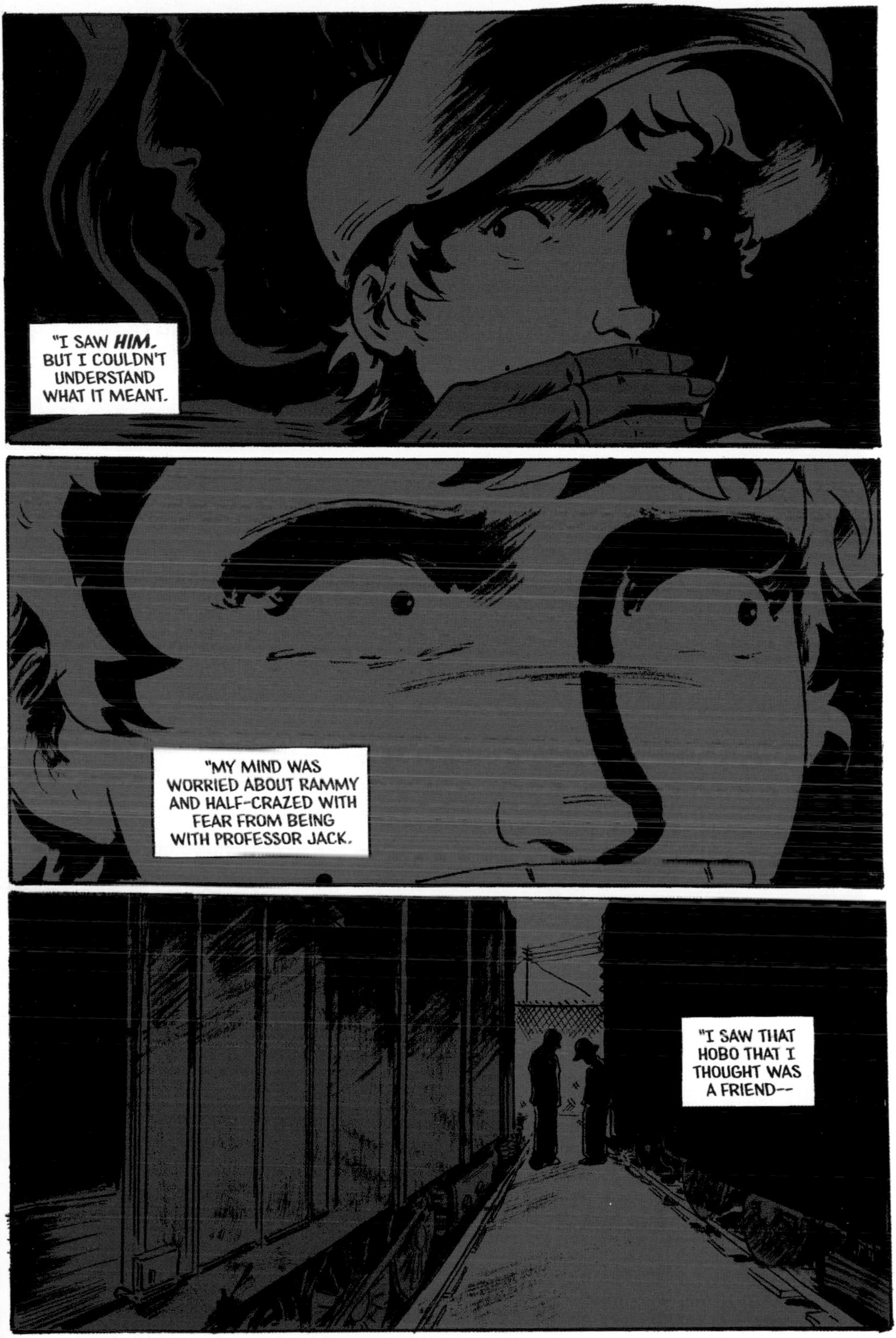
"I SAW HIM. BUT I COULDN'T UNDERSTAND WHAT IT MEANT.
"MY MIND WAS WORRIED ABOUT RAMMY AND HALF-CRAZED WITH FEAR FROM BEING WITH PROFESSOR JACK.
"I SAW THAT HOBO THAT I THOUGHT WAS A FRIEND--

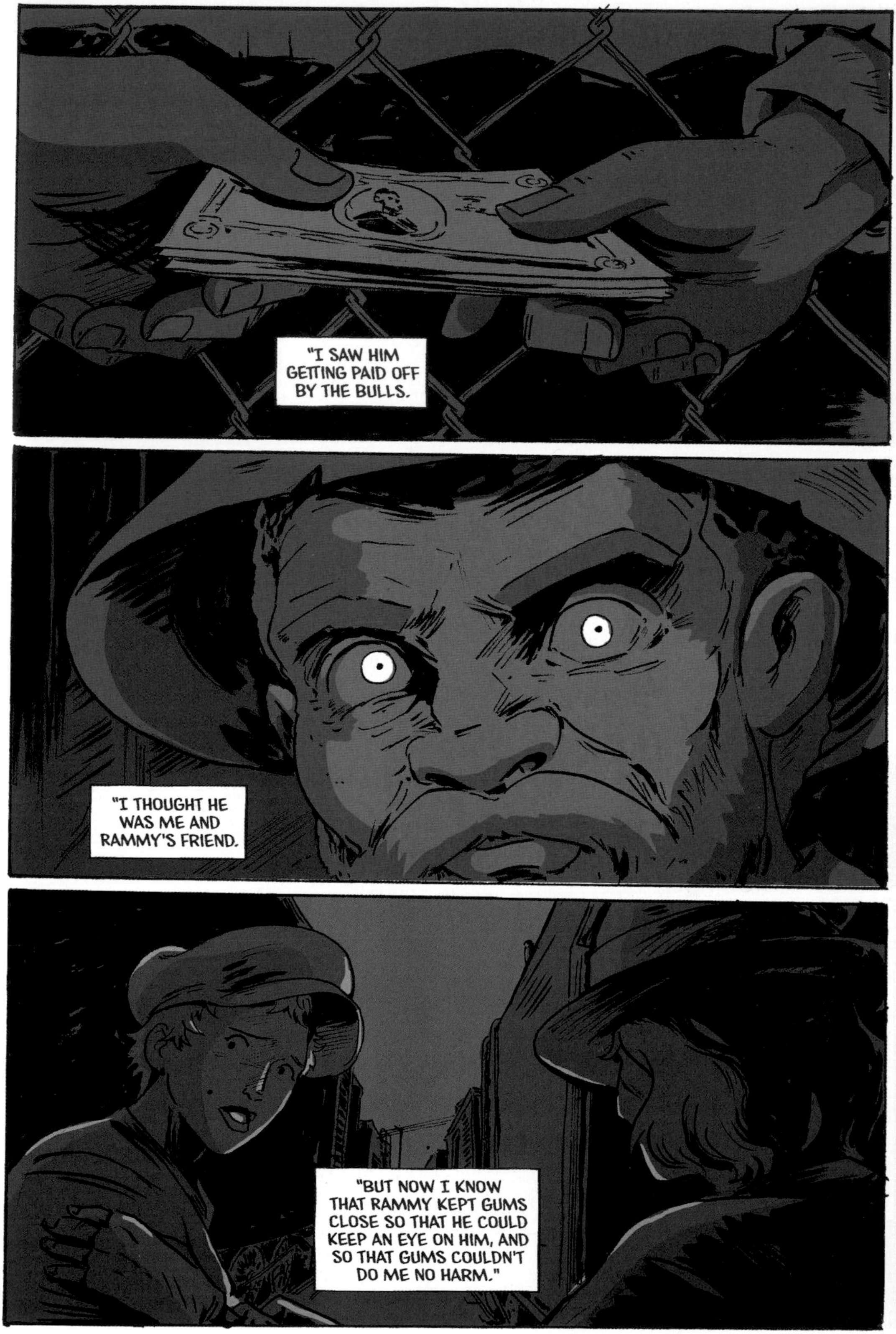
"I SAW HIM GETTING PAID OFF BY THE BULLS.
"I THOUGHT HE WAS ME AND RAMMY'S FRIEND.
"BUT NOW I KNOW THAT RAMMY KEPT GUMS CLOSE SO THAT HE COULD KEEP AN EYE ON HIM, AND SO THAT GUMS COULDN'T DO ME NO HARM."

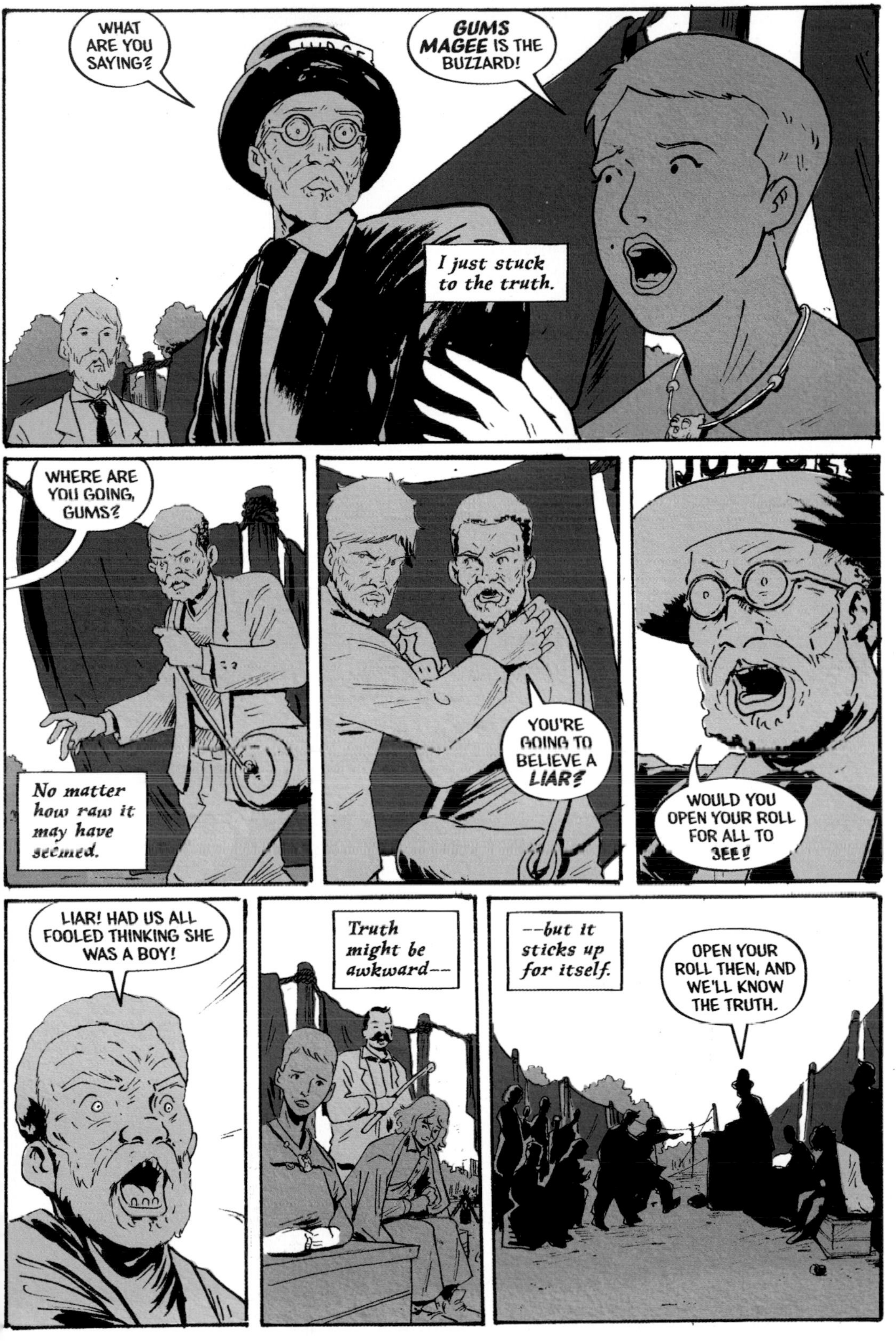
WHAT ARE YOU SAYING?
GUMS MAGEE IS THE BUZZARD!
I just stuck to the truth.
WHERE ARE YOU GOING, GUMS?
No matter how raw it may have seemed.
YOU'RE GOING TO BELIEVE A LIAR?
WOULD YOU OPEN YOUR ROLL FOR ALL TO SEE!
LIAR! HAD US ALL FOOLED THINKING SHE WAS A BOY!
Truth might be awkward--
--but it sticks up for itself.
OPEN YOUR ROLL THEN, AND WE'LL KNOW THE TRUTH.

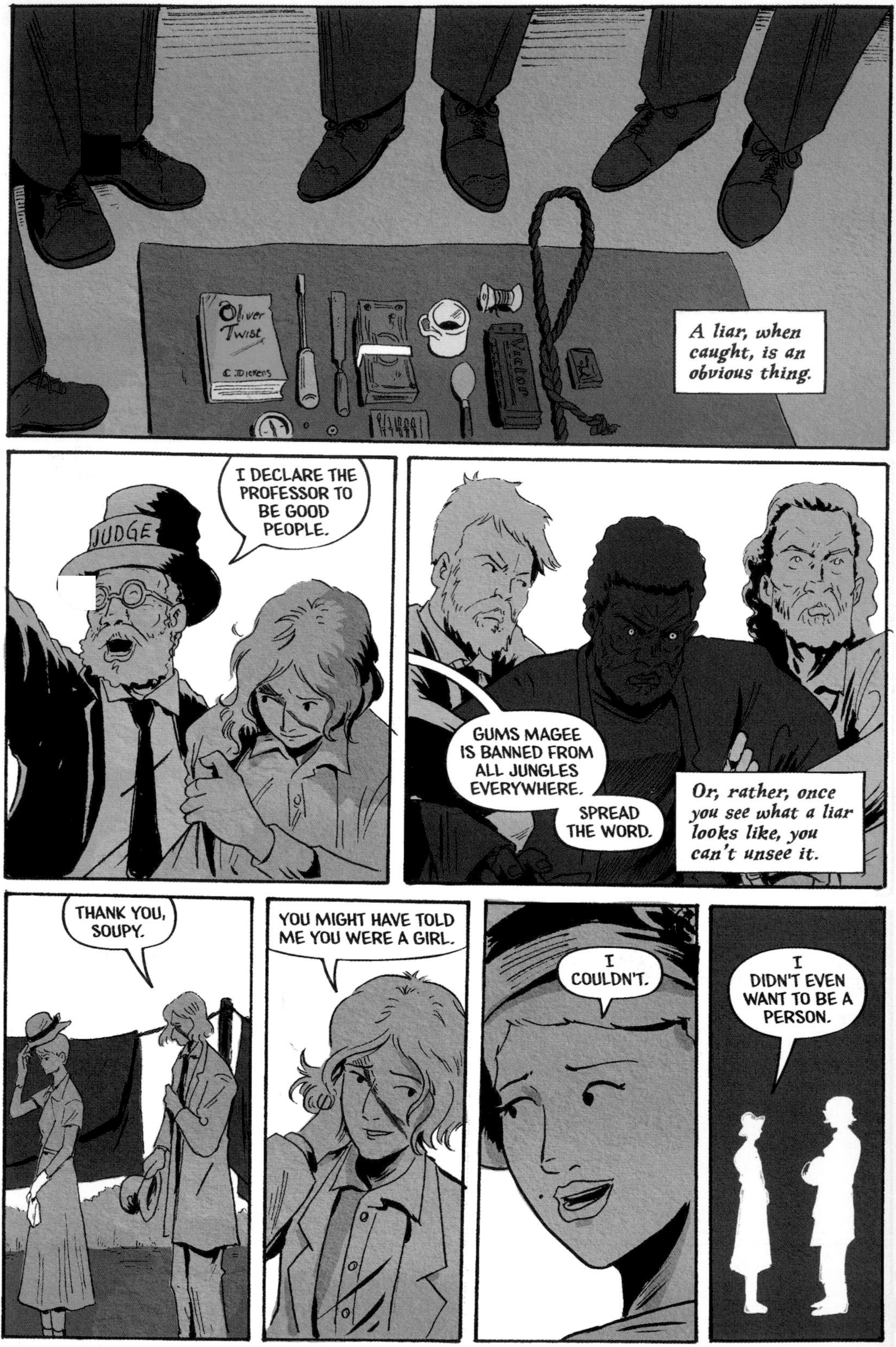
Oliver Twist
C. Dickens
A liar, when caught, is an obvious thing.
JUDGE
I DECLARE THE PROFESSOR TO BE GOOD PEOPLE.
GUMS MAGEE IS BANNED FROM ALL JUNGLES EVERYWHERE.
SPREAD THE WORD.
Or, rather, once you see what a liar looks like, you can't unsee it.
THANK YOU, SOUPY.
YOU MIGHT HAVE TOLD ME YOU WERE A GIRL.
I COULDN'T.
I DIDN'T EVEN WANT TO BE A PERSON.

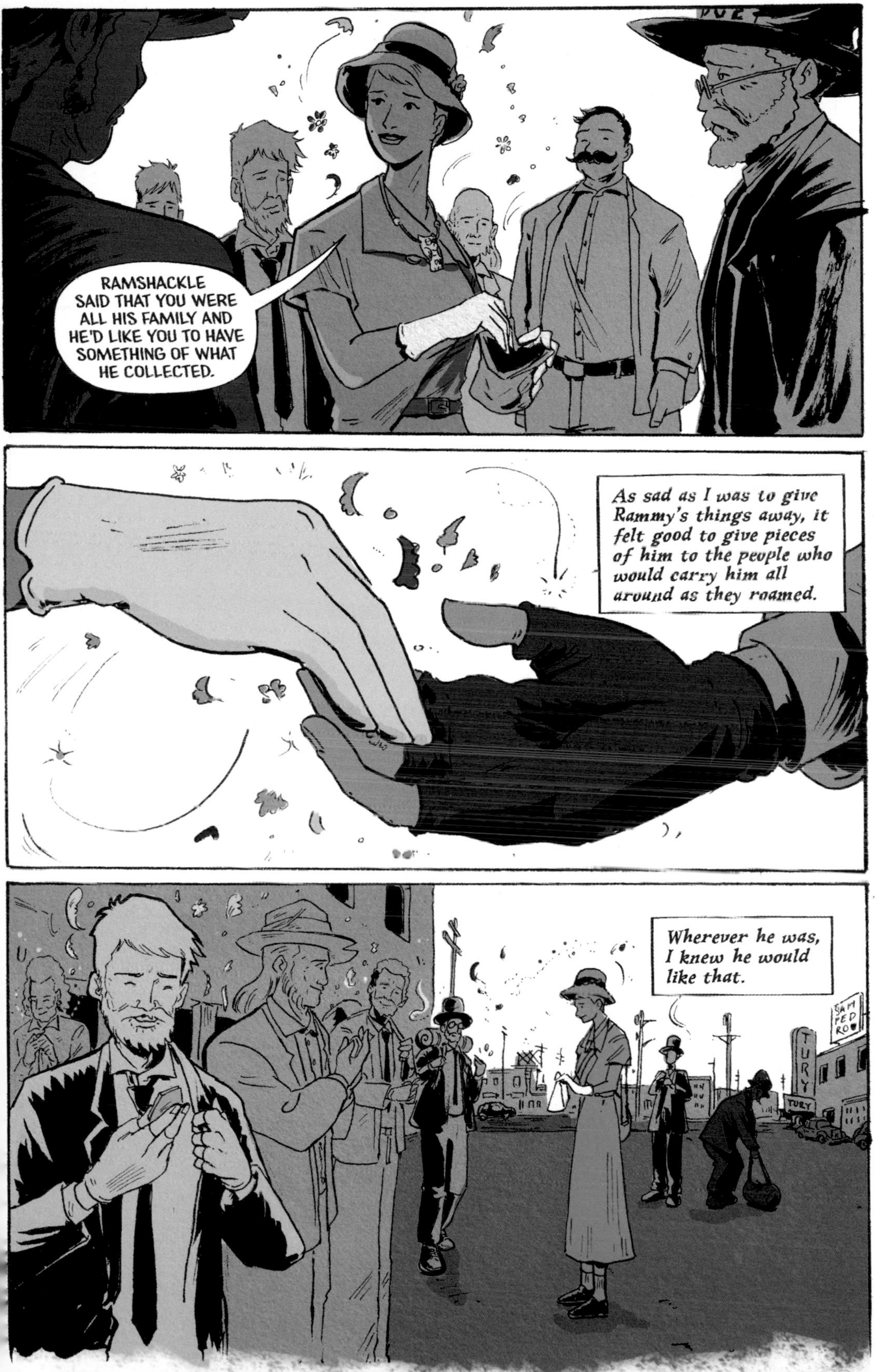
RAMSHACKLE SAID THAT YOU WERE ALL HIS FAMILY AND HE'D LIKE YOU TO HAVE SOMETHING OF WHAT HE COLLECTED.
As sad as I was to give Rammy's things away, it felt good to give pieces of him to the people who would carry him all around as they roamed.
Wherever he was, I knew he would like that.
SAN PEDRO
TURY
TURY

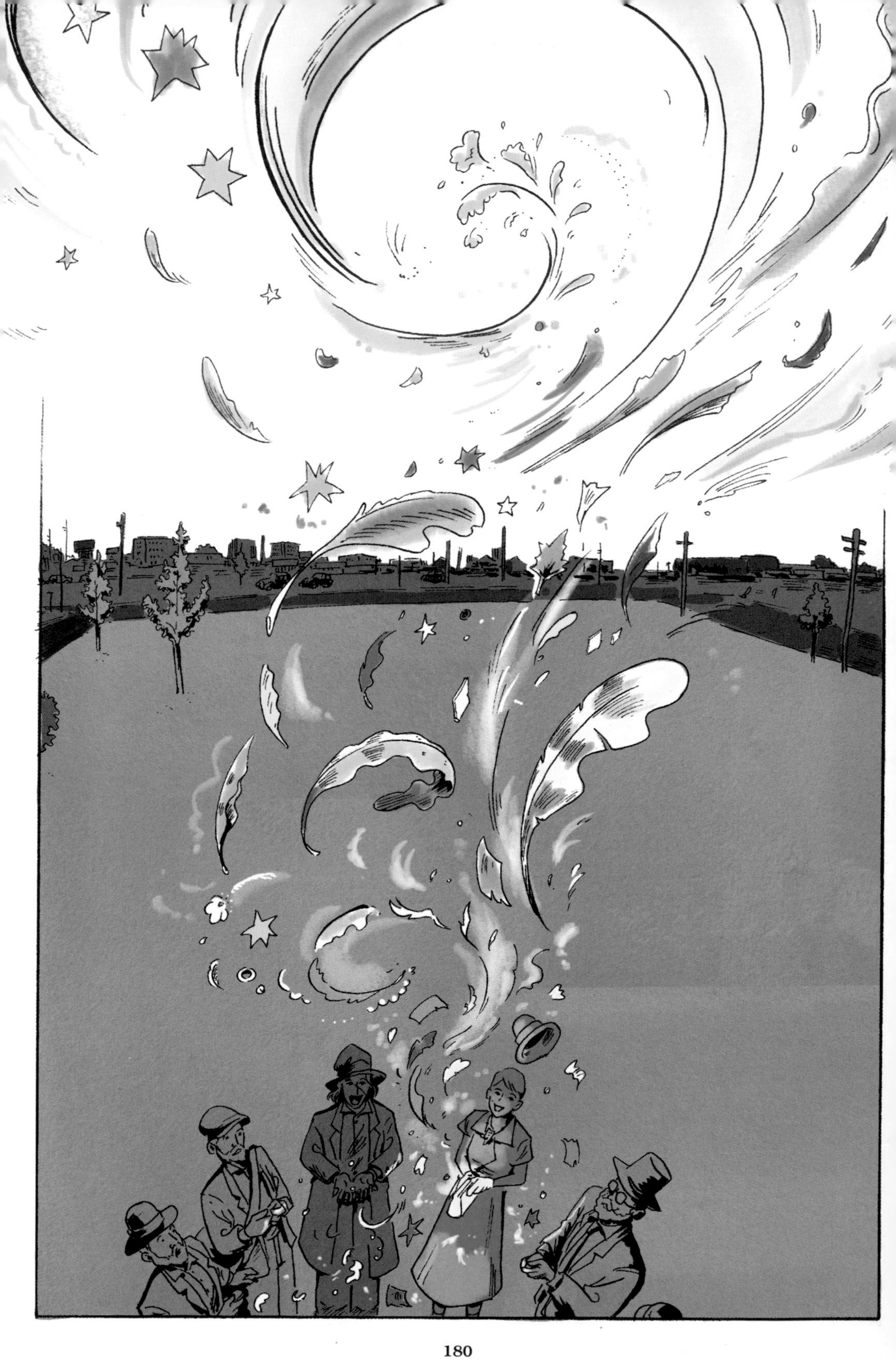

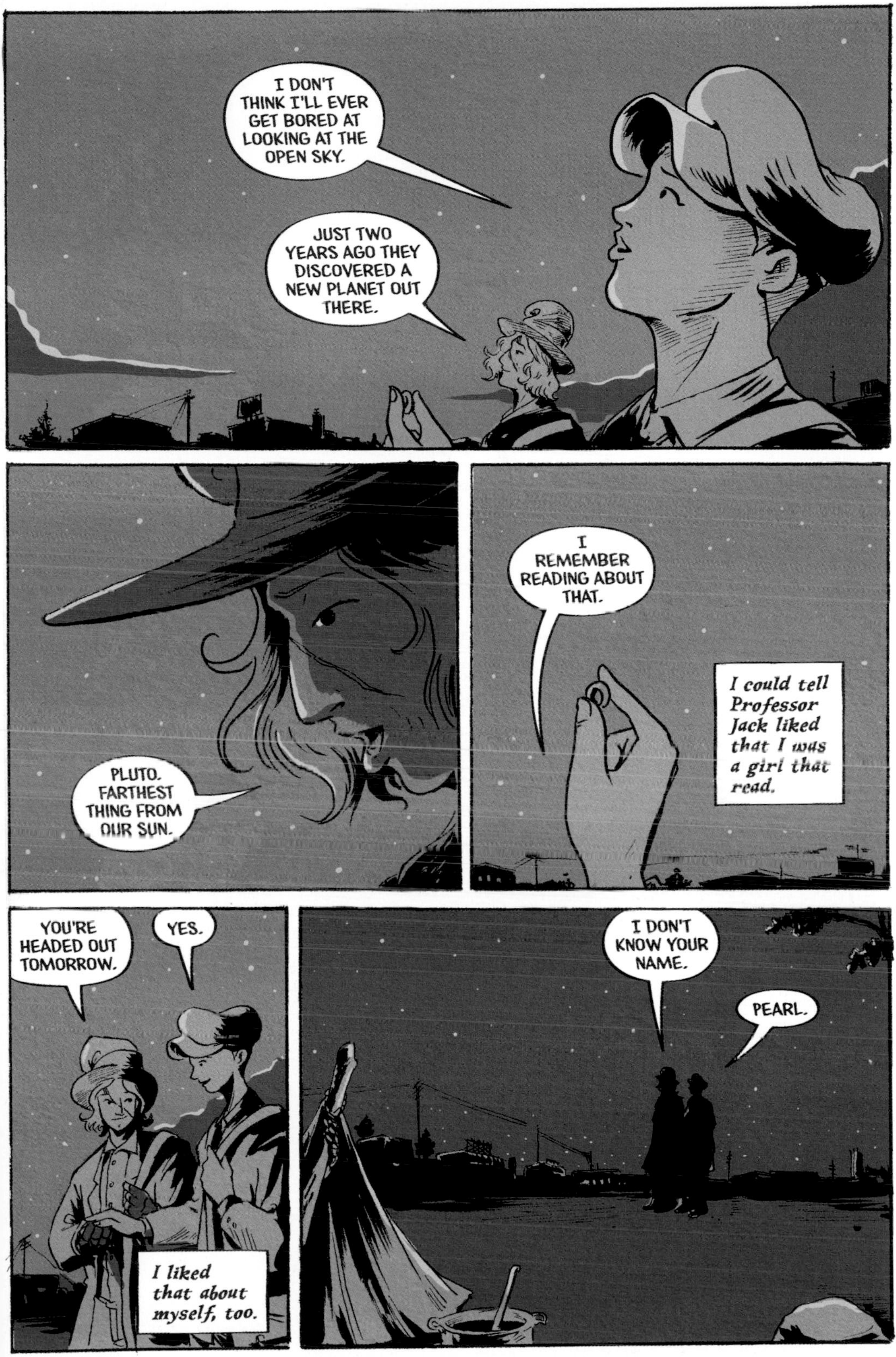
I DON'T THINK I'LL EVER GET BORED AT LOOKING AT THE OPEN SKY.
JUST TWO YEARS AGO THEY DISCOVERED A NEW PLANET OUT THERE.
PLUTO. FARTHEST THING FROM OUR SUN.
I REMEMBER READING ABOUT THAT.
I could tell Professor Jack liked that I was a girl that read.
YOU'RE HEADED OUT TOMORROW.
YES.
I liked that about myself, too.
I DON'T KNOW YOUR NAME.
PEARL.

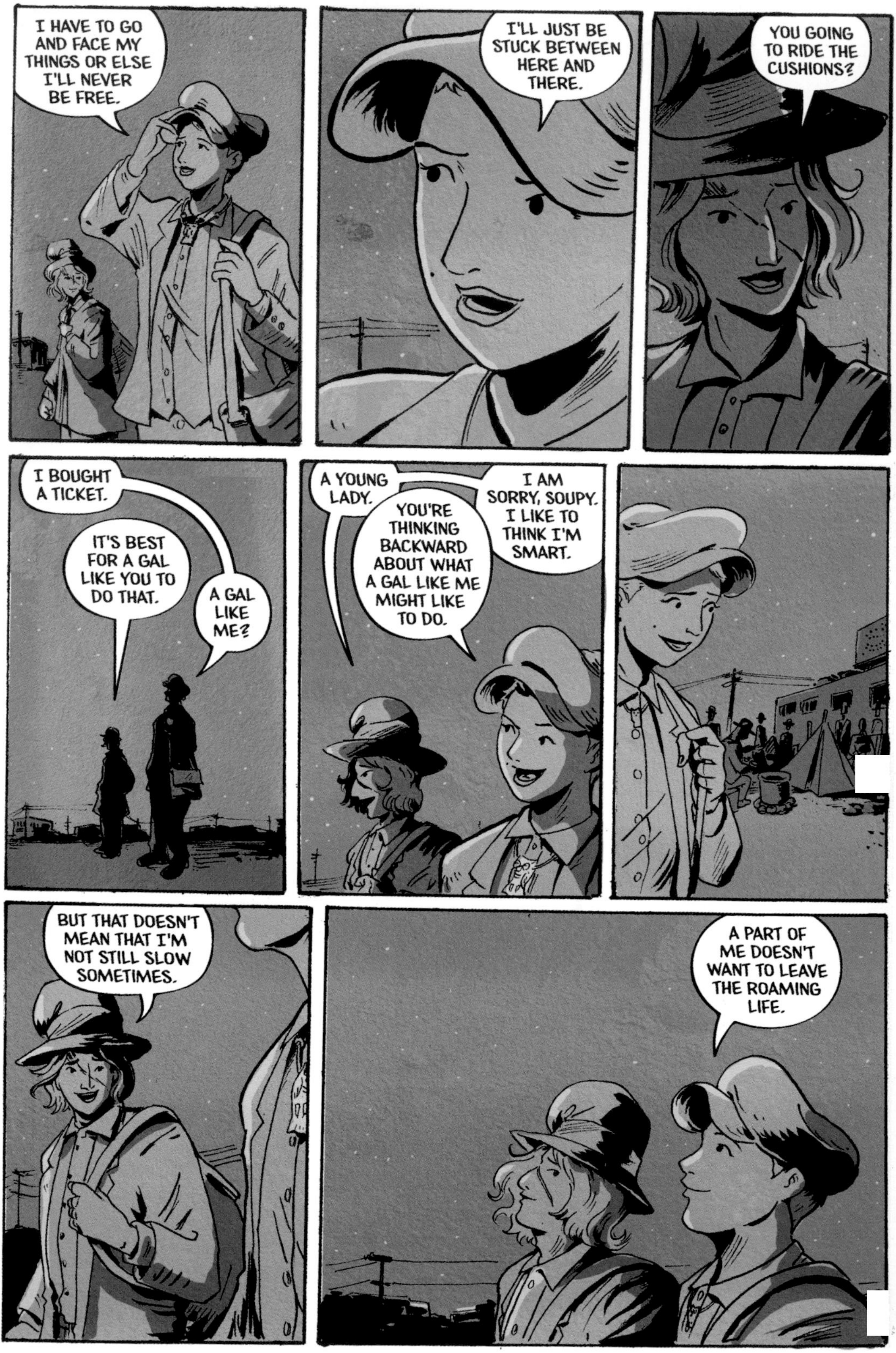
I HAVE TO GO AND FACE MY THINGS OR ELSE I'LL NEVER BE FREE.
I'LL JUST BE STUCK BETWEEN HERE AND THERE.
YOU GOING TO RIDE THE CUSHIONS?
I BOUGHT A TICKET.
IT'S BEST FOR A GAL LIKE YOU TO DO THAT.
A GAL LIKE ME?
A YOUNG LADY.
YOU'RE THINKING BACKWARD ABOUT WHAT A GAL LIKE ME MIGHT LIKE TO DO.
I AM SORRY, SOUPY. I LIKE TO THINK I'M SMART.
BUT THAT DOESN'T MEAN THAT I'M NOT STILL SLOW SOMETIMES.
A PART OF ME DOESN'T WANT TO LEAVE THE ROAMING LIFE.

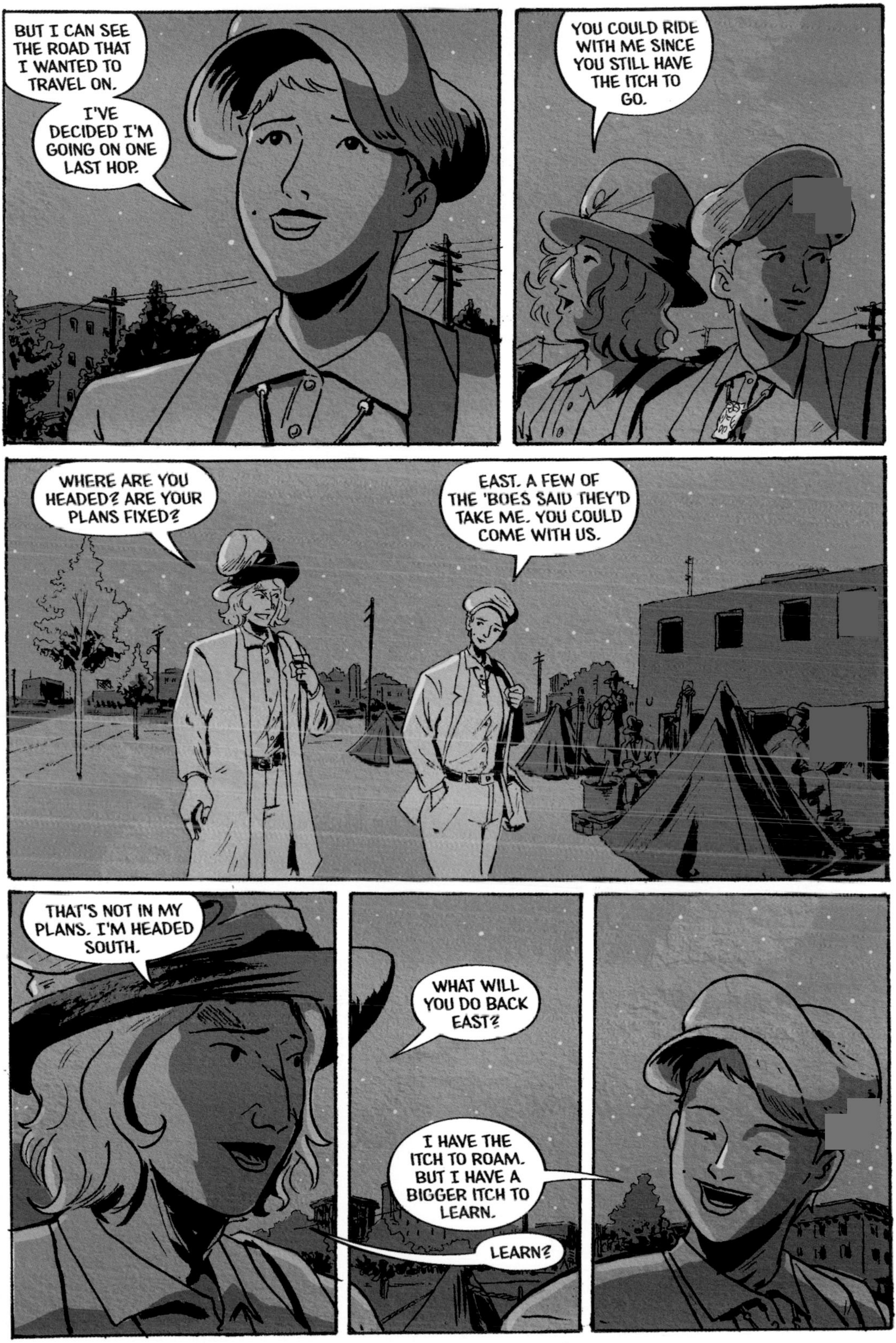
BUT I CAN SEE THE ROAD THAT I WANTED TO TRAVEL ON.
I'VE DECIDED I'M GOING ON ONE LAST HOP.
YOU COULD RIDE WITH ME SINCE YOU STILL HAVE THE ITCH TO GO.
WHERE ARE YOU HEADED? ARE YOUR PLANS FIXED?
EAST. A FEW OF THE 'BOES SAID THEY'D TAKE ME. YOU COULD COME WITH US.
THAT'S NOT IN MY PLANS. I'M HEADED SOUTH.
WHAT WILL YOU DO BACK EAST?
I HAVE THE ITCH TO ROAM. BUT I HAVE A BIGGER ITCH TO LEARN.
LEARN?

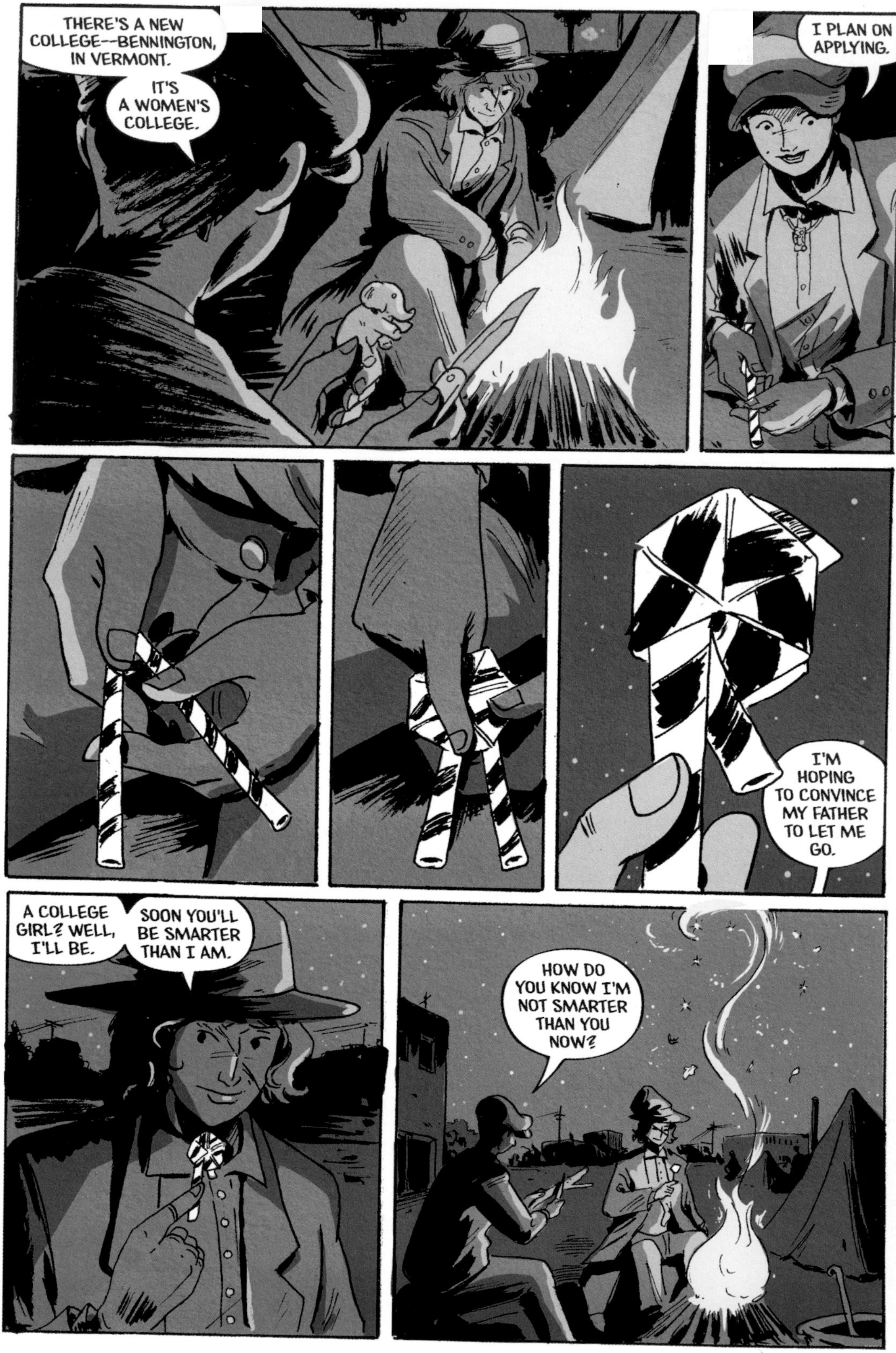
THERE'S A NEW COLLEGE--BENNINGTON, IN VERMONT.
IT'S A WOMEN'S COLLEGE.
I PLAN ON APPLYING.
I'M HOPING TO CONVINCE MY FATHER TO LET ME GO.
A COLLEGE GIRL? WELL, I'LL BE.
SOON YOU'LL BE SMARTER THAN I AM.
HOW DO YOU KNOW I'M NOT SMARTER THAN YOU NOW?

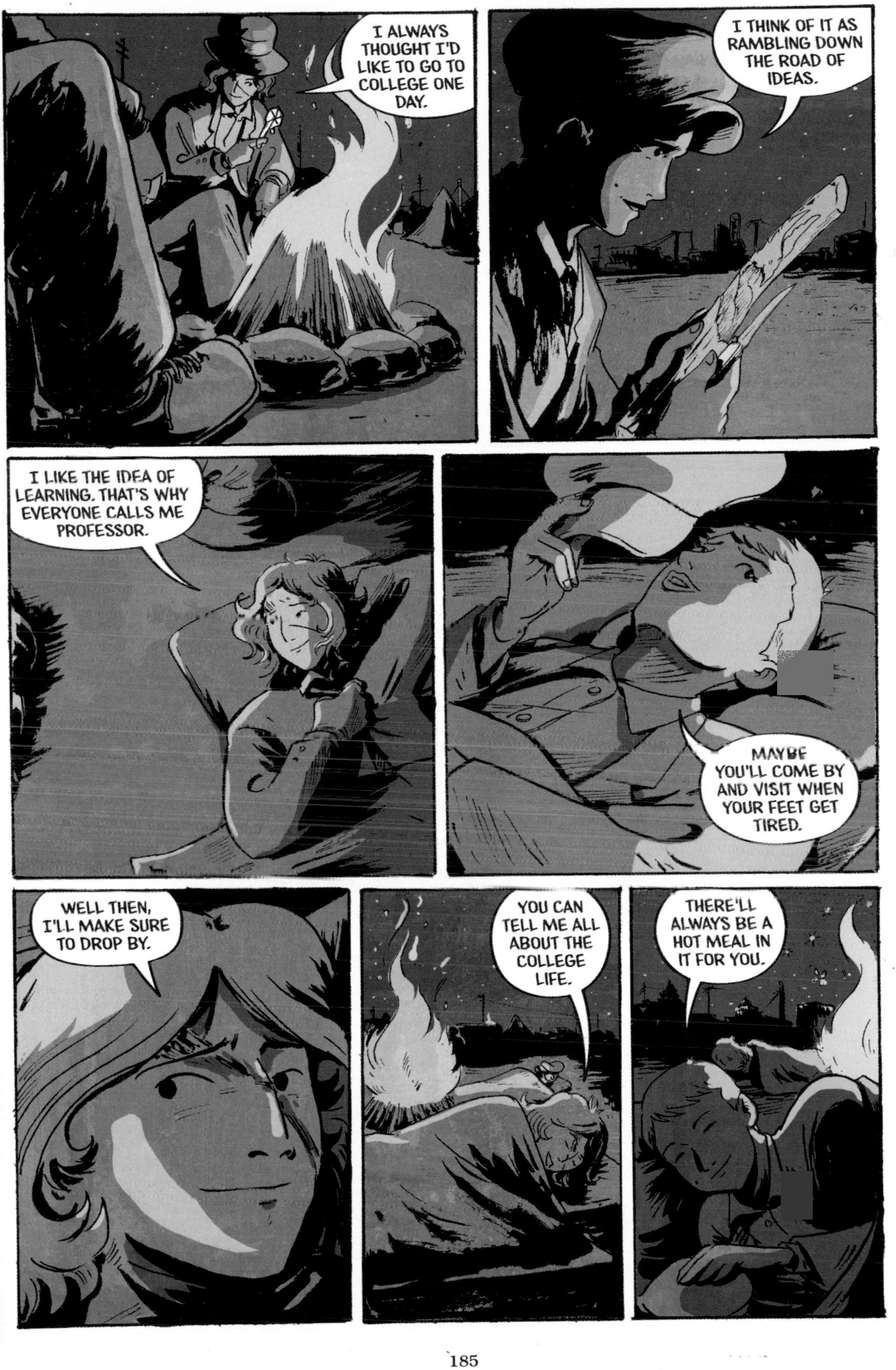
I ALWAYS THOUGHT I'D LIKE TO GO TO COLLEGE ONE DAY.
I THINK OF IT AS RAMBLING DOWN THE ROAD OF IDEAS.
I LIKE THE IDEA OF LEARNING. THAT'S WHY EVERYONE CALLS ME PROFESSOR.
MAYBE YOU'LL COME BY AND VISIT WHEN YOUR FEET GET TIRED.
WELL THEN, I'LL MAKE SURE TO DROP BY.
YOU CAN TELL ME ALL ABOUT THE COLLEGE LIFE.
THERE'LL ALWAYS BE A HOT MEAL IN IT FOR YOU.

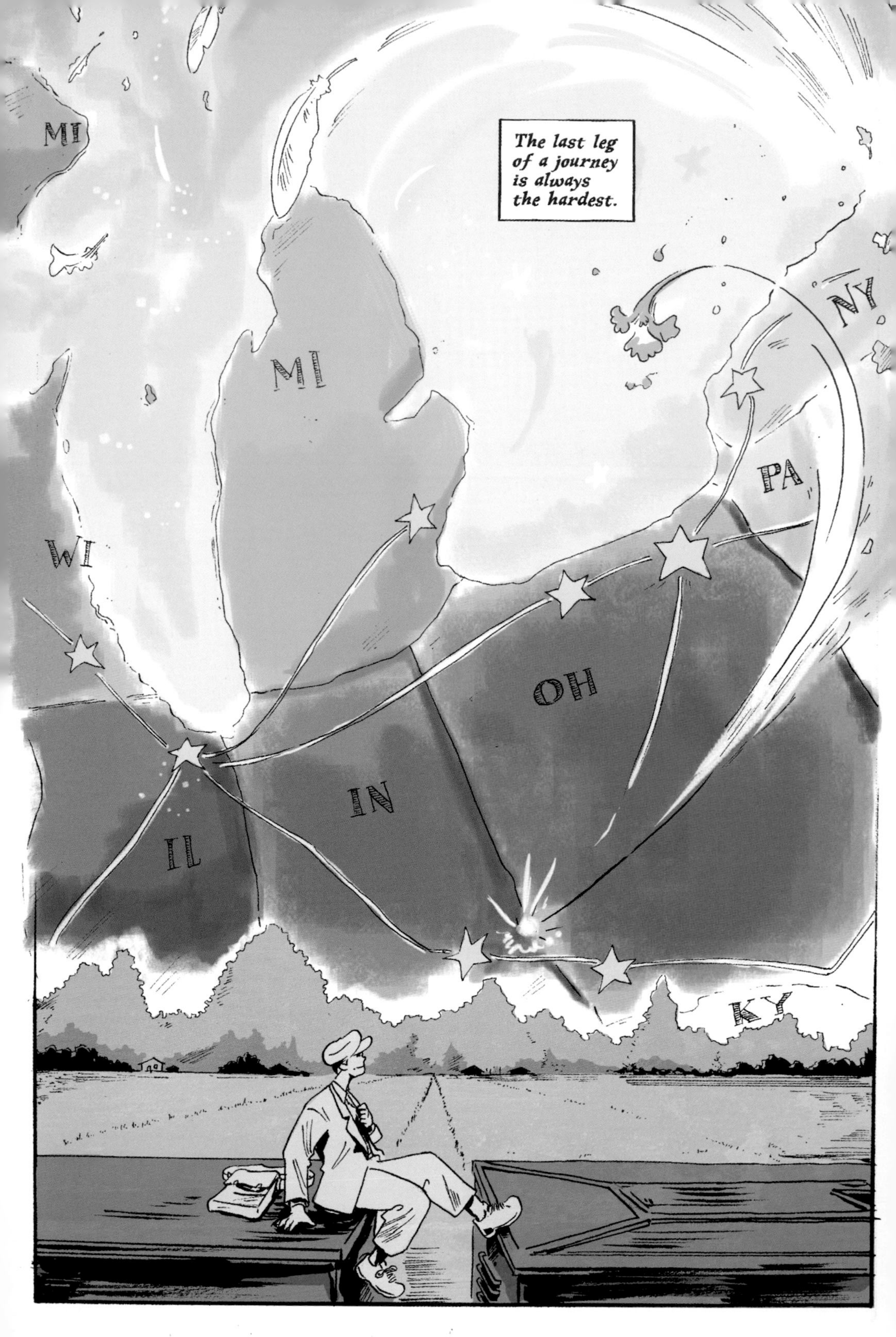
The last leg
of a journey
is always
the hardest.
MI
MI
WI
NY
PA
OH
IN
IL
KY

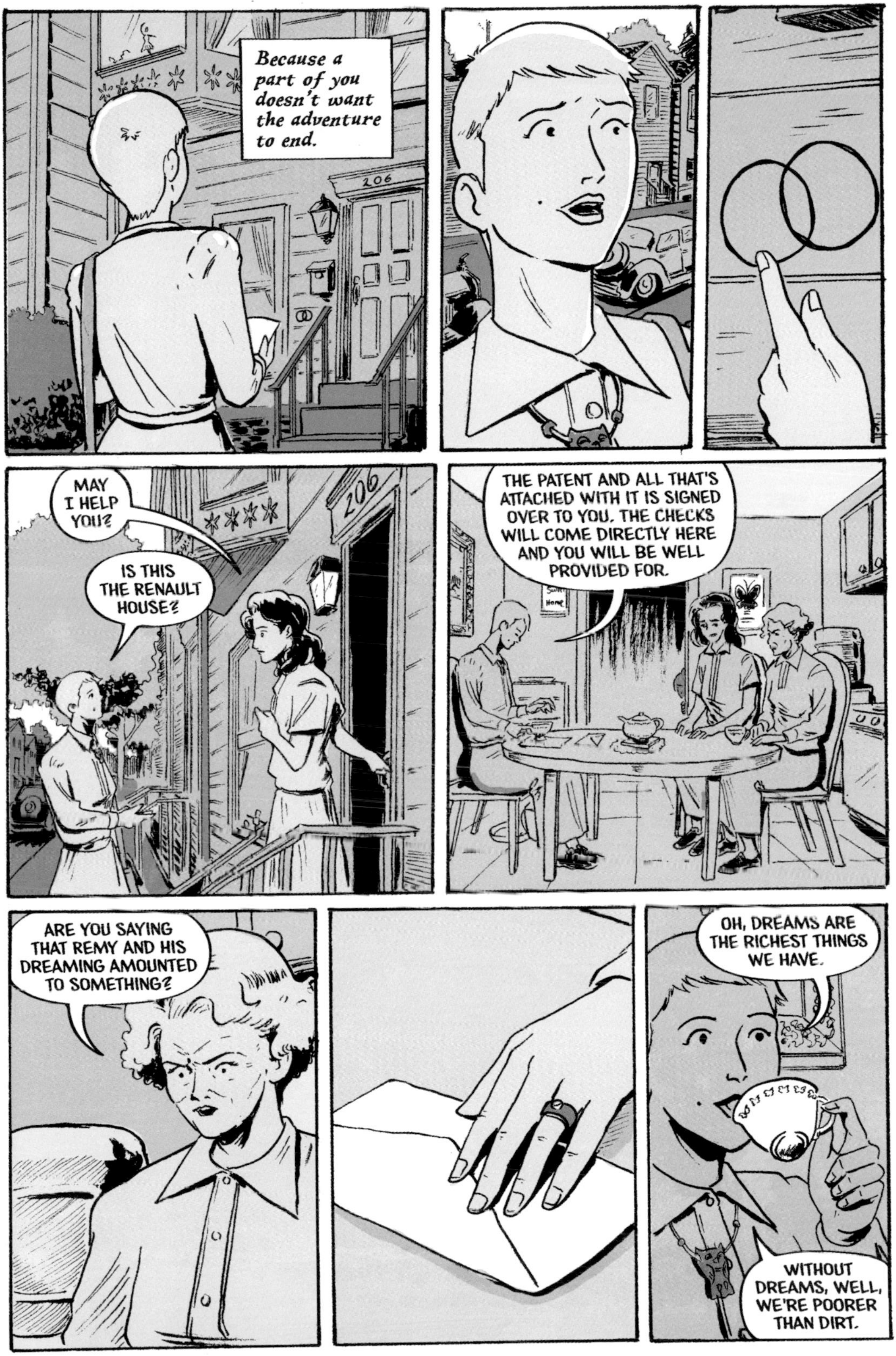
Because a part of you doesn't want the adventure to end.
206
MAY I HELP YOU?
IS THIS THE RENAULT HOUSE?
206
THE PATENT AND ALL THAT'S ATTACHED WITH IT IS SIGNED OVER TO YOU. THE CHECKS WILL COME DIRECTLY HERE AND YOU WILL BE WELL PROVIDED FOR.
ARE YOU SAYING THAT REMY AND HIS DREAMING AMOUNTED TO SOMETHING?
OH, DREAMS ARE THE RICHEST THINGS WE HAVE.
WITHOUT DREAMS, WELL, WE'RE POORER THAN DIRT.

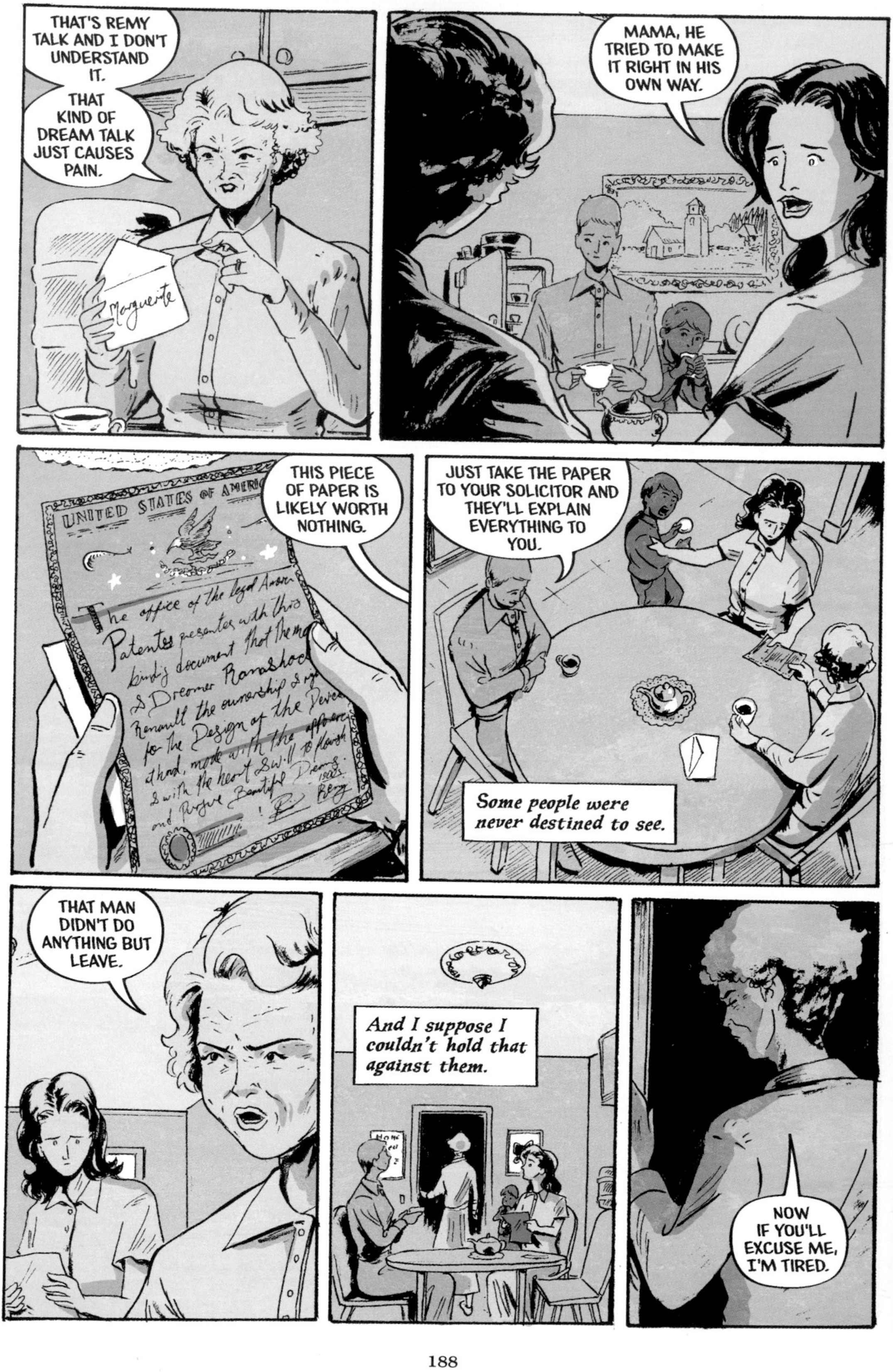
THAT'S REMY TALK AND I DON'T UNDERSTAND IT.
THAT KIND OF DREAM TALK JUST CAUSES PAIN.
Marguerite
MAMA, HE TRIED TO MAKE IT RIGHT IN HIS OWN WAY.
THIS PIECE OF PAPER IS LIKELY WORTH NOTHING.
JUST TAKE THE PAPER TO YOUR SOLICITOR AND THEY'LL EXPLAIN EVERYTHING TO YOU.
Some people were never destined to see.
THAT MAN DIDN'T DO ANYTHING BUT LEAVE.
And I suppose I couldn't hold that against them.
NOW IF YOU'LL EXCUSE ME, I'M TIRED.

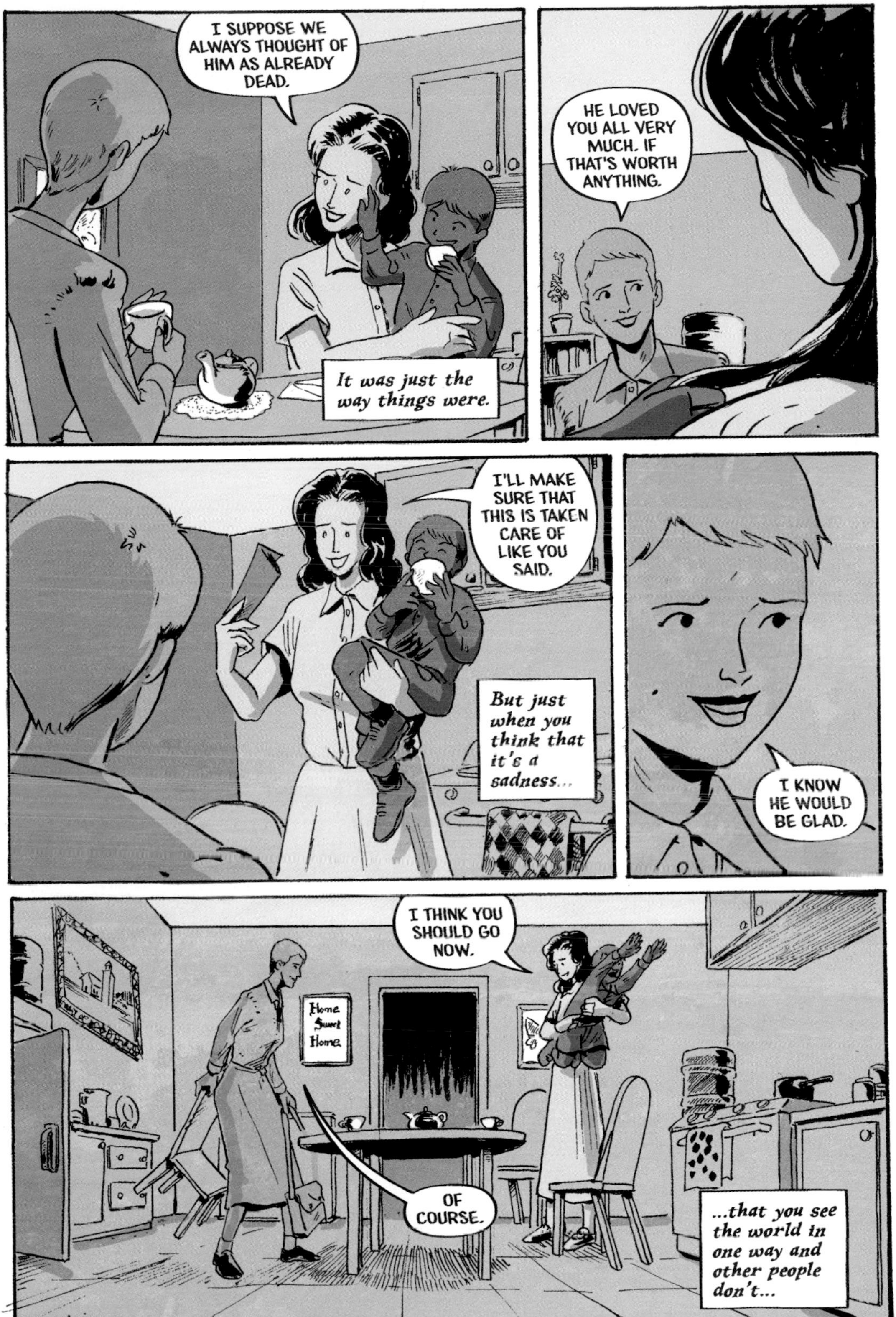

I SUPPOSE WE ALWAYS THOUGHT OF HIM AS ALREADY DEAD.
It was just the way things were.
HE LOVED YOU ALL VERY MUCH. IF THAT'S WORTH ANYTHING.
I'LL MAKE SURE THAT THIS IS TAKEN CARE OF LIKE YOU SAID.
But just when you think that it's a sadness...
I KNOW HE WOULD BE GLAD.
I THINK YOU SHOULD GO NOW.
Home Sweet Home
OF COURSE.
...that you see the world in one way and other people don't...

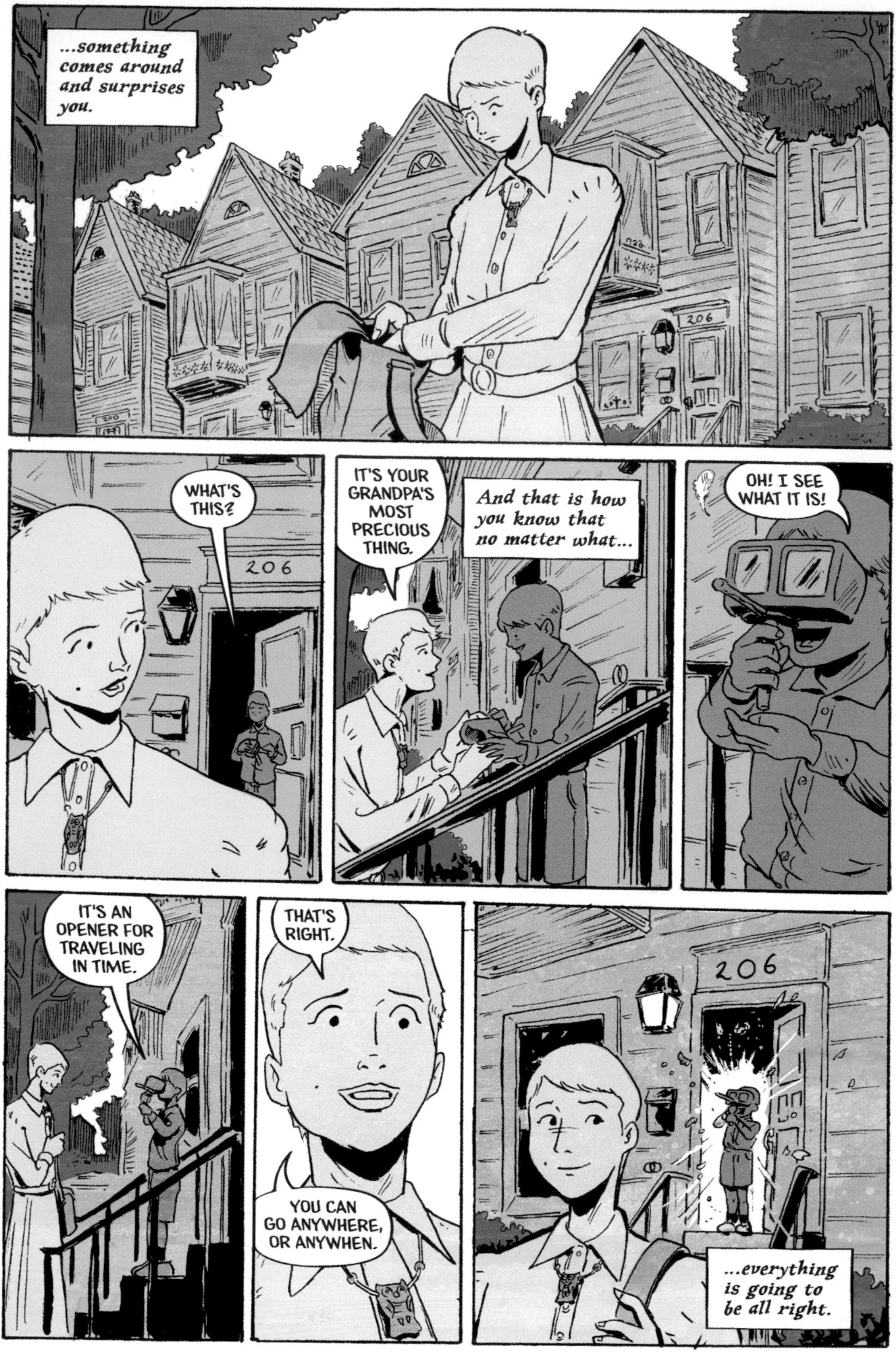
...something comes around and surprises you.
206
WHAT'S THIS?
206
IT'S YOUR GRANDPA'S MOST PRECIOUS THING.
And that is how you know that no matter what...
OH! I SEE WHAT IT IS!
IT'S AN OPENER FOR TRAVELING IN TIME.
THAT'S RIGHT.
YOU CAN GO ANYWHERE, OR ANYWHEN.
206
...everything is going to be all right.

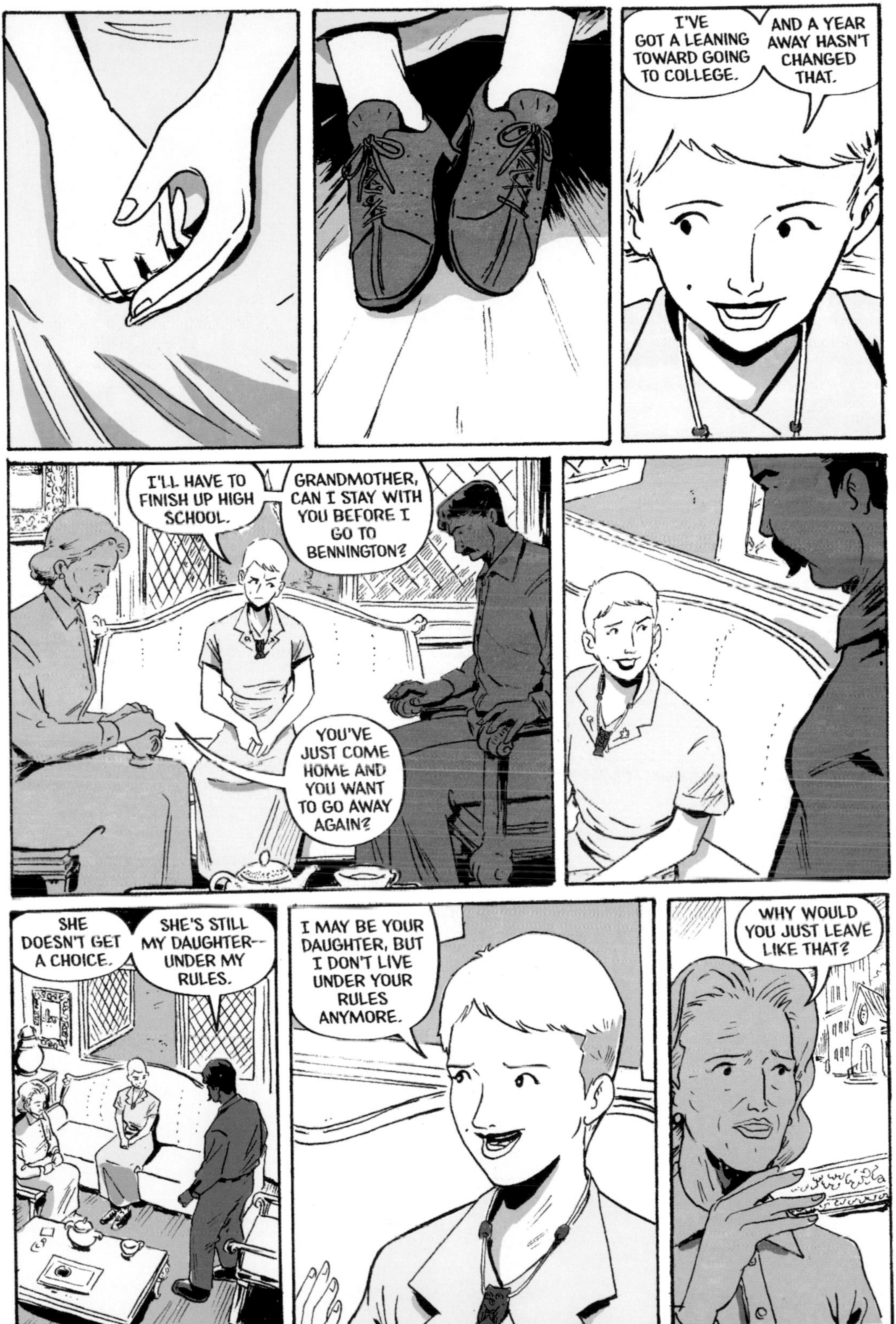
I'VE GOT A LEANING TOWARD GOING TO COLLEGE.
AND A YEAR AWAY HASN'T CHANGED THAT.
I'LL HAVE TO FINISH UP HIGH SCHOOL.
GRANDMOTHER, CAN I STAY WITH YOU BEFORE I GO TO BENNINGTON?
YOU'VE JUST COME HOME AND YOU WANT TO GO AWAY AGAIN?
SHE DOESN'T GET A CHOICE.
SHE'S STILL MY DAUGHTER-- UNDER MY RULES.
I MAY BE YOUR DAUGHTER, BUT I DON'T LIVE UNDER YOUR RULES ANYMORE.
WHY WOULD YOU JUST LEAVE LIKE THAT?

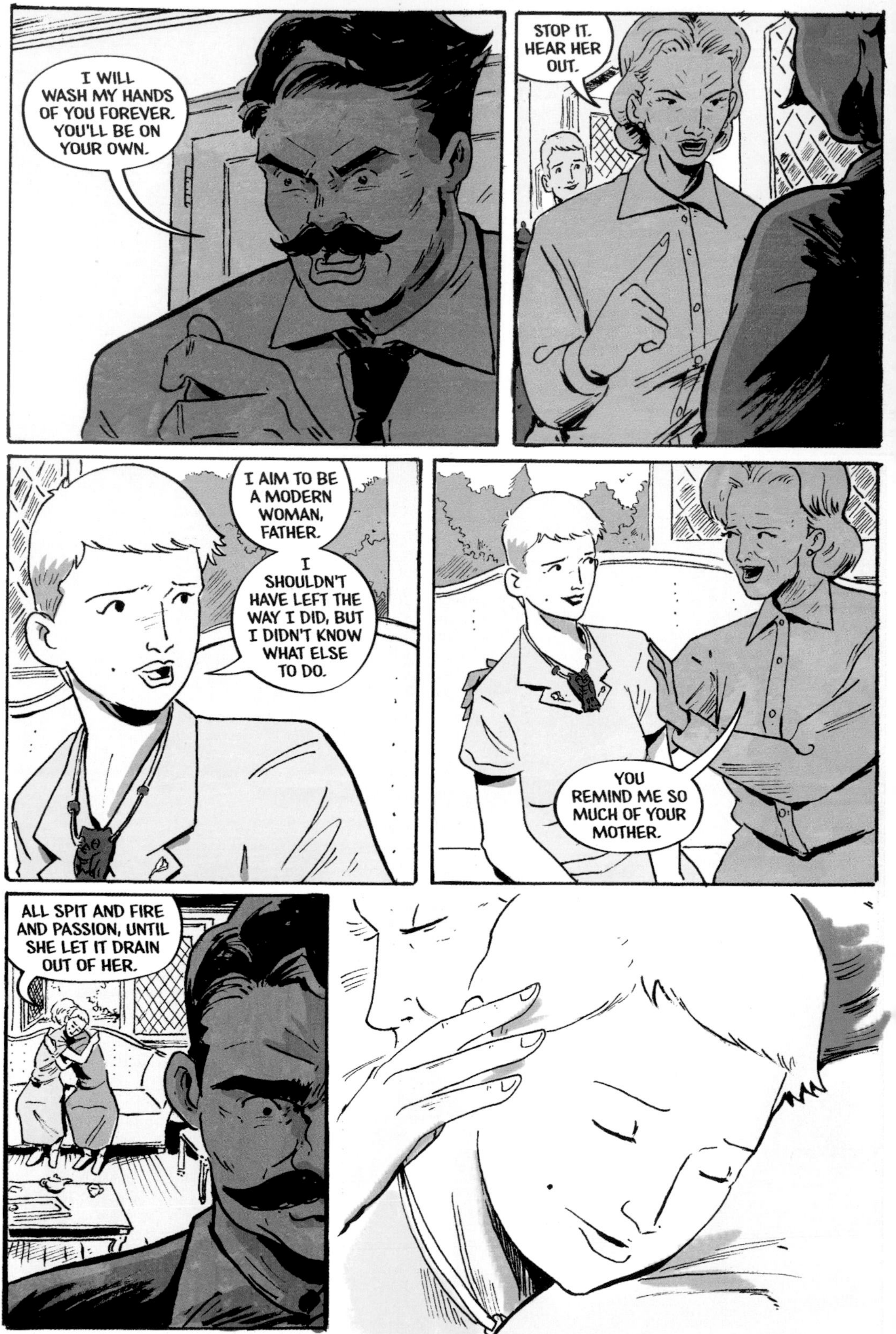
I WILL WASH MY HANDS OF YOU FOREVER. YOU'LL BE ON YOUR OWN.
STOP IT. HEAR HER OUT.
I AIM TO BE A MODERN WOMAN, FATHER.
I SHOULDN'T HAVE LEFT THE WAY I DID, BUT I DIDN'T KNOW WHAT ELSE TO DO.
YOU REMIND ME SO MUCH OF YOUR MOTHER.
ALL SPIT AND FIRE AND PASSION, UNTIL SHE LET IT DRAIN OUT OF HER.

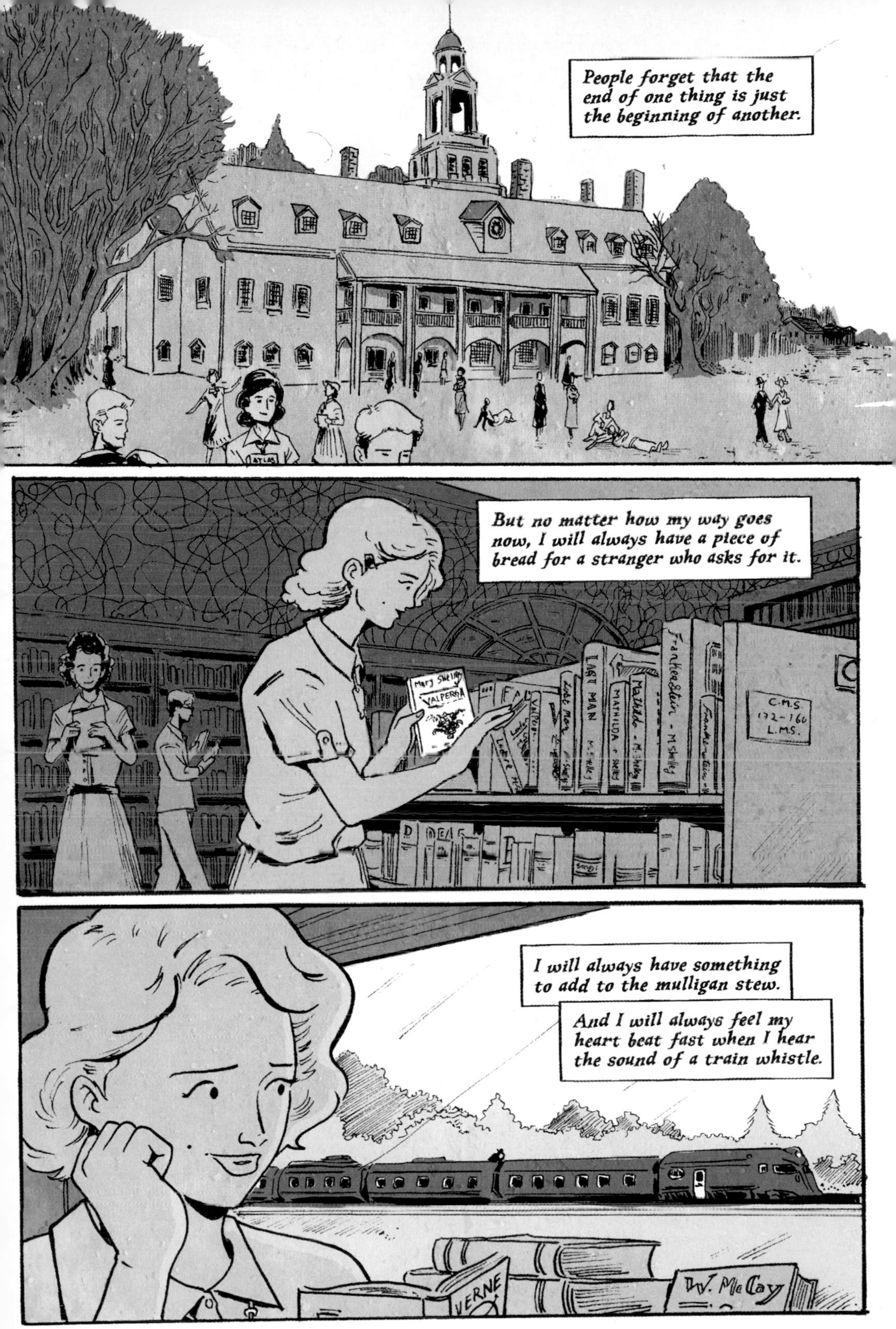
People forget that the end of one thing is just the beginning of another.
But no matter how my way goes now, I will always have a piece of bread for a stranger who asks for it.
I will always have something to add to the mulligan stew.
And I will always feel my heart beat fast when I hear the sound of a train whistle.
VERNE
W. McCay

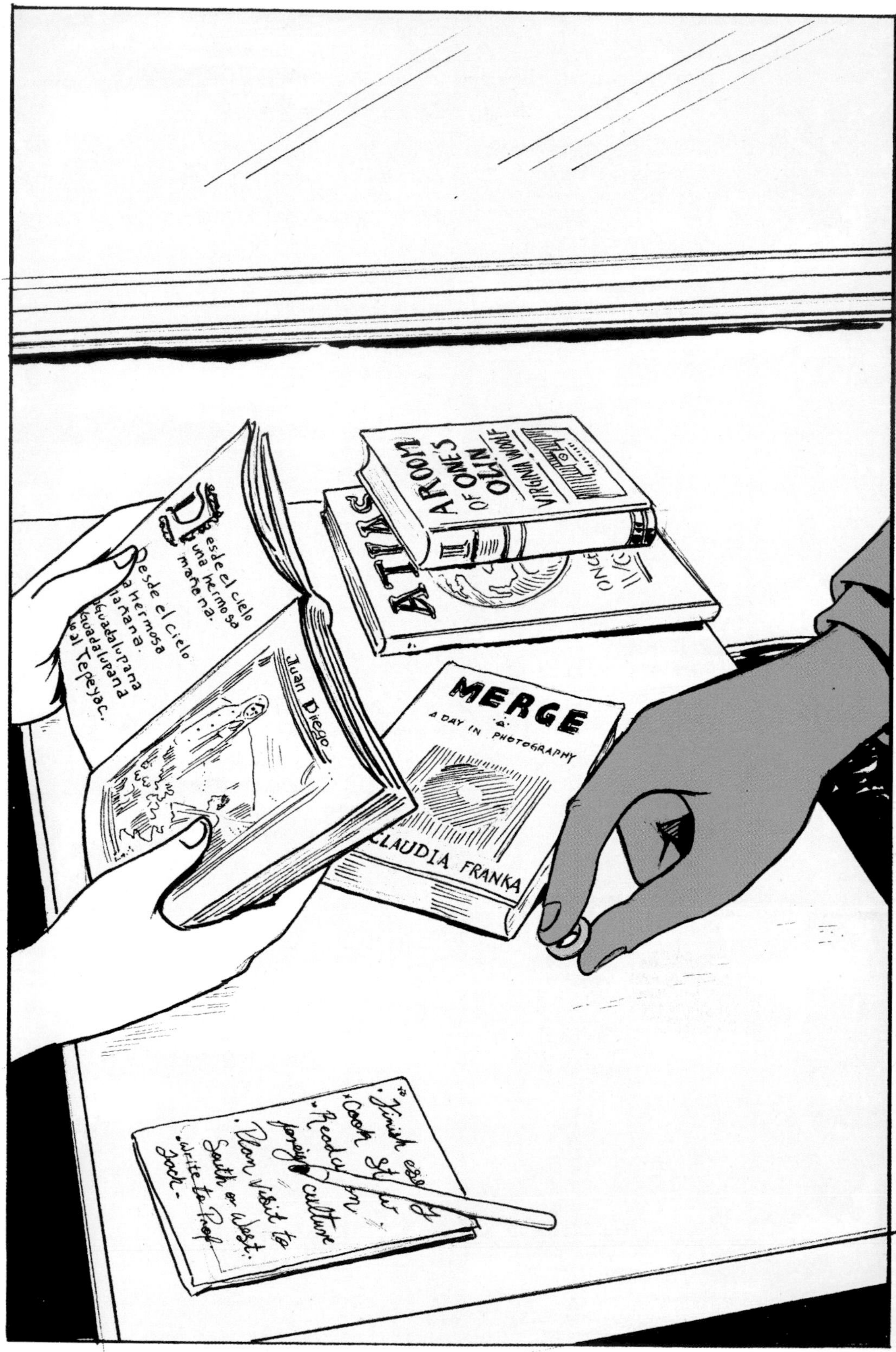
Desde el cielo una hermosa mañana.
Juan Diego
A ROOM OF ONE'S OWN
VIRGINIA WOOLF
ATLAS
MERGE
A DAY IN PHOTOGRAPHY
CLAUDIA FRANKA
Cook stew
culture
Plan visit to
South or West.
write to Prof.
Jack-

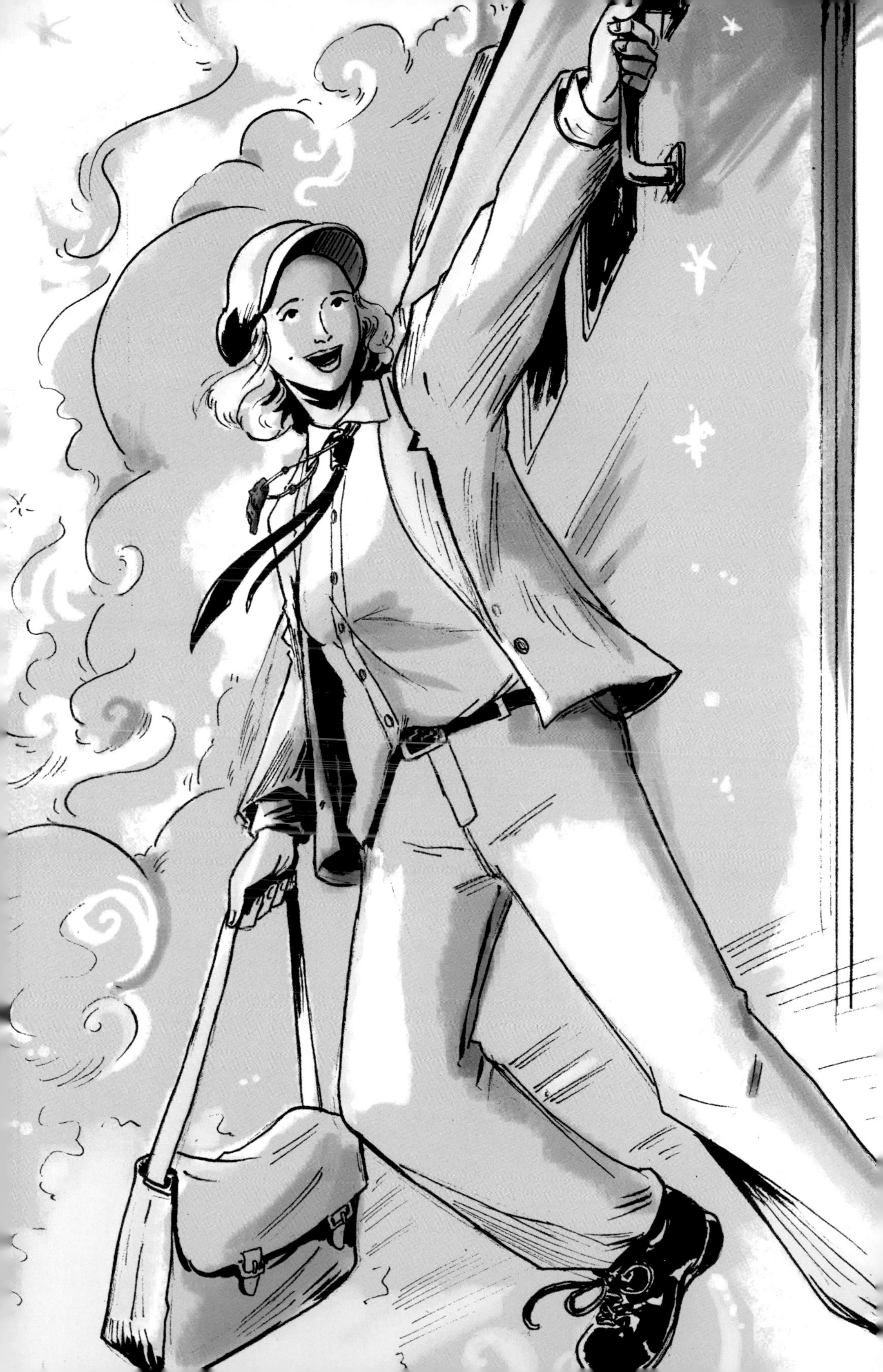

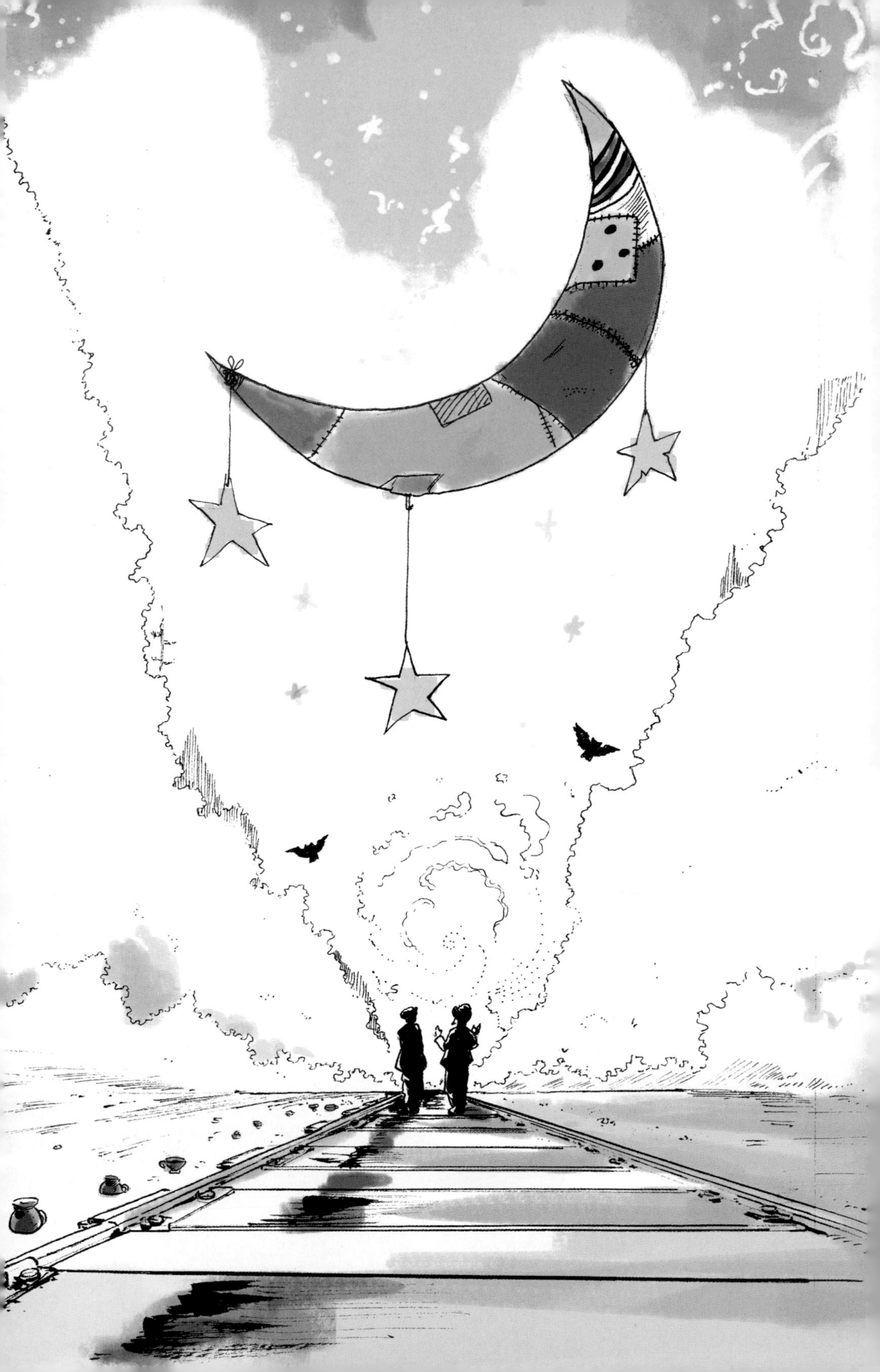

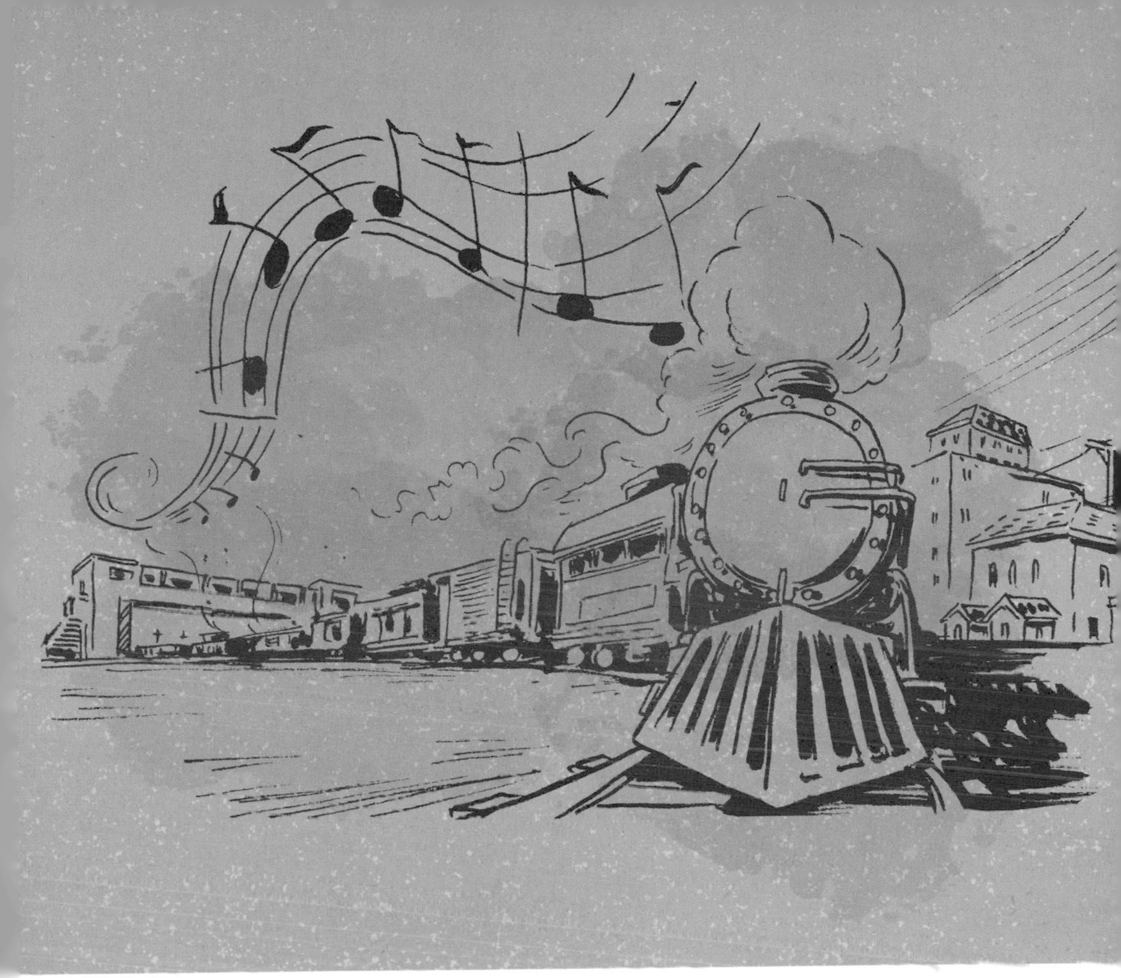

SOUPY AND THE RAILS LEADING HOME

Soupy's journey took her all across the United States of America—riding trains from upstate New York down to Pennsylvania, North Carolina, and South Carolina. She then traveled farther south to Louisiana and all along the southern border until she reached Los Angeles, California.

After reaching the west coast and discovering her truth, Soupy begins on a new path . . . traveling the rails once again to Chicago, Illinois and to her dream of going to college in Vermont.

Follow along on her adventures with the following map.

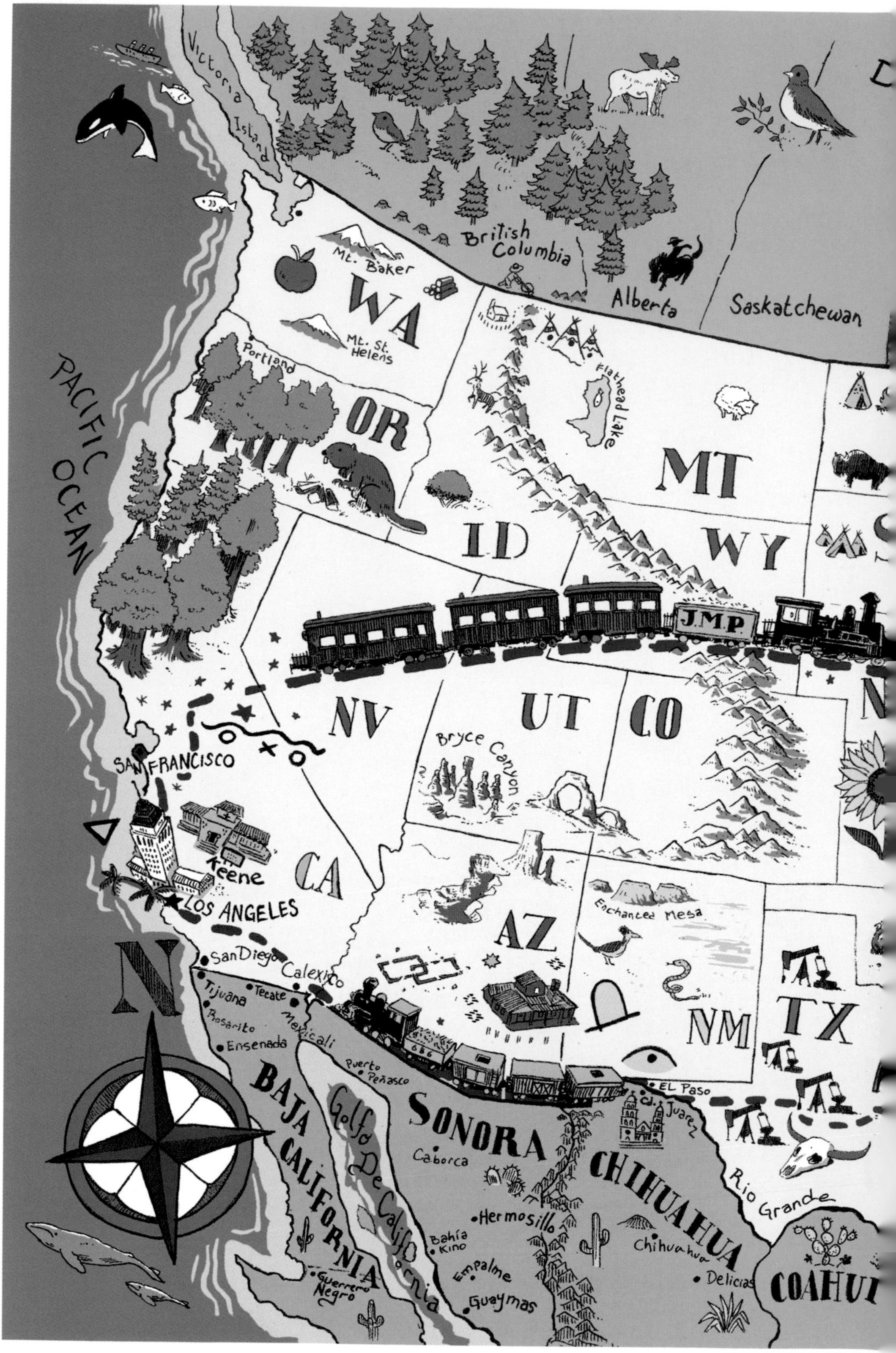
Victoria Island
British Columbia
Alberta
Saskatchewan
Mt. Baker
WA
Mt. St. Helens
Portland
OR
Flathead Lake
MT
ID
WY
PACIFIC OCEAN
J.M.P.
NV
UT
CO
Bryce Canyon
SAN FRANCISCO
Keene
CA
LOS ANGELES
AZ
Enchanted Mesa
N
San Diego
Calexico
Tijuana
Tecate
Rosarito
Mexicali
Ensenada
NM
TX
686
Puerto Peñasco
El Paso
Cd. Juarez
BAJA CALIFORNIA
Golfo De California
SONORA
Caborca
CHIHUAHUA
Rio Grande
Hermosillo
Bahía Kino
Chihuahua
Empalme
Delicias
COAHUI
Guerrero Negro
Guaymas

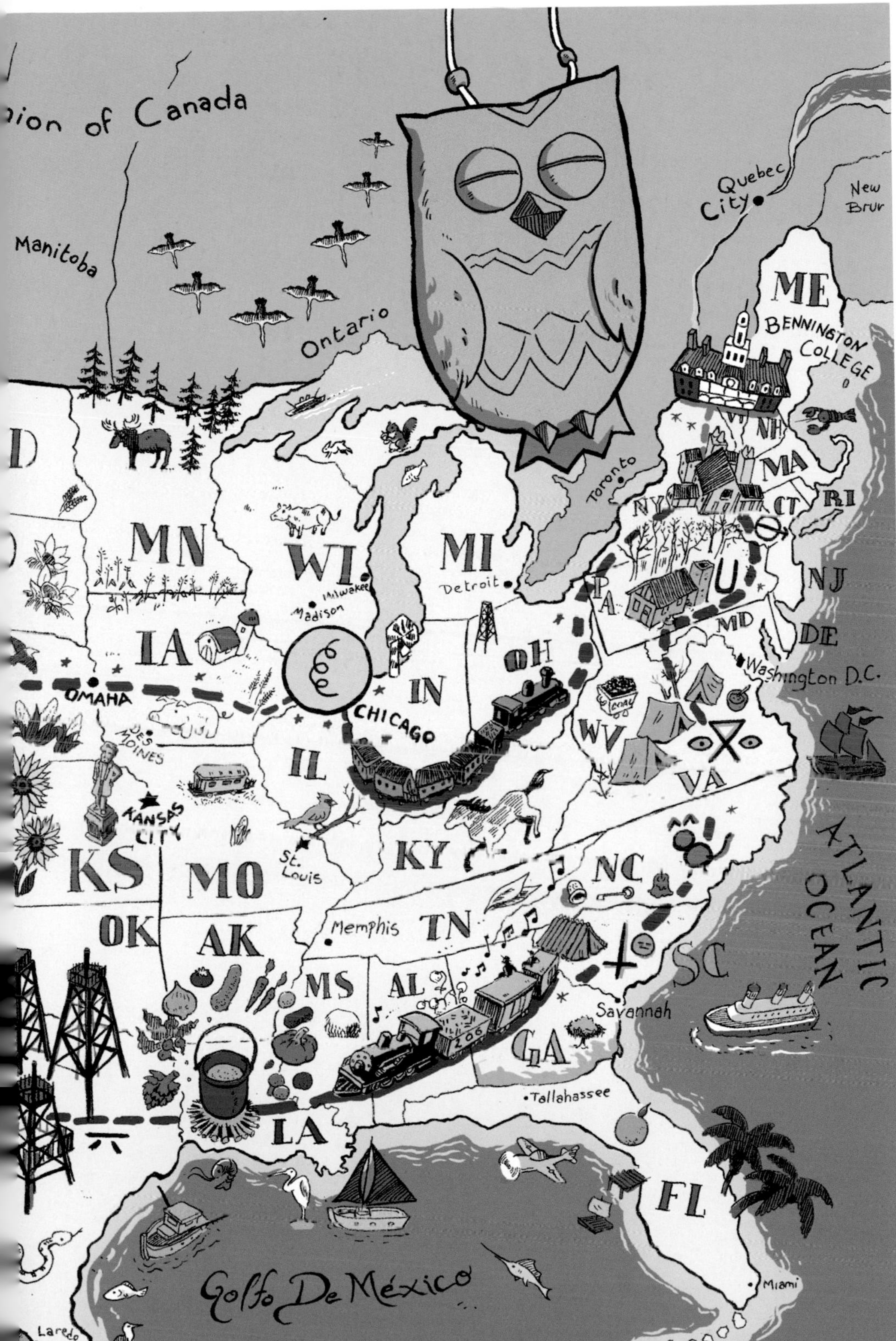

nion of Canada
Manitoba
Ontario
Quebec City
New Brur
ME
BENNINGTON COLLEGE
NH
MA
RI
CT
NY
Toronto
NJ
PA
MD
DE
Washington D.C.
MN
WI
Milwakee
Madison
MI
Detroit
IA
OMAHA
DES MOINES
CHICAGO
IN
OH
IL
WV
VA
KANSAS CITY
St. Louis
KY
KS
MO
NC
OK
AK
Memphis
TN
SC
ATLANTIC OCEAN
MS
AL
Savannah
GA
206
Tallahassee
LA
FL
Miami
Golfo De México
Laredo

HOBO SIGNS

During the Great Depression, hoboes developed a visual code they used to communicate. Though some were unable to read, all could recognize and remember the symbols. Hoboes would write this code with chalk or coal to provide directions, information, and warnings to others coming down the line. Symbols could indicate many different things. Here are some that show up in *Soupy Leaves Home*.

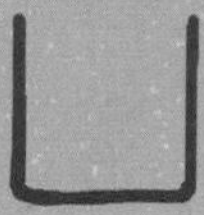

Camp here

Safe camp

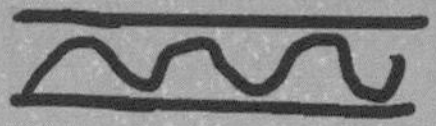

Bad (or dangerous) water

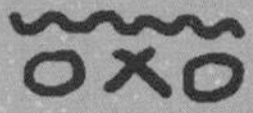

Good (or safe) water

Cops active

Cops inactive

No-alcohol town

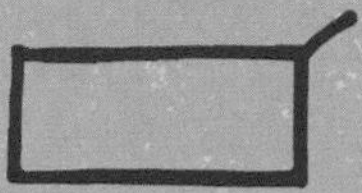

Town allows alcohol

Go

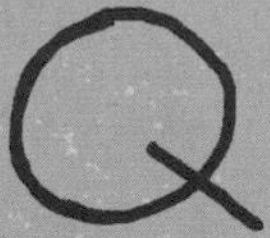

At crossroads go this way

Straight ahead

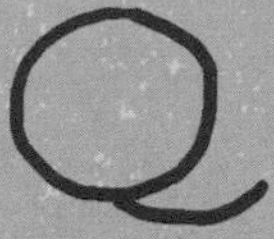

Turn right here

Stop

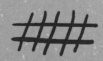

Unsafe place

Get out fast

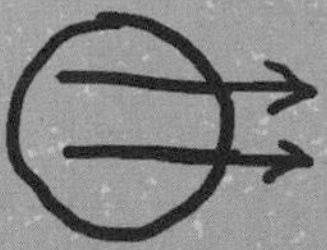

Get out fast

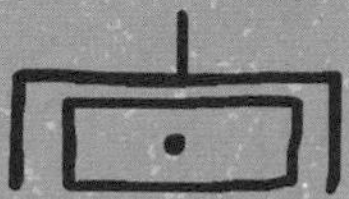

Dangerous neighborhood

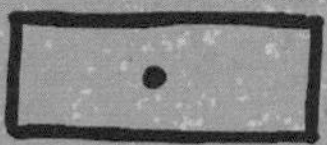

Danger

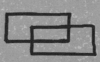

Afraid

Don't go this way

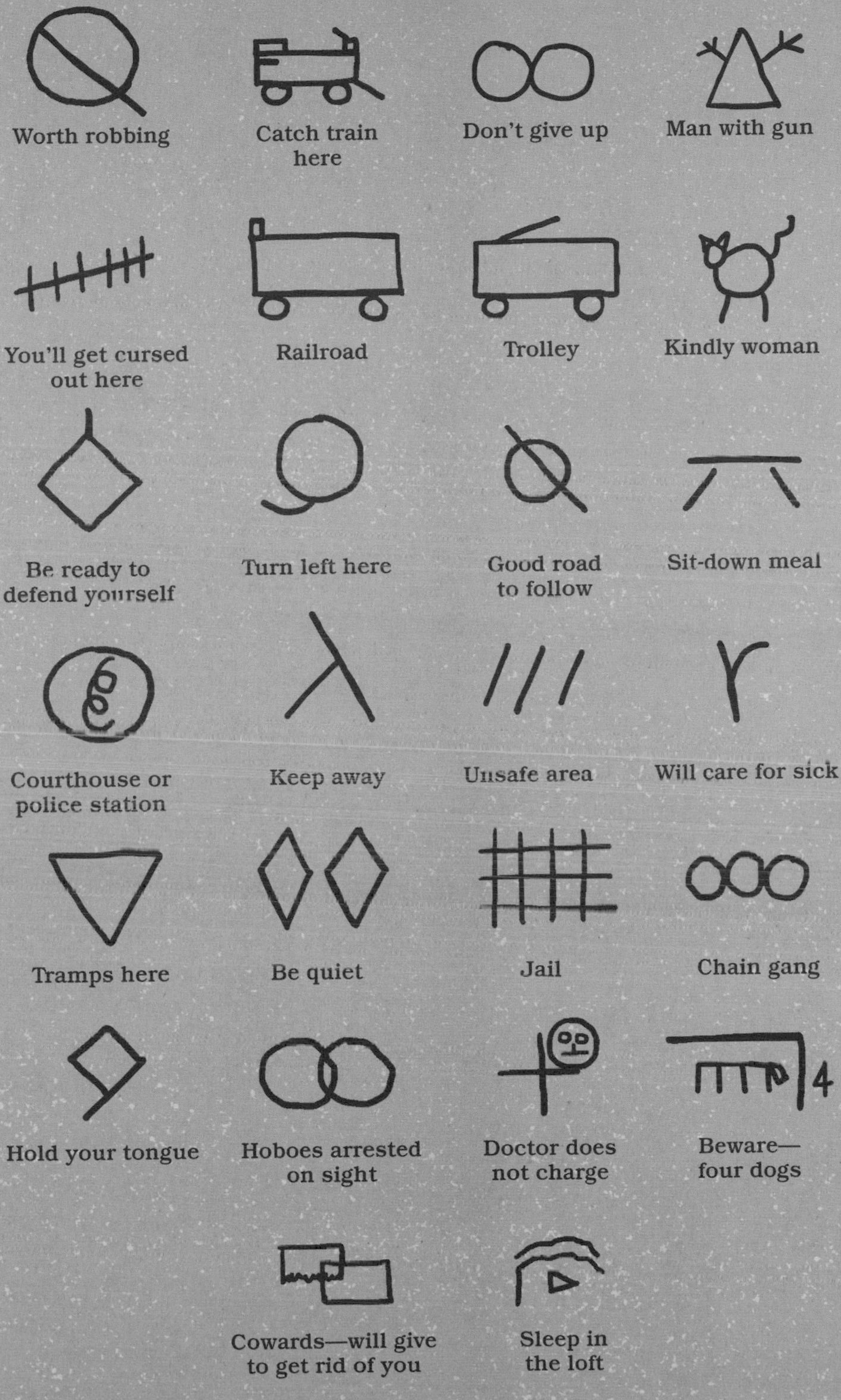
Worth robbing
Catch train here
Don't give up
Man with gun
You'll get cursed out here
Railroad
Trolley
Kindly woman
Be ready to defend yourself
Turn left here
Good road to follow
Sit-down meal
Courthouse or police station
Keep away
Unsafe area
Will care for sick
Tramps here
Be quiet
Jail
Chain gang
Hold your tongue
Hoboes arrested on sight
Doctor does not charge
4
Beware—four dogs
Cowards—will give to get rid of you
Sleep in the loft

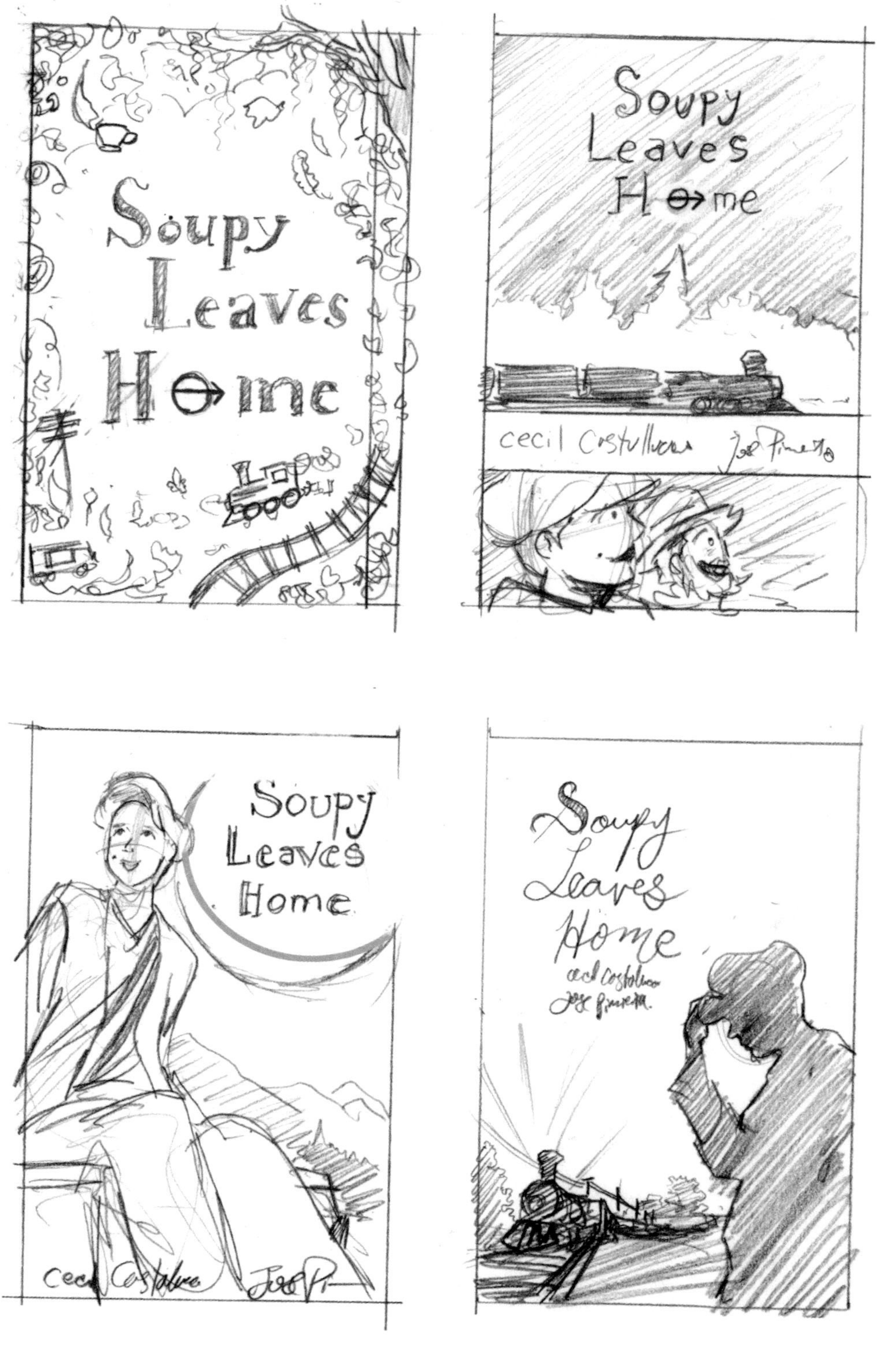
Soupy Leaves Home
Soupy Leaves Home
Soupy Leaves Home
Soupy Leaves Home

Cover sketches and final pencils (*facing*) for first edition by Jose

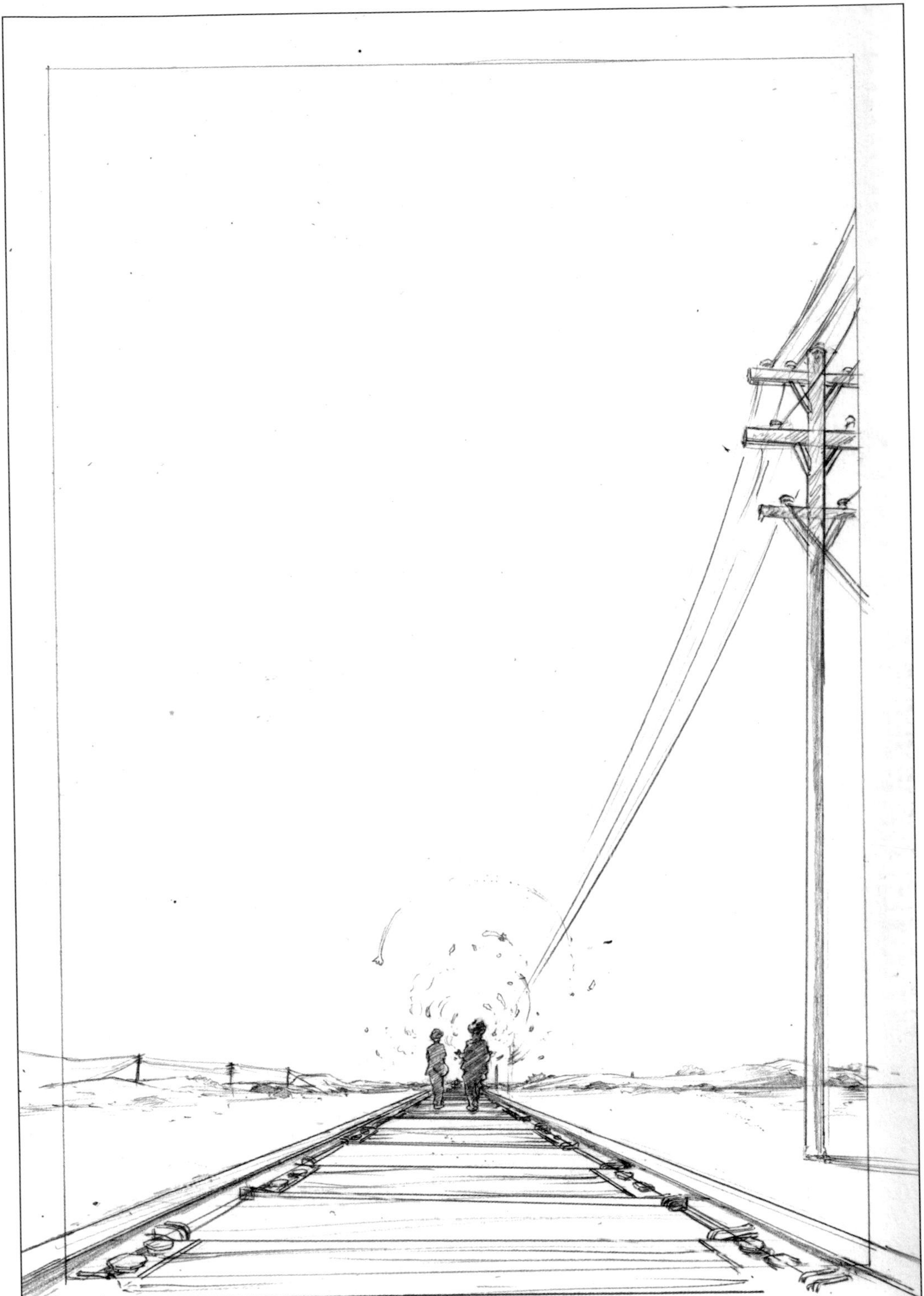

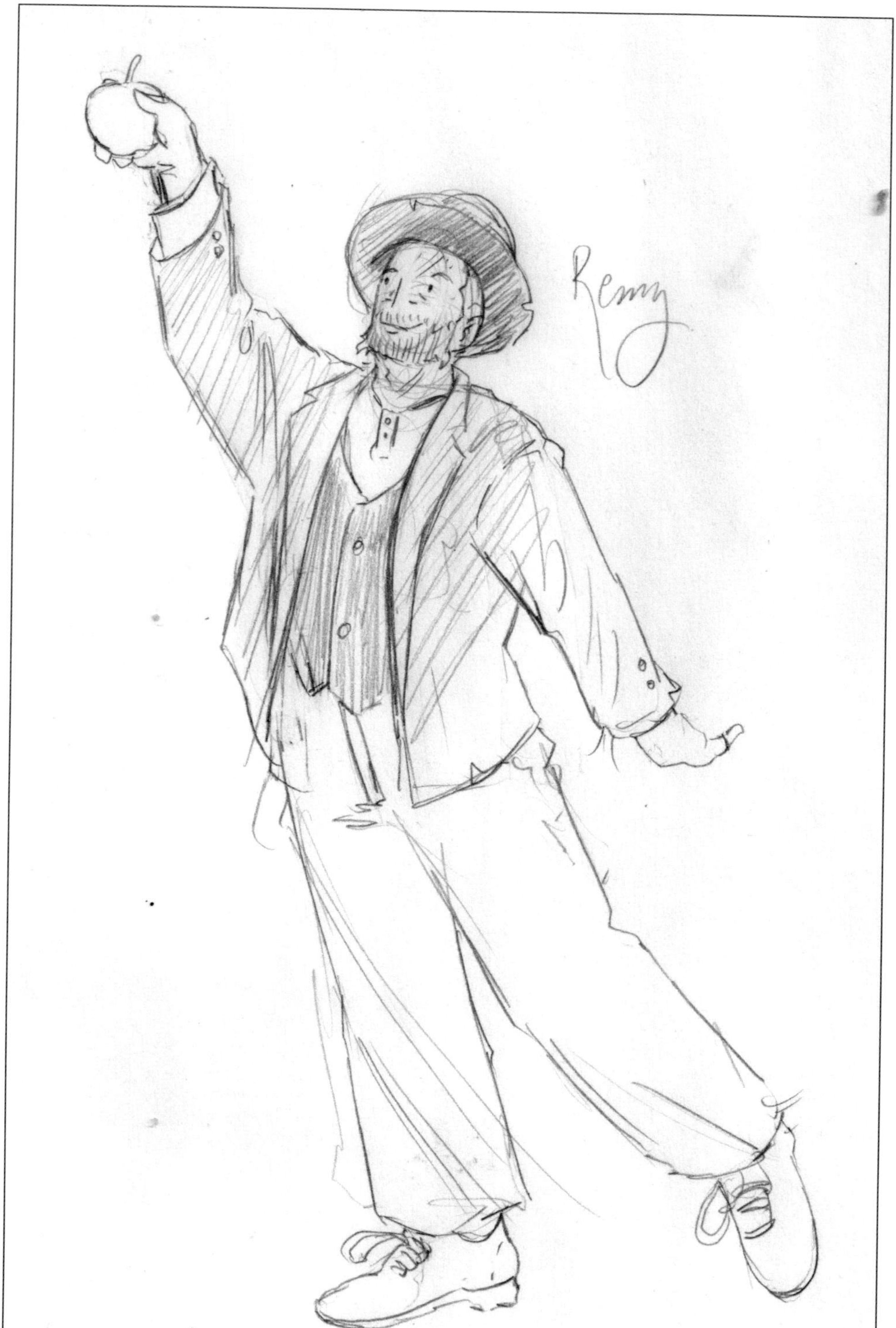
Remy

Remy "Ramshackle" Renault

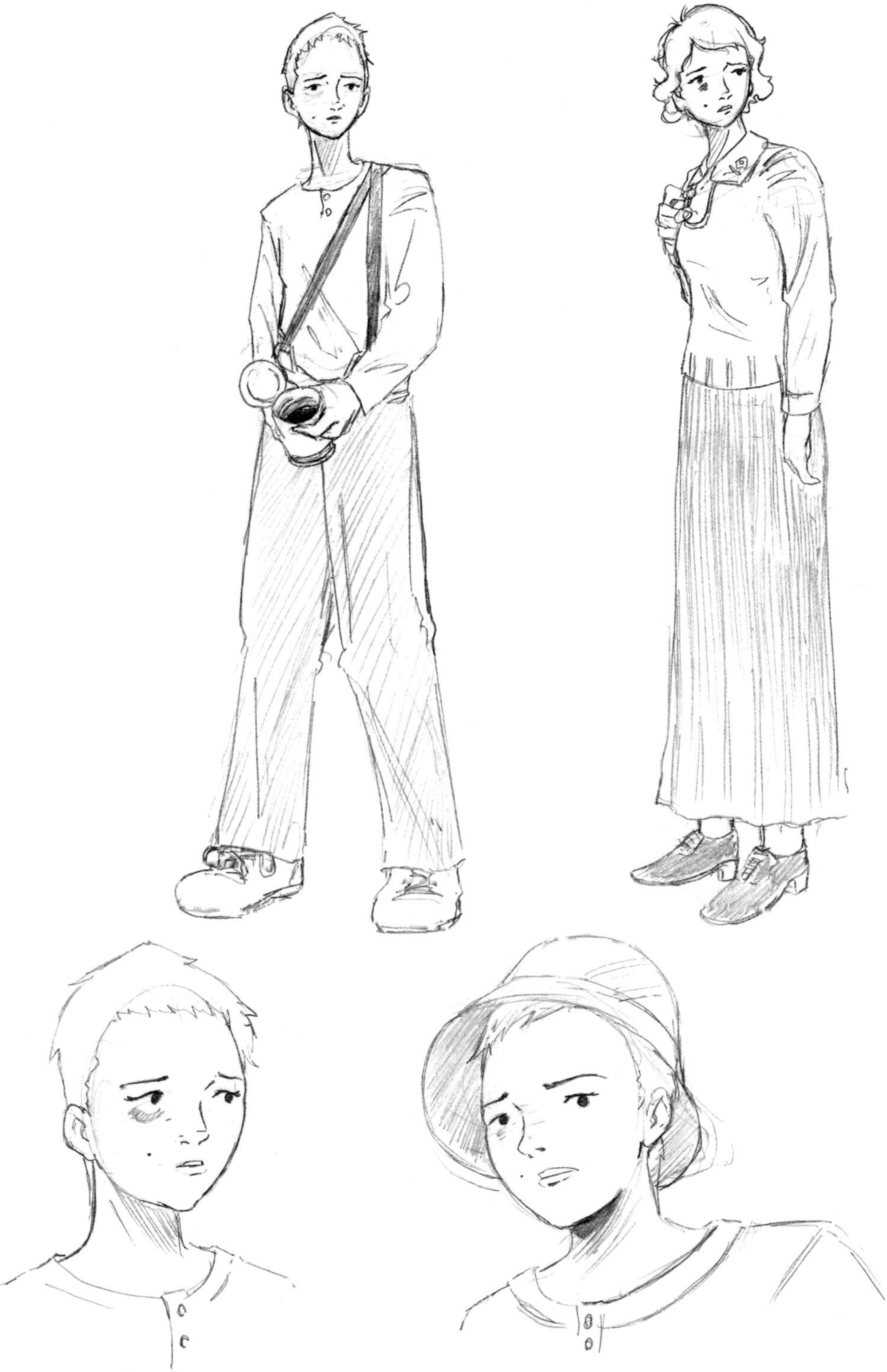

Pearl "Soupy" Plankette

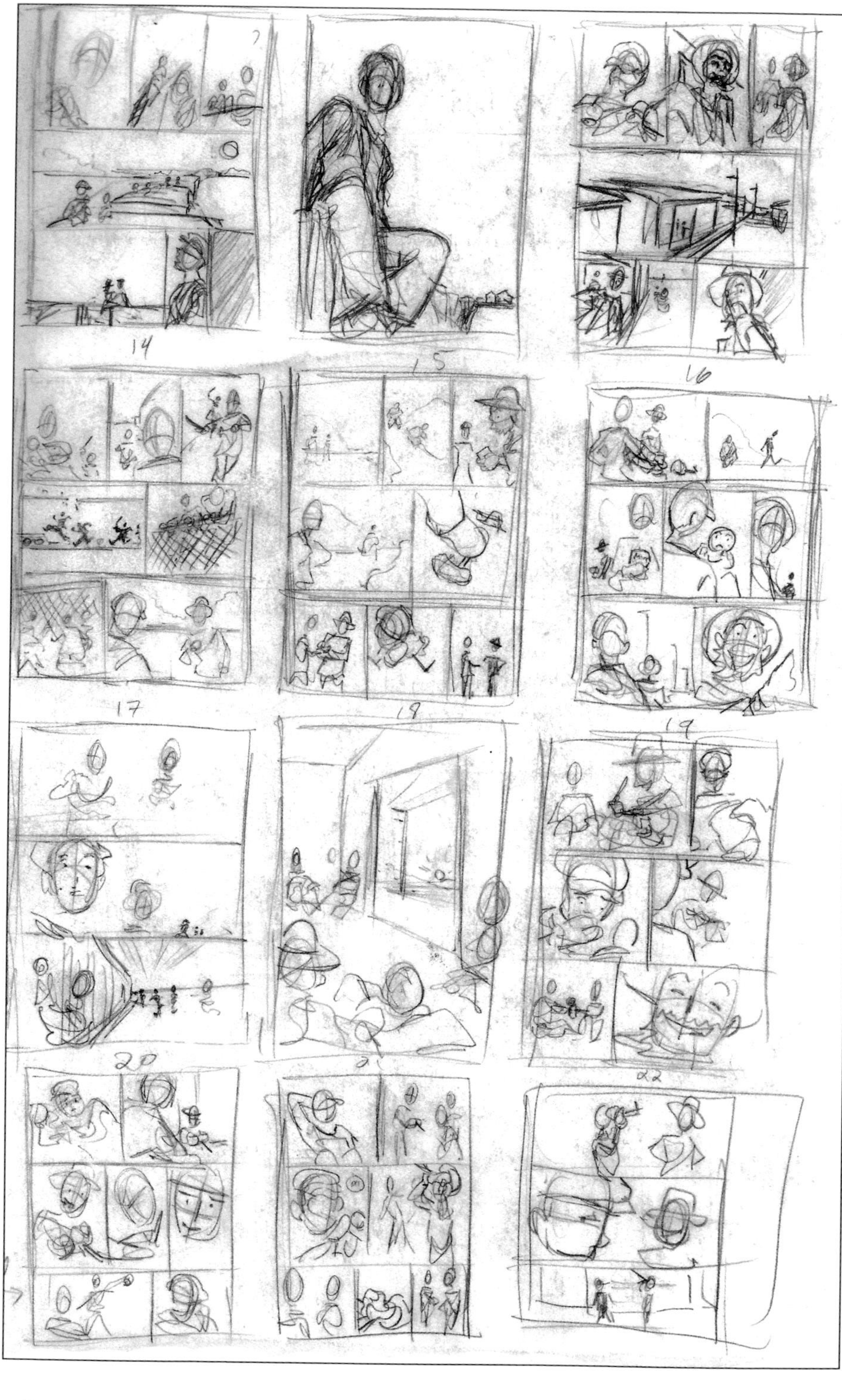
14
15
16
17
18
19
20
22

Layouts for pages 17-28 and 121-132, 136-145, 147-149 (*facing*) by Jose

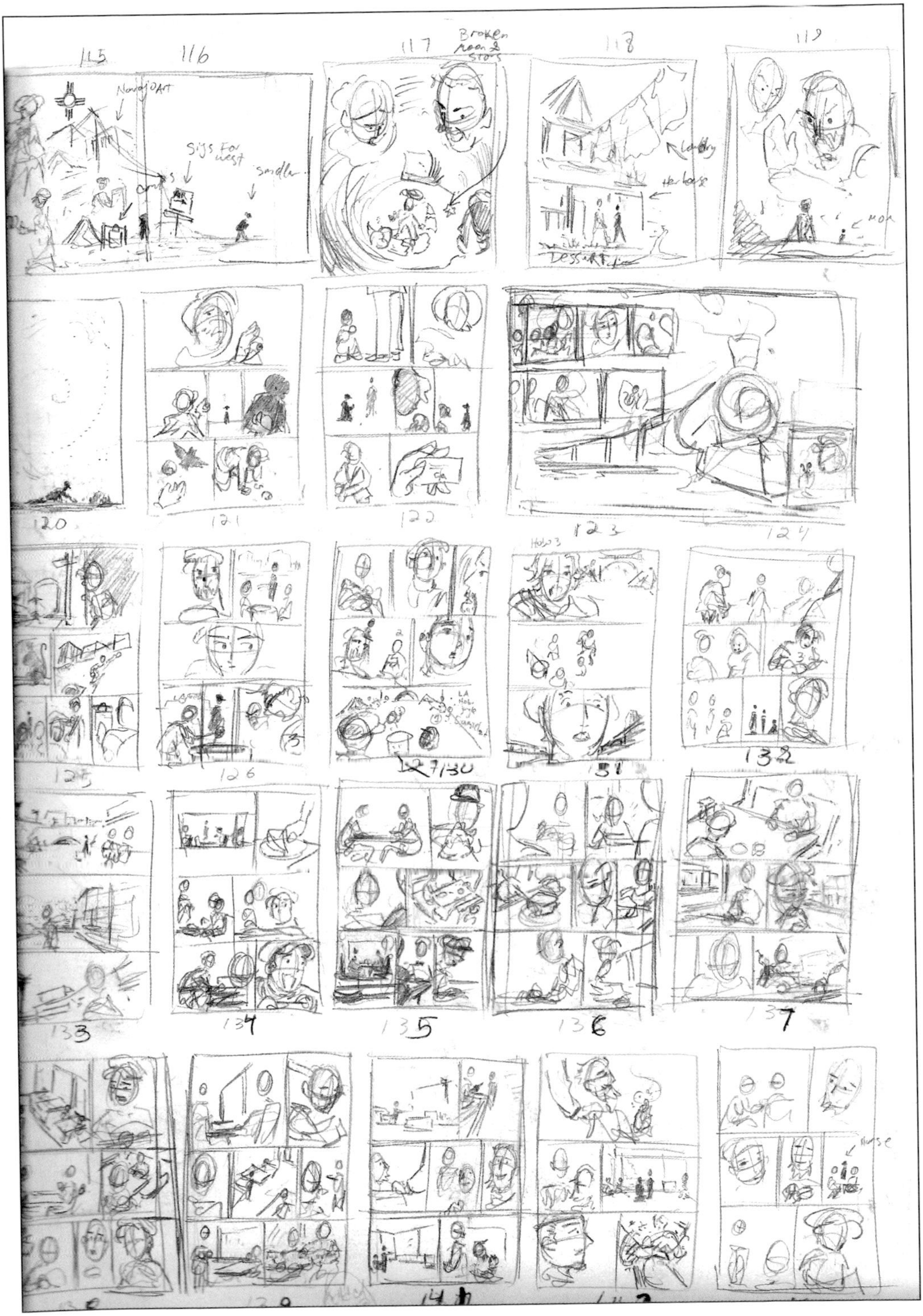

115
116
117
118
119
120
121
122
123
124
126
127/130
132
133
134
135
136
137

Check out the books that Soupy is reading and the stories that inspired Cecil and Jose!

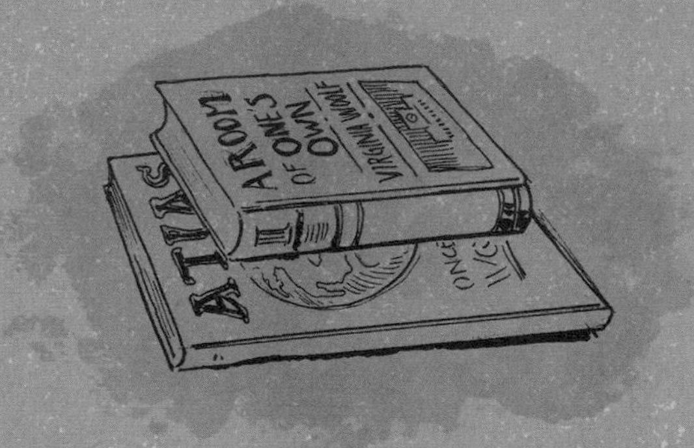
A ROOM OF ONE'S OWN
VIRGINIA WOOLF
ATLAS

Farthest North by **Fridtjof Nansen**

Valperga; or, The Life and Adventures of Castruccio, Prince of Lucca and *Frankenstein; or, The Modern Prometheus* by **Mary Shelley**

Little Nemo in Slumberland by **Winsor McCay**

Journey to the Center of the Earth by **Jules Verne**

A Room of One's Own by **Virginia Woolf**

The tale of Juan Diego and the Virgin of Guadalupe

Citizen Hobo by **Todd Depastino**

Tramping with Tramps by **Josiah Flynt**

Hoboes by **Mark Wyman**

I Was Looking for a Street by **Charles Willeford**

Beggars of Life by **Jim Tully**

You Can't Win by **Jack Black**

"*Soupy Leaves Home* tells the story of a time no longer familiar to us—a time of living the rails and simmering Mulligan Soup, a time of chosen names and secret languages—yet a tale that anyone with a longing heart and a restless spirit can relate to. It transports you magically to a place long gone, but its tale of poverty and survival are still as relevant as they ever were—the characters may be penniless, but they are so emotionally wealthy that this book leaves you filled with warmth, hope, and love."

—Gerard Way

CECIL CASTELLUCCI is the author of books and graphic novels for young adults including *Boy Proof*, *The Plain Janes*, *First Day on Earth*, *The Year of the Beasts*, *Tin Star*, *Stone in the Sky* and the Eisner nominated *Odd Duck*. In 2015 she co-authored *Moving Target: A Princess Leia Adventure* and in 2016 she worked on *Shade, The Changing Girl* an ongoing comic on Gerard Way's Young Animal imprint at DC Comics. Her picture book, *Grandma's Gloves*, won the California Book Award Gold Medal. Her short stories have been published in Strange Horizons, YARN, Tor.com, and various anthologies including, *Teeth*, *After*, and *Interfictions 2*. She is the Children's Correspondence Coordinator for The Rumpus, a two time Macdowell Fellow and the founding YA Editor at the LA Review of Books. She lives in Los Angeles.

JOSE PIMIENTA grew up in Mexicali, Mexico, watching a lot of cartoons and listening to as much music as possible. After finishing high school, he studied visual storytelling in Georgia, where he made friends and drank a lot of coffee. Eventually, he headed back to Southern California, where he currently resides. He draws on a regular basis and still listens to as much music as he can. He also enjoys recreational walks and whistling. Sometimes he goes by "Joe."

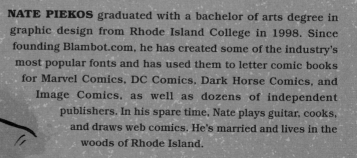

NATE PIEKOS graduated with a bachelor of arts degree in graphic design from Rhode Island College in 1998. Since founding Blambot.com, he has created some of the industry's most popular fonts and has used them to letter comic books for Marvel Comics, DC Comics, Dark Horse Comics, and Image Comics, as well as dozens of independent publishers. In his spare time, Nate plays guitar, cooks, and draws web comics. He's married and lives in the woods of Rhode Island.

CECIL CASTELLUCCI JOSE PIMIENTA

SOUPY LEAVES HOME

Educator's Guide

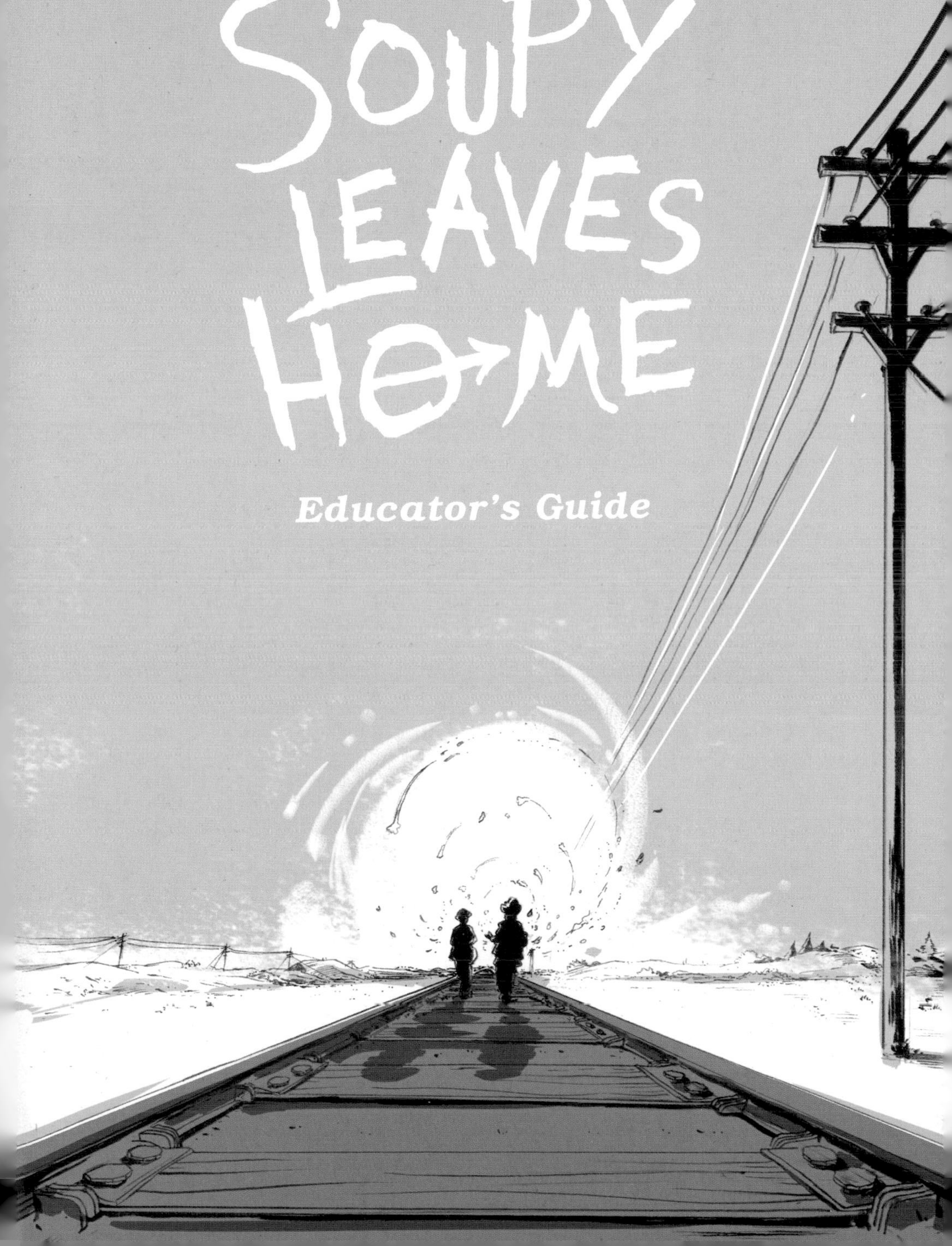

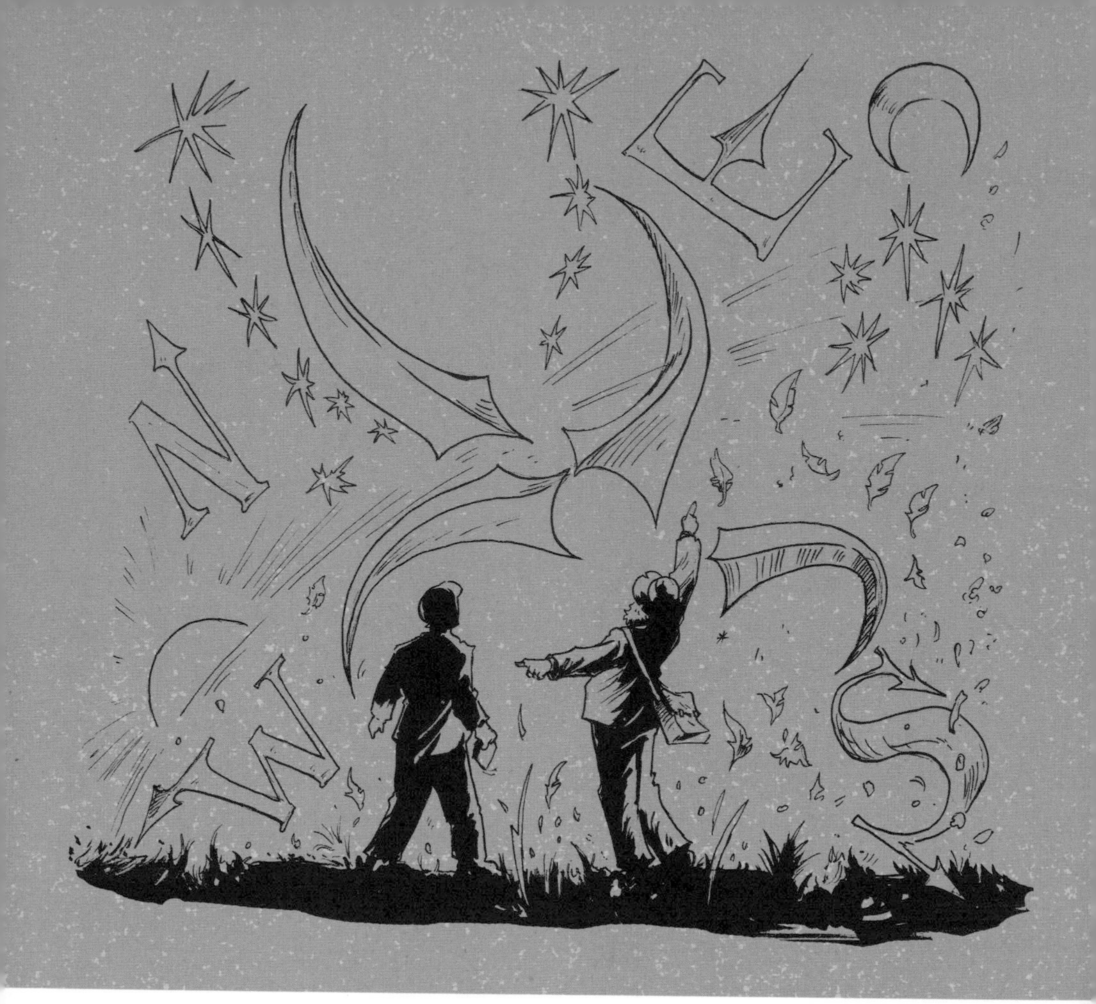

S*oupy Leaves Home* is a graphic novel written by Cecil Castellucci and illustrated by Jose Pimienta. Set in the early 1930s in the heart of the Great Depression, this is a story about two hoboes: one young named "Soupy," and one much older named "Ramshackle." Together they journey south and then "Westward" while healing their hearts, facing their respective demons, and evaluating their paths and dreams.

Soupy (whose given name is Pearl Plankette) is running away from home and her abusive father. After cutting her hair and "taking" men's clothing she poses as a boy and heads for the train tracks in the hope of catching a train to anywhere. It's on the tracks that Soupy meets Ramshackle, or "Rammy." She thinks he's "some kind of strange beast. Like a yeti. Or a Sasquatch. But of course, looks can be deceiving."

From cover to cover, readers travel with these larger-than-life characters, feeling their pains and their hopes as they grapple with the world around them. In the end, we realize that Soupy, Rammy, and even Professor Jack are a lot like us and that their dreams aren't much different from ours. As such, this is a book about humanity, about heart and empathy, and the quests we all must travel (whether on trains, by foot, or simply with time) as we find our own truths and love along our individual paths while figuring out who we really are.

While only out a few months, this book received a starred review from *Kirkus Reviews*, which describes this as "a compelling graphic offering that explores relevant gender roles and self-identity through a historical lens." This book is an outstanding read for readers 12+.

SUMMARY

Just as we hold on to our pains and secrets only gradually allowing them to surface, so too this story holds pain and secrets that surface with growing trust and healing. It opens with the image of a girl walking through the gates of a home explaining:

> "Sometimes a house starts out one way, filled with love, and then something happens. And suddenly, you can't find the warmth, no matter how hard you try . . . I'm leaving home . . . This is the story of how I became warm again."

As Pearl leaves home she physically transforms herself trying to hide who she is both inside and outside. While her physical transformation is immediate and convincing, her emotional and personal transformations come later as she and Ramshackle help each other find their inner peace.

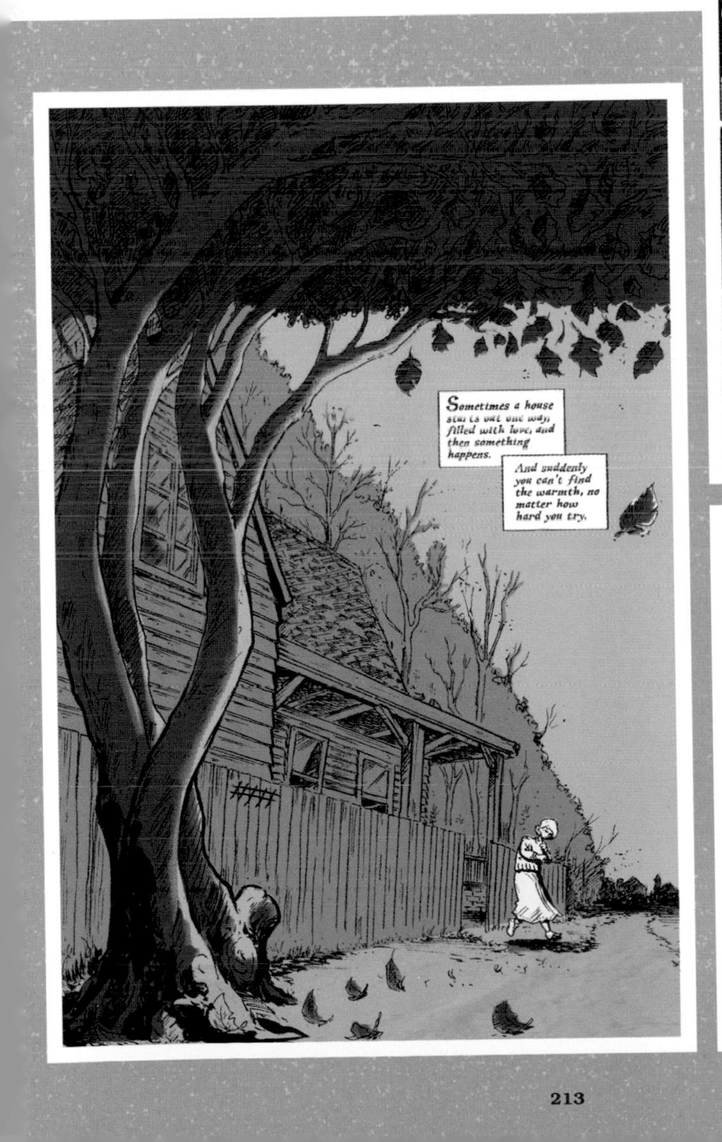
Sometimes a house
filled with love, and then something happens.
And suddenly you can't find the warmth, no matter how hard you try.

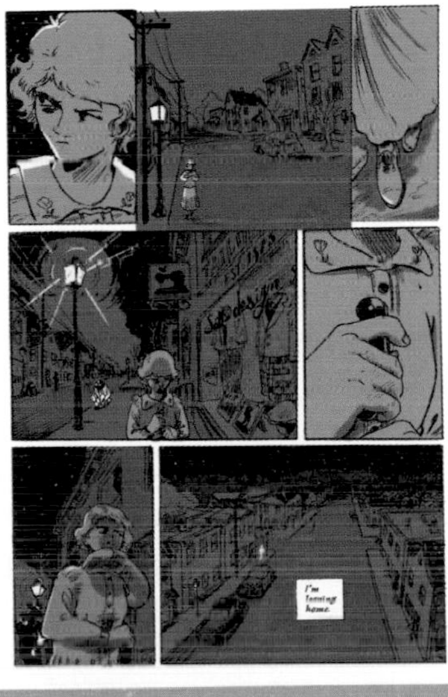
I'm leaving home.

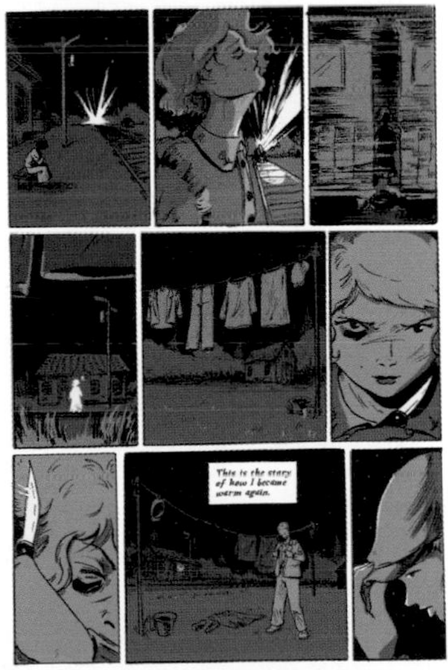
This is the story of how I became warm again.

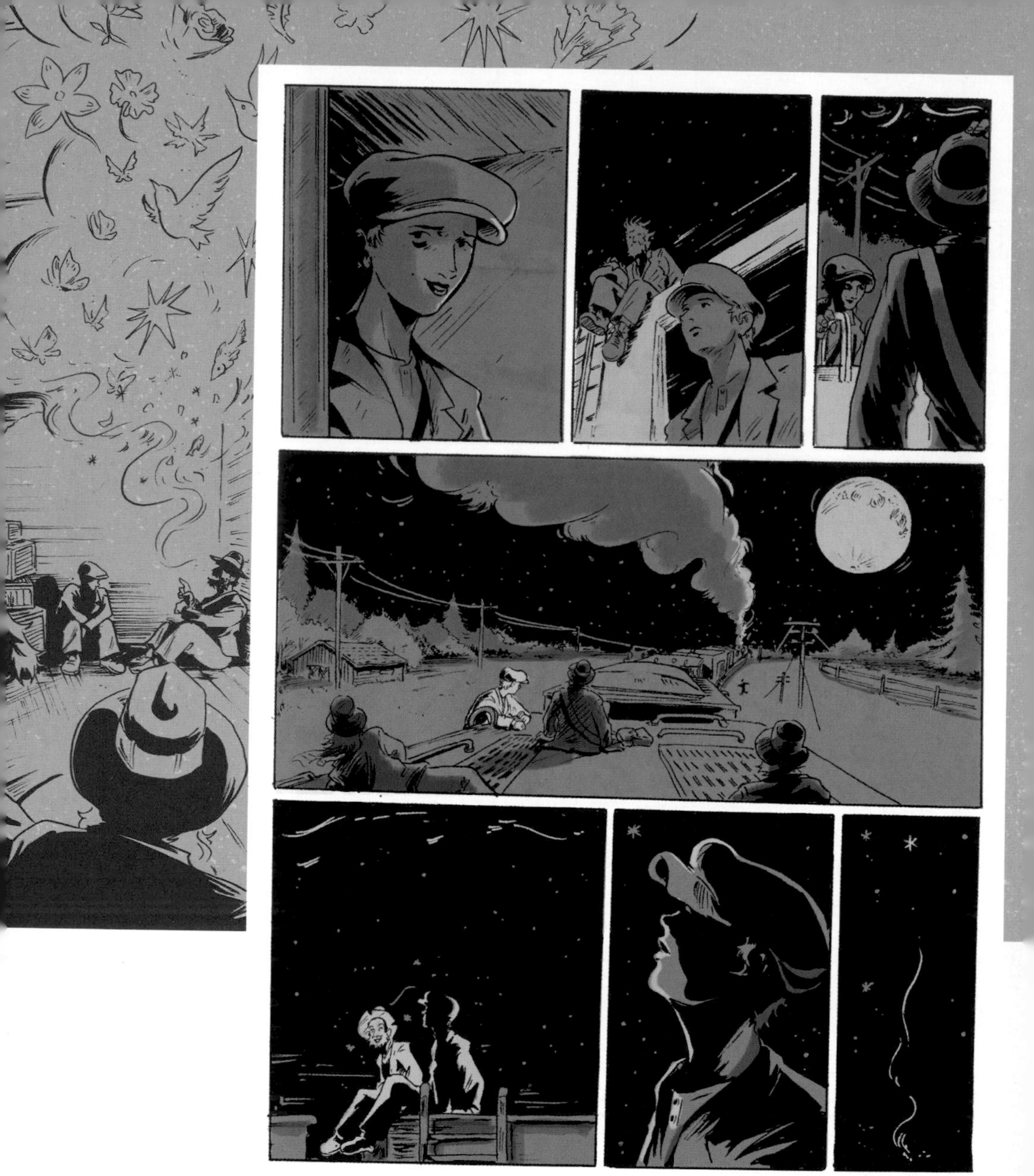

The tragedy of Soupy's life (at least initially) is somewhat balanced by Ramshackle's magic. It is this inner magic that draws Soupy to him. Ramshackle seems to see through people's defenses. He sees their inner beauty and he can make the simplest things (what others might consider garbage or worthless) seem magically special. We learn to trust Ramshackle and his insights as Soupy does. He teaches Soupy how to survive as a 'bo—how to find defend herself and read hobo signs warning of danger or showing were one might find food or temporary work. And as they travel, Ramshackle helps Soupy find purpose, inner strength, and beauty in the world around her. Soupy, in return, gives Ramshackle strength, love, and purpose when he needs it most.

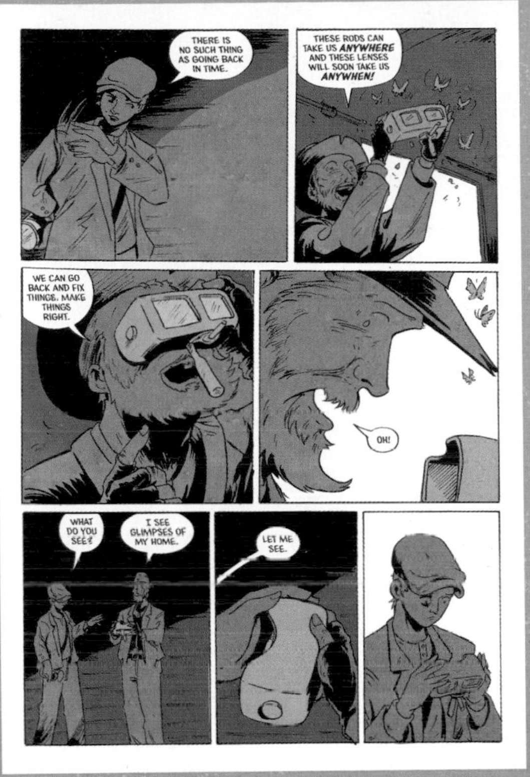
THERE IS NO SUCH THING AS GOING BACK IN TIME.
THESE RODS CAN TAKE US ANYWHERE AND THESE LENSES WILL SOON TAKE US ANYWHEN!
WE CAN GO BACK AND FIX THINGS, MAKE THINGS RIGHT.
OH!
WHAT DO YOU SEE?
I SEE GLIMPSES OF MY HOME.
LET ME SEE.

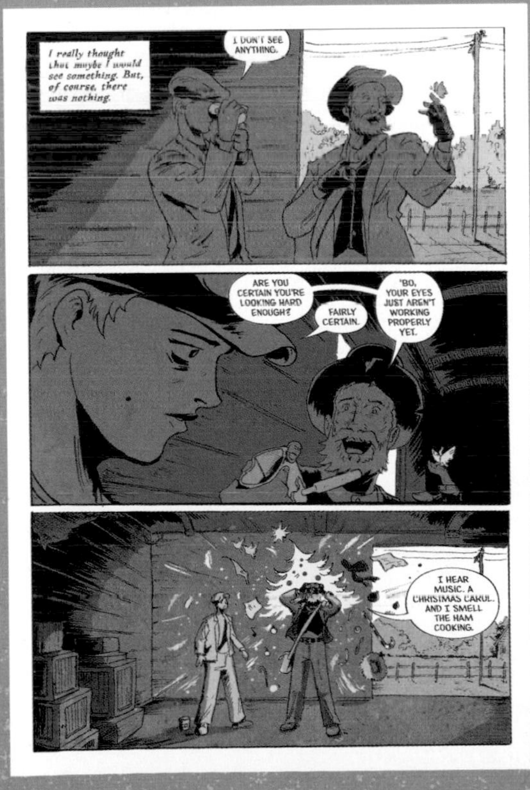
I really thought that maybe I would see something. But, of course, there was nothing.
I DON'T SEE ANYTHING.
ARE YOU CERTAIN YOU'RE LOOKING HARD ENOUGH?
FAIRLY CERTAIN.
'BO, YOUR EYES JUST AREN'T WORKING PROPERLY YET.
I HEAR MUSIC. A CHRISTMAS CAROL. AND I SMELL THE HAM COOKING.

While crossing the country we learn more about Soupy, Ramshackle, and hobo life during the Great Depression. We learn that after her mother died, Soupy's father was so grief-stricken he couldn't contain his anger, which he took out on Soupy. We learn of Ramshackle's life—of his wife and child whom he left years ago. We learn that while he tried to return to them, it just didn't work, and to find his own inner peace, he finds solace by helping others.

We also meet other supporting characters on the trains or in "hobo jungles" that are equally mysterious and faceted. One character in particular is "the Professor," a young hobo scarred inside and out, ostracized after being accused of breaking the Hobo Code for stealing and ratting on others. It is Ramshackle, however, who sees the Professor (and Soupy) for who they are and who helps guide all to see the truth. Unfortunately, Ramshackle is ill and must head "westward"—he leaves his unfinished "work" to Pearl and Professor Jack.

Soupy's story is told through sensitive, insightful dialogue and narrative as well as through image, color, and page/panel design. While clearly and convincingly set in the 1930s, the story, character, and dialogue, are timeless. Castellucci's text is moving, engaging, and weighty with nuance and meaning. Along with the narrative and dialogue, Castellucci introduces wonderful pieces of history, adding depth to the story and its characters—from the Hobo Signs and slang, to the Code of the Road (the ethical code created by Tourist Union #63 at the Annual Hobo Convention in the late 1880s), and snippets of songs from the 1930s, reflecting the trials tribulations of the Great Depression. These contributions make Soupy's story truly come to life.

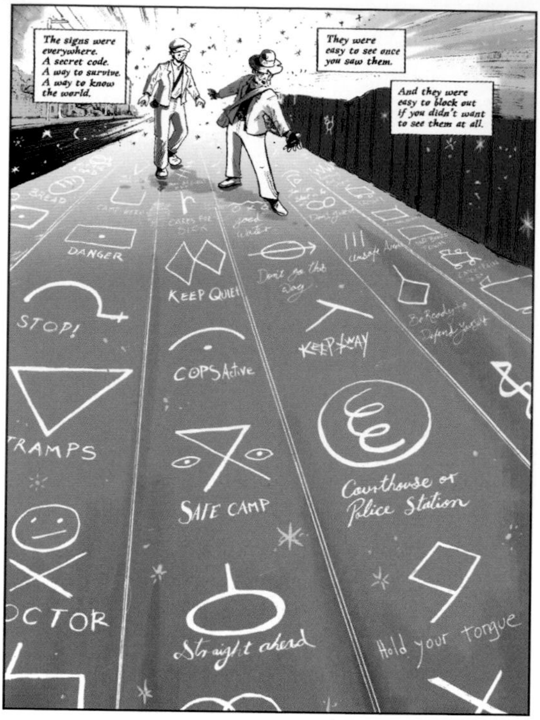
The signs were everywhere. A secret code. A way to survive. A way to know the world.
They were easy to see once you saw them.
And they were easy to block out if you didn't want to see them at all.
DANGER
KEEP QUIET
STOP!
KEEP AWAY
COPS Active
TRAMPS
SAFE CAMP
Courthouse or Police Station
Straight ahead
Hold your tongue

Then there are Pimienta's images and brilliant use of color. While most of the panels are monochromatic, color is inserted with great intention and effect. Nights are dark and olive green when depicting melancholy; dark and purple when depicting the majesty of the great outdoors and nature; dark and blue when depicting sadness or cold fear; or dark and red when depicting or alluding to danger and/or violent thoughts or actions. Days are equally depicted in light shades of drab olive, depicting dust, dirt and destitution, or icy whites and blues signifying cold, fear, or loneliness. And then there is Ramshackle's magic when he relays memories, insights, love, or special thoughts. At these times bursts of colors, shapes, and flying swirling images set against a bright white background truly support the magical feelings they elicit.

The book's power lies both in its moving story and its insights into life. The fact that things are rarely as they seem—from initial impressions, to stereotypes about hoboes and tramps, to relationships or expectations of what girls and boys can or cannot do. We learn to see people as diverse and multifaceted, and we learn the powers of love, trust, and helping others.

In short, *Soupy Leaves Home* is about friendship, survival, the power or "sight," of finding oneself and following dreams—even (or especially) when they're not what is "expected." Through nuanced characters, the use and layers of art, design, and color, and pithy, touching dialogue, Castellucci and Pimienta relay:

- Different ways we all struggle to find and follow our inner voices as we figure out who we are
- Gender stereotyping and gender equality issues
- Finding ways to be oneself—even when it breaks with others' expectations
- Dealing with fear
- Dealing with abusive relationships
- The power of friendship, especially when things get tough
- The power and perils of dreams
- Finding ways to "see" truths in life and within the people around us
- The difficulties of being uprooted and finding oneself and one's place in the world

TEACHING: DISCUSSION SUGGESTIONS AND/OR WRITING PROMPTS

Plot, Themes, and Values Related

- Discuss what might make a young person run away from home. Discuss the dangers involved. Discuss what other options Pearl might have had and/or options one might have today.

- Discuss the characters' choice of Hobo names (for example: Soupy, Ramshackle/Rammy, Gums Magee, Tom Cat Tuna, and Professor Jack). Discuss why hoboes might have chosen to create new names. Have students come up with names for themselves, explaining (as a writing assignment) why they've chosen that particular name. You may also want to have them create a visual sign or "crest" the visually expresses who they are.

- Discuss why Pearl hid her gender and what might have happened if she hadn't. Why did she feel she had to? Are things different today? Why and why not?

- Compare and contrast hobo life in the 1930s versus homeless life today. What has changed? What hasn't? What might you and your students do to help? (Note: there two articles in the resources below to help with this.)

- On page 127 Pearl's mother tells her, "Being a woman is such a disappointment. I had dreams when I was young. I thought when we won the vote there could be a new kind of woman. But . . ." Discuss Pearl's mother's options when she was a young woman. Discuss Pearl's options. Discuss how things did and did not change from mother to daughter. Discuss how things did and did not change in our culture today. Analyze and compare gender equality of the 1930s versus gender equality issues today.

- On pages 7–9 Pearl tells us, "Sometimes a house starts out one way, filled with love, and then something happens. And suddenly you can't find the warmth, no matter how hard you try . . . This is the story of how I became warm again." Discuss what makes a house warm, and what makes it cold, frightening, uninhabitable. Discuss what one might do to make things better.

- On page 187 Pearl tells Rammy's wife, ". . . Dreams are the richest things we have. Without dreams, well, we're poorer than dirt." Discuss what she means. Discuss the power and perils of dreams.

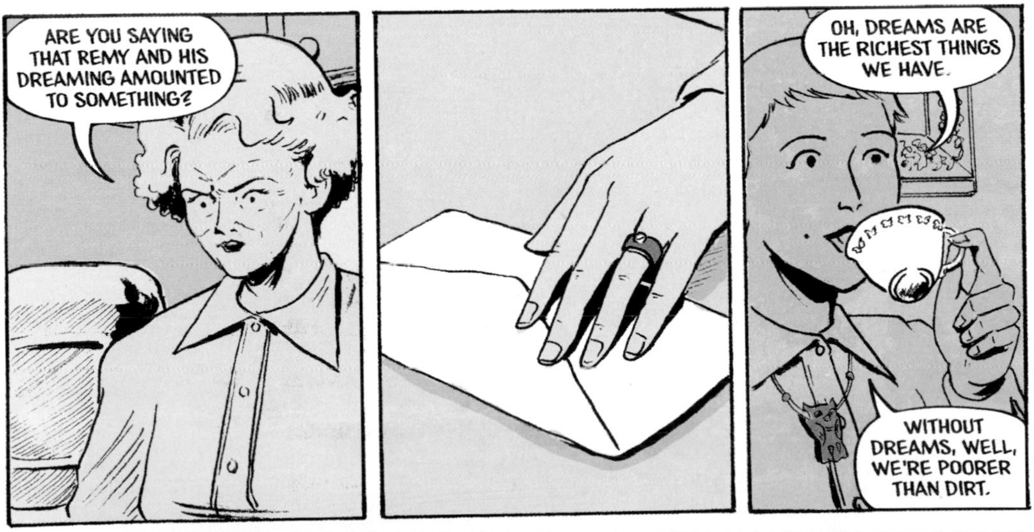

ARE YOU SAYING THAT REMY AND HIS DREAMING AMOUNTED TO SOMETHING?
OH, DREAMS ARE THE RICHEST THINGS WE HAVE.
WITHOUT DREAMS, WELL, WE'RE POORER THAN DIRT.

Critical Reading and Making Inferences

- On pages 26–27 Rammy finds a broken ViewMaster with which he pictures all kinds of Christmas wonders. Pearl can't seem to see anything through the ViewMaster. Then, on page 29, she thinks, "*Maybe the way to see starts by sneaking into your dreams.*" Discuss what she means by this. How might dreams help us see?

- On pages 32–33 Rammy asks, "Do you know how to defend yourself? . . . Well, I'm not saying to throw the first punch . . . You prepare your mind so that you don't crumble." Discuss what Rammy means and how one might best "prepare" to defend oneself?

- Research and discuss the "Code of the Road" ethical code (mentioned on pages 39–43) created by Tourist Union #63 at the Annual Hobo Convention in the late 1880s. Discuss the purpose and intent of this code and how it may or may not be applicable to life today.

- On page 58 Rammy says, "Nothing is ever garbage unless you say it's so. You're just looking at this wrong." Discuss what Rammy is trying to tell Pearl and how Pearl (and others) might look at various things ("garbage," "life") differently. Discuss why and when it is beneficial to look at things differently. Discuss why it is that Rammy sees things so differently from others.

- Trust is an important theme throughout this book. Discuss how some trust more and trust differently than others. Discuss why, for example, Pearl says to the doctor on page 73, "It's hard to trust people to do anything," and the doctor responds, "I hope you grow out of that one day, boy. Trust in trust. It's a fine thing." Evaluate and discuss the different characters' levels of trust.

- Discuss about how lying can hurt. Discuss for example what Pearl says on page 178: "A liar, when caught, is an obvious thing. Or, rather, once you see what a liar looks like, you can't unsee it." Discuss how lying can erode trust.

- Discuss what Pearl means when she says on pages 79–80, "Folded into the worst news, or the worst days, there are still moments of beauty . . . Small things like a piece of kindness . . ." Have students brainstorm and evaluate moments of beauty in their lives and/or stories or history.

- On page 136 Pearl realizes, "Once someone is considered bad people, no matter what they do, it looks bad." Discuss and evaluate this with your students. You may want to use this to look at historical and/or fictional characters. Discuss how one might change opinions.

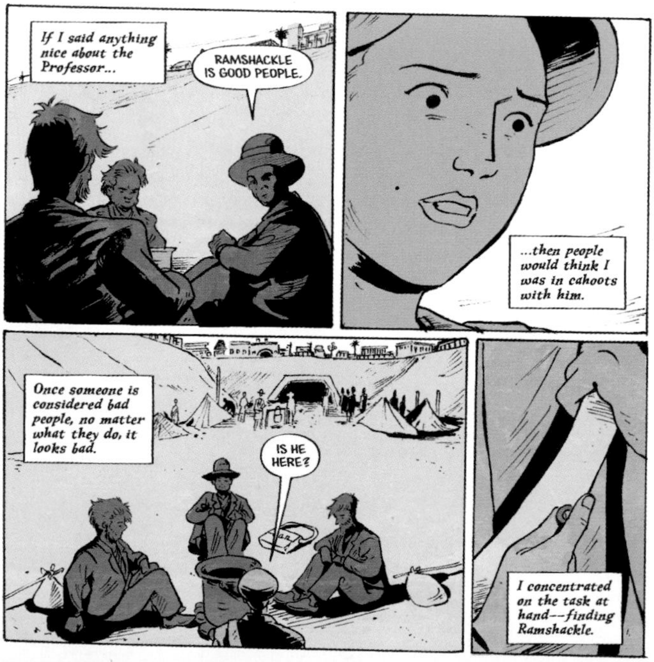

If I said anything nice about the Professor...
RAMSHACKLE IS GOOD PEOPLE.
...then people would think I was in cahoots with him.
Once someone is considered bad people, no matter what they do, it looks bad.
IS HE HERE?
I concentrated on the task at hand--finding Ramshackle.

Language, Literature, and Language Usage

- Have students search for and reflect upon Castellucci's uses of language, literary devices, and imagery to tell the story

- Castellucci includes a lot of period-related hobo signs and language/ jargon. Have students search for instances of this jargon (for example: jungling, jungle buzzards, flop bum versus hobo versus tramp, etc.) while creating their own Hobo Dictionaries (optional: these can include images as well as words to define the jargon).

- Have students study and evaluate the language of hobo signs Castellucci and Pimienta introduce us to (as found throughout the book and through links provided in the resources below).

- Discuss Castellucci's and Pimienta's uses of language and imagery on page 17 as she writes, "I drank in all the beauty I could."

- On page 55, Castellucci provides us with various descriptions of how hungry Pearl was. Have students think about times when they were really, really hungry. Have them try to describe it.

- On pages 104–105 Soupy tells us, "I think the saddest lands have the most beautiful sunsets. The rocks and the dirt, they don't have much else. Just like the saddest hearts are warmed by the tiniest and brightest of moments, just to get through the next one . . . . The land is just so sad it breaks my heart." Evaluate and discuss Soupy's sentiments—evaluating "the saddest lands" and "the saddest hearts." You may also want to discuss how these sentiments are relayed in text versus image (with just whites, greens, and a hint of violet). Why did they decide to use these specific colors? You may want to follow this up by having students describe and/or draw their saddest moments.

- Discuss Castellucci's and Pimienta's uses of language and imagery on page 169 as she writes, "There's a moment in every person's life when they emerge, like a chrysalis from a cocoon. They are formed and steady and who they truly are." Discuss why Pearl thinks this. Discuss whether you think it's true or not. When/how is it true? When/how is it not always true?

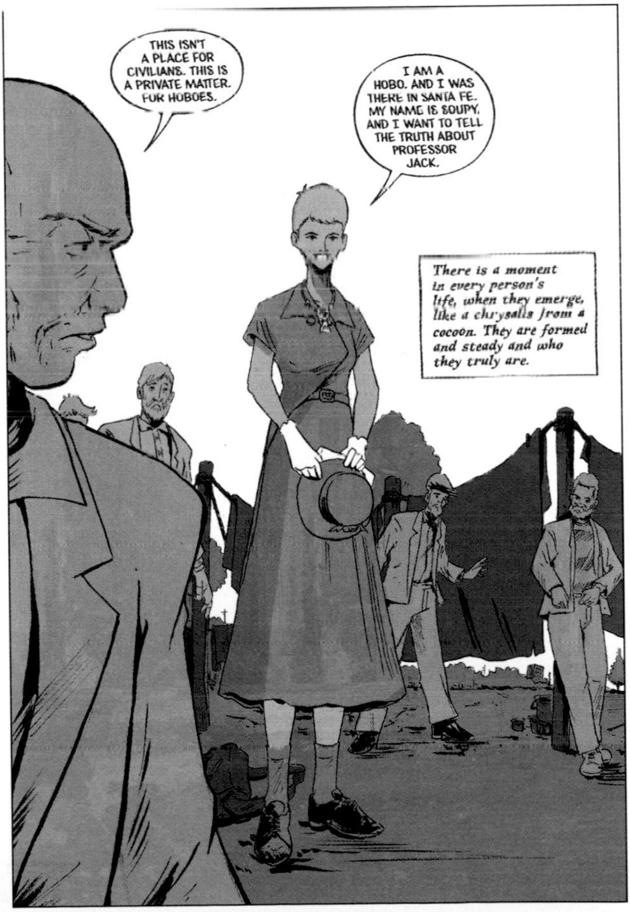
THIS ISN'T A PLACE FOR CIVILIANS. THIS IS A PRIVATE MATTER. FOR HOBOES.
I AM A HOBO. AND I WAS THERE IN SANTA FE. MY NAME IS SOUPY, AND I WANT TO TELL THE TRUTH ABOUT PROFESSOR JACK.
There is a moment in every person's life, when they emerge, like a chrysalis from a cocoon. They are formed and steady and who they truly are.

Cultural Diversity, Civic Responsibilities, and Social Issues

- In *Soupy Leaves Home* most of the hoboes have an opinion of Professor Jack based on the way he looks. Discuss this with students along with a discussion on how cultural differences play into this as well.
- Research, discuss, and/or debate homelessness in our world today. [Note there are some links in the resources below that may help.]
- Discuss how different cultures have dealt with runaways and with the homeless.
- Discuss how this book may have helped your students better understand the impact of abuse and the plight of the homeless.
- Discuss what civic responsibilities we have for our homeless and how you and your students might be able to contribute and help.

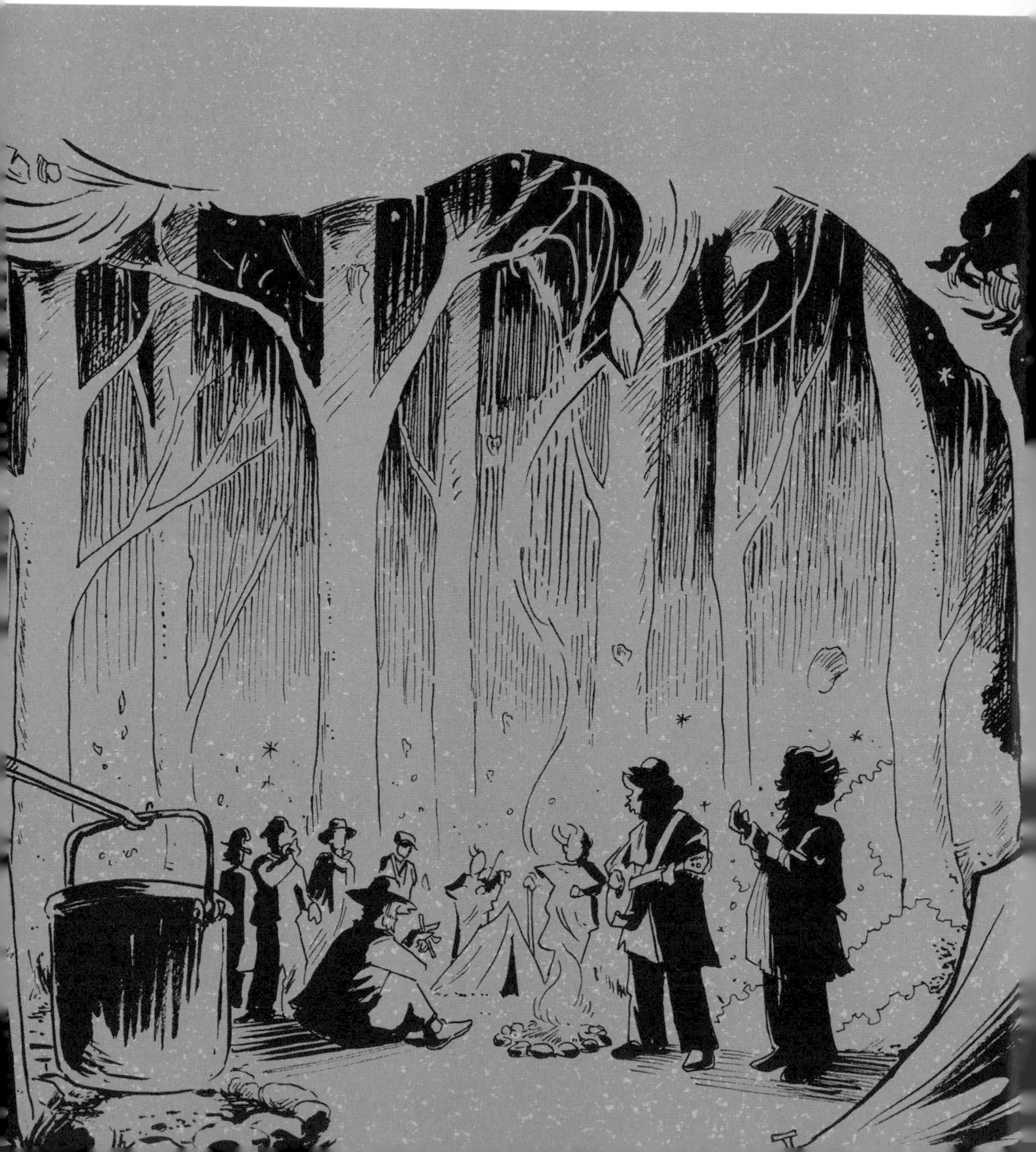

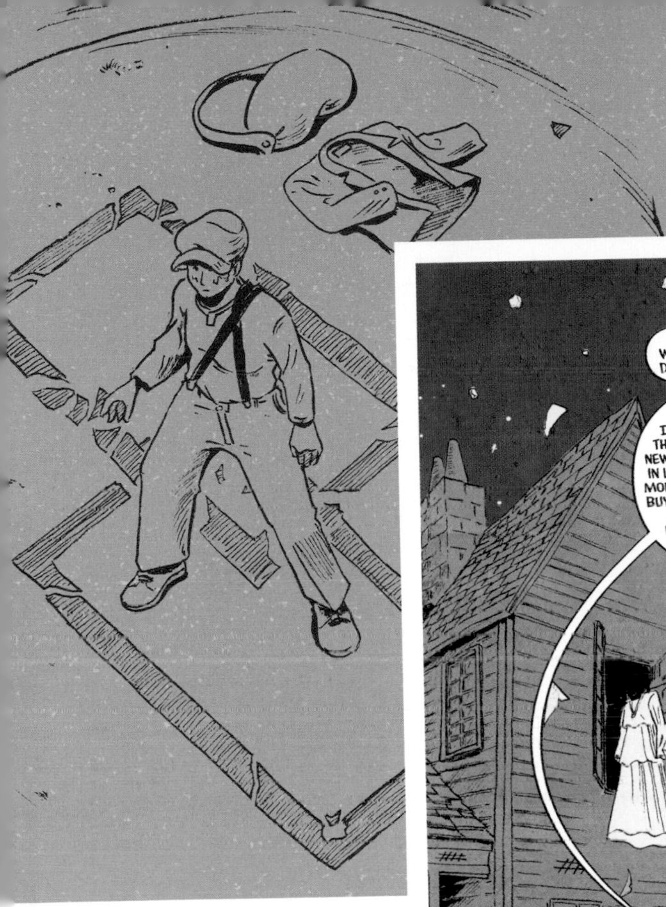

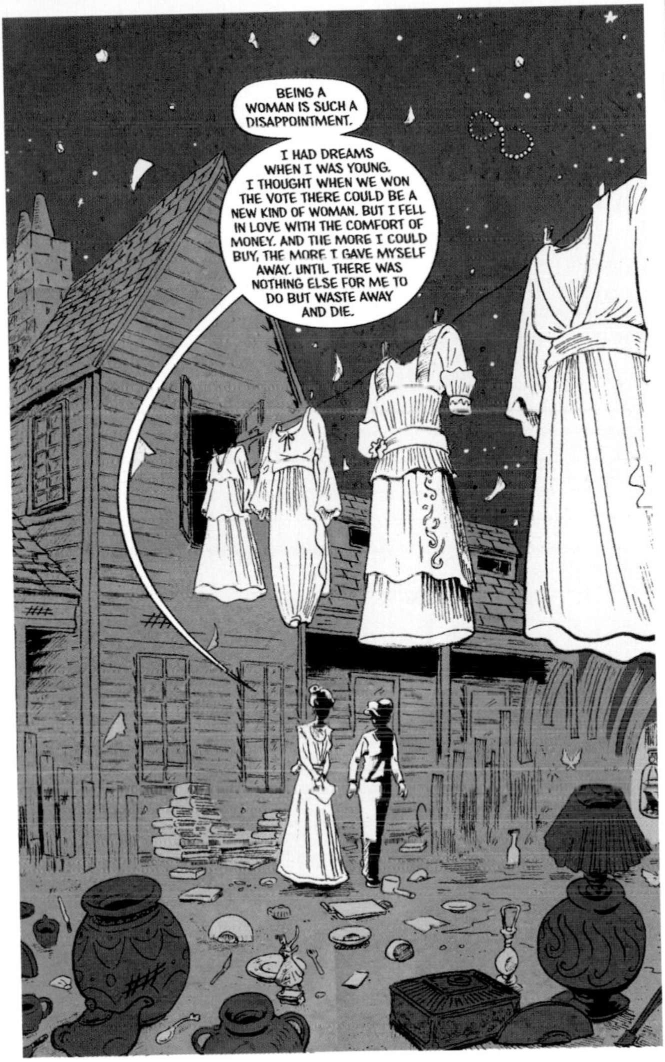
BEING A WOMAN IS SUCH A DISAPPOINTMENT.
I HAD DREAMS WHEN I WAS YOUNG. I THOUGHT WHEN WE WON THE VOTE THERE COULD BE A NEW KIND OF WOMAN. BUT I FELL IN LOVE WITH THE COMFORT OF MONEY. AND THE MORE I COULD BUY, THE MORE I GAVE MYSELF AWAY. UNTIL THERE WAS NOTHING ELSE FOR ME TO DO BUT WASTE AWAY AND DIE.

Social Studies Correlates

- Research and discuss how the Great Depression affected families and family life. [See suggested resource links below.] How was Pearl's life similar/different?

- Research the incidents and demographics of hoboes in the 1930s. Note that while there were women, a bobbed haircut (like Soupy's) was considered scandalous, as was wearing men's clothing. Even going a woman going to college was "weird" (or at best progressive). Discuss women's roles and fashions in the 1930s. What was a "Modern Woman" (and "Modern Man") in the 1930s? How have Modern Men and Women changed/not changed today?

- Discuss the Great Depression of the late 1920s through 1930s. Research and discuss the fate and lifestyles of hoboes and their "Code of the Road."

- Research women "getting the vote." Discuss Pearl's mother's reference to how women thought things might change when they "got the vote."

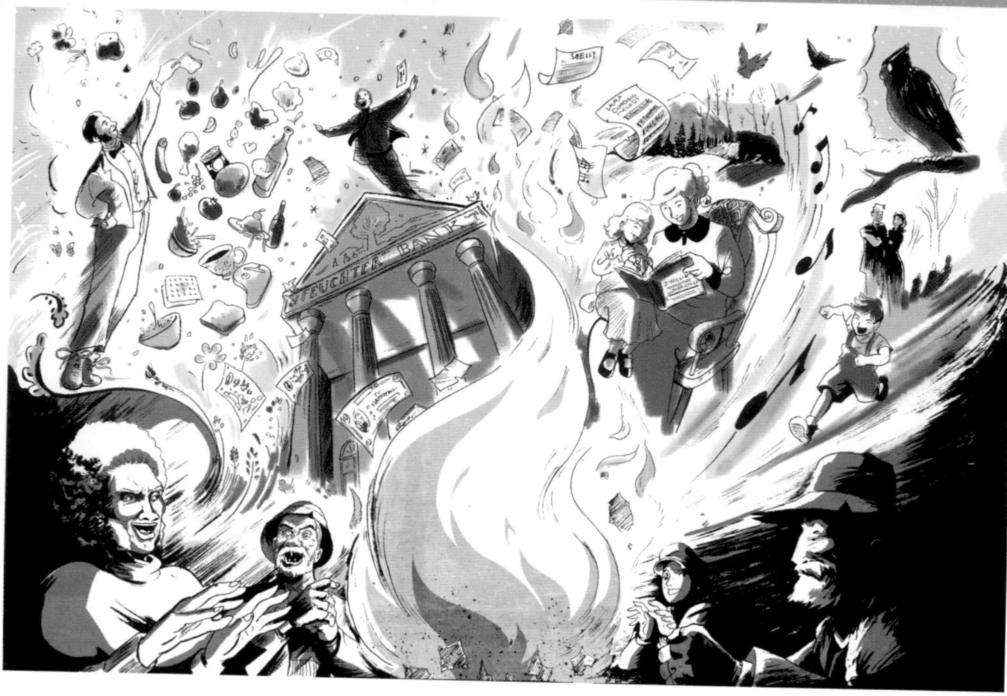
STEUCHTER BANK

Modes of Storytelling and Visual Literacy

In graphic novels, images are used to relay content with and without accompanying text, adding additional dimension to the story. Compare, contrast, and discuss with students how images can be used to relay complex messages. For example:

- *Soupy Leaves Home* is a perfect example of **visual storytelling**—how art/image/and design can tell the story as effectively as the words do. It is an excellent collaboration of verbal and visual storytelling. From the olive and sepia-tone colors reflecting the 1930s depression (along with Soupy and Rammy's depression) to the fantastical magical trips Rammy takes (along with Soupy), to the hobo signs left throughout the book—*Soupy Leaves Home* truly engages the graphic novel format. As such, this offers a perfect opportunity to study visual and verbal storytelling. To do this:
    - Set up a chart with five columns: Page; Panel; Verbal Storytelling; Visual Storytelling (use of color, design, images); Silent Storytelling (i.e. characters thinking, emoting, reflecting).
    - You may want to define and discuss the power of this silent storytelling that allows readers—along with Soupy—to rethink and review the world around her.
    - Have students chart what is told through words and what is told through image, color, and page/panel design. You may want to break your students into groups and divide the book among those groups—or you may want to simply begin the exercise and see how far they get. Note that if you have students evaluating the same pages, you may get more opinions and deeper follow-up discussion based on their different perspectives.
    - Review what students found. Discuss the nuances found along with the pros and cons of verbal and of visual storytelling.

- **Color** plays a huge role in the storytelling here. While the color palette is often limited (often using just one color as background), there are moments when the color bursts (often relaying Rammy's whimsy and fantastical look at life). Throughout the book color is used to relay mood, whimsy, and magical realism. Discuss the different moods, emotions, and information the colors relay. Discuss how the magical realism of Rammy's world and of his character (as a visionary, a dreamer, and a man at the end of his life coming to terms with the past and the future). Discuss /evaluate how color here is almost like a character in the book.

- **Art and design:** Regarding Jose Pimienta's work and contributions, Castellucci notes in an interview: "Jose brought so much heart and love to the table . . . Emotions and story just burst off the page . . ." Evaluate and discuss what Castellucci means and how the emotions and story burst off the page. ("Cecil Castellucci Explores Depression-Era Teen Wanderlust *Soupy Leaves Home* with Jose Pimienta" by Steve Foxe, Paste magazine, posted online April 17, 2017, 2:00pm and found at: https://www.pastemagazine.com/articles/2017/04/cecil-castellucci-hits-the-road-in-soupy-leaves-ho.html)

- **Silent storytelling:** In the same interview Castellucci notes that: "One thing that comics does so well is silence. There can be pages or panels with no words, and still the entire feeling that you want to convey is there. For Soupy's story, those moments of silence were essential . . ." Evaluate and discuss what Castellucci means. Find, evaluate, and discuss moments of silence and how powerfully they relay content. ("Cecil Castellucci Explores Depression-Era Teen Wanderlust *Soupy Leaves Home* with Jose Pimienta" by Steve Foxe, Paste magazine, posted online April 17, 2017, 2:00pm and found at: https://www.pastemagazine.com/articles/2017/04/cecil-castellucci-hits-the-road-in-soupy-leaves-ho.html)

- **Evaluate and discuss specific instances of visual storytelling.** For example:

  ◦ As Pearl first meets Rammy she thinks, ". . . [H]e's some kind of strange beast. Like a yeti. Or a Sasquatch. But of course, looks can be deceiving." Discuss the power of appearances and images and how they often shape first (and at times lasting) impressions. Have students consider what different "looks" mean and how these "looks" are used to judge people, places, books, toys, food, etc. You may want to chart their responses for these different categories to consider underlying themes or trends.

  ◦ Evaluate and discuss the instances of magical realism. You may want students to search and find these instances themselves or assign them specific pages (such as pages: 15, 23, 25 29, 52–53, 60, 65, 79, 86–87, 113, 152–153, and 180—to list just a few).

  ◦ Note how text, art, and design are used to relay the Hobo Code of the Road on pages 39–43. Evaluate and discuss how each of these storytelling mediums tells the story and helps us relate more closely to the characters and content.

  ◦ Pages 128–129 explode with passion as Soupy reveals and faces her demons. For example, her father and grandmother are huge, larger than life, and cannot fit completely on the page; her dad's hand is raised to hit her; on one page, their faces ooze rage, and on the other we see the hope in Soupy's heart as she struggles to come to terms with everything. Discuss the use of text and image to relay this very powerful scene and how the visual and verbal storytelling allow us not only to understand, but to feel Soupy's state of mind.

Suggested Prose and Graphic Novel Pairings

For greater discussion on literary style and/or content here are some prose novels and poetry you may want to read with *Soupy Leaves Home*:

- Look through/read/pair the list of books found in the back of the book that inspired Castellucci and Pimienta and that "Soupy is reading." You may want to discuss how Soupy might react to them and you might want to evaluate who they may have influenced/inspired *Soupy Leaves Home*.

- Songs and poems about hoboes including the song presented in the book—"The Wayfaring Stranger" (also known as "The Poor Wayfaring Stranger") versus some others listed below:

  ○ Don McLean's "Homeless Brother" (song title from the album of the same name 1974 and on the Album *Solo* in 1976) found at: https://youtu.be/EBj2L4E2KJo

  ○ "Hobo Life" by Dave McCarn (1930). Lyrics can be found at: http://www.folkarchive.de/hobolife.html , and song can be heard (along with subtitles of the text) on YouTube at: https://www.youtube.com/watch?v=pgYrsBqOq2M

  ○ "Man of Constant Sorrow" by The Stanley Brothers (1950s). Lyrics and song can be found at: https://genius.com/The-stanley-brothers-im-a-man-of-constant-sorrow-lyrics There is a version by Bob Dylan that can be heard here: https://www.youtube.com/watch?v=0dr-N9uZbaQ

  ○ "Mysteries of a Hobo's Life (The Job I Left Behind Me)" by T-Bone Slim (1910s)—lyrics can be found at: http://www.folkarchive.de/jobleft.html

  ○ "The Reckless Hobo" by Richard (Dick) Burnett and Leonard Rutherford (c. 1913) Lyrics can be found at: http://www.folkarchive.de/recklhob.html and song (with lyrics) can be heard at: https://www.youtube.com/watch?v=BWNp1o9EJSQ

  ○ "Freight Train Blues" by Roy Acuff (1947) can be heard at: https://www.youtube.com/watch?v=TmclgyXIrYY A later remake by Bob Dylan (1962) with lyrics found at: https://genius.com/Bob-dylan-freight-train-blues-lyrics

  ○ "The Boxer" by Simon and Garfunkel. Song and lyrics found at: https://www.youtube.com/watch?v=MYPJOCxSUFc

  ○ Walt Whitman

- *Nowhere to Call Home* by Cynthia DeFelice is about Frances who must cope with the hardships of the Great Depression. After losing the family's money and assets to the crash, Frances's dad takes his life. Devastated and bereft, Frances trades in her dress and railway ticket to her aunt's house for trousers, a cap, and a chance to ride the rails. There she meets hoboes Frankie Blue and Stewpot. Frances learns how to survive but eventually realizes that life traveling the rails is not anywhere near as glamorous or fulfilling as it initially appeared to be.

- *Kings in Disguise* by James Vance is an award winning graphic novel (winner of Eisner and Harvey Awards), a coming of age story about 12-year-old Freddie Bloch who finds himself homeless in Detroit's winter of 1932 after his dad disappears and his brother gets arrested. Hitting the railcars in search of his father, Freddie meets Sam, a hobo, and together they explore America.

- *The Grapes of Wrath* by John Steinbeck, about migrant workers, footloose lifestyles, and a classic, heartbreaking look at life in Great Depression America.

- *The Plain Janes*, *Odd Duck*, and *Shade the Changing Girl*, all graphic novels by Cecil Castellucci about being different, and/or containing strong female characters. Compare and contrast Castellucci's stories, the language, and the use of art.

- *A Room of One's Own* by Virginia Woolf, containing Ms. Woolf's thoughts and reflections on what women need to become professional writers of fiction. Note that this book is listed in the back of *Soupy Leaves Home* as inspiration for this story, and discussions can easily center around the obvious influences it had.

- Books about hoboes:

    - *Rolling Nowhere: Riding the Rails with America's Hoboes* by Ted Conover. First Vintage Departures Edition, 2001. Nonfiction concerning the author in the early 1980s riding the trains and interviewing hoboes. In his second edition the preface discusses the death of hoboes and how/why things changed.

    - *Citizen Hobo: How a Century of Homelessness Shaped America* by Todd DePastino. This book grew out of the author's dissertation, which discusses how hoboes (and homelessness) were the impetus for significant social reforms in 20th Century America including Roosevelt's New Deal and the post-war GI bill. DePastino also explores the literary treatment (and romanticism) of the open road.

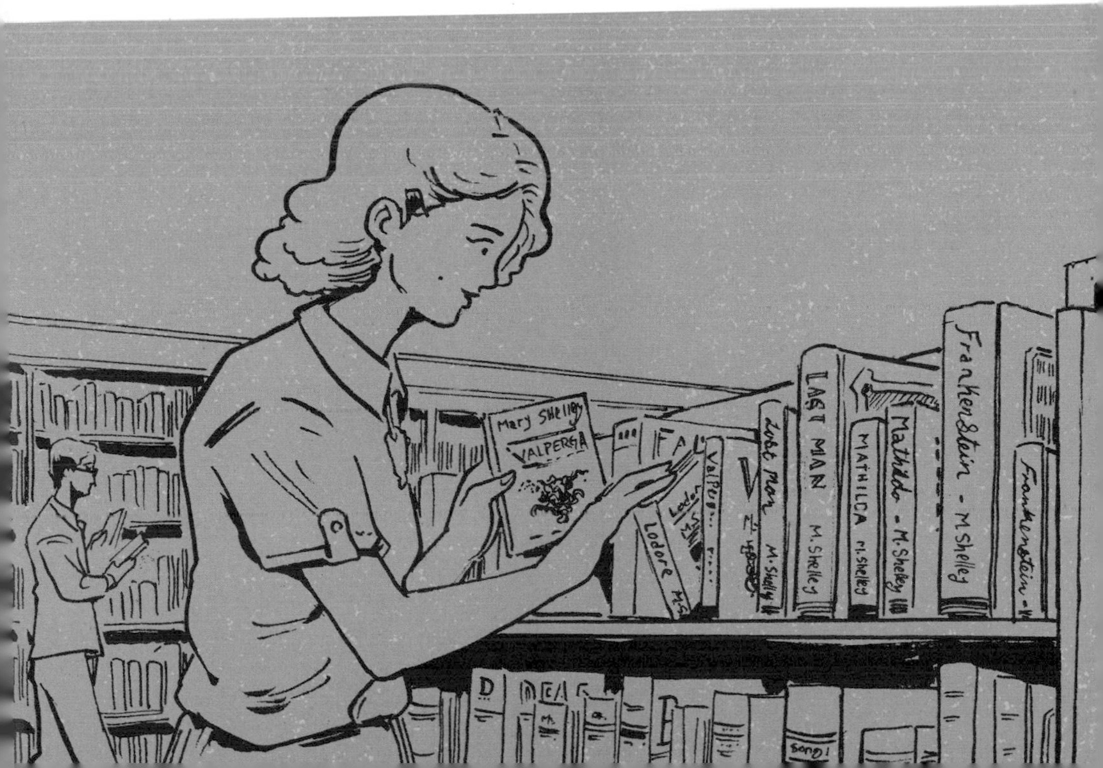
Mary Shelley
VALPERGA
Lodore
LAST MAN
M. Shelley
MATHILDA
Mathilda - M. Shelley
Frankenstein - M.Shelley

Common Core State Standards

Soupy Leaves Home is full of literary devices, verbal imagery, wordplay, inferences, nuanced characters, and humor. It deals with issues of identity, stereotyping and setting/breaking expectations. It sensitively deals with issues that permeated the 1930s as many still do today (home-lessness, domestic abuse, stereotyping, etc.). It can be deftly and effectively integrated into middle and high school language arts and social studies classrooms. It promotes critical thinking, relays issues of civic and ethical responsibilities, describes the language (verbal and sign) and lifestyles of hoboes (past and present), and its graphic novel format provides verbal and visual storytelling that addresses multi-modal teaching. As a result it meets Common Core State Standards for language arts as well as for social studies. As it can be used for a range of ages and grade levels, the section below explores its use in en-acting Common Core Anchor standards and with social studies standards identified by The National Council for the Social Studies.

Common Core Anchor Standards

- **Knowledge of Language:** Apply knowledge of language to understand how language functions in different contexts, to make effective choices for meaning or style, and to comprehend more fully when reading or listening. Not only can this book be used to analyze and reinforce modern vocabulary and word use, it can be used to evaluate hobo signs and language as well for a discussion on the role of words and images for effective communication.

  ◦ CCSS.ELA-Literacy.CCRA.L.3

- **Vocabulary Acquisition and Use:** Determine or clarify the meaning of unknown and multiple-meaning words and phrases by using context clues, analyzing meaningful word parts, and consulting general and specialized reference materials; demonstrate understanding of figurative language, word relationships, and nuances in word meaning; acquire and use accurately a range of general academic and domain-

specific words and phrases sufficient for reading, writing, speaking and listening at the college and career readiness level. This can also be explored using Castellucci's modern language as well as exploring hobo jargon.

  ◦ CCSS.ELA-Literacy.CCRA.L.4
  ◦ CCSS.ELA-Literacy.CCRA.L.5
  ◦ CCSS.ELA-Literacy.CCRA.L.6

- **Key ideas and details:** Reading closely to determine what the text says explicitly and making logical inferences from it; citing specific textual evidence when writing or speaking to support conclusions drawn from the text; determining central ideas or themes and analyzing their development; sum-marizing the key supporting details and ideas; analyzing how and why individuals, events, or ideas develop and interact over the course of the text. Due to the limited amount of text and prominent use of color and image, *Soupy Leaves Home* provides a concrete medium and unlimited opportunities for students to explore the differences between key ideas and details.

  ◦ CCSS.ELA-Literacy.CCRA.R.1
  ◦ CCSS.ELA-Literacy.CCRA.R.2
  ◦ CCSS.ELA-Literacy.CCRA.R.3

- **Craft and structure:** Interpreting words and phrases as they are used in a text, including determining technical, connotative, and figurative meanings and analyzing how specific word choices shape meaning or tone; analyzing the structure of texts, including how specific sentences, paragraphs, and larger portions of the text relate to each other and the whole; assessing how point of view or purpose shapes the content and style of a text. Here too, because the storytelling in *Soupy Leaves Home* employs limited amounts of text and prominent use of color and image, this provides a concrete medium and unlimited opportunities for students to explore the craft and structure of its storytelling.

  ◦ CCSS.ELA-Literacy.CCRA.R.4
  ◦ CCSS.ELA-Literacy.CCRA.R.5
  ◦ CCSS.ELA-Literacy.CCRA.R.6

- **Integration of knowledge and ideas:** Integrate and evaluate content presented in diverse media and formats, including visually, as well as in words; delineate and evaluate the argument and specific claims in a text, including the validity of the reasoning as well as the relevance and sufficiency of the evidence; analyze how two or more texts address similar themes or topics in order to build knowledge or to compare the approaches the authors take. Graphic novels by definition explore the use of diverse media formats. *Soupy Leaves Home*, with its use of hobo language and signs, provides an even more diverse format.

  - CCSS.ELA-Literacy.CCRA.R.7
  - CCSS.ELA-Literacy.CCRA.R.8
  - CCSS.ELA-Literacy.CCRA.R.9

- **Range of reading and level of text complexity:** Read and comprehend complex literary and informational texts independently and proficiently. While there is a limited amount of text, the vocabulary, text complexity, and language usage in *Soupy Leaves Home* is quite sophisticated. As a result it appeals to a wide range of student language learners.

  - CCSS.ELA-Literacy.CCRA.R.10

- **Comprehension and collaboration:** Prepare for and participate effectively in a range of conversations and collaborations with diverse partners, building on others' ideas and expressing their own clearly and persuasively; integrate and evaluate information presented in diverse media and formats, including visually, quantitatively, and orally; evaluate a speaker's point of view, reasoning, and use of evidence and rhetoric. These skills are addressed both in the book itself, as we see various forms and formats for collaboration among and between characters, as well as in many of the discussion/writing prompts above.

  - CCSS.ELA-Literacy.CCRA.SL.1
  - CCSS.ELA-Literacy.CCRA.SL.2
  - CCSS.ELA-Literacy.CCRA.SL.3

Social Studies Standards and following themes identified by The National Council for the Social Studies

- **Culture and Cultural Diversity** – ". . . [S]tudents need to comprehend multiple perspectives . . . to consider the strengths and advantages that this diversity offers to the society in general and to their own growth . . . to analyze the ways that a people's cultural ideas and actions influence its members . . ." In *Soupy Leaves Home* not only are the characters diverse but the theme of cultural/gender differences are a major theme of the book.

- **Time, Continuity, and Change** – ". . . [F]acilitate the understanding and appreciation of differences in historical perspectives and the recognition that interpretations are influenced by individual experiences, societal values, and cultural traditions . . . examine the relationship of the past to the present and extrapolating into the future . . . provide learners with opportunities to investigate, interpret, and analyze multiple historical and contemporary viewpoints within and across cultures related to important events, recurring dilemmas, and persistent issues, while employing empathy, skepticism, and critical judgment . . ." As *Soupy Leaves Home* depicts hoboes in the early twentieth century, it provides an excellent format to evaluate time, continuity and cultural change.

- **Individual Development and Identity**– ". . . [D]escribe how family, religion, gender, ethnicity, nationality, socio-economic status, and other group and cultural influences contribute to the development of a sense of self . . . [H]ave learners compare and evaluate the impact of stereotyping, conformity, acts of altruism, discrimination, and other behaviors on individuals and groups . . ." *Soupy Leaves Home* is all about how characters grow and change as they face their own dreams and realities. Individual development and identity are major themes of the book.

Social Studies Standards and following themes identified by **The National Council for the Social Studies** *(Cont'd)*

- **Power, Authority, and Governance** – ". . . [U]nderstanding the historical development of structures of power, authority, and governance and their evolving functions in contemporary American society . . . enable learners to examine the rights and responsibilities of the individual in relation to their families, their social groups, their community, and their nation . . . examine issues involving the rights, roles, and status of individuals in relation to the general welfare . . . explain conditions, actions, and motivations that contribute to conflict and cooperation within and among nations . . . challenge learners to apply concepts such as power, role, status, justice, democratic values, and

influence . . ." After reading *Soupy Leaves Home* readers can evaluate not only how hoboes governed themselves, but how government institutions helped and/or failed hoboes, particularly in the 1930s.

- Civic Ideals and Practices – "[A]ssist learners in understanding the origins and continuing influence of key ideals of the democratic republican form of government, such as individual human dignity, liberty, justice, equality, and the rule of law . . . analyze and evaluate the influence of various forms of citizen action on public policy . . . evaluate the effectiveness of public opinion in influencing and shaping public policy development and decision-making . . ." Here too, civic ideals and practices (in the 1930s versus now) are also major themes found in this book.

ADDITIONAL RESOURCES

- Resources around "The Wayfaring Stranger" song:
  - Nice background history/renditions can be found at: https://en.wikipedia.org/wiki/The_Wayfaring_Stranger_(song)
  - Twenty different versions (and recordings) can be found at: https://thebluegrasssituation.com/read/i-am-a-poor-wayfaring-stranger-20-versions-of-an-american-classic

- On Hoboes:
  - Wonderful background on the rise of hoboes, where they gathered, and the hobo jungle. See: "Hoboes: Denizens of the Jungle" by Sheena Morrison at: http://ultimatehistoryproject.com/hobo.html
  - Don McLean's "Homeless Brother" (song title from the album of the same name 1974) https://youtu.be/EBj2L4E2KJo
  - "The Vanishing American Hobo" published in the magazine *Holiday* in 1960 and reprinted in Kerouac's book *Lonesome Traveler*, published by McGraw-Hill in 1960. Reprinted in *Jack Kerouac, Road Novels, 1957–1960*; New York: Library of America, 2007. Available online at: http://www.hermitary.com/lorc/kerouac.html

  - Hoboes today:
    - "Riding the rails: A Report from the National Hobo Convention" *The Economist*, August 17, 2013 found online at: https://www.economist.com/news/united-states/21583673-report-national-hobo-convention-riding-rails
    - "Homeless Millennials are Transforming Hobo Culture" by Betsy Isaacson, *Newsweek* posted online 4/9/15 and found at: http://www.newsweek.com/2015/05/01/homeless-millennials-are-transforming-hobo-culture 323151.html

  - Hobo signs: their form, their purpose, and hobo life has changed over the years:
    - https://weburbanist.com/2010/06/03/hoboglyphs-secret-transient-symbols-modern-nomad-codes/
    - https://owlcation.com/humanities/All-things-HOBO-signs-and-symbols

- On Homelessness:
  - Homelessness in America: sponsored by National Coalition for the Homeless and found at: http://nationalhomeless.org/about-homelessness/ detailing why people are homeless, with additional links for factsheets; for those who need help; with research on homelessness; and how to take action and help.
  - National Coalition for the Homeless Report: No Safe Street—A Survey of Hate Crimes and Violence Committed Against Homeless People in 2014 and 2015, found at: http://nationalhomeless.org/wp-content/uploads/2016/07/HCR-2014-151.pdf
  - "How America counts its homeless—and why so many are overlooked" by Alastair Gee, homelessness editor in Los Angeles, Liz Barney in Honolulu, and Julia O'Malley in Anchorage, *The Guardian*, posted online February 16, 2017 and found at: https://www.theguardian.com/us-news/2017/feb/16/homeless-count-population-america-shelters-people
  - General homelessness facts: http://www.greendoors.org/facts/general-data.php

- On Abuse and Domestic Violence:

  ○ Website discussing what abuse is (different types), how to recognize abuse, why abuse happens, effects of abuse, and what one can do about it. From *TeensHealth* found at: http://kidshealth.org/en/teens/family-abuse.html

  ○ The National Domestic Violence Hotline http://www.thehotline.org/is-this-abuse/abuse-defined/, defining domestic abuse with an excellent infographic on how issues of power and control can lead to various forms of physical and sexual violence.

- On the Great Depression:

  ○ National Education Association's New Deal Network houses print documents, photographs, cartoons, quizzes, scripts, (primary source) letters, and lesson plans for middle and high school students about the Great Depression and FDR's New Deal. Found at: http://www.nea.org/tools/lessons/65482.htm

  ○ "PBS Presentation: The Great Depression" (video) found at: https://www.youtube.com/watch?v=IQ_lizW5zSI

  ○ "The Great Depression (1929–1939)" video sponsored by The History Channel and ABC News, found at: https://www.youtube.com/watch?v=TtttXC9tFPU

  ○ A brief synopsis with additional links to explore archives of the FDR Presidential Library, an overview of the 1930s, and more. Found at: https://www2.gwu.edu/~erpapers/teachinger/glossary/great-depression.cfm

  ○ History.com articles, videos, speeches and numerous resources (with advertisements): http://www.history.com/topics/great-depression

  ○ Depression-related articles found in *The New York Times* https://www.nytimes.com/topic/subject/the-great-depression

Meryl Jaffe, PhD teaches visual literacy and critical reading at Johns Hopkins University Center for Talented Youth Online Program. She is the author of *Worth A Thousand Words: Using Graphic Novels to Teach Visual and Verbal Literacy* (Wiley, 2018), *Raising a Reader: How Comics and Graphic Novels Can Help Your Kids Love to Read* (Comic Book Legal Defense Fund, 2013), and *Using Content-Area Graphic Texts for Learning* (Capstone, 2011). She used to encourage the "classics" to the exclusion of comics, but with her kids' intervention, Meryl has become an avid graphic novel fan. She now incorporates them in her work, believing that the educational process must reflect the imagination and intellectual flexibility it hopes to nurture. Please visit Dr. Jaffe at meryljaffe.com with your own comments or questions.

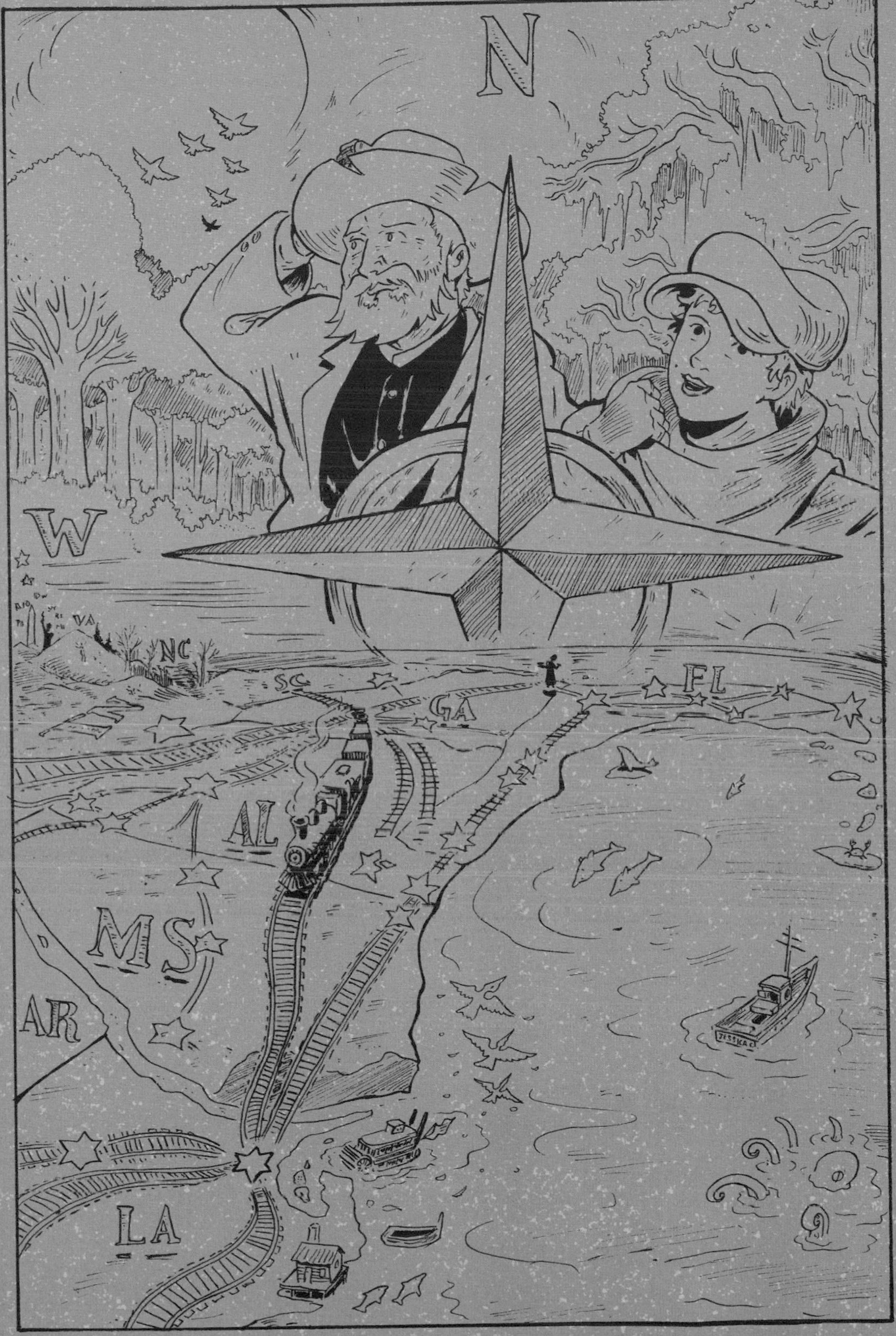
N
W
VA
NC
SC
GA
FL
AL
MS
AR
LA

Dark Horse ♥ Reading!

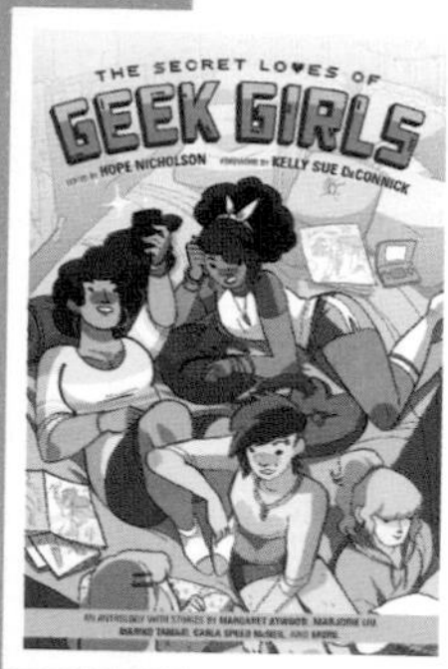
THE SECRET LOVES OF
GEEK GIRLS

THE SECRET LOVES OF GEEK GIRLS

Margaret Atwood, Hope Larson, Mariko Tamaki, Marjorie Liu, and more!

A nonfiction anthology mixing prose, comics, and illustrated stories on the lives and loves of an amazing cast of female creators. *The Secret Loves of Geek Girls* is a compilation of tales told from both sides of the tables: from the fans who love video games, comics, and sci-fi to those that work behind the scenes as creators and industry insiders.

$14.99 | ISBN 978-1-50670-099-1

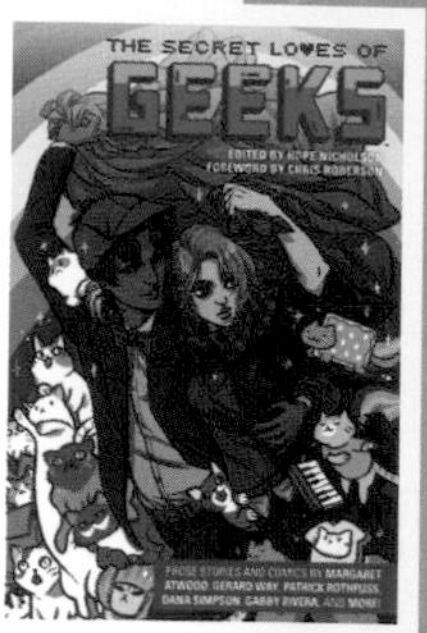
THE SECRET LOVES OF
GEEKS

THE SECRET LOVES OF GEEKS

Cecil Castellucci, Margaret Atwood, Gerard Way, Dana Simpson, Hope Larson, and more!

The follow-up to the smash-hit *The Secret Loves of Geek Girls*, this anthology features comic and prose stories from cartoonists and professional geeks about their most intimate, heartbreaking, and inspiring tales of love, sex, and dating. This volume includes creators of diverse genders, orientations, and cultural backgrounds.

$14.99 | ISBN 978-1-50670-473-9

STEPHEN MCCRANIE'S SPACE BOY

Stephen McCranie

A sci-fi drama of a high school aged girl who belongs in a different time, a boy possessed by emptiness as deep as space, an alien artifact, mysterious murder, and a love that crosses light years.

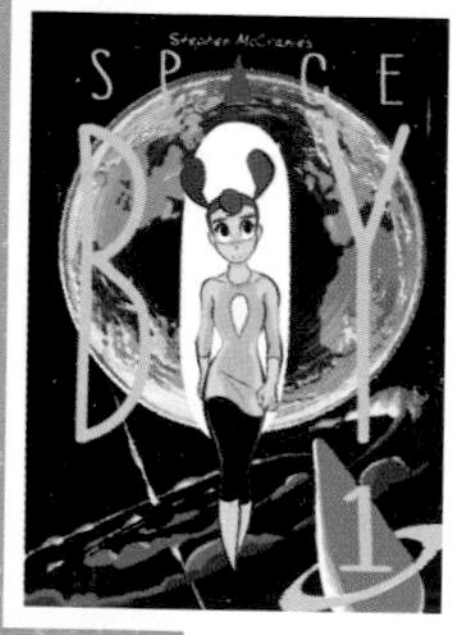
Stephen McCranie's
SPACE
BOY
1

$10.99 each!

Volume 1 | ISBN 978-1-50670-648-1
Volume 2 | ISBN 978-1-50670-680-1
Volume 3 | ISBN 978-1-50670-842-3
Volume 4 | ISBN 978-1-50670-843-0
Volume 5 | ISBN 978-1-50671-399-1
Volume 6 | ISBN 978-1-50671-400-4
Volume 7 | ISBN 978-1-50671-401-1

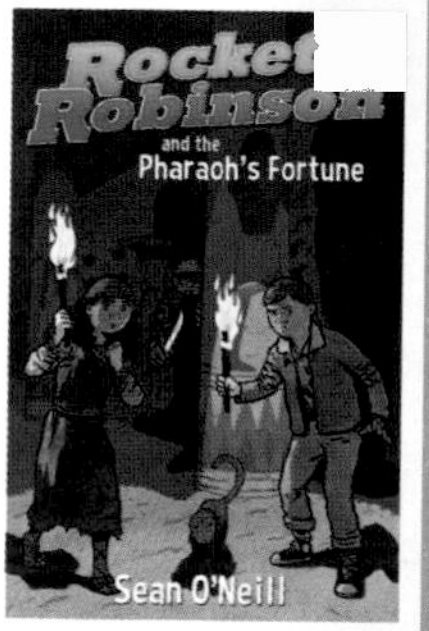
Rocket Robinson
and the
Pharaoh's Fortune
Sean O'Neill

ROCKET ROBINSON

Sean O'Neill

The only son of an American diplomat, 12-year-old Ronald "Rocket" Robinson travels from city to city with his monkey, Screech, never staying in one place long enough to call it home, but when Rocket finds a strange note, he stumbles into an adventure more incredible than anything he's ever dreamt of.

$14.99 each!

The Pharaoh's Fortune
ISBN 978-1-50670-618-4

The Secret of the Saint
ISBN 978-1-50670-679-5

The Jade Dragon
ISBN 978-1-50672-145-3

EXTRAORDINARY: A STORY OF AN ORDINARY PRINCESS

Cassie Anderson

While her sisters were blessed at birth with exceptional skills, Princess Basil's "gift" is to be ordinary. After escaping an unconventional kidnapping, Princess Basil finds herself far from her castle and must take fate into her own hands. She tracks down the fairy godmother who "blessed" her, and finds the solution to her ordinariness might be as simple as finding a magic ring. With an unlikely ally in tow, she takes on gnomes, a badger, and a couple of snarky foxes in her quest for a less ordinary life.

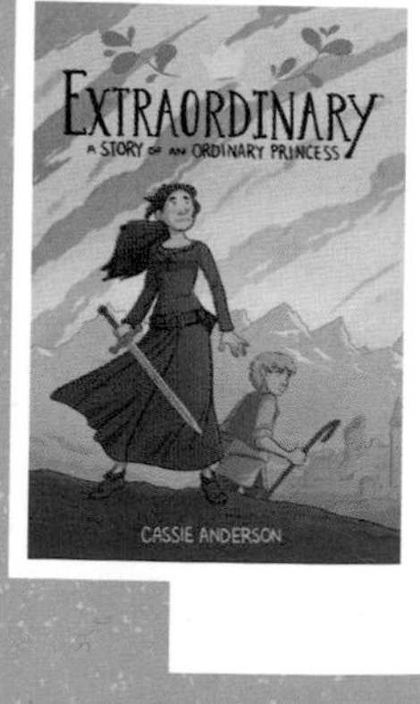
EXTRAORDINARY
A STORY OF AN ORDINARY PRINCESS
CASSIE ANDERSON

$12.99 | ISBN 978-1-50671-027-3

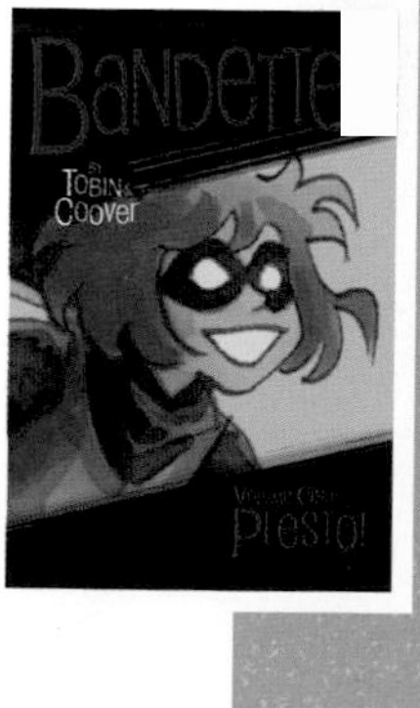
Bandette
Tobin & Coover
Presto!

BANDETTE

Paul Tobin, Colleen Coover

The world's greatest thief is a costumed teen burglar by the *nome d'arte* of Bandette! Gleefully plying her skills on either side of the law alongside her network of street urchins, Bandette is a thorn in the side of both Police Inspector Belgique and the criminal underworld.

Volume 1 TPB
$14.99 | ISBN 978-1-50671-923-8

Volume 2 TPB
$14.99 | ISBN 978-1-50671-924-5

Volume 3 TPB
$14.99 | ISBN 978-1-50671-925-2

Volume 4 HC
$17.99 | ISBN 978-1-50671-926-9

DARKHORSE.COM

Available at your local comics shop or bookstore. To find a comics shop in your area, visit comicshoplocator.com

For more information or to order direct, visit DarkHorse.com

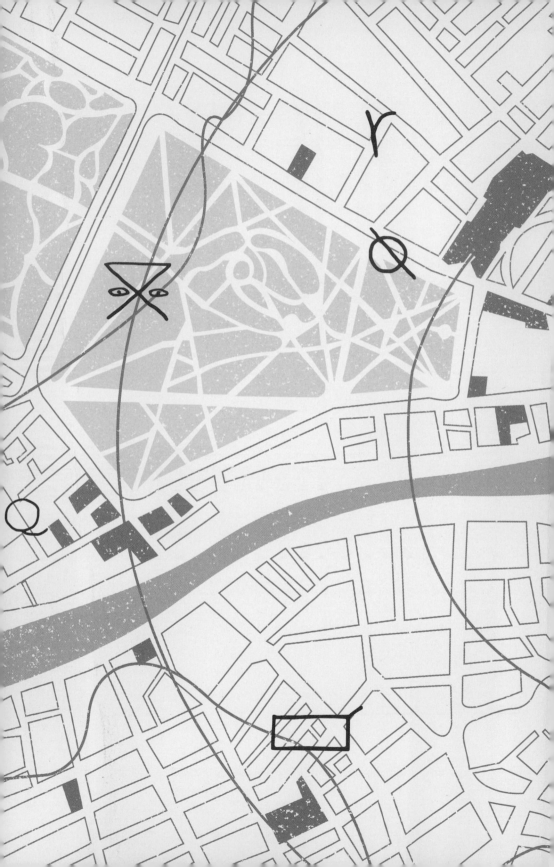